THE LOVELY BONES

Alice Sebold is the author of the memoir *Lucky*. She lives in California with her husband, Glen David Gold.

ALSO BY ALICE SEBOLD

Lucky

THE LOVELY BONES

a novel

Alice Sebold

PICADOR

Always, Glen

First published 2002 by Little, Brown and Company, USA

First published in Great Britain 2002 by Picador

This edition published 2003 by Picador
an imprint of Pan Macmillan Ltd
Pan Macmillan, 20 New Wharf Road, London N1 9RR
Basingstoke and Oxford
Associated companies throughout the world
www.panmacmillan.com

ISBN 0 330 48538 5

41 43 45 47 49 48 46 44 42 40

A CIP catalogue record for this book is available from
the British Library.

Printed and bound in Great Britain by
Mackays of Chatham plc, Chatham, Kent

THE LOVELY BONES

Inside the snow globe on my father's desk, there was a penguin wearing a red-and-white-striped scarf. When I was little my father would pull me into his lap and reach for the snow globe. He would turn it over, letting all the snow collect on the top, then quickly invert it. The two of us watched the snow fall gently around the penguin. The penguin was alone in there, I thought, and I worried for him. When I told my father this, he said, "Don't worry, Susie; he has a nice life. He's trapped in a perfect world."

ONE

My name was Salmon, like the fish; first name, Susie. I was fourteen when I was murdered on December 6, 1973. In newspaper photos of missing girls from the seventies, most looked like me: white girls with mousy brown hair. This was before kids of all races and genders started appearing on milk cartons or in the daily mail. It was still back when people believed things like that didn't happen.

In my junior high yearbook I had a quote from a Spanish poet my sister had turned me on to, Juan Ramón Jiménez. It went like this: "If they give you ruled paper, write the other way." I chose it both because it expressed my contempt for my structured surroundings à la the classroom and because, not being some dopey quote from a rock group, I thought it marked me as literary. I was a member of the Chess Club and Chem Club and burned everything I tried to make in Mrs. Delminico's home ec class. My favorite teacher was Mr. Botte, who taught biology and liked to animate the frogs and crawfish we had to dissect by making them dance in their waxed pans.

I wasn't killed by Mr. Botte, by the way. Don't think every person you're going to meet in here is suspect. That's the problem. You never know. Mr. Botte came to my memorial (as, may I add, did almost the entire junior high school—I was never so popular) and cried quite a bit. He had a sick kid. We all knew this, so when he laughed at his own jokes, which were rusty way before I had him, we laughed too, forcing it sometimes just to make him happy. His daughter died a year and a half after I did. She had leukemia, but I never saw her in my heaven.

My murderer was a man from our neighborhood. My mother liked his border flowers, and my father talked to him once about fertilizer. My murderer believed in old-fashioned things like eggshells and coffee grounds, which he said his own mother had used. My father came home smiling, making jokes about how the man's garden might be beautiful but it would stink to high heaven once a heat wave hit.

But on December 6, 1973, it was snowing, and I took a shortcut through the cornfield back from the junior high. It was dark out because the days were shorter in winter, and I remember how the broken cornstalks made my walk more difficult. The snow was falling lightly, like a flurry of small hands, and I was breathing through my nose until it was running so much that I had to open my mouth. Six feet from where Mr. Harvey stood, I stuck my tongue out to taste a snowflake.

"Don't let me startle you," Mr. Harvey said.

Of course, in a cornfield, in the dark, I was startled. After I was dead I thought about how there had been the light scent of cologne in the air but that I had not been paying attention, or thought it was coming from one of the houses up ahead.

"Mr. Harvey," I said.

"You're the older Salmon girl, right?"

"Yes."

"How are your folks?"

Although the eldest in my family and good at acing a science quiz, I had never felt comfortable with adults.

"Fine," I said. I was cold, but the natural authority of his age, and the added fact that he was a neighbor and had talked to my father about fertilizer, rooted me to the spot.

"I've built something back here," he said. "Would you like to see?"

"I'm sort of cold, Mr. Harvey," I said, "and my mom likes me home before dark."

"It's after dark, Susie," he said.

I wish now that I had known this was weird. I had never told him my name. I guess I thought my father had told him one of the embarrassing anecdotes he saw merely as loving testaments to his children. My father was the kind of dad who kept a nude photo of you when you were three in the downstairs bathroom, the one that guests would use. He did this to my little sister, Lindsey, thank God. At least I was spared that indignity. But he liked to tell a story about how, once Lindsey was born, I was so jealous that one day while he was on the phone in the other room, I moved down the couch—he could see me from where he stood—and tried to pee on top of Lindsey in her carrier. This story humiliated me every time he told it, to the pastor of our church, to our neighbor Mrs. Stead, who was a therapist and whose take on it he wanted to hear, and to everyone who ever said "Susie has a lot of spunk!"

"Spunk!" my father would say. "Let me tell you about spunk," and he would launch immediately into his Susie-peed-on-Lindsey story.

But as it turned out, my father had not mentioned us to Mr. Harvey or told him the Susie-peed-on-Lindsey story.

Mr. Harvey would later say these words to my mother when he

ran into her on the street: "I heard about the horrible, horrible tragedy. What was your daughter's name, again?"

"Susie," my mother said, bracing up under the weight of it, a weight that she naively hoped might lighten someday, not knowing that it would only go on to hurt in new and varied ways for the rest of her life.

Mr. Harvey told her the usual: "I hope they get the bastard. I'm sorry for your loss."

I was in my heaven by that time, fitting my limbs together, and couldn't believe his audacity. "The man has no shame," I said to Franny, my intake counselor. "Exactly," she said, and made her point as simply as that. There wasn't a lot of bullshit in my heaven.

Mr. Harvey said it would only take a minute, so I followed him a little farther into the cornfield, where fewer stalks were broken off because no one used it as a shortcut to the junior high. My mom had told my baby brother, Buckley, that the corn in the field was inedible when he asked why no one from the neighborhood ate it. "The corn is for horses, not humans," she said. "Not dogs?" Buckley asked. "No," my mother answered. "Not dinosaurs?" Buckley asked. And it went like that.

"I've made a little hiding place," said Mr. Harvey.

He stopped and turned to me.

"I don't see anything," I said. I was aware that Mr. Harvey was looking at me strangely. I'd had older men look at me that way since I'd lost my baby fat, but they usually didn't lose their marbles over me when I was wearing my royal blue parka and yellow elephant bell-bottoms. His glasses were small and round with gold frames, and his eyes looked out over them and at me.

"You should be more observant, Susie," he said.

I felt like observing my way out of there, but I didn't. Why didn't I? Franny said these questions were fruitless: "You didn't and that's that. Don't mull it over. It does no good. You're dead and you have to accept it."

"Try again," Mr. Harvey said, and he squatted down and knocked against the ground.

"What's that?" I asked.

My ears were freezing. I wouldn't wear the multicolored cap with the pompom and jingle bells that my mother had made me one Christmas. I had shoved it in the pocket of my parka instead.

I remember that I went over and stomped on the ground near him. It felt harder even than frozen earth, which was pretty hard.

"It's wood," Mr. Harvey said. "It keeps the entrance from collapsing. Other than that it's all made out of earth."

"What is it?" I asked. I was no longer cold or weirded out by the look he had given me. I was like I was in science class: I was curious.

"Come and see."

It was awkward to get into, that much he admitted once we were both inside the hole. But I was so amazed by how he had made a chimney that would draw smoke out if he ever chose to build a fire that the awkwardness of getting in and out of the hole wasn't even on my mind. You could add to that that escape wasn't a concept I had any real experience with. The worst I'd had to escape was Artie, a strange-looking kid at school whose father was a mortician. He liked to pretend he was carrying a needle full of embalming fluid around with him. On his notebooks he would draw needles spilling dark drips.

"This is neato!" I said to Mr. Harvey. He could have been the hunchback of Notre Dame, whom we had read about in French class. I didn't care. I completely reverted. I was my brother Buckley on our day-trip to the Museum of Natural History in New York, where he'd fallen in love with the huge skeletons on display. I hadn't used the word *neato* in public since elementary school.

"Like taking candy from a baby," Franny said.

* * *

I can still see the hole like it was yesterday, and it was. Life is a perpetual yesterday for us. It was the size of a small room, the mud room in our house, say, where we kept our boots and slickers and where Mom had managed to fit a washer and dryer, one on top of the other. I could almost stand up in it, but Mr. Harvey had to stoop. He'd created a bench along the sides of it by the way he'd dug it out. He immediately sat down.

"Look around," he said.

I stared at it in amazement, the dug-out shelf above him where he had placed matches, a row of batteries, and a battery-powered fluorescent lamp that cast the only light in the room—an eerie light that would make his features hard to see when he was on top of me.

There was a mirror on the shelf, and a razor and shaving cream. I thought that was odd. Wouldn't he do that at home? But I guess I figured that a man who had a perfectly good split-level and then built an underground room only half a mile away had to be kind of loo-loo. My father had a nice way of describing people like him: "The man's a character, that's all."

So I guess I was thinking that Mr. Harvey was a character, and I liked the room, and it was warm, and I wanted to know how he had built it, what the mechanics of the thing were and where he'd learned to do something like that.

But by the time the Gilberts' dog found my elbow three days later and brought it home with a telling corn husk attached to it, Mr. Harvey had closed it up. I was in transit during this. I didn't get to see him sweat it out, remove the wood reinforcement, bag any evidence along with my body parts, except that elbow. By the time I popped up with enough wherewithal to look down at the goings-on on Earth, I was more concerned with my family than anything else.

My mother sat on a hard chair by the front door with her mouth open. Her pale face paler than I had ever seen it. Her blue eyes staring. My father was driven into motion. He wanted to know details and to comb the cornfield along with the cops. I still thank God for a small detective named Len Fenerman. He assigned two uniforms to take my dad into town and have him point out all the places I'd hung out with my friends. The uniforms kept my dad busy in one mall for the whole first day. No one had told Lindsey, who was thirteen and would have been old enough, or Buckley, who was four and would, to be honest, never fully understand.

Mr. Harvey asked me if I would like a refreshment. That was how he put it. I said I had to go home.

"Be polite and have a Coke," he said. "I'm sure the other kids would."

"What other kids?"

"I built this for the kids in the neighborhood. I thought it could be some sort of clubhouse."

I don't think I believed this even then. I thought he was lying, but I thought it was a pitiful lie. I imagined he was lonely. We had read about men like him in health class. Men who never married and ate frozen meals every night and were so afraid of rejection that they didn't even own pets. I felt sorry for him.

"Okay," I said, "I'll have a Coke."

In a little while he said, "Aren't you warm, Susie? Why don't you take off your parka."

I did.

After this he said, "You're very pretty, Susie."

"Thanks," I said, even though he gave me what my friend Clarissa and I had dubbed the skeevies.

"Do you have a boyfriend?"

"No, Mr. Harvey," I said. I swallowed the rest of my Coke, which was a lot, and said, "I got to go, Mr. Harvey. This is a cool place, but I have to go."

He stood up and did his hunchback number by the six dug-in

steps that led to the world. "I don't know why you think you're leaving."

I talked so that I would not have to take in this knowledge: Mr. Harvey was no character. He made me feel skeevy and icky now that he was blocking the door.

"Mr. Harvey, I really have to get home."

"Take off your clothes."

"What?"

"Take your clothes off," Mr. Harvey said. "I want to check that you're still a virgin."

"I am, Mr. Harvey," I said.

"I want to make sure. Your parents will thank me."

"My parents?"

"They only want good girls," he said.

"Mr. Harvey," I said, "please let me leave."

"You aren't leaving, Susie. You're mine now."

Fitness was not a big thing back then; *aerobics* was barely a word. Girls were supposed to be soft, and only the girls we suspected were butch could climb the ropes at school.

I fought hard. I fought as hard as I could not to let Mr. Harvey hurt me, but my hard-as-I-could was not hard enough, not even close, and I was soon lying down on the ground, in the ground, with him on top of me panting and sweating, having lost his glasses in the struggle.

I was so alive then. I thought it was *the worst thing in the world* to be lying flat on my back with a sweating man on top of me. To be trapped inside the earth and have no one know where I was.

I thought of my mother.

My mother would be checking the dial of the clock on her oven. It was a new oven and she loved that it had a clock on it. "I can time things to the minute," she told her own mother, a mother who couldn't care less about ovens.

She would be worried, but more angry than worried, at my

lateness. As my father pulled into the garage, she would rush about, fixing him a cocktail, a dry sherry, and put on an exasperated face: "You know junior high," she would say. "Maybe it's Spring Fling." "Abigail," my father would say, "how can it be Spring Fling when it's snowing?" Having failed with this, my mother might rush Buckley into the room and say, "Play with your father," while she ducked into the kitchen and took a nip of sherry for herself.

Mr. Harvey started to press his lips against mine. They were blubbery and wet and I wanted to scream but I was too afraid and too exhausted from the fight. I had been kissed once by someone I liked. His name was Ray and he was Indian. He had an accent and was dark. I wasn't supposed to like him. Clarissa called his large eyes, with their half-closed lids, "freak-a-delic," but he was nice and smart and helped me cheat on my algebra exam while pretending he hadn't. He kissed me by my locker the day before we turned in our photos for the yearbook. When the yearbook came out at the end of the summer, I saw that under his picture he had answered the standard "My heart belongs to" with "Susie Salmon." I guess he had had plans. I remember that his lips were chapped.

"Don't, Mr. Harvey," I managed, and I kept saying that one word a lot. *Don't.* And I said *please* a lot too. Franny told me that almost everyone begged "please" before dying.

"I want you, Susie," he said.

"Please," I said. "Don't," I said. Sometimes I combined them. "Please don't" or "Don't please." It was like insisting that a key works when it doesn't or yelling "I've got it, I've got it, I've got it" as a softball goes sailing over you into the stands.

"Please don't."

But he grew tired of hearing me plead. He reached into the pocket of my parka and balled up the hat my mother had made me, smashing it into my mouth. The only sound I made after that was the weak tinkling of bells.

As he kissed his wet lips down my face and neck and then began to shove his hands up under my shirt, I wept. I began to leave my body; I began to inhabit the air and the silence. I wept and struggled so I would not feel. He ripped open my pants, not having found the invisible zipper my mother had artfully sewn into their side.

"Big white panties," he said.

I felt huge and bloated. I felt like a sea in which he stood and pissed and shat. I felt the corners of my body were turning in on themselves and out, like in cat's cradle, which I played with Lindsey just to make her happy. He started working himself over me.

"Susie! Susie!" I heard my mother calling. "Dinner is ready."

He was inside me. He was grunting.

"We're having string beans and lamb."

I was the mortar, he was the pestle.

"Your brother has a new finger painting, and I made apple crumb cake."

Mr. Harvey made me lie still underneath him and listen to the beating of his heart and the beating of mine. How mine skipped like a rabbit, and how his thudded, a hammer against cloth. We lay there with our bodies touching, and, as I shook, a powerful knowledge took hold. He had done this thing to me and I had lived. That was all. I was still breathing. I heard his heart. I smelled his breath. The dark earth surrounding us smelled like what it was, moist dirt where worms and animals lived their daily lives. I could have yelled for hours.

I knew he was going to kill me. I did not realize then that I was an animal already dying.

"Why don't you get up?" Mr. Harvey said as he rolled to the side and then crouched over me.

His voice was gentle, encouraging, a lover's voice on a late morning. A suggestion, not a command.

I could not move. I could not get up.

When I would not—was it only that, only that I would not follow his suggestion?—he leaned to the side and felt, over his head, across the ledge where his razor and shaving cream sat. He brought back a knife. Unsheathed, it smiled at me, curving up in a grin.

He took the hat from my mouth.

"Tell me you love me," he said.

Gently, I did.

The end came anyway.

TWO

When I first entered heaven I thought everyone saw what I saw. That in everyone's heaven there were soccer goalposts in the distance and lumbering women throwing shot put and javelin. That all the buildings were like suburban northeast high schools built in the 1960s. Large, squat buildings spread out on dismally landscaped sandy lots, with overhangs and open spaces to make them feel modern. My favorite part was how the colored blocks were turquoise and orange, just like the blocks in Fairfax High. Sometimes, on Earth, I had made my father drive me by Fairfax High so I could imagine myself there.

Following the seventh, eighth, and ninth grades of middle school, high school would have been a fresh start. When I got to Fairfax High I would insist on being called Suzanne. I would wear my hair feathered or up in a bun. I would have a body that the boys wanted and the girls envied, but I'd be so nice on top of it all that they would feel too guilty to do anything but worship me. I liked to think of myself—having reached a sort of queenly status—as protecting misfit kids in the cafeteria. When someone taunted Clive Saunders for walking like a girl, I would deliver swift vengeance with my foot to the taunter's less-protected parts. When the boys teased Phoebe Hart for her sizable breasts, I would give a speech on why boob jokes weren't funny. I had to forget that I too had made lists in the margins of my notebook when Phoebe walked by: Winnebagos, Hoo-has, Johnny Yellows. At the end of my reveries, I sat in the back of the car as my father drove. I was beyond reproach. I would overtake high school in a matter of days, not years, or, inexplicably, earn an Oscar for Best Actress during my junior year.

These were my dreams on Earth.

After a few days in heaven, I realized that the javelin-throwers and the shot-putters and the boys who played basketball on the cracked blacktop were all in their own version of heaven. Theirs just fit with mine—didn't duplicate it precisely, but had a lot of the same things going on inside.

I met Holly, who became my roommate, on the third day. She was sitting on the swing set. (I didn't question that a high school had swing sets: that's what made it heaven. And no flat-benched swings—only bucket seats made out of hard black rubber that cradled you and that you could bounce in a bit before swinging.) Holly sat reading a book in a weird alphabet that I associated with the pork-fried rice my father brought home from Hop Fat Kitchen, a place Buckley loved the name of, loved so much he yelled "Hop Fat!" at the top of his lungs. Now I know Vietnamese, and I know that Vietnamese is not what Herman Jade, who owned Hop Fat, was, and that Herman Jade was not Herman Jade's real name but one he adopted when he came to the U.S. from China. Holly taught me all this.

"Hi," I said. "My name is Susie."

Later she would tell me she picked her name from a movie, *Breakfast at Tiffany's*. But that day it rolled right off her tongue.

"I'm Holly," she said. Because she wanted no trace of an accent in her heaven, she had none.

I stared at her black hair. It was shiny like the promises in magazines. "How long have you been here?" I asked.

"Three days."

"Me too."

I sat down on the swing next to her and twisted my body around and around to tie up the chains. Then I let go and spun until I stopped.

"Do you like it here?" she asked.

"No."

"Me either."

So it began.

We had been given, in our heavens, our simplest dreams. There were no teachers in the school. We never had to go inside except for art class for me and jazz band for Holly. The boys did not pinch our backsides or tell us we smelled; our textbooks were *Seventeen* and *Glamour* and *Vogue*.

And our heavens expanded as our relationship grew. We wanted many of the same things.

Franny, my intake counselor, became our guide. Franny was old enough to be our mother—mid-forties—and it took Holly and me a while to figure out that this had been something we wanted: our mothers.

In Franny's heaven, she served and was rewarded by results and gratitude. On Earth she had been a social worker for the homeless and destitute. She worked out of a church named Saint Mary's that served meals to women and children only, and she did everything there from manning the phones to swatting the roaches—karate-chop style. She was shot in the face by a man looking for his wife.

Franny walked over to Holly and me on the fifth day. She

handed us two Dixie Cups of lime Kool-Aid and we drank. "I'm here to help," she said.

I looked into her small blue eyes surrounded by laugh lines and told her the truth. "We're bored."

Holly was busy trying to reach her tongue out far enough to see if it had turned green.

"What do you want?" Franny asked.

"I don't know," I said.

"All you have to do is desire it, and if you desire it enough and understand why—really know—it will come."

It seemed so simple and it was. That's how Holly and I got our duplex.

I hated our split-level on Earth. I hated my parents' furniture, and how our house looked out onto another house and another house and another—an echo of sameness riding up over the hill. Our duplex looked out onto a park, and in the distance, just close enough to know we weren't alone, but not too close, we could see the lights of other houses.

Eventually I began to desire more. What I found strange was how much I desired to know what I had not known on Earth. I wanted to be allowed to grow up.

"People grow up by living," I said to Franny. "I want to live."

"That's out," she said.

"Can we at least watch the living?" asked Holly.

"You already do," she said.

"I think she means whole lives," I said, "from beginning to end, to see how they did it. To know the secrets. Then we can pretend better."

"You won't experience it," Franny clarified.

"Thank you, Brain Central," I said, but our heavens began to grow.

There was the high school still, all the Fairfax architecture, but now there were roads leading out.

"Walk the paths," Franny said, "and you'll find what you need."

So that's when Holly and I set out. Our heaven had an ice cream shop where, when you asked for peppermint stick ice cream, no one ever said, "It's seasonal"; it had a newspaper where our pictures appeared a lot and made us look important; it had real men in it and beautiful women too, because Holly and I were devoted to fashion magazines. Sometimes Holly seemed like she wasn't paying attention, and other times she was gone when I went looking for her. That was when she went to a part of heaven we didn't share. I missed her then, but it was an odd sort of missing because by then I knew the meaning of forever.

I could not have what I wanted most: Mr. Harvey dead and me living. Heaven wasn't perfect. But I came to believe that if I watched closely, and desired, I might change the lives of those I loved on Earth.

My father was the one who took the phone call on December ninth. It was the beginning of the end. He gave the police my blood type, had to describe the lightness of my skin. They asked him if I had any identifying features. He began to describe my face in detail, getting lost in it. Detective Fenerman let him go on, the next news too horrible to interrupt with. But then he said it: "Mr. Salmon, we have found only a body part."

My father stood in the kitchen and a sickening shiver overtook him. How could he tell that to Abigail?

"So you can't be certain that she's dead?" he asked.

"Nothing is ever certain," Len Fenerman said.

That was the line my father said to my mother: "Nothing is ever certain."

For three nights he hadn't known how to touch my mother or what to say. Before, they had never found themselves broken together. Usually, it was one needing the other but not both needing each other, and so there had been a way, by touching, to borrow from the stronger one's strength. And they had never understood, as they did now, what the word *horror* meant.

"Nothing is ever certain," my mother said, clinging to it as he had hoped she might.

My mother had been the one who knew the meaning of each charm on my bracelet—where we had gotten it and why I liked it. She made a meticulous list of what I'd carried and worn. If found miles away and in isolation along a road, these clues might lead a policeman there to link it to my death.

In my mind I had wavered between the bittersweet joy of seeing my mother name all the things I carried and loved and her futile hope that these things mattered. That a stranger who found a cartoon character eraser or a rock star button would report it to the police.

After Len's phone call, my father reached out his hand and the two of them sat in the bed together, staring straight in front of them. My mother numbly clinging to this list of things, my father feeling as if he were entering a dark tunnel. At some point, it began to rain. I could feel them both thinking the same thing then, but neither of them said it. That I was out there somewhere, in the rain. That they hoped I was safe. That I was dry somewhere, and warm.

Neither of them knew who fell asleep first; their bones aching with exhaustion, they drifted off and woke guiltily at the same time. The rain, which had changed several times as the temperature dropped, was now hail, and the sound of it, of small stones of ice hitting the roof above them, woke them together.

They did not speak. They looked at each other in the small light cast from the lamp left on across the room. My mother began to cry, and my father held her, wiped her tears with the pad of his thumbs as they crested her cheekbones, and kissed her very gently on the eyes.

I looked away from them then, as they touched. I moved my

eyes into the cornfield, seeing if there was anything that in the morning the police might find. The hail bent the stalks and drove all the animals into their holes. Not so deep beneath the earth were the warrens of the wild rabbits I loved, the bunnies that ate the vegetables and flowers in the neighborhood nearby and that sometimes, unwittingly, brought poison home to their dens. Then, inside the earth and so far away from the man or woman who had laced a garden with toxic bait, an entire family of rabbits would curl into themselves and die.

On the morning of the tenth, my father poured the Scotch down the kitchen sink. Lindsey asked him why.

"I'm afraid I might drink it," he said.

"What was the phone call?" my sister asked.

"What phone call?"

"I heard you say that thing you always say about Susie's smile. About stars exploding."

"Did I say that?"

"You got kind of goofy. It was a cop, wasn't it?"

"No lies?"

"No lies," Lindsey agreed.

"They found a body part. It might be Susie's."

It was a hard sock in the stomach. "What?"

"Nothing is ever certain," my father tried.

Lindsey sat down at the kitchen table. "I'm going to be sick," she said.

"Honey?"

"Dad, I want you to tell me what it was. Which body part, and then I'm going to need to throw up."

My father got down a large metal mixing bowl. He brought it to the table and placed it near Lindsey before sitting down.

"Okay," she said. "Tell me."

"It was an elbow. The Gilberts' dog found it."

He held her hand and then she threw up, as she had promised, into the shiny silver bowl.

Later that morning the weather cleared, and not too far from my house the police roped off the cornfield and began their search. The rain, sleet, snow, and hail melting and mixing had left the ground sodden; still, there was an obvious area where the earth had been freshly manipulated. They began there and dug.

In places, the lab later found, there was a dense concentration of my blood mixed with the dirt, but at the time, the police grew more and more frustrated, plying the cold wet ground and looking for girl.

Along the border of the soccer field, a few of my neighbors kept a respectful distance from the police tape, wondering at the men dressed in heavy blue parkas wielding shovels and rakes like medical tools.

My father and mother remained at home. Lindsey stayed in her room. Buckley was nearby at his friend Nate's house, where he spent a lot of time these days. They had told him I was on an extended sleepover at Clarissa's.

I knew where my body was but I could not tell them. I watched and waited to see what they would see. And then, like a thunderbolt, late in the afternoon, a policeman held up his earth-caked fist and shouted.

"Over here!" he said, and the other officers ran to surround him.

The neighbors had gone home except for Mrs. Stead. After conferring around the discovering policeman, Detective Fenerman broke their dark huddle and approached her.

"Mrs. Stead?" he said over the tape that separated them.

"Yes."

"You have a child in the school?"

"Yes."

"Could you come with me, please?"

A young officer led Mrs. Stead under the police tape and over the bumpy, churned-up cornfield to where the rest of the men stood.

"Mrs. Stead," Len Fenerman said, "does this look familiar?" He held up a paperback copy of *To Kill a Mockingbird.* "Do they read this at the school?"

"Yes," she said, her face draining of color as she said the small word.

"Do you mind if I ask you . . ." he began.

"Ninth grade," she said, looking into Len Fenerman's slate blue eyes. "Susie's grade." She was a therapist and relied on her ability to hear bad news and discuss rationally the difficult details of her patients' lives, but she found herself leaning into the young policeman who had led her over. I could feel her wishing that she had gone home when the other neighbors had left, wishing that she was in the living room with her husband, or out in the backyard with her son.

"Who teaches the class?"

"Mrs. Dewitt," Mrs. Stead said. "The kids find it a real relief after *Othello.*"

"*Othello?*"

"Yes," she said, her knowledge of the school suddenly very important right now—all the policemen listening. "Mrs. Dewitt likes to modulate her reading list, and she does a big push right before Christmas with Shakespeare. Then she passes out Harper Lee as a reward. If Susie was carrying around *To Kill a Mockingbird* it means she must have turned in her paper on *Othello* already."

All of this checked out.

The police made calls. I watched the circle widen. Mrs. Dewitt had my paper. Eventually, she sent it back to my parents, unmarked, through the mail. "Thought you would want to have this," Mrs.

Dewitt had written on a note attached to it. "I'm so very very sorry." Lindsey inherited the paper because it was too painful for my mother to read. "The Ostracized: One Man Alone," I had called it. Lindsey had suggested "The Ostracized," and I made up the other half. My sister punched three holes down the side of it and fastened each carefully handwritten page into an empty notebook. She put it in her closet under her Barbie case and the box that held her perfect-condition Raggedy Ann and Andy that I'd envied.

Detective Fenerman called my parents. They had found a schoolbook, they believed, that might have been given to me that last day.

"But it could be anyone's," my father said to my mother as they began another restless vigil. "Or she could have dropped it along the way."

Evidence was mounting, but they refused to believe.

Two days later, on December twelfth, the police found my notes from Mr. Botte's class. Animals had carried off the notebook from its original burial site—the dirt did not match the surrounding samples, but the graph paper, with its scribbled theories that I could never understand but still dutifully recorded, had been found when a cat knocked down a crow's nest. Shreds of the paper were laced among the leaves and twigs. The police unbraided the graph paper, along with strips of another kind of paper, thinner and brittle, that had no lines.

The girl who lived in the house where the tree stood recognized some of the handwriting. It was not my writing, but the writing of the boy who had a crush on me: Ray Singh. On his mother's special rice paper Ray had written me a love note, which I never read. He had tucked it into my notebook during our Wednesday lab. His hand was distinct. When the officers came they had to piece together the scraps of my biology notebook and of Ray Singh's love note.

"Ray is not feeling well," his mother said when a detective called his house and asked to speak to him. But they found out what they needed from her. Ray nodded to her as she repeated the policeman's questions to her son. Yes, he had written Susie Salmon a love note. Yes, he had put it in her notebook after Mr. Botte had asked her to collect the pop quiz. Yes, he had called himself the Moor.

Ray Singh became the first suspect.

"That sweet boy?" my mother said to my father.

"Ray Singh is nice," my sister said in a monotone at dinner that night.

I watched my family and knew they knew. It was not Ray Singh.

The police descended on his house, leaning heavily on him, insinuating things. They were fueled by the guilt they read into Ray's dark skin, by the rage they felt at his manner, and by his beautiful yet too exotic and unavailable mother. But Ray had an alibi. A whole host of nations could be called to testify on his behalf. His father, who taught postcolonial history at Penn, had urged his son to represent the teenage experience at a lecture he gave at the International House on the day I died.

At first Ray's absence from school had been seen as evidence of his guilt, but once the police were presented with a list of forty-five attendees who had seen Ray speak at "Suburbia: The American Experience," they had to concede his innocence. The police stood outside the Singh house and snapped small twigs from the hedges. It would have been so easy, so magical, their answer literally falling out of the sky from a tree. But rumors spread and, in school, what little headway Ray had made socially was reversed. He began to go home immediately after school.

All this made me crazy. Watching but not being able to steer the police toward the green house so close to my parents, where Mr. Harvey sat carving finials for a gothic dollhouse he was building. He watched the news and scanned the papers, but he wore his own innocence like a comfortable old coat. There had been a riot inside him and now there was calm.

I tried to take solace in Holiday, our dog. I missed him in a way

I hadn't yet let myself miss my mother and father, my sister and brother. That way of missing would mean that I had accepted that I would never be with them again; it might sound silly but I didn't believe it, would not believe it. Holiday stayed with Lindsey at night, stood by my father each time he answered the door to a new unknown. Gladly partook of any clandestine eating on the part of my mother. Let Buckley pull his tail and ears inside the house of locked doors.

There was too much blood in the earth.

On December fifteenth, among the knocks on the door that signaled to my family that they must numb themselves further before opening their house to strangers—the kind but awkward neighbors, the bumbling but cruel reporters—came the one that made my father finally believe.

It was Len Fenerman, who had been so kind to him, and a uniform.

They came inside, by now familiar enough with the house to know that my mother preferred them to come in and say what they had to say in the living room so that my sister and brother would not overhear.

"We've found a personal item that we believe to be Susie's," Len said. Len was careful. I could see him calculating his words. He made sure to specify so that my parents would be relieved of their first thought—that the police had found my body, that I was, for certain, dead.

"What?" my mother said impatiently. She crossed her arms and braced for another inconsequential detail in which others invested meaning. She was a wall. Notebooks and novels were nothing to her. Her daughter might survive without an arm. A lot of blood was a lot of blood. It was not a body. Jack had said it and she believed: Nothing is ever certain.

But when they held up the evidence bag with my hat inside, something broke in her. The fine wall of leaden crystal that had protected her heart—somehow numbed her into disbelief—shattered.

"The pompom," Lindsey said. She had crept into the living room from the kitchen. No one had seen her come in but me.

My mother made a sound and reached out her hand. The sound was a metallic squeak, a human-as-machine breaking down, uttering last sounds before the whole engine locks.

"We've tested the fibers," Len said. "It appears whoever accosted Susie used this during the crime."

"What?" my father asked. He was powerless. He was being told something he could not comprehend.

"As a way to keep her quiet."

"What?"

"It is covered with her saliva," the uniformed officer, who had been silent until now, volunteered. "He gagged her with it."

My mother grabbed it out of Len Fenerman's hands, and the bells she had sewn into the pompom sounded as she landed on her knees. She bent over the hat she had made me.

I saw Lindsey stiffen at the door. Our parents were unrecognizable to her; everything was unrecognizable.

My father led the well-meaning Len Fenerman and the uniformed officer to the front door.

"Mr. Salmon," Len Fenerman said, "with the amount of blood we've found, and the violence I'm afraid it implies, as well as other material evidence we've discussed, we must work with the assumption that your daughter has been killed."

Lindsey overheard what she already knew, had known since five days before, when my father told her about my elbow. My mother began to wail.

"We'll be working with this as a murder investigation from this point out," Fenerman said.

"But there is no body," my father tried.

"All evidence points to your daughter's death. I'm very sorry."

The uniformed officer had been staring to the right of my father's pleading eyes. I wondered if that was something they'd taught him in school. But Len Fenerman met my father's gaze. "I'll call to check in on you later today," he said.

By the time my father turned back to the living room, he was too devastated to reach out to my mother sitting on the carpet or my sister's hardened form nearby. He could not let them see him. He mounted the stairs, thinking of Holiday on the rug in the study. He had last seen him there. Into the deep ruff of fur surrounding the dog's neck, my father would let himself cry.

That afternoon the three of them crept forward in silence, as if the sound of footsteps might confirm the news. Nate's mother knocked on the door to return Buckley. No one answered. She stepped away, knowing something had changed inside the house, which looked exactly like the ones on either side of it. She made herself my brother's co-conspirator, telling him they would go out for ice cream and ruin his appetite.

At four, my mother and father ended up standing in the same room downstairs. They had come in from opposite doorways.

My mother looked at my father: "Mother," she said, and he nodded his head. He made the phone call to my only living grandparent, my mother's mother, Grandma Lynn.

I worried that my sister, left alone, would do something rash. She sat in her room on the old couch my parents had given up on and worked on hardening herself. *Take deep breaths and hold them. Try to stay still for longer and longer periods of time. Make yourself small and like a stone. Curl the edges of yourself up and fold them under where no one can see.*

My mother told her it was her choice whether she wanted to return to school before Christmas—there was only one week left—but Lindsey chose to go.

On Monday, in homeroom, everyone stared at her as she approached the front of the classroom.

"The principal would like to see you, dear," Mrs. Dewitt confided in a hush.

My sister did not look at Mrs. Dewitt when she was speaking. She was perfecting the art of talking to someone while looking through them. That was my first clue that something would have to give. Mrs. Dewitt was also the English teacher, but more importantly she was married to Mr. Dewitt, who coached boys' soccer and had encouraged Lindsey to try out for his team. My sister liked the Dewitts, but that morning she began looking into the eyes of only those people she could fight against.

As she gathered her things, she heard whispers everywhere. She was certain that right before she left the room Danny Clarke had whispered something to Sylvia Henley. Someone had dropped something near the back of the classroom. They did this, she believed, so that on their way to pick it up and back again, they could say a word or two to their neighbor about the dead girl's sister.

Lindsey walked through the hallways and in and out of the rows of lockers—dodging anyone who might be near. I wished I could walk with her, mimic the principal and the way he always started out a meeting in the auditorium: "Your principal is your pal with principles!" I would whine in her ear, cracking her up.

But while she was blessed with empty halls, when she reached the main office she was cursed with the drippy looks of consoling secretaries. No matter. She had prepared herself at home in her bedroom. She was armed to the teeth for any onslaught of sympathy.

"Lindsey," Principal Caden said, "I received a call from the police this morning. I'm sorry to hear of your loss."

She looked right at him. It was not so much a look as a laser. "What exactly is my loss?"

Mr. Caden felt he needed to address issues of children's crises directly. He walked out from behind his desk and ushered Lindsey onto what was commonly referred to by the students as The Sofa. Eventually he would replace The Sofa with two chairs, when politics swept through the school district and told him, *"It is not good to have a sofa here—chairs are better. Sofas send the wrong message."*

Mr. Caden sat on The Sofa and so did my sister. I like to think she was a little thrilled, in that moment, no matter how upset, to be on The Sofa itself. I like to think I hadn't robbed her of everything.

"We're here to help in any way we can," Mr. Caden said. He was doing his best.

"I'm fine," she said.

"Would you like to talk about it?"

"What?" Lindsey asked. She was being what my father called "petulant," as in, "Susie, don't speak to me in that petulant tone."

"Your loss," he said. He reached out to touch my sister's knee. His hand was like a brand burning into her.

"I wasn't aware I had lost anything," she said, and in a Herculean effort she made the motions of patting her shirt and checking her pockets.

Mr. Caden didn't know what to say. He had had Vicki Kurtz fall apart in his arms the year before. It had been difficult, yes, but now, in hindsight, Vicki Kurtz and her dead mother seemed an artfully handled crisis. He had led Vicki Kurtz to the couch—no, no, Vicki had just gone right over and sat down on it—he had said, "I'm sorry for your loss," and Vicki Kurtz had burst like an overinflated balloon. He held her in his arms as she sobbed, and sobbed, and that night he brought his suit to the dry cleaner's.

But Lindsey Salmon was another thing altogether. She was

gifted, one of the twenty students from his school who had been selected for the statewide Gifted Symposium. The only trouble in her file was a slight altercation early in the year when a teacher reprimanded her for bringing obscene literature—*Fear of Flying*—into the classroom.

"Make her laugh," I wanted to say to him. "Bring her to a Marx Brothers movie, sit on a fart cushion, show her the boxers you have on with the little devils eating hot dogs on them!" All I could do was talk, but no one on Earth could hear me.

The school district made everyone take tests and then decided who was gifted and who was not. I liked to suggest to Lindsey that I was much more pissed off by her hair than by my dumbo status. We had both been born with masses of blond hair, but mine quickly fell out and was replaced with a grudging growth of mousy brown. Lindsey's stayed and acquired a sort of mythical place. She was the only true blonde in our family.

But once called gifted, it had spurred her on to live up to the name. She locked herself in her bedroom and read big books. When I read *Are You There God? It's Me, Margaret,* she read Camus's *Resistance, Rebellion, and Death.* She might not have gotten most of it, but she carried it around, and that made people—including teachers—begin to leave her alone.

"What I'm saying, Lindsey, is that we all miss Susie," Mr. Caden said.

She did not respond.

"She was very bright," he tried.

She stared blankly back at him.

"It's on your shoulders now." He had no idea what he was saying, but he thought the silence might mean he was getting somewhere. "You're the only Salmon girl now."

Nothing.

"You know who came in to see me this morning?" Mr. Caden had held back his big finish, the one he was sure would work. "Mr. Dewitt. He's considering coaching a girls' team," Mr. Caden said. "The idea is all centered around you. He's watched how good you are, as competitive as his boys, and he thinks other girls would come out if you led the charge. What do you say?"

Inside, my sister's heart closed like a fist. "I'd say it would be pretty hard to play soccer on the soccer field when it's approximately twenty feet from where my sister was supposedly murdered."

Score!

Mr. Caden's mouth opened and he stared at her.

"Anything else?" Lindsey asked.

"No, I . . ." Mr. Caden reached out his hand again. There was a thread still—a desire to understand. "I want you to know how sorry we are," he said.

"I'm late for first period," she said.

In that moment she reminded me of a character in the Westerns my father loved, the ones we watched together on late-night TV. There was always a man who, after he shot his gun, raised the pistol to his lips and blew air across the opening.

Lindsey got up and took the walk out of Principal Caden's office slow. The walks away were her only rest time. Secretaries were on the other side of the door, teachers were at the front of the class, students in every desk, our parents at home, police coming by. She would not break. I watched her, felt the lines she repeated over and over again in her head. *Fine. All of it is fine.* I was dead, but that was something that happened all the time—people died. As she left the outer office that day, she appeared to be looking into the eyes of the secretaries, but she was focusing on their misapplied lipstick or two-piece paisley crepe de chine instead.

At home that night she lay on the floor of her room and braced her feet under her bureau. She did ten sets of sit-ups. Then she got into push-up position. Not the girl's kind. Mr. Dewitt had told her about the kind he had done in the Marines, head-up, or one-handed, clapping between. After she did ten push-ups, she went to her shelf and chose the two heaviest books—her dictionary and a world almanac. She did bicep curls until her arms ached. She focused only on her breathing. The in. The out.

I sat in the gazebo in the main square of my heaven (our neighbors, the O'Dwyers, had had a gazebo; I had grown up jealous for one), and watched my sister rage.

Hours before I died, my mother hung on the refrigerator a picture that Buckley had drawn. In the drawing a thick blue line separated the air and ground. In the days that followed I watched my family walk back and forth past that drawing and I became convinced that that thick blue line was a real place—an Inbetween, where heaven's horizon met Earth's. I wanted to go there into the cornflower blue of Crayola, the royal, the turquoise, the sky.

Often I found myself desiring simple things and I would get them. Riches in furry packages. Dogs.

Every day in my heaven tiny dogs and big dogs, dogs of every kind, ran through the park outside my room. When I opened the door I saw them fat and happy, skinny and hairy, lean and hairless even. Pitbulls rolled on their backs, the nipples of the females distended and dark, begging for their pups to come and suckle them, happy in the sun. Bassets tripped over their ears, ambling forward, nudging the rumps of dachshunds, the ankles of greyhounds, and the heads of the Pekingese. And when Holly took her tenor sax, set herself up outside the door that looked onto the park, and played the blues, the hounds all ran to form her chorus.

On their haunches they sat wailing. Other doors opened then, and women stepped out from where they lived alone or with roommates. I would step outside, Holly would go into an endless encore, the sun going down, and we would dance with the dogs—all of us together. We chased them, they chased us. We circled tail to tail. We wore spotted gowns, flowered gowns, striped gowns, plain. When the moon was high the music would stop. The dancing stopped. We froze.

Mrs. Bethel Utemeyer, the oldest resident of my heaven, would bring out her violin. Holly tread lightly on her horn. They would do a duet. One woman old and silent, one woman not past girl yet. Back and forth, a crazy schizoid solace they'd create.

All the dancers would slowly go inside. The song reverberated until Holly, for a final time, passed the tune over, and Mrs. Utemeyer, quiet, upright, historical, finished with a jig.

The house asleep by then; this was my Evensong.

THREE

The odd thing about Earth was what we saw when we looked down. Besides the initial view that you might suspect, the old ants-from-the-skyscraper phenomenon, there were souls leaving bodies all over the world.

Holly and I could be scanning Earth, alighting on one scene or another for a second or two, looking for the unexpected in the most mundane moment. And a soul would run by a living being, touch them softly on the shoulder or cheek, and continue on its way to heaven. The dead are never exactly seen by the living, but many people seem acutely aware of something changed around them. They speak of a chill in the air. The mates of the deceased wake from dreams and see a figure standing at the end of their bed, or in a doorway, or boarding, phantomlike, a city bus.

On my way out of Earth, I touched a girl named Ruth. She went to my school but we'd never been close. She was standing in my path that night when my soul shrieked out of Earth. I could not help but graze her. Once released from life, having lost it in such violence, I couldn't calculate my steps. I didn't have time for contemplation. In violence, it is the getting away that you concentrate on. When you begin to go over the edge, life receding from you as a boat recedes inevitably from shore, you hold on to death tightly, like a rope that will transport you, and you swing out on it, hoping only to land away from where you are.

Like a phone call from the jail cell, I brushed by Ruth Connors—wrong number, accidental call. I saw her standing there near Mr. Botte's red and rusted Fiat. When I streaked by her, my hand leapt out to touch her, touch the last face, feel the last connection to Earth in this not-so-standard-issue teenage girl.

On the morning of December seventh, Ruth complained to her mother about having had a dream that seemed too real to be a dream. When her mother asked her what she meant, Ruth said, "I was crossing through the faculty parking lot, and suddenly, down out of the soccer field, I saw a pale running ghost coming toward me."

Mrs. Connors stirred the hardening oatmeal in its pot. She watched her daughter gesticulating with the long thin fingers of her hands—hands she had inherited from her father.

"It was female, I could sense that," Ruth said. "It flew up out of the field. Its eyes were hollow. It had a thin white veil over its body, as light as cheesecloth. I could see its face through it, the features coming up through it, the nose, the eyes, the face, the hair."

Her mother took the oatmeal off the stove and lowered the flame. "Ruth," she said, "you're letting your imagination get the best of you."

Ruth took the cue to shut up. She did not mention the dream that was not a dream again, even ten days later, when the story of my death began to travel through the halls of the school, receiving add-on nuances as all good horror stories do. They were hard-pressed, my peers, to make the horror any more horrible than it was. But the details were still missing—the what and when and who became hollow bowls to fill with their conjectures. Devil Worship. Midnight. Ray Singh.

Try as I might, I could not point Ruth strongly enough to what no one had found: my silver charm bracelet. I thought it might help her. It lay exposed, waiting for a hand to reach out, a hand that would recognize it and think, *Clue*. But it was no longer in the cornfield.

Ruth began writing poetry. If her mother or her more approachable teachers did not want to hear the darker reality she had experienced, she would cloak this reality in poetry.

How I wished Ruth could have gone to my family and talked to them. In all likelihood, no one but my sister would have even known her name. Ruth was the girl who got chosen next to last in gym. She was the girl who, when a volleyball sailed in her direction, cowered where she stood while the ball hit the gymnasium floor beside her, and her teammates and the gym teacher tried hard not to groan.

As my mother sat in the straight-backed chair in our hallway, watching my father run in and out on his various errands of responsibility—he would now be hyperaware of the movements and the whereabouts of his young son, of his wife, and of his remaining daughter—Ruth took our accidental meeting in the school parking lot and went underground.

She went through old yearbooks and found my class photos, as well as any activities photos like Chem Club, and cut them out with her mother's swan-shaped embroidery scissors. Even as her obsession grew I remained wary of her, until that last week before Christmas when she saw something in the hallway of our school.

It was my friend Clarissa and Brian Nelson. I'd dubbed Brian "the scarecrow" because even though he had incredible shoulders that all the girls mooned over, his face reminded me of a burlap sack stuffed with straw. He wore a floppy leather hippie hat and smoked hand-rolled cigarettes in the student smoking lounge. According to my mother, Clarissa's penchant for baby blue eye shadow was an early warning sign, but I'd always liked her for just this reason. She did things I wasn't allowed to do: she lightened her long hair, she wore platform shoes, she smoked cigarettes after school.

Ruth came upon the two of them, but they didn't see her. She had a pile of huge books she had borrowed from Mrs. Kaplan, the social science teacher. They were all early feminist texts, and she held them with their spines resting against her stomach so that no one could see what they were. Her father, a building contractor, had made her a gift of two super-strong elastic book bands. Ruth had placed two of them around the volumes she planned to read over vacation.

Clarissa and Brian were giggling. His hand was inside her shirt. As he inched it up, her giggling increased, but she thwarted his advances each time by twisting or moving an inch or two away. Ruth stood apart from this, as she did most things. She would have passed it in her usual manner, head down/eyes averted, but everyone knew Clarissa had been my friend. So she watched.

"Come on, honey," Brian said, "just a little mound of love. Just one."

I noticed Ruth's lip curl in disgust. Mine was curling up in heaven.

"Brian, I can't. Not here."

"How 'bout out in the cornfield?" he whispered.

Clarissa giggled nervously but nuzzled the space between his neck and shoulder. For now, she would deny him.

After that, Clarissa's locker was burgled.

Gone were her scrapbook, random photos stuck to the inside of her locker, and Brian's stash of marijuana, which he had hidden there without Clarissa's knowledge.

Ruth, who had never been high, spent that night emptying out the tobacco from her mother's long brown More 100s and stuffing them with pot. She sat in the toolshed with a flashlight, looking at photos of me and smoking more grass than even the potheads at school could suck down.

Mrs. Connors, standing at the kitchen window doing dishes, caught a whiff of the scent coming from the toolshed.

"I think Ruth is making friends at school," she said to her husband, who sat over his copy of the *Evening Bulletin* with a cup of coffee. At the end of his workday he was too tired even to speculate.

"Good," he said.

"Maybe there's hope for her yet."

"Always," he said.

When Ruth tottered in later that night, her eyes bleary from using the flashlight and from the eight More cigarettes she'd smoked, her mother greeted her with a smile and told her there was blueberry pie in the kitchen. It took a few days and some non-Susie-Salmon-focused research, but Ruth discovered why she had eaten the entire pie in one sitting.

The air in my heaven often smelled like skunk—just a hint of it. It was a smell that I had always loved on Earth. When I breathed it in, I could feel the scent as well as smell it. It was the animal's fear and power mixed together to form a pungent, lingering musk. In Franny's heaven it smelled like pure, grade-A tobacco. In Holly's it smelled like kumquats.

I would sit whole days and nights in the gazebo and watch. See Clarissa spin away from me, toward the comfort of Brian. See Ruth staring at her from behind a corner near the home ec room or outside the cafeteria near the nurse's station. At the start, the freedom I had to see the whole school was intoxicating. I would watch the assistant football coach leave anonymous chocolates for the married science teacher, or the head of the cheerleading squad trying to capture the attention of the kid who had been expelled so many times, from so many schools, even he had lost count. I watched the art teacher make love to his girlfriend in the kiln room and the principal moon over the assistant football coach. I concluded that this assistant football coach was a stud in the world of Kennet Junior High, even if his square jaw left me cold.

On the way back to the duplex each night I would pass under old-time street lamps that I had seen once in a play of *Our Town.* The globes of light hung down in an arc from an iron post. I had remembered them because when I saw the play with my family, I thought of them as giant, heavy berries full of light. I made a game in heaven of positioning myself so that my shadow plucked the berries as I made my way home.

After watching Ruth one night I met Franny in the midst of this. The square was deserted, and leaves began to swirl around in an eddy up ahead. I stood and looked at her—at the laugh lines that were clustered near her eyes and mouth.

"Why are you shivering?" Franny asked.

And though the air was damp and chilly I could not say that that was why.

"I can't help thinking of my mother," I said.

Franny took my left hand in both of hers and smiled.

I wanted to kiss her lightly on the cheek or have her hold me, but instead I watched her walk off in front of me, saw her blue dress trail away. I knew that she was not my mother; I could not play pretend.

I turned around and went back to the gazebo. I felt the moist air lace its way up along my legs and arms, lifting, ever so slightly, the ends of my hair. I thought of spider webs in the morning, how they held small jewels of dew, how, with a light movement of the wrist, I used to destroy them without thinking.

On the morning of my eleventh birthday I had woken up very early. No one else was up, or so I thought. I crept downstairs and looked into the dining room, where I assumed my presents would be. But there was nothing there. Same table as yesterday. But as I turned around I saw it lying on my mother's desk in the living room. The fancy desk with an always-clean surface. "The bill-paying desk" was what they called it. Swaddled in tissue paper but not yet wrapped was a camera—what I had asked for with a tinge of whining in my voice, so sure they would not get it for me. I went over to it and stared down. It was an Instamatic, and lying beside it were three cartridges of film and a box of four square flashbulbs. It was my first machine, my starter kit to becoming what I wanted to be. A wildlife photographer.

I looked around. No one. I saw through the front blinds, which my mother always kept at a half-slant—"inviting but discreet"—that Grace Tarking, who lived down the street and went to a private school, was walking with ankle weights strapped to her feet. Hurriedly I loaded the camera and I began to stalk Grace Tarking as I would, I imagined, when I grew older, stalk wild elephants and rhinos. Here I hid behind blinds and windows, there it would be high reeds. I was quiet, what I thought of as stealthy, gathering the long hem of my flannel nightgown up in my free hand. I traced her movements past our living room, front hall, into the den on the other side. As I watched her receding form I had a brainstorm—I would run into the backyard, where I could see her with no barriers.

So I ran on tiptoe into the back of the house, only to find the door to the porch wide open.

When I saw my mother, I forgot all about Grace Tarking. I wish I could explain it better than this, but I had never seen her sitting so still, so *not there* somehow. Outside the screened-in porch she was sitting on an aluminum fold-out chair that was facing the backyard. In her hand she held a saucer and in the saucer was her customary cup of coffee. That morning there were no lipstick marks because there was no lipstick until she put it on for . . . who? I had never thought to ask the question. My father? Us?

Holiday was sitting near the birdbath, panting happily, but he did not notice me. He was watching my mother. She had a stare that stretched to infinity. She was, in that moment, not my mother but something separate from me. I looked at what I had never seen as anything but Mom and saw the soft powdery skin of her face—powdery without makeup—soft without help. Her eyebrows and eyes were a set-piece together. "Ocean Eyes," my father called her when he wanted one of her chocolate-covered cherries, which she kept hidden in the liquor cabinet as her private treat. And now I understood the name. I had thought it was because they were blue, but now I saw it was because they were bottomless in a way that I found frightening. I had an instinct then, not a developed thought, and it was that, before Holiday saw and smelled me, before the dewy mist hovering over the grass evaporated and the mother inside her woke as it did every morning, I should take a photograph with my new camera.

When the roll came back from the Kodak plant in a special heavy envelope, I could see the difference immediately. There was only one picture in which my mother was Abigail. It was that first one, the one taken of her unawares, the one captured before the click startled her into the mother of the birthday girl, owner of the happy dog, wife to the loving man, and mother again to another girl and a cherished boy. Homemaker. Gardener. Sunny neighbor. My mother's eyes were oceans, and inside them there was loss. I thought I had my whole life to understand them, but that was the only day I had. Once upon Earth I saw her as Abigail, and then I let it slip effortlessly back—my fascination held in check by wanting her to be that mother and envelop me as that mother.

I was in the gazebo thinking of the photo, thinking of my mother, when Lindsey got up in the middle of the night and crept across the hall. I watched her as I would a burglar circling a house in a movie. I knew when she turned the knob to my room it would give. I knew she would get in, but what would she do in there? Already my private territory had become a no man's land in the middle of our house. My mother had not touched it. My bed was still unmade from the hurried morning of my death. My flowered hippo lay among the sheets and pillows, and so did an outfit I'd discarded before I chose the yellow bell-bottoms.

Lindsey walked across the soft rug and touched the navy skirt and red and blue crocheted vest that were two separate, heatedly despised balls. She had an orange and green vest made from the same pattern. She took the vest and spread it out flat on the bed, smoothing it. It was ugly and precious all at once. I could see that. She petted it.

Lindsey traced the outline of the gold tray I kept on my dresser, filled with pins from elections and school. My favorite was a pink pin that said "Hippy-Dippy Says Love," which I'd found in the school parking lot but had had to promise my mother I wouldn't wear. I kept a lot of pins on that tray and pinned to a giant felt banner from Indiana University, where my father had gone to school. I thought she would steal them—take one or two to wear—but she didn't. She didn't even pick them up. She just swept her fingertips over everything on the tray. Then she saw it, a tiny white corner sticking out from underneath. She pulled.

It was the picture.

A deep breath rushed out of her, and she sat down on the floor, her mouth still open and her hand still holding the picture. The tethers were rushing and whipping around her, like a canvas tent come loose from its stakes. She too, like me until the morning of that photograph, had never seen the mother-stranger. She had seen the photos right after. My mother looking tired but smiling. My mother and Holiday standing in front of the dogwood tree as the sun shot through her robe and gown. But I had wanted to be the only one in the house that knew my mother was also someone else—someone mysterious and unknown to us.

The first time I broke through, it was an accident. It was December 23, 1973.

Buckley was sleeping. My mother had taken Lindsey to the dentist. That week they had agreed that each day, as a family, they would spend time trying to move forward. My father had assigned himself the task of cleaning the upstairs guest room, which long ago had become his den.

His own father had taught him how to build ships in bottles. They were something my mother, sister, and brother couldn't care less about. It was something I adored. The den was full of them.

All day at work he counted numbers—due diligence for a Chadds Ford insurance firm—and at night he built the ships or read Civil War books to unwind. He would call me in whenever he was ready to raise the sail. By then the ship would have been glued fast to the bottom of the bottle. I would come in and my father would ask me to shut the door. Often, it seemed, the dinner bell rang immediately, as if my mother had a sixth sense for things that didn't include her. But when this sense failed her, my job was to hold the bottle for him.

"Stay steady," he'd say. "You're my first mate."

Gently he would draw the one string that still reached out of the bottle's neck, and, voilà, the sails all rose, from simple mast to clipper ship. We had our boat. I couldn't clap because I held the bottle, but I always wanted to. My father worked quickly then, burning the end of the string off inside the bottle with a coat hanger he'd heated over a candle. If he did it improperly, the ship would be ruined, or, worse still, the tiny paper sails would catch on fire and suddenly, in a giant whoosh, I would be holding a bottle of flames in my hands.

Eventually my father built a balsa wood stand to replace me. Lindsey and Buckley didn't share my fascination. After trying to create enough enthusiasm for all three of them, he gave up and retreated to his den. One ship in a bottle was equal to any other as far as the rest of my family was concerned.

But as he cleaned that day he talked to me.

"Susie, my baby, my little sailor girl," he said, "you always liked these smaller ones."

I watched him as he lined up the ships in bottles on his desk, bringing them over from the shelves where they usually sat. He used an old shirt of my mother's that had been ripped into rags and began dusting the shelves. Under his desk there were empty bottles—rows and rows of them we had collected for our future shipbuilding. In the closet were more ships—the ships he had built with his own father, ships he had built alone, and then those we had made together. Some were perfect, but their sails browned; some had sagged or toppled over after years. Then there was the one that had burst into flames in the week before my death.

He smashed that one first.

My heart seized up. He turned and saw all the others, all the years they marked and the hands that had held them. His dead father's, his dead child's. I watched him as he smashed the rest. He christened the walls and wooden chair with the news of my death, and afterward he stood in the guest room/den surrounded by green glass. The bottles, all of them, lay broken on the floor, the sails and boat bodies strewn among them. He stood in the wreckage. It was then that, without knowing how, I revealed myself. In every piece of glass, in every shard and sliver, I cast my face. My father glanced down and around him, his eyes roving across the room. Wild. It was just for a second, and then I was gone. He was quiet for a moment, and then he laughed—a howl coming up from the bottom of his stomach. He laughed so loud and deep, I shook with it in my heaven.

He left the room and went down the two doors to my bedroom. The hallway was tiny, my door like all the others, hollow enough to easily punch a fist through. He was about to smash the mirror over my dresser, rip the wallpaper down with his nails, but instead he fell against my bed, sobbing, and balled the lavender sheets up in his hands.

"Daddy?" Buckley said. My brother held the doorknob with his hand.

My father turned but was unable to stop his tears. He slid to the floor with the sheets still in his fists, and then he opened up his arms. He had to ask my brother twice, which he had never had to do before, but Buckley came to him.

My father wrapped my brother inside the sheets that smelled of me. He remembered the day I'd begged him to paint and paper my room purple. Remembered moving in the old *National Geographics* to the bottom shelves of my bookcases. (I had wanted to steep myself in wildlife photography.) Remembered when there was just one child in the house for the briefest of time until Lindsey arrived.

"You are so special to me, little man," my father said, clinging to him.

Buckley drew back and stared at my father's creased face, the fine bright spots of tears at the corners of his eyes. He nodded seriously and kissed my father's cheek. Something so divine that no one up in heaven could have made it up; the care a child took with an adult.

My father draped the sheets around Buckley's shoulders and remembered how I would fall out of the tall four-poster bed and onto the rug, never waking up. Sitting in his study in his green chair and reading a book, he would be startled by the sound of my body landing. He would get up and walk the short distance to my bedroom. He liked to watch me sleeping soundly, unchecked by nightmare or even hardwood floor. He swore in those moments that his children would be kings or rulers or artists or doctors or wildlife photographers. Anything they dreamed they could be.

A few months before I died, he had found me like this, but tucked inside my sheets with me was Buckley, in his pajamas, with his bear, curled up against my back, sucking sleepily on his thumb. My father had felt in that moment the first flicker of the strange sad mortality of being a father. His life had given birth to three children, so the number calmed him. No matter what happened to Abigail or to him, the three would have one another. In that way the line he had begun seemed immortal to him, like a strong steel filament threading into the future, continuing past him no matter where he might fall off. Even in deep snowy old age.

He would find his Susie now inside his young son. Give that love to the living. He told himself this—spoke it aloud inside his brain—but my presence was like a tug on him, it dragged him back back back. He stared at the small boy he held in his arms. *"Who are you?"* he found himself asking. *"Where did you come from?"*

I watched my brother and my father. The truth was very different from what we learned in school. The truth was that the line between the living and the dead could be, it seemed, murky and blurred.

FOUR

In the hours after I was murdered, as my mother made phone calls and my father began going door to door in the neighborhood looking for me, Mr. Harvey had collapsed the hole in the cornfield and carried away a sack filled with my body parts. He passed within two houses of where my father stood talking to Mr. and Mrs. Tarking. He kept to the property line in between two rows of warring hedge—the O'Dwyers' boxwood and the Steads' goldenrod. His body brushed past the sturdy green leaves, leaving traces of me behind him, smells the Gilberts' dog would pick up and follow to find my elbow, smells the sleet and rain of the next three days would wash away before police dogs could even be thought of. He carried me back to his house, where, while he went inside to wash up, I waited for him.

After the house changed hands, the new owners tsk-tsked at the dark spot on the floor of their garage. As she brought prospective buyers through, the realtor said it was an oil stain, but it was me, seeping out of the bag Mr. Harvey carried and spilling onto the concrete. The beginning of my secret signals to the world.

It would be some time before I realized what you've undoubtedly already assumed, that I wasn't the first girl he'd killed. He knew to remove my body from the field. He knew to watch the weather and to kill during an arc of light-to-heavy precipitation because that would rob the police of evidence. But he was not as fastidious as the police liked to think. He forgot my elbow, he used a cloth sack for a bloody body, and if someone, anyone, had been watching, maybe they would have thought it strange to see their neighbor walk a property line that was a tight fit, even for children who liked to pretend the warring hedges were a hideout.

As he scoured his body in the hot water of his suburban bathroom—one with the identical layout to the one Lindsey, Buckley, and I shared—his movements were slow, not anxious. He felt a calm flood him. He kept the lights out in the bathroom and felt the warm water wash me away and he felt thoughts of me then. My muffled scream in his ear. My delicious death moan. The glorious white flesh that had never seen the sun, like an infant's, and then split, so perfectly, with the blade of his knife. He shivered under the heat, a prickling pleasure creating goose bumps up and down his arms and legs. He had put me in the waxy cloth sack and thrown in the shaving cream and razor from the mud ledge, his book of sonnets, and finally the bloody knife. They were tumbled together with my knees, fingers, and toes, but he made a note to extract them before my blood grew too sticky later that night. The sonnets and the knife, at least, he saved.

At Evensong, there were all sorts of dogs. And some of them, the ones I liked best, would lift their heads when they smelled an interesting scent in the air. If it was vivid enough, if they couldn't identify it immediately, or if, as the case may be, they knew exactly what it was—their brains going, "Um steak tartare"—they'd track it until they came to the object itself. In the face of the real article, the true story, they decided then what to do. That's how they operated. They didn't shut down their desire to know just because the smell was bad or the object was dangerous. They hunted. So did I.

Mr. Harvey took the waxy orange sack of my remains to a sinkhole eight miles from our neighborhood, an area that until recently had been desolate save for the railroad tracks and a nearby motorcycle repair shop. In his car he played a radio station that looped Christmas carols during the month of December. He whistled inside his huge station wagon and congratulated himself, felt full-up. Apple pie, cheeseburger, ice cream, coffee. Full. Better and better he was getting now, never using an old pattern that would bore him but making each kill a surprise to himself, a gift to himself.

The air inside the station wagon was cold and fragile. I could see the moist air when he exhaled, and this made me want to palpate my own stony lungs.

He drove the reed-thin road that cut between two new industrial lots. The wagon fishtailed coming up out of a particularly deep pothole, and the safe that held the sack that held my body smashed against the inside hub of the wagon's back wheel, cracking the plastic. "Damn," Mr. Harvey said. But he picked up his whistling again without pause.

I had a memory of going down this road with my father at the wheel and Buckley sitting nestled against me—one seat belt serving the two of us—in an illegal joyride away from the house.

My father had asked if any of us kids wanted to watch a refrigerator disappear.

"The earth will swallow it!" he said. He put on his hat and the dark cordovan gloves I coveted. I knew gloves meant you were an adult and mittens meant you weren't. (For Christmas 1973, my mother had bought me a pair of gloves. Lindsey ended up with them, but she knew they were mine. She left them at the edge of the cornfield one day on her way home from school. She was always doing that—bringing me things.)

"The earth has a mouth?" Buckley asked.

"A big round mouth but with no lips," my father said.

"Jack," my mother said, laughing, "stop it. Do you know I caught him outside growling at the snapdragons?"

"I'll go," I said. My father had told me that there was an abandoned underground mine and it had collapsed to create a sinkhole. I didn't care; I liked to see the earth swallow something as much as the next kid.

So when I watched Mr. Harvey take me out to the sinkhole, I couldn't help but think how smart he was. How he put the bag in a metal safe, placing me in the middle of all that weight.

It was late when he got there, and he left the safe in his Wagoneer while he approached the house of the Flanagans, who lived on the property where the sinkhole was. The Flanagans made their living by charging people to dump their appliances.

Mr. Harvey knocked on the door of the small white house and a woman came to answer it. The scent of rosemary and lamb filled my heaven and hit Mr. Harvey's nose as it trailed out from the back of the house. He could see a man in the kitchen.

"Good evening, sir," Mrs. Flanagan said. "Got an item?"

"Back of my wagon," Mr. Harvey said. He was ready with a twenty-dollar bill.

"What you got in there, a dead body?" she joked.

It was the last thing on her mind. She lived in a warm if small house. She had a husband who was always home to fix things and to be sweet on her because he never had to work, and she had a son who was still young enough to think his mother was the only thing in the world.

Mr. Harvey smiled, and, as I watched his smile break across his face, I would not look away.

"Old safe of my father's, finally got it out here," he said. "Been meaning to do it for years. No one remembers the combination."

"Anything in it?" she asked.

"Stale air."

"Back her up then. You need any help?"

"That would be lovely," he said.

The Flanagans never suspected for a moment that the girl they read about in the papers over the next few years—MISSING, FOUL PLAY SUSPECTED; ELBOW FOUND BY NEIGHBORING DOG; GIRL, 14, BELIEVED KILLED IN STOLFUZ CORNFIELD; WARNINGS TO OTHER YOUNG WOMEN; TOWNSHIP TO REZONE ADJOINING LOTS TO HIGH SCHOOL; LINDSEY SALMON, SISTER OF DEAD GIRL, GIVES VALEDICTORIAN SPEECH—could have been in the gray metal safe that a lonely man brought over one night and paid them twenty dollars to sink.

On the way back to the wagon Mr. Harvey put his hands in his pockets. There was my silver charm bracelet. He couldn't remember taking it off my wrist. Had no memory of thrusting it into the pocket of his clean pants. He fingered it, the fleshy pad of his index finger finding the smooth gold metal of the Pennsylvania keystone, the back of the ballet slipper, the tiny hole of the minuscule thimble, and the spokes of the bicycle with wheels that worked. Down Route 202, he pulled over on the shoulder, ate a liverwurst sandwich he'd prepared earlier that day, then drove to an industrial park they were building south of Downingtown. No one was on the construction lot. In those days there was no security in the suburbs. He parked his car near a Port-o-John. His excuse was prepared in the unlikely event that he needed one.

It was this part of the aftermath that I thought of when I thought of Mr. Harvey—how he wandered the muddy excavations and got lost among the dormant bulldozers, their monstrous bulk frightening in the dark. The sky of the earth was dark blue on the night following my death, and out in this open area Mr. Harvey could see for miles. I chose to stand with him, to see those miles ahead as he saw them. I wanted to go where he would go. The snow had stopped. There was wind. He walked into what his builder's instincts told him would soon be a false pond, and he stood there and fingered the charms one last time. He liked the Pennsylvania keystone, which my father had had engraved with my initials—my favorite was the tiny bike—and he pulled it off and placed it in his pocket. He threw the bracelet, with its remaining charms, into the soon-to-be man-made lake.

Two days before Christmas, I watched Mr. Harvey read a book on the Dogon and Bambara of Mali. I saw the bright spark of an idea when he was reading of the cloth and ropes they used to build shelters. He decided he wanted to build again, to experiment as he had with the hole, and he settled on a ceremonial tent like the ones described in his reading. He would gather the simple materials and raise it in a few hours in his backyard.

After smashing all the ships in bottles, my father found him there.

It was cold out, but Mr. Harvey wore only a thin cotton shirt. He had turned thirty-six that year and was experimenting with hard contacts. They made his eyes perpetually bloodshot, and many people, my father among them, believed he had taken to drink.

"What's this?" my father asked.

Despite the Salmon men's heart disease, my father was hardy. He was a bigger man than Mr. Harvey, so when he walked around the front of the green shingled house and into the backyard, where he saw Harvey erecting things that looked like goalposts,

FIVE

of me wished swift vengeance, wanted my father to turn
e man he could never have been—a man violent in rage.
what you see in movies, that's what happens in the books peo-
d. An everyman takes a gun or a knife and stalks the mur-
f his family; he does a Bronson on them and everyone cheers.
t it *was* like:
y day he got up. Before sleep wore off, he was who he used
hen, as his consciousness woke, it was as if poison seeped in.
e couldn't even get u
only movement co
d he moved, no mo
lt on him, the hand
ot there when your

father left for Mr. H
front hall next to

he seemed bluff and able. He was buzzing from having seen me in the shattered glass. I watched him cut through the lawn, ambling as school kids did on their way toward the high school. He stopped just short of brushing Mr. Harvey's elderberry hedge with his palm.

"What's this?" he asked again.

Mr. Harvey stopped long enough to look at him and then turned back to his work.

"A mat tent."

"What's that?"

"Mr. Salmon," he said, "I'm sorry for your loss."

Drawing himself up, my father gave back what the ritual demanded.

"Thank you." It was like a rock perched in his throat.

There was a moment of quiet, and then Mr. Harvey, sensing my father had no intention of leaving, asked him if he wanted to help.

So it was that, from heaven, I watched my father build a tent with the man who'd killed me.

My father did not learn much. He learned how to lash arch pieces onto pronged posts and to weave more slender rods through these pieces to form semiarches in the other direction. He learned to gather the ends of these rods and lash them to the crossbars. He learned he was doing this because Mr. Harvey had been reading about the Imezzureg tribe and had wanted to replicate their tents. He stood, confirmed in the neighborhood opinion that the man was odd. So far, that was all.

But when the basic structure was done—a one-hour job—Mr. Harvey went toward the house without giving a reason. My father assumed it was breaktime. That Mr. Harvey had gone in to get coffee or brew a pot of tea.

He was wrong. Mr. Harvey went into the house and up the stairs to check on the carving knife that he had put in his bedroom. It was still in the nightstand, on top of which he kept his sketch pad where, often, in the middle of the night, he drew the designs in his dreams. He looked inside a crumpled paper grocery sack. My blood on the blade had turned black. Remembering it, remembering his act in the hole, made him remember what he had read about a particular tribe in southern Ayr. How, when a tent was made for a newly married couple, the women of the tribe made the sheet that would cover it as beautiful as they could.

It had begun to snow outside. It was the first snow since my death, and this was not lost on my father.

"I can hear you, honey," he said to me, even though I wasn't talking. "What is it?"

I focused very hard on the dead geranium in his line of vision. I thought if I could make it bloom he would have his answer. In my heaven it bloomed. In my heaven geranium petals swirled in eddies up to my waist. On Earth nothing happened.

But through the snow I noticed this: my father was looking toward the green house in a new way. He had begun to wonder.

Inside, Mr. Harvey had donned a heavy flannel shirt, but what my father noticed first was what he carried in his arms: a stack of white cotton sheets.

"What are those for?" my father asked. Suddenly he could not stop seeing my face.

"Tarps," said Mr. Harvey. When he handed a stack to my father, the back of his hand touched my father's fingers. It was like an electric shock.

"You know something," my father said.

He met my father's eyes, held them, but did not speak.

They worked together, the snow falling, almost wafting, down. And as my father moved, his adrenaline raced. He checked what he knew. Had anyone asked this man where he was the day I disappeared? Had anyone seen this man in the cornfield? He knew his neighbors had been questioned. Methodically, the police had gone from door to door.

My father and Mr. Harvey sprea
arch, anchoring them along the sq
that linked the forked posts. Then t
straight down from these crossbar
sheets brushed the ground.

By the time they had finished, the
ered arches. It filled in the hollows
a line across the top of his belt. I ach
rush out into the snow with Holida
Lindsey on a sled, would never teach,
my little brother how to compact sn
base of his palm. I stood alone in a se
the snowflakes fell soft and blameless,

Standing inside the tent, Mr. Harve
bride would be brought to a memb
camel. When my father made a move t
his palm up.

"That's enough now," he said. "Why
The time had come for my father to thi
But all he could think of was this: "Susie," h
ond syllable whipped like a snake.

"We've just built a tent," Mr. Harve
us. We're friends now."

"You know something," my fathe
"Go home. I can't help you."

Mr. Harvey did not smile or ste
bridal tent and let the final mon
own.

he seemed bluff and able. He was buzzing from having seen me in the shattered glass. I watched him cut through the lawn, ambling as school kids did on their way toward the high school. He stopped just short of brushing Mr. Harvey's elderberry hedge with his palm.

"What's this?" he asked again.

Mr. Harvey stopped long enough to look at him and then turned back to his work.

"A mat tent."

"What's that?"

"Mr. Salmon," he said, "I'm sorry for your loss."

Drawing himself up, my father gave back what the ritual demanded.

"Thank you." It was like a rock perched in his throat.

There was a moment of quiet, and then Mr. Harvey, sensing my father had no intention of leaving, asked him if he wanted to help.

So it was that, from heaven, I watched my father build a tent with the man who'd killed me.

My father did not learn much. He learned how to lash arch pieces onto pronged posts and to weave more slender rods through these pieces to form semiarches in the other direction. He learned to gather the ends of these rods and lash them to the crossbars. He learned he was doing this because Mr. Harvey had been reading about the Imezzureg tribe and had wanted to replicate their tents. He stood, confirmed in the neighborhood opinion that the man was odd. So far, that was all.

But when the basic structure was done—a one-hour job—Mr. Harvey went toward the house without giving a reason. My father assumed it was breaktime. That Mr. Harvey had gone in to get coffee or brew a pot of tea.

He was wrong. Mr. Harvey went into the house and up the stairs to check on the carving knife that he had put in his bedroom. It was still in the nightstand, on top of which he kept his sketch pad where, often, in the middle of the night, he drew the designs in his dreams. He looked inside a crumpled paper grocery sack. My blood on the blade had turned black. Remembering it, remembering his act in the hole, made him remember what he had read about a particular tribe in southern Ayr. How, when a tent was made for a newly married couple, the women of the tribe made the sheet that would cover it as beautiful as they could.

It had begun to snow outside. It was the first snow since my death, and this was not lost on my father.

"I can hear you, honey," he said to me, even though I wasn't talking. "What is it?"

I focused very hard on the dead geranium in his line of vision. I thought if I could make it bloom he would have his answer. In my heaven it bloomed. In my heaven geranium petals swirled in eddies up to my waist. On Earth nothing happened.

But through the snow I noticed this: my father was looking toward the green house in a new way. He had begun to wonder.

Inside, Mr. Harvey had donned a heavy flannel shirt, but what my father noticed first was what he carried in his arms: a stack of white cotton sheets.

"What are those for?" my father asked. Suddenly he could not stop seeing my face.

"Tarps," said Mr. Harvey. When he handed a stack to my father, the back of his hand touched my father's fingers. It was like an electric shock.

"You know something," my father said.

He met my father's eyes, held them, but did not speak.

They worked together, the snow falling, almost wafting, down. And as my father moved, his adrenaline raced. He checked what he knew. Had anyone asked this man where he was the day I disappeared? Had anyone seen this man in the cornfield? He knew his neighbors had been questioned. Methodically, the police had gone from door to door.

My father and Mr. Harvey spread the sheets over the domed arch, anchoring them along the square formed by the crossbars that linked the forked posts. Then they hung the remaining sheets straight down from these crossbars so that the bottoms of the sheets brushed the ground.

By the time they had finished, the snow sat gingerly on the covered arches. It filled in the hollows of my father's shirt and lay in a line across the top of his belt. I ached. I realized I would never rush out into the snow with Holiday again, would never push Lindsey on a sled, would never teach, against my better judgment, my little brother how to compact snow by shaping it against the base of his palm. I stood alone in a sea of bright petals. On Earth the snowflakes fell soft and blameless, a curtain descending.

Standing inside the tent, Mr. Harvey thought of how the virgin bride would be brought to a member of the Imezzureg on a camel. When my father made a move toward him, Mr. Harvey put his palm up.

"That's enough now," he said. "Why don't you go on home?"

The time had come for my father to think of something to say. But all he could think of was this: "Susie," he whispered, the second syllable whipped like a snake.

"We've just built a tent," Mr. Harvey said. "The neighbors saw us. We're friends now."

"You know something," my father said.

"Go home. I can't help you."

Mr. Harvey did not smile or step forward. He retreated into the bridal tent and let the final monogrammed white cotton sheet fall down.

FIVE

Part of me wished swift vengeance, wanted my father to turn into the man he could never have been—a man violent in rage. That's what you see in movies, that's what happens in the books people read. An everyman takes a gun or a knife and stalks the murderer of his family; he does a Bronson on them and everyone cheers.

What it *was* like:

Every day he got up. Before sleep wore off, he was who he used to be. Then, as his consciousness woke, it was as if poison seeped in. At first he couldn't even get up. He lay there under a heavy weight. But then only movement could save him, and he moved and he moved and he moved, no movement being enough to make up for it. The guilt on him, the hand of God pressing down on him, saying, *You were not there when your daughter needed you.*

Before my father left for Mr. Harvey's, my mother had been sitting in the front hall next to the statue they'd bought of St.

Francis. She was gone when he came back. He'd called for her, said her name three times, said it like a wish that she would not appear, and then he ascended the steps to his den to jot things down in a small spiral notebook: "A drinker? Get him drunk. Maybe he's a talker." He wrote this next: "I think Susie watches me." I was ecstatic in heaven. I hugged Holly, I hugged Franny. My father knew, I thought.

Then Lindsey slammed the front door more loudly than usual, and my father was glad for the noise. He was afraid of going further in his notes, of writing the words down. The slamming door echoed down the strange afternoon he'd spent and brought him into the present, into activity, where he needed to be so he would not drown. I understood this—I'm not saying I didn't resent it, that it didn't remind me of sitting at the dinner table and having to listen to Lindsey tell my parents about the test she'd done so well on, or about how the history teacher was going to recommend her for the district honors council, but Lindsey was living, and the living deserved attention too.

She stomped up the stairs. Her clogs slammed against the pine boards of the staircase and shook the house.

I may have begrudged her my father's attention, but I respected her way of handling things. Of everyone in the family, it was Lindsey who had to deal with what Holly called the Walking Dead Syndrome—when other people see the dead person and don't see you.

When people looked at Lindsey, even my father and mother, they saw me. Even Lindsey was not immune. She avoided mirrors. She now took her showers in the dark.

She would leave the dark shower and feel her way over to the towel rack. She would be safe in the dark—the moist steam from the shower still rising off the tiles encased her. If the house was quiet or if she heard murmurs below her, she knew she would be undisturbed. This was when she could think of me and she did so in two ways: she either thought *Susie,* just that one word, and cried there, letting her tears roll down her already damp cheeks, knowing no one would see her, no one would quantify this dangerous substance as grief, or she would imagine me running, imagine me getting away, imagine herself being taken instead, fighting until she was free. She fought back the constant question, *Where is Susie now?*

My father listened to Lindsey in her room. Bang, the door was slammed shut. Thump, her books were thrown down. Squeak, she fell onto her bed. Her clogs, boom, boom, were kicked off onto the floor. A few minutes later he stood outside her door.

"Lindsey," he said upon knocking.

There was no answer.

"Lindsey, can I come in?"

"Go away," came her resolute answer.

"Come on now, honey," he pleaded.

"Go away!"

"Lindsey," my father said, sucking in his breath, "why can't you let me in?" He placed his forehead gently against the bedroom door. The wood felt cool and, for a second, he forgot the pounding of his temples, the suspicion he now held that kept repeating itself. *Harvey, Harvey, Harvey.*

In sock feet, Lindsey came silently to the door. She unlocked it as my father drew back and prepared a face that he hoped said "Don't run."

"What?" she said. Her face was rigid, an affront. "What is it?"

"I want to know how you are," he said. He thought of the curtain falling between him and Mr. Harvey, how a certain capture, a lovely blame, was lost to him. He had his family walking through the streets, going to school, passing, on their way, Mr. Harvey's green-shingled house. To get the blood back in his heart he needed his child.

"I want to be alone," Lindsey said. "Isn't that obvious?"

"I'm here if you need me," he said.

"Look, Dad," my sister said, making her one concession for him, "I'm handling this alone."

What could he do with that? He could have broken the code and said, "I'm not, I can't, don't make me," but he stood there for a second and then retreated. "I understand," he said first, although he didn't.

I wanted to lift him up, like statues I'd seen in art history books. A woman lifting up a man. The rescue in reverse. Daughter to father saying, "It's okay. You're okay. Now I won't let anything hurt."

Instead, I watched him as he went to place a call to Len Fenerman.

The police in those first weeks were almost reverent. Missing dead girls were not a common occurrence in the suburbs. But with no leads coming in on where my body was or who had killed me, the police were getting nervous. There was a window of time during which physical evidence was usually found; that window grew smaller every day.

"I don't want to sound irrational, Detective Fenerman," my father said.

"Len, please." Tucked in the corner of his desk blotter was the school picture Len Fenerman had taken from my mother. He had known, before anyone said the words, that I was already dead.

"I'm certain there's a man in the neighborhood who knows something," my father said. He was staring out the window of his upstairs den, toward the cornfield. The man who owned it had told the press he was going to let it sit fallow for now.

"Who is it, and what led you to believe this?" Len Fenerman asked. He chose a stubby, chewed pencil from the front metal lip of his desk drawer.

My father told him about the tent, about how Mr. Harvey had told him to go home, about saying my name, about how weird the neighborhood thought Mr. Harvey was with no regular job and no kids.

"I'll check it out," Len Fenerman said, because he had to. That was the role he played in the dance. But what my father had given him offered him little or nothing to work with. "Don't talk to anyone and don't approach him again," Len warned.

When my father hung up the phone he felt strangely empty. Drained, he opened the door to his den and closed it quietly behind him. In the hallway, for the second time, he called my mother's name: "Abigail."

She was in the downstairs bathroom, sneaking bites from the macaroons my father's firm always sent us for Christmas. She ate them greedily; they were like suns bursting open in her mouth. The summer she was pregnant with me, she wore one gingham maternity dress over and over, refusing to spend money on another, and ate all she wanted, rubbing her belly and saying, "Thank you, baby," as she dribbled chocolate on her breasts.

There was a knock down low on the door.

"Momma?" She stuffed the macaroons back in the medicine cabinet, swallowing what was already in her mouth.

"Momma?" Buckley repeated. His voice was sleepy.

"Mommmmm-maaa!"

She despised the word.

When my mother opened the door, my little brother held on to her knees. Buckley pressed his face into the flesh above them.

Hearing movement, my father went to meet my mother in the kitchen. Together they took solace in attending to Buckley.

"Where's Susie?" Buckley asked as my father spread Fluffernutter on wheat bread. He made three. One for himself, one for my mother, and one for his four-year-old son.

"Did you put away your game?" my father asked Buckley,

wondering why he persisted in avoiding the topic with the one person who approached it head-on.

"What's wrong with Mommy?" Buckley asked. Together they watched my mother, who was staring into the dry basin of the sink.

"How would you like to go to the zoo this week?" my father asked. He hated himself for it. Hated the bribe and the tease—the deceit. But how could he tell his son that, somewhere, his big sister might lie in pieces?

But Buckley heard the word *zoo* and all that it meant—which to him was largely *Monkeys!*—and he began on the rippling path to forgetting for one more day. The shadow of years was not as big on his small body. He knew I was away, but when people left they always came back.

When Len Fenerman had gone door to door in the neighborhood he had found nothing remarkable at George Harvey's. Mr. Harvey was a single man who, it was said, had meant to move in with his wife. She had died sometime before this. He built dollhouses for specialty stores and kept to himself. That was all anyone knew. Though friendships had not exactly blossomed around him, the sympathy of the neighborhood had always been with him. Each split-level contained a narrative. To Len Fenerman especially, George Harvey's seemed a compelling one.

No, Harvey said, he didn't know the Salmons well. Had seen the children. Everyone knew who had children and who didn't, he noted, his head hanging down and to the left a bit. "You can see the toys in the yard. The houses are always more lively," he noted, his voice halting.

"I understand you had a conversation with Mr. Salmon recently," Len said on his second trip to the dark green house.

"Yes, is there something wrong?" Mr. Harvey asked. He

squinted at Len but then had to pause. "Let me get my glasses," he said. "I was doing some close work on a Second Empire."

"Second Empire?" Len asked.

"Now that my Christmas orders are done, I can experiment," Mr. Harvey said. Len followed him into the back, where a dining table was pushed against a wall. Dozens of small lengths of what looked like miniature wainscoting were lined up on top of it.

A little strange, Fenerman thought, *but it doesn't make the man a murderer.*

Mr. Harvey got his glasses and immediately opened up. "Yes, Mr. Salmon was on one of his walks and he helped me build the bridal tent."

"The bridal tent?"

"Each year it's something I do for Leah," he said. "My wife. I'm a widower."

Len felt he was intruding on this man's private rituals. "So I understand," he said.

"I feel terrible about what happened to that girl," Mr. Harvey said. "I tried to express that to Mr. Salmon. But I know from experience that nothing makes sense at a time like this."

"So you erect this tent every year?" Len Fenerman asked. This was something he could get confirmation on from neighbors.

"In the past, I've done it inside, but I tried to do it outside this year. We were married in the winter. Until the snow picked up, I thought it would work."

"Where inside?"

"The basement. I can show you if you want. I have all of Leah's things down there still."

But Len did not go further.

"I've intruded enough," he said. "I just wanted to sweep the neighborhood a second time."

"How's your investigation coming?" Mr. Harvey asked. "Are you finding anything?"

Len never liked questions like this, though he supposed they were the right of the people whose lives he was invading.

"Sometimes I think clues find their way in good time," he said. "If they want to be found, that is." It was cryptic, sort of a Confucius-says answer, but it worked on almost every civilian.

"Have you talked to the Ellis boy?" Mr. Harvey asked.

"We talked to the family."

"He's hurt some animals in the neighborhood, I hear."

"He sounds like a bad kid, I grant you," said Len, "but he was working in the mall at the time."

"Witnesses?"

"Yes."

"That's my only idea," Mr. Harvey said. "I wish I could do more."

Len felt him to be sincere.

"He's certainly a bit tweaked at an angle," Len said when he called my father, "but I have nothing on him."

"What did he say about the tent?"

"That he built it for Leah, his wife."

"I remember Mrs. Stead told Abigail his wife's name was Sophie," my father said.

Len checked his notes. "No, Leah. I wrote it down."

My father doubted himself. Where had he gotten the name Sophie? He was sure he had heard it too, but that was years ago, at a block party, where the names of children and wives flew about like confetti between the stories people told to be neighborly and the introductions to infants and strangers too vague to remember the following day.

He did remember that Mr. Harvey had not come to the block party. He had never come to any of them. This went to his strangeness by the standards of many in the neighborhood but not by my father's own standards. He had never felt completely comfortable at these forced efforts of conviviality himself.

My father wrote "Leah?" in his book. Then he wrote, "Sophie?" Though unaware of it, he had begun a list of the dead.

On Christmas Day, my family would have been more comfortable in heaven. Christmas was largely ignored in my heaven. Some people dressed all in white and pretended they were snowflakes, but other than that, nothing.

That Christmas, Samuel Heckler came to our house on an unexpected visit. He was not dressed like a snowflake. He wore his older brother's leather jacket and a pair of ill-fitting army fatigues.

My brother was in the front room with his toys. My mother blessed the fact that she had gone early to buy his gifts. Lindsey got gloves and cherry-flavored lip gloss. My father got five white handkerchiefs that she'd ordered months ago in the mail. Save Buckley, no one wanted anything anyway. In the days before Christmas the lights on the tree were not plugged in. Only the candle that my father kept in the window of his den burned. He lit it after dark, but my mother, sister, and brother had stopped leaving the house after four o'clock. Only I saw it.

"There's a man outside!" my brother shouted. He'd been playing Skyscraper and it had yet to collapse. "He's got a suitcase."

My mother left her eggnog in the kitchen and came to the front of the house. Lindsey was suffering the mandatory presence in the family room that all holidays required. She and my father played Monopoly, ignoring the more brutal squares for each other's sake. There was no Luxury Tax, and a bad Chance wasn't recognized.

In the front hall my mother pressed her hands down along her skirt. She placed Buckley in front of her and put her arms on his shoulders.

"Wait for the man to knock," she said.

"Maybe it's Reverend Strick," my father said to Lindsey,

collecting his fifteen dollars for winning second prize in a beauty contest.

"For Susie's sake, I hope not," Lindsey ventured.

My father held on to it, on to my sister saying my name. She rolled doubles and moved to Marvin Gardens.

"That's twenty-four dollars," my father said, "but I'll take ten."

"Lindsey," my mother called. "It's a visitor for you."

My father watched my sister get up and leave the room. We both did. I sat with my father then. I was the ghost on the board. He stared at the old shoe lying on its side in the box. If only I could have lifted it up, made it hop from Boardwalk to Baltic, where I always claimed the better people lived. "That's because you're a purple freak," Lindsey would say. My father would say, "I'm proud I didn't raise a snob."

"Railroads, Susie," he said. "You always liked owning those railroads."

To accentuate his widow's peak and tame his cowlick, Samuel Heckler insisted on combing his hair straight back. This made him look, at thirteen and dressed in black leather, like an adolescent vampire.

"Merry Christmas, Lindsey," he said to my sister, and held out a small box wrapped in blue paper.

I could see it happen: Lindsey's body began to knot. She was working hard keeping everyone out, everyone, but she found Samuel Heckler cute. Her heart, like an ingredient in a recipe, was reduced, and regardless of my death she was thirteen, he was cute, and he had visited her on Christmas Day.

"I heard you made gifted," he said to her, because no one was talking. "Me too."

My mother remembered then, and she switched on her autopilot hostess. "Would you like to come sit?" she managed. "I have some eggnog in the kitchen."

"That would be wonderful," Samuel Heckler said and, to Lindsey's amazement and mine, offered my sister his arm.

"What's that?" asked Buckley, trailing behind and pointing to what he thought was a suitcase.

"An alto," Samuel Heckler said.

"What?" asked Buckley.

Lindsey spoke then. "Samuel plays the alto saxophone."

"Barely," Samuel said.

My brother did not ask what a saxophone was. He knew what Lindsey was being. She was being what I called snooty-wooty, as in "Buckley, don't worry, Lindsey's being snooty-wooty." Usually I'd tickle him as I said the word, sometimes burrowing into his stomach with my head, butting him and saying "snooty-wooty" over and over until his trills of laughter flowed down over me.

Buckley followed the three of them into the kitchen and asked, as he had at least once a day, "Where's Susie?"

They were silent. Samuel looked at Lindsey.

"Buckley," my father called from the adjoining room, "come play Monopoly with me."

My brother had never been invited to play Monopoly. Everyone said he was too young, but this was the magic of Christmas. He rushed into the family room, and my father picked him up and sat him on his lap.

"See this shoe?" my father said.

Buckley nodded his head.

"I want you to listen to everything I say about it, okay?"

"Susie?" my brother asked, somehow connecting the two.

"Yes, I'm going to tell you where Susie is."

I began to cry up in heaven. What else was there for me to do?

"This shoe was the piece Susie played Monopoly with," he said. "I play with the car or sometimes the wheelbarrow. Lindsey plays with the iron, and when your mother plays, she likes the cannon."

"Is that a dog?"

"Yes, that's a Scottie."

"Mine!"

"Okay," my father said. He was patient. He had found a way to explain it. He held his son in his lap, and as he spoke, he felt Buckley's small body on his knee—the very human, very warm, very alive weight of it. It comforted him. "The Scottie will be your piece from now on. Which piece is Susie's again?"

"The shoe," Buckley said.

"Right, and I'm the car, your sister's the iron, and your mother is the cannon."

My brother concentrated very hard.

"Now let's put all the pieces on the board, okay? You go ahead and do it for me."

Buckley grabbed a fist of pieces and then another, until all the pieces lay between the Chance and Community Chest cards.

"Let's say the other pieces are our friends."

"Like Nate?"

"Right, we'll make your friend Nate the hat. And the board is the world. Now if I were to tell you that when I rolled the dice, one of the pieces would be taken away, what would that mean?"

"They can't play anymore?"

"Right."

"Why?" Buckley asked.

He looked up at my father; my father flinched.

"Why?" my brother asked again.

My father did not want to say "because life is unfair" or "because that's how it is." He wanted something neat, something that could explain death to a four-year-old. He placed his hand on the small of Buckley's back.

"Susie is dead," he said now, unable to make it fit in the rules of any game. "Do you know what that means?"

Buckley reached over with his hand and covered the shoe. He looked up to see if his answer was right.

My father nodded. "You won't see Susie anymore, honey. None of us will." My father cried. Buckley looked up into the eyes of our father and did not fully understand.

Buckley kept the shoe on his dresser, until one day it wasn't there anymore and no amount of looking for it could turn it up.

In the kitchen my mother finished her eggnog and excused herself. She went into the dining room and counted silverware, methodically laying out the three kinds of forks, the knives, and the spoons, making them "climb the stairs" as she'd been taught when she worked in Wanamaker's bridal shop before I was born. She wanted a cigarette and for her children who were living to disappear for a little while.

"Are you going to open your gift?" Samuel Heckler asked my sister.

They stood at the counter, leaning against the dishwasher and the drawers that held napkins and towels. In the room to their right sat my father and brother; on the other side of the kitchen, my mother was thinking Wedgwood Florentine, Cobalt Blue; Royal Worcester, Mountbatten; Lenox, Eternal.

Lindsey smiled and pulled at the white ribbon on top of the box.

"My mom did the ribbon for me," Samuel Heckler said.

She tore the blue paper away from the black velvet box. Carefully she held it in her palm once the paper was off. In heaven I was excited. When Lindsey and I played Barbies, Barbie and Ken got married at sixteen. To us there was only one true love in everyone's life; we had no concept of compromise, or retrys.

"Open it," Samuel Heckler said.

"I'm scared."

"Don't be."

He put his hand on her forearm and—Wow!—what I felt

when he did that. Lindsey had a cute boy in the kitchen, vampire or no! This was news, this was a bulletin—I was suddenly privy to everything. She never would have told me any of this stuff.

What the box held was typical or disappointing or miraculous depending on the eye. It was typical because he was a thirteen-year-old boy, or it was disappointing because it was not a wedding ring, or it was miraculous. He'd given her a half a heart. It was gold and from inside his Hukapoo shirt, he pulled out the other side. It hung around his neck on a rawhide cord.

Lindsey's face flushed; mine flushed up in heaven.

I forgot my father in the family room and my mother counting silver. I saw Lindsey move toward Samuel Heckler. She kissed him; it was glorious. I was almost alive again.

SIX

Two weeks before my death, I left the house later than usual, and by the time I reached the school, the blacktop circle where the school buses usually hovered was empty.

A hall monitor from the discipline office would write down your name if you tried to get in the front doors after the first bell rang, and I didn't want to be paged during class to come and sit on the hard bench outside Mr. Peterford's room, where, it was widely known, he would bend you over and paddle your behind with a board. He'd asked the shop teacher to drill holes into it for less wind resistance on the downstroke and more pain when it landed against your jeans.

I had never been late enough or done anything bad enough to meet the board, but in my mind as in every other kid's I could visualize it so well my butt would sting. Clarissa had told me that the baby stoners, as they were called in junior high, used the back door to the stage, which was always left open by Cleo, the janitor, who had dropped out of high school as a full-blown stoner.

So that day I crept into the backstage area, watching my step, careful not to trip over the various cords and wires. I paused near some scaffolding and put down my book bag to brush my hair. I'd taken to leaving the house in the jingle-bell cap and then switching, as soon as I gained cover behind the O'Dwyers' house, to an old black watch cap of my father's. All this left my hair full of static electricity, and my first stop was usually the girls' room, where I would brush it flat.

"You are beautiful, Susie Salmon."

I heard the voice but could not place it immediately. I looked around me.

"Here," the voice said.

I looked up and saw the head and torso of Ray Singh leaning out over the top of the scaffold above me.

"Hello," he said.

I knew Ray Singh had a crush on me. He had moved from England the year before but Clarissa said he was born in India. That someone could have the face of one country and the voice of another and then move to a third was too incredible for me to fathom. It made him immediately cool. Plus, he seemed eight hundred times smarter than the rest of us, and he had a crush on me. What I finally realized were affectations—the smoking jacket that he sometimes wore to school and his foreign cigarettes, which were actually his mother's—I thought were evidence of his higher breeding. He knew and saw things that the rest of us didn't see. That morning when he spoke to me from above, my heart plunged to the floor.

"Hasn't the first bell rung?" I asked.

"I have Mr. Morton for homeroom," he said. This explained everything. Mr. Morton had a perpetual hangover, which was at its peak during homeroom. He never called roll.

"What are you doing up there?"

"Climb up and see," he said, removing his head and shoulders from my view.

I hesitated.

"Come on, Susie."

It was my one day in life of being a bad kid—of at least feigning the moves. I placed my foot on the bottom rung of the scaffold and reached my arms up to the first crossbar.

"Bring your stuff," Ray advised.

I went back for my book bag and then climbed unsteadily up.

"Let me help you," he said and put his hands under my armpits, which, even though covered by my winter parka, I was self-conscious about. I sat for a moment with my feet dangling over the side.

"Tuck them in," he said. "That way no one will see us."

I did what he told me, and then I stared at him for a moment. I felt suddenly stupid—unsure of why I was there.

"Will you stay up here all day?" I asked.

"Just until English class is over."

"You're cutting English!" It was as if he said he'd robbed a bank.

"I've seen every Shakespeare play put on by the Royal Shakespeare Company," Ray said. "That bitch has nothing to teach me."

I felt sorry for Mrs. Dewitt then. If part of being bad was calling Mrs. Dewitt a bitch, I wasn't into it.

"I like *Othello,*" I ventured.

"It's condescending twaddle the way she teaches it. A sort of *Black Like Me* version of the Moor."

Ray was smart. This combined with being an Indian from England had made him a Martian in Norristown.

"That guy in the movie looked pretty stupid with black makeup on," I said.

"You mean Sir Laurence Olivier."

Ray and I were quiet. Quiet enough to hear the bell for the end of homeroom ring and then, five minutes later, the bell that meant we should be on the first floor in Mrs. Dewitt's class. As each second passed after that bell, I could feel my skin heat up and Ray's look lengthen out over my body, taking in my royal blue parka and my kelly green miniskirt with my matching Danskin tights. My real shoes sat beside me inside my bag. On my feet I had a pair of fake sheepskin boots with dirty synthetic shearing spilling out like animal innards around the tops and seams. If I had known this was to be the sex scene of my life, I might have prepared a bit, reapplied my Strawberry-Banana Kissing Potion as I came in the door.

I could feel Ray's body leaning toward me, the scaffolding underneath us squeaking from his movement. *He is from England,* I was thinking. His lips moved closer, the scaffold listed. I was dizzy—about to go under the wave of my first kiss, when we both heard something. We froze.

Ray and I lay down side by side and stared at the lights and wires overhead. A moment later, the stage door opened and in walked Mr. Peterford and the art teacher, Miss Ryan, who we recognized by their voices. There was a third person with them.

"We are not taking disciplinary action at this time, but we will if you persist," Mr. Peterford was saying. "Miss Ryan, did you bring the materials?"

"Yes." Miss Ryan had come to Kennet from a Catholic school and taken over the art department from two ex-hippies who had been fired when the kiln exploded. Our art classes had gone from wild experiments with molten metals and throwing clay to day after day of drawing profiles of wooden figures she placed in stiff positions at the beginning of each class.

"I'm only doing the assignments." It was Ruth Connors. I recognized the voice and so did Ray. We all had Mrs. Dewitt's English class first period.

"This," Mr. Peterford said, "was not the assignment."

Ray reached for my hand and squeezed. We knew what they

were talking about. A xeroxed copy of one of Ruth's drawings had been passed around in the library until it had reached a boy at the card catalog who was overtaken by the librarian.

"If I'm not mistaken," said Miss Ryan, "there are no breasts on our anatomy model."

The drawing had been of a woman reclining with her legs crossed. And it was no wooden figure with eyehooks connecting the limbs. It was a real woman, and the charcoal smudges of her eyes—whether by accident or intent—had given her a leering look that made every kid who saw it either highly uncomfortable or quite happy, thank you.

"There isn't a nose or mouth on that wooden model either," Ruth said, "but you encouraged us to draw in faces."

Again Ray squeezed my hand.

"That's enough, young lady," Mr. Peterford said. "It is the attitude of repose in this particular drawing that clearly made it something the Nelson boy would xerox."

"Is that my fault?"

"Without the drawing there would be no problem."

"So it's my fault?"

"I invite you to realize the position this puts the school in and to assist us by drawing what Miss Ryan instructs the class to draw without making unnecessary additions."

"Leonardo da Vinci drew cadavers," Ruth said softly.

"Understood?"

"Yes," said Ruth.

The stage doors opened and shut, and a moment later Ray and I could hear Ruth Connors crying. Ray mouthed the word *go,* and I moved to the end of the scaffold, dangling my foot over the side to find a hold.

That week Ray would kiss me by my locker. It didn't happen up on the scaffold when he'd wanted it to. Our only kiss was like an accident—a beautiful gasoline rainbow.

I climbed down off the scaffold with my back to her. She didn't move or hide, just looked at me when I turned around. She was sitting on a wooden crate near the back of the stage. A pair of old curtains hung to her left. She watched me walk toward her but didn't wipe her eyes.

"Susie Salmon," she said, just to confirm it. The possibility of my cutting first period and hiding backstage in the auditorium was, until that day, as remote as the smartest girl in our class being bawled out by the discipline officer.

I stood in front of her, hat in hand.

"That's a stupid hat," she said.

I lifted the jingle-bell cap and looked at it. "I know. My mom made it."

"So you heard?"

"Can I see?"

Ruth unfolded the much-handled xerox and I stared.

Using a blue ballpoint pen, Brian Nelson had made an obscene hole where her legs were crossed. I recoiled and she watched me. I could see something flicker in her eyes, a private wondering, and then she leaned over and brought out a black leather sketchbook from her knapsack.

Inside, it was beautiful. Drawings of women mostly, but of animals and men too. I'd never seen anything like it before. Each page was covered in her drawings. I realized how subversive Ruth was then, not because she drew pictures of nude women that got misused by her peers, but because she was more talented than her teachers. She was the quietest kind of rebel. Helpless, really.

"You're really good, Ruth," I said.

"Thank you," she said, and I kept looking through the pages of her book and drinking it in. I was both frightened and excited by what existed underneath the black line of the navel in those drawings—what my mother called the "baby-making machinery."

I told Lindsey I'd never have one, and when I was ten I'd spent the better part of six months telling any adult who would listen that I intended on getting my tubes tied. I didn't know what this meant, exactly, but I knew it was drastic, required surgery, and it made my father laugh out loud.

Ruth went from weird to special for me then. The drawings were so good that in that moment I forgot the rules of school, all the bells and whistles, which as kids we were supposed to respond to.

After the cornfield was roped off, searched, then abandoned, Ruth went walking there. She would wrap a large wool shawl of her grandmother's around her under the ratty old peacoat of her father's. Soon she noted that teachers in subjects besides gym didn't report her if she cut. They were happy not to have her there: her intelligence made her a problem. It demanded attention and rushed their lesson plans forward.

And she began to take rides from her father in the mornings to avoid the bus. He left very early and brought his red metal, sloped-top lunchbox, which he had allowed her to pretend was a barn for her Barbies when she was little, and in which he now tucked bourbon. Before he let her out in the empty parking lot, he would stop his truck but keep the heater running.

"Going to be okay today?" he always asked.

Ruth nodded.

"One for the road?"

And without nodding this time she handed him the lunchbox. He opened it, unscrewed the bourbon, took a deep swallow, and then passed it to her. She threw her head back dramatically and either placed her tongue against the glass so very little would make it to her mouth, or took a small, wincing gulp if he was watching her.

She slid out of the high cab. It was cold, bitterly cold, before the sun rose. Then she remembered a fact from one of our classes:

people moving are warmer than people at rest. So she began to walk directly to the cornfield, keeping a good pace. She talked to herself, and sometimes she thought about me. Often she would rest a moment against the chain-link fence that separated the soccer field from the track, while she watched the world come alive around her.

So we met each morning in those first few months. The sun would come up over the cornfield and Holiday, let loose by my father, would come to chase rabbits in and out of the tall dry stalks of dead corn. The rabbits loved the trimmed lawns of the athletic fields, and as Ruth approached she'd see their dark forms line up along the white chalk of the farthest boundaries like some sort of tiny sports team. She liked the idea of this and I did too. She believed stuffed animals moved at night when humans went to sleep. She still thought in her father's lunchbox there might be minute cows and sheep that found time to graze on the bourbon and baloney.

When Lindsey left the gloves from Christmas for me, in between the farthest boundary of the soccer field and the cornfield, I looked down one morning to see the rabbits investigate: sniff at the corners of the gloves lined with their own kin. Then I saw Ruth pick them up before Holiday grabbed them. She turned the bottom of one glove so the fur faced out and held it up to her cheek. She looked up to the sky and said, "Thank you." I liked to think she was talking to me.

I grew to love Ruth on those mornings, feeling that in some way we could never explain on our opposite sides of the Inbetween, we were born to keep each other company. Odd girls who had found each other in the strangest way—in the shiver she had felt when I passed.

Ray was a walker, like me, living at the far end of our development, which surrounded the school. He had seen Ruth Connors walking alone out on the soccer fields. Since Christmas he had come and gone to school as quickly as he could, never lingering. He wanted my killer to be caught almost as much as my parents did. Until he was, Ray could not wipe the traces of suspicion off himself, despite his alibi.

He chose a morning when his father was not going to work at the university and filled his father's thermos with his mother's sweet tea. He left early to wait for Ruth and made a little camp of the cement shot-put circle, sitting on the metal curve against which the shot-putters braced their feet.

When he saw her walking on the other side of the chain-link fence that separated the school from the soccer field and inside which was the most revered of the sports fields—the football one—he rubbed his hands together and prepared what he wanted to say. His bravery this time came not from having kissed me—a goal he'd set himself a full year before its completion—but from being, at fourteen, intensely lonely.

I watched Ruth approach the soccer field, thinking she was alone. In an old home her father had gone to scavenge, he had found her a treat to go along with her new hobby—an anthology of poems. She held them close.

She saw Ray stand up when she was still some distance away.

"Hello, Ruth Connors!" he called and waved his arms.

Ruth looked over, and his name came into her head: Ray Singh. But she didn't know much more than that. She had heard the rumors about the police being over at his house, but she believed what her father had said—"No kid did that"—and so she walked over to him.

"I prepared tea and have it in my thermos here," Ray said. I blushed for him up in heaven. He was smart when it came to *Othello,* but now he was acting like a geek.

"No thank you," Ruth said. She stood near him but with a definite few feet more than usual still in between. Her fingernails were pressed into the worn cover of the poetry anthology.

"I was there that day, when you and Susie talked backstage," Ray said. He held the thermos out to her. She made no move closer and didn't respond.

"Susie Salmon," he clarified.

"I know who you mean," she said.

"Are you going to the memorial service?"

"I didn't know there was one," she said.

"I don't think I'm going."

I was staring hard at his lips. They were redder than usual from the cold. Ruth took a step forward.

"Do you want some lip balm?" Ruth asked.

Ray lifted his wool gloves up to his lips, where they snagged briefly on the chapped surface that I had kissed. Ruth dug her hands in the peacoat pocket and pulled out her Chap Stick. "Here," she said, "I have tons of them. You can keep it."

"That's so nice," he said. "Will you at least sit with me until the buses come?"

They sat together on the shot-putters' cement platform. Again I was seeing something I never would have seen: the two of them together. It made Ray more attractive to me than he had ever been. His eyes were the darkest gray. When I watched him from heaven I did not hesitate to fall inside of them.

It became a ritual for the two of them. On the days that his father taught, Ruth brought him a little bourbon in her father's flask; otherwise they had sweet tea. They were cold as hell, but that didn't seem to matter to them.

They talked about what it was like to be a foreigner in Norristown. They read poems aloud from Ruth's anthology. They talked about how to become what they wanted to be. A doctor for Ray. A painter/poet for Ruth. They made a secret club of the other oddballs they could point out in our class. There were the obvious ones like Mike Bayles, who had taken so much acid no one understood how he was still in school, or Jeremiah, who was from Louisiana and so just as much a foreigner as Ray. Then there were the quiet ones. Artie, who talked excitedly to anyone about the effects of formaldehyde. Harry Orland, who was so painfully shy he wore his gym shorts over his jeans. And Vicki Kurtz, who everyone thought was okay after the death of her mother, but whom Ruth had seen sleeping in a bed of pine needles behind the junior high's regulating plant. And, sometimes, they would talk about me.

"It's so strange," Ruth said. "I mean, it's like we were in the same class since kindergarten but that day backstage in the auditorium was the first time we ever looked at each other."

"She was great," Ray said. He thought of our lips brushing past one another as we stood alone in a column of lockers. How I had smiled with my eyes closed and then almost run away. "Do you think they'll find him?"

"I guess so. You know, we're only like one hundred yards away from where it happened."

"I know," he said.

They both sat on the thin metal rim of the shot-putters' brace, holding tea in their gloved hands. The cornfield had become a place no one went. When a ball strayed from the soccer field, a boy took a dare to go in and get it. That morning the sun was slicing right through the dead stalks as it rose, but there was no heat from it.

"I found these here," she said, indicating the leather gloves.

"Do you ever think about her?" he asked.

They were quiet again.

"All the time," Ruth said. A chill ran down my spine. "Sometimes I think she's lucky, you know. I hate this place."

"Me too," Ray said. "But I've lived other places. This is just a temporary hell, not a permanent one."

"You're not implying . . ."

"She's in heaven, if you believe in that stuff."

"You don't?"

"I don't think so, no."

"I do," Ruth said. "I don't mean la-la angel-wing crap, but I do think there's a heaven."

"Is she happy?"

"It *is* heaven, right?"

"But what does that mean?"

The tea was stone-cold and the first bell had already rung. Ruth smiled into her cup. "Well, as my dad would say, it means she's out of this shithole."

When my father knocked on the door of Ray Singh's house, he was struck dumb by Ray's mother, Ruana. It was not that she was immediately welcoming, and she was far from sunny, but something about her dark hair, and her gray eyes, and even the strange way she seemed to step back from the door once she opened it, all of these things overwhelmed him.

He had heard the offhand comments the police made about her. To their mind she was cold and snobbish, condescending, odd. And so that was what he imagined he would find.

"Come in and sit," she'd said to him when he pronounced his name. Her eyes, on the word *Salmon,* had gone from closed to open doorways—dark rooms where he wanted to travel firsthand.

He almost lost his balance as she led him into the small cramped front room of their house. There were books on the floor with their spines facing up. They came out three rows deep from the wall. She was wearing a yellow sari and what looked like gold lamé capri pants underneath. Her feet were bare. She padded across the wall-to-wall and stopped at the couch. "Something to drink?" she asked, and he nodded his head.

"Hot or cold?"

"Hot."

As she turned the corner into a room he couldn't see, he sat down on the brown plaid couch. The windows across from him under which the books were lined were draped with long muslin curtains, which the harsh daylight outside had to fight to filter through. He felt suddenly very warm, almost close to forgetting why that morning he had double-checked the Singhs' address.

A little while later, as my father was thinking of how tired he was and how he had promised my mother to pick up some long-held dry cleaning, Mrs. Singh returned with tea on a tray and put it down on the carpet in front of him.

"We don't have much furniture, I'm afraid. Dr. Singh is still looking for tenure."

She went into an adjoining room and brought back a purple floor pillow for herself, which she placed on the floor to face him.

"Dr. Singh is a professor?" my father asked, though he knew this already, knew more than he was comfortable with about this beautiful woman and her sparsely furnished home.

"Yes," she said, and poured the tea. It was quiet. She held out a cup to him, and as he took it she said, "Ray was with him the day your daughter was killed."

He wanted to fall over into her.

"That must be why you've come," she continued.

"Yes," he said, "I want to talk to him."

"He's at school right now," she said. "You know that." Her legs in the gold pants were tucked to her side. The nails on her toes were long and unpolished, their surface gnarled from years of dancing.

"I wanted to come by and assure you I mean him no harm," my father said. I watched him. I had never seen him like this before. The words fell out of him like burdens he was delivering, back-logged verbs and nouns, but he was watching her feet curl against the dun-colored rug and the way the small pool of numbed light from the curtains touched her right cheek.

"He did nothing wrong and loved your little girl. A schoolboy crush, but still."

Schoolboy crushes happened all the time to Ray's mother. The teenager who delivered the paper would pause on his bike, hoping that she would be near the door when she heard the thump of the *Philadelphia Inquirer* hit the porch. That she would come out and, if she did, that she would wave. She didn't even have to smile, and she rarely did outside her house—it was the eyes, her dancer's carriage, the way she seemed to deliberate over the smallest movement of her body.

When the police had come they had stumbled into the dark front hall in search of a killer, but before Ray even reached the top of the stairs, Ruana had so confused them that they were agreeing to tea and sitting on silk pillows. They had expected her to fall into the grooves of the patter they relied on with all attractive women, but she only grew more erect in posture as they tried harder and harder to ingratiate themselves, and she stood upright by the windows while they questioned her son.

"I'm glad Susie had a nice boy like her," my father said. "I'll thank your son for that."

She smiled, not showing teeth.

"He wrote her a love note," he said.

"Yes."

"I wish I had known enough to do the same," he said. "Tell her I loved her on that last day."

"Yes."

"But your son did."

"Yes."

They stared at each other for a moment.

"You must have driven the policemen nuts," he said and smiled more to himself than to her.

"They came to accuse Ray," she said. "I wasn't concerned with how they felt about me."

"I imagine it's been hard for him," my father said.

"No, I won't allow that," she said sternly and placed her cup back on the tray. "You cannot have sympathy for Ray or for us."

My father tried to stutter out a protest.

She placed her hand in the air. "You have lost a daughter and come here for some purpose. I will allow you that and that only, but trying to understand our lives, no."

"I didn't mean to offend," he said. "I only . . ."

Again, the hand up.

"Ray will be home in twenty minutes. I will talk to him first and prepare him, then you may talk to my son about your daughter."

"What did I say?"

"I like that we don't have much furniture. It allows me to think that someday we might pack up and leave."

"I hope you'll stay," my father said. He said it because he had been trained to be polite from an early age, a training he passed on to me, but he also said it because part of him wanted more of her, this cold woman who was not exactly cold, this rock who was not stone.

"With all gentleness," she said, "you don't even know me. We'll wait together for Ray."

My father had left our house in the midst of a fight between Lindsey and my mother. My mother was trying to get Lindsey to go with her to the Y to swim. Without thinking, Lindsey had blared, "I'd rather die!" at the top of her lungs. My father watched as my mother froze, then burst, fleeing to their bedroom to wail behind the door. He quietly tucked his notebook in his jacket pocket, took the car keys off the hook by the back door, and snuck out.

In those first two months my mother and father moved in opposite directions from each other. One stayed in, the other went out. My father fell asleep in his den in the green chair, and when he woke he crept carefully into the bedroom and slid into bed. If my mother had most of the sheets he would lie without them, his body curled up tight, ready to spring at a moment's notice, ready for anything.

"I know who killed her," he heard himself say to Ruana Singh.

"Have you told the police?"

"Yes."

"What do they say?"

"They say that for now there is nothing but my suspicion to link him to the crime."

"A father's suspicion . . ." she began.

"Is as powerful as a mother's intuition."

This time there were teeth in her smile.

"He lives in the neighborhood."

"What are you doing?"

"I'm investigating all leads," my father said, knowing how it sounded as he said it.

"And my son . . ."

"Is a lead."

"Perhaps the other man frightens you too much."

"But I have to do something," he protested.

"Here we are again, Mr. Salmon," she said. "You misinterpret me. I am not saying you are doing the wrong thing by coming here. It is the right thing in its way. You want to find something soft, something warm in all this. Your searching led you here. That's a good thing. I am only concerned that it be good, too, for my son."

"I mean no harm."

"What is the man's name?"

"George Harvey." It was the first time he'd said it aloud to anyone but Len Fenerman.

She paused and stood. Turning her back to him, she walked over to first one window and then the other and drew the curtains back. It was the after-school light that she loved. She watched for Ray as he walked up the road.

"Ray will come now. I will go to meet him. If you'll excuse me I need to put on my coat and boots." She paused. "Mr. Salmon," she said, "I would do exactly what you are doing: I would talk to everyone I needed to, I would not tell too many people his name. When I was sure," she said, "I would find a quiet way, and I would kill him."

He could hear her in the hallway, the metal clank of hangers as she got her coat. A few minutes later the door was opened and closed. A cold breeze came in from the outside and then out on the road he could see a mother greet her son. Neither of them smiled. Their heads bent low. Their mouths moved. Ray took in the fact that my father was waiting for him inside his home.

At first my mother and I thought it was just the obvious that marked Len Fenerman as different from the rest of the force. He was smaller than the hulking uniforms who frequently accompanied him. Then there were the less obvious traits too—the way he often seemed to be thinking to himself, how he wasn't much for joking or trying to be anything but serious when he talked about me and the circumstances of the case. But, talking with my mother, Len Fenerman had shown himself for what he was: an optimist. He believed my killer would be caught.

"Maybe not today or tomorrow," he said to my mother, "but someday he'll do something uncontrollable. They are too uncontrolled in their habits not to."

My mother was left to entertain Len Fenerman until my father arrived home from the Singhs'. On the table in the family room Buckley's crayons were scattered across the butcher paper my mother had laid down. Buckley and Nate had drawn until their heads began to nod like heavy flowers, and my mother had plucked them up in her arms, first one and then the other, and brought them over to the couch. They slept there end to end with their feet almost touching in the center.

Len Fenerman knew enough to talk in hushed whispers, but he wasn't, my mother noted, a worshiper of children. He watched her carry the two boys but did not stand to help or comment on them the way the other policemen always did, defining her by her children, both living and dead.

"Jack wants to talk to you," my mother said. "But I'm sure you're too busy to wait."

"Not too busy."

I saw a black strand of her hair fall from where she had tucked it behind her ear. It softened her face. I saw Len see it too.

"He went over to that poor Ray Singh's house," she said and tucked the fallen hair back in its proper place.

"I'm sorry we had to question him," Len said.

"Yes," she said. "No young boy is capable of . . ." She couldn't say it, and he didn't make her.

"His alibi was airtight."

My mother took up a crayon from the butcher paper.

Len Fenerman watched my mother draw stick figures and stick dogs. Buckley and Nate made quiet sounds of sleep on the couch. My brother curled up into a fetal position and a moment later placed his thumb in his mouth to suck. It was a habit my mother had told us all we must help him break. Now she envied such easy peace.

"You remind me of my wife," Len said after a long silence, during which my mother had drawn an orange poodle and what looked like a blue horse undergoing electroshock treatment.

"She can't draw either?"

"She wasn't much of a talker when there was nothing to say."

A few more minutes passed. A yellow ball of sun. A brown house with flowers outside the door—pink, blue, purple.

"You used the past tense."

They both heard the garage door. "She died soon after we were married," he said.

"Daddy!" Buckley yelled, and leapt up, forgetting Nate and everyone else.

"I'm sorry," she said to Len.

"I am too," he said, "about Susie. Really."

In the back hall my father greeted Buckley and Nate with high cheers and calls for "Oxygen!" as he always did when we besieged him after a long day. Even if it felt false, elevating his mood for my brother was often the favorite part of his day.

My mother stared at Len Fenerman while my father walked toward the family room from the back. *Rush to the sink,* I felt like saying to her, stare down the hole and look into the earth. I'm down there waiting; I'm up here watching.

Len Fenerman had been the one that first asked my mother for my school picture when the police thought I might be found alive. In his wallet, my photo sat in a stack. Among these dead children and strangers was a picture of his wife. If a case had been solved he had written the date of its resolution on the back of the photo. If the case was still open—in his mind if not in the official files of the police—it was blank. There was nothing on the back of mine. There was nothing on his wife's.

"Len, how are you?" my father asked. Holiday up and wiggling back and forth for my father to pet him.

"I hear you went to see Ray Singh," Len said.

"Boys, why don't you go play up in Buckley's room?" my mother suggested. "Detective Fenerman and Daddy need to talk."

SEVEN

"Do you see her?" Buckley asked Nate as they climbed the stairs, Holiday in tow. "That's my sister."

"No," Nate said.

"She was gone for a while, but now she's back. Race!"

And the three of them—two boys and a dog—raced the rest of the way up the long curve of the staircase.

I had never even let myself yearn for Buckley, afraid he might see my image in a mirror or a bottle cap. Like everyone else I was trying to protect him. "Too young," I said to Franny. "Where do you think imaginary friends come from?" she said.

For a few minutes the two boys sat under the framed grave rubbing outside my parents' room. It was from a tomb in a London graveyard. My mother had told Lindsey and me the story of how my father and she had wanted things to hang on their walls and an old woman they met on their honeymoon had taught them how to do grave rubbings. By the time I was in double digits most of the grave rubbings had been put down in the basement for storage, the spots on our suburban walls replaced with bright graphic prints meant to stimulate children. But Lindsey and I loved the grave rubbings, particularly the one under which Nate and Buckley sat that afternoon.

Lindsey and I would lie down on the floor underneath it. I would pretend to be the knight that was pictured, and Holiday was the faithful dog curled up at his feet. Lindsey would be the wife he'd left behind. It always dissolved into giggles no matter how solemn the start. Lindsey would tell the dead knight that a wife had to move on, that she couldn't be trapped for the rest of her life by a man who was frozen in time. I would act stormy and mad, but it never lasted. Eventually she would describe her new lover: the fat butcher who gave her prime cuts of meat, the agile blacksmith who made her hooks. "You are dead, knight," she would say. "Time to move on."

"Last night she came in and kissed me on the cheek," Buckley said.

"Did not."

"Did too."

"Really?"

"Yeah."

"Have you told your mom?"

"It's a secret," Buckley said. "Susie told me she isn't ready to talk to them yet. Do you want to see something else?"

"Sure," said Nate.

The two of them stood up to go to the children's side of the house, leaving Holiday asleep under the grave rubbing.

"Come look," Buckley said.

They were in my room. The picture of my mother had been taken by Lindsey. After reconsideration, she had come back for the "Hippy-Dippy Says Love" button too.

"Susie's room," Nate said.

Buckley put his fingers to his lips. He'd seen my mother do this when she wanted us to be quiet, and now he wanted that from Nate. He got down on his belly and gestured for Nate to follow, and they wriggled like Holiday as they made their way beneath the dust ruffle of my bed into my secret storage space.

In the material that was stretched on the underside of the box spring, there was a hole, and stuffed up inside were things I didn't want anyone else to see. I had to guard it from Holiday or he would scratch at it to try and pry the objects loose. This had been exactly what happened twenty-four hours after I went missing. My parents had searched my room hoping to find a note of explanation and then left the door open. Holiday had carried off the licorice I kept there. Strewn beneath my bed were the objects I'd kept hidden, and one of them only Buckley and Nate would recognize. Buckley unwrapped an old handkerchief of my father's and there it was, the stained and bloody twig.

The year before, a three-year-old Buckley had swallowed it. Nate and he had been shoving rocks up their noses in our backyard, and Buckley had found a small twig under the oak tree where my mother strung one end of the clothesline. He put the stick in his mouth like a cigarette. I watched him from the roof outside my bedroom window, where I was sitting painting my toenails with Clarissa's Magenta Glitter and reading *Seventeen.*

I was perpetually assigned the job of watching out for little brother. Lindsey was not thought to be old enough. Besides, she was a burgeoning brain, which meant she got to be free to do things like spend that summer afternoon drawing detailed pictures of a fly's eye on graph paper with her 130-pack of Prisma Colors.

It was not too hot out and it was summer, and I was going to spend my internment at home beautifying. I had begun the morning by showering, shampooing, and steaming myself. On the roof I air-dried and applied lacquer.

I had on two coats of Magenta Glitter when a fly landed on the bottle's applicator. I heard Nate making dare and threat sounds, and I squinted at the fly to try to make out all the quadrants of his eyes that Lindsey was coloring inside the house. A breeze came up, blowing the fringe on my cutoffs against my thighs.

"Susie, Susie!" Nate was yelling.

I looked down to see Buckley on the ground.

It was this day that I always told Holly about when we talked about rescue. I believed it was possible; she did not.

I swung my legs around and scrambled through my open window, one foot landing on the sewing stool and the other immediately in front of that one and on the braided rug and then down on my knees and out of the blocks like an athlete. I ran down the hall and slid down the banister as we'd been forbidden to do. I called Lindsey's name and then forgot her, ran out to the backyard through the screened-in porch, and jumped over the dog fence to the oak tree.

Buckley was choking, his body bucking, and I carried him with Nate trailing into the garage, where my father's precious Mustang sat. I had watched my parents drive, and my mother had shown me how a car went from park to reverse. I put Buckley in the back and grabbed the keys from the unused terra-cotta pots where my father hid them. I sped all the way to the hospital. I burned out the emergency brake, but no one seemed to care.

"If she hadn't been there," the doctor later told my mother, "you would have lost your little boy."

Grandma Lynn predicted I'd have a long life because I had saved my brother's. As usual, Grandma Lynn was wrong.

"Wow," Nate said, holding the twig and marveling at how over time red blood turned black.

"Yeah," said Buckley. His stomach felt queasy with the memory of it. How much pain he had been in, how the faces of the adults changed as they surrounded him in the huge hospital bed. He had seen them that serious only one other time. But whereas in the hospital, their eyes had been worried and then later not, shot through with so much light and relief that they'd enveloped him, now our parents' eyes had gone flat and not returned.

I felt faint in heaven that day. I reeled back in the gazebo, and my eyes snapped open. It was dark, and across from me stood a large building that I had never been in.

I had read *James and the Giant Peach* when I was little. The building looked like the house of his aunts. Huge and dark and Victorian. It had a widow's walk. For a moment, as I readjusted to the darkness, I thought I saw a long row of women standing on the widow's walk and pointing my way. But a moment later, I saw differently. Crows were lined up, their beaks holding crooked twigs. As I stood to go back to the duplex, they took wing and followed me. Had my brother really seen me somehow, or was he merely a little boy telling beautiful lies?

EIGHT

For three months Mr. Harvey dreamed of buildings. He saw a slice of Yugoslavia where thatched-roofed dwellings on stilts gave way to rushing torrents of water from below. There were blue skies overhead. Along the fjords and in the hidden valley of Norway, he saw wooden stave churches, the timbers of which had been carved by Viking boat-builders. Dragons and local heroes made from wood. But there was one building, from the Vologda, that he dreamed about most: the Church of the Transfiguration. And it was this dream—his favorite—that he had on the night of my murder and on the nights following until the others came back. The *not still* dreams—the ones of women and children.

I could see all the way back to Mr. Harvey in his mother's arms, staring out over a table covered with pieces of colored glass. His father sorted them into piles by shape and size, depth and weight. His father's jeweler's eyes looked deeply into each specimen for cracks and flaws. And George Harvey would turn his attention to the single jewel that hung from his mother's neck, a large oval-shaped piece of amber framed by silver, inside of which sat a whole and perfect fly.

"A builder" was all Mr. Harvey said when he was young. Then he stopped answering the question of what his father did. How could he say he worked in the desert, and that he built shacks of broken glass and old wood? He lectured George Harvey on what made a good building, on how to make sure you were constructing things to last.

So it was his father's old sketchbooks that Mr. Harvey looked at when the not still dreams came back. He would steep himself in the images of other places and other worlds, trying to love what he did not. And then he would begin to dream dreams of his mother the last time he had seen her, running through a field on the side of the road. She had been dressed in white. White capri pants and a tight white boat-neck shirt, and his father and she had fought for the last time in the hot car outside of Truth or Consequences, New Mexico. He had forced her out of the car. George Harvey sat still as stone in the back seat—eyes wide, no more afraid than a stone, watching it all as he did everything by then—in slow-mo. She had run without stopping, her white body thin and fragile and disappearing, while her son clung on to the amber necklace she had torn from her neck to hand him. His father had watched the road. "She's gone now, son," he said. "She won't be coming back."

NINE

My grandmother arrived on the evening before my memorial in her usual style. She liked to hire limousines and drive in from the airport sipping champagne while wearing what she called her "thick and fabulous animal"—a mink she had gotten secondhand at the church bazaar. My parents had not so much invited her as included her if she wanted to be there. In late January, Principal Caden had initiated the idea. "It will be good for your children and all the students at school," he had said. He took it upon himself to organize the event at our church. My parents were like sleepwalkers saying yes to his questions, nodding their heads to flowers or speakers. When my mother mentioned it on the phone to her mother, she was surprised to hear the words "I'm coming."

"But you don't have to, Mother."

There was a silence on my grandmother's end. "Abigail," she said, "this is Susan's funeral."

* * *

Grandma Lynn embarrassed my mother by insisting on wearing her used furs on walks around the block and by once attending a block party in high makeup. She would ask my mother questions until she knew who everyone was, whether or not my mother had seen the inside of their house, what the husband did for a living, what cars they drove. She made a solid catalog of the neighbors. It was a way, I now realized, to try to understand her daughter better. A miscalculated circling, a sad, partnerless dance.

"Jack-y," my grandmother said as she approached my parents on the front porch, "we need some stiff drinks!" She saw Lindsey then, trying to sneak up the stairs and gain a few more minutes before the required visitation. "Kid hates me," Grandma Lynn said. Her smile was frozen, her teeth perfect and white.

"Mother," my mother said. And I wanted to rush into those ocean eyes of loss. "I'm sure Lindsey is just going to make herself presentable."

"An impossibility in this house!" said my grandmother.

"Lynn," said my father, "this is a different house than last time you were here. I'll get you a drink, but I ask you to respect that."

"Still handsome as hell, Jack," my grandmother said.

My mother took my grandmother's coat. Holiday had been closed up in my father's den as soon as Buckley had yelled from his post at the upstairs window—"It's Grandma!" My brother bragged to Nate or anyone who would listen that his grandmother had the biggest cars in the whole wide world.

"You look lovely, Mother," my mother said.

"Hmmmm." While my father was out of earshot, my grandmother said, "How is he?"

"We're all coping, but it's hard."

"Is he still muttering about that man having done it?"

"He still thinks so, yes."

"You'll be sued, you know," she said.

"He hasn't told anyone but the police."

What they couldn't see was that my sister was sitting above them on the top step.

"And he shouldn't. I realize he has to blame someone, but . . ."

"Lynn, seven and seven or a martini?" my father said, coming back out into the hallway.

"What are you having?"

"I'm not drinking these days, actually," my father said.

"Now there's your problem. I'll lead the way. No one has to tell me where the liquor is!"

Without her thick and fabulous animal, my grandmother was rail thin. "Starved down" was how she put it when she'd counseled me at age eleven. "You need to get yourself starved down, honey, before you keep fat on for too long. Baby fat is just another way to say ugly." She and my mother had fought about whether I was old enough for benzedrine—her own personal savior, she called it, as in, "I am offering your daughter my own personal savior and you deny her?"

When I was alive, everything my grandmother did was bad. But an odd thing happened when she arrived in her rented limo that day, opened up our house, and barged in. She was, in all her obnoxious finery, dragging the light back in.

"You need help, Abigail," my grandmother said after having eaten the first real meal my mother had cooked since my disappearance. My mother was stunned. She had donned her blue dishwashing gloves, filled the sink with sudsy water, and was preparing to do every dish. Lindsey would dry. Her mother, she assumed, would call upon Jack to pour her an after-dinner drink.

"Mother, that is so nice of you."

"Don't mention it," she said. "I'll just run out to the front hall and get my bag o' magic."

"Oh no," I heard my mother say under her breath.

"Ah, yes, the bag o' magic," said Lindsey, who had not spoken the whole meal.

"Please, Mother!" my mother protested when Grandma Lynn came back.

"Okay, kids, clear off the table and get your mother over here. I'm doing a makeover."

"Mother, that's crazy. I have all these dishes to do."

"Abigail," my father said.

"Oh no. She may get you to drink, but she's not getting those instruments of torture near me."

"I'm not drunk," he said.

"You're smiling," my mother said.

"So sue him," Grandma Lynn said. "Buckley, grab your mother's hand and drag her over here." My brother obliged. It was fun to see his mother be bossed and prodded.

"Grandma Lynn?" Lindsey asked shyly.

My mother was being led by Buckley to a kitchen chair my grandmother had turned to face her.

"What?"

"Could you teach me about makeup?"

"My God in heaven, praise the Lord, yes!"

My mother sat down and Buckley climbed up into her lap. "What's wrong, Mommy?"

"Are you laughing, Abbie?" My father smiled.

And she was. She was laughing and she was crying too.

"Susie was a good girl, honey," Grandma Lynn said. "Just like you." There was no pause. "Now lift up your chin and let me have a look at those bags under your eyes."

Buckley got down and moved onto a chair. "This is an eyelash curler, Lindsey," my grandmother instructed. "I taught your mother all of these things."

"Clarissa uses those," Lindsey said.

My grandmother set the rubber curler pads on either side of my mother's eyelashes, and my mother, knowing the ropes, looked upward.

"Have you talked to Clarissa?" my father asked.

"Not really," said Lindsey. "She's hanging out a lot with Brian Nelson. They cut class enough times to get a three-day suspension."

"I don't expect that of Clarissa," my father said. "She may not have been the brightest apple in the bunch, but she was never a troublemaker."

"When I ran into her she reeked of pot."

"I hope you're not getting into that," Grandma Lynn said. She finished the last of her seven and seven and slammed the highball glass down on the table. "Now, see this, Lindsey, see how when the lashes are curled it opens up your mother's eyes?"

Lindsey tried to imagine her own eyelashes, but instead saw the star-clumped lashes of Samuel Heckler as his face neared hers for a kiss. Her pupils dilated, pulsing in and out like small, ferocious olives.

"I stand amazed," Grandma Lynn said, and put her hands, one still twisted into the awkward handles of the eyelash curler, on her hips.

"What?"

"Lindsey Salmon, you have a boyfriend," my grandmother announced to the room.

My father smiled. He was liking Grandma Lynn suddenly. I was too.

"Do not," Lindsey said.

My grandmother was about to speak when my mother whispered, "Do too."

"Bless you, honey," my grandmother said, "you should have a boyfriend. As soon as I'm done with your mother, I'm giving you the grand Grandma Lynn treatment. Jack, make me an apéritif."

"An apéritif is something you . . ." my mother began.

"Don't correct me, Abigail."

My grandmother got sloshed. She made Lindsey look like a

clown or, as Grandma Lynn said herself, "a grade-A 'tute." My father got what she called "finely drunkened." The most amazing thing was that my mother went to bed and left the dirty dishes in the sink.

While everyone else slept, Lindsey stood at the mirror in the bathroom, looking at herself. She wiped off some of the blush, blotted her lips, and ran her fingers over the swollen, freshly plucked parts of her formerly bushy eyebrows. In the mirror she saw something different and so did I: an adult who could take care of herself. Under the makeup was the face she'd always known as her own, until very recently, when it had become the face that reminded people of me. With lip pencil and eyeliner, she now saw, the edges of her features were delineated, and they sat on her face like gems imported from some far-off place where the colors were richer than the colors in our house had ever been. It was true what our grandmother said—the makeup brought out the blue of her eyes. The plucking of the eyebrows changed the shape of her face. The blush highlighted the hollows beneath her cheekbones ("The hollows that could stand some more hollowing," our grandmother pointed out). And her lips—she practiced her facial expressions. She pouted, she kissed, she smiled wide as if she too had had a cocktail, she looked down and pretended to pray like a good girl but cocked one eye up to see how she looked being good. She went to bed and slept on her back so as not to mess up her new face.

Mrs. Bethel Utemeyer was the only dead person my sister and I ever saw. She moved in with her son to our development when I was six and Lindsey five.

My mother said that she had lost part of her brain and that

sometimes she left her son's house and didn't know where she was. She would often end up in our front yard, standing under the dogwood tree and looking out at the street as if waiting for a bus. My mother would sit her down in the kitchen and make tea for the two of them, and after she calmed her she would call her son's house to tell them where she was. Sometimes no one was home and Mrs. Utemeyer would sit at our kitchen table and stare into the centerpiece for hours. She would be there when we came home from school. Sitting. She smiled at us. Often she called Lindsey "Natalie" and reached out to touch her hair.

When she died, her son encouraged my mother to bring Lindsey and me to the funeral. "My mother seemed to have a special fondness for your children," he wrote.

"She didn't even know my name, Mom," Lindsey whined, as our mother buttoned up the infinite number of round buttons on Lindsey's dress coat. *Another impractical gift from Grandma Lynn,* my mother thought.

"At least she *called* you a name," I said.

It was after Easter, and a spring heat wave had set in that week. All but the most stubborn of that winter's snow had seeped into the earth, and in the graveyard of the Utemeyers' church snow clung to the base of the headstones, while, nearby, buttercup shoots were making their way up.

The Utemeyers' church was fancy. "High Catholic," my father had said in the car. Lindsey and I thought this was very funny. My father hadn't wanted to come but my mother was so pregnant that she couldn't drive. For the last few months of her pregnancy with Buckley she was unable to fit behind the wheel. She was so uncomfortable most of the time that we avoided being near her for fear we'd be thrown into servitude.

But her pregnancy allowed her to get out of what Lindsey and I couldn't stop talking about for weeks and what I kept dreaming about for long after that: viewing the body. I could tell my father and mother didn't want this to happen, but Mr. Utemeyer made a beeline for the two of us when it was time to file past the casket. "Which one of you is the one she called Natalie?" he asked. We stared at him. I pointed to Lindsey.

"I'd like you to come say goodbye," he said. He smelled of a perfume sweeter than what my mother sometimes wore, and the sting of it in my nose, and my sense of exclusion, made me want to cry. "You can come too," he said to me, extending his hands so we would flank him in the aisle.

It wasn't Mrs. Utemeyer. It was something else. But it *was* Mrs. Utemeyer too. I tried to keep my eyes focused on the gleaming gold rings on her fingers.

"Mother," Mr. Utemeyer said, "I brought the little girl you called Natalie."

Lindsey and I both admitted later that we expected Mrs. Utemeyer to speak and that we had decided, individually, that if she did we were going to grab the other one and run like hell.

An excruciating second or two and it was over and we were released back to our mother and father.

I wasn't very surprised when I first saw Mrs. Bethel Utemeyer in my heaven, nor was I shocked when Holly and I found her walking hand in hand with a small blond girl she introduced as her daughter, Natalie.

The morning of my memorial Lindsey stayed in her room for as long as she could. She didn't want my mother to see the still-applied makeup until it would be too late to make her wash it off. She had also told herself it would be okay to take a dress from my closet. That I wouldn't mind.

But it was weird to watch.

She opened the door to my room, a vault that by February was being disturbed more and more, though no one, not my mother or father, nor Buckley or Lindsey, confessed to entering, nor to taking things that they didn't plan on returning. They were blind to the clues that each of them came and visited me there. Any disturbance, even if it could not possibly be blamed on Holiday, was blamed on him.

Lindsey wanted to look nice for Samuel. She opened the double doors to my closet and reviewed the mess. I hadn't been exactly orderly, so every time my mother told us to clean up, I'd shoved whatever was on the floor or bed into my closet.

Lindsey had always wanted the clothes I owned first-run but had gotten them all as hand-me-downs.

"Gosh," she said, whispering into the darkness of my closet. She realized with guilt and glee that everything she saw before her was hers now.

"Hello? Knock-knock," said Grandma Lynn.

Lindsey jumped.

"Sorry to disturb you, hon," she said. "I thought I heard you in here."

My grandmother stood in what my mother called one of her Jackie Kennedy dresses. She had never understood why unlike the rest of us her mother had no hips—she could slide into a straight-cut dress and fill it out just enough, even at sixty-two, to look perfect in it.

"What are you doing in here?" Lindsey asked.

"I need help with this zipper." Grandma Lynn turned, and Lindsey could see what she had never seen on our own mother. The back of Grandma Lynn's black bra, the top of her half-slip. She walked the step or two over to our grandmother and, trying not to touch anything but the zipper tab, zipped her up.

"How about that hook and eye up there," said Grandma Lynn. "Can you get that?"

There were powdery smells and Chanel No. 5 sprinkled all around our grandmother's neck.

"It's one of the reasons for a man—you can't do this stuff yourself."

Lindsey was as tall as our grandmother and still growing. As she took the hook and eye in either hand, she saw the fine wisps of dyed blond hair at the base of my grandmother's skull. She saw the downy gray hair trailing along her back and neck. She hooked the dress and then stood there.

"I've forgotten what she looked like," Lindsey said.

"What?" Grandma Lynn turned.

"I can't remember," Lindsey said. "I mean her neck, you know, did I ever look at it?"

"Oh honey," Grandma Lynn said, "come here." She opened up her arms, but Lindsey turned into the closet.

"I need to look pretty," she said.

"You are pretty," Grandma Lynn said.

Lindsey couldn't get her breath. One thing Grandma Lynn never did was dole out compliments. When they came, they were unexpected gold.

"We'll find you a nice outfit in here," Grandma Lynn said and strode toward my clothes. No one could shop a rack like Grandma Lynn. On the rare occasions that she visited near the start of the school year she would take the two of us out. We marveled at her as we watched her nimble fingers play the hangers like so many keys. Suddenly, hesitating only for a moment, she would pull out a dress or shirt and hold it up to us. "What do you think?" she'd ask. It was always perfect.

As she considered my separates, plucked and posed them against my sister's torso, she talked:

"Your mother's a wreck, Lindsey. I've never seen her like this before."

"Grandma."

"Hush, I'm thinking." She held up my favorite church dress. It was blackwatch wool with a Peter Pan collar. I liked it mostly because the skirt was so big I could sit in the pew cross-legged and flounce the hem down to the ground. "Where did she get *this* sack?" my grandmother asked. "Your dad, he's a mess too, but he's mad about it."

"Who was that man you asked Mom about?"

She stiffened on the question. "What man?"

"You asked Mom if Dad still was saying that *that* man did it. What man?"

"Voilà!" Grandma Lynn held up a dark blue minidress that my sister had never seen. It was Clarissa's.

"It's so short," Lindsey said.

"I'm shocked at your mother," Grandma Lynn said. "She let the kid get something stylish!"

My father called up from the hallway that he expected everyone downstairs in ten minutes.

Grandma Lynn went into preparation overdrive. She helped Lindsey get the dark blue dress over her head, and then they ran back to Lindsey's room for shoes, and then, finally, in the hallway, under the overhead light, she fixed the smudged eyeliner and mascara on my sister's face. She finished her off with firmly pressed powder, whisking the cotton pad lightly in an upward direction along either side of Lindsey's face. It wasn't until my grandmother came downstairs and my mother commented on the shortness of Lindsey's dress while looking suspiciously at Grandma Lynn that my sister and I realized Grandma Lynn didn't have a spot of makeup on her own face. Buckley rode between them in the back seat, and as they neared the church he looked at Grandma Lynn and asked what she was doing.

"When you don't have time for rouge, this puts a little life into them," she said, and so Buckley copied her and pinched his cheeks.

* * *

Samuel Heckler was standing by the stone posts that marked the path to the church door. He was dressed all in black, and beside him his older brother, Hal, stood wearing the beat-up leather jacket Samuel had worn on Christmas Day.

His brother was like a darker print of Samuel. He was tanned, and his face was weathered from riding his motorcycle full-tilt down country roads. As my family approached, Hal turned quickly and walked away.

"This must be Samuel," my grandmother said. "I'm the evil grandma."

"Shall we go in?" my father said. "It's nice to see you, Samuel."

Lindsey and Samuel led the way, while my grandmother dropped back and walked on the other side of my mother. A united front.

Detective Fenerman was standing by the doorway in an itchy-looking suit. He nodded at my parents and seemed to linger on my mother. "Will you join us?" my father asked.

"Thank you," he said, "but I just want to be in the vicinity."

"We appreciate that."

They walked into the cramped vestibule of our church. I wanted to snake up my father's back, circle his neck, whisper in his ear. But I was already there in his every pore and crevice.

He had woken up with a hangover and turned over on his side to watch my mother's shallow breathing against the pillow. His lovely wife, his lovely girl. He wanted to place his hand on her cheek, smooth her hair back from her face, kiss her—but sleeping, she was at peace. He hadn't woken a day since my death when the day wasn't something to get through. But the truth was, the memorial service day was not the worst kind. At least it was honest. At least it was a day shaped around what they were so pre-occupied by: my absence. Today he would not have to pretend he was getting back to normal—whatever normal was. Today he could walk tall with grief and so could Abigail. But he knew that as soon as she woke up he would not really look at her for the rest of the day, not really look into her and see the woman he had known her to be before the day they had taken in the news of my death. At nearly two months, the idea of it as news was fading away in the hearts of all but my family—and Ruth.

She came with her father. They were standing in the corner near the glass case that held a chalice used during the Revolutionary War, when the church had been a hospital. Mr. and Mrs. Dewitt were making small talk with them. At home on her desk, Mrs. Dewitt had a poem of Ruth's. On Monday she was going to the guidance counselor with it. It was a poem about me.

"My wife seems to agree with Principal Caden," Ruth's father was saying, "that the memorial will help allow the kids to accept it."

"What do you think?" Mr. Dewitt asked.

"I think let bygones be bygones and leave the family to their own. But Ruthie wanted to come."

Ruth watched my family greet people and noted in horror my sister's new look. Ruth did not believe in makeup. She thought it demeaned women. Samuel Heckler was holding Lindsey's hand. A word from her readings popped into her head: *subjugation.* But then I saw her notice Hal Heckler through the window. He was standing out by the oldest graves in the front and pulling on a cigarette butt.

"Ruthie," her father asked, "what is it?"

She focused again and looked at him. "What's what?"

"You were staring off into space just now," he said.

"I like the way the graveyard looks."

"Ah kid, you're my angel," he said. "Let's grab a seat before the good ones get taken."

Clarissa was there, with a sheepish-looking Brian Nelson, who was wearing a suit of his father's. She made her way up to my family, and when Principal Caden and Mr. Botte saw her they fell away and let her approach.

She shook hands with my father first.

"Hello, Clarissa," he said. "How are you?"

"Okay," she said. "How are you and Mrs. Salmon?"

"We're fine, Clarissa," he said. *What an odd lie,* I thought. "Would you like to join us in the family pew?"

"Um"—she looked down at her hands—"I'm with my boyfriend."

My mother had entered some trancelike state and was staring hard at Clarissa's face. Clarissa was alive and I was dead. Clarissa began to feel it, the eyes boring into her, and she wanted to get away. Then Clarissa saw the dress.

"Hey," she said, reaching out toward my sister.

"What is it, Clarissa?" my mother snapped.

"Um, nothing," she said. She looked at the dress again, knew she could never ask for it back now.

"Abigail?" my father said. He was attuned to her voice, her anger. Something was off.

Grandma Lynn, who stood just a bit behind my mother, winked at Clarissa.

"I was just noticing how good Lindsey looked," Clarissa said.

My sister blushed.

The people in the vestibule began to stir and part. It was the Reverend Strick, walking in his vestments toward my parents.

Clarissa faded back to look for Brian Nelson. When she found him, she joined him out among the graves.

Ray Singh stayed away. He said goodbye to me in his own way: by looking at a picture—my studio portrait—that I had given him that fall.

He looked into the eyes of that photograph and saw right through them to the backdrop of marbleized suede every kid had to sit in front of under a hot light. What did dead mean, Ray wondered. It meant lost, it meant frozen, it meant gone. He knew that no one ever really looked the way they did in photos. He knew he didn't look as wild or as frightened as he did in his own. He came to realize something as he stared at my photo—that it was not me. I was in the air around him, I was in the cold mornings he had now with Ruth, I was in the quiet time he spent alone between studying. I was the girl he had chosen to kiss. He wanted, somehow, to set me free. He didn't want to burn my photo or toss it away, but he didn't want to look at me anymore, either. I watched him as he placed the photograph in one of the giant volumes of Indian poetry in which he and his mother had pressed dozens of fragile flowers that were slowly turning to dust.

At the service they said nice things about me. Reverend Strick. Principal Caden. Mrs. Dewitt. But my father and mother sat through it numbed. Samuel kept squeezing Lindsey's hand, but she didn't seem to notice him. She barely blinked. Buckley sat in a small suit borrowed for the occasion from Nate, who had attended a wedding that year. He fidgeted and watched my father. It was Grandma Lynn who did the most important thing that day.

During the final hymn, as my family stood, she leaned over to Lindsey and whispered, "By the door, that's him."

Lindsey looked over.

Standing just behind Len Fenerman, who was now inside the doorway and singing along, stood a man from the neighborhood. He was dressed more casually than anyone else, wearing flannel-lined khaki trousers and a heavy flannel shirt. For a moment Lindsey thought she recognized him. Their eyes locked. Then she passed out.

In all the commotion of attending to her, George Harvey slipped between the Revolutionary War gravestones behind the church and walked away without being noticed.

TEN

At the statewide Gifted Symposium each summer, the gifted kids from seventh to ninth grade would get together for a four-week retreat to, as I always thought of it, hang out in the trees and pick one another's brains. Around the campfire they sang oratorios instead of folk songs. In the girls' showers they would swoon over the physique of Jacques d'Amboise or the frontal lobe of John Kenneth Galbraith.

But even the gifted had their cliques. There were the Science Nerds and the Math Brains. They formed the superior, if somewhat socially crippled, highest rung of the gifted ladder. Then came the History Heads, who knew the birth and death dates of every historical figure anyone had ever heard of. They would pass by the other campers voicing cryptic, seemingly meaningless life spans: "1769 to 1821," "1770 to 1831." When Lindsey passed the History Heads she would think the answers to herself. "Napoleon." "Hegel."

There were also the Masters of Arcane Knowledge. Everyone begrudged their presence among the gifteds. These were the kids that could break down an engine and build it back again—no diagrams or instructions needed. They understood things in a real, not theoretical, way. They seemed not to care about their grades.

Samuel was a Master. His heroes were Richard Feynman and his brother, Hal. Hal had dropped out of high school and now ran the bike shop near the sinkhole, where he serviced everyone from Hell's Angels to the elderly who rode motorized scooters around the parking lots of their retirement homes. Hal smoked, lived at home over the Hecklers' garage, and conducted a variety of romances in the back of his shop.

When people asked Hal when he was going to grow up, he said, "Never." Inspired by this, when the teachers asked Samuel what he wanted to be, he would say: "I don't know. I just turned fourteen."

Almost fifteen now, Ruth Connors knew. Out in the aluminum toolshed behind her house, surrounded by the doorknobs and hardware her father had found in old houses slated for demolition, Ruth sat in the darkness and concentrated until she came away with a headache. She would run into the house, past the living room, where her father sat reading, and up to her room, where in fits and bursts she would write her poetry. "Being Susie," "After Death," "In Pieces," "Beside Her Now," and her favorite—the one she was most proud of and carried with her to the symposium folded and refolded so often that the creases were close to cuts—"The Lip of the Grave."

Ruth had to be driven to the symposium because that morning, when the bus was leaving, she was still at home with an acute attack of gastritis. She was trying weird all-vegetable regimes and the night before had eaten a whole head of cabbage for dinner. Her mother refused to kowtow to the vegetarianism Ruth had taken up after my death.

"This is not Susie, for Chrissakes!" her mother would say, plunking down an inch-thick sirloin in front of her daughter.

Her father drove her first to the hospital at three A.M. and then to the symposium, stopping home on the way to pick up the bag her mother had packed and left at the end of their driveway.

As the car pulled up into the camp, Ruth scanned the crowd of kids lining up for nametags. She spotted my sister among an all-male group of Masters. Lindsey had avoided putting her last name on her nametag, choosing to draw a fish instead. She wasn't exactly lying that way, but she hoped to meet a few kids from the surrounding schools who didn't know the story of my death or at least wouldn't connect her to it.

All spring she'd worn the half-a-heart pendant while Samuel wore the other half. They were shy about their affection for each other. They did not hold hands in the hallways at school, and they did not pass notes. They sat together at lunch; Samuel walked her home. On her fourteenth birthday he brought her a cupcake with a candle in it. Other than that, they melted into the gender-subdivided world of their peers.

The following morning Ruth was up early. Like Lindsey, Ruth was a floater at gifted camp. She didn't belong to any one group. She had gone on a nature walk and collected plants and flowers she needed help naming. When she didn't like the answers one of the Science Nerds provided, she decided to start naming the plants and flowers herself. She drew a picture of the leaf or blossom in her journal, and then what sex she thought it was, and then gave it a name like "Jim" for a simple-leaved plant and "Pasha" for a more downy flower.

By the time Lindsey stumbled in to the dining hall, Ruth was in line for a second helping of eggs and sausage. She had made a big stink about no meat at home and she had to hold to it, but no one at the symposium knew of the oath she'd sworn.

Ruth hadn't talked to my sister since before my death, and then it was only to excuse herself in the hallway at school. But she'd seen Lindsey walking home with Samuel and seen her smile with him. She watched as my sister said yes to pancakes and no to everything else. She had tried to imagine herself being my sister as she had spent time imagining being me.

As Lindsey walked blindly to the next open spot in line, Ruth interceded. "What's the fish for?" Ruth asked, nodding her head toward my sister's nametag. "Are you religious?"

"Notice the direction of the fish," Lindsey said, wishing simultaneously that they had vanilla puddings at breakfast. They would go great with her pancakes.

"Ruth Connors, poet," Ruth said, by way of introduction.

"Lindsey," Lindsey said.

"Salmon, right?"

"Please don't," Lindsey said, and for a second Ruth could feel the feeling a little more vividly—what it was like to claim me. How people looked at Lindsey and imagined a girl covered in blood.

Even among the gifteds, who distinguished themselves by doing things differently, people paired off within the first few days. It was mostly pairs of boys or pairs of girls—few serious relationships had begun by fourteen—but there was one exception that year. Lindsey and Samuel.

"K-I-S-S-I-N-G!" greeted them wherever they went. Unchaperoned, and with the heat of the summer, something grew in them like weeds. It was lust. I'd never felt it so purely or seen it move so hotly into someone I knew. Someone whose gene pool I shared.

They were careful and followed the rules. No counselor could say he had flashed a light under the denser shrubbery by the boys' dorm and found Salmon and Heckler going at it. They set up little meetings outside in back of the cafeteria or by a certain tree that they'd marked up high with their initials. They kissed. They wanted to do more but couldn't. Samuel wanted it to be special. He was aware that it should be perfect. Lindsey just wanted to get it over with. Have it behind her so she could achieve adulthood—transcend the place and the time. She thought of sex as the *Star Trek* transport. You vaporized and found yourself navigating another planet within the second or two it took to realign.

"They're going to do it," Ruth wrote in her journal. I had pinned hopes on Ruth's writing everything down. She told her journal about me passing by her in the parking lot, about how on that night I had touched her—literally, she felt, reached out. What I had looked like then. How she dreamed about me. How she had fashioned the idea that a spirit could be a sort of second skin for someone, a protective layer somehow. How maybe if she was assiduous she could free us both. I would read over her shoulder as she wrote down her thoughts and wonder if anyone might believe her one day.

When she was imagining me, she felt better, less alone, more connected to something out there. To someone out there. She saw the cornfield in her dreams, and a new world opening, a world where maybe she could find a foothold too.

"You're a really good poet, Ruth," she imagined me saying, and her journal would release her into a daydream of being such a good poet that her words had the power to resurrect me.

I could see back to an afternoon when Ruth watched her teenage cousin undress to take a bath while Ruth sat on the bathroom rug, locked in the bathroom so her cousin could babysit her as she'd been told. Ruth had longed to touch her cousin's skin and hair, longed to be held. I wondered if this longing in a three-year-old had sparked what came at eight. That fuzzy feeling of difference, that her crushes on female teachers or her cousin were more real than the other girls' crushes. Hers contained a desire beyond sweetness and attention, it fed a longing, beginning to flower green and yellow into a crocuslike lust, the soft petals opening into her awkward adolescence. It was not so much, she would write in her journal, that she wanted to have sex with women, but that she wanted to disappear inside of them forever. To hide.

The last week of the symposium was always spent developing a final project, which the various schools would present in competition on the night before the parents returned to pick the students up. The competition wasn't announced until the Saturday breakfast of that final week, but the kids had already begun planning for it anyway. It was always a better-mousetrap competition, and so the stakes were raised year after year. No one wanted to repeat a mousetrap that had already been built.

Samuel went in search of the kids with braces. He needed the tiny rubber bands orthodontists doled out. They would work to keep the tension tight on the guiding arm of his mousetrap. Lindsey begged clean tinfoil from the retired army cook. Their trap involved reflecting light in order to confuse the mice.

"What happens if they like the way they look?" Lindsey asked Samuel.

"They can't see that clearly," Samuel said. He was stripping the paper off the wire twists from the camp garbage bag supply. If a kid looked strangely at ordinary objects around the camp, he or she was most likely thinking of how it would serve the ultimate mousetrap.

"They're pretty cute," Lindsey said one afternoon.

Lindsey had spent the better part of the night before gathering field mice with string lures and putting them under the wire mesh of an empty rabbit hutch.

Samuel watched them intently. "I could be a vet, I guess," he said, "but I don't think I'd like cutting them open."

"Do we have to kill them?" Lindsey asked. "It's a better mouse*trap,* not a better mouse death camp."

"Artie's contributing little coffins made out of balsa wood," Samuel said, laughing.

"That's sick."

"That's Artie."

"He supposedly had a crush on Susie," Lindsey said.

"I know."

"Does he talk about her?" Lindsey took a long thin stick and poked it through the mesh.

"He's asked about you, actually," Samuel said.

"What did you tell him?"

"That you're okay, that you'll be okay."

The mice kept running from the stick into the corner, where they crawled on top of one another in a useless effort to flee. "Let's build a mousetrap with a little purple velvet couch in it and we can rig up a latch so that when they sit on the couch, a door drops and little balls of cheese fall down. We can call it Wild Rodent Kingdom."

Samuel didn't press my sister like the adults did. He would talk in detail about mouse couch upholstery instead.

By that summer I had begun to spend less time watching from the gazebo because I could still see Earth as I walked the fields of heaven. The night would come and the javelin-throwers and shot-putters would leave for other heavens. Heavens where a girl like me didn't fit in. Were they horrific, these other heavens? Worse than feeling so solitary among one's living, growing peers? Or were they the stuff I dreamed about? Where you could be caught in a Norman Rockwell world forever. Turkey constantly being brought to a table full of family. A wry and twinkling relative carving up the bird.

If I walked too far and wondered loud enough the fields would change. I could look down and see horse corn and I could hear it then—singing—a kind of low humming and moaning warning me back from the edge. My head would throb and the sky would darken and it would be that night again, that perpetual yesterday lived again. My soul solidifying, growing heavy. I came up to the lip of my grave this way many times but had yet to stare in.

I did begin to wonder what the word *heaven* meant. I thought, if this were heaven, truly heaven, it would be where my grandparents lived. Where my father's father, my favorite of them all, would lift me up and dance with me. I would feel only joy and have no memory, no cornfield and no grave.

"You can have that," Franny said to me. "Plenty of people do."

"How do you make the switch?" I asked.

"It's not as easy as you might think," she said. "You have to stop desiring certain answers."

"I don't get it."

"If you stop asking why you were killed instead of someone else, stop investigating the vacuum left by your loss, stop wondering what everyone left on Earth is feeling," she said, "you can be free. Simply put, you have to give up on Earth."

This seemed impossible to me.

Ruth crept into Lindsey's dorm that night.

"I had a dream about her," she whispered to my sister.

Lindsey blinked sleepily at her. "Susie?" she asked.

"I'm sorry about the incident in the dining hall," Ruth said.

Lindsey was on the bottom of a three-tiered aluminum bunk bed. Her neighbor directly above her stirred.

"Can I get into bed with you?" Ruth asked.

Lindsey nodded.

Ruth crawled in next to Lindsey in the narrow sliver of the bed.

"What happened in your dream?" Lindsey whispered.

Ruth told her, turning her face so that Lindsey's eyes could make out the silhouette of Ruth's nose and lips and forehead. "I was inside the earth," Ruth said, "and Susie walked over me in the cornfield. I could feel her walking over me. I called out to her but my mouth filled with dirt. She couldn't hear me no matter how much I tried to yell. Then I woke up."

"I don't dream about her," Lindsey said. "I have nightmares about rats nibbling at the ends of my hair."

Ruth liked the comfort she felt next to my sister—the heat their bodies created.

"Are you in love with Samuel?"

"Yes."

"Do you miss Susie?"

Because it was dark, because Ruth was facing away from her, because Ruth was almost a stranger, Lindsey said what she felt. "More than anyone will ever know."

The principal of Devon Junior High was called away on a family matter, and it was left up to the newly appointed assistant principal of Chester Springs School to create, overnight, that year's challenge. She wanted to do something different from mousetraps.

CAN YOU GET AWAY WITH CRIME? HOW TO COMMIT THE PERFECT MURDER, announced her hurriedly drawn-up flier.

The kids loved it. The musicians and poets, the History Heads and artists, were teeming and bubbling about how to begin. They shoveled down their bacon and eggs at breakfast and compared the great unsolved murders of the past or thought of ordinary objects that could be used for fatal wounds. They began to think of whom they could plot to kill. It was all in good fun until 7:15, when my sister walked in.

Artie watched her get in line. She was still unaware, just picking up on the excitement in the air—figuring the mousetrap competition had been announced.

He kept his eye on Lindsey and saw the closest flier was posted at the end of the food line over the utensils tray. He was listening to a story about Jack the Ripper that someone at the table was relaying. He stood to return his tray.

When he reached my sister, he cleared his throat. All my hopes were pinned on this wobbly boy. "Catch her," I said. A prayer going down to Earth.

"Lindsey," Artie said.

Lindsey looked at him. "Yes?"

Behind the counter the army cook held out a spoon full of scrambled eggs to plop on her tray.

"I'm Artie, from your sister's grade."

"I don't need any coffins," Lindsey said, moving her tray down the metalwork to where there was orange juice and apple juice in big plastic pitchers.

"What?"

"Samuel told me you were building balsa wood coffins for the mice this year. I don't want any."

"They changed the competition," he said.

That morning Lindsey had decided she would take the bottom off of Clarissa's dress. It would be perfect for the mouse couch.

"To what?"

"Do you want to go outside?" Artie used his body to shadow her and block her passage to the utensils. "Lindsey," he blurted. "The competition is about murder."

She stared at him.

Lindsey held on to her tray. She kept her eyes locked on Artie.

"I wanted to tell you before you read the flier," he said.

Samuel rushed into the tent.

"What's going on?" Lindsey looked helplessly at Samuel.

"This year's competition is how to commit the perfect murder," Samuel said.

Samuel and I saw the tremor. The inside shakeoff of her heart. She was getting so good the cracks and fissures were smaller and smaller. Soon, like a sleight-of-hand trick perfected, no one would see her do it. She could shut out the whole world, including herself.

"I'm fine," she said.

But Samuel knew she wasn't.

He and Artie watched her back as she departed.

"I was trying to warn her," Artie said weakly.

Artie returned to his table. He drew hypodermics, one after another. His pen pressed harder and harder as he colored in the embalming fluid inside, as he perfected the trajectory of the three drops squirting out.

Lonely, I thought, *on Earth as it is in heaven.*

"You kill people by stabbing and cutting and shooting," Ruth said. "It's sick."

"Agreed," Artie said.

Samuel had taken my sister away to talk. Artie had seen Ruth at one of the outside picnic tables with her big blank book.

"But there are good reasons to kill," Ruth said.

"Who do you think did it?" Artie asked. He sat on the bench and braced his feet up under the table on the crossbar.

Ruth sat almost motionless, right leg crossed over left, but her foot jiggled ceaselessly.

"How did you hear?" she asked.

"My father told us," Artie said. "He called my sister and me into the family room and made us sit down."

"Shit, what did he say?"

"First he said that horrible things happened in the world and my sister said, 'Vietnam,' and he was quiet because they always fight about that whenever it comes up. So he said, 'No, honey, horrible things happen close to home, to people we know.' She thought it was one of her friends."

Ruth felt a raindrop.

"Then my dad broke down and said a little girl had been killed. I was the one who asked who. I mean, when he said 'little girl,' I pictured *little,* you know. Not us."

It was a definite drop, and they began to land on the redwood tabletop.

"Do you want to go in?" Artie asked.

"Everyone else will be inside," Ruth said.

"I know."

"Let's get wet."

They sat still for a while and watched the drops fall around them, heard the sound against the leaves of the tree above.

"I knew she was dead. I sensed it," Ruth said, "but then I saw a mention of it in my dad's paper and I was sure. They didn't use her name at first. Just 'Girl, fourteen.' I asked my dad for the page but he wouldn't give it to me. I mean, who else and her sister hadn't been in school all week?"

"I wonder who told Lindsey?" Artie said. The rain picked up. Artie slipped underneath the table. "We're going to get soaked," he yelled up.

And then as quickly as the rain had started, it ceased. Sun came through the branches of the tree above her, and Ruth looked up past them. "I think she listens," she said, too softly to be heard.

It became common knowledge at the symposium who my sister was and how I had died.

"Imagine being stabbed," someone said.

"No thanks."

"I think it's cool."

"Think of it—she's famous."

"Some way to get famous. I'd rather win the Nobel Prize."

"Does anyone know what she wanted to be?"

"I dare you to ask Lindsey."

And they listed the dead they knew.

Grandmother, grandfather, uncle, aunt, some had a parent, rarer was a sister or brother lost young to an illness—a heart irregularity—leukemia—an unpronounceable disease. No one knew anyone who had been murdered. But now they knew me.

Under a rowboat that was too old and worn to float, Lindsey lay down on the earth with Samuel Heckler, and he held her.

"You know I'm okay," she said, her eyes dry. "I think Artie was trying to help me," she offered.

"You can stop now, Lindsey," he said. "We'll just lie here and wait until things quiet down."

Samuel's back was flush against the ground, and he brought my sister close into his body to protect her from the dampness of the quick summer rain. Their breath began to heat the small space beneath the boat, and he could not stop it—his penis stiffened inside his jeans.

Lindsey reached her hand over.

"I'm sorry . . ." he began.

"I'm ready," my sister said.

At fourteen, my sister sailed away from me into a place I'd never been. In the walls of my sex there was horror and blood, in the walls of hers there were windows.

"How to Commit the Perfect Murder" was an old game in heaven. I always chose the icicle: the weapon melts away.

ELEVEN

When my father woke up at four A.M., the house was quiet. My mother lay beside him, lightly snoring. My brother, the only child, what with my sister attending the symposium, was like a rock with a sheet pulled up over him. My father marveled at what a sound sleeper he was—just like me. While I was still alive, Lindsey and I had had fun with that, clapping, dropping books, and even banging pot lids to see if Buckley would wake up.

Before leaving the house, my father checked on Buckley—to make sure, to feel the warm breath against his palm. Then he suited up in his thin-soled sneakers and light jogging outfit. His last task was to put Holiday's collar on.

It was still early enough that he could almost see his breath. He could pretend at that early hour that it was still winter. That the seasons had not advanced.

The morning dog walk gave him an excuse to pass by Mr. Harvey's house. He slowed only slightly—no one would have noticed save me or, if he had been awake, Mr. Harvey. My father was sure that if he just stared hard enough, just looked long enough, he would find the clues he needed in the casements of the windows, in the green paint coating the shingles, or along the driveway, where two large stones sat, painted white.

By late summer 1974, there had been no movement on my case. No body. No killer. Nothing.

My father thought of Ruana Singh: "When I was sure, I would find a quiet way, and I would kill him." He had not told this to Abigail because the advice made a sort of baseline sense that would frighten her into telling someone, and he suspected that someone might be Len.

Ever since the day he'd seen Ruana Singh and then had come home to find Len waiting for him, he'd felt my mother leaning heavily on the police. If my father said something that contradicted the police theories—or, as he saw them, the lack of them—my mother would immediately rush to fill the hole left open by my father's idea. "Len says that doesn't mean anything," or, "I trust the police to find out what happened."

Why, my father wondered, did people trust the police so much? Why not trust instinct? It was Mr. Harvey and he knew it. But what Ruana had said was *when I was sure.* Knowing, the deep-soul knowing that my father had, was not, in the law's more literal mind, incontrovertible proof.

The house that I grew up in was the same house where I was born. Like Mr. Harvey's, it was a box, and because of this I nurtured useless envies whenever I visited other people's homes. I dreamed about bay windows and cupolas, balconies, and slanted attic ceilings in a bedroom. I loved the idea that there could be trees in a yard taller and stronger than people, slanted spaces under stairs, thick hedges grown so large that inside there were hollows of dead branches where you could crawl and sit. In my heaven there were verandas and circular staircases, window ledges with iron rails, and a campanile housing a bell that tolled the hour.

I knew the floor plan of Mr. Harvey's by heart. I had made a warm spot on the floor of the garage until I cooled. He had brought my blood into the house with him on his clothes and skin. I knew the bathroom. Knew how in my house my mother had tried to decorate it to accommodate Buckley's late arrival by stenciling battleships along the top of the pink walls. In Mr. Harvey's house the bathroom and kitchen were spotless. The porcelain was yellow and the tile on the floor was green. He kept it cold. Upstairs, where Buckley, Lindsey, and I had our rooms, he had almost nothing. He had a straight chair where he would go to sit sometimes and stare out the window over at the high school, listen for the sound of band practice wafting over from the field, but mostly he spent his hours in the back on the first floor, in the kitchen building dollhouses, in the living room listening to the radio or, as his lust set in, sketching blueprints for follies like the hole or the tent.

No one had bothered him about me for several months. By that summer he only occasionally saw a squad car slow in front of his house. He was smart enough not to alter his pattern. If he was walking out to the garage or the mailbox, he kept on going.

He set several clocks. One to tell him when to open the blinds, one when to close them. In conjunction with these alarms, he would turn lights on and off throughout the house. When an occasional child happened by to sell chocolate bars for a school competition or inquire if he would like to subscribe to the *Evening Bulletin,* he was friendly but businesslike, unremarkable.

He kept things to count, and this counting reassured him. They were simple things. A wedding ring, a letter sealed in an envelope, the heel of a shoe, a pair of glasses, an eraser in the shape of a cartoon character, a small bottle of perfume, a plastic bracelet, my Pennsylvania keystone charm, his mother's amber pendant. He would take them out at night long after he was certain that no newsboy or neighbor would knock on his door. He would count them like the beads on a rosary. For some he had forgotten the names. I knew the names. The heel of the shoe was from a girl named Claire, from Nutley, New Jersey, whom he had convinced to walk into the back of a van. She was littler than me. (I like to think I wouldn't have gone into a van. Like to think it was my curiosity about how he could make a hole in the earth that wouldn't collapse.) He had ripped the heel off her shoe before he let Claire go. That was all he did. He got her into the van and took her shoes off. She started crying, and the sound drove into him like screws. He pleaded with her to be quiet and just leave. Step magically out of the van barefoot and uncomplaining while he kept her shoes. But she wouldn't. She cried. He started working on one of the heels of the shoes, prying it loose with his penknife, until someone pounded on the back of the van. He heard men's voices and a woman yelling something about calling the police. He opened the door.

"What the hell are you doing to that kid?" one of the men yelled. This man's buddy caught the little girl as she flew, bawling, out of the back.

"I'm trying to repair her shoe."

The little girl was hysterical. Mr. Harvey was all reason and calm. But Claire had seen what I had—his look bearing down—his wanting something unspoken that to give him would equal our oblivion.

Hurriedly, as the men and woman stood confused, unable to see what Claire and I knew, Mr. Harvey handed the shoes to one of the men and said his goodbyes. He kept the heel. He liked to hold the small leather heel and rub it between his thumb and forefinger—a perfect worry stone.

* * *

I knew the darkest place in our house. I had climbed inside of it and stayed there for what I told Clarissa was a whole day but was really about forty-five minutes. It was the crawlspace in the basement. Inside ours there were pipes coming down that I could see with a flashlight and tons and tons of dust. That was it. There were no bugs. My mother, like her own, employed an exterminator for the slightest infestation of ants.

When the alarm had gone off to tell him to shut the blinds and then the next alarm, which told him to shut off most of the lights because the suburbs were asleep after that, Mr. Harvey would go down into the basement, where there were no cracks that light could peek through and people could point to, to say he was strange. By the time he killed me he had tired of visiting the crawlspace, but he still liked to hang out in the basement in an easy chair that faced the dark hole beginning halfway up the wall and reaching to the exposed baseboards of his kitchen floor. He would often drift off to sleep there, and there he was asleep when my father passed the green house at around 4:40 A.M.

Joe Ellis was an ugly little tough. He had pinched Lindsey and me under water in the pool and kept us from going to swim parties because we hated him so much. He had a dog that he dragged around no matter what the dog wanted. It was a small dog and couldn't run very fast, but Ellis didn't care. He would hit it or lift it painfully by the tail. Then one day it was gone, and so was a cat that Ellis had been seen taunting. And then animals from all over the neighborhood began disappearing.

What I discovered, when I followed Mr. Harvey's stare to the crawlspace, were these animals that had gone missing for more than a year. People thought it stopped because the Ellis boy had been sent to military school. When they let their pets loose in the morning, they returned in the evening. This they held as proof. No one could imagine an appetite like the one in the green house. Someone who would spread quicklime on the bodies of cats and dogs, the sooner for him to have nothing left but their bones. By counting the bones and staying away from the sealed letter, the wedding ring, the bottle of perfume, he tried to stay away from what he wanted most—from going upstairs in the dark to sit in the straight chair and look out toward the high school, from imagining the bodies that matched the cheerleaders' voices, which pulsated in waves on fall days during football games, or from watching the buses from the grammar school unload two houses down. Once he had taken a long look at Lindsey, the lone girl on the boys' soccer team out running laps in our neighborhood near dark.

What I think was hardest for me to realize was that he had tried each time to stop himself. He had killed animals, taking lesser lives to keep from killing a child.

By August, Len wanted to establish some boundaries for his sake and for my father's. My father had called the precinct too many times and frustrated the police into irritation, which wouldn't help anyone be found and just might make the whole place turn against him.

The final straw had been a call that came in the first week of July. Jack Salmon had detailed to the operator how, on a morning walk, his dog had stopped in front of Mr. Harvey's house and started howling. No matter what Salmon had done, went the story, the dog wouldn't budge from the spot and wouldn't stop howling. It became a joke at the station: Mr. Fish and his Huckleberry Hound.

Len stood on the stoop of our house to finish his cigarette. It was still early, but the humidity from the day before had intensified. All week rain had been promised, the kind of thunder and lightning rainstorm the area excelled at, but so far the only moisture of which Len was aware was that covering his body in a damp sweat. He had made his last easy visit to my parents' house.

Now he heard humming—a female voice from inside. He stubbed out his cigarette against the cement under the hedge and lifted the heavy brass knocker. The door opened before he let go.

"I smelled your cigarette," Lindsey said.

"Was that you humming?"

"Those things will kill you."

"Is your father home?"

Lindsey stood aside to let him in.

"Dad!" my sister yelled into the house. "It's Len!"

"You were away, weren't you?" Len asked.

"I just got back."

My sister was wearing Samuel's softball shirt and a pair of strange sweatpants. My mother had accused her of returning home without one single item of her own clothing.

"I'm sure your parents missed you."

"Don't bet on it," Lindsey said. "I think they were happy to have me out of their hair."

Len knew she was right. He was certainly sure my mother had seemed less frantic when he had visited the house.

Lindsey said, "Buckley's made you the head of the police squad in the town he built under his bed."

"That's a promotion."

The two of them heard my father's footsteps in the hallway above and then the sounds of Buckley begging. Lindsey could tell that whatever he'd asked for our father had finally granted.

My father and brother descended the stairs, all smiles.

"Len," he said, and he shook Len's hand.

"Good morning, Jack," Len said. "And how are you this morning, Buckley?"

My father took Buckley's hand and stood him in front of Len, who solemnly bent down to my brother.

"I hear you've made me chief of police," Len said.

"Yes sir."

"I don't think I deserve the job."

"You more than anyone," my father said breezily. He loved it when Len Fenerman dropped by. Each time he did, it verified for my father that there was a consensus—a group behind him—that he wasn't alone in all this.

"I need to talk to your father, kids."

Lindsey took Buckley back into the kitchen with the promise of cereal. She herself was thinking of what Samuel had shown her; it was a drink called a jellyfish, which involved a maraschino cherry at the bottom of some sugar and gin. Samuel and Lindsey had sucked the cherries up through the sugar and booze until their heads hurt and their lips were stained red.

"Should I get Abigail? Can I make you some coffee or something?"

"Jack," Len said, "I'm not here with any news—just the opposite. Can we sit?"

I watched my father and Len head into the living room. The living room seemed to be where no living ever actually occurred. Len sat on the edge of a chair and waited for my father to take a seat.

"Listen, Jack," he said. "It's about George Harvey."

My father brightened. "I thought you said you had no news."

"I don't. I have something I need to say on behalf of the station and myself."

"Yes."

"We need you to stop making calls about George Harvey."

"But . . ."

"*I* need you to stop. There is nothing, no matter how much we stretch it, to connect him to Susie's death. Howling dogs and bridal tents are not evidence."

"I know he did it," my father said.

"He's odd, I agree, but as far as we know he isn't a killer."

"How could you possibly know that?"

Len Fenerman talked, but all my father could hear was Ruana Singh saying what she had to him, and of standing outside Mr. Harvey's house and feeling the energy radiating out to him, the coldness at the core of the man. Mr. Harvey was at once unknowable and the only person in the world who could have killed me. As Len denied it, my father grew more certain.

"You are stopping your investigation of him," my father said flatly.

Lindsey was in the doorway, hovering as she'd done on the day Len and the uniformed officer had brought my hat with the jingle bell, the twin of which she owned. That day she had quietly shoved this second hat into a box of old dolls in the back of her closet. She never wanted my mother to hear the sound of those beadlike bells again.

There was our father, the heart we knew held all of us. Held us heavily and desperately, the doors of his heart opening and closing with the rapidity of stops on an instrument, the quiet felt closures, the ghostly fingering, practice and practice and then, incredibly, sound and melody and warmth. Lindsey stepped forward from her place by the door.

"Hello again, Lindsey," Len said.

"Detective Fenerman."

"I was just telling your father . . ."

"That you're giving up."

"If there was any good reason to suspect the man . . ."

"Are you done?" Lindsey asked. She was suddenly the wife to our father, as well as the oldest, most responsible child.

"I just want you all to know that we've investigated every lead."

My father and Lindsey heard her, and I saw her. My mother coming down the stairs. Buckley raced out of the kitchen and charged, propelling his full weight into my father's legs.

"Len," my mother said, pulling her terry-cloth robe tighter when she saw him, "has Jack offered you coffee?"

My father looked at his wife and Len Fenerman.

"The cops are punting," Lindsey said, taking Buckley gently by the shoulders and holding him against her.

"Punting?" Buckley asked. He always rolled a sound around in his mouth like a sourball until he had its taste and feel.

"What?"

"Detective Fenerman is here to tell Dad to stop bugging them."

"Lindsey," Len said, "I wouldn't put it like that."

"Whatever," she said. My sister wanted out, now, into a place where gifted camp continued, where Samuel and she, or even Artie, who at the last minute had won the Perfect Murder competition by entering the icicle-as-murder-weapon idea, ruled her world.

"Come on, Dad," she said. My father was slowly fitting something together. It had nothing to do with George Harvey, nothing to do with me. It was in my mother's eyes.

That night, as he had more and more often, my father stayed up by himself in his study. He could not believe the world falling down around him—how unexpected it all was after the initial blast of my death. "I feel like I'm standing in the wake of a volcano eruption," he wrote in his notebook. "Abigail thinks Len Fenerman is right about Harvey."

As he wrote, the candle in the window kept flickering, and despite his desk lamp the flickering distracted him. He sat back in the old wooden school chair he'd had since college and heard the reassuring squeak of the wood under him. At the firm he was failing to even register what was needed of him. Daily now he faced column after column of meaningless numbers he was supposed to make square with company claims. He was making mistakes with a frequency that was frightening, and he feared, more than he had in the first days following my disappearance, that he would not be able to support his two remaining children.

He stood up and stretched his arms overhead, trying to concentrate on the few exercises that our family doctor had suggested. I watched his body bend in uneasy and surprising ways I had never seen before. He could have been a dancer rather than a businessman. He could have danced on Broadway with Ruana Singh.

He snapped off the desk light, leaving only the candle.

In his low green easy chair he now felt the most comfortable. It was where I often saw him sleep. The room like a vault, the chair like a womb, and me standing guard over him. He stared at the candle in the window and thought about what to do; how he had tried to touch my mother and she had pulled away over to the edge of the bed. But how in the presence of the police she seemed to bloom.

He had grown used to the ghostly light behind the candle's flame, that quivering reflection in the window. He stared at the two of them—real flame and ghost—and began to work toward a doze, dozing in thought and strain and the events of the day.

As he was about to let go for the night, we both saw the same thing: another light. Outside.

It looked like a penlight from that distance. One white beam slowly moving out across the lawns and toward the junior high. My father watched it. It was after midnight now, and the moon was not full enough, as it often was, to see the outlines of the trees and houses. Mr. Stead, who rode his bike late at night with a flashing light on the front powered by his pedals, would never degrade the lawns of his neighbors that way. It was too late for Mr. Stead anyway.

My father leaned forward in the green chair in his study and watched the flashlight move in the direction of the fallow cornfield.

"Bastard," he whispered. "You murderous bastard."

He dressed quickly from the storage closet in his study, putting on a hunting jacket that he hadn't had on since an ill-fated hunting trip ten years earlier. Downstairs he went into the front hall closet and found the baseball bat he'd bought for Lindsey before she favored soccer.

First he shut off the porch light they kept on all night for me and that, even though it had been eight months since the police said I would not be found alive, they could not bring themselves to stop leaving on. With his hand on the doorknob, he took a deep breath.

He turned the knob and found himself out on the dark front porch. Closed the door and found himself standing in his front yard with a baseball bat and these words: *find a quiet way.*

He walked through his front yard and across the street and then into the O'Dwyers' yard, where he had first seen the light. He passed their darkened swimming pool and the rusted-out swing set. His heart was pumping, but he could not feel anything but the knowledge in his brain. George Harvey had killed his last little girl.

He reached the soccer field. To his right, far into the cornfield but not in the vicinity he knew by heart—the area that had been roped off and cleared and combed and bulldozed—he saw the small light. He clenched his fingers tighter around the bat by his side. For just a second he could not believe what he was about to do, but then, with everything in him, he knew.

The wind helped him. It swept along the soccer field alongside the cornfield and whipped his trousers around the front of his legs; it pushed him forward despite himself. Everything fell away. Once he was among the rows of corn, his focus solely on the light, the wind disguised his presence. The sound of his feet crushing the stalks was swept up in the whistle and bustle of the wind against the broken plants.

Things that made no sense flooded his head—the hard rubber sound of children's roller skates on pavement, the smell of his father's pipe tobacco, Abigail's smile when he met her, like light piercing his confused heart—and then the flashlight shut off and everything went equal and dark.

He took a few more steps, then stopped.

"I know you're here," he said.

I flooded the cornfield, I flashed fires through it to light it up, I sent storms of hail and flowers, but none of it worked to warn him. I was relegated to heaven: I watched.

"I'm here for it," my father said, his voice trembling. That heart bursting in and out, blood gorging the rivers of his chest and then cinching up. Breath and fire and lungs seizing, releasing, adrenaline saving what was left. My mother's smile in his mind gone, mine taking its place.

"Nobody's awake," my father said. "I'm here to finish it."

He heard whimpering. I wanted to cast down a spotlight like they did in the school auditorium, awkwardly, the light not always hitting the right place on the stage. There she would be, crouching and whimpering and now, despite her blue eye shadow and Western-style boots from Bakers', wetting her pants. A child.

She didn't recognize my father's voice infused with hate. "Brian?" Clarissa's quavering voice came out. "Brian?" It was hope like a shield.

My father's hand loosened on the bat, letting it fall.

"Hello? Who's there?"

With wind in his ears, Brian Nelson, the beanstalk scarecrow, parked his older brother's Spyder Corvette in the school lot. Late, always late, sleeping in class and at the dinner table but never when a boy had a *Playboy* or a cute girl walked by, never on a night when he had a girl waiting for him out in the cornfield. Still, he took his time. The wind, glorious blanket and cover for what he had planned, whipped past his ears.

Brian moved toward the cornfield with his giant torch light from his mother's under-the-sink disaster kit. Finally he heard what he would later say were Clarissa's cries for help.

My father's heart was like a stone there, heavy, carried inside his chest as he ran and fumbled toward the sound of the girl's whimpering. His mother was knitting him mittens, Susie was asking for gloves, so cold in the cornfield in winter. Clarissa! Susie's silly friend. Makeup, prissy jam sandwiches, and her tropical tan skin.

He ran blind into her and knocked her down in the darkness. Her screaming filled his ear and poured into the empty spaces, ricocheting inside of him. "Susie!" he screamed back.

Brian ran when he heard my name—full-speed-ahead awake. His light hopped over the cornfield, and, for one bright second, there was Mr. Harvey. No one but me saw him. Brian's light hit his back as he crawled into the high stalks and listened, again, for the sound of whimpering.

And then the light hit target and Brian dragged my father up and off Clarissa to hit him. Hit him on the head and back and face with the survival-kit flashlight. My father shouted and yelped and moaned.

And then Brian saw the bat.

I pushed and pushed against the unyielding borders of my heaven. I wanted to reach out and lift my father up, away, to me.

Clarissa ran and Brian swung. My father's eyes caught Brian's but he could barely breathe.

"You fucker!" Brian was black and white with blame.

I heard mumblings in the dirt. I heard my name. I thought I could taste the blood on my father's face, reach out to draw my fingers across his cut lips, lie down with him in my grave.

But I had to turn my back in heaven. I could do nothing—

trapped in my perfect world. The blood I tasted was bitter. Acid. I wanted my father's vigil, his tight love for me. But also I wanted him to go away and leave me be. I was granted one weak grace. Back in the room where the green chair was still warm from his body, I blew that lonely, flickering candle out.

TWELVE

I stood in the room beside him and watched him sleep. During the night the story had come unwound and spun down so that the police understood: Mr. Salmon was crazy with grief and had gone out to the cornfield seeking revenge. It fit what they knew of him, his persistent phone calls, his obsession with the neighbor, and Detective Fenerman having visited that same day to tell my parents that for all intents and purposes my murder investigation had entered a sort of hiatus. No clues were left to pursue. No body had been found.

The surgeon had to operate on his knee to replace the cap with a purselike suture that partially disabled the joint. As I watched the operation I thought of how much like sewing it seemed, and I hoped that my father was in more capable hands than if he had been brought to me. In home ec my hands had been clumsy. Zipper foot or baster, I got them all confused.

But the surgeon had been patient. A nurse had filled him in on the story as he washed and scrubbed his hands. He remembered reading about what had happened to me in the papers. He was my father's age and had children of his own. He shivered as he stretched his gloves out over his hands. How alike he and this man were. How very different.

In the dark hospital room, a fluorescent bar light buzzed just behind my father's bed. As dawn approached it was the only light in the room until my sister walked in.

My mother and sister and brother woke to the sounds of the police sirens and came down into the dark kitchen from their bedrooms.

"Go wake your father," my mother said to Lindsey. "I can't believe he slept through this."

And so my sister had gone up. Everyone now knew where to look for him: in only six months, the green chair had become his true bed.

"Dad's not here!" my sister yelled as soon as she realized. "Dad's gone. Mom! Mom! Dad's gone!" For a rare moment Lindsey was a frightened child.

"Damn!" my mother said.

"Mommy?" Buckley said.

Lindsey rushed into the kitchen. My mother faced the stove. Her back was a riddled mass of nerves as she went about making tea.

"Mom?" Lindsey asked. "We have to do something."

"Don't you see . . . ?" my mother said, stopping for a moment with a box of Earl Grey suspended in the air.

"What?"

She put the tea down, switched on the burner, and turned around. She saw something herself then: Buckley had gone to cling to my sister as he anxiously sucked his thumb.

"He's gone off after that man and gotten himself in trouble."

"We should go out, Mom," Lindsey said. "We should go help him."

"No."

"Mom, we have to help Daddy."

"Buckley, stop milking your thumb!"

My brother burst into hot panicked tears, and my sister reached her arms down to pull him in tighter. She looked at our mother.

"I'm going out to find him," Lindsey said.

"You are doing no such thing," my mother said. "He'll come home in good time. We're staying out of this."

"Mom," Lindsey said, "what if he's hurt?"

Buckley stopped crying long enough to look back and forth from my sister to my mother. He knew what hurt meant and who was missing from the house.

My mother gave Lindsey a meaningful look. "We are not discussing this further. You can go up to your room and wait or wait with me. Your choice."

Lindsey was dumbfounded. She stared at our mother and knew what she wanted most: to flee, to run out into the cornfield where my father was, where I was, where she felt suddenly that the heart of her family had moved. But Buckley stood warm against her.

"Buckley," she said, "let's go back upstairs. You can sleep in my bed."

He was beginning to understand: you were treated special and, later, something horrible would be told to you.

When the call came from the police, my mother went immediately to the front closet. "He's been hit with our own baseball bat!" she said, grabbing her coat and keys and lipstick. My sister felt more alone than she had ever been but also more responsible. Buckley couldn't be left by himself, and Lindsey wasn't even able to drive. Besides, it made the clearest sense in the world. Didn't the wife belong most at the husband's side?

But when my sister was able to get Nate's mother on the line—after all, the commotion in the cornfield had awakened the whole neighborhood—she knew what she would do. She called Samuel next. Within an hour, Nate's mother arrived to take Buckley, and Hal Heckler pulled up to our house on his motorcycle. It should have been exciting—clutching on to Samuel's gorgeous older brother, riding on a motorcycle for the first time—but all she could think of was our father.

My mother was not in his hospital room when Lindsey entered; it was just my father and me. She came up and stood on the other side of his bed and started to cry quietly.

"Daddy?" she said. "Are you okay, Daddy?"

The door opened a crack. It was Hal Heckler, a tall handsome slash of a man.

"Lindsey," he said, "I'll wait for you out in the visitors' area in case you need a ride home."

He saw her tears when she turned around. "Thanks, Hal. If you see my mother . . ."

"I'll tell her you're in here."

Lindsey took my father's hand and watched his face for movement. My sister was growing up before my eyes. I listened as she whispered the words he had sung to the two of us before Buckley was born:

> Stones and bones;
> snow and frost;
> seeds and beans and polliwogs.
> Paths and twigs, assorted kisses,
> We all know who Daddy misses!

His two little frogs of girls, that's who.
They know where they are, do you, do you?

I wish a smile had come curling up onto my father's face, but he was deep under, swimming against drug and nightmare and waking dream. For a time leaden weights had been tied by anesthesia to the four corners of his consciousness. Like a firm waxen cover it had locked him away tight into the hard-blessed hours where there was no dead daughter and no gone knee, and where there was also no sweet daughter whispering rhymes.

"When the dead are done with the living," Franny said to me, "the living can go on to other things."

"What about the dead?" I asked. "Where do we go?"

She wouldn't answer me.

Len Fenerman had rushed to the hospital as soon as they put the call through. Abigail Salmon, the dispatcher said, requesting him.

My father was in surgery, and my mother was pacing back and forth near the nurses' station. She had driven to the hospital in her raincoat with only her thin summer nightgown beneath it. She had her beating-around-the-yard ballet flats on her feet. She hadn't bothered to pull her hair back, and there hadn't been any hair elastics in her pockets or purse. In the dark foggy parking lot of the hospital she had stopped to check her face and applied her stock red lipstick with a practiced hand.

When she saw Len approaching from the end of the long white corridor, she relaxed.

"Abigail," he said when he grew closer.

"Oh, Len," she said. Her face puzzled up on what she could say next. His name had been the sigh she needed. Everything that came next was not words.

The nurses at their station turned their heads away as Len and my mother touched hands. They extended this privacy veil habitually, as a matter of course, but even so they could see this man meant something to this woman.

"Let's talk in the visitors' area," Len said and led my mother down the corridor.

As they walked she told him my father was in surgery. He filled her in on what had happened in the cornfield.

"Apparently he said he thought the girl was George Harvey."

"He thought Clarissa was George Harvey?" My mother stopped, incredulous, just outside the visitors' area.

"It was dark out, Abigail. I think he only saw the girl's flashlight. My visit today couldn't have helped much. He's convinced that Harvey is involved."

"Is Clarissa all right?"

"She was treated for scratches and released. She was hysterical. Crying and screaming. It was a horrible coincidence, her being Susie's friend."

Hal was slumped down in a darkened corner of the visitors' area with his feet propped up on the helmet he'd brought for Lindsey. When he heard the voices approaching he stirred.

It was my mother and a cop. He slumped back down and let his shoulder-length hair obscure his face. He was pretty sure my mother wouldn't remember him.

But she recognized the jacket as Samuel's and for a moment thought, *Samuel's here,* but then thought, *His brother.*

"Let's sit," Len said, indicating the connected modular chairs on the far side of the room.

"I'd rather keep walking," my mother said. "The doctor said it will be an hour at least before they have anything to tell us."

"Where to?"

"Do you have cigarettes?"

"You know I do," Len said, smiling guiltily. He had to seek out her eyes. They weren't focusing on him. They seemed to be preoccupied, and he wished he could reach up and grab them and train them on the here and now. On him.

"Let's find an exit, then."

They found a door to a small concrete balcony near my father's room. It was a service balcony for a heating unit, so even though it was cramped and slightly chilly, the noise and the hot exhaust of the humming hydrant beside them shut them into a capsule that felt far away. They smoked cigarettes and looked at each other as if they had suddenly and without preparation moved on to a new page, where the pressing business had already been highlighted for prompt attention.

"How did your wife die?" my mother asked.

"Suicide."

Her hair was covering most of her face, and watching her I was reminded of Clarissa at her most self-conscious. The way she behaved around boys when we went to the mall. She would giggle too much and flash her eyes over at them to see where they were looking. But I was also struck by my mother's red mouth with the cigarette going up and away from it and smoke trailing out. I had seen this mother only once before—in the photograph. This mother had never had us.

"Why did she kill herself?"

"That's the question that preoccupies me most when I'm not preoccupied by things like your daughter's murder."

A strange smile came across my mother's face.

"Say that again," she said.

"What?" Len looked at her smile, wanted to reach out and trace the corners of it with his fingertips.

"My daughter's murder," my mother said.

"Abigail, are you okay?"

"No one says it. No one in the neighborhood talks about it. People call it the 'horrible tragedy' or some variation on that. I just want it to be spoken out loud by somebody. To have it said aloud. I'm ready—I wasn't ready before."

My mother dropped her cigarette onto the concrete and let it burn. She took Len's face in her hands.

"Say it," she said.

"Your daughter's murder."

"Thank you."

And I watched that flat red mouth move across an invisible line that separated her from the rest of the world. She pulled Len in to her and slowly kissed him on the mouth. He seemed to hesitate at first. His body tensed, telling him NO, but that NO became vague and cloudy, became air sucked into the intake fan of the humming hydrant beside them. She reached up and unbuttoned her raincoat. He placed his hand against the thin gauzy material of her summer gown.

My mother was, in her need, irresistible. As a child I had seen her effect on men. When we were in grocery stores, stockers volunteered to find the items on her list and would help us out to the car. Like Ruana Singh, she was known as one of the pretty mothers in the neighborhood; no man who met her could help but smile. When she asked a question, their beating hearts gave in.

But still, it had only ever been my father who stretched her laughter out into the rooms of the house and made it okay, somehow, for her to let go.

By tacking on extra hours here and there and skipping lunches, my father had managed to come home early from work every Thursday when we were little. But whereas the weekends were family time, they called that day "Mommy and Daddy time." Lindsey and I thought of it as good-girl time. It meant no peeps out of us as we stayed quiet on the other side of the house, while we used my father's then sparsely filled den as our playroom.

My mother would start preparing us around two.

"Bath time," she sang, as if she were saying we could go out to play. And in the beginning that was how it felt. All three of us would rush up to our rooms and put on bathrobes. We would meet in the hallway—three girls—and my mother would take us by the hands and lead us into our pink bathroom.

Back then she talked to us about mythology, which she had studied in school. She liked to tell us stories about Persephone and Zeus. She bought us illustrated books on the Norse gods, which gave us nightmares. She had gotten her master's in English—having fought tooth and nail with Grandma Lynn to go so far in school—and still held on to vague ideas of teaching when the two of us were old enough to be left on our own.

Those bath times blur together, as do all the gods and goddesses, but what I remember most is watching things hit my mother while I looked at her, how the life she had wanted and the loss of it reached her in waves. As her firstborn, I thought it was me who took away all those dreams of what she had wanted to be.

My mother would lift Lindsey out of the tub first, dry her, and listen to her chatter about ducks and cuts. Then she would get me out of the tub and though I tried to be quiet the warm water made my sister and me drunk, and we talked to my mother about everything that mattered to us. Boys that teased us or how another family down the block had a puppy and why couldn't we have one too. She would listen seriously as if she were mentally noting the points of our agenda on a steno pad to which she would later refer.

"Well, first things first," she summed up. "Which means a nice nap for the two of you!"

She and I would tuck Lindsey in together. I stood by the bed as she kissed my sister on her forehead and brushed back her hair from her face. I think competition started there for me. Who got the better kiss, the longer time after the bath with Mom.

Luckily, I always won this. When I look back now I see that my mother had become—and very quickly after they moved into that house—lonely. Because I was the oldest, I became her closest friend.

I was too little to know what she was really saying to me, but I loved to be hushed to sleep by the soft lullaby of her words. One of the blessings of my heaven is that I can go back to these moments, live them again, and be with my mother in a way I never could have been. I reach my hand across the Inbetween and take the hand of that young lonely mother in mine.

What she said to a four-year-old about Helen of Troy: "A feisty woman who screwed things up." About Margaret Sanger: "She was judged by her looks, Susie. Because she looked like a mouse, no one expected her to last." Gloria Steinem: "I feel horrible, but I wish she'd trim those nails." Our neighbors: "An idiot in tight pants; oppressed by that prig of a husband; typically provincial and judgmental of everyone."

"Do you know who Persephone is?" she asked me absently one Thursday. But I didn't answer. By then I'd learned to hush when she brought me into my room. My sister's and my time was in the bathroom as we were being toweled off. Lindsey and I could talk about anything then. In my bedroom it was Mommy's time.

She took the towel and draped it over the spindle knob of my four-poster bed. "Imagine our neighbor Mrs. Tarking as Persephone," she said. She opened the drawer of the dresser and handed me my underpants. She always doled out my clothes piecemeal, not wanting to pressure me. She understood my needs early. If I was aware I would have to tie laces I would not have been able to put my feet into socks.

"She's wearing a long white robe, like a sheet draped over her shoulders, but made out of some nice shiny or light fabric, like silk. And she has sandals made of gold and she's surrounded by torches which are light made out of flames . . ."

She went to the drawer to get my undershirt and absentmindedly put it over my head instead of leaving it to me. Once my mother was launched I could take advantage of it—be the baby again. I never protested and claimed to be grown up or a big girl. Those afternoons were about listening to my mysterious mother.

She pulled back the tough-cord Sears bedspread, and I scooted over to the far side along the wall. She always checked her watch then and afterward she would say, "Just for a little while," and slide off her shoes and slip in between the sheets with me.

For both of us it was about getting lost. She got lost in her story. I got lost in her talk.

She would tell me about Persephone's mother, Demeter, or Cupid and Psyche, and I would listen to her until I fell asleep. Sometimes my parents' laughter in the room beside me or the sounds of their late-afternoon lovemaking would wake me up. I would lie there in half-sleep, listening. I liked to pretend that I was in the warm hold of a ship from one of the stories my father read to us, and that all of us were on the ocean and the waves were rolling gently up against the sides of the ship. The laughter, the small sounds of muffled moaning, would usher me back under into sleep.

But then my mother's escape, her half-measure return to the outside world, had been smashed when I was ten and Lindsey nine. She'd missed her period and had taken the fateful car trip to the doctor. Underneath her smile and exclamations to my sister and me were fissures that led somewhere deep inside her. But because I didn't want to, because I was a child, I chose not to follow them. I grabbed the smile like a prize and entered the land of wonder of whether I would be the sister to a little boy or to a little girl.

If I had paid attention, I would have noticed signs. Now I see the shifting, how the stack of books on my parents' bedside table changed from catalogs for local colleges, encyclopedias of mythology, novels by James, Eliot, and Dickens, to the works of Dr. Spock. Then came gardening books and cookbooks until for her birthday two months before I died, I thought the perfect gift was *Better Homes and Gardens Guide to Entertaining*. When she realized she was pregnant the third time, she sealed the more mysterious mother off. Bottled up for years behind that wall, that needy part of her had grown, not shrunk, and in Len, the need to get out, to smash, destroy, rescind, overtook her. Her body led, and in its wake would be the pieces left to her.

It was not easy for me to witness, but I did.

Their first embrace was hurried, fumbled, passionate.

"Abigail," Len said, his two hands now on either side of her waist underneath the coat, the gauzy gown barely a veil between them. "Think of what you're doing."

"I'm tired of thinking," she said. Her hair was floating above her head because of the fan beside them—in an aureole. Len blinked as he looked at her. Marvelous, dangerous, wild.

"Your husband," he said.

"Kiss me," she said. "Please."

I was watching a beg for leniency on my mother's part. My mother was moving physically through time to flee from me. I could not hold her back.

Len kissed her forehead hard and closed his eyes. She took his hand and placed it on her breast. She whispered in his ear. I knew what was happening. Her rage, her loss, her despair. The whole life lost tumbling out in an arc on that roof, clogging up her being. She needed Len to drive the dead daughter out.

He pushed her back into the stucco surface of the wall as they kissed, and my mother held on to him as if on the other side of his kiss there could be a new life.

* * *

On my way home from the junior high, I would sometimes stop at the edge of our property and watch my mother ride the ride-on mower, looping in and out among the pine trees, and I could remember then how she used to whistle in the mornings as she made her tea and how my father, rushing home on Thursdays, would bring her marigolds and her face would light up yellowy in delight. They had been deeply, separately, wholly in love—apart from her children my mother could reclaim this love, but with them she began to drift. It was my father who grew toward us as the years went by; it was my mother who grew away.

Beside his hospital bed, Lindsey had fallen asleep while holding our father's hand. My mother, still mussed, passed by Hal Heckler in the visitors' area, and a moment later so did Len. Hal didn't need more than this. He grabbed his helmet and went off down the hall.

After a brief visit to the ladies' room, my mother was heading in the direction of my father's room when Hal stopped her.

"Your daughter's in there," Hal called out. She turned.

"Hal Heckler," he said, "Samuel's brother. I was at the memorial service."

"Oh, yes, I'm sorry. I didn't recognize you."

"Not your job," he said.

There was an awkward pause.

"So, Lindsey called me and I brought her here an hour ago."

"Oh."

"Buckley's with a neighbor," he said.

"Oh." She was staring at him. In her eyes she was climbing back to the surface. She used his face to climb back to.

"Are you okay?"

"I'm a little upset—that's understandable, right?"

"Perfectly," he said, speaking slowly. "I just wanted to let you know that your daughter is in there with your husband. I'll be in the visitors' area if you need me."

"Thank you," she said. She watched him turn away and paused for a moment to listen to the worn heels of his motorcycle boots reverberate down the linoleum hall.

She caught herself then, shook herself back to where she was, never guessing for a second that that had been Hal's purpose in greeting her.

Inside the room it was dark now, the fluorescent light behind my father flickering so slightly it lit only the most obvious masses in the room. My sister was in a chair pulled up alongside the bed, her head resting on the side of it with her hand extended out to touch my father. My father, deep under, was lying on his back. My mother could not know that I was there with them, that here were the four of us so changed now from the days when she tucked Lindsey and me into bed and went to make love to her husband, our father. Now she saw the pieces. She saw that my sister and father, together, had become a piece. She was glad of it.

I had played a hide-and-seek game of love with my mother as I grew up, courting her attention and approval in a way that I had never had to with my father.

I didn't have to play hide-and-seek anymore. As she stood in the darkened room and watched my sister and father, I knew one of the things that heaven meant. I had a choice, and it was not to divide my family in my heart.

Late at night the air above hospitals and senior citizen homes was often thick and fast with souls. Holly and I watched sometimes on the nights when sleep was lost to us. We came to realize how these deaths seemed choreographed from somewhere far away. Not our heaven. And so we began to suspect that there was a place more all-encompassing than where we were.

Franny came to watch with us in the beginning.

"It's one of my secret pleasures," she admitted. "After all these years I still love to watch the souls that float and spin in masses, all of them clamoring at once inside the air."

"I don't see anything," I said that first time.

"Watch closely," she said, "and hush."

But I felt them before I saw them, small warm sparks along my arms. Then there they were, fireflies lighting up and expanding in howls and swirls as they abandoned human flesh.

"Like snowflakes," Franny said, "none of them the same and yet each one, from where we stand, exactly like the one before."

THIRTEEN

When she returned to junior high in the fall of 1974, Lindsey was not only the sister of the murdered girl but the child of a "crackpot," "nutcase," "looney-tunes," and the latter hurt her more because it wasn't true.

The rumors Lindsey and Samuel heard in the first weeks of the school year wove in and out of the rows of student lockers like the most persistent of snakes. Now the swirl had grown to include Brian Nelson and Clarissa who, thankfully, had both entered the high school that year. At Fairfax Brian and Clarissa clung to each other, exploiting what had happened to them, using my father's debasement as a varnish of cool they could coat themselves with by retelling throughout the school what had happened that night in the cornfield.

Ray and Ruth walked by on the inside of the glass wall that looked out on the outdoor lounge. On the false boulders where the supposed bad kids sat, they would see Brian holding court. His walk that year went from anxious scarecrow to masculine strut. Clarissa, giggly with both fear and lust, had unlocked her privates and slept with Brian. However haphazardly, everyone I'd known was growing up.

Buckley entered kindergarten that year and immediately arrived home with a crush on his teacher, Miss Koekle. She held his hand so gently whenever she had to lead him to the bathroom or help explain an assignment that her force was irresistible. In one way he profited—she would often sneak him an extra cookie or a softer sit-upon—but in another he was held aloft and apart from his fellow kindergartners. By my death he was made different among the one group—children—in which he might have been anonymous.

Samuel would walk Lindsey home and then go down the main road and thumb his way to Hal's bike shop. He counted on buddies of his brother's to recognize him, and he reached his destination in various pasted-together bikes and trucks that Hal would fine-tune for the driver when they pulled up.

He did not go inside our house for a while. No one but family did. By October my father was just beginning to get up and around. His doctors had told him that his right leg would always be stiff, but if he stretched and stayed limber it wouldn't present too much of an obstacle. "No running bases, but everything else," the surgeon said the morning after his surgery, when my father woke to find Lindsey beside him and my mother standing by the window staring out at the parking lot.

Buckley went right from basking in the shine of Miss Koekle home to burrow in the empty cave of my father's heart. He asked ceaseless questions about the "fake knee," and my father warmed to him.

"The knee came from outer space," my father would say. "They brought pieces of the moon back and carved them up and now they use them for things like this."

"Wow," Buckley would say, grinning. "When can Nate see?"

"Soon, Buck, soon," my father said. But his smile grew weak.

When Buckley took these conversations and brought them to our mother—"Daddy's knee is made out of moonbone," he would tell her, or "Miss Koekle said my colors were really good"—she would nod her head. She had become aware of what she did. She cut carrots and celery into edible lengths. She washed out thermoses and lunchboxes, and when Lindsey decided she was too old for a lunchbox, my mother caught herself actually happy when she found wax-lined bags that would keep her daughter's lunch from seeping through and staining her clothes. Which she washed. Which she folded. Which she ironed when necessary and which she straightened on hangers. Which she picked up from the floor or retrieved from the car or untangled from the wet towel left on the bed that she made every morning, tucking the corners in, and fluffing the pillows, and propping up stuffed animals, and opening the blinds to let the light in.

In the moments when Buckley sought her out, she often made a barter of it. She would focus on him for a few minutes, and then she would allow herself to drift away from her house and home and think of Len.

By November, my father had mastered what he called an "adroit hobble," and when Buckley egged him on he would do a contorted skip that, as long as it made his son laugh, didn't make him think of how odd and desperate he might look to an outsider or to my mother. Everyone save Buckley knew what was coming: the first anniversary.

Buckley and my father spent the crisp fall afternoons out in the fenced-in yard with Holiday. My father would sit in the old iron lawn chair with his leg stretched out in front of him and propped up slightly on an ostentatious boot scraper that Grandma Lynn had found in a curio shop in Maryland.

Buckley threw the squeaky cow toy while Holiday ran to get it. My father took pleasure in the agile body of his five-year-old son and Buckley's peals of delight when Holiday knocked him over and nudged him with his nose or licked his face with his long pink tongue. But he couldn't rid himself of one thought: this too—this perfect boy—could be taken from him.

It had been a combination of things, his injury not the least among them, that had made him stay inside the house on an extended sick leave from his firm. His boss acted differently around him now, and so did his coworkers. They trod gently outside his office and would stop a few feet from his desk as if, should they be too relaxed in his presence, what had happened to him would happen to them—as if having a dead child were contagious. No one knew how he continued to do what he did, while simultaneously they wanted him to shut all signs of his grief away, place it in a file somewhere and tuck it in a drawer that no one would be asked to open again. He called in regularly, and his boss just as easily agreed that he could take another week, another month if he had to, and he counted this as a blessing of always having been on time or willing to work late. But he stayed away from Mr. Harvey and tried to curb even the thought of him. He would not use his name except in his notebook, which he kept hidden in his study, where it was surprisingly easily agreed with my mother that she would no longer clean. He had apologized to me in his notebook. "I need to rest, honey. I need to understand how to go after this man. I hope you'll understand."

But he had set his return to work for December 2, right after Thanksgiving. He wanted to be back in the office by the anniversary of my disappearance. Functioning and catching up on work—in as public and distracting a place as he could think of. And away from my mother, if he was honest with himself.

How to swim back to her, how to reach her again. She was pulling and pulling away—all her energy was against the house, and all his energy was inside it. He settled on building back his strength and finding a strategy to pursue Mr. Harvey. Placing blame was easier than adding up the mounting figures of what he'd lost.

Grandma Lynn was due for Thanksgiving, and Lindsey had kept to a beautifying regime Grandma had set up for her through letters. She'd felt silly when she first put cucumbers on her eyes (to diminish puffiness), or oatmeal on her face (to cleanse the pores and absorb excess oils), or eggs yolks in her hair (to make it shine). Her use of groceries had even made my mother laugh, then wonder if she too should start to beautify. But that was only for a second, because she was thinking of Len, not because she was in love with him but because being with him was the fastest way she knew to forget.

Two weeks before Grandma Lynn's arrival, Buckley and my father were out in the yard with Holiday. Buckley and Holiday were romping from one large pile of burnished oak leaves to another in an increasingly hyper game of tag. "Watch out, Buck," my father said. "You'll make Holiday nip." And sure enough.

My father said he wanted to try something out.

"We have to see if your old dad can carry you piggyback style again. Soon you'll be too big."

So, awkwardly, in the beautiful isolation of the yard, where if my father fell only a boy and a dog who loved him would see, the two of them worked together to make what they both wanted—this return to father/son normalcy—happen. When Buckley stood on the iron chair—"Now scoot up my back," my father said, stooping forward, "and grab on to my shoulders," not knowing if he'd have the strength to lift him up from there—I crossed my fingers hard in heaven and held my breath. In the cornfield, yes, but, in this moment, repairing the most basic fabric of their previous day-to-day lives, challenging his injury to take a moment like this back, my father became my hero.

"Duck, now duck again," he said as they galumphed through the downstairs doorways and up the stairs, each step a balance my father negotiated, a wincing pain. And with Holiday rushing past them on the stairs, and Buckley joyous on his mount, he knew that in this challenge to his strength he had done the right thing.

When the two of them—with dog—discovered Lindsey in the upstairs bathroom, she whined a loud complaint.

"Daaaaddd!"

My father stood up straight. Buckley reached up and touched the light fixture with his hand.

"What are you doing?" my father said.

"What does it look like I'm doing?"

She sat on the toilet lid wrapped in a large white towel (the towels my mother bleached, the towels my mother hung on the line to dry, the towels she folded, and placed in a basket and brought up to the linen closet . . .). Her left leg was propped up on the edge of the tub, covered with shaving cream. In her hand she held my father's razor.

"Don't be petulant," my father said.

"I'm sorry," my sister said, looking down. "I just want a little privacy is all."

My father lifted Buckley up and over his head. "The counter, the counter, son," he said, and Buckley thrilled at the illegal halfway point of the bathroom counter and how his muddy feet soiled the tile.

"Now hop down." And he did. Holiday tackled him.

"You're too young to shave your legs, sweetie," my father said.

"Grandma Lynn started shaving at eleven."

"Buckley, will you go in your room and take the dog? I'll be in in a while."

"Yes, Daddy."

Buckley was still a little boy who my father could, with patience and a bit of maneuvering, get up on his shoulders so they could be a typical father and son. But he now saw in Lindsey what brought a double pain. I was a little girl in the tub, a toddler being held up to the sink, a girl who had forever stopped just short of sitting as my sister did now.

When Buckley was gone, he turned his attention to my sister. He would care for his two daughters by caring for one: "Are you being careful?" he asked.

"I just started," Lindsey said. "I'd like to be alone, Dad."

"Is that the same blade that was on it when you got it from my shaving kit?"

"Yes."

"Well, my beard stubble dulls the blade. I'll go get you a fresh one."

"Thanks, Dad," my sister said, and again she was his sweet, piggyback-riding Lindsey.

He left the room and went down the hallway to the other side of the house and the master bathroom that he and my mother still shared, though they no longer slept in the same room together. As he reached up into the cabinet for the package of fresh razors, he felt a tear in his chest. He ignored it and focused on the task. There was only a flicker of a thought then: *Abigail should be doing this.*

He brought the razor blades back, showed Lindsey how to change them, and gave her a few pointers on how best to shave. "Watch out for the ankle and the knee," he said. "Your mother always called those the danger spots."

"You can stay if you want," she said, ready now to let him in.

"But I might be a bloody mess." She wanted to hit herself. "Sorry, Dad," she said. "Here, I'll move—you sit."

She got up and went to sit on the edge of the tub. She ran the tap, and my father lowered himself onto the toilet lid.

"It's okay, honey," he said. "We haven't talked about your sister in a while."

"Who needs to?" my sister said. "She's everywhere."

"Your brother seems to be all right."

"He's glued to you."

"Yes," he said, and he realized he liked it, this father-courting his son was doing.

"Ouch," Lindsey said, a fine trickle of blood beginning to spread into the white foam of the shaving cream. "This is a total hassle."

"Press down on the nick with your thumb. It stops the bleeding. You could do just to the top of your knee," he offered. "That's what your mother does unless we're going to the beach."

Lindsey paused. "You guys never go to the beach."

"We used to."

My father had met my mother when they were both working at Wanamaker's during the summer break from college. He had just made a nasty comment about how the employee's lounge reeked of cigarettes when she smiled and brought out her then-habitual pack of Pall Malls. "Touché," he said, and he stayed beside her despite the reeking stink of her cigarettes enveloping him from head to toe.

"I've been trying to decide who I look like," Lindsey said, "Grandma Lynn or Mom."

"I've always thought both you and your sister looked like my mother," he said.

"Dad?"

"Yes."

"Are you still convinced that Mr. Harvey had something to do with it?"

It was like a stick finally sparking against another stick—the friction took.

"There is no doubt in my mind, honey. None."

"Then why doesn't Len arrest him?"

She drew the razor sloppily up and finished her first leg. She hesitated there, waiting.

"I wish it was easy to explain," he said, the words coiling out of him. He had never talked at length about his suspicion to anyone. "When I met him that day, in his backyard, and we built that tent—the one he claimed he built for his wife, whose name I thought was Sophie and Len took down as Leah—there was something about his movements that made me sure."

"Everyone thinks he's kind of weird."

"True, I understand that," he said. "But then everyone hasn't had much to do with him either. They don't know whether his weirdness is benign or not."

"Benign?"

"Harmless."

"Holiday doesn't like him," Lindsey offered.

"Exactly. I've never seen that dog bark so hard. The fur on his back stood straight up that morning."

"But the cops think you're nuts."

" 'No evidence' is all they can say. Without evidence and without—excuse me, honey—a body, they have nothing to move on and no basis for an arrest."

"What would be a basis?"

"I guess something to link him to Susie. If someone had seen him in the cornfield or even lurking around the school. Something like that."

"Or if he had something of hers?" Both my father and Lindsey were heatedly talking, her second leg lathered but left unshaved, because what radiated as the two sticks of their interest sparked flame was that I was in that house somewhere. My body—in the basement, first floor, second floor, attic. To keep from acknowledging that horrible—but oh, if it were true, so blatant so perfect so conclusive as evidence—thought, they remembered what I wore that day, remembered what I carried, the Frito Bandito eraser I prized, the David Cassidy button I'd pinned inside my bag, the David Bowie one I had pinned on the outside. They named all the clutter and accessories that surrounded what would be the best, most hideous evidence anyone could find—my corpse cut up, my blank and rotting eyes.

My eyes: the makeup Grandma Lynn had given her helped but did not solve the problem of how much everyone could see my eyes in Lindsey's. When they presented themselves—a compact flashing past her when in use by a girl at a neighboring desk, or an unexpected reflection in the window of a store—she looked away. It was particularly painful with my father. What she realized as they talked was that as long as they were on this subject—Mr. Harvey, my clothes, my book bag, my body, me—the vigilance to my memory made my father see her as Lindsey and not as a tragic combination of his two daughters.

"So you would want to be able to get in his house?" she said.

They stared at each other, a flicker of recognition of a dangerous idea. In his hesitation, before he finally said that that would be illegal, and no, he hadn't thought of that, she knew he was lying. She also knew he needed someone to do it for him.

"You should finish shaving, honey," he said.

She agreed with him and turned away, knowing what she'd been told.

Grandma Lynn arrived on the Monday before Thanksgiving. With the same laser-beam eyes that immediately sought out any unsightly blemish on my sister, she now saw something beneath the surface of her daughter's smile, in her placated, tranquilized movements and in how her body responded whenever Detective Fenerman or the police work came up.

When my mother refused my father's help in cleaning up after dinner that night, the laser eyes were certain. Adamantly, and to the shock of everyone at the table and the relief of my sister—Grandma Lynn made an announcement.

"Abigail, I am going to help you clean up. It will be a mother/daughter thing."

"What?"

My mother had calculated that she could let Lindsey off easily and early and then she would spend the rest of the night over the sink, washing slowly and staring out the window until the darkness brought her own reflection back to her. The sounds of the TV would fade away and she would be alone again.

"I just did my nails yesterday," Grandma Lynn said after tying on an apron over her camel-colored A-line dress, "so I'll dry."

"Mother, really. This isn't necessary."

"It is necessary, believe me, sweetie," my grandmother said. There was something sober and curt in that *sweetie.*

Buckley led my father by the hand into the adjoining room where the TV sat. They took up their stations and Lindsey, having been given a reprieve, went upstairs to call Samuel.

It was such a strange thing to see. So out of the ordinary. My grandmother in an apron, holding a dish towel up like a matador's red flag in anticipation of the first dish coming her way.

They were quiet as they worked, and the silence—the only sounds being the splash of my mother's hands plunging into the scalding water, the squeak of plates, and the clank of the silver—made a tension fill the room which grew unbearable. The noises of the game from the nearby room were just as odd to me. My father had never watched football; basketball his only sport. Grandma Lynn had never done dishes; frozen meals and takeout menus were her weapons of choice.

"Oh Christ," she finally said. "Take this." She handed the just-washed dish back to my mother. "I want to have a real conversation but I'm afraid I'm going to drop these things. Let's take a walk."

"Mother, I need to . . ."

"You need to take a walk."

"After the dishes."

"Listen," my grandmother said, "I know I'm whatever I am and you're whatever you are, which isn't me, which makes you happy, but I know some things when I see them and I know something is going on that isn't kosher. *Capisce?*"

My mother's face was wavering, soft and malleable—almost as soft and malleable as the image of her that floated on the sullied water in the sink.

"What?"

"I have suspicions and I don't want to talk about them here."

Ten-four, Grandma Lynn, I thought. I'd never seen her nervous before.

It would be easy for the two of them to leave the house alone. My father, with his knee, would never think to join them, and, these days, where my father went or did not go, my brother, Buckley, followed.

My mother was silent. She saw no other option. As an afterthought they removed their aprons in the garage and piled them on the roof of the Mustang. My mother bent down and lifted the garage door.

It was still early enough so the light would hold for the beginning of their walk. "We could take Holiday," my mother tried.

"Just you and your mother," my grandmother said. "The most frightening pairing imaginable."

They had never been close. They both knew it, but it wasn't something they acknowledged very much. They joked around it like two children who didn't particularly like each other but were the only children in a large, barren neighborhood. Now, never having tried to before, having always let her daughter run as fast as she could in whatever direction she wished, my grandmother found that she was suddenly catching up.

They had passed by the O'Dwyers' and were near the Tarkings' before my grandmother said what she had to say.

"My humor buried my acceptance," my grandmother said. "Your father had a long-term affair in New Hampshire. Her first initial was F and I never knew what it stood for. I found a thousand options for it over the years."

"Mother?"

My grandmother kept walking, didn't turn. She found that the crisp fall air helped, filling her lungs until they felt cleaner than they had just minutes before.

"Did you know that?"

"No."

"I guess I never told you," she said. "I didn't think you needed to know. Now you do, don't you think?"

"I'm not sure why you're telling me this."

They had come to the bend in the road that would lead them back around the circle. If they went that way and did not stop, eventually they would find themselves in front of Mr. Harvey's house. My mother froze.

"My poor, poor sweetie," my grandmother said. "Give me your hand."

They were awkward. My mother could count on her fingers how many times her tall father had leaned down and kissed her as a child. The scratchy beard that smelled of a cologne that, after years of searching, she could never identify. My grandmother took her hand and held on as they walked the other way.

They walked into an area of the neighborhood where newer families seemed to be moving in more and more. The anchor houses, I remembered my mother calling them, because they lined the street that led into the whole development—anchored the neighborhood to an original road built before the township was a township. The road that led to Valley Forge, to George Washington and the Revolution.

"Susie's death brought your father's back to me," my grandmother said. "I never let myself mourn him properly."

"I know," my mother said.

"Do you resent me for it?"

My mother paused. "Yes."

My grandmother patted the back of my mother's hand with her free one. "Good, see, that's a nugget."

"A nugget?"

"Something that's coming out of all this. You and me. A nugget of truth between us."

They passed the one-acre lots on which trees had been growing for twenty years. If not exactly towering, they were still twice as tall as the fathers who had first held them and stomped the dirt around them with their weekend work shoes.

"Do you know how alone I've always felt?" my mother asked her mother.

"That's why we're walking, Abigail," Grandma Lynn said.

My mother focused her eyes in front of her but stayed connected to her mother with her hand. She thought of the solitary nature of her childhood. How, when she had watched her two daughters tie string between paper cups and go to separate rooms to whisper secrets to each other, she could not really say she knew how that felt. There had been no one else in the house with her but her mother and father, and then her father had gone.

She stared at the tops of the trees, which, miles from our development, were the tallest things around. They stood on a high hill that had never been cleared for houses and on which a few old farmers still dwelled.

"I can't describe what I'm feeling," she said. "To anyone."

They reached the end of the development just as the sun was going down over the hill in front of them. A moment passed without either of them turning around. My mother watched the last light flicker in a drain-off puddle at the end of the road.

"I don't know what to do," she said. "It's all over now."

My grandmother was not sure what she meant by "it," but she did not press harder.

"Shall we head back?" my grandmother offered.

"How?" my mother said.

"To the house, Abigail. Head back to the house."

They turned and began walking again. The houses one after another, identical in structure. Only what my grandmother thought of as their accessories marked them as different. She had never understood places like this—places where her own child had chosen to live.

"When we get to the turn to the circle," my mother said, "I want to walk past it."

"His house?"

"Yes."

I watched Grandma Lynn turn when my mother turned.

"Would you promise me not to see the man anymore?" my grandmother asked.

"Who?"

"The man you're involved with. That's what I've been talking about."

"I'm not involved with anyone," my mother said. Her mind flew like a bird from one rooftop to the next. "Mother?" she said, and turned.

"Abigail?"

"If I needed to get away for a while, could I use Daddy's cabin?"

"Have you been listening to me?"

They could smell something in the air, and again my mother's anxious, agile mind slipped away. "Someone is smoking," she said.

Grandma Lynn was staring at her child. The pragmatic, prim mistress that my mother had always been was gone. She was flighty and distracted. My grandmother had nothing left to say to her.

"They're foreign cigarettes," my mother said. "Let's go find them!"

And in the fading light my grandmother stared, flabbergasted, as my mother began to follow the scent to its source.

"I'm heading back," my grandmother said.

But my mother kept walking.

She found the source of the smoke soon enough. It was Ruana Singh, standing behind a tall fir tree in her backyard.

"Hello," my mother said.

Ruana did not start as I thought she would. Her calmness had become something practiced. She could make a breath last through the most startling event, whether it was her son being accused of murder by the police or her husband running their dinner party as if it were an academic committee meeting. She had told Ray he could go upstairs, and then she had disappeared out the back door and not been missed.

"Mrs. Salmon," Ruana said, exhaling the heady smell of her cigarettes. In a rush of smoke and warmth my mother met Ruana's extended hand. "I'm so glad to see you."

"Are you having a party?" my mother asked.

"My husband is having a party. I am the hostess."

My mother smiled.

"This is a weird place we both live," Ruana said.

Their eyes met. My mother nodded her head. Back on the road somewhere was her own mother, but for right now she, like Ruana, was on a quiet island off the mainland.

"Do you have another cigarette?"

"Absolutely, Mrs. Salmon, yes." Ruana fished into the pocket of her long black cardigan and held out the pack and her lighter. "Dunhills," she said. "I hope that's all right."

My mother lit her cigarette and handed the blue package with its golden foil back to Ruana. "Abigail," she said as she exhaled. "Please call me Abigail."

Up in his room with his lights off, Ray could smell his mother's cigarettes, which she never accused him of pilfering, just as he never let on that he knew she had them. He heard voices downstairs—the loud sounds of his father and his colleagues speaking six different languages and laughing delightedly over the oh-so-American holiday to come. He did not know that my mother was out on the lawn with his mother or that I was watching him sit in his window and smell their sweet tobacco. Soon he would turn away from the window and switch on the small light by his bed to read. Mrs. McBride had told them to find a sonnet they'd like to write a paper on, but as he read the lines of those available to him in his *Norton Anthology* he kept drifting back to the moment he wished he could take back and do over again. If he had just kissed me on the scaffold, maybe everything would have turned out differently.

Grandma Lynn kept on the course she had set with my mother, and, eventually, there it was—the house they tried to forget while living two houses down. *Jack was right,* my grandmother thought. She could even feel it in the dark. The place radiated something malevolent. She shivered and began to hear the crickets and see the fireflies gathering in a swarm above his front flower beds. She thought suddenly that she would do nothing but sympathize with her daughter. Her child was living inside the middle of a ground zero to which no affair on her own husband's part could offer her insight. She would tell my mother in the morning that the keys to the cabin would always be there for her if she needed them.

That night my mother had what she considered a wonderful

dream. She dreamed of the country of India, where she had never been. There were orange traffic cones and beautiful lapis lazuli insects with mandibles of gold. A young girl was being led through the streets. She was taken to a pyre where she was wound in a sheet and placed up on a platform built from sticks. The bright fire that consumed her brought my mother into that deep, light, dreamlike bliss. The girl was being burned alive, but, first, there had been her body, clean and whole.

FOURTEEN

For a week Lindsey cased my killer's house. She was doing exactly what he did to everyone else.

She had agreed to train with the boys' soccer team all year in preparation for the challenge Mr. Dewitt and Samuel encouraged her to take on: qualifying to play in the all-male high school soccer league. And Samuel, to show his support, trained alongside her with no hope of qualifying for anything, he said, other than "fastest guy in shorts."

He could run, even if kicking and fielding and noticing a ball anywhere within his vicinity were all beyond him. And so, while they did laps around the neighborhood, each time Lindsey shot a look toward Mr. Harvey's house, Samuel was out in front, setting the pace for her—unaware of anything else.

Inside the green house, Mr. Harvey was looking out. He saw her watching and he began to itch. It had been almost a year now, but the Salmons remained bent on crowding him.

It had happened before in other towns and states. The family of a girl suspected him but no one else did. He had perfected his patter to the police, a certain obsequious innocence peppered with wonder about their procedures or useless ideas that he presented as if they might help. Bringing up the Ellis boy with Fenerman had been a good stroke, and the lie that he was a widower always helped. He fashioned a wife out of whichever victim he'd recently been taking pleasure in in his memory, and to flesh her out there was always his mother.

He left the house every day for an hour or two in the afternoon. He would pick up any supplies he needed and then drive out to Valley Forge Park and walk the paved roads and the unpaved trails and find himself suddenly surrounded by school tours at George Washington's log cabin or the Washington Memorial Chapel. This would buoy him up—these moments when the children were eager to see history, as if they might actually find a long silver hair from Washington's wig caught on the rough end of a log post.

Occasionally one of the tour guides or teachers would notice him standing there, unfamiliar even if amiable, and he would be met with a questioning stare. He had a thousand lines to give them: "I used to bring my children here." "This is where I met my wife." He knew to ground whatever he said in connection to some imagined family, and then the women would smile at him. Once an attractive, heavy woman tried to engage him in conversation while the park guide told the children about the winter of 1776 and the Battle of the Clouds.

He had used the story of widowhood and talked about a woman named Sophie Cichetti, making her his now-deceased wife and true love. It had been like luscious food to this woman, and, as he listened to her tell him about her cats and her brother, who had three children, whom she loved, he pictured her sitting on the chair in his basement, dead.

After that, when he met a teacher's questioning glare he would shyly back off and go somewhere else inside the park. He watched mothers with their children still in strollers walk briskly along the exposed paths. He saw teenagers who were cutting school necking in the uncut fields or along the interior trails. And at the highest point of the park was a small wood beside which he sometimes parked. He would sit in his Wagoneer and watch lonely men pull up beside him and get out of their cars. Men in suits on their lunch hour or men in flannel and jeans would walk quickly into that wood. Sometimes they would cast a look back in his direction—an inquiry. If they were close enough, these men could see, through his windshield, what his victims saw—his wild and bottomless lust.

On November 26, 1974, Lindsey saw Mr. Harvey leaving the green house, and she began to hang back from the pack of running boys. Later she could claim she had gotten her period and all of them would hush up, even be satisfied that this was proof that Mr. Dewitt's unpopular plan—a girl at regionals!—would never work out.

I watched my sister and marveled. She was becoming everything all at once. A woman. A spy. A jock. The Ostracized: One Man Alone.

She walked, clutching her side in a false cramp, and waved the boys on when they turned to notice her. She kept walking with her hand on her waist until they turned the corner at the far end of the block. At the edge of Mr. Harvey's property was a row of tall, thick pines that had been left untrimmed for years. She sat down by one of them, still feigning exhaustion in case any neighbor was looking out, and then, when she felt the moment was right, she curled up in a ball and rolled in between two pines. She waited. The boys had one more lap. She watched them pass her and followed them with her eyes as they cut up through the vacant lot and back to the high school. She was alone. She calculated she had forty-five minutes before our father would begin to wonder when she'd be home. The agreement had been that if she trained with the boys' soccer team, Samuel would escort her home and have her back by five o'clock.

The clouds had hung heavy in the sky all day, and the late-fall cold raised goose bumps along her legs and arms. The team runs always warmed her, but when she reached the locker room where she shared the showers with the field hockey team, she would begin to shiver until the hot water hit her body. But on the lawn of the green house, her goose bumps were also from fear.

When the boys cut up the path, she scrambled over to the basement window at the side of Mr. Harvey's house. She had already thought of a story if she was caught. She was chasing a kitten that she'd seen dart in between the pine trees. She would say it was gray, that it was fast, that it had run toward Mr. Harvey's house and she'd followed it without thinking.

She could see inside to the basement, where it was dark. She tried the window, but the latch lock was pushed in. She would have to break the glass. Her mind racing, she worried about the noise, but she was too far along to stop now. She thought of my father at home, ever mindful of the clock near his chair, and took her sweatshirt off and balled it around her feet. Sitting down, she braced her body with her arms and then kicked once, twice, three times with both feet until the window smashed—a muffled cracking.

Carefully, she lowered herself down, searching the wall for a foothold but having to jump the final few feet onto the broken glass and concrete.

The room appeared tidy and swept, different from our own basement, where heaps of holiday-marked boxes—EASTER EGGS AND GREEN GRASS, CHRISTMAS STAR/ORNAMENTS—never made it back on the shelves my father had built.

The cold air from outside came in, and she felt the draft along her neck pushing her out of the shimmering semicircle of shattered glass and into the rest of the room. She saw the easy chair and a little table beside it. She saw the large alarm clock with luminous numbers sitting on the metal shelving. I wanted to guide her eyes to the crawlspace, where she would find the bones of the animals, but I knew, too, that regardless of drawing a fly's eyes on graph paper and excelling that fall in Mr. Botte's biology class, she would imagine the bones were mine. For this, I was glad she went nowhere near them.

Despite my inability to appear or whisper, push or usher, Lindsey, all alone, felt something. Something charged the air in the cold, dank basement and made her cringe. She stood only a few feet from the open window, knowing that she would, no matter what, be walking farther in and that she had to, no matter what, calm and focus herself to look for clues; but right then, for one moment, she thought of Samuel running ahead, having thought he would find her on his last lap, then running back toward the school, thinking he would find her outside, and then assuming, but with the first trace of a doubt, that she was showering, and so he too would be showering now, and then waiting for her before he did anything else. How long would he wait? As her eyes mounted the stairs to the first floor before her feet followed, she wished that Samuel were there to climb down after her and trace her movements, erasing her solitude as he went, fitting into her limbs. But she had not told him on purpose—had told no one. What she was doing was beyond the pale—criminal—and she knew it.

If she thought about it later, she would say that she had needed air and so that was what had gotten her up the stairs. Small flecks of white dust collected at the tips of her shoes as she mounted the stairs, but she didn't notice them.

She twisted the knob of the basement door and reached the

first floor. Only five minutes had passed. She had forty left, or so she thought. There was still a bit of light seeping in through the closed blinds. As she stood, again, hesitating, in this house identical to our own, she heard the thwack of the *Evening Bulletin* hit the stoop and the delivery boy ring the bell on his bike as he passed.

My sister told herself that she was inside a series of rooms and spaces that, gone through methodically, might yield what she needed, provide her the trophy she could take home to our father, earning her freedom from me that way. Competition always, even between the living and the dead. She saw the flagstones in the hall—the same dark green and gray as ours—and imagined crawling after me when she was a baby and I was just learning to walk. Then she saw my toddler body running delightedly away from her and into the next room, and she remembered her own sense of reaching out, of taking her first steps as I teased her from the living room.

But Mr. Harvey's house was much emptier than ours, and there were no rugs to lend warmth to the decor. Lindsey stepped from the flagstones onto the polished pine floors of what in our house was the living room. She made echoes up the open front hall, the sound of every movement reaching back for her.

She couldn't stop the memories slamming into her. Every one had a brutal report. Buckley riding piggyback on my shoulders down the stairs. Our mother steadying me as Lindsey looked on, jealous that I could reach, with the silver star in my hands, the top of the Christmas tree. Me sliding down the banister and asking her to join. Both of us begging the comics off our father after dinner. All of us running after Holiday as he barked and barked. And the countless exhausted smiles awkwardly dressing our faces for photos at birthdays, and holidays, and after school. Two sisters dressed identically in velvet or plaid or Easter yellows. We held baskets of bunnies and eggs we had sunk in dye. Patent leather shoes with straps and hard buckles. Smiling hard as our mother tried to focus her camera. The photos always fuzzy, our eyes bright red spots. None of them, these artifacts left to my sister, would hold for posterity the moments before and the moments after, when we two girls played in the house or fought over toys. When we were sisters.

Then she saw it. My back darting into the next room. Our dining room, the room that held his finished dollhouses. I was a child running just ahead of her.

She hurried after me.

She chased me through the downstairs rooms and though she was training hard for soccer, when she returned to the front hall she was unable to catch her breath. She grew dizzy.

I thought of what my mother had always said about a boy at our bus stop who was twice as old as us but still in the second grade. "He doesn't know his own strength, so you need to be careful around him." He liked to give bear hugs to anyone who was nice to him, and you could see this dopey love drop into his features and ignite his desire to touch. Before he was removed from regular school and sent somewhere else no one talked about, he had picked up a little girl named Daphne and squeezed her so hard that she fell into the road when he let go. I was pushing so hard on the Inbetween to get to Lindsey that I suddenly felt I might hurt her when I meant to help.

My sister sat down on the wide steps at the bottom of the front hall and closed her eyes, focused on regaining her breath, on why she was in Mr. Harvey's house in the first place. She felt encased in something heavy, a fly trapped in a spider's funnel web, the thick silk binding up around her. She knew that our father had walked into the cornfield possessed by something that was creeping into her now. She had wanted to bring back clues he could use as rungs to climb back to her on, to anchor him with facts, to ballast his sentences to Len. Instead she saw herself falling after him into a bottomless pit.

She had twenty minutes.

Inside that house my sister was the only living being, but she was not alone, and I was not her only company. The architecture of my murderer's life, the bodies of the girls he'd left behind, began to reveal itself to me now that my sister was in that house. I stood in heaven. I called their names:

Jackie Meyer. Delaware, 1967. Thirteen.

A chair knocked over, its underside facing the room. Lying curled toward it, she wore a striped T-shirt and nothing else. Near her head, a small pool of blood.

Flora Hernandez. Delaware, 1963. Eight.

He'd only wanted to touch her, but she screamed. A small girl for her age. Her left sock and shoe were found later. The body, unrecovered. The bones lay in the earthen basement of an old apartment house.

Leah Fox. Delaware, 1969. Twelve.

On a slipcovered couch under a highway on-ramp, he killed her, very quietly. He fell asleep on top of her, lulled by the sound of cars rushing above them. Not until ten hours later, when a vagrant knocked on the small shack Mr. Harvey had built out of discarded doors—did he begin to pack himself and Leah Fox's body up.

Sophie Cichetti, Pennsylvania, 1960. Forty-nine.

A landlady, she had divided her upstairs apartment into two by erecting a Sheetrock wall. He liked the half-circle window this created, and the rent was cheap. But she talked too much about her son and insisted on reading him poems from a book of sonnets. He made love to her on her side of the divided room, smashed her skull in when she started to talk, and brought her body to the bank of a creek nearby.

Leidia Johnson. 1960. Six.

Buck's County, Pennsylvania. He dug an arched cave inside a hill near the quarry and waited. She was the youngest one.

Wendy Richter. Connecticut, 1971. Thirteen.

She was waiting for her father outside a bar. He raped her in the bushes and then strangled her. That time, as he grew conscious, coming up out of the stupor that often clung on, he heard noises. He turned the dead girl's face toward his, and as the voices grew closer he bit down on her ear. "Sorry, man," he heard two drunk men say as they walked into the nearby bushes to take a leak.

I saw now that town of floating graves, cold and whipped by winds, where the victims of murder went in the minds of the living. I could see his other victims as they occupied his house—those trace memories left behind before they fled this earth—but I let them go that day and went to my sister.

Lindsey stood up the moment I focused back on her. Together the two of us walked the stairs. She felt like the zombies in the movies Samuel and Hal loved. One foot in front of the other and staring blankly straight ahead. She reached what was my parents' bedroom in our house and found nothing. She circled the hallway upstairs. Nothing. Then she went into what had been my bedroom in our house, and she found my killer's.

It was the least barren room in the house, and she did her best not to displace anything. To move her hand in between the sweaters stacked on the shelf, prepared to find anything in their warm insides—a knife, a gun, a Bic pen chewed on by Holiday. Nothing. But then, as she heard something but could not identify what it was, she turned toward the bed and saw the bedside table and, lying in the circle of light from a reading lamp left on, his sketchbook. She walked toward it and heard another sound, again, not putting the sounds together. Car pulling up. Car braking with a squeak. Car door slamming shut.

She turned the pages of the sketchbook and looked at the inky drawings of crossbeams and braces or turrets and buttresses, and she saw the measurements and notes, none of which meant anything to her. Then, as she flipped a final page, she thought she heard footsteps outside and very close.

As Mr. Harvey turned the key in the lock of his front door, she saw the light pencil sketch on the page in front of her. It was a small drawing of stalks above a sunken hole, a detail off to the side of a shelf and how a chimney could draw out smoke from a fire, and the thing that sunk into her: in a spidery hand he had written "Stolfuz cornfield." If it were not for the articles in the paper after the discovery of my elbow, she would not have known that the cornfield was owned by a man named Stolfuz. Now she saw what I wanted her to know. I had died inside that hole; I had screamed and fought and lost.

She ripped out the page. Mr. Harvey was in the kitchen making something to eat—the liverwurst he favored, a bowl of sweet green grapes. He heard a board creak. He stiffened. He heard another and his back rose and blossomed with sudden understanding.

The grapes dropped on the floor to be crushed by his left foot, while my sister in the room above sprang to the aluminum blinds and unlocked the stubborn window. Mr. Harvey mounted the stairs two at a time, and my sister smashed out the screen, scrambling onto the porch roof and rolling down it as he gained the upstairs hall and came barreling toward her. The gutter broke when her body tipped past it. As he reached his bedroom, she fell into the bushes and brambles and muck.

But she was not hurt. Gloriously not hurt. Gloriously young. She stood up as he reached the window to climb out. But he stopped. He saw her running toward the elderberry. The silk-screened number on her back screamed out at him. 5! 5! 5!

Lindsey Salmon in her soccer shirt.

Samuel was sitting with my parents and Grandma Lynn when Lindsey reached the house.

"Oh my God," my mother said, the first to see her through the small square windows that lined either side of our front door.

And by the time my mother opened it Samuel had rushed to fill the space, and she walked, without looking at my mother or even my father hobbling forward, right into Samuel's arms.

"My God, my God, my God," my mother said as she took in the dirt and the cuts.

My grandmother came to stand beside her.

Samuel put his hand on my sister's head and smoothed her hair back.

"Where have you been?"

But Lindsey turned to our father, lessened so now—smaller, weaker, than this child who raged. How alive she was consumed me whole that day.

"Daddy?"

"Yes, sweetheart."

"I did it. I broke into his house." She was shaking slightly and trying not to cry.

My mother balked: "You what?"

But my sister didn't look at her, not once.

"I brought you this. I think it might be important."

She had kept the drawing in her hand, crumpled tightly into a ball. It had made her landing harder, but she had come away anyway.

A phrase my father had read that day appeared in his mind now. He spoke it aloud as he looked into Lindsey's eyes.

"There is no condition one adjusts to so quickly as a state of war."

Lindsey handed him the drawing.

"I'm going to pick up Buckley," my mother said.

"Don't you even want to look at this, Mom?"

"I don't know what to say. Your grandmother is here. I have shopping to do, a bird to cook. No one seems to realize that we have a family. We have a family, a family and a son, and I'm going."

Grandma Lynn walked my mother to the back door but did not try to stop her.

My mother gone, my sister reached her hand out to Samuel. My father saw what Lindsey did in Mr. Harvey's spidery hand: the possible blueprint of my grave. He looked up.

"Do you believe me now?" he asked Lindsey.

"Yes, Daddy."

My father—so grateful—had a call to make.

"Dad," she said.

"Yes."

"I think he saw me."

I could never have imagined a blessing greater to me than the physical safety of my sister that day. As I walked back from the gazebo I shivered with the fear that had held me, the possibility of her loss on Earth not just to my father, my mother, Buckley, and Samuel, but, selfishly, the loss of her on Earth to me.

Franny walked toward me from the cafeteria. I barely raised my head.

"Susie," she said. "I have something to tell you."

She drew me under one of the old-fashioned lampposts and then out of the light. She handed me a piece of paper folded into four.

"When you feel stronger, look at it and go there."

Two days later, Franny's map led me to a field that I had always walked by but which, though beautiful, I'd left unexplored. The drawing had a dotted line to indicate a path. Searching nervously, I looked for an indentation in the rows and rows of wheat. Just ahead I saw it, and as I began to walk between the rows the paper dissolved in my hand.

I could see an old and beautiful olive tree just up ahead.

The sun was high, and in front of the olive tree was a clearing. I waited only a moment until I saw the wheat on the other side begin to pulse with the arrival of someone who did not crest the stalks.

She was small for her age, as she had been on Earth, and she wore a calico dress that was frayed at the hem and the cuffs.

She paused and we stared at each other.

"I come here almost every day," she said. "I like to listen to the sounds."

All around us, I realized, the wheat was rustling as it moved against itself in the wind.

"Do you know Franny?" I asked.

The little girl nodded solemnly.

"She gave me a map to this place."

"Then you must be ready," she said, but she was in *her* heaven too, and that called for twirling and making her skirt fly out in a circle. I sat on the ground under the tree and watched her.

When she was done she came toward me and breathlessly sat herself down. "I was Flora Hernandez," she said. "What was your name?"

I told her, and then I began to cry with comfort, to know another girl he had killed.

"The others will be here soon," she said.

And as Flora twirled, other girls and women came through the field in all directions. Our heartache poured into one another like water from cup to cup. Each time I told my story, I lost a bit, the smallest drop of pain. It was that day that I knew I wanted to tell the story of my family. Because horror on Earth is real and it is every day. It is like a flower or like the sun; it cannot be contained.

FIFTEEN

At first no one stopped them, and it was something his mother enjoyed so much, the trill of her laughter when they ducked around the corner from whatever store and she uncovered and presented the pilfered item to him, that George Harvey joined in her laughter and, spying an opportunity, would hug her while she was occupied with her newest prize.

It was a relief for both of them, getting away from his father for the afternoon and driving into the nearby town to get food or other supplies. They were scavengers at best and made their money by collecting scrap metal and old bottles and hauling them into town on the back of the elder Harvey's ancient flatbed truck.

When his mother and he were caught for the first time, the two of them were treated graciously by the woman at the cash register. "If you can pay for it, do. If you can't, leave it on the counter as good as new," she said brightly and winked at the eight-year-old George Harvey. His mother took the small glass bottle of aspirin out of her pocket and placed it sheepishly on the counter.

Her face sank. "No better than the child," his father often reprimanded her.

Getting caught became another moment in his life that brought fear—that sick feeling curling into his stomach like eggs being folded into a bowl—and he could tell by the closed faces and hard eyes when the person walking down the aisle toward them was a store employee who had seen a woman stealing.

And she began handing him the stolen items to hide on his body, and he did it because she wanted him to. If they got outside and away in the truck, she would smile and bang the steering wheel with the flat of her hand and call him her little accomplice. The cab would fill with her wild, unpredictable love, and for a little while—until it wore off and they spied something glinting on the side of the road that they would have to investigate for what his mother called its "possibilities"—he did feel free. Free and warm.

He remembered the advice she gave him the first time they drove a stretch of road in Texas and saw a white wooden cross along the road. Around the base of it were clusters of fresh and dead flowers. His scavenger's eye had been drawn immediately by the colors.

"You have to be able to look past the dead," his mother said. "Sometimes there are good trinkets to take away from them."

Even then, he could sense they were doing something wrong. The two of them got out of the truck and went up to the cross, and his mother's eyes changed into the two black points that he was used to seeing when they were searching. She found a charm in the shape of an eye and one in the shape of a heart and held them out for George Harvey to see.

"Don't know what your father would make of them, but we can keep them, just you and me."

She had a secret stash of things that she never showed his father.

"Do you want the eye or the heart?"

"The eye," he said.

"I think these roses are fresh enough to save, nice for the truck."

That night they slept in the truck, unable to make the drive back to where his father was working a temporary job splitting and riving boards by hand.

The two of them slept curled into each other as they did with some frequency, making the inside of the cab an awkward nest. His mother, like a dog worrying a blanket, moved around in her seat and fidgeted. George Harvey had realized after earlier struggles that it was best to go limp and let her move him as she wished. Until his mother was comfortable, no one slept.

In the middle of the night, as he was dreaming about the soft insides of the palaces in picture books he'd seen in public libraries, someone banged on the roof, and George Harvey and his mother sat bolt upright. It was three men, looking through the windows in a way George Harvey recognized. It was the way his own father looked when he was drunk sometimes. It had a double effect: the whole gaze was leveled at his mother and simultaneously absented his son.

He knew not to cry out.

"Stay quiet. They aren't here for you," she whispered to him. He began to shiver underneath the old army blankets that covered them.

One of the three men was standing in front of the truck. The other two were banging on either side of the truck's roof, laughing and lolling their tongues.

His mother shook her head vehemently, but this only enraged them. The man blocking the truck started rocking his hips back and forth against the front end, which caused the other two men to laugh harder.

"I'm going to move slow," his mother whispered, "and pretend I'm getting out of the truck. I want you to reach forward and turn the keys in the ignition when I say so."

He knew he was being told something very important. That she needed him. Despite her practiced calm, he could hear the metal in her voice, the iron breaking up through fear now.

She smiled at the men, and as they sent up whoops and their bodies relaxed, she used her elbow to knock the gear shift into place. "Now," she said in a flat monotone, and George Harvey reached forward and turned the keys. The truck came to life with its rumbling old engine.

The faces of the men changed, fading from an acquisitive joy and then, as she reversed back to a good degree and they stared after her, uncertainty. She switched into drive and screamed, "On the floor!" to her son. He could feel the bump of the man's body hitting the truck only a few feet from where he lay curled up inside. Then the body was pitched up onto the roof. It lay there for a second until his mother reversed again. He had had a moment of clarity about how life should be lived: not as a child or as a woman. They were the two worst things to be.

His heart had beat wildly as he watched Lindsey make for the elderberry hedge, but then immediately he had calmed. It was a skill his mother, not his father, had taught him—to take action only after calculating the worst possible outcome of each choice available. He saw the notebook disturbed and the missing page in his sketchbook. He checked the bag with the knife. He took the knife with him to the basement and dropped it down the square hole that was drilled through the foundation. From the metal shelving, he retrieved the group of charms that he kept from the women. He took the Pennsylvania keystone charm from my bracelet and held it in his hand. Good luck. The others he spread out on his white handkerchief, and then he brought the four ends together to form a small hobo sack. He put his hand inside the hole under the foundation and got down on the floor on his stomach to push his arm in all the way to the shoulder. He groped, feeling with the free fingers of his hand as the other held the hobo sack, until he found a rusty jut of a metal support over which the workmen had poured the cement. He hung his trophy bag there and then withdrew his arm and stood. The book of sonnets he had buried earlier that summer in the woods of Valley Forge Park, shedding evidence slowly as he always did; now, he had to hope, not too slowly.

Five minutes at the most had gone by. That could be accounted for by shock and anger. By checking what everyone else thought to be valuables—his cuff links, his cash, his tools. But he knew no more time than that could be overlooked. He had to call the police.

He worked himself up. He paced briefly, drew his breath in and out rapidly, and when the operator answered he set his voice on edge.

"My home has been broken into. I need the police," he said, scripting the opening of his version of the story as inside he calculated how quickly he could leave and what he would carry with him.

When my father called the station, he requested Len Fenerman. But Fenerman couldn't be located. My father was informed that two uniforms had already been sent out to investigate. What they found when Mr. Harvey answered his door was a man who was tearfully upset and who in every aspect, save a certain repellent quality that the officers attributed to the sight of a man allowing himself to cry, seemed to be responding rationally to the reported events.

Even though the information about the drawing Lindsey had taken had come in over the radio, the officers were more impressed by Mr. Harvey's readily volunteering to have his home searched. He also seemed sincere in his sympathy for the Salmon family.

The officers grew uncomfortable. They searched the house perfunctorily and found nothing except both the evidence of what they took to be extreme loneliness and a room full of beautiful dollhouses on the second floor, where they switched topics and asked him how long he had been building them.

They noticed, they said later, an immediate and friendly change in his demeanor. He went into his bedroom and got the sketchbook, not mentioning any stolen drawing. The police took note of his increasing warmth as he showed them the sketches for the dollhouses. They asked their next question delicately.

"Sir," an officer said, "we can take you down to the station for further questioning, and you do have the right to have a lawyer present but—"

Mr. Harvey interrupted him. "I would be happy to answer anything here. I am the wronged party, though I have no wish to press charges against that poor girl."

"The young woman that broke in," the other officer began, "she did take something. It was a drawing of the cornfield and a sort of structure in it . . ."

The way it hit Harvey, the officers would tell Detective Fenerman, was all at once and very convincing. He had an explanation that fit so perfectly, they did not see him as a flight risk—largely because they did not see him first and foremost as a murderer.

"Oh, the poor girl," he said. He placed his fingers to his pursed lips. He turned to his sketchbook and flipped through it until he came to a drawing that was very much like the one Lindsey had taken.

"There, it was a drawing similar to this one, correct?" The officers—now audience—nodded. "I was trying to figure it out," Mr. Harvey confessed. "I admit the horror of it has obsessed me. I think everyone in the neighborhood has tried to think how they could have prevented it. Why they didn't hear something, see something. I mean, surely the girl screamed.

"Now here," he said to the two men, pointing to his drawing with a pen. "Forgive me, but I think in structures, and after hearing about how much blood there was in the cornfield and the churned-up nature of that area where it was found, I decided that perhaps . . ." He looked at them, checking their eyes. Both officers were following him. They wanted to follow him. They had had no leads, no body, no clues. Perhaps this strange man had a workable theory. "Well, that the person who did it had built something underground, a hole, and then I confess I began to worry at it and detail it the way I do the dollhouses, and I gave it a chimney and a shelf, and, well, that's just my habit." He paused. "I have a lot of time to myself."

"So, did it work out?" one of the two officers asked.

"I always did think I had something there."

"Why didn't you call us?"

"I wasn't bringing back their daughter. When Detective Fenerman interviewed me I mentioned how I suspected the Ellis boy, and I turned out to be dead wrong. I didn't want to meddle with any more of my amateur theories."

The officers apologized for the fact that the following day Detective Fenerman would be calling again, most likely wanting to go over the same material. See the sketchbook, hear Mr. Harvey's assertions about the cornfield. All of this Mr. Harvey took as part of being a dutiful civilian, even if it had been he who was victimized. The officers documented my sister's path of break-in from the basement window and then out through the bedroom window. They discussed the damages, which Mr.

Harvey said he would take care of out-of-pocket, stressing his awareness of the overwhelming grief the Salmon father had displayed several months ago, and how it now seemed to be infecting the poor girl's sister.

I saw the chances of Mr. Harvey's capture diminish as I watched the end of my family as I had known it ignite.

After picking up Buckley from Nate's house, my mother stopped at a payphone outside the 7-Eleven on Route 30. She told Len to meet her at a loud and raucous store in the mall near the grocery store. He left immediately. As he pulled out of his driveway, the phone in his house was ringing but he didn't hear it. He was inside the capsule of his car, thinking of my mother, of how wrong it all was and then of how he could not say no to her for reasons he couldn't hold on to long enough to analyze or disclaim.

My mother drove the short distance from the grocery store to the mall and led Buckley by the hand through the glass doors to a sunken circle where parents could leave their children to play while they shopped.

Buckley was elated. "The circle! Can I?" he said, as he saw his peers jumping off the jungle gym and turning somersaults on the rubber-covered floor.

"Do you really want to, honey?" she asked him.

"Please," he said.

She phrased it as a motherly concession. "All right," she said. And he went off in the direction of a red metal slide. "Be good," she called after him. She had never allowed him to play there without her.

She left his name with the monitor who watched over the play circle and said that she would be shopping on the lower level near Wanamaker's.

While Mr. Harvey was explaining his theory of my murder, my mother felt a hand brush across the back of her shoulders inside a trashy store called Spencer's. She turned with expectant relief, only to see Len Fenerman's back as he made his way out of the store. Passing glow-in-the-dark masks, black plastic eight balls, fuzzy troll keychains, and a large laughing skull, my mother followed after him.

He did not turn around. She kept following him, at first excited and then annoyed. In between footfalls there was enough time to think, and she did not want to think.

Finally, she saw him unlock a white door that was set flush into the wall, which she had never noticed before.

She could tell by the noises up ahead in the dark corridor that Len had brought her into the inner workings of the mall—the air filtration system or the water pumping plant. She didn't care. In the darkness she imagined herself to be within her own heart, and a vision of the enlarged drawing from her doctor's office entered her head and simultaneously she saw my father, in his paper gown and black socks, perched on the edge of the examining table as the doctor had explained to them the dangers of congestive heart failure. Just as she was about to let go into grief, cry out, and stumble and fall into confusion, she came to the end of the corridor. It opened into a huge room three stories high that throbbed and buzzed and throughout which there were tiny lights mounted higgledy-piggledy on metal tanks and drums. She paused and listened for any sound other than the deafening thrumming of air being sucked out of the mall and reconditioned to be pushed back in. Nothing.

I saw Len before she did. Standing alone in the almost-darkness he watched her for a moment, locating the need in her eyes. He was sorry for my father, for my family, but he fell into those eyes. "I could drown in those eyes, Abigail," he wanted to say to her, but he knew that this he would not be allowed.

My mother began to make out more and more shapes within the bright interconnected jumble of metal, and for a moment I could feel the room begin to be enough for her, the foreign territory enough to soothe her. It was the feeling of being unreachable.

If it had not been for Len's hand stretching out and grazing her fingers with the tips of his own, I might have kept her to myself there. The room could have remained simply a brief vacation from her life as Mrs. Salmon.

But he did touch her, and she did turn. Still, she could not really look at him. He accepted this absence on her part.

I swirled as I watched it and held on to the bench in the gazebo, gulping air. She could never know, I thought, that while she was clutching Len's hair and he was reaching his hand around to the small of her back, bringing her in closer, that the man who had murdered me was escorting two officers out his front door.

I felt the kisses as they came down my mother's neck and onto her chest, like the small, light feet of mice, and like the flower petals falling that they were. Ruinous and marvelous all at once. They were whispers calling her away from me and from her family and from her grief. She followed with her body.

While Len took her hand and brought her away from the wall into the tangle of pipes where the noise overhead added its chorus, Mr. Harvey began to pack his belongings; my brother met a small girl playing Hula-Hoop in the circle; my sister and Samuel lay beside each other on her bed, fully dressed and nervous; my grandmother downed three shots in the empty dining room. My father watched the phone.

My mother grabbed at Len's coat and shirt greedily, and he helped her. He watched as she tugged at her own clothes, pulling her sweater over her head, then her mother-jumper, and her turtleneck, until she was left in her underpants and camisole. He stared at her.

Samuel kissed the back of my sister's neck. She smelled of soap and Bactine, and he wanted, even then, never to leave her.

Len was about to say something; I could see my mother notice his lips just as they parted. She shut her eyes and commanded the world to shut up—screaming the words inside her skull. She opened her eyes again and looked at him. He was silent, his mouth set. She took her cotton camisole over the top of her head and stepped out of her underwear. My mother had my body as it would never become. But she had her own moonlit skin, her ocean eyes. She was hollow and lost and abandoned up.

Mr. Harvey left his house for the final time while my mother was granted her most temporal wish. To find a doorway out of her ruined heart, in merciful adultery.

SIXTEEN

A year to the day after my death, Dr. Singh called to say he would not be home for dinner. But Ruana would do her exercises no matter what. If, as she stretched out on the rug in the one warm spot that the house seemed to hold in the winter, she could not help but turn over and over again her husband's absences in her mind, she would let them consume her until her body pled for her to let him go and to focus—as she leaned forward, her arms outstretched toward her toes now—and move, to shut her brain off and forget everything but the slight and pleasant yearning of muscles stretching and her own body bending.

Reaching almost to the floor, the window in the dining room was interrupted only by the metal baseboard for the heat, which Ruana liked to keep turned off because the noises it made disturbed her. Outside, she could see the cherry tree, its leaves and flowers all gone. The empty bird feeder swung slightly on its branch.

She stretched until she was quite warm and she'd forgotten herself, and the home she stood in fell away from her. Her age.

Her son. But still, creeping in on her was the figure of her husband. She had a premonition. She did not believe it was a woman, or even a student who worshiped him, that made him late more and more often. She knew what it was because it was something she too had had and had severed herself from after having been injured long ago. It was ambition.

She heard sounds now. Holiday barking two streets over and the Gilberts' dog answering him and Ray moving around upstairs. Blessedly, in another moment, Jethro Tull erupted again, shutting out all else.

Except for the occasional cigarette, which she smoked as secretly as she could so as not to give Ray license, she had kept herself in good health. Many of the women in the neighborhood commented on how well she kept herself and some had asked her if she would mind showing them how, though she had always taken these entreaties merely as their way of making conversation with their lone foreign-born neighbor. But as she sat in Sukhasana and her breath slowed to a deep rhythm, she could not fully release and let go. The niggling idea of what she would do as Ray grew older and her husband worked increasingly long hours crept up the inside of her foot and along her calf to the back of her knee and began to climb into her lap.

The doorbell rang.

Ruana was happy for the escape, and though she was someone to whom order was also a sort of meditation, she hopped up, wrapped a shawl that was hanging on the back of a chair around her waist, and, with Ray's music barreling down the stairs, walked to the door. She thought only for a moment that it might be a neighbor. A complaining neighbor—the music—and she, dressed in a red leotard and shawl.

Ruth stood on the stoop, holding a grocery sack.

"Hello," Ruana said. "May I help you?"

"I'm here to see Ray."

"Come in."

All of this had to be half-shouted over the noise coming from upstairs. Ruth stepped into the front hall.

"Go on up," Ruana shouted, pointing to the stairs.

I watched Ruana take in Ruth's baggy overalls, her turtleneck, her parka. *I could start with her,* Ruana thought to herself.

Ruth had been standing in the grocery store with her mother when she saw the candles among the paper plates and plastic forks and spoons. At school that day she had been acutely aware of what day it was and even though what she had done so far—lain in bed reading *The Bell Jar,* helped her mother clean out what her father insisted on calling his toolshed and what she thought of as the poetry shed, and tagged along to the grocery store—hadn't consisted of anything that might mark the anniversary of my death, she had been determined to do something.

When she saw the candles she knew immediately that she would find her way over to Ray's house and ask him to come with her. Because of their meetings at the shot-put circle, the kids at school had made them a couple despite all evidence to the contrary. Ruth could draw as many female nudes as she might wish and fashion scarves on her head and write papers on Janis Joplin and loudly protest the oppression of shaving her legs and armpits. In the eyes of her classmates at Fairfax, she remained a weird girl who had been found K-I-S-S-I-N-G a weird boy.

What no one understood—and they could not begin to tell anyone—was that it had been an experiment between them. Ray had kissed only me, and Ruth had never kissed anyone, so, united, they had agreed to kiss each other and see.

"I don't feel anything," Ruth had said afterward, as they lay in the maple leaves under a tree behind the teachers' parking lot.

"I don't either," Ray admitted.

"Did you feel something when you kissed Susie?"

"Yes."

"What?"

"That I wanted more. That night I dreamed of kissing her again and wondered if she was thinking the same thing."

"And sex?"

"I hadn't really gotten that far yet," Ray said. "Now I kiss you and it's not the same."

"We could keep trying," Ruth said. "I'm game if you don't tell anyone."

"I thought you liked girls," Ray said.

"I'll make you a deal," Ruth said. "You can pretend I'm Susie and I will too."

"You are so entirely screwed up," Ray said, smiling.

"Are you saying you don't want to?" Ruth teased.

"Show me your drawings again."

"I may be screwed up," Ruth said, dragging out her sketchbook from her book bag—it was now full of nudes she'd copied out of *Playboy,* scaling various parts up or down and adding hair and wrinkles where they had been airbrushed out—"but at least I'm not a perv for charcoal."

Ray was dancing around his bedroom when Ruth walked in. He wore his glasses, which at school he tried to do without because they were thick and his father had only sprung for the least expensive, hard-to-break frames. He had on a pair of jeans that were baggy and stained and a T-shirt that Ruth imagined, and I knew, had been slept in.

He stopped dancing as soon as he saw her standing at the doorway holding the grocery bag. His hands went up immediately and collected his glasses, and then, not knowing what to do with them, he waved them at her and said, "Hello."

"Can you turn it down?" Ruth screamed.

"Sure!"

When the noise ceased her ears rang for a second, and in that second she saw something flicker across Ray's eyes.

He now stood on the other side of the room, and in between them was his bed, where sheets were rumpled and balled and over which hung a drawing Ruth had done of me from memory.

"You hung it up," Ruth said.

"I think it's really good."

"You and me and nobody else."

"My mom thinks it's good."

"She's intense, Ray," Ruth said, putting down the bag. "No wonder you're so freak-a-delic."

"What's in the bag?"

"Candles," said Ruth. "I got them at the grocery store. It's December sixth."

"I know."

"I thought we might go to the cornfield and light them. Say goodbye."

"How many times can you say it?"

"It was an idea," Ruth said. "I'll go alone."

"No," Ray said. "I'll go."

Ruth sat down in her jacket and overalls and waited for him to change his shirt. She watched him with his back toward her, how thin he was but also how the muscles seemed to pop on his arms the way they were supposed to and the color of his skin, like his mother's, so much more inviting than her own.

"We can kiss for a while if you want."

And he turned, grinning. He had begun to like the experiments. He was not thinking of me anymore—though he couldn't tell that to Ruth.

He liked the way she cursed and hated school. He liked how smart she was and how she tried to pretend that it didn't matter to her that his father was a doctor (even though not a real doctor, as she pointed out) and her father scavenged old houses, or that the Singhs had rows and rows of books in their house while she was starved for them.

He sat down next to her on the bed.

"Do you want to take your parka off?"

She did.

And so on the anniversary of my death, Ray mashed himself against Ruth and the two of them kissed and at some point she looked him in the face. "Shit!" she said. "I think I feel something."

When Ray and Ruth arrived at the cornfield, they were silent and he was holding her hand. She didn't know whether he was holding it because they were observing my death together or because he liked her. Her brain was a storm, her usual insight gone.

Then she saw she had not been the only one to think of me. Hal and Samuel Heckler were standing in the cornfield with their hands jammed in their pockets and their backs turned toward her. Ruth saw yellow daffodils on the ground.

"Did you bring those?" Ruth asked Samuel.

"No," Hal said, answering for his brother. "They were already here when we got here."

Mrs. Stead watched from her son's upstairs bedroom. She decided to throw on her coat and walk out to the field. It was not something she even tried to judge, whether or not she belonged there.

Grace Tarking was walking around the block when she saw Mrs. Stead leaving her house with a poinsettia. They talked briefly in the street. Grace said that she was going to stop at home but she would come and join them.

Grace made two phone calls, one to her boyfriend, who lived a short distance away in a slightly richer area, and one to the

Gilberts. They had not yet recovered from their strange role in the discovery of my death—their faithful lab having found the first evidence. Grace offered to escort them, since they were older and cutting across neighbors' lawns and over the bumpy earth of the cornfield would be a challenge to them, but yes, Mr. Gilbert had said, he wanted to come. They needed this, he told Grace Tarking, his wife particularly—though I could see how crushed he was. He always covered his pain by being attentive to his wife. Though they had thought briefly of giving their dog away, he was too much comfort to both of them.

Mr. Gilbert wondered if Ray, who ran errands for them and was a sweet boy who had been badly judged, knew, and so he called the Singh household. Ruana said she suspected her son must already be there but that she would be along herself.

Lindsey was looking out the window when she saw Grace Tarking with her arm in Mrs. Gilbert's and Grace's boyfriend steadying Mr. Gilbert as the four of them cut across the O'Dwyers' lawn.

"Something's going on in the cornfield, Mom," she said.

My mother was reading Molière, whom she had studied so intensely in college but hadn't looked at since. Beside her were the books that had marked her as an avant-garde undergraduate: Sartre, Colette, Proust, Flaubert. She had pulled them off the shelves in her bedroom and promised herself she would reread them that year.

"I'm not interested," she said to Lindsey, "but I'm sure your father will be when he gets home. Why don't you go up and play with your brother?"

My sister had dutifully hovered for weeks now, paying court to our mother regardless of the signals she gave. There was something on the other side of the icy surface. Lindsey was sure of it. She stayed by my mother, sitting by her chair and watching our neighbors outside the window.

* * *

By the time darkness fell, the candles the latecomers had had the foresight to bring lit the cornfield. It seemed like everyone I'd ever known or sat next to in a classroom from kindergarten to eighth grade was there. Mr. Botte saw that something was happening when he'd come out of the school after preparing his classroom for the next day's annual animal digestion experiment. He'd strolled over, and, when he realized what it was, he let himself back into the school and made some calls. There had been a secretary who had been overcome by my death. She came with her son. There had been some teachers who hadn't come to the official school memorial.

The rumors of Mr. Harvey's suspected guilt had begun to make their way from neighbor to neighbor on Thanksgiving night. By the next afternoon it was the only thing the neighbors could talk about—was it possible? Could that strange man who had lived so quietly among them have killed Susie Salmon? But no one had dared approach my family to find out the details. Cousins of friends or fathers of the boys who cut their lawn were asked if they knew anything. Anyone who might know what the police were doing had been buddied up to in the past week, and so my memorial was both a way to mark my memory and a way for the neighbors to seek comfort from one another. A murderer had lived among them, passed them on the street, bought Girl Scout cookies from their daughters and magazine subscriptions from their sons.

In my heaven I buzzed with heat and energy as more and more people reached the cornfield and lit their candles and began to hum a low, dirgelike song for which Mr. O'Dwyer called back to the distant memory of his Dublin grandfather. My neighbors were awkward at first, but the secretary from the school clung to Mr. O'Dwyer as his voice gave forth, and she added her less melodious one. Ruana Singh stood stiffly in an outer circle away from her son. Dr. Singh had called as she was leaving to say he would be sleeping overnight in his office. But other fathers, coming home from their offices, parked their cars in their driveways only to get out and follow their neighbors. How could they both work to support their families and watch their children to make sure they were safe? As a group they would learn it was impossible, no matter how many rules they laid down. What had happened to me could happen to anyone.

No one had called my house. My family was left undisturbed. The impenetrable barrier that surrounded the shingles, the chimney, the woodpile, the driveway, the fence, was like a layer of clear ice that coated the trees when it rained and then froze. Our house looked the same as every other one on the block, but it was not the same. Murder had a blood red door on the other side of which was everything unimaginable to everyone.

When the sky had turned a dappled rose, Lindsey realized what was happening. My mother never lifted her eyes from her book.

"They're having a ceremony for Susie," Lindsey said. "Listen." She cracked the window open. In rushed the cold December air and the distant sound of singing.

My mother used all her energy. "We've had the memorial," she said. "That's done for me."

"What's done?"

My mother's elbows were on the armrests of the yellow winged-back chair. She leaned slightly forward and her face moved into shadow, making it harder for Lindsey to see the expression on her face. "I don't believe she's waiting for us out there. I don't think lighting candles and doing all that stuff is honoring her memory. There are other ways to honor it."

"Like what?" Lindsey said. She sat cross-legged on the rug in front of my mother, who sat in her chair with her finger marking her place in Molière.

"I want to be more than a mother."

Lindsey thought she could understand this. She wanted to be more than a girl.

My mother put the Molière book on top of the coffee table and scooted forward on the chair until she lowered herself down onto the rug. I was struck by this. My mother did not sit on the floor, she sat at the bill-paying desk or in the wing chairs or sometimes on the end of the couch with Holiday curled up beside her.

She took my sister's hand in hers.

"Are you going to leave us?" Lindsey asked.

My mother wobbled. How could she say what she already knew? Instead, she told a lie. "I promise I won't leave you."

What she wanted most was to be that free girl again, stacking china at Wanamaker's, hiding from her manager the Wedgwood cup with the handle she broke, dreaming of living in Paris like de Beauvoir and Sartre, and going home that day laughing to herself about the nerdy Jack Salmon, who was pretty cute even if he hated smoke. The cafés in Paris were full of cigarettes, she'd told him, and he'd seemed impressed. At the end of that summer when she invited him in and they had, both for the first time, made love, she'd smoked a cigarette, and for the joke he said he'd have one too. When she handed him the damaged blue china to use as an ashtray, she used all her favorite words to embellish the story of breaking and then hiding, inside her coat, the now homely Wedgwood cup.

"Come here, baby," my mother said, and Lindsey did. She leaned her back into my mother's chest, and my mother rocked her awkwardly on the rug. "You are doing so well, Lindsey; you are keeping your father alive." And they heard his car pull into the drive.

Lindsey let herself be held while my mother thought of Ruana Singh out behind her house, smoking. The sweet scent of Dunhills had drifted out onto the road and taken my mother far away. Her last boyfriend before my father had loved Gauloises. He had been a pretentious little thing, she thought, but he had also been oh-so-serious in a way that let her be oh-so-serious as well.

"Do you see the candles, Mom?" Lindsey asked, as she stared out the window.

"Go get your father," my mother said.

My sister met my father in the mud room, hanging up his keys and coat. Yes, they would go, he said. Of course they would go.

"Daddy!" My brother called from the second floor, where my sister and father went to meet him.

"Your call," my father said as Buckley bodychecked him.

"I'm tired of protecting him," Lindsey said. "It doesn't feel real not to include him. Susie's gone. He knows that."

My brother stared up at her.

"There is a party for Susie," Lindsey said. "And me and Daddy are taking you."

"Is Mommy sick?" Buckley asked.

Lindsey didn't want to lie to him, but she also felt it was an accurate description of what she knew.

"Yes."

Lindsey agreed to meet our father downstairs while she brought Buckley into his room to change his clothes.

"I see her, you know," Buckley said, and Lindsey looked at him.

"She comes and talks to me, and spends time with me when you're at soccer."

Lindsey didn't know what to say, but she reached out and grabbed him and squeezed him to her, the way he often squeezed Holiday.

"You are so special," she said to my brother. "I'll always be here, no matter what."

My father made his slow way down the stairs, his left hand tightening on the wooden banister, until he reached the flagstone landing.

His approach was loud. My mother took her Molière book and crept into the dining room, where he wouldn't see her. She read her book, standing in the corner of the dining room and hiding from her family. She waited for the front door to open and close.

My neighbors and teachers, friends and family, circled an arbitrary spot not far from where I'd been killed. My father, sister, and brother heard the singing again once they were outside. Everything in my father leaned and pitched toward the warmth and light. He wanted so badly to have me remembered in the minds and hearts of everyone. I knew something as I watched: almost everyone was saying goodbye to me. I was becoming one of many little-girl-losts. They would go back to their homes and put me to rest, a letter from the past never reopened or reread. And I could say goodbye to them, wish them well, bless them somehow for their good thoughts. A handshake in the street, a dropped item picked up and retrieved and handed back, or a friendly wave from a distant window, a nod, a smile, a moment when the eyes lock over the antics of a child.

Ruth saw my three family members first, and she tugged on Ray's sleeve. "Go help him," she whispered. And Ray, who had met my father on his first day of what would prove a long journey to try to find my killer, moved forward. Samuel came away too. Like youthful pastors, they brought my father and sister and brother into the group, which made a wide berth for them and grew silent.

My father had not been outside the house except to drive back and forth to work or sit out in the backyard, for months, nor had he seen his neighbors. Now he looked at them, from face to face, until he realized I had been loved by people he didn't even recognize. His heart filled up, warm again as it had not been in what seemed so long to him—save small forgotten moments with Buckley, the accidents of love that happened with his son.

He looked at Mr. O'Dwyer. "Stan," he said, "Susie used to stand at the front window during the summer and listen to you singing in your yard. She loved it. Will you sing for us?"

And in the kind of grace that is granted, but rarely, and not when you wish it most—to save a loved one from dying—Mr. O'Dwyer wobbled only a moment on his first note, then sang loud and clear and fine.

Everyone joined in.

I remembered those summer nights my father spoke of. How the darkness would take forever to come and with it I always hoped for it to cool down. Sometimes, standing at the open window in the front hall, I would feel a breeze, and on that breeze was the music coming from the O'Dwyers' house. As I listened to Mr. O'Dwyer run through all the Irish ballads he had ever learned, the breeze would begin to smell of earth and air and a mossy scent that meant only one thing: a thunderstorm.

There was a wonderful temporary hush then, as Lindsey sat in her room on the old couch studying, my father sat in his den reading his books, my mother downstairs doing needlepoint or washing up.

I liked to change into a long cotton nightgown and go out onto the back porch, where, as the rain began falling in heavy drops against the roof, breezes came in the screens from all sides and swept my gown against me. It was warm and wonderful and the lightning would come and, a few moments later, the thunder.

My mother would stand at the open porch door, and, after she said her standard warning, "You're going to catch your death of cold," she grew quiet. We both listened together to the rain pour down and the thunder clap and smelled the earth rising to greet us.

"You look invincible," my mother said one night.

I loved these times, when we seemed to feel the same thing. I turned to her, wrapped in my thin gown, and said:

"I am."

SNAPSHOTS

With the camera my parents gave me, I took dozens of candids of my family. So many that my father forced me to choose which rolls I thought should be developed. As the cost of my obsession mounted, I began keeping two boxes in my closet. "Rolls to be sent out" and "Rolls to hold back." It was, my mother said, the only hint of any organizational skills I possessed.

I loved the way the burned-out flashcubes of the Kodak Instamatic marked a moment that had passed, one that would now be gone forever except for a picture. When they were spent, I took the cubed four-corner flashbulbs and passed them from hand to hand until they cooled. The broken filaments of the flash would turn a molten marble blue or sometimes smoke the thin glass black. I had rescued the moment by using my camera and in that way had found a way to stop time and hold it. No one could take that image away from me because I owned it.

* * *

On a summer evening in 1975, my mother turned to my father and said:

"Have you ever made love in the ocean?"

And he said, "No."

"Neither have I," my mother said. "Let's pretend it is the ocean and that I am going away and we might never see each other again."

The next day she left for her father's cabin in New Hampshire.

That same summer, Lindsey or Buckley or my father would open the front door and find a casserole or a bundt cake on the front stoop. Sometimes an apple pie—my father's favorite. The food was unpredictable. The casseroles Mrs. Stead made were horrible. The bundt cakes Mrs. Gilbert made were overly moist but bearable. The apple pies from Ruana: heaven on Earth.

In his study during the long nights after my mother left, my father would try to lose himself by rereading passages from the Civil War letters of Mary Chestnut to her husband. He tried to let go of any blame, of any hope, but it was impossible. He did manage a small smile once.

"Ruana Singh bakes a mean apple pie," he wrote in his notebook.

In the fall he picked up the phone one afternoon to hear Grandma Lynn.

"Jack," my grandmother announced, "I am thinking of coming to stay."

My father was silent, but the line was riddled with his hesitation.

"I would like to make myself available to you and the children. I've been knocking around in this mausoleum long enough."

"Lynn, we're just beginning to start over again," he stammered. Still, he couldn't depend on Nate's mother to watch Buckley forever. Four months after my mother left, her temporary absence was beginning to take on the feel of permanence.

My grandmother insisted. I watched her resist the remaining slug of vodka in her glass. "I will contain my drinking until"—she thought hard here—"after five o'clock, and," she said, "what the hell, I'll stop altogether if you should find it necessary."

"Do you know what you're saying?"

My grandmother felt a clarity from her phone hand down to her pump-encased feet. "Yes, I do. I think."

It was only after he got off the phone that he let himself wonder, *Where will we PUT her?*

It was obvious to everyone.

By December 1975, a year had passed since Mr. Harvey had packed his bags, but there was still no sign of him. For a while, until the tape dirtied or the paper tore, store owners kept a scratchy sketch of him taped to their windows. Lindsey and Samuel walked in the neighborhood or hung out at Hal's bike shop. She wouldn't go to the diner where the other kids went. The owner of the diner was a law and order man. He had blown up the sketch of George Harvey to twice its size and taped it to the front door. He willingly gave the grisly details to any customer who asked—young girl, cornfield, found only an elbow.

Finally Lindsey asked Hal to give her a ride to the police station. She wanted to know what exactly they were doing.

They bid farewell to Samuel at the bike shop and Hal gave Lindsey a ride through a wet December snow.

From the start, Lindsey's youth and purpose had caught the police off guard. As more and more of them realized who she was, they gave her a wider and wider berth. Here was this girl, focused, mad, fifteen. Her breasts were perfect small cups, her legs gangly but curved, her eyes like flint and flower petals.

While Lindsey and Hal waited outside the captain's office on a wooden bench, she thought she saw something across the room that she recognized. It was on Detective Fenerman's desk and it stood out in the room because of its color. What her mother had always distinguished as Chinese red, a harsher red than rose red, it was the red of classic lipsticks, rarely found in nature. Our mother was proud of her ability to wear Chinese red, noting each time she tied a particular scarf around her neck that it was a color even Grandma Lynn dared not wear.

"Hal," she said, every muscle tense as she stared at the increasingly familiar object on Fenerman's desk.

"Yes."

"Do you see that red cloth?"

"Yes."

"Can you go and get it for me?"

When Hal looked at her, she said: "I think it's my mother's."

As Hal stood to retrieve it, Len entered the squad room from behind where Lindsey sat. He tapped her on the shoulder just as he realized what Hal was doing. Lindsey and Detective Fenerman stared at each other.

"Why do you have my mother's scarf?"

He stumbled. "She might have left it in my car one day."

Lindsey stood and faced him. She was clear-eyed and driving fast toward the worst news yet. "What was she doing in your car?"

"Hello, Hal," Len said.

Hal held the scarf in his hand. Lindsey grabbed it away, her voice growing angry. "Why do you have my mother's scarf?"

And though Len was the detective, Hal saw it first—it arched over her like a rainbow—Prisma Color understanding. The way it happened in algebra class or English when my sister was the first person to figure out the sum of *x* or point out the double entendres to her peers. Hal put his hand on Lindsey's shoulder to guide her. "We should go," he said.

And later she cried out her disbelief to Samuel in the back room of the bike shop.

When my brother turned seven, he built a fort for me. It was something the two of us had said we would always do together and something my father could not bring himself to do. It reminded him too much of building the tent with the disappeared Mr. Harvey.

A family with five little girls had moved into Mr. Harvey's house. Laughter traveled over into my father's study from the built-in pool they had poured the spring after George Harvey ran. The sound of little girls — girls to spare.

The cruelty of it became like glass shattering in my father's ears. In the spring of 1976, with my mother gone, he would shut the window of his den on even the hottest evenings to avoid the sound. He watched his solitary little boy in among the three pussy-willow bushes, talking to himself. Buckley had brought empty terra-cotta pots from the garage. He hauled the boot scraper out from where it lay forgotten at the side of the house. Anything to make walls for the fort. With the help of Samuel and Hal and Lindsey, he edged two huge boulders from the front of the driveway into the backyard. This was such an unexpected windfall that it prompted Samuel to ask, "How are you going to make a roof?"

And Buckley looked at him in wonder as Hal mentally scanned the contents of his bike shop and remembered two scrap sheets of corrugated tin he had leaning up against the back wall.

So one hot night my father looked down and didn't see his son anymore. Buckley was nestled inside his fort. On his hands and knees, he would pull the terra-cotta pots in after him and then prop a board against them that reached almost up to the wavy roof. Just enough light came in to read by. Hal had obliged him and painted in big black spray paint letters KEEP OUT on one side of the plywood door.

Mostly he read the Avengers and the X-Men. He dreamed of being Wolverine, who had a skeleton made of the strongest metal in the universe and who could heal from any wound overnight. At the oddest moments he would think about me, miss my voice, wish I would come out from the house and pound on the roof of his fort and demand to be let in. Sometimes he wished Samuel and Lindsey hung out more or that my father would play with him as he once had. Play without that always-worried look underneath the smile, that desperate worry that surrounded everything now like an invisible force field. But my brother would not let himself miss my mother. He tunneled into stories where weak men changed into strong half-animals or used eye beams or magic hammers to power through steel or climb up the sides of skyscrapers. He was the Hulk when angry and Spidey the rest of the time. When he felt his heart hurt he turned into something stronger than a little boy, and he grew up this way. A heart that flashed from heart to stone, heart to stone. As I watched I thought of what Grandma Lynn liked to say when Lindsey and I rolled our eyes or grimaced behind her back. "Watch out what faces you make. You'll freeze that way."

One day, Buckley came home from the second grade with a story he'd written: "Once upon a time there was a kid named Billy. He liked to explore. He saw a hole and went inside but he never came out. The End."

My father was too distracted to see anything in this. Mimicking my mother, he taped it to the fridge in the same place Buckley's long-forgotten drawing of the Inbetween had been. But my brother knew something was wrong with his story. Knew it by how his teacher had reacted, doing a double take like they did in his comic books. He took the story down and brought it to my old room while Grandma Lynn was downstairs. He folded it into a tiny square and put it inside the now-empty insides of my four-poster bed.

On a hot day in the fall of 1976, Len Fenerman visited the large safety box in the evidence room. The bones of the neighborhood animals he had found in Mr. Harvey's crawlspace were there, along with the lab confirmation of evidence of quicklime. He had supervised the investigation, but no matter how much they dug, or how deep, no other bones or bodies had been found on his property. The blood stain on the floor of his garage was my only calling card. Len had spent weeks, then months, poring over a xerox of the sketch Lindsey had stolen. He had led a team back into the field, and they had dug and then dug again. Finally they found an old Coke bottle at the opposite end of the field. There it was, a solid link: fingerprints matching Mr. Harvey's prints, which were all over his house, and fingerprints matching those on my birth certificate. There was no question in his mind: Jack Salmon had been right from the beginning.

But no matter how hard he looked for the man himself, it was as if George Harvey had evaporated into thin air when he hit the property line. He could find no records with that name attached. Officially, he did not exist.

What he had left behind were his dollhouses. So Len called the man who sold them for him, and who took commissions from select stores, and the wealthy people who ordered replicas of their own homes. Nothing. He had called the makers of the miniature chairs, the tiny doors and windows with beveled glass and brass hardware, and the manufacturer of the cloth shrubs and trees. Nothing.

He sat down among the evidence at a barren communal desk in the basement of the station. He looked through the stack of extra fliers that my father had made up. He had memorized my face, but still he looked at them. He had come to believe that the best hope in my case might be the recent rise in development in the area. With all the land churning and changing, perhaps other clues would be found that would provide the answer he needed.

In the bottom of the box was the bag with my jingle-bell hat. When he'd handed it to my mother, she had collapsed on the rug. He still couldn't pinpoint the moment he'd fallen in love with her. I knew it was the day he'd sat in our family room while my mother drew stick figures on butcher paper and Buckley and Nate slept toe to toe on the couch. I felt sorry for him. He had tried to solve my murder and he had failed. He had tried to love my mother and he had failed.

Len looked at the drawing of the cornfield that Lindsey had stolen and forced himself to acknowledge this: in his cautiousness, he had allowed a murderer to get away. He could not shake his guilt. He knew, if no one else did, that by being with my mother in the mall that day he was the one to blame for George Harvey's freedom.

He took his wallet out of his back pocket and laid down the photos of all the unsolved cases he had ever worked on. Among them was his wife's. He turned them all face-down. "Gone," he wrote on each one of them. He would no longer wait for a date to mark an understanding of who or why or how. He would never understand all the reasons why his wife had killed herself. He would never understand how so many children went missing. He placed these photos in the box with my evidence and turned the lights off in the cold room.

But he did not know this:

In Connecticut on September 10, 1976, a hunter on his way back to his car saw something shiny on the ground. My

Pennsylvania keystone charm. Then he saw that the ground nearby had been partially dug up by a bear. Exposed by the bear were the unmistakable bones of a child's foot.

My mother made it through only one winter in New Hampshire before she got the idea of driving all the way to California. It was something she had always thought she would do but had never done. A man she met in New Hampshire had told her about the work to be had in wineries in the valleys above San Francisco. It was easy to get, it was physical, and it could be, if you wanted it to be, very anonymous. All three sounded good to her.

This man had also wanted to sleep with her, but she said no. By then, she knew this wasn't the road out anymore. From the first night with Len in the innards of the mall she had known the two of them weren't building anything. She could not even really feel him.

She packed her bags for California and sent cards to my brother and sister from every town she stopped in. "Hello, I'm in Dayton. Ohio's state bird is the cardinal." "Reached the Mississippi last night at sunset. It certainly is a big river."

In Arizona, when she was eight states beyond the farthest she had ever been, she paid for her room and brought a bucket of ice with her from the machine outside. The next day she would reach California, and to celebrate she had bought herself a bottle of champagne. She thought of what the man in New Hampshire had said, how he had spent one whole year scraping the mold out of the giant casks that held wine. He had lain flat on his back and had to use a knife to peel back the layers of mold. The mold had the color and consistency of liver, and no matter how hard he bathed he would still attract fruit flies for hours afterward.

She sipped champagne from a plastic cup and looked at herself in the mirror. She forced herself to look.

She remembered sitting in our living room then, with me and my sister, my brother and father, on the first New Year's Eve that all five of us had stayed up. She had shaped the day around making sure Buckley got enough sleep.

When he woke up after dark he was sure that someone better than Santa would come that night. In his mind he held a big bang image of the ultimate holiday, when he would be transported to toyland.

Hours later, as he yawned and leaned into my mother's lap and she finger-combed his hair, my father ducked into the kitchen to make cocoa and my sister and I served German chocolate cake. When the clock struck twelve and there was only distant screaming and a few guns shot into the air in our neighborhood, my brother was unbelieving. Disappointment so swiftly and thoroughly overtook him that my mother was at a loss for what to do. She thought of it as sort of an infant Peggy Lee's "Is that all there is?" and then bawling.

She remembered my father had lifted Buckley up into his arms and started singing. The rest of us joined in. "Let ole acquaintance be forgot and never brought to mind, should ole acquaintance be forgot and days of auld lang syne!"

And Buckley had stared at us. He captured the foreign words like bubbles floating above him in the air. "Lang syne?" he said with a look of wonder.

"What does that mean?" I asked my parents.

"The old days," my father said.

"Days long past," my mother said. But then, suddenly, she had started pinching the crumbs of her cake together on her plate.

"Hey, Ocean Eyes," my father said. "Where'd you go on us?"

And she remembered that she had met his question with a closing off, as though her spirit had a tap—twist to the right and she was up on her feet asking me to help her clean up.

In the fall of 1976, when she reached California, she drove

directly to the beach and stopped her car. She felt like she had driven through nothing but families for four days—squabbling families, bawling families, screaming families, families under the miraculous strain of the day by day—and she was relieved to see the waves from the windshield of her car. She couldn't help thinking of the books she had read in college. *The Awakening.* And what had happened to one writer, Virginia Woolf. It all seemed so wonderful back then—filmy and romantic—stones in the pocket, walk into the waves.

She climbed down the cliffs after tying her sweater loosely around her waist. Down below she could see nothing but jagged rocks and waves. She was careful, but I watched her feet more than the view she saw—I worried about her slipping.

My mother's desire to reach those waves, touch her feet to another ocean on the other side of the country, was all she was thinking of—the pure baptismal goal of it. Whoosh and you can start over again. Or was life more like the horrible game in gym that has you running from one side of an enclosed space to another, picking up and setting down wooden blocks without end? She was thinking *reach the waves, the waves, the waves,* and I was watching her feet navigate the rocks, and when we heard her we did so together—looking up in shock.

It was a baby on the beach.

In among the rocks was a sandy cove, my mother now saw, and crawling across the sand on a blanket was a baby in knitted pink cap and singlet and boots. She was alone on the blanket with a stuffed white toy—my mother thought a lamb.

With their backs to my mother as she descended were a group of adults—very official and frantic-looking—wearing black and navy with cool slants to their hats and boots. Then my wildlife photographer's eye saw the tripods and silver circles rimmed by wire, which, when a young man moved them left or right, bounced light off or on the baby on her blanket.

My mother started laughing, but only one assistant turned to notice her up among the rocks; everyone else was too busy. This was an ad for something, I imagined, but what? New fresh infant girls to replace your own? As my mother laughed and I watched her face light up, I also saw it fall into strange lines.

She saw the waves behind the girl child and how both beautiful and intoxicating they were—they could sweep up so softly and remove this girl from the beach. All the stylish people could chase after her, but she would drown in a moment—no one, not even a mother who had every nerve attuned to anticipate disaster, could have saved her if the waves leapt up, if life went on as usual and freak accidents peppered a calm shore.

That same week she found work at the Krusoe Winery, in a valley above the bay. She wrote my sister and brother postcards filled with the bright fragments of her life, hoping in a postcard's limited space she would sound cheery.

On her days off, she would walk down the streets of Sausalito or Santa Rosa—tiny upscale towns where everyone was a stranger—and, no matter how hard she tried to focus on the hopeful unfamiliar, when she walked inside a gift shop or café the four walls around her would begin to breathe like a lung. She would feel it then, creeping up the side of her calves and into her gut, the onslaught, the grief coming, the tears like a small relentless army approaching the front lines of her eyes, and she would breathe in, taking a large gulp of air to try to stop herself from crying in a public place. She asked for coffee and toast in a restaurant and buttered it with tears. She went into a flower shop and asked for daffodils, and when there were none she felt robbed. It was such a small wish—a bright yellow flower.

The first impromptu memorial in the cornfield opened in my father the need for more. Yearly now, he organized a memorial, to which fewer and fewer neighbors and friends came. There were the regulars, like Ruth, and the Gilberts, but more and more the group was filled out by kids from the high school who, as time went by, knew only my name and even that only as a large dark rumor invoked as a warning to any student that might prove too much a loner. Especially girls.

Each time my name was said by these strangers it felt like a pinprick. It was not the pleasant sensation that it could be when my father said it or when Ruth wrote it in her journal. It was the sensation of being simultaneously resurrected and buried within the same breath. As if in an economics class I had been ushered over into a column of transmutable commodities: the Murdered. A few teachers, like Mr. Botte, remembered me as a real girl. Sometimes on his lunch hour he would go and sit in his red Fiat and think about the daughter he had lost to leukemia. In the distance, out past his window, the cornfield loomed. Often, he would say a prayer for me.

In just a few short years, Ray Singh grew so handsome that a spell radiated from him when he walked into a crowd. His adult face had still not settled on him, but, now that he was seventeen, it was just around the corner. He exuded a dreamy asexuality that made him attractive to both men and women, with his long lashes and hooded eyelids, his thick black hair, and the same delicate features that were still a boy's.

I would watch Ray with a longing different from that which I had for anyone else. A longing to touch and hold him, to understand the very body that he examined with the coldest of eyes. He would sit at his desk and read his favorite book—*Gray's Anatomy*—and depending on what he was reading about he would use his fingers to palpate his carotid artery or his thumb to press down and follow the longest muscle in his body—the sartorius, which ran from the outside of his hip to the inside of his knee. His thinness was a boon to him then, the bones and muscles clearly distinguished beneath the skin.

By the time he packed his bags for Penn, he had committed so many words and their definitions to memory that I grew worried. With all that, how could his mind contain anything else? Ruth's friendship, his mother's love, my memory would be pushed to the back as he made way for the eye's crystalline lens and its capsule, the semicircular canals of the ear, or my favorite, the qualities of the sympathetic nervous system.

I need not have worried. Ruana cast about the house for something, anything, that her son might bring with him that was equal in heft and weight to *Gray's* and that would, she hoped, keep the flower-gathering side of him alive. Without his knowing, she tucked the book of Indian poetry into his luggage. Inside was the long-forgotten photo of me. When he unpacked inside Hill House dormitory, my picture fell on the floor by his bed. Despite how he could dissect it—the vessels of the globe of my eye, the surgical anatomy of my nasal fossae, the light tincture of my epidermis—he could not avoid them, the lips he had once kissed.

In June 1977, on the day of what would have been my graduation, Ruth and Ray were already gone. The day classes ended at Fairfax, Ruth moved to New York City with her mother's old red suitcase full of new black clothes. Having graduated early, Ray was already at the end of his freshman year at Penn.

In our kitchen that same day, Grandma Lynn gave Buckley a book on gardening. She told him about how plants came from seeds. That radishes, which he hated, grew fastest, but that flowers, which he loved, could grow from seeds as well. And she began to teach him the names: zinnias and marigolds, pansies and lilacs, carnations and petunias, and morning glory vines.

* * *

Occasionally my mother called from California. My parents had hurried and difficult conversations. She asked after Buckley and Lindsey and Holiday. She asked how the house was holding up and whether there was anything he needed to tell her.

"We still miss you," he said in December 1977, when the leaves had all fallen and been blown or raked away but even still, with the ground waiting to receive it, there had been no snow.

"I know that," she said.

"What about teaching? I thought that was your plan."

"It was," she conceded. She was on the phone in the office of the winery. Things had slowed up after the lunch crowd, but five limos of old ladies, three sheets to the wind, were soon due in. She was silent and then she said something that no one, least of all my father, could have argued with. "Plans change."

In New York, Ruth was living in an old woman's walk-in closet on the Lower East Side. It was the only thing she could afford, and she had no intention of spending much time there anyway. Daily she rolled her twin-sized futon into the corner so she could have a little floor space in which to dress. She visited the closet only once a day, and she never spent any time there if she could help it. The closet was for sleeping and having an address, a solid if tiny perch in the city.

She worked service bar and walked every inch of Manhattan on her off hours. I watched her pound the cement in her defiant boots, sure that women were being murdered wherever she went. Down in stairwells and up inside beautiful highrises. She would linger at streetlights and scan the facing street. She wrote small prayers in her journal at the cafés and the bars, where she stopped to use the bathroom after ordering the cheapest thing on the menu.

She had become convinced that she had a second sight that no one else had. She didn't know what she would do with it, save taking copious notes for the future, but she had grown unafraid. The world she saw of dead women and children had become as real to her as the world in which she lived.

In the library at Penn, Ray read about the elderly under the boldface heading "The Conditions of Death." It described a study done in nursing homes in which a large percentage of patients reported to the doctors and nurses that they saw someone standing at the end of their bed at night. Often this person tried to talk to them or call their name. Sometimes the patients were in such a high state of agitation during these delusions that they had to be given a sedative or strapped to their beds.

The text went on to explain that these visions were a result of small strokes that often preceded death. "What is commonly thought of by the layman as the Angel of Death, when discussed at all with the patient's family, should be presented to them as a small series of strokes compounding an already precipitous state of decline."

For a moment, with his finger marking the place in the book, Ray imagined what it would be like if, standing over the bed of an elderly patient, remaining as open as he could to possibility, he might feel something brush past him as Ruth had so many years ago in the parking lot.

Mr. Harvey had been living wild within the Northeast Corridor from the outlying areas of Boston down to the northern tips of the southern states, where he would go to find easier work and fewer questions and make an occasional attempt to reform. He had always liked Pennsylvania and had crisscrossed the long state, camping sometimes behind the 7-Eleven just down the local highway from our development, where a ridge of woods survived between the all-night store and the railroad tracks, and where he found more and more tin cans and cigarette butts each time he passed through. He still liked to drive close to the old neighborhood when he could. He took these risks early in the morning or late at night, when the wild pheasants that had once been plentiful still traversed the road and his headlights would catch the hollow glowing of their eye sockets as they skittered from one side of the road to the other. There were no longer teenagers and young children sent to pick blackberries just up to the edge of our development, because the old farm fence that had hung so heavily with them had been torn down to make room for more houses. He had learned to pick wild mushrooms over time and gorged on them sometimes when staying overnight in the overgrown fields of Valley Forge Park. On a night like this I saw him come upon two novice campers who had died after eating the mushrooms' poisonous look-alikes. He tenderly stripped their bodies of any valuables and then moved on.

Hal and Nate and Holiday were the only ones Buckley had ever allowed into his fort. The grass died underneath the boulders and when it rained, the insides of the fort were a fetid puddle, but it stayed there, though Buckley went there less and less, and it was Hal who finally begged him to make improvements.

"We need to waterproof it, Buck," Hal said one day. "You're ten—that's old enough to work a caulking gun."

And Grandma Lynn couldn't help herself, she loved men. She encouraged Buck to do what Hal said, and when she knew Hal would be coming to visit, she dressed up.

"What are you doing?" my father said one Saturday morning, lured out of his den by the sweet smell of lemons and butter and golden batter rising in pans.

"Making muffins," Grandma Lynn said.

My father did a sanity check, staring at her. He was still in his robe and it was almost ninety degrees at ten in the morning, but she had pantyhose and makeup on. Then he noticed Hal in an undershirt out in the yard.

"My God, Lynn," he said. "That boy is young enough . . ."

"But he's de-lec-ta-ble!"

My father shook his head and sat down at the kitchen table. "When will the love muffins be done, Mata Hari?"

In December 1981, Len did not want to get the call he got from Delaware, where a murder in Wilmington had been connected to a girl's body found in 1976 in Connecticut. A detective, working overtime, had painstakingly traced the keystone charm in the Connecticut case back to a list of lost property from my murder.

"It's a dead file," Len told the man on the other end.

"We'd like to see what you have."

"George Harvey," Len said out loud, and the detectives at neighboring desks turned toward him. "The crime was in December 1973. The murder victim was Susie Salmon, fourteen."

"Any body for the Simon girl?"

"Salmon, like the fish. We found an elbow," Len said.

"She have a family?"

"Yes."

"Connecticut has teeth. Do you have her dentals?"

"Yes."

"That may save the family some grief," the man told Len.

Len trekked back to the evidence box he had hoped never to look at again. He would have to make a phone call to my family. But he would wait as long as possible, until he was certain the detective in Delaware had something.

* * *

For almost eight years after Samuel told Hal about the drawing Lindsey had stolen, Hal had quietly worked through his network of biker friends to track George Harvey down. But he, like Len, had vowed not to report anything until he was sure it might be a lead. And he had never been sure. When late one night a Hell's Angel named Ralph Cichetti, who admitted freely he had spent some time in prison, said that he thought his mother had been killed by a man she rented a room to, Hal began asking his usual questions. Questions that held elements of elimination about height and weight and preoccupations. The man hadn't gone by the name George Harvey, though that didn't mean anything. But the murder itself seemed too different. Sophie Cichetti was forty-nine. She was killed in her home with a blunt object and her body had been found intact nearby. Hal had read enough crime books to know that killers had patterns, peculiar and important ways they did things. So as Hal adjusted the timing chain of Cichetti's cranky Harley, they moved on to other topics, then fell silent. It was only when Cichetti mentioned something else that every hair on Hal's neck stood up.

"The guy built dollhouses," Ralph Cichetti said.

Hal placed a call to Len.

•

Years passed. The trees in our yard grew taller. I watched my family and my friends and neighbors, the teachers whom I'd had or imagined having, the high school I had dreamed about. As I sat in the gazebo I would pretend instead that I was sitting on the topmost branch of the maple under which my brother had swallowed a stick and still played hide-and-seek with Nate, or I would perch on the railing of a stairwell in New York and wait for Ruth to pass near. I would study with Ray. Drive the Pacific Coast Highway on a warm afternoon of salty air with my mother. But I would end each day with my father in his den.

I would lay these photographs down in my mind, those gathered from my constant watching, and I could trace how one thing—my death—connected these images to a single source. No one could have predicted how my loss would change small moments on Earth. But I held on to those moments, hoarded them. None of them were lost as long as I was there watching.

At Evensong one night, while Holly played her sax and Mrs. Bethel Utemeyer joined in, I saw him: Holiday, racing past a fluffy white Samoyed. He had lived to a ripe old age on Earth and slept at my father's feet after my mother left, never wanting to let him out of his sight. He had stood with Buckley while he built his fort and had been the only one permitted on the porch while Lindsey and Samuel kissed. And in the last few years of his life, every Sunday morning, Grandma Lynn had made him a skillet-sized peanut butter pancake, which she would place flat on the floor, never tiring of watching him try to pick it up with his snout.

I waited for him to sniff me out, anxious to know if here, on the other side, I would still be the little girl he had slept beside. I did not have to wait long: he was so happy to see me, he knocked me down.

SEVENTEEN

At twenty-one Lindsey was many things I would never become, but I barely grieved this list anymore. Still, I roved where she roved. I collected my college diploma and rode on the back of Samuel's bike, clinging on to him with my arms wrapped around his waist, pressing into his back for warmth . . .

Okay, it was Lindsey. I realized that. But in watching her I found I could get lost more than with anyone else.

On the night of their graduation from Temple University, she and Samuel rode his bike back to my parents' house, having promised my father and Grandma Lynn repeatedly that they would not touch the champagne tucked inside the bike's pannard until they reached the house. "After all, we're college graduates!" Samuel had said. My father was soft in his trust with Samuel—years had gone by when the boy had done nothing but right by his surviving daughter.

But on the ride back from Philadelphia down Route 30, it began to rain. Lightly at first, small pinpricks flashing into my sister and Samuel at fifty miles per hour. The cool rain hit the hot dry tar of the road and lifted up smells that had been baked in all day under the hot June sun. Lindsey liked to rest her head between Samuel's shoulder blades and take in the scent of the road and the scrappy shrubs and bushes on either side. She had been remembering how the breeze in the hours before the storm had filled all the white gowns of the graduating seniors as they stood outside Macy Hall. Everyone looked poised, for just a moment, to float away.

Finally, eight miles away from the turnoff that led to our house, the rain grew heavy enough to hurt, and Samuel shouted back to Lindsey that he was going to pull off.

They passed into a slightly more overgrown stretch of road, the kind that existed between two commercial areas and that gradually, by accretion, would be eliminated by another strip mall or auto parts store. The bike wobbled but did not fall on the wet gravel of the shoulder. Samuel used his feet to help brake the bike, then waited, as Hal had taught him, for my sister to get off and step a few feet away before he got off himself.

He opened the visor of his helmet to yell to her. "This is no good," he said, "I'm going to roll her under those trees."

Lindsey followed behind him, the sound of rain hushed inside her padded helmet. They picked their way through the gravel and mud, stepping over branches and litter that had gathered at the side of the road. The rain seemed to be getting heavier still, and my sister was glad she had changed out of the dress she'd worn to commencement and into the leather pants and jacket that Hal had insisted on getting her despite her protests that she looked like a pervert.

Samuel wheeled the bike into the stand of oaks close to the road, and Lindsey followed. They had gone the week before to get haircuts at the same barber shop on Market Street, and though Lindsey's hair was lighter and finer than Samuel's, the barber had given them identical short, spiky cuts. Within a moment of removing their helmets their hair caught the large drops that filtered through the trees, and Lindsey's mascara began to bleed. I watched as Samuel used his thumb to wipe the traces from Lindsey's cheek. "Happy graduation," he said in the darkness, and stooped to kiss her.

Since their first kiss in our kitchen two weeks after my death, I had known that he was—as my sister and I had giggled with our Barbies or while watching Bobby Sherman on TV—her one and only. Samuel had pressed himself into her need, and the cement between the two of them had begun to set immediately. They had gone to Temple together, side by side. He had hated it and she had pushed him through. She had loved it and this had allowed him to survive.

"Let's try and find the densest part of this underbrush," he said.

"What about the bike?"

"Hal will probably have to rescue us when the rain stops."

"Shit!" Lindsey said.

Samuel laughed and grabbed her hand to start walking. The moment they did, they heard the first thunderclap and Lindsey jumped. He tightened his hold on her. The lightning was in the distance still, and the thunder would grow louder on its heels. She had never felt about it the way I did. It made her jumpy and nervous. She imagined trees split down the middle and houses on fire and dogs cowering in basements throughout the suburbs.

They walked through the underbrush, which was getting soaked despite the trees. Even though it was the middle of the afternoon, it was dark except for Samuel's safety light. Still they felt the evidence of people. Their boots crunched down on top of tin cans and pushed up against empty bottles. And then, through the thick weeds and darkness both of them saw the broken window panes that ran along the top of an old Victorian house. Samuel shut off the safety light immediately.

"Do you think there's someone inside?" Lindsey asked.

"It's dark."

"It's spooky."

They looked at each other, and my sister said what they both were thinking. "It's dry!"

They held hands in the heavy rain and ran toward the house as fast as they could, trying not to trip or slide in the increasing mud.

As they drew closer, Samuel could make out the steep pitch of the roof and the small wooden cross work that hung down from the gables. Most of the windows on the bottom floor had been covered over with wood, but the front door swung back and forth on its hinges, banging against the plaster wall on the inside. Though part of him wanted to stand outside in the rain and stare up at the eaves and cornices, he rushed into the house with Lindsey. They stood a few feet inside the doorway, shivering and staring out into the pre-suburban forest that surrounded them. Quickly I scanned the rooms of the old house. They were alone. No scary monsters lurked in corners, no wandering men had taken root.

More and more of these undeveloped patches were disappearing, but they, more than anything, had marked my childhood. We lived in one of the first developments to be built on the converted farmland in the area—a development that became the model and inspiration for what now seemed a limitless number—but my imagination had always rested on the stretch of road that had not been filled in with the bright colors of shingles and drainpipes, paved driveways and super-size mailboxes. So too had Samuel's.

"Wow!" Lindsey said. "How old do you think this is?"

Lindsey's voice echoed off the walls as if they stood alone in a church.

"Let's explore," said Samuel.

The boarded-up windows on the first floor made it hard to see anything, but with the help of Samuel's safety light they could pick out both a fireplace and the chair rail along the walls.

"Look at the floor," Samuel said. He knelt down, taking her with him. "Do you see the tongue and groove work? These people had more money than their neighbors."

Lindsey smiled. Just as Hal cared only for the inner workings of motorcycles, Samuel had become obsessed with carpentry.

He ran his fingers over the floor and had Lindsey do it too. "This is a gorgeous old wreck," he said.

"Victorian?" Lindsey asked, making her best guess.

"It blows my mind to say this," Samuel said, "but I think it's gothic revival. I noticed cross-bracing on the gable trim, so that means it was after 1860."

"Look," said Lindsey.

In the center of the floor someone had once, long ago, set a fire.

"And *that* is a tragedy," Samuel said.

"Why didn't they use the fireplace? There's one in every room."

But Samuel was busy looking up through the hole the fire had burned into the ceiling, trying to make out the patterns of the woodwork along the window frames.

"Let's go upstairs," he said.

"I feel like I'm in a cave," said Lindsey as they climbed the stairs. "It's so quiet in here you can barely hear the rain."

Samuel bounced the soft side of his fist off the plaster as he went. "You could wall someone into this place."

And suddenly it was one of those awkward moments that they had learned to let pass and I lived to anticipate. It begged a central question. Where was I? Would I be mentioned? Brought up and discussed? Usually now the answer was a disappointing no. It was no longer a Susie-fest on Earth.

But something about the house and the night—markers like graduations and birthdays always meant that I was more alive, higher up in the register of thoughts—made Lindsey dwell on me more in that moment than she normally might. Still, she didn't mention it. She remembered the heady feeling she had had in Mr.

Harvey's house and that she had often felt since—that I was with her somehow, in her thoughts and limbs—moving with her like a twin.

At the top of the stairs they found the entrance to the room they had stared up at.

"I want this house," Samuel said.

"What?"

"This house needs me, I can feel it."

"Maybe you should wait until the sun comes out to decide," she said.

"It's the most beautiful thing I've ever seen," he said.

"Samuel Heckler," my sister said, "fixer of broken things."

"One to talk," he said.

They stood for a moment in silence and smelled the damp air coming through the chimney and flooding the room. Even with the sound of rain, Lindsey still felt hidden away, tucked safely in an outside corner of the world with the one person she loved more than anyone else.

She took his hand, and I traveled with them up to the doorway of a small room at the very front. It jutted out over what would be the entrance hall of the floor below and was octagonal in shape.

"Oriels," Samuel said. "The windows"—he turned to Lindsey—"when they're built out like that, like a tiny room, that's called an oriel."

"Do they turn you on?" Lindsey asked, smiling.

I left them in the rain and darkness. I wondered if Lindsey noticed that when she and Samuel began to unzip their leathers the lightning stopped and the rumble in the throat of God—that scary thunder—ceased.

In his den, my father reached out to hold the snow globe in his hand. The cold glass against his fingers comforted him, and he shook it to watch the penguin disappear and then slowly be uncovered by the gently falling snow.

Hal had made it back from the graduation ceremonies on his motorcycle but instead of calming my father—providing some assurance that if one motorcycle could maneuver the storm and deliver its rider safe to his door, another one could too—it seemed to stack the probabilities in the reverse in his mind.

He had taken what could be called a painful delight in Lindsey's graduation ceremony. Buckley had sat beside him, dutifully prompting him when to smile and react. He often *knew* when, but his synapses were never as quick now as normal people's—or at least that was how he explained it to himself. It was like reaction time in the insurance claims he reviewed. There was an average number of seconds for most people between when they saw something coming—another car, a rock rolling down an embankment—and when they reacted. My father's response times were slower than most, as if he moved in a world where a crushing inevitability had robbed him of any hope of accurate perception.

Buckley tapped on the half-open door of my father's den.

"Come in," he said.

"They'll be okay, Dad." At twelve, my brother had become serious and considerate. Even if he didn't pay for the food or cook the meals, he managed the house.

"You looked good in your suit, son," my father said.

"Thanks." This mattered to my brother. He had wanted to make my father proud and had taken time with his appearance, even asking Grandma Lynn that morning to help trim the bangs that fell in his eyes. My brother was in the most awkward stage of adolescence—not boy, not man. Most days he hid his body in big T-shirts and sloppy jeans, but he had liked wearing the suit that day. "Hal and Grandma are waiting for us downstairs," he said.

"I'll be down in a minute."

Buckley closed the door all the way this time, letting the latch snap into place.

That fall my father had developed the last roll of film that I'd kept in my closet in my "rolls to hold back" box, and now, as he often did when he begged just a minute before dinner or saw something on TV or read an article in the paper that made his heart ache, he drew back his desk drawer and gingerly lifted the photos in his hand.

He had lectured me repeatedly that what I called my "artistic shots" were foolhardy, but the best portrait he ever had was one I took of him at an angle so his face filled the three-by-three square when you held it so it was a diamond.

I must have been listening to his hints on camera angles and composition when I took the pictures he held now. He had had no idea what order the rolls were in or what they were of when he had them developed. There were an inordinate number of photos of Holiday, and many a shot of my feet or the grass. Gray balls of blurs in the air which were birds, and a grainy attempt at a sunset over the pussy-willow tree. But at some point I had decided to take portraits of my mother. When he'd picked the roll up at the photo lab my father sat in the car staring at photos of a woman he felt he barely knew anymore.

Since then he had taken these photos out too many times to count, but each time he looked into the face of this woman he had felt something growing inside him. It took him a long time to realize what it was. Only recently had his wounded synapses allowed him to name it. He had been falling in love all over again.

He didn't understand how two people who were married, who saw each other every day, could forget what each other looked like, but if he had had to name what had happened—this was it. And the last two photos in the roll provided the key. He had come home from work—I remember trying to keep my mother's attention as Holiday barked when he heard the car pull into the garage.

"He'll come out," I said. "Stay still." And she did. Part of what I loved about photography was the power it gave me over the people on the other side of the camera, even my own parents.

Out of the corner of my eye I saw my father walk through the side door into the yard. He carried his slim briefcase, which, years before, Lindsey and I had heatedly investigated only to find very little of interest to us. As he set it down I snapped the last solitary photo of my mother. Already her eyes had begun to seem distracted and anxious, diving under and up into a mask somehow. In the next photo, the mask was almost, but not quite, in place and the final photo, where my father was leaning slightly down to give her a kiss on the cheek—there it was.

"Did I do that to you?" he asked her image as he stared at the pictures of my mother, lined up in a row. "How did that happen?"

"The lightning stopped," my sister said. The moisture of the rain on her skin had been replaced by sweat.

"I love you," Samuel said.

"I know."

"No, I mean I love you, and I want to marry you, and I want to live in this house!"

"What?"

"That hideous, hideous college shit is over!" Samuel screamed. The small room absorbed his voice, barely bouncing back an echo from its thick walls.

"Not for me, it isn't," my sister said.

Samuel got up off the floor, where he had been lying beside my sister, and came to his knees in front of her. "Marry me."

"Samuel?"

"I'm tired of doing all the right things. Marry me and I'll make this house gorgeous."

"Who will support us?"

"We will," he said, "somehow."

She sat up and then joined him kneeling. They were both half-dressed and growing colder as their heat began to dissipate.

"Okay."

"Okay?"

"I think I can," my sister said. "I mean, yes!"

Some clichés I understood only when they came into my heaven full speed. I had never seen a chicken with its head cut off. It had never meant much to me except something else that had been treated much the same as me. But that moment I ran around my heaven like . . . a chicken with its head cut off! I was so happy I screamed over and over and over again. My sister! My Samuel! My dream!

She was crying, and he held her in his arms, rocking her against him.

"Are you happy, sweetheart?" he asked.

She nodded against his bare chest. "Yes," she said, then froze. "My dad." She raised her head and looked at Samuel. "I know he's worried."

"Yes," he said, trying to switch gears with her.

"How many miles is it to the house from here?"

"Ten maybe," Samuel said. "Maybe eight."

"We could do that," she said.

"You're nuts."

"We have sneakers in the other pannard."

They could not run in leather, so they wore their underwear and T-shirts, as close to streakers as anyone in my family would ever be. Samuel, as he had for years, set a pace just ahead of my sister to keep her going. There were hardly any cars on the road, but when one passed by a wall of water would come up from the puddles near the side of the road and make the two of them gasp to get air back in their lungs. Both of them had run in rain before but never rain this heavy. They made a game of who could gain the most shelter as they ran the miles, waltzing in and out to gain cover under any overhanging trees, even as the dirt and grime of the road covered their legs. But by mile three they were silent, pushing their feet forward in a natural rhythm they had both known for years, focusing on the sound of their own breath and the sound of their wet shoes hitting the pavement.

At some point as she splashed through a large puddle, no longer trying to avoid them, she thought of the local pool of which we had been members until my death brought the comfortably public existence of my family to a close. It had been somewhere along this road, but she did not lift her head to find the familiar chain-link fence. Instead, she had a memory. She and I were under water in our bathing suits with their small ruffled skirts. Both of our eyes were open under water, a new skill—newer for her—and we were looking at each other, our separate bodies suspended under water. Hair floating, small skirts floating, our cheeks bulging with captured air. Then, together, we would grab on to each other and shoot up out of the water, breaking the surface. We sucked air into our lungs—ears popping—and laughed together.

I watched my beautiful sister running, her lungs and legs pumping, and the skill from the pool still there—fighting to see through the rain, fighting to keep her legs lifting at the pace set by Samuel, and I knew she was not running away from me or toward me. Like someone who has survived a gut-shot, the wound had been closing, closing—braiding into a scar for eight long years.

By the time the two of them were within a mile of my house, the rain had lightened and people were beginning to look out their windows toward the street.

Samuel slowed his pace and she joined him. Their T-shirts were locked onto their bodies like paste.

Lindsey had fought off a cramp in her side, but as the cramp lifted she ran with Samuel full-out. Suddenly she was covered in goose bumps and smiling ear to ear.

"We're getting married!" she said, and he stopped short, grabbed her up in his arms, and they were still kissing when a car passed them on the road, the driver honking his horn.

When the doorbell rang at our house it was four o'clock and Hal was in the kitchen wearing one of my mother's old white chef's aprons and cutting brownies for Grandma Lynn. He liked being put to work, feeling useful, and my grandmother liked to use him. They were a simpatico team. While Buckley, the boy-guard, loved to eat.

"I'll get it," my father said. He had been propping himself up during the rain with highballs, mixed, not measured, by Grandma Lynn.

He was spry now with a thin sort of grace, like a retired ballet dancer who favored one leg over the other after long years of one-footed leaps.

"I was so worried," he said when he opened the door.

Lindsey was holding her arms over her chest, and even my father had to laugh while he looked away and hurriedly got the extra blankets kept in the front closet. Samuel draped one around Lindsey first, as my father covered Samuel's shoulders as best he could and puddles collected on the flagstone floor. Just as Lindsey had covered herself up, Buckley and Hal and Grandma Lynn came forward into the hallway.

"Buckley," Grandma Lynn said, "go get some towels."

"Did you manage the bike in this?" Hal asked, incredulous.

"No, we ran," Samuel said.

"You what?"

"Get into the family room," my father said. "We'll set a fire going."

* * *

While the two of them sat with their backs to the fire, shivering at first and drinking the brandy shots Grandma Lynn had Buckley serve them on a silver tray, everyone heard the story of the bike and the house and the octagonal room with windows that had made Samuel euphoric.

"And the bike's okay?" Hal asked.

"We did the best we could," Samuel said, "but we'll need a tow."

"I'm just happy that the two of you are safe," my father said.

"We ran home for you, Mr. Salmon."

My grandmother and brother had taken seats at the far end of the room, away from the fire.

"We didn't want anyone to worry," Lindsey said.

"Lindsey didn't want you to worry, specifically."

The room was silent for a moment. What Samuel had said was true, of course, but it also pointed too clearly to a certain fact—that Lindsey and Buckley had come to live their lives in direct proportion to what effect it would have on a fragile father.

Grandma Lynn caught my sister's eye and winked. "Hal and Buckley and I made brownies," she said. "And I have some frozen lasagna I can break out if you'd like." She stood and so did my brother—ready to help.

"I'd love some brownies, Lynn," Samuel said.

"Lynn? I like that," she said. "Are you going to start calling Jack 'Jack'?"

"Maybe."

Once Buckley and Grandma Lynn had left the room, Hal felt a new nervousness in the air. "I think I'll pitch in," he said.

Lindsey, Samuel, and my father listened to the busy noises of the kitchen. They could all hear the clock ticking in the corner, the one my mother had called our "rustic colonial clock."

"I know I worry too much," my father said.

"That's not what Samuel meant," Lindsey said.

Samuel was quiet and I was watching him.

"Mr. Salmon," he finally said—he was not quite ready to try "Jack." "I've asked Lindsey to marry me."

Lindsey's heart was in her throat, but she wasn't looking at Samuel. She was looking at my father.

Buckley came in with a plate of brownies, and Hal followed him with champagne glasses hanging from his fingers and a bottle of 1978 Dom Perignon. "From your grandmother, on your graduation day," Hal said.

Grandma Lynn came through next, empty-handed except for her highball. It caught the light and glittered like a jar of icy diamonds.

For Lindsey, it was as if no one but herself and my father were there. "What do you say, Dad?" she asked.

"I'd say," he managed, standing up to shake Samuel's hand, "that I couldn't wish for a better son-in-law."

Grandma Lynn exploded on the final word. "My God, oh, honey! Congratulations!"

Even Buckley let loose, slipping out of the knot that usually held him and into a rare joy. But I saw the fine, wavering line that still tied my sister to my father. The invisible cord that can kill.

The champagne cork popped.

"Like a master!" my grandmother said to Hal, who was pouring.

It was Buckley, as my father and sister joined the group and listened to Grandma Lynn's countless toasts, who saw me. He saw me standing under the rustic colonial clock and stared. He was drinking champagne. There were strings coming out from all around me, reaching out, waving in the air. Someone passed him a brownie. He held it in his hands but did not eat. He saw my shape and face, which had not changed—the hair still parted down the middle, the chest still flat and hips undeveloped—and wanted to call out my name. It was only a moment, and then I was gone.

* * *

Over the years, when I grew tired of watching, I often sat in the back of the trains that went in and out of Suburban Station in Philadelphia. Passengers would get on and off as I listened to their conversations mix with the sounds of the train doors opening and closing, the conductors yelling their stops, and the shuffle and staccato of shoe soles and high heels going from pavement to metal to the soft *thump thump* on the carpeted train aisles. It was what Lindsey, in her workouts, called an active rest; my muscles were still engaged but my focus relaxed. I listened to the sounds and felt the train's movement and sometimes, by doing this, I could hear the voices of those who no longer lived on Earth. Voices of others like me, the watchers.

Almost everyone in heaven has someone on Earth they watch, a loved one, a friend, or even a stranger who was once kind, who offered warm food or a bright smile when one of us had needed it. And when I wasn't watching I could hear the others talking to those they loved on Earth: just as fruitlessly as me, I'm afraid. A one-sided cajoling and coaching of the young, a one-way loving and desiring of their mates, a single-sided card that could never be signed.

The train would be still or stop-starting from 30th Street to near Overbrook, and I could hear them say names and sentences: "Now be careful with that glass." "Mind your father." "Oh, look how big she looks in that dress." "I'm with you, Mother," ". . . Esmeralda, Sally, Lupe, Keesha, Frank . . ." So many names. And then the train would gain speed, and as it did the volume of all these unheard phrases coming from heaven would grow louder and louder; at its height between stations, the noise of our longing became so deafening that I had to open my eyes.

I saw women hanging or collecting wash as I peered from the windows of the suddenly silent trains. They stooped over baskets and then spread white or yellow or pink sheets along the line. I counted men's underwear and boys' underwear and the familiar lollipop cotton of little girls' drawers. And the sound of it that I craved and missed—the sound of life—replaced the endless calling of names.

Wet laundry: the snap, the yank, the wet heaviness of double- and queen-sized sheets. The real sounds bringing back the remembered sounds of the past when I had lain under the dripping clothes to catch water on my tongue or run in between them as if they were traffic cones through which I chased Lindsey or was chased by Lindsey back and forth. And this would be joined by the memory of our mother attempting to lecture us about the peanut butter from our hands getting on the good sheets, or the sticky lemon-candy patches she had found on our father's shirts. In this way the sight and smell of the real, of the imagined, and of the remembered all came together for me.

After I turned away from Earth that day, I rode the trains until I could think of only one thing:

"Hold still," my father would say, while I held the ship in the bottle and he burned away the strings he'd raised the mast with and set the clipper ship free on its blue putty sea. And I would wait for him, recognizing the tension of that moment when the world in the bottle depended, solely, on me.

EIGHTEEN

When her father mentioned the sinkhole on the phone, Ruth was in the walk-in closet that she rented on First Avenue. She twirled the phone's long black cord around her wrist and arm and gave short, clipped answers of acknowledgment. The old woman that rented her the closet liked to listen in, so Ruth tried not to talk much on the phone. Later, from the street, she would call home collect and plan a visit.

She had known she would make a pilgrimage to see it before the developers closed it up. Her fascination with places like the sinkhole was a secret she kept, as was my murder and our meeting in the faculty parking lot. They were all things she would not give away in New York, where she watched others tell their drunken bar stories, prostituting their families and their traumas for popularity and booze. These things, she felt, were not to be passed around like disingenuous party favors. She kept an honor code with her journals and her poems. "Inside, inside," she would whisper quietly to herself when she felt the urge to tell, and she would end up taking long walks through the city, seeing instead the Stolfuz cornfield or an image of her father staring at his pieces of rescued antique molding. New York provided a perfect background for her thoughts. Despite her willed stomping and pitching in its streets and byways, the city itself had very little to do with her interior life.

She no longer looked haunted, as she had in high school, but still, if you looked closely at her eyes you could see the skittery rabbit energy that often made people nervous. She had an expression of someone who was constantly on the lookout for something or someone that hadn't yet arrived. Her whole body seemed to slant forward in inquiry, and though she had been told at the bar where she worked that she had beautiful hair or beautiful hands or, on the rare occasions when any of her patrons saw her come out from behind the bar, beautiful legs, people never said anything about her eyes.

She dressed hurriedly in black tights, a short black skirt, black boots, and a black T-shirt, all of them stained from serving double-duty as work clothes and real clothes. The stains could be seen only in the sunlight, so Ruth was never really aware of them until later, when she would stop at an outdoor café for a cup of coffee and look down at her skirt and see the dark traces of spilled vodka or whiskey. The alcohol had the effect of making the black cloth blacker. This amused her; she had noted in her journal: "booze affects material as it does people."

Once outside the apartment, on her way for a cup of coffee on First Avenue, she made up secret conversations with the bloated lap dogs—Chihuahuas and Pomeranians—that the Ukrainian women held on their laps as they sat on their stoops. Ruth liked the antagonistic little dogs, who barked ardently as she passed.

Then she walked, walked flat out, walked with an ache coming up through the earth and into the heel of her striking foot. No one said hello to her except creeps, and she made a game of how many streets she could navigate without having to stop for traffic. She would not slow down for another person and would vivisect crowds of NYU students or old women with their laundry carts, creating a wind on either side of her. She liked to imagine that when she passed the world looked after her, but she also knew how anonymous she was. Except when she was at work, no one knew where she was at any time of day and no one waited for her. It was an immaculate anonymity.

She would not know that Samuel had proposed to my sister and, unless it trickled down to her through Ray, the sole person she had kept in touch with from school, she would never find out. While still at Fairfax she had heard my mother had left. A fresh ripple of whispers had gone through the high school, and Ruth had watched my sister cope with them as best she could. Occasionally the two of them would meet up in the hallway. Ruth would say a few words of support if she could manage them without doing what she thought of as harming Lindsey by talking to her. Ruth knew her status as a freak at school and knew that their one night at the gifted symposium had been exactly what it felt like—a dream, where elements let loose came together unbidden outside the damning rules of school.

But Ray was different. Their kisses and early pushing and rubbings were objects under glass to her—memories that she kept preserved. She saw him every time she visited her parents and had known immediately that it would be Ray she took when she went back to see the sinkhole. He would be happy for the vacation from his constant studying grind, and, if she was lucky, he would describe, as he often did, a medical procedure that he had observed. Ray's way of describing such things made her feel as if she knew exactly what it felt like—not just what it looked like. He could evoke everything for her, with small verbal pulse points of which he was completely unaware.

Heading north on First, she could tick off all the places she'd formerly stopped and stood, certain that she had found a spot where a woman or girl had been killed. She tried to list them in her journal at the end of each day, but often she was so consumed with what she thought might have happened in this or that dark overhang or tight alleyway that she neglected the simpler, more obvious ones, where she had read about a death in the paper and visited what had been a woman's grave.

She was unaware that she was somewhat of a celebrity up in heaven. I had told people about her, what she did, how she observed moments of silence up and down the city and wrote small individual prayers in her journal, and the story had traveled so quickly that women lined up to know if she had found where they'd been killed. She had fans in heaven, even though she would have been disappointed to know that often these fans, when they gathered, resembled more a bunch of teenagers poring over an issue of *TeenBeat* than Ruth's image of low dirgelike whisperings set to a celestial timpani.

I was the one who got to follow and watch, and, as opposed to the giddy choir, I often found these moments as painful as they were amazing. Ruth would get an image and it would burn into her memory. Sometimes they were only bright flashes—a fall down the stairs, a scream, a shove, the tightening of hands around a neck—and at other times it was as if an entire scenario spun out in her head in just the amount of time that it took the girl or woman to die.

No one on the street thought anything of the downtown girl dressed in black who had paused in the middle of midtown foot traffic. In her art student camouflage she could walk the entire length of Manhattan and, if not blend in, be classified and therefore ignored. Meanwhile, for us, she was doing important work, work that most people on Earth were too frightened even to contemplate.

The day after Lindsey and Samuel's graduation I joined her on her walk. By the time she got up to Central Park it was well past lunchtime, but the park was still busy. Couples sat on the clipped grass of the sheep meadow. Ruth peered at them. Her ardentness was off-putting on a sunny afternoon, and when the open faces of young men caught sight of her they closed down or looked away.

She zigzagged up and across the park. There were obvious places where she could go, like the rambles, to document the history of violence there without even leaving the trees, but she preferred those places people considered safe. The cool shimmering surface of the duck pond tucked into the busy southeast corner of the park, or the placid man-made lake, where old men sailed beautiful hand-carved boats.

She sat on a bench on a path leading to the Central Park Zoo and looked out across the gravel at children with their nannies and lone adults reading books in various patches of shade or sun. She was tired from the walk uptown, but still she took her journal out from her bag. She placed it open on her lap, holding the pen as her thinking prop. It was better to look like you were doing something when you stared into the distance, Ruth had learned. Otherwise it was likely that strange men would come over and try to talk to you. Her journal was her closest and most important relationship. It held everything.

Across from her a little girl had strayed from the blanket where her nanny slept. She was making her way for the bushes that lined a small rise before giving way to a fence separating the park from Fifth Avenue. Just as Ruth was about to enter the world of human beings whose lives impinged on one another by calling out to the nanny, a thin cord, which Ruth had not seen, warned the nanny to wake. She immediately sat bolt upright and barked an order at the little girl to return.

In moments like this she thought of all the little girls who grew into adulthood and old age as a sort of cipher alphabet for all of those who didn't. Their lives would somehow be inextricably attached to all the girls who had been killed. It was then, as the nanny packed up her bag and rolled up the blanket, preparing for whatever came next in their day, that Ruth saw her—a little girl who had strayed for the bushes one day and disappeared.

She could tell by the clothes that it had happened some time ago, but that was all. There was nothing else—no nanny or mother, no idea of night or day, only a little girl gone.

I stayed with Ruth. Her journal open, she wrote it down. "Time? Little girl in C.P. strays toward bushes. White lace collar, fancy." She closed the journal and tucked it into her bag. Close at hand was a place that soothed her. The penguin house at the zoo.

We spent the afternoon together there, Ruth sitting on the carpeted seat that ran the length of the exhibit, her black clothes making only her face and hands visible in the room. The penguins tottered and clucked and dived, slipping off the habitat rocks like amiable hams but living under water like tuxedoed muscles. Children shouted and screamed and pressed their faces against the glass. Ruth counted the living just as much as she counted the dead, and in the close confines of the penguin house the joyous screams of the children echoed off the walls with such vibrancy that, for a little while, she could drown out the other kinds of screams.

That weekend my brother woke early, as he always did. He was in the seventh grade and bought his lunch at school and was on the debate team and, like Ruth had been, was always picked either last or second to last in gym. He had not taken to athletics as Lindsey had. He practiced instead what Grandma Lynn called his "air of dignification." His favorite teacher was not really a teacher at all but the school librarian, a tall, frail woman with wiry hair who drank tea from her thermos and talked about having lived in England when she was young. After this he had affected an

English accent for a few months and shown a heightened interest when my sister watched *Masterpiece Theatre.*

When he had asked my father that year if he could reclaim the garden my mother had once kept, my father had said, "Sure, Buck, go crazy."

And he had. He had gone extraordinarily, insanely crazy, reading old Burpee catalogs at night when he was unable to sleep and scanning the few books on gardening that the school library kept. Where my grandmother had suggested respectful rows of parsley and basil and Hal had suggested "some plants that really matter"—eggplants, cantaloupes, cucumbers, carrots, and beans—my brother had thought they were both right.

He didn't like what he read in books. He saw no reason to keep flowers separated from tomatoes and herbs segregated in a corner. He had slowly planted the whole garden with a spade, daily begging my father to bring him seeds and taking trips to the grocery with Grandma Lynn, where the price of his extreme helpfulness in fetching things would be a quick stop at the greenhouse for a small flowering plant. He was now awaiting his tomatoes, his blue daisies, his petunias, and pansies and salvias of all kinds. He had made his fort a sort of work shed for the garden, where he kept his tools and supplies.

But my grandmother was preparing for the moment when he realized that they couldn't grow all together and that some seeds would not come up at certain times, that the fine downy tendrils of cucumber might be abruptly stopped by the thickening underground bosses of carrot and potato, that the parsley might be camouflaged by the more recalcitrant weeds, and bugs that hopped about could blight the tender flowers. But she was waiting patiently. She no longer believed in talk. It never rescued anything. At seventy she had come to believe in time alone.

Buckley was hauling up a box of clothes from the basement and into the kitchen when my father came down for his coffee.

"What ya got there, Farmer Buck?" my father said. He had always been at his best in the morning.

"I'm making stakes for my tomato plants," my brother said.

"Are they even above ground yet?"

My father stood in the kitchen in his blue terry-cloth robe and bare feet. He poured his coffee from the coffee maker that Grandma Lynn set up each morning, and sipped at it as he looked at his son.

"I just saw them this morning," my brother said, beaming. "They curl up like a hand unfolding."

It wasn't until my father was repeating this description to Grandma Lynn as he stood at the counter that he saw, through the back window, what Buckley had taken from the box. They were my clothes. My clothes, which Lindsey had picked through for anything she might save. My clothes, which my grandmother, when she had moved into my room, had quietly boxed while my father was at work. She had put them down in the basement with a small label that said, simply, SAVE.

My father put down his coffee. He walked out through the screened-in porch and strode forward, calling Buckley's name.

"What is it, Dad?" He was alert to my father's tone.

"Those clothes are Susie's," my father said calmly when he reached him.

Buckley looked down at my blackwatch dress that he held in his hand.

My father stepped closer, took the dress from my brother, and then, without speaking, he gathered the rest of my clothes, which Buckley had piled on the lawn. As he turned in silence toward the house, hardly breathing, clutching my clothes to him, it sparked.

I was the only one to see the colors. Just near Buckley's ears and on the tips of his cheeks and chin he was a little orange somehow, a little red.

"Why can't I use them?" he asked.

It landed in my father's back like a fist.

"Why can't I use those clothes to stake my tomatoes?"

My father turned around. He saw his son standing there, behind him the perfect plot of muddy, churned-up earth spotted with tiny seedlings. "How can you ask me that question?"

"You have to choose. It's not fair," my brother said.

"Buck?" My father held my clothes against his chest.

I watched Buckley flare and light. Behind him was the sun of the goldenrod hedge, twice as tall as it had been at my death.

"I'm tired of it!" Buckley blared. "Keesha's dad died and she's okay!"

"Is Keesha a girl at school?"

"Yes!"

My father was frozen. He could feel the dew that had gathered on his bare ankles and feet, could feel the ground underneath him, cold and moist and stirring with possibility.

"I'm sorry. When did this happen?"

"That's not the point, Dad! You don't get it." Buckley turned around on his heel and started stomping the tender tomato shoots with his foot.

"Buck, stop!" my father cried.

My brother turned.

"You don't get it, Dad," he said.

"I'm sorry," my father said. "These are Susie's clothes and I just . . . It may not make sense, but they're hers—something she wore."

"You took the shoe, didn't you?" my brother said. He had stopped crying now.

"What?"

"You took the shoe. You took it from my room."

"Buckley, I don't know what you're talking about."

"I saved the Monopoly shoe and then it was gone. You took it! You act like she was yours only!"

"Tell me what you want to say. What's this about your friend Keesha's dad?"

"Put the clothes down."

My father laid them gently on the ground.

"It isn't about Keesha's dad."

"Tell me what it is about." My father was now all immediacy. He went back to the place he had been after his knee surgery, coming up out of the druggie sleep of painkillers to see his then-five-year-old son sitting near him, waiting for his eyes to flicker open so he could say, "Peek-a-boo, Daddy."

"She's dead."

It never ceased to hurt. "I know that."

"But you don't act that way. Keesha's dad died when she was six. Keesha said she barely even thinks of him."

"She will," my father said.

"But what about us?"

"Who?"

"Us, Dad. Me and Lindsey. Mom left because she couldn't take it."

"Calm down, Buck," my father said. He was being as generous as he could as the air from his lungs evaporated out into his chest. Then a little voice in him said, *Let go, let go, let go*. "What?" my father said.

"I didn't say anything."

Let go. Let go. Let go.

"I'm sorry," my father said. "I'm not feeling very well." His feet had grown unbelievably cold in the damp grass. His chest felt hollow, bugs flying around an excavated cavity. There was an echo in there, and it drummed up into his ears. *Let go.*

My father dropped down to his knees. His arm began to tingle on and off as if it had fallen asleep. Pins and needles up and down. My brother rushed to him.

"Dad?"

"Son." There was a quaver in his voice and a grasping outward toward my brother.

"I'll get Grandma." And Buckley ran.

My father whispered faintly as he lay on his side with his face twisted in the direction of my old clothes: "You can never choose. I've loved all three of you."

That night my father lay in a hospital bed, attached to monitors that beeped and hummed. Time to circle around my father's feet and along his spine. Time to hush and usher him. But where?

Above his bed the clock ticked off the minutes and I thought of the game Lindsey and I had played in the yard together: "he loves me/he loves me not" picked out on a daisy's petals. I could hear the clock casting my own two greatest wishes back to me in this same rhythm: "Die for me/don't die for me, die for me/don't die for me." I could not help myself, it seemed, as I tore at his weakening heart. If he died, I would have him forever. Was this so wrong to want?

At home, Buckley lay in bed in the dark and pulled the sheet up to his chin. He had not been allowed past the emergency room where Lindsey had driven them, following the shrieking ambulance inside which lay our father. My brother had felt a huge burden of guilt descend in the silences from Lindsey. In her two repeated questions: "What were you talking about? Why was he so upset?"

My little brother's greatest fear was that the one person who meant so much to him would go away. He loved Lindsey and Grandma Lynn and Samuel and Hal, but my father kept him stepping lightly, son gingerly monitoring father every morning and every evening as if, without such vigilance, he would lose him.

We stood—the dead child and the living—on either side of my father, both wanting the same thing. To have him to ourselves forever. To please us both was an impossibility.

My father had only missed nighttimes twice in Buckley's life. Once after he had gone into the cornfield at night looking for Mr. Harvey and now as he lay in the hospital and they monitored him in case of a second heart attack.

Buckley knew he should be too old for it to matter, but I sympathized with him. The good-night kiss was something at which my father excelled. As my father stood at the end of the bed after closing the venetian blinds and running his hands down them to make sure they were all down at the same slant—no rebel venetian stuck to let the sunlight in on his son before he came to wake him—my brother would often get goose bumps on his arms and legs. The anticipation was so sweet.

"Ready, Buck?" my father would say, and sometimes Buckley said "Roger," or sometimes he said "Takeoff," but when he was most frightened and giddy and waiting for peace he just said "Yes!" And my father would take the thin cotton top sheet and bunch it up in his hands while being careful to keep the two corners between his thumb and forefinger. Then he would snap it out so the pale blue (if they were using Buckley's) or lavender (if they were using mine) sheet would spread out like a parachute above him and gently, what felt wonderfully slowly, it would waft down and touch along his exposed skin—his knees, his forearms, his cheeks and chin. Both air and cover somehow there in the same space at the same time—it felt like the ultimate freedom and protection. It was lovely, left him vulnerable and quivering on some edge and all he could hope was that if he begged him, my father would oblige and do it again. Air and cover, air and cover—sustaining the unspoken connection between them: little boy, wounded man.

That night his head lay on the pillow while his body was curled in the fetal position. He had not thought to close the blinds himself, and the lights from the nearby houses spotted the hill. He stared across his room at the louvered doors of his closet, out of which he had once imagined evil witches would escape to join the dragons beneath his bed. He no longer feared these things.

"Please don't let Daddy die, Susie," he whispered. "I need him."

When I left my brother, I walked out past the gazebo and under the lights hanging down like berries, and I saw the brick paths branching out as I advanced.

I walked until the bricks turned to flat stones and then to small, sharp rocks and then to nothing but churned earth for miles and miles around me. I stood there. I had been in heaven long enough to know that something would be revealed. And as the light began to fade and the sky turn a dark, sweet blue as it had on the night of my death, I saw someone walking into view, so far away I could not at first make out if it was man or woman, child or adult. But as moonlight reached this figure I could make out a man and, frightened now, my breathing shallow, I raced just far enough to see. Was it my father? Was it what I had wanted all this time so desperately?

"Susie," the man said as I approached and then stopped a few feet from where he stood. He raised his arms up toward me.

"Remember?" he said.

I found myself small again, age six and in a living room in Illinois. Now, as I had done then, I placed my feet on top of his feet.

"Grandaddy," I said.

And because we were all alone and both in heaven, I was light enough to move as I had moved when I was six and he was fifty-six and my father had taken us to visit. We danced so slowly to a song that on Earth had always made my grandfather cry.

"Do you remember?" he asked.

"Barber!"

"Adagio for Strings," he said.

But as we danced and spun—none of the herky-jerky awkwardness of Earth—what I remembered was how I'd found him crying to this music and asked him why.

"Sometimes you cry, Susie, even when someone you love has been gone a long time." He had held me against him then, just briefly, and then I had run outside to play again with Lindsey in what seemed like my grandfather's huge backyard.

We didn't speak any more that night, but we danced for hours in that timeless blue light. I knew as we danced that something was happening on Earth and in heaven. A shifting. The sort of slow-to-sudden movement that we'd read about in science class one year. Seismic, impossible, a rending and tearing of time and space. I pressed myself into my grandfather's chest and smelled the old-man smell of him, the mothball version of my own father, the blood on Earth, the sky in heaven. The kumquat, skunk, grade-A tobacco.

When the music stopped, it could have been forever since we'd begun. My grandfather took a step back, and the light grew yellow at his back.

"I'm going," he said.

"Where?" I asked.

"Don't worry, sweetheart. You're so close."

He turned and walked away, disappearing rapidly into spots and dust. Infinity.

NINETEEN

When she reached Krusoe Winery that morning, my mother found a message waiting for her, scrawled in the imperfect English of the caretaker. The word *emergency* was clear enough, and my mother bypassed her morning ritual of an early coffee drunk while staring out at the grapevines grafted on row upon row of sturdy white crosses. She opened up the part of the winery reserved for public tastings. Without turning on the overhead, she located the phone behind the wooden bar and dialed the number in Pennsylvania. No answer.

Then she dialed the operator in Pennsylvania and asked for the number of Dr. Akhil Singh.

"Yes," Ruana said, "Ray and I saw an ambulance pull up a few hours ago. I imagine they're all at the hospital."

"Who was it?"

"Your mother, perhaps?"

But she knew from the note that her mother had been the one who *called.* It was one of the children or it was Jack. She thanked

Ruana and hung up. She grabbed the heavy red phone and lifted it up from underneath the bar. A ream of color sheets that they passed out to customers—"Lemon Yellow = Young Chardonnay, Straw-colored = Sauvignon Blanc . . ."—fell down and around her feet from where they had been kept weighted by the phone. She had habitually arrived early ever since taking the job, and now she gave a quick thanks that this was so. After that, all she could think of were the names of the local hospitals, so she called the ones to which she had rushed her young children with unexplained fevers or possible broken bones from falls. At the same hospital where I had once rushed Buckley: "A Jack Salmon was seen in emergency and is still here."

"Can you tell me what happened?"

"What is your relationship to Mr. Salmon?"

She said the words she had not said in years: "I'm his wife."

"He had a heart attack."

She hung up the phone and sat down on the rubber-and-cork mats that covered the floor on the employee side. She sat there until the shift manager arrived and she repeated the strange words: *husband, heart attack.*

When she looked up later she was in the caretaker's truck, and he, this quiet man who barely ever left the premises, was barreling toward San Francisco International Airport.

She paid for her ticket and boarded a flight that would connect to another in Chicago and finally land her in Philadelphia. As the plane gained height and they were buried in the clouds, my mother listened distantly to the signature bells of the plane which told the crew what to do or what to prepare for, and she heard the cocktail cart jiggling past, but instead of her fellow passengers she saw the cool stone archway at the winery, behind which the empty oak barrels were stored, and instead of the men who often sat inside there to get out of the sun she imagined my father sitting there, holding the broken Wedgwood cup out toward her.

By the time she landed in Chicago with a two-hour wait, she had steadied herself enough to buy a toothbrush and a pack of cigarettes and place a call to the hospital, this time asking to speak to Grandma Lynn.

"Mother," my mother said. "I'm in Chicago and on my way."

"Abigail, thank God," my grandmother said. "I called Krusoe again and they said you were headed for the airport."

"How is he?"

"He's asking for you."

"Are the kids there?"

"Yes, and Samuel. I was going to call you today and tell you. Samuel has asked Lindsey to marry him."

"That's wonderful," my mother said.

"Abigail?"

"Yes." She could hear her mother's hesitation, which was always rare.

"Jack's asking for Susie, too."

She lit a cigarette as soon as she walked outside the terminal at O'Hare, a school tour flooding past her with small overnight bags and band instruments, each of which had a bright yellow nametag on the side of the case. HOME OF THE PATRIOTS, they read.

It was muggy and humid in Chicago, and the smoky exhaust of double-parked cars made the heavy air noxious.

She burned through the cigarette in record time and lit another, keeping one arm tucked hard across her chest and the other one extended on each exhale. She was wearing her winery outfit: a pair of faded but clean jeans and a pale orange T-shirt with KRUSOE WINERY embroidered over the pocket. Her skin was darker now, which made her pale blue eyes seem even bluer in contrast, and she had taken to wearing her hair in a loose ponytail at the base of her neck. I could see small wisps of salt and pepper hair near her ears and at her temples.

She held on to two sides of an hourglass and wondered how this could be possible. The time she'd had alone had been gravitationally circumscribed by when her attachments would pull her back. And they had pulled now—double-fisted. A marriage. A heart attack.

Standing outside the terminal, she reached into the back pocket of her jeans, where she kept the man's wallet she had started carrying when she got the job at Krusoe because it was easier not to worry about stowing a purse beneath the bar. She flicked her cigarette into the cab lane and turned to find a seat on the edge of a concrete planter, inside of which grew weeds and one sad sapling choked by fumes.

In her wallet were pictures, pictures she looked at every day. But there was one that she kept turned upside down in a fold of leather meant for a credit card. It was the same one that rested in the evidence box at the police station, the same one Ray had put in his mother's book of Indian poetry. My class photo that had made the papers and been put on police fliers and in mailboxes.

After eight years it was, even for my mother, like the ubiquitous photo of a celebrity. She had encountered it so many times that I had been neatly buried inside of it. My cheeks never redder, my eyes never bluer than they were in the photograph.

She took the photo out and held it face-up and slightly cupped in her hand. She had always missed my teeth—their small rounded serrations had fascinated her as she watched me grow. I had promised my mother a wide-open smile for that year's picture, but I was so self-conscious in front of the photographer that I had barely managed a close-lipped grin.

She heard the announcement for the connecting flight over the outdoor speaker. She stood. Turning around she saw the tiny, struggling tree. She left my class portrait propped up against its trunk and hurried inside the automatic doors.

On the flight to Philadelphia, she sat alone in the middle of a row of three seats. She could not help but think of how, if she were a mother traveling, there would be two seats filled beside her. One for Lindsey. One for Buckley. But though she was, by definition, a mother, she had at some point ceased to be one too. She couldn't claim that right and privilege after missing more than half a decade of their lives. She now knew that being a mother was a calling, something plenty of young girls dreamed of being. But my mother had never had that dream, and she had been punished in the most horrible and unimaginable way for never having wanted me.

I watched her on the plane, and I sent a wish into the clouds for her release. Her body grew heavy with the dread of what would come but in this heaviness was at least relief. The stewardess handed her a small blue pillow and for a little while she fell asleep.

When they reached Philadelphia, the airplane taxied down the runway and she reminded herself both where she was and what year it was. She hurriedly clicked through all the things she might say when she saw her children, her mother, Jack. And then, when they finally shivered to a halt, she gave up and focused only on getting off the plane.

She barely recognized her own child waiting at the end of the long ramp. In the years that had passed, Lindsey had become angular, thin, every trace of body fat gone. And standing beside my sister was what looked like her male twin. A bit taller, a little more meat. Samuel. She was staring so hard at the two of them, and they were staring back, that at first she didn't even see the chubby boy sitting off to the side on the arm of a row of waiting-area seats.

And then, just before she began walking toward them—for they all seemed suspended and immobile for the first few moments, as if they had been trapped in a viscous gelatin from which only her movement might free them—she saw him.

She began walking down the carpeted ramp. She heard announcements being made in the airport and saw passengers, with their more normal greetings, rushing past her. But it was as if she were entering a time warp as she took him in. 1944 at Camp Winnekukka. She was twelve, with chubby cheeks and heavy legs—all the things she'd felt grateful her daughters had escaped had been her son's to endure. So many years she had been away, so much time she could never recover.

If she had counted, as I did, she would have known that in seventy-three steps she had accomplished what she had been too afraid to do for almost seven years.

It was my sister who spoke first:

"Mom," she said.

My mother looked at my sister and flashed forward thirty-eight years from the lonely girl she'd been at Camp Winnekukka.

"Lindsey," my mother said.

Lindsey stared at her. Buckley was standing now, but he looked first down at his shoes and then over his shoulder, out past the window to where the planes were parked, disgorging their passengers into accordioned tubes.

"How is your father?" my mother asked.

My sister had spoken the word *Mom* and then frozen. It tasted soapy and foreign in her mouth.

"He's not in the greatest shape, I'm afraid," Samuel said. It was the longest sentence anyone had said, and my mother found herself disproportionately grateful for it.

"Buckley?" my mother said, preparing no face for him. Being who she was—whoever that was.

He turned his head toward her like a racheted gun. "Buck," he said.

"Buck," she repeated softly and looked down at her hands.

Lindsey wanted to ask, *Where are your rings?*

"Shall we go?" Samuel asked.

The four of them entered the long carpeted tunnel that would bring them from her gate into the main terminal. They were headed toward the cavernous baggage claim when my mother said, "I didn't bring any bags."

They stood in an awkward cluster, Samuel looking for the right signs to redirect them back to the parking garage.

"Mom," my sister tried again.

"I lied to you," my mother said before Lindsey could say anything further. Their eyes met, and in that hot wire that went from one to the other I swore I saw it, like a rat bulging, undigested, inside a snake: the secret of Len.

"We go back up the escalator," Samuel said, "and then we can take the overhead walkway into the parking lot."

Samuel called for Buckley, who had drifted off in the direction of a cadre of airport security officers. Uniforms had never lost the draw they held for him.

They were on the highway when Lindsey spoke next. "They won't let Buckley in to see Dad because of his age."

My mother turned around in her seat. "I'll try and do something about that," she said, looking at Buckley and attempting her first smile.

"Fuck you," my brother whispered without looking up.

My mother froze. The car opened up. Full of hate and tension—a riptide of blood to swim through.

"Buck," she said, remembering the shortened name just in time, "will you look at me?"

He glared over the front seat, boring his fury into her.

Eventually my mother turned back around and Samuel, Lindsey, and my brother could hear the sounds from the passenger seat that she was trying hard not to make. Little peeps and a choked sob. But no amount of tears would sway Buckley. He had been keeping, daily, weekly, yearly, an underground storage room of hate. Deep inside this, the four-year-old sat, his heart flashing. Heart to stone, heart to stone.

"We'll all feel better after seeing Mr. Salmon," Samuel said, and then, because even he could not bear it, he leaned forward toward the dash and turned on the radio.

It was the same hospital that she had come to eight years ago in the middle of the night. A different floor painted a different color, but she could feel it encasing her as she walked down the hall—what she'd done there. The push of Len's body, her back pressed into the sharp stucco wall. Everything in her wanted to run—fly back to California, back to her quiet existence working among strangers. Hiding out in the folds of tree trunks and tropical petals, tucked away safely among so many foreign plants and people.

Her mother's ankles and oxford pumps, which she saw from the hallway, brought her back. One of the many simple things she'd lost by moving so far away, just the commonplace of her mother's feet—their solidity and humor—seventy-year-old feet in ridiculously uncomfortable shoes.

But as she walked forward into the room, everyone else—her son, her daughter, her mother—fell away.

My father's eyes were weak but fluttered open when he heard her enter. He had tubes and wires coming out of his wrist and shoulder. His head seemed so fragile on the small square pillow.

She held his hand and cried silently, letting the tears come freely.

"Hello, Ocean Eyes," he said.

She nodded her head. This broken, beaten man—her husband.

"My girl," he breathed out heavily.

"Jack."

"Look what it took to get you home."

"Was it worth it?" she said, smiling bleakly.

"We'll have to see," he said.

To see them together was like a tenuous belief made real.

My father could see glimmers, like the colored flecks inside my mother's eyes—things to hold on to. These he counted among the broken planks and boards of a long-ago ship that had struck something greater than itself and sunk. There were only remnants and artifacts left to him now. He tried to reach up and touch her cheek, but his arm felt too weak. She moved closer and laid her cheek in his palm.

My grandmother knew how to move silently in heels. She tiptoed out of the room. As she resumed her normal stride and approached the waiting area, she intercepted a nurse with a message for Jack Salmon in Room 582. She had never met the man but knew his name. "Len Fenerman, will visit soon. Wishes you well." She folded the note neatly. Just before she came upon Lindsey and Buckley, who had gone to join Samuel in the waiting room, she popped open the metal lip of her purse and placed it between her powder and comb.

TWENTY

By the time Mr. Harvey reached the tin-roofed shack in Connecticut that night, it promised rain. He had killed a young waitress inside the shack several years before and then bought some new slacks with the tips he'd found in the front pocket of her apron. By now the rot would have been eclipsed, and it was true, as he approached the area, that no rank smell greeted him. But the shack was open and inside he could see the earth had been dug up. He breathed in and approached the shack warily.

He fell asleep beside her empty grave.

At some point, to counter the list of the dead, I had begun keeping my own list of the living. It was something I noticed Len Fenerman did too. When he was off duty he would note the young girls and elderly women and every other female in the rainbow in between and count them among the things that sustained him. That young girl in the mall whose pale legs had grown too long for her now-too-young dress and who had an aching vulnerability that went straight to both Len's and my own heart. Elderly women, wobbling with walkers, who insisted on dyeing their hair unnatural versions of the colors they had in youth. Middle-aged single mothers racing around in grocery stores while their children pulled bags of candy off the shelves. When I saw them, I took count. Living, breathing women. Sometimes I saw the wounded—those who had been beaten by husbands or raped by strangers, children raped by their fathers—and I would wish to intervene somehow.

Len saw these wounded women all the time. They were regulars at the station, but even when he went somewhere outside his jurisdiction he could sense them when they came near. The wife in the bait-'n'-tackle shop had no bruises on her face but cowered like a dog and spoke in apologetic whispers. The girl he saw walk the road each time he went upstate to visit his sisters. As the years passed she'd grown leaner, the fat from her cheeks had drained, and sorrow had loaded her eyes in a way that made them hang heavy and hopeless inside her mallowed skin. When she was not there it worried him. When she was there it both depressed and revived him.

He had not had much to write in my file for a long time, but a few items had joined the log of old evidence in the last few months: the name of another potential victim, Sophie Cichetti, the name of her son, and an alias of George Harvey's. There was also what he held in his hands: my Pennsylvania keystone charm. He moved it around inside the evidence bag, using his fingers, and found, again, my initials. The charm had been checked for any clues it could provide, and, besides its presence at the scene of another girl's murder, it had come up clean under the microscope.

He had wanted to give the charm back to my father from the first moment he was able to confirm it was mine. Doing so was breaking the rules, but he had never had a body for them, just a sodden schoolbook and the pages from my biology book mixed in with a boy's love note. A Coke bottle. My jingle-bell hat. These he had cataloged and kept. But the charm was different, and he meant to give it back.

A nurse he'd dated in the years after my mother left had called him when she noticed the name Jack Salmon on a list of patients admitted. Len had determined that he would visit my father in the hospital and bring my charm along with him. In Len's mind he saw the charm as a talisman that might speed my father's recovery.

I couldn't help but think, as I watched him, of the barrels of toxic fluids that had accrued behind Hal's bike shop where the scrub lining the railroad tracks had offered local companies enough cover to dump a stray container or two. Everything had been sealed up, but things were beginning to leak out. I had come to both pity and respect Len in the years since my mother left. He followed the physical to try to understand things that were impossible to comprehend. In that, I could see, he was like me.

Outside the hospital, a young girl was selling small bouquets of daffodils, their green stems tied with lavender ribbons. I watched as my mother bought out the girl's whole stock.

Nurse Eliot, who remembered my mother from eight years ago, volunteered to help her when she saw her coming down the hall, her arms full of flowers. She rounded up extra water pitchers from a supply closet and together she and my mother filled them with water and placed the flowers around my father's room while he slept. Nurse Eliot thought that if loss could be used as a measure of beauty in a woman, my mother had grown even more beautiful.

Lindsey, Samuel, and Grandma Lynn had taken Buckley home

earlier in the evening. My mother was not ready to see the house yet. She focused solely on my father. Everything else would have to wait, from the house and its silent reproach to her son and daughter. She needed something to eat and time to think. Instead of going to the hospital cafeteria, where the bright lights made her think only of all the futile efforts that hospitals contained to keep people awake for more bad news—the weak coffee, the hard chairs, the elevators that stopped on every floor—she left the building and walked down the sloped sidewalk leading away from the entrance.

It was dark out now, and the parking lot where she had once driven in the middle of the night in her nightgown was spotted with only a few cars. She hugged the cardigan her mother had left behind tightly to her.

She crossed the parking lot, looking into the dark cars for signs of who the people inside the hospital were. There were cassette tapes spread out on the passenger seat of one car, the bulky shape of a baby's carseat in another. It became a game to her then, seeing what she could in each car. A way not to feel so alone and alien, as if she were a child playing a spy game in the house of her parents' friends. Agent Abigail to Mission Control. I see a fuzzy dog toy, I see a soccer ball, I see a woman! There she was, a stranger sitting in the driver's side behind the wheel. The woman did not see my mother looking at her, and as soon as she saw her face my mother turned her attention away, focusing on the bright lights of the old diner she had as her goal. She did not have to look back to know what the woman was doing. She was girding herself up to go inside. She knew the face. It was the face of someone who wanted more than anything to be anywhere but where she was.

She stood on the landscaped strip between the hospital and the emergency room entrance and wished for a cigarette. She had not questioned anything that morning. Jack had had a heart attack;

she would go home. But now here, she didn't know what she was supposed to do anymore. How long would she have to wait, what would have to happen, before she could leave again? Behind her in the parking lot, she heard the sound of a car door opening and closing—the woman going in.

The diner was a blur to her. She sat in a booth alone and ordered the kind of food—chicken-fried steak—that didn't seem to exist in California.

She was thinking about this when a man directly across from her gave her the eye. She registered every detail of his appearance. It was automatic and something she didn't do out west. While living in Pennsylvania after my murder, when she saw a strange man whom she didn't trust, she did an immediate breakdown in her mind. It was quicker—honoring the pragmatics of fear—than pretending she shouldn't think this way. Her dinner arrived, the chicken-fried steak and tea, and she focused on her food, on the gritty breading around the rubbery meat, on the metallic taste of old tea. She did not think she could handle being home more than a few days. Everywhere she looked she saw me, and at the booth across from her she saw the man who could have murdered me.

She finished the food, paid for it, and walked out of the diner without raising her eyes above waist level. A bell mounted on the door jingled above her, and she started, her heart jumping up in her chest.

She made it back across the highway in one piece, but she was breathing shallowly as she passed back across the parking lot. The car of the apprehensive visitor was still there.

In the main lobby, where people rarely sat, she decided to sit down and wait for her breathing to come back again.

She would spend a few hours with him and when he woke, she would say goodbye. As soon as her decision was made, a welcome coolness flew through her. The sudden relief of responsibility. Her ticket to a far-away land.

It was late now, after ten, and she took an empty elevator to the fifth floor, where the hall lights had been dimmed. She passed the nurses' station, behind which two nurses were quietly gossiping. She could hear the lilt and glee of nuanced rumors being exchanged between them, the sound of easy intimacy in the air. Then, just as one nurse was unable to suppress a high-pitched laugh, my mother opened my father's door and let it swing shut again.

Alone.

It was as if there was a vacuum hush when the door closed. I felt I did not belong, that I should go too. But I was glued.

Seeing him sleeping in the dark, with only the low-wattage fluorescent light on at the back of the bed, she remembered standing in this same hospital and taking steps to sever herself from him.

As I saw her take my father's hand, I thought of my sister and me sitting underneath the grave rubbing in the upstairs hallway. I was the dead knight gone to heaven with my faithful dog and she was the live wire of a wife. "How can I be expected to be trapped for the rest of my life by a man frozen in time?" Lindsey's favorite line.

My mother sat with my father's hand in hers for a long while. She thought how wonderful it would be to climb up on the fresh hospital sheets and lie beside him. And how impossible.

She leaned close. Even under the smells of antiseptics and alcohol, she could smell the grassy smell of his skin. When she'd left, she had packed her favorite shirt of my father's and would sometimes wrap it around her just to have something of his on. She never wore it outside, so it kept his scent longer than it might have. She remembered one night, when she missed him most, buttoning it over a pillow and hugging it to her as if she were still a high school girl.

In the distance beyond the closed window she could hear the hum of far-off traffic on the highway, but the hospital was shutting down for the night. Only the rubber soles of the night nurses' shoes made sounds as they passed in the hallway.

Just that winter she had found herself saying to a young woman who worked with her at the tasting bar on Saturdays that between a man and a woman there was always one person who was stronger than the other one. "That doesn't mean the weaker one doesn't love the stronger," she'd pleaded. The girl looked at her blankly. But for my mother what mattered was that as she spoke, she had suddenly identified herself as the weaker one. This revelation sent her reeling. What had she thought all those years but the opposite?

She pulled her chair as close to his head as she could and laid her face on the edge of his pillow to watch him breathing, to see the flutter of his eye beneath his eyelid when he dreamed. How could it be that you could love someone so much and keep it secret from yourself as you woke daily so far from home? She had put billboards and roads in between them, throwing roadblocks behind her and ripping off the rearview mirror, and thought that that would make him disappear? erase their life and children?

It was so simple, as she watched him, as his regular breathing calmed her, that she did not even see it happening at first. She began to think of the rooms in our house and the hours that she had worked so hard to forget spent inside of them. Like fruit put up in jars and forgotten about, the sweetness seemed even more distilled as she returned. There on that shelf were all the dates and silliness of their early love, the braid that began to form of their dreams, the solid root of a burgeoning family. The first solid evidence of it all. Me.

She traced a new line on my father's face. She liked the silvering of his temples.

Shortly after midnight, she fell asleep after trying as hard as she could to keep her eyes open. To hold on to everything all at once while she looked at that face, so that when he woke she could say goodbye.

When her eyes were closed and they both slept silently together, I whispered to them:

> Stones and bones;
> snow and frost;
> seeds and beans and polliwogs.
> Paths and twigs, assorted kisses,
> We all know who Susie misses . . .

Around two A.M. it began to rain, and it rained down on the hospital and on my old home and in my heaven. On the tin-roofed shack where Mr. Harvey slept, it was raining too. As the rain beat its tiny hammers above his head, he dreamed. He did not dream of the girl whose remains had been removed and were now being analyzed but of Lindsey Salmon, of the 5! 5! 5! hitting the border of elderberry. He had this dream whenever he felt threatened. It had been in the flash of her soccer shirt that his life had begun to spin out of control.

It was near four when I saw my father's eyes open and saw him feel the warmth of my mother's breath on his cheek even before he knew she was asleep. We wished together that he could hold her, but he was too weak. There was another way and he took it. He would tell her the things he had felt after my death—the things that came into his mind so frequently but that no one knew but me.

But he did not want to wake her. The hospital was silent except for the sound of rain. Rain was following him, he felt, darkness and damp—he thought of Lindsey and Samuel at the doorway, soaked and smiling, having run all that way to relieve him. He often found himself repeatedly commanding himself back to center. Lindsey. Lindsey. Lindsey. Buckley. Buckley. Buckley.

The way the rain looked outside the windows, lit up in circular patches by the lights in the hospital parking lot, reminded him of the movies he had gone to see as a boy—Hollywood rain. He closed his eyes with the breath of my mother reassuringly exhaling against his cheek and listened to it, the slight patter on the slim metal window sills, and then he heard the sound of birds—small birds chirping, but he could not see them. And the idea of this, that there might be a nest right outside his window where baby birds had woken in the rain and found their mother gone, made him want to rescue them. He felt my mother's limp fingers, which had loosened their hold on his hand in sleep. She was here, and this time, despite all, he was going to let her be who she was.

It was then that I slipped inside the room with my mother and father. I was present somehow, as a person, in a way I had never been. I had always hovered but had never stood beside them.

I made myself small in the darkness, unable to know if I could be seen. I had left him for hours every day for eight and a half years as I had left my mother or Ruth and Ray, my brother and sister, and certainly Mr. Harvey, but he, I now saw, had never left me. His devotion to me had made me know again and again that I had been beloved. In the warm light of my father's love I had remained Susie Salmon—a girl with my whole life in front of me.

"I thought if I was very quiet I would hear you," he whispered. "If I was still enough you might come back."

"Jack?" my mother said, waking. "I must have fallen asleep."

"It's wonderful to have you back," he said.

And my mother looked at him. Everything stripped away. "How do you do it?" she asked.

"There's no choice, Abbie," he said. "What else can I do?"

"Go away, start over again," she said.

"Did it work?"

They were silent. I reached out my hand and faded away.

"Why don't you come lie down up here?" my father said. "We have a little time before the enforcers come on duty and kick you out."

She didn't move.

"They've been nice to me," she said. "Nurse Eliot helped me put all the flowers in water while you slept."

He looked around him and made out their shapes. "Daffodils," he said.

"It's Susie's flower."

My father smiled beautifully. "See," he said, "that's how. You live in the face of it, by giving her a flower."

"That's so sad," my mother said.

"Yes," he said, "it is."

My mother had to balance somewhat precariously on one hip near the edge of his hospital bed, but they managed. They managed to stretch out together beside each other so they could stare into each other's eyes.

"How was it seeing Buckley and Lindsey?"

"Incredibly hard," she said.

They were silent for a moment and he squeezed her hand.

"You look so different," he said.

"You mean older."

I watched him reach up and take a strand of my mother's hair and loop it around her ear. "I fell in love with you again while you were away," he said.

I realized how much I wished I could be where my mother was. His love for my mother wasn't about looking back and loving something that would never change. It was about loving my mother for everything—for her brokenness and her fleeing, for her being there right then in that moment before the sun rose and the hospital staff came in. It was about touching that hair with the side of his fingertip, and knowing yet plumbing fearlessly the depths of her ocean eyes.

My mother could not bring herself to say "I love you."

"Will you stay?" he asked.

"For a while."

This was something.

"Good," he said. "So what did you say when people asked you about family in California?"

"Out loud I said I had two children. Silently I said three. I always felt like apologizing to her for that."

"Did you mention a husband?" he asked.

And she looked at him. "No."

"Man," he said.

"I didn't come back to pretend, Jack," she said.

"Why did you come back?"

"My mother called me. She said it was a heart attack and I thought about your father."

"Because I might die?"

"Yes."

"You were sleeping," he said. "You didn't see her."

"Who?"

"Someone came in the room and then left. I think it was Susie."

"Jack?" my mother asked, but her alarm was only at half-mast.

"Don't tell me you don't see her."

She let go.

"I see her everywhere," she said, breathing out her relief. "Even in California she was everywhere. Boarding buses or on the streets outside schools when I drove by. I'd see her hair but it didn't match the face or I'd see her body or the way she moved. I'd see older sisters and their little brothers, or two girls that looked like sisters and I imagined what Lindsey wouldn't have in her life—the whole relationship gone for her and for Buckley, and then that would just hit me, because I had left too. It would just spin onto you and even to my mother."

"She's been great," he said, "a rock. A spongelike rock, but a rock."

"So I gather."

"So if I tell you that Susie was in the room ten minutes ago, what would you say?"

"I'd say you were insane and you were probably right."

My father reached up and traced the line of my mother's nose and brought his finger over her two lips. As he did, the lips parted ever so slightly.

"You have to lean down," he said, "I'm still a sick man."

And I watched as my parents kissed. They kept their eyes open as they did, and my mother was the one to cry first, the tears dropping down onto my father's cheeks until he wept too.

TWENTY-ONE

After I left my parents in the hospital, I went to watch Ray Singh. We had been fourteen together, he and I. Now I saw his head on his pillow, dark hair on yellow sheets, dark skin on yellow sheets. I had always been in love with him. I counted the lashes of each closed eye. He had been my almost, my might-have-been, and I did not want to leave him any more than I did my family.

On the listing scaffold behind the stage, with Ruth below us, Ray Singh had gotten close enough to me so that his breath was near mine. I could smell the mixture of cloves and cinnamon that I imagined he topped his cereal with each morning, and a dark smell too, the human smell of the body coming at me where deep inside there were organs suspended by a chemistry separate from mine.

From the time I knew it would happen until the time it did, I had made sure not to be alone with Ray Singh inside or outside school. I was afraid of what I wanted most—his kiss. That it would not be good enough to match the stories everyone told or those I read in *Seventeen* and *Glamour* and *Vogue.* I feared that I would not be good enough—that my first kiss would equal rejection, not love. Still, I collected kiss stories.

"Your first kiss is destiny knocking," Grandma Lynn said over the phone one day. I was holding the phone while my father went to get my mother. I heard him in the kitchen say "three sheets to the wind."

"If I had it to do over again I would have worn something stupendous—like Fire and Ice, but Revlon didn't make that lipstick back then. I would have left my mark on the man."

"Mother?" my mother said into the bedroom extension.

"We're talking kiss business, Abigail."

"How much have you had?"

"See, Susie," Grandma Lynn said, "if you kiss like a lemon, you make lemonade."

"What was it like?"

"Ah, the kiss question," my mother said. "I'll leave you to it." I had been making my father and her tell it over and over again to hear their different takes. What I came away with was an image of my parents behind a cloud of cigarette smoke—the lips only vaguely touching inside the cloud.

A moment later Grandma Lynn whispered, "Susie, are you still there?"

"Yes, Grandma."

She was quiet for a while longer. "I was your age, and my first kiss came from a grown man. A father of a friend."

"Grandma!" I said, honestly shocked.

"You're not going to tell on me, are you?"

"No."

"It was wonderful," Grandma Lynn said. "He knew how to kiss. The boys who kissed me I couldn't even tolerate. I'd put my hand flat against their chests and push them away. Mr. McGahern knew how to use his lips."

"So what happened?"

"Bliss," she said. "I knew it wasn't right, but it was wonderful—at least for me. I never asked him how he felt about it, but then I never saw him alone after that."

"But did you want to do it again?"

"Yes, I was always searching for that first kiss."

"How about Grandaddy?"

"Not much of a kisser," she said. I could hear the clink of ice cubes on the other end of the phone. "I've never forgotten Mr. McGahern, even though it was just for a moment. Is there a boy who wants to kiss you?"

Neither of my parents had asked me this. I now know that they knew this already, could tell, smiled at each other when they compared notes.

I swallowed hard on my end. "Yes."

"What's his name?"

"Ray Singh."

"Do you like him?"

"Yes."

"Then what's the holdup?"

"I'm afraid I won't be good at it."

"Susie?"

"Yes?"

"Just have fun, kid."

But when I stood by my locker that afternoon and I heard Ray's voice say my name—this time behind me and not above me—it felt like anything but fun. It didn't feel not fun either. The easy states of black and white that I had known before did not apply.

I felt, if I were to say any word, churned. Not as a verb but as an adjective. Happy + Frightened = Churned.

"Ray," I said, but before the name had left my mouth, he leaned into me and caught my open mouth in his. It was so unexpected, even though I had waited weeks for it, that I wanted more. I wanted so badly to kiss Ray Singh again.

The following morning Mr. Connors cut out an article from the paper and saved it for Ruth. It was a detailed drawing of the Flanagan sinkhole and how it was going to be filled in. While Ruth dressed, he penned a note to her. "This is a crock of shit," it said. "Someday some poor sap's car is going to fall into it all over again."

"Dad says this is the death knell for him," Ruth said to Ray, waving the clipping at him as she got into Ray's ice blue Chevy at the end of her driveway. "Our place is going to be swallowed up in subdivision land. Get this. In this article they have four blocks like the cubes you draw in beginning art class, and it's supposed to show how they're going to patch the sinkhole up."

"Nice to see you too, Ruth," Ray said, reversing out of the driveway while making eyes at Ruth's unbuckled seat belt.

"Sorry," Ruth said. "Hello."

"What does the article say?" Ray asked.

"Nice day today, beautiful weather."

"Okay, okay. Tell me about the article."

Every time he saw Ruth after a few months had passed, he was reminded of her impatience and her curiosity—two traits that had both made and kept them friends.

"The first three are the same drawing only with different arrows pointing to different places and saying 'topsoil,' 'cracked limestone,' and 'dissolving rock.' The last one has a big headline that says, 'Patching it' and underneath it says, 'Concrete fills the throat and grout fills the cracks.'"

"Throat?" Ray said.

"I know," said Ruth. "Then there's this other arrow on the other side as if this was such a huge project that they had to pause a second so readers could understand the concept, and this one says, 'Then the hole is filled with dirt.' "

Ray started laughing.

"Like a medical procedure," Ruth said. "Intricate surgery is needed to patch up the planet."

"I think holes in the earth draw on some pretty primal fears."

"I'll say," Ruth said. "They have throats, for God's sake! Hey, let's check this out."

A mile or so down the road there were signs of new construction. Ray took a left and drove into the circles of freshly paved roads where the trees had been cleared and small red and yellow flags waved at intervals from the tops of waist-high wire markers.

Just as they had lulled themselves into thinking that they were alone, exploring the roads laid out for a territory as yet uninhabited, they saw Joe Ellis walking up ahead.

Ruth didn't wave and neither did Ray, nor did Joe make a move to acknowledge them.

"My mom says he still lives at home and can't get a job."

"What does he do all day?" Ray asked.

"Look creepy, I guess."

"He never got over it," Ray said, and Ruth stared out into the rows and rows of vacant lots until Ray connected with the main road again and they crossed back over the railroad tracks moving toward Route 30, which would take them in the direction of the sinkhole.

Ruth floated her arm out the window to feel the moist air of the morning after rain. Although Ray had been accused of being involved in my disappearance, he had understood why, knew that the police were doing their job. But Joe Ellis had never recovered from being accused of killing the cats and dogs Mr. Harvey had killed. He wandered around, keeping a good distance from his neighbors and wanting so much to take solace in the love of cats and dogs. For me the saddest thing was that these animals smelled the brokenness in him—the human defect—and kept away.

Down Route 30 near Eels Rod Pike, at a spot that Ray and Ruth were about to pass, I saw Len coming out of an apartment over Joe's barbershop. He carried a lightly stuffed student knapsack out to his car. The knapsack had been the gift of the young woman who owned the apartment. She had asked him out for coffee one day after they met down at the station as part of a criminology course at West Chester College. Inside the knapsack he had a combination of things—some of which he would show my father and some that no child's parent needed to see. The latter included the photos of the graves of the recovered bodies—both elbows there in each case.

When he had called the hospital, the nurse had told him Mr. Salmon was with his wife and family. Now his guilt thickened as he pulled his car into the hospital parking lot and sat for a moment with the hot sun coming through the windshield, baking in the heat.

I could see Len working on how to state what he had to say. He could work with only one assumption in his head—after almost seven years of ever more dwindling contact since late 1975, what my parents would hope for most was a body or the news that Mr. Harvey had been found. What he had to give them was a charm.

He grabbed his knapsack and locked up the car, passing by the girl outside with her replenished buckets of daffodils. He knew the number of my father's room, so he did not bother announcing himself to the fifth-floor nurses' station but merely tapped lightly on my father's open door before walking in.

My mother was standing with her back toward him. When she turned, I could see the force of her presence hit him. She was holding my father's hand. I suddenly felt terribly lonely.

My mother wobbled a bit when she met Len's eyes, and then she led with what came easiest.

"Is it *ever* wonderful to see you?" she tried to joke.

"Len," my father managed. "Abbie, will you tilt me up?"

"How are you feeling, Mr. Salmon?" Len asked as my mother pressed the up arrow button on the bed.

"Jack, please," my father insisted.

"Before you get your hopes up," Len said, "we haven't caught him."

My father visibly deflated.

My mother readjusted the foam pillows behind my father's back and neck. "Then why are you here?" she asked.

"We found an item of Susie's," Len said.

He had used almost the same sentence when he'd come to the house with the jingle-bell hat. It was a distant echo in her head.

The night before, as first my mother watched my father sleeping and then my father woke to see her head beside his on his pillow, they had both been staving off the memory of that first night of snow and hail and rain and how they had clung to each other, neither of them voicing aloud their greatest hope. Last night it had been my father who'd finally said it: "She's never coming home." A clear and easy piece of truth that everyone who had ever known me had accepted. But he needed to say it, and she needed to hear him say it.

"It's a charm off her bracelet," Len said. "A Pennsylvania keystone with her initials on it."

"I bought that for her," my father said. "At Thirtieth Street Station when I went into the city one day. They had a booth, and a man wearing safety glasses etched in initials for free. I brought Lindsey one too. Remember, Abigail?"

"I remember," my mother said.

"We found it near a grave in Connecticut."

My parents were suddenly still for a moment—like animals trapped in ice—their eyes frozen open and beseeching whoever walked above them to release them now, please.

"It wasn't Susie," Len said, rushing to fill the space. "What it means is that Harvey has been linked to other murders in Delaware and Connecticut. It was at the grave site outside Hartford where we found Susie's charm."

My father and mother watched as Len fumbled to open the slightly jammed zipper of his knapsack. My mother smoothed my father's hair back and tried to catch his eye. But my father was focused on the prospect Len presented—my murder case reopening. And my mother, just when she was beginning to feel on more solid ground, had to hide the fact that she'd never wanted it to begin again. The name George Harvey silenced her. She had never known what to say about him. For my mother, connecting her life to his capture and punishment spoke more about choosing to live with the enemy than about having to learn to live in the world without me.

Len pulled out a large Ziploc bag. At the bottom corner of the bag my parents could see the glint of gold. Len handed it to my mother, and she held it in front of her, slightly away from her body.

"Don't you need this, Len?" my father asked.

"We did all the tests on it," he said. "We've documented where it was found and taken the required photographs. The time may come when I would have to ask for it back, but until then, it's yours to keep."

"Open it, Abbie," my father said.

I watched my mother hold open the bag and lean over the bed. "It's for you, Jack," she said. "It was a gift from you."

As my father reached in, his hand shook, and it took him a

second to feel the small, sharp edges of the keystone against the flesh of his fingers. The way he drew it out of the bag reminded me of playing the game Operation with Lindsey when we were little. If he touched the sides of the Ziploc bag an alarm would go off and he would have to forfeit.

"How can you be sure he killed these other girls?" my mother asked. She stared at the tiny ember of gold in my father's palm.

"Nothing is ever certain," Len said.

And the echo rang in her ears again. Len had a fixed set of phrases. It was this same phrase that my father had borrowed to soothe his family. It was a cruel phrase that preyed on hope.

"I think I want you to leave now," she said.

"Abigail?" my father queried.

"I can't hear anymore."

"I'm very glad to have the charm, Len," my father said.

Len doffed an imaginary cap to my father before turning to go. He had made a certain kind of love to my mother before she went away. Sex as an act of willful forgetting. It was the kind he made more and more in the rooms above the barbershop.

I headed south toward Ruth and Ray, but I saw Mr. Harvey instead. He was driving an orange patchwork car that had been pieced together from so many different versions of the same make and model that it looked like Frankenstein's monster on wheels. A bungee cord held the front hood, which fluttered up and down as it caught the oncoming air.

The engine had resisted anything but a shimmer above the speed limit no matter how hard he pressed the gas pedal. He had slept next to an empty grave, and while he'd been sleeping he had dreamed of the 5! 5! 5!, waking near dawn to make the drive to Pennsylvania.

The edges of Mr. Harvey seemed oddly blurred. For years he

had kept at bay the memories of the women he killed, but now, one by one, they were coming back.

The first girl he'd hurt was by accident. He got mad and couldn't stop himself, or that was how he began to weave it into sense. She stopped going to the high school that they were both enrolled in, but this didn't seem strange to him. By that time he had moved so many times that he assumed that was what the girl had done. He had regretted it, this quiet, muffled rape of a school friend, but he didn't see it as something that would stay with either one of them. It was as if something outside him had resulted in the collision of their two bodies one afternoon. For a second afterward, she'd stared. It was bottomless. Then she put on her torn underpants, tucking them into her skirt's waistband to keep them in place. They didn't speak, and she left. He cut himself with his penknife along the back of his hand. When his father asked about the blood, there would be a plausible explanation. "See," he could say, and point to the place on his hand. "It was an accident."

But his father didn't ask, and no one came around looking for him. No father or brother or policeman.

Then what I saw was what Mr. Harvey felt beside him. This girl, who had died only a few years later when her brother fell asleep smoking a cigarette. She was sitting in the front seat. I wondered how long it would take before he began to remember me.

The only signs of change since the day Mr. Harvey had delivered me up to the Flanagans' were the orange pylons set around the lot. That and the evidence that the sinkhole had expanded. The house's southeast corner sloped downward, and the front porch was quietly sinking into the earth.

As a precaution, Ray parked on the other side of Flat Road,

under a section of overgrown shrubbery. Even so, the passenger side skimmed the edge of the pavement. "What happened to the Flanagans?" Ray asked as they got out of his car.

"My father said the corporation that bought the property gave them a settlement and they took off."

"It's spooky around here, Ruth," Ray said.

They crossed the empty road. Above them the sky was a light blue, a few smoky clouds dotting the air. From where they stood they could just make out the back of Hal's bike shop on the other side of the railroad tracks.

"I wonder if Hal Heckler still owns that?" Ruth said. "I had a crush on him when we were growing up."

Then she turned toward the lot. They were quiet. Ruth moved in ever-diminishing circles, with the hole and its vague edge as their goal. Ray trailed just behind Ruth as she led the way. If you saw it from a distance, the sinkhole seemed innocuous—like an overgrown mud puddle just starting to dry out. There were spots of grass and weeds surrounding it and then, if you looked close enough, it was as if the earth stopped and a light cocoa-colored flesh began. It was soft and convex, and it drew in items placed on top of it.

"How do you know it won't swallow us?" Ray asked.

"We're not heavy enough," Ruth said.

"Stop if you feel yourself sinking."

Watching them I remembered holding on to Buckley's hand the day we went to bury the refrigerator. While my father was talking to Mr. Flanagan, Buckley and I walked up to the point where the earth sloped down and softened, and I swore I felt it give ever so slightly beneath my feet. It had been the same sensation as walking in the graveyard of our church and suddenly sinking into the hollow tunnels that the moles had dug among the headstones.

Ultimately it was the memory of those very moles—and the

pictures of their blind, nosy, toothsome selves that I sought out in books — that had made me accept more readily being sunk inside the earth in a heavy metal safe. I was mole-proof, anyway.

Ruth tiptoed up to what she took to be the edge, while I thought of the sound of my father's laughter on that long-ago day. I made up a story for my brother on the way home. How underneath the sinkhole there was a whole village inside the earth that no one knew about and the people who lived there greeted these appliances like gifts from an Earthly heaven. "When our refrigerator reaches them," I said, "they will praise us, because they are a race of tiny repairmen who love to put things back together again." My father's laughter filled the car.

"Ruthie," Ray said, "that's close enough."

Ruth's toes were on the soft part, her heels were on the hard, and there was a sense as I watched her that she might point her fingers and raise her arms and dive right in to be beside me. But Ray came up behind her.

"Apparently," he said, "the earth's throat burps."

All three of us watched the corner of something metal as it rose.

"The great Maytag of 'sixty-nine," Ray said.

But it was not a washer or a safe. It was an old red gas stove, moving slow.

"Do you ever think about where Susie Salmon's body ended up?" asked Ruth.

I wanted to walk out from underneath the overgrown shrubs that half-hid their ice blue car and cross the road and walk down into the hole and back up and tap her gently on the shoulder and say, "It's me! You've done it! Bingo! Score!"

"No," Ray said. "I leave that to you."

"Everything is changing here now. Every time I come back something is gone that made it not just every other place in the country," she said.

"Do you want to go inside the house?" Ray asked, but he was thinking of me. How his crush had come when he was thirteen. He had seen me walking home from school ahead of him, and it was a series of simple things: my awkward plaid skirt, my peacoat covered in Holiday's fur, the way what I thought of as my mousy brown hair caught the afternoon sun so that the light moved fluidly from spot to spot as we walked home, one behind the other. And then, a few days later, when he had stood in social science class and accidentally read from his paper on *Jane Eyre* instead of the War of 1812—I had looked at him in a way he thought was nice.

Ray walked toward the house that would soon be demolished, and that had already been stripped of any valuable doorknobs and faucets late one night by Mr. Connors, but Ruth stayed by the sinkhole. Ray was already inside the house when it happened. As clear as day, she saw me standing there beside her, looking at the spot Mr. Harvey had dumped me.

"Susie," Ruth said, feeling my presence even more solidly when she said my name.

But I said nothing.

"I've written poems for you," Ruth said, trying to get me to stay with her. What she had wished for her whole life happening, finally. "Don't you want anything, Susie?" she asked.

Then I vanished.

Ruth stood there reeling, waiting in the gray light of the Pennsylvania sun. And her question rang in my ears: "Don't you want anything?"

On the other side of the railroad tracks, Hal's shop was deserted. He had taken the day off and brought Samuel and Buckley to a bike show in Radnor. I could see Buckley's hands move over the curved front-wheel casing of a red minibike. It would be his birthday soon, and Hal and Samuel watched him. Hal had wanted to give Samuel's old alto sax to my brother, but my Grandma Lynn had intervened. "He needs to bang on things, honey," she said. "Save the subtle stuff." So Hal and Samuel had chipped in together and bought my brother a secondhand set of drums.

Grandma Lynn was at the mall trying to find simple yet elegant clothes that she might convince my mother to wear. With fingers made dexterous from years of practice, she pulled a near-navy dress from a rack of black. I could see the woman near her alight on the dress in greenish envy.

At the hospital, my mother was reading aloud to my father from a day-old *Evening Bulletin,* and he was watching her lips move and not really listening. Wanting to kiss her instead.

And Lindsey.

I could see Mr. Harvey take the turn into my old neighborhood in broad daylight, past caring who spotted him, even depending on his standard invisibility—here, in the neighborhood where so many had said they would never forget him, had always thought of him as strange, had come easily to suspect that the dead wife he spoke of by alternate names had been one of his victims.

Lindsey was at home alone.

Mr. Harvey drove by Nate's house inside the anchor area of the development. Nate's mother was picking the wilted blossoms from her front kidney-shaped flower bed. She looked up when the car passed. She saw the unfamiliar, patched-together car and imagined it was a college friend of one of the older children home for the summer. She had not seen Mr. Harvey in the driver's seat. He turned left onto the lower road, which circled around to his old street. Holiday whined at my feet, the same kind of sick, low moan he would let out when we drove him to the vet.

Ruana Singh had her back to him. I saw her through the dining room window, alphabetizing stacks of new books and placing them in carefully kept bookshelves. There were children out in their yards on swings and pogo sticks and chasing one another with water pistols. A neighborhood full of potential victims.

He rounded the curve at the bottom of our road and passed the small municipal park across from where the Gilberts lived. They were both inside, Mr. Gilbert now infirm. Then he saw his old house, no longer green, though to my family and me it would always be "the green house." The new owners had painted it a lavendery mauve and installed a pool and, just off to the side, near the basement window, a gazebo made out of redwood, which overflowed with hanging ivy and children's toys. The front flower beds had been paved over when they expanded their front walk, and they had screened in the front porch with frost-resistant glass, behind which he saw an office of some sort. He heard the sound of girls laughing out in the backyard, and a woman came out of the front door carrying a pair of pruning shears and wearing a sun hat. She stared at the man sitting in his orange car and felt something kick inside her — the queasy kick of an empty womb. She turned abruptly and went back inside, peering at him from behind her window. Waiting.

He drove down the road a few houses further.

There she was, my precious sister. He could see her in the upstairs window of our house. She had cut all her hair off and grown thinner in the intervening years, but it was her, sitting at the drafting board she used as a desk and reading a psychology book.

It was then that I began to see them coming down the road.

While he scanned the windows of my old house and wondered where the other members of my family were — whether my father's leg still made him hobble — I saw the final vestiges of the animals and the women taking leave of Mr. Harvey's house. They straggled forward together. He watched my sister and thought of the sheets he had draped on the poles of the bridal tent. He had stared right in my father's eyes that day as he said my name. And the dog — the one that barked outside his house — the dog was surely dead by now.

Lindsey moved in the window, and I watched him watching her. She stood up and turned around, going farther into the room to a floor-to-ceiling bookshelf. She reached up and brought another book down. As she came back to the desk and he lingered on her face, his rearview mirror suddenly filled with a black-and-white cruising slowly up the street behind him.

He knew he could not outrace them. He sat in his car and prepared the last vestiges of the face he had been giving authorities for decades—the face of a bland man they might pity or despise but never blame. As the officer pulled alongside him, the women slipped in the windows and the cats curled around his ankles.

"Are you lost?" the young policeman asked when he was flush with the orange car.

"I used to live here," Mr. Harvey said. I shook with it. He had chosen to tell the truth.

"We got a call, suspicious vehicle."

"I see they're building something in the old cornfield," Mr. Harvey said. And I knew that part of me could join the others then, swoop down in pieces, each body part he had claimed raining down inside his car.

"They're expanding the school."

"I thought the neighborhood looked more prosperous," he said wistfully.

"Perhaps you should move along," the officer said. He was embarrassed for Mr. Harvey in his patched-up car, but I saw him jot the license plate down.

"I didn't mean to scare anyone."

Mr. Harvey was a pro, but in that moment I didn't care. With each section of road he covered, I focused on Lindsey inside reading her textbooks, on the facts jumping up from the pages and into her brain, on how smart she was and how whole. At Temple she had decided to be a therapist. And I thought of the mix of air that was our front yard, which was daylight, a queasy mother and a cop—it was a convergence of luck that had kept my sister safe so far. Every day a question mark.

Ruth did not tell Ray what had happened. She promised herself she would write it in her journal first. When they crossed the road back to the car, Ray saw something violet in the scrub halfway up a high dirt berm that had been dumped there by a construction crew.

"That's periwinkle," he said to Ruth. "I'm going to clip some for my mom."

"Cool, take your time," Ruth said.

Ray ducked into the underbrush by the driver's side and climbed up to the periwinkle while Ruth stood by the car. Ray wasn't thinking of me anymore. He was thinking of his mother's smiles. The surest way to get them was to find her wildflowers like this, to bring them home to her and watch her as she pressed them, first opening their petals flat against the black and white of dictionaries or reference books. Ray walked to the top of the berm and disappeared over the side in hopes of finding more.

It was only then that I felt a prickle along my spine, when I saw his body suddenly vanish on the other side. I heard Holiday, his fear lodged low and deep in his throat, and realized it could not have been Lindsey for whom he had whined. Mr. Harvey crested the top of Eels Rod Pike and saw the sinkhole and the orange pylons that matched his car. He had dumped a body there. He remembered his mother's amber pendant, and how when she had handed it to him it was still warm.

Ruth saw the women stuffed in the car in blood-colored gowns. She began walking toward them. On that same road where I had been buried, Mr. Harvey passed by Ruth. All she could see were the women. Then: blackout.

That was the moment I fell to Earth.

TWENTY-TWO

Ruth collapsing into the road. Of this I was aware. Mr. Harvey sailing away unwatched, unloved, unbidden—this I lost.

Helplessly I tipped, my balance gone. I fell through the open doorway of the gazebo, across the lawn and out past the farthest boundary of the heaven I had lived in all these years.

I heard Ray screaming in the air above me, his voice shouting in an arc of sound. "Ruth, are you okay?" And then he reached her and grabbed on.

"Ruth, Ruth," he yelled. "What happened?"

And I was in Ruth's eyes and I was looking up. I could feel the arch of her back against the pavement, and scrapes inside her clothes where flesh had been torn away by the gravel's sharp edges. I felt every sensation—the warmth of the sun, the smell of the asphalt—but I could not see Ruth.

I heard Ruth's lungs bubbling, a giddiness there in her stomach, but air still filling her lungs. Then tension stretching out the body. Her body. Ray above, his eyes—gray, pulsing, looking up and down the road hopelessly for help that was not coming. He had not seen the car but had come through the scrub delighted, carrying a bouquet of wildflowers for his mother, and there was Ruth, lying in the road.

Ruth pushed up against her skin, wanting out. She was fighting to leave and I was inside now, struggling with her. I willed her back, willed that divine impossible, but she wanted out. There was nothing and no one that could keep her down. Flying. I watched as I had so many times from heaven, but this time it was a blur beside me. It was lust and rage yearning upward.

"Ruth," Ray said. "Can you hear me, Ruth?"

Right before she closed her eyes and all the lights went out and the world was frantic, I looked into Ray Singh's gray eyes, at his dark skin, at his lips I had once kissed. Then, like a hand unclasping from a tight lock, Ruth passed by him.

Ray's eyes bid me forward while the watching streamed out of me and gave way to a pitiful desire. To be alive again on this Earth. Not to watch from above but to be—the sweetest thing—beside.

Somewhere in the blue blue Inbetween I had seen her—Ruth streaking by me as I fell to Earth. But she was no shadow of a human form, no ghost. She was a smart girl breaking all the rules.

And I was in her body.

I heard a voice calling me from heaven. It was Franny's. She ran toward the gazebo, calling my name. Holiday was barking so loud that his voice would catch and round in the base of his throat with no break. Then, suddenly, Franny and Holiday were gone and all was silent. I felt something holding me down, and I felt a hand in mine. My ears were like oceans in which what I had known, voices, faces, facts, began to drown. I opened my eyes for the first time since I had died and saw gray eyes looking back at me. I was still as I came to realize that the marvelous weight weighing me down was the weight of the human body.

I tried to speak.

"Don't," Ray said. "What happened?"

I died, I wanted to tell him. How do you say, "I died and now I'm back among the living"?

Ray had kneeled down. Scattered around him and on top of me were the flowers he'd been gathering for Ruana. I could pick out their bright elliptical shapes against Ruth's dark clothes. And then Ray leaned his ear to my chest to listen to me breathing. He placed a finger on the inside of my wrist to check my pulse.

"Did you faint?" he asked when these checked out.

I nodded. I knew I would not be granted this grace on Earth forever, that Ruth's wish was only temporary.

"I think I'm fine," I tried, but my voice was too faint, too far away, and Ray did not hear me. My eyes locked on to his then, opening as wide as I could make them. Something urged me to lift up. I thought I was floating back to heaven, returning, but I was trying to stand up.

"Ruth," Ray said. "Don't move if you feel weak. I can carry you to the car."

I smiled at him, one-thousand-watted. "I'm okay," I said.

Tentatively, watching me carefully, he released my arm but continued to hold on to my other hand. He went with me as I stood, and the wildflowers fell to the pavement. In heaven, women were throwing rose petals as they saw Ruth Connors.

I watched his beautiful face break into a stunned smile. "So you're all right," he said. Cautious, he came close enough to kiss me, but he told me he was checking my pupils to see if they were equal in size.

I was feeling the weight of Ruth's body, both the luscious bounce of breasts and thighs but also an awesome responsibility. I was a soul back on Earth. AWOL a little while from heaven, I had been given a gift. By force of will I stood as straight as I could.

"Ruth?"

I tried to get used to the name. "Yes," I said.

"You've changed," he said. "Something's changed."

We stood near the center of the road, but this was my moment. I wanted so much to tell him, but what could I say then? "I'm Susie, I have only a little time." I was too afraid.

"Kiss me," I said instead.

"What?"

"Don't you want to?" I reached my hands up to his face and felt the light stubble of a beard that had not been there eight years ago.

"What's happened to you?" he said, bewildered.

"Sometimes cats fall ten flights out of the windows of highrises and land on their feet. You only believe it because you've seen it in print."

Ray stared at me, mystified. He leaned his head down and our lips touched, tender. At the roots I felt his cool lips deep down inside me. Another kiss, precious package, stolen gift. His eyes were so close to me I saw the green flecks in the gray.

I took his hand, and we walked back to the car in silence. I was aware that he dragged behind, stretching my arm out behind me as we held hands and scanning Ruth's body to make sure she was walking fine.

He opened the door of the passenger side, and I slid into the seat and placed my feet on the carpeted floor. When he came around to his side and ducked inside he looked hard at me once more.

"What's wrong?" I asked.

He kissed me lightly again, on the lips. What I had wanted for so long. The moment slowed down, and I drank it in. The brush of his lips, the slight stubble of his beard as it grazed me, and the sound of the kiss—the small smack of suction as our lips parted after the pushing together and then the more brutal breaking away. It reverberated, this sound, down the long tunnel of loneliness and making do with watching the touch and caress of others on Earth. I had never been touched like this. I had only been hurt by hands past all tenderness. But spreading out into my heaven after death had been a moonbeam that swirled and blinked on and off—Ray Singh's kiss. Somehow Ruth knew this.

My head throbbed then, with the thought of it, with me hiding inside Ruth in every way but this—that when Ray kissed me or as our hands met it was my desire, not Ruth's, it was *me* pushing out at the edges of her skin. I could see Holly. She was laughing, her head tilted back, and then I heard Holiday howling plaintively, for I was back where we had both once lived.

"Where do you want to go?" Ray asked.

And it was such a wide question, the answer so vast. I knew I did not want to chase after Mr. Harvey. I looked at Ray and knew why I was there. To take back a piece of heaven I had never known.

"Hal Heckler's bike shop," I stated firmly.

"What?"

"You asked," I said.

"Ruth?"

"Yes?"

"Can I kiss you again?"

"Yes," I said, my face flushing.

He leaned over as the engine warmed and our lips met once more and there she was, Ruth, lecturing a group of old men in berets and black turtlenecks while they held glowing lighters in the air and called her name in a rhythmic chant.

Ray sat back and looked at me. "What is it?" he asked.

"When you kiss me I see heaven," I said.

"What does it look like?"

"It's different for everyone."

"I want details," he said, smiling. "Facts."

"Make love to me," I said, "and I'll tell you."

"Who are you?" he asked, but I could tell he didn't know what he was asking yet.

"The car is warmed up," I said.

His hand grabbed the shiny chrome stick on the side of the steering wheel and then we drove—normal as day—a boy and a girl together. The sun caught the broken mica in the old patched pavement as he made the U-turn.

We drove down to the bottom of Flat Road, and I pointed to the dirt path on the other side of Eels Rod Pike, which led up to a place where we could cross the railroad tracks.

"They'll have to change this soon," Ray said as he shot across the gravel and up onto the dirt path. The railroad stretched to Harrisburg in one direction and Philadelphia in the other, and all along it buildings were being razed and old families were moving out and industrial tenants in.

"Will you stay here," I asked, "after you're done with school?"

"No one does," Ray said. "You know that."

I was almost blinded by it, this choice; the idea that if I'd remained on Earth I could have left this place to claim another, that I could go anywhere I wanted to. And I wondered then, was it the same in heaven as on Earth? What I'd been missing was a wanderlust that came from letting go?

We drove onto the slim patch of cleared earth that ran along either side of Hal's bike shop. Ray stopped and braked the car.

"Why here?" Ray asked.

"Remember," I said, "we're exploring."

I led him around to the back of the shop and reached up over the doorjamb until I felt the hidden key.

"How do you know about that?"

"I've watched hundreds of people hide keys," I said. "It doesn't take a genius to guess."

Inside it was as I remembered it, the smell of bike grease heavy in the air.

I said, "I think I need to shower. Why not make yourself at home?"

I walked past the bed and turned on the light switch on the cord—all the tiny white lights above Hal's bed glittered then, the only light save the dusty light coming from the small back window.

"Where are you going?" Ray asked. "How do you know about this place?" His voice had a frantic sound it hadn't just a moment before.

"Give me just a little time, Ray," I said. "Then I'll explain."

I walked into the small bathroom but kept the door slightly ajar. As I took Ruth's clothes off and waited for the hot water to heat up, I hoped that Ruth could see me, could see her body as I saw it, its perfect living beauty.

It was damp and musty in the bathroom, and the tub was stained from years of having anything but water poured down its drain. I stepped up into the old claw-foot tub and stood under the water. Even at the hottest I could make it, I still felt cold. I called Ray's name. I begged him to step inside the room.

"I can see you through the curtain," he said, averting his eyes.

"It's okay," I said. "I like it. Take your clothes off and join me."

"Susie," he said, "you know I'm not like that."

My heart seized up. "What did you say?" I asked. I focused my eyes on his through the white translucent liner Hal kept for a curtain—he was a dark shape with a hundred small pinpoints of light surrounding him.

"I said I'm not that kind."

"You called me Susie."

There was silence, and then a moment later he drew back the curtain, being careful to look only at my face.

"Susie?"

"Join me," I said, my eyes welling up. "Please, join me."

I closed my eyes and waited. I put my head under the water

and felt the heat of it prickling my cheeks and neck, my breasts and stomach and groin. Then I heard him fumbling, heard his belt buckle hit the cold cement floor and his pockets lose their change.

I had the same sense of anticipation then as I sometimes had as a child when I lay down in the back seat and closed my eyes while my parents drove, sure we would be home when the car stopped, that they would lift me up and carry me inside. It was an anticipation born of trust.

Ray drew back the curtain. I turned to face him and opened my eyes. I felt a marvelous draft on the inside of my thighs.

"It's okay," I said.

He stepped slowly into the tub. At first he did not touch me, but then, tentatively, he traced a small scar along my side. We watched together as his finger moved down the ribbony wound.

"Ruth's volleyball incident, nineteen seventy-five," I said. I shivered again.

"You're not Ruth," he said, his face full of wonder.

I took the hand that had reached the end of the cut and placed it under my left breast.

"I've watched you both for years," I said. "I want you to make love to me."

His lips parted to speak, but what was on his lips now was too strange to say out loud. He brushed my nipple with his thumb, and I pulled his head toward me. We kissed. The water came down between our bodies and wet the sparse hair along his chest and stomach. I kissed him because I wanted to see Ruth and I wanted to see Holly and I wanted to know if they could see me. In the shower I could cry and Ray could kiss my tears, never knowing exactly why I shed them.

I touched every part of him and held it in my hands. I cupped his elbow in my palm. I dragged his pubic hair out straight between my fingers. I held that part of him that Mr. Harvey had forced inside me. Inside my head I said the word *gentle,* and then I said the word *man.*

"Ray?"

"I don't know what to call you."

"Susie."

I put my fingers up to his lips to stop his questioning. "Remember the note you wrote me? Remember how you called yourself the Moor?"

For a moment we both stood there, and I watched the water bead along his shoulders, then slip and fall.

Without saying anything further, he lifted me up and I wrapped my legs around him. He turned out of the path of the water to use the edge of the tub for support. When he was inside of me, I grabbed his face in my hands and kissed him as hard as I could.

After a full minute, he pulled away. "Tell me what it looks like."

"Sometimes it looks like the high school did," I said, breathless. "I never got to go there, but in my heaven I can make a bonfire in the classrooms or run up and down the halls yelling as loud as I want. But it doesn't always look like that. It can look like Nova Scotia, or Tangiers, or Tibet. It looks like anything you've ever dreamed."

"Is Ruth there?"

"Ruth is doing spoken word, but she'll come back."

"Can you see yourself there?"

"I'm here right now," I said.

"But you'll be gone soon."

I would not lie. I bowed my head. "I think so, Ray. Yes."

We made love then. We made love in the shower and in the bedroom and under the lights and fake glow-in-the-dark stars. While he rested, I kissed him across the line of his backbone and blessed each knot of muscle, each mole and blemish.

"Don't go," he said, and his eyes, those shining gems, shut and I could feel the shallow breath of sleep from him.

"My name is Susie," I whispered, "last name Salmon, like the fish." I leaned my head down to rest on his chest and sleep beside him.

When I opened my eyes, the window across from us was dark red and I could feel that there was not much time left. Outside, the world I had watched for so long was living and breathing on the same earth I now was. But I knew I would not go out. I had taken this time to fall in love instead—in love with the sort of helplessness I had not felt in death—the helplessness of being alive, the dark bright pity of being human—feeling as you went, groping in corners and opening your arms to light—all of it part of navigating the unknown.

Ruth's body was weakening. I leaned on one arm and watched Ray sleeping. I knew that I was going soon.

When his eyes opened a short while later, I looked at him and traced the edge of his face with my fingers.

"Do you ever think about the dead, Ray?"

He blinked his eyes and looked at me.

"I'm in med school."

"I don't mean cadavers, or diseases, or collapsed organs, I mean what Ruth talks about. I mean us."

"Sometimes I do," he said. "I've always wondered."

"We're here, you know," I said. "All the time. You can talk to us and think about us. It doesn't have to be sad or scary."

"Can I touch you again?" He shook the sheets from his legs to sit up.

It was then that I saw something at the end of Hal's bed. It was cloudy and still. I tried to convince myself that it was an odd trick of light, a mass of dust motes trapped in the setting sun. But when Ray reached out to touch me, I didn't feel anything.

Ray leaned close to me and kissed me lightly on the shoulder. I didn't feel it. I pinched myself under the blanket. Nothing.

The cloudy mass at the end of the bed began to take shape now. As Ray slipped out of the bed and stood, I saw men and women filling the room.

"Ray," I said, just before he reached the bathroom. I wanted to say "I'll miss you," or "don't go," or "thank you."

"Yes."

"You have to read Ruth's journals."

"You couldn't pay me not to," he said.

I looked through the shadowy figures of the spirits forming a mass at the end of the bed and saw him smile at me. Saw his lovely fragile body turn and walk through the doorway. A tenuous and sudden memory.

As the steam began to billow out from the bathroom, I made my way, slowly, to the small child's desk where Hal stacked bills and records. I began to think of Ruth again, how I hadn't seen any of it coming—the marvelous possibility that Ruth had dreamed of since our meeting in the parking lot. Instead, I saw how hope was what I had traded on in heaven and on Earth. Dreams of being a wildlife photographer, dreams of winning an Oscar in junior year, dreams of kissing Ray Singh once more. Look what happens when you dream.

In front of me I saw a phone and picked it up. Without thinking, I punched in the number to my house, like a lock whose combination you know only when you spin the dial in your hand.

On the third ring, someone picked up.

"Hello?"

"Hello, Buckley," I said.

"Who is this?"

"It's me, Susie."

"Who's there?"

"Susie, honey, your big sister."

"I can't hear you," he said.

I stared at the phone for a minute, and then I felt them. The room was full now of these silent spirits. Among them were children as well as adults. "Who are you? Where did you all come from?" I asked, but what had been my voice made no noise in the room. It was then that I noticed it. I was sitting up and watching the others, but Ruth was lying sprawled across the desk.

"Can you throw me a towel?" Ray yelled after shutting off the water. When I did not answer he pulled back the curtain. I heard him get out of the tub and come to the doorway. He saw Ruth and ran toward her. He touched her shoulder and, sleepily, she roused. They looked at each other. She did not have to say anything. He knew that I was gone.

I remembered once, with my parents and Lindsey and Buckley, riding backward on a train into a dark tunnel. That was how it felt to leave Earth the second time. The destination somehow inevitable, the sights seen in passing so many times. But this time I was accompanied, not ripped away, and I knew we were taking a long trip to a place very far away.

Leaving Earth again was easier than coming back had been. I got to see two old friends silently holding each other in the back of Hal's bike shop, neither of them ready to say aloud what had happened to them. Ruth was both more tired and more happy than she had ever been. For Ray, what he had been through and the possibilities this opened up for him were just starting to sink in.

TWENTY-THREE

The next morning the smell of his mother's baking had sneaked up the stairs and into Ray's room where he and Ruth lay together. Overnight, their world had changed. It was that simple.

After leaving Hal's bike shop, being careful to cover any trace that they had ever been there, Ray and Ruth drove in silence back to Ray's house. Later that night, when Ruana found the two of them curled up together asleep and fully clothed, she was glad that Ray had at least this one weird friend.

Around three A.M., Ray had stirred. He sat up and looked at Ruth, at her long gangly limbs, at the beautiful body to which he had made love, and felt a sudden warmth infuse him. He reached out to touch her, and just then a bit of moonlight fell across the floor from the window where I had watched him sit and study for so many years. He followed it. There on the floor was Ruth's bag.

Careful not to wake her, he slid off the bed and walked over to it. Inside was her journal. He lifted it out and began to read:

"At the tips of feathers there is air and at their base: blood. I hold up bones; I wish like broken glass they could court light . . . still I try to place these pieces back together, to set them firm, to make murdered girls live again."

He skipped ahead:

"Penn Station, bathroom stall, struggle which led to the sink. Older woman.

"Domestic. Ave. C. Husband and wife.

"Roof on Mott Street, a teenage girl, gunshot.

"Time? Little girl in C.P. strays toward bushes. White lace collar, fancy."

He grew incredibly cold in the room but kept reading, looking up only when he heard Ruth stir.

"I have so much to tell you," she said.

Nurse Eliot helped my father lower himself into the wheelchair while my mother and sister fussed about the room, collecting the daffodils to take home.

"Nurse Eliot," he said, "I'll remember your kindness but I hope it will be a long time before I see you again."

"I hope so too," she said. She looked at my family gathered in the room, standing awkwardly about. "Buckley, your mother's and sister's hands are full. It's up to you."

"Steer her easy, Buck," my father said.

I watched the four of them begin to trail down the hall to the elevator, Buckley and my father first while Lindsey and my mother followed behind, their arms full of dripping daffodils.

In the elevator going down, Lindsey stared into the throats of the bright yellow flowers. She remembered that Samuel and Hal had found yellow daffodils lying in the cornfield on the afternoon of the first memorial. They had never known who placed them there. My sister looked at the flowers and then my mother. She could feel my brother's body touching hers, and our father, sitting in the shiny hospital chair, looking tired but happy to be going home. When they reached the lobby and the doors opened I knew they were meant to be there, the four of them together, alone.

While Ruana's hands grew wet and swollen paring apple after apple, she began to say the word in her mind, the one she had avoided for years: *divorce.* It had been something about the crumpled, clinging postures of her son and Ruth that finally freed her. She could not remember the last time she had gone to bed at the same time as her husband. He walked in the room like a ghost and like a ghost slipped in between the sheets, barely creasing them. He was not unkind in the ways that the television and newspapers were full of. His cruelty was in his absence. Even when he came and sat at her dinner table and ate her food, he was not there.

She heard the sound of water running in the bathroom above her and waited what she thought was a considerate interval before calling up to them. My mother had called that morning to thank her for having talked to her when she called from California, and Ruana had decided to drop off a pie.

After handing a mug of coffee each to Ruth and Ray, Ruana announced that it was already late and she wanted Ray to accompany her to the Salmons', where she intended to run quietly to the door and place a pie on their doorstep.

"Whoa, pony," Ruth managed.

Ruana stared at her.

"Sorry, Mom," Ray said. "We had a pretty intense day yesterday." But he wondered, might his mother ever believe him?

Ruana turned toward the counter and brought one of two pies she had baked to the table, where the scent of it rose in a steamy mist from the holes cut into the crust. "Breakfast?" she said.

"You're a goddess!" said Ruth.

Ruana smiled.

"Eat your fill and then get dressed and both of you can come with me."

Ruth looked at Ray while she said, "Actually, I have somewhere to go, but I'll drop by later."

Hal brought the drum set over for my brother. Hal and my grandmother had agreed. Though it was still weeks before Buckley turned thirteen, he needed them. Samuel had let Lindsey and Buckley meet my parents at the hospital without him. It would be a double homecoming for them. My mother had stayed with my father for forty-eight hours straight, during which the world had changed for them and for others and would, I saw now, change again and again and again. There was no way to stop it.

"I know we shouldn't start too early," Grandma Lynn said, "but what's your poison, boys?"

"I thought we were set up for champagne," Samuel said.

"We are later," she said. "I'm offering an apéritif."

"I think I'm passing," Samuel said. "I'll have something when Lindsey does."

"Hal?"

"I'm teaching Buck the drums."

Grandma Lynn held her tongue about the questionable sobriety of known jazz greats. "Well, how about three scintillating tumblers of water?"

My grandmother stepped back into the kitchen to get their drinks. I had come to love her more after death than I ever had on Earth. I wish I could say that in that moment in the kitchen she decided to quit drinking, but I now saw that drinking was part of what made her who she was. If the worst of what she left on Earth was a legacy of inebriated support, it was a good legacy in my book.

She brought the ice over to the sink from the freezer and splurged on cubes. Seven in each tall glass. She ran the tap to make the water as cold as it would come. Her Abigail was coming home again. Her strange Abigail, whom she loved.

But when she looked up and through the window, she swore she saw a young girl wearing the clothes of her youth sitting outside Buckley's garden-shed fort and staring back at her. The next moment the girl was gone. She shook it off. The day was busy. She would not tell anyone.

When my father's car pulled into the drive, I was beginning to wonder if this had been what I'd been waiting for, for my family to come home, not to me anymore but to one another with me gone.

In the afternoon light my father looked smaller somehow, thinner, but his eyes looked grateful in a way they had not in years.

My mother, for her part, was thinking moment by moment that she might be able to survive being home again.

All four of them got out at once. Buckley came forward from the rear passenger seat to assist my father perhaps more than he needed assistance, perhaps protecting him from my mother. Lindsey looked over the hood of the car at our brother—her habitual check-in mode still operating. She felt responsible, just as my brother did, just as my father did. And then she turned back and saw my mother looking at her, her face lit by the yellowy light of the daffodils.

"What?"

"You are the spitting image of your father's mother," my mother said.

"Help me with the bags," my sister said.

They walked to the trunk together as Buckley led my father up the front path.

Lindsey stared into the dark space of the trunk. She wanted to know only one thing.

"Are you going to hurt him again?"

"I'm going to do everything I can not to," my mother said, "but no promises this time." She waited until Lindsey glanced up and looked at her, her eyes a challenge now as much as the eyes of a child who had grown up fast, run fast since the day the police had said too much blood in the earth, your daughter/sister/child is dead.

"I know what you did."

"I stand warned."

My sister hefted the bag.

They heard shouting. Buckley ran out onto the front porch. "Lindsey!" he said, forgetting his serious self, his heavy body buoyant. "Come see what Hal got me!"

He banged. And he banged and he banged and he banged. And Hal was the only one still smiling after five minutes of it. Everyone else had glimpsed the future and it was loud.

"I think now would be a good time to introduce him to the brush," Grandma Lynn said. Hal obliged.

My mother had handed the daffodils to Grandma Lynn and gone upstairs almost immediately, using the bathroom as an excuse. Everyone knew where she was going: my old room.

She stood at the edge of it, alone, as if she were standing at the edge of the Pacific. It was still lavender. The furniture, save for a reclining chair of my grandmother's, was unchanged.

"I love you, Susie," she said.

I had heard these words so many times from my father that it shocked me now; I had been waiting, unknowingly, to hear it from my mother. She had needed the time to know that this love would not destroy her, and I had, I now knew, given her that time, could give it, for it was what I had in great supply.

She noticed a photograph on my old dresser, which Grandma Lynn had put in a gold frame. It was the very first photograph I'd ever taken of her—my secret portrait of Abigail before her family woke and she put on her lipstick. Susie Salmon, wildlife photographer, had captured a woman staring out across her misty suburban lawn.

She used the bathroom, running the tap noisily and disturbing the towels. She knew immediately that her mother had bought these towels—cream, a ridiculous color for towels—and monogrammed—also ridiculous, my mother thought. But then, just as quickly, she laughed at herself. She was beginning to wonder how useful her scorched-earth policy had been to her all these years. Her mother was loving if she was drunk, solid if she was vain. When was it all right to let go not only of the dead but of the living—to learn to accept?

I was not in the bathroom, in the tub, or in the spigot; I did not hold court in the mirror above her head or stand in miniature at the tip of every bristle on Lindsey's or Buckley's toothbrush. In some way I could not account for—had they reached a state of bliss? were my parents back together forever? had Buckley begun to tell someone his troubles? would my father's heart truly heal?—I was done yearning for them, needing them to yearn for me. Though I still would. Though they still would. Always.

Downstairs Hal was holding Buckley's wrist as it held the brush stick. "Just pass it over the snare lightly." And Buckley did and looked up at Lindsey sitting across from him on the couch.

"Pretty cool, Buck," my sister said.

"Like a rattlesnake."

Hal liked that. "Exactly," he said, visions of his ultimate jazz combo dancing in his head.

My mother arrived back downstairs. When she entered the room she saw my father first. Silently she tried to let him know she was okay, that she was still breathing the air in, coping with the altitude.

"Okay, everyone!" my grandmother shouted from the kitchen, "Samuel has an announcement to make, so sit down!"

Everyone laughed and before they realigned into their more closed selves—this being together so hard for them even if it was what they all had wanted—Samuel came into the room along with Grandma Lynn. She held a tray of champagne flutes ready to be filled. He glanced at Lindsey briefly.

"Lynn is going to assist me by pouring," he said.

"Something she's quite good at," my mother said.

"Abigail?" Grandma Lynn said.

"Yes?"

"It's nice to see you too."

"Go ahead, Samuel," my father said.

"I wanted to say that I'm happy to be here with you all."

But Hal knew his brother. "You're not done, wordsmith. Buck, give him some brush." This time Hal let Buckley do it without assistance, and my brother backed Samuel up.

"I wanted to say that I'm glad that Mrs. Salmon is home, and that Mr. Salmon is home too, and that I'm honored to be marrying their beautiful daughter."

"Hear! Hear!" my father said.

My mother stood to hold the tray for Grandma Lynn, and together they distributed the glasses across the room.

As I watched my family sip champagne, I thought about how their lives trailed backward and forward from my death and then, I saw, as Samuel took the daring step of kissing Lindsey in a room full of family, became borne aloft away from it.

These were the lovely bones that had grown around my absence: the connections—sometimes tenuous, sometimes made at great cost, but often magnificent—that happened after I was gone. And I began to see things in a way that let me hold the world without me in it. The events that my death wrought were merely the bones of a body that would become whole at some unpredictable time in the future. The price of what I came to see as this miraculous body had been my life.

My father looked at the daughter who was standing there in front of him. The shadow daughter was gone.

With the promise that Hal would teach him to do drum rolls after dinner, Buckley put up his brush and drumsticks; and the seven of them began to trail through the kitchen into the dining room, where Samuel and Grandma Lynn had used the good plates to serve her trademark Stouffer's frozen ziti and Sara Lee frozen cheesecake.

"Someone's outside," Hal said, spotting a man through the window. "It's Ray Singh!"

"Let him in," my mother said.

"He's leaving."

All of them save my father and grandmother, who stayed together in the dining room, began to go after him.

"Hey, Ray!" Hal said, opening the door and nearly stepping directly in the pie. "Wait up!"

Ray turned. His mother was in the car with the engine running.

"We didn't mean to interrupt," Ray said now to Hal. Lindsey and Samuel and Buckley and a woman he recognized as Mrs. Salmon were all crowded together on the porch.

"Is that Ruana?" my mother called. "Please ask her in."

"Really, that's fine," Ray said and made no move to come closer. He wondered, *Is Susie watching this?*

Lindsey and Samuel broke away from the group and came toward him.

By that time my mother had walked down the front path to the driveway and was leaning in the car window talking to Ruana.

Ray glanced at his mother as she opened the car door to go inside the house. "Anything but pie for the two of us," she said to my mother as they walked up the path.

"Is Dr. Singh working?" my mother asked.

"As usual," Ruana said. She watched to see Ray walking, with Lindsey and Samuel, through the door of the house. "Will you come smoke stinky cigarettes with me again?"

"It's a date," my mother said.

"Ray, welcome, sit," my father said when he saw him coming through the living room. He had a special place in his heart for the boy who had loved his daughter, but Buckley swooped into the chair next to my father before anyone else could get to him.

Lindsey and Samuel found two straight chairs from the living room and brought them in to sit by the sideboard. Ruana sat between Grandma Lynn and my mother and Hal sat alone on one end.

I realized then that they would not know when I was gone, just as they could not know sometimes how heavily I had hovered in a particular room. Buckley had talked to me and I had talked back. Even if I hadn't thought I'd been talking to him, I had. I became manifest in whatever way they wanted me to be.

And there she was again, alone and walking out in the cornfield while everyone else I cared for sat together in one room. She would always feel me and think of me. I could see that, but there was no longer anything I could do. Ruth had been a girl haunted and now she would be a woman haunted. First by accident and now by choice. All of it, the story of my life and death, was hers if she chose to tell it, even to one person at a time.

* * *

It was late in Ruana and Ray's visit when Samuel started talking about the gothic revival house that Lindsey and he had found along an overgrown section of Route 30. As he told Abigail about it in detail, describing how he had realized he wanted to propose to Lindsey and live there with her, Ray found himself asking, "Does it have a big hole in the ceiling of the back room and cool windows above the front door?"

"Yes," Samuel said, as my father grew alarmed. "But it can be fixed, Mr. Salmon. I'm sure of it."

"Ruth's dad owns that," Ray said.

Everyone was quiet for a moment and then Ray continued.

"He took out a loan on his business to buy up old places that aren't already slated for destruction. He wants to restore them," Ray said.

"My God," Samuel said.

And I was gone.

BONES

You don't notice the dead leaving when they really choose to leave you. You're not meant to. At most you feel them as a whisper or the wave of a whisper undulating down. I would compare it to a woman in the back of a lecture hall or theater whom no one notices until she slips out. Then only those near the door themselves, like Grandma Lynn, notice; to the rest it is like an unexplained breeze in a closed room.

Grandma Lynn died several years later, but I have yet to see her here. I imagine her tying it on in her heaven, drinking mint juleps with Tennessee Williams and Dean Martin. She'll be here in her own sweet time, I'm sure.

If I'm to be honest with you, I still sneak away to watch my family sometimes. I can't help it, and sometimes they still think of me. They can't help it.

After Lindsey and Samuel got married they sat in the empty house on Route 30 and drank champagne. The branches of the overgrown trees had grown into the upstairs windows, and they huddled beneath them, knowing the branches would have to be cut. Ruth's father had promised he would sell the house to them only if Samuel paid him in labor as his first employee in a restoration business. By the end of that summer, Mr. Connors had cleared the lot with the help of Samuel and Buckley and set up a trailer, which during the day would be his work quarters and at night could be Lindsey's study room.

In the beginning it was uncomfortable, the lack of plumbing and electricity, and having to go home to either one of their parents' houses to take showers, but Lindsey buried herself in school work and Samuel buried himself in tracking down the right era doorknobs and light pulls. It was a surprise to everyone when Lindsey found out she was pregnant.

"I thought you looked fatter," Buck said, smiling.

"You're one to talk," Lindsey said.

My father dreamed that one day he might teach another child to love ships in bottles. He knew there would be both sadness and joy in it; that it would always hold an echo of me.

I would like to tell you that it is beautiful here, that I am, and you will one day be, forever safe. But this heaven is not about safety just as, in its graciousness, it isn't about gritty reality. We have fun.

We do things that leave humans stumped and grateful, like Buckley's garden coming up one year, all of its crazy jumble of plants blooming all at once. I did that for my mother who, having stayed, found herself facing the yard again. Marvel was what she did at all the flowers and herbs and budding weeds. Marveling was what she mostly did after she came back—at the twists life took.

And my parents gave my leftover possessions to the Good Will, along with Grandma Lynn's things.

They kept sharing when they felt me. Being together, thinking and talking about the dead, became a perfectly normal part of their life. And I listened to my brother, Buckley, as he beat the drums.

Ray became Dr. Singh, "the real doctor in the family," as Ruana liked to say. And he had more and more moments that he chose not to disbelieve. Even if surrounding him were the serious surgeons and scientists who ruled over a world of black and white, he maintained this possibility: that the ushering strangers that sometimes appeared to the dying were not the results of strokes, that he had called Ruth by my name, and that he had, indeed, made love to me.

If he ever doubted, he called Ruth. Ruth, who had graduated from a closet to a closet-sized studio on the Lower East Side. Ruth, who was still trying to find a way to write down whom she saw and what she had experienced. Ruth, who wanted everyone to believe what she knew: that the dead truly talk to us, that in the air between the living, spirits bob and weave and laugh with us. They are the oxygen we breathe.

Now I am in the place I call this wide wide Heaven because it includes all my simplest desires but also the most humble and grand. The word my grandfather uses is *comfort.*

So there are cakes and pillows and colors galore, but underneath this more obvious patchwork quilt are places like a quiet room where you can go and hold someone's hand and not have to say anything. Give no story. Make no claim. Where you can live at the edge of your skin for as long as you wish. This wide wide Heaven is about flathead nails and the soft down of new leaves, wild roller coaster rides and escaped marbles that fall then hang then take you somewhere you could never have imagined in your small-heaven dreams.

* * *

One afternoon I was scanning Earth with my grandfather. We were watching birds skip from top to top of the very tallest pines in Maine and feeling the bird's sensations as they landed then took flight then landed again. We ended up in Manchester, visiting a diner my grandfather remembered from his days traveling up and down the East Coast on business. It had gotten seedier in the fifty intervening years and after taking stock we left. But in the instant I turned away, I saw him: Mr. Harvey coming out of the doors of a Greyhound bus.

He went into the diner and ordered a cup of coffee at the counter. To the uninitiated, he still looked every bit as ordinary as he could, except around the eyes, but he no longer wore his contacts and no one took the time to look past his thick lenses anymore.

As an older waitress passed him a Styrofoam cup full of boiling coffee, he heard a bell over the door behind him tinkle and felt a cold blast of air.

It was a teenage girl who had sat a few rows ahead of him for the last few hours, playing her Walkman and humming along with the songs. He sat at the counter until she was done using the bathroom, and then he followed her out.

I watched him trail her in the dirty snow along the side of the diner and out to the back of the bus station, where she would be out of the wind for a smoke. While she stood there, he joined her. She wasn't even startled. He was another boring old man in bad clothes.

He calculated his business in his mind. The snow and cold. The pitched ravine that dropped off immediately in front of them. The blind woods on the other side. And he engaged her in conversation.

"Long ride," he said.

She looked at him at first as if she couldn't believe he was talking to her.

"Um hmmm," she said.

"Are you traveling alone?"

It was then that I noticed them, hanging above their heads in a long and plentiful row. Icicles.

The girl put out her cigarette on the heel of her shoe and turned to go.

"Creep," she said, and walked fast.

A moment later, the icicle fell. The heavy coldness of it threw him off balance just enough for him to stumble and pitch forward. It would be weeks before the snow in the ravine melted enough to uncover him.

But now let me tell you about someone special:

Out in her yard, Lindsey made a garden. I watched her weed the long thick flower bed. Her fingers twisted inside the gloves as she thought about the clients she saw in her practice each day—how to help them make sense of the cards life had dealt them, how to ease their pain. I remembered that the simplest things were the ones that often eluded what I thought of as her big brain. It took her forever to figure out that I always volunteered to clip the grass inside the fence so I could play with Holiday while we did yard work. She remembered Holiday then, and I followed her thoughts. How in a few years it would be time to get her child a dog, once the house was settled and fenced-in. Then she thought about how there were now machines with whipcords that could trim a fence post to post in minutes—what it had taken us hours of grumbling to achieve.

Samuel walked out to Lindsey then, and there she was in his arms, my sweet butterball babe, born ten years after my fourteen years on Earth: Abigail Suzanne. Little Susie to me. Samuel placed Susie on a blanket near the flowers. And my sister, my Lindsey, left me in her memories, where I was meant to be.

* * *

And in a small house five miles away was a man who held my mud-encrusted charm bracelet out to his wife.

"Look what I found at the old industrial park," he said. "A construction guy said they were bulldozing the whole lot. They're afraid of more sinkholes like that one that swallowed the cars."

His wife poured him some water from the sink as he fingered the tiny bike and the ballet shoe, the flower basket and the thimble. He held out the muddy bracelet as she set down his glass.

"This little girl's grown up by now," she said.

Almost.

Not quite.

I wish you all a long and happy life.

ACKNOWLEDGMENTS

I owe a debt to my passionate early readers: Judith Grossman, Wilton Barnhardt, Geoffrey Wolff, Margot Livesey, Phil Hay, and Michelle Latiolais. As well as the workshop at the University of California, Irvine.

To those who joined the party late but brought the most awesome refreshments: Teal Minton, Joy Johannessen, and Karen Joy Fowler.

To the pros: Henry Dunow, Jennifer Carlson, Bill Contardi, Ursula Doyle, Michael Pietsch, Asya Muchnick, Ryan Harbage, Laura Quinn, and Heather Fain.

Abiding thanks to: Sarah Burnes, Sarah Crichton, and the glorious MacDowell Colony.

A smarty-pants badge of honor to my informants: Dee Williams, Orren Perlman, Dr. Carl Brighton, and the essential facts-on-file team of Bud and Jane.

And to my continuing troika, whose sustaining friendship and rigorous reading and rereading are, next to tapioca and coffee, what keep me going on a day-to-day basis: Aimee Bender, Kathryn Chetkovich, Glen David Gold.

And a *woof!* to Lilly.

FROM PLOUGHTAIL TO PARLIAMENT

An Autobiography

The Cresset Library

The Best Circles
Leonore Davidoff

Britain by Mass Observation
Arranged and written by Tom Harrison and Charles Madge

China: A Short Cultural History
C. P. Fitzgerald

From Ploughtail to Parliament
An Autobiography
Joseph Arch

A Short History of Ireland
J. C. Beckett

Wittgenstein
W. W. Bartley III

From Ploughtail to Parliament

An Autobiography

Joseph Arch

PREFACE BY Norman Willis

NEW INTRODUCTION BY Alun Howkins

THE CRESSET LIBRARY

London Melbourne Sydney Auckland Johannesburg

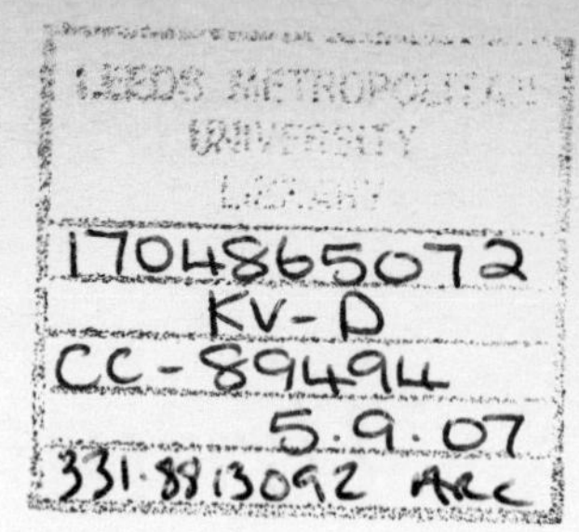

The Cresset Library

An imprint of Century Hutchinson Ltd

62–65 Chandos Place, London WC2N 4NW

Century Hutchinson Publishing Group (Australia) Pty Ltd
16–22 Church Street, Hawthorn, Melbourne, Victoria 3122

Century Hutchinson Group (NZ) Ltd
32–34 View Road, PO Box 40–086, Glenfield, Auckland 10

Century Hutchinson (SA) (Pty) Ltd
PO Box 337, Bergvlei 2012, South Africa

This edition first published 1986

Printed and bound in Great Britain by
Richard Clay (The Chaucer Press) Ltd, Bungay, Suffolk

British Library Cataloguing in Publication Data

Arch, Joseph
From ploughtail to parliament: an autobiography—
(The Cresset library; 4)
1. Arch, Joseph 2. Trade unions—
Agricultural labourers—Great Britain—
History—19th century 3. Trade unions—
Great Britain—Officials and employees
—Biography
331.88′13′0924 HD6665.A73

ISBN 0 09 168791 8

cover
Front: courtesy of the John Gorman collection
Back: courtesy of the National Museum of Labour History
The Old Limehouse Town Hall, Commercial Road, London E14

CONTENTS

Contents

PREFACE TO THE CRESSET LIBRARY EDITION

To view the life of Joseph Arch and the battles he fought for the agricultural workers from the standpoint of the late twentieth century is to be both inspired and somewhat chastened.

We cannot help but be inspired by Arch's determination and vision. What began as no more than a handful of labourers meeting under the shelter of a chestnut tree in the gloom of a February evening became in time a force which made its presence felt the length and breadth of rural England. Its achievements were mighty. Simply to have organized the agricultural workers would have been enough, given the nature of the industry and the character of the times. But to have organized them, to have gained significantly higher wages, and to have eventually in 1884 forced Parliament to grant them the vote, were mighty feats indeed. Against bitter opposition – opposition that did not scruple on one occasion to have sixteen women sent to prison with hard labour for picketting – Joseph Arch and the union doggedly struggled to help lay the foundations for not only the economic advances we enjoy today, but also for the political and social benefits.

As for the chastening effects of reading this work – it is tempting always to suppose that our struggles are the fiercest, and our foes the bitterest. Without underestimating the struggles trade unionists face today, it is worth remembering that the agricultural workers were fighting for the very right to organize at a time when they had no political power whatsoever. When wages were at starvation level, and when their employers often held over them the power of life and death itself.

Their success, and the inspiration they drew from Joseph Arch, should make us all the more determined to proclaim that what we have we hold. The right to belong to a trade union, to enjoy a decent standard of living and a safe working environment have become inalienable by the fact that so many have suffered and struggled for them.

There are many battles still to be fought on all these fronts. Joseph Arch and others like him have given today's trade unionists a good start.

Norman Willis
General Secretary
Trades Union Congress
1986

INTRODUCTION TO THE CRESSET LIBRARY EDITION

Joseph Arch was born, as this autobiography tells us, in Barford Warwickshire on 10 November 1826. His parents were poor but deeply respectable country people. His mother had been, prior to her first marriage, a servant at Warwick Castle. She was widowed in 1816 and married Joseph's father, John Arch, a farm labourer. To her marriage she bought the freehold of a cottage which put the family a little 'above' the ordinary labourers as well as giving the family a crucial independence.

Like most of England's labouring men in this period, Joseph's father lived an increasingly hand-to-mouth existence. The days of hiring by the year and regular employment were long gone as agriculture came to demand an increasingly casual workforce employed by the week or even the day. Winter presented the villager with weeks of unemployment when parish doles and the charity of parson and squire (if it was there) were all a family had. Barford was no exception. Like many Southern and Midland villages its Poor Relief payments crept up through the 1820s and into the early 1830s. Arch's family, although better off than most, felt this want. Joseph proudly says 'I never went to the rectory for soup' (p. 15) but many years saw his mother's work, in and out of the home, provide the barley bread which was their winter diet.

Yet it was poverty in the midst of plenty. From the mid 1830s the fortunes of English agriculture increased. As the labourer was ever more impoverished so the farmers and the landlords apparently grew richer. Wealth separated them more and more from those they employed. 'Work was all they wanted from him; he was to work and hold his tongue, year in and year out, early and late, and if he could not work, why, what was the use of him?' (p. 11) In many areas of England a bitter, and growing, antagonism developed between 'master and man' which is at odds with our often idyllic view of nineteenth-century rural life.

It was Arch, and many like him, who came to speak for that antagonism. For all his later moderation he never lost his deep hatred of the rural elite as a class, even if he came to admit of exceptions. When the autobiography was first published in 1898 this aspect was picked up by hostile reviewers. As *The Times* put it the book 'is marred here and there by a needless acrimony of tone [and] crude invectives as to the country clergy, "Squarsons" and Squires. . . .' But such hatred was not enough, what was needed was organization. Through his chapel connections, his membership of friendly societies and his contacts with Warwickshire Liberalism the young Arch learnt this skill. Free from fear of victimization because of his mother's cottage and his own talents as hedger and ditcher, Arch had, by the early 1870s emerged as a local figure of some importance.

Quite how important is difficult to assess. He himself plays down this aspect in the autobiography, seeking to present himself as an 'ordinary man' who was 'called' by his fellow labourers but it is clear that he had contacts with local Liberalism from at the least the early 1860s. Even in the 1840s he had saved his pence to buy old newspapers where he could read the speeches of Cobden and Bright, and by 1868, he took an active part in the general election in Warwickshire both in canvassing and on polling day. Contacts from these years were to prove vital later. At this stage of equal importance was his religion. By his early 20s he was an active member of, and a lay preacher in, the Primitive Methodists. This was a sect which had been expelled from the Wesleyan Methodists in 1811 because of the adherence to open air preaching and their insistence that they were the 'real' successors to Wesley. They were an intensely democratic sect which appealed, anyway until the 1870s, overwhelmingly to the poor. Their organization relied heavily on lay workers and they encouraged working men and women to become preachers and 'exhorters'. This training in public speaking and organization, as well as a belief in a 'democratic' gospel, made the Primitive Methodists natural leaders of their fellows.

In February 1872 'the call' came. In the previous few years the despised and impoverished farm labourers had shown signs of awakening. In Norfolk, Herefordshire, Buckinghamshire and elsewhere trades unions had appeared among the rural poor. Most were short lived; a few relied upon the support of gentry or urban sympathizers – but change was in the air. To the labourers of the Barford district Arch must have seemed a natural choice as spokesman. His radicalism was probably well known and his speaking and organizing abilities certainly were. Further, he was 'safe', he had his own cottage and his skills were in demand even among those who were the enemies of trades unions. In this he was similar to many of the local leaders who emerged in the next eighteen months all over England. The crucial difference at this stage seems to have been that Joseph Arch had a vision of a national union, where others saw things in village or at best county terms, and that he was able to draw sympathetic support from Liberalism, at first locally, but then very quickly nationally.

Arch's own account of the rise and fall of agricultural trades unionism forms the main part of the second half of the book. In this account, not surprisingly, he himself figures large. Although some of his supporters get a mention one often gets the impression that the union was simply the creation of one man. Such an account has elements of truth. There can be little doubt that Arch was a charismatic figure. His followers frequently referred to him as a 'Moses' and compared the union to the Children of Israel and the escape from Egypt. At another level his enormous energy and commitment in the early years and his continued personal power on the union's executive certainly made him a unique figure within the labourers' union.

Yet there were others who never get mentioned in the autobiography, or whose real local power and influence is either minimalized by Arch or simply seen as malign since it opposed his own. George Rix in Norfolk who split with Arch in 1878 taking with him one of the union's most powerful districts, or Alfred Simmons who organized most of Kent and Sussex outside the National, simply do not appear despite the fact that Rix had been close to Arch politically and personally in the early years. Similarly, those who opposed his increasingly arrogant and even despotic rule within the union get short shrift and their objections are put down to personal spite.

Perhaps this is inevitable in an autobiography yet it has important consequences. Arch's book is one of the few contemporary accounts of the labourer's movement and as such it has dominated historical writing on the subject. This has meant that Arch's account has very much determined how historians have judged the movement. In one way that is as it should be. Arch comes through the biography as a powerful, if puritanical, figure. His abilities cannot be doubted, nor can his achievements. Yet this has meant that many important local (and even national) figures have until recently simply not figured in accounts of the unions of the 1870s and 1880s.

The autobiography was written in 1897–8 at the behest of the radical Countess of Warwick who, in his words, 'offered to edit the work'. Quite what this means is unclear. Most of the book clearly was written by Arch and some of it appears in articles he wrote on the history of the movement in the 1870s. The material on the period before 1872 and after 1890 also bear the unmistakable anger and bitterness of one who has lived through success and defeat. This tone is strongly present in an interview between Arch and Tom Higdon, one of the leaders of the new union founded in 1906, and published in the *Labour Leader*, the newspaper of the Independent Labour Party.

Other parts clearly must have been copied either from newspaper reports of his own speeches or, as in the case of the Game Law material, from transcripts or other printed sources. But again they are clearly 'genuine'. Arch probably kept press cuttings, although they are not mentioned, and all have the ring of real speech.

The overall structure of the autobiography is characteristic of many written by Victorian working men and, very rarely, women. Its model is ultimately Bunyan's *Pilgrim's Progress*. In the 'secular' model the world, like that of Christian, is a constant series of struggles, each overcome in turn by the writer's own beliefs and abilities. Finally, as in the original, the 'Holy City' is reached. In Arch's case, as with others, this was election to Parliament as the 'Labourer's champion'.

Parliament may have been the 'Holy City' of Arch's life but his career there, from 1885–6 and then 1892–1900, was not auspicious. His speeches and interventions were restricted to topics of rural life and his real power as a speaker seems not to have worked in the chambers of Westminster. Although it must be said that in this he was better than many an elite political figure.

He was a loyal and uncritical Liberal who saw the emergence of socialism as being against the interests of working people. It was to be the next generation of labourer's leaders who took the farm worker into the Labour Party. London also played to his vanity. He was feted by sections of the Liberal Party, for a time at least, and took a slightly pathetic pride in being 'the Prince of Wales' M.P.' (Sandringham was in his constituency).

In 1900 he retired from Parliament to Barford where he lived in the cottage of his mother and grandparents on a small annuity provided by wealthy Liberal friends.

Perhaps the saddest change of all was his alienation from the labourers. He blamed the farm workers for 'deserting him' and for the collapse of the union in 1896. When the union was reformed in 1906, led by many who had been his comrades in the 1870s and 1880s, he refused to have anything to do with it. At one level this was perhaps understandable. He was an old man and his bitterness was shared by many of the leaders of the 1870s, but many did support the new union as they had supported the old. In the 1911 interview with Tom Higdon there is an overwhelming sense of disbelief about the new union and its hopes, as well as the old Arch vanity about its admittedly limited gains at that point.

He died in the cottage where he was born on 12 February 1919. His health had deteriorated during the Great War and he suffered a series of strokes leaving him increasingly incapacitated. He was buried in Barford churchyard where his grave is now marked by an impressive obelisk erected by the 'new' union about which he was so scathing in 1911. His burial by an Anglican parson was the final sign of the fact that the Primitive Methodism of his youth had effectively been abandoned in the 1890s.

In some respects Joseph Arch was not unique. That almost millennial spring of 1872 generated hundreds like him throughout the length and breadth of England. But nor is he just 'typical'. To the labourers he had a special importance and place. Few of them left their opinions – seldom do the poor speak through historical records – but occasionally they are heard. The proud and unrecalcitrant 'King of the Norfolk Poachers' says in his remarkable life story, 'at last wen (*sic*) things were as bad as they could be, Joseph Arch came along to be a champion for Labour. . . . He stood up in Norfolk and gathered the men round him, and told them they must Orgernise (*sic*). . . . Arch spent his whole life pleading the Worker's cause'. Josiah Sage, who was active in Arch's union and in its successor the National Union of Agricultural Workers, put clearly what many English labourers of the last quarter of the nineteenth century felt. 'Never before the days of Arch, nor yet since, have the ranks of the agricultural labourers produced such a man.'

Alun Howkins
University of Sussex, 1986

FURTHER READING

Those interested in Arch and his world will find Pamela Horn's *Joseph Arch: the Farm Workers' Leader* (1971) interesting. The history of the union and its successors is told in Reg Groves, *Sharpen the Sickle* (1948) and Alun Howkins *Poor Labouring Men* (1985). A good account of farming in the 1890s can be found in Henry Rider Haggard's *A Farmers Year* also published in the Cresset Library; the 'other side' can be found in 'The King of the Norfolk Poachers', *I Walked By Night* (1983).

PREFACE.

BY THE COUNTESS OF WARWICK.

"To couple my name with that of Joseph Arch gives me no displeasure. I believe him to be an honest and good man. I believe, too, that the cause he has in hand is well founded, and I confide in his using no means to promote it but such as are sanctioned by the law of God and the law of the land." *

These words of the late Cardinal Manning, uttered more than a quarter of a century ago, at a time when Arch and the Union were fiercely assailed, express my own sentiments to-day, when he and the Union have accomplished their work. Joseph Arch is a Warwickshire man, and his people have been connected with Warwick Castle for generations. It seemed to me a pity that the story of his life-work should remain

* "Life of Cardinal Manning."

untold, and I am glad to have been some small help to him in the telling of it. In doing this, I have been careful not to over-edit ; I have judged it best that he should speak for himself and express his opinions quite frankly in his own way. The chapters which deal with his early struggles, aspirations, and difficulties—aye, and his early jealousies and prejudices, too—give us an insight to the forces silently working in many an agricultural labourer's breast, and show us with what travail the Union was brought forth. It is good for us to see things sometimes through another's eyes. But it will, of course, be understood that with all the opinions expressed in his pages I do not necessarily agree.

If it were possible to separate the man from the work (which it is not), I should regard the history of the National Agricultural Labourers' Union as far more important than any personal record. I look upon the Union as one of the most remarkable movements of modern times. The phrase is commonplace, but it is true ; the Union was remarkable alike in its inception, progress, and achievement ; and in the social history of England it must henceforth fill a prominent place. I know of no movement, *working always within the four corners of the law*, which accomplished so much in so short a time. For, what are the facts ? A

Warwickshire peasant, at first alone and unaided, started and led an organisation which revolutionised the condition of the agricultural labourer. From small beginnings—a handful of labourers, a hurried meeting under an old chestnut tree in the gloom of a February evening—an agitation was set on foot, which rapidly grew from strength to strength until it permeated the length and breadth of rural England. It was no barren agitation merely; for coincident with its growth was a visible improvement in the moral and material condition of those for whom it was organised. The Union is known by its fruits. We have only to compare the condition of the agricultural labourer before the Union was started, with his condition to-day, to see that these fruits are manifold. The late Dr. Fraser, the well-known Bishop of Manchester, then vicar of a country parish, bore eloquent witness before a Royal Commission in the sixties as to the deplorable state of things existing at that time in many rural districts. Bread was dear, and wages down to starvation point; the labourers were uneducated, underfed, underpaid; their cottages were often unfit for human habitation, the sleeping and sanitary arrangements were appalling. Naturally, they took colour from their environment. How could any of the things which make for the beauty and the joy of life, morality, or even common decency, exist in such inhuman homes? In many a country village the condition of the labourer and his family was but little removed from that of the cattle they tended.

If we ask how these things came about and were suffered to continue, we are sorrowfully constrained to admit that the agricultural labourer in those days had few friends, either in his own class or in any other. He had no organisation, the Trades Unions let him alone; he had no money, the professional agitator ignored him; he had no vote, the politician passed him by. His lot was indeed a hard one; and, though of course there were many places where it had ameliorations—villages where the poor were well looked after; estates where the owners made it their duty to see their labourers were well housed and fairly paid—yet the ameliorations were comparatively few; and even they came, not as a right—the right of every honest working-man to a fair wage and decent condition of life—but rather as a charity, and so helped to weaken that spirit of independence which is an Englishman's birthright. Agricultural depression (a very real obstacle now) could hardly then be urged as an excuse; for at the time when wheat was dearest and land most valuable, the lot of the agricultural labourer was at its worst. These are unpleasant facts, but it is idle to blink at them, since they were the things which made the Union possible—and desirable.

The natural result of this state of affairs was a rankling sense of injustice among the agricultural labourers. The discontent was sullen, inchoate, voiceless, hardly apparent on the surface; but it was there all the same. The tide of social betterment was beginning to flow strongly in the towns, and it agitated even the stagnant backwaters of remote agricultural districts. The peasant, ignorant and illiterate though he was, could hardly remain insensible to the fact that, while the condition of workmen in other industries was improving, his remained the same. And this thought added to his dumb discontent. People have said it was the Union which caused discontent; on the contrary, it was discontent which caused the Union. In the Union the legitimate discontent of the agricultural labourer found its legitimate outlet. The labourers were crying for a man to lead them, to organise them, to voice their needs. The time was ripe and the man came; fortunately he was an honest and law-abiding one. One trembles to think what might have happened if the movement had been in less capable hands. The situation had in it all the elements of danger; inflammatory appeals to the prejudices of an ignorant and suffering peasantry would have lighted a fire difficult to quench, and would probably have put back the movement for their betterment at least a generation. Arch was no firebrand, but rather a "village Hampden," who put the welfare of the cause he had espoused before any personal ambition. In my opinion he was the man of the moment, the indispensable man. As Lord Rosebery said recently :

"There are junctures in the affairs of men when what is wanted is a man : not treasures, not fleets, not legends, but a man, the man of the moment, the man of the occasion, the man of destiny, whose spirit attracts, binds and inspires, whose capacity is congenial to the crisis, whose powers are equal to the convulsion. . . . The crisis is the travail, the birth of the man ends or assuages it."*

Such a man was Joseph Arch. The Union was his and he led it ; and I think we owe him gratitude—not the labourer only but every one connected with the land—that he led it wisely and well.

It is very difficult for us now, when the turmoil has ended, to realise the state of affairs when Arch came to the front, or the tempest of feeling which his coming raised. Yet we must try to do so, if we

* Lord Rosebery on Sir William Wallace.

are to form a just estimate of his work. In this connexion a friend writes to me :

"I well remember the immense surprise which the revolt of Hodge occasioned in the North. It was as if the dead had come to life. We regarded the movement with intense expectation and hope. It had seemed to us impossible that there should be any stirring of the dry bones. The agricultural labourer had seemed hopeless. The serfs of the plough had lost even the aspiration to be free men. Such at least was the prevailing opinion when Joseph Arch arose.

"We hailed him as another Moses, and rejoiced exceedingly in the belief that his advent heralded the dawn of a happier social system, more compatible with the natural dignity of man.

"Several things combined to interest the public in the movement. It was a time ot unrest. The town workmen had only a few years before received the franchise. The French Empire had just gone down under the blows of the German Army. The Education Act was just getting into working order. Everywhere there was a ferment in the minds of men. That it had at last affected even the Midland peasants proved how deep and wide the leaven of change was working.

"The old order was indeed changing and giving place to the new, and those who believed in progress, and were perhaps more alive to the evils and abuses of the old, than to the danger of the new, were loud in rejoicings over the revolt of Hodge.

"One thing that much helped the movement was the

direct and unmistakeable religious sentiment which found expression at the early meetings of the labourers. The revolt was thereby linked on to the old Civil Wars, when the Puritan preacher was the soul of the army of the Commonwealth. Most of the leaders of the strike were Methodist local preachers. In no instance, I am told by one who was in the midst of the movement, was one of the agitators trained for the work in the Established Church. This linked the movement on to Nonconformists everywhere, and when Bishop Ellicott uttered his famous remark about the horsepond the Midland Dissenters felt that the hour of victory was nigh.

"Another thing that appealed to the imagination was the extent to which the meetings of the strikers were inspired by song. The hymn tunes were easily linked to the verses in which the labourers expressed their hopes, and embodied their demands. The industrial revolt had in it some of the elements of a religious revival, and one of the most conspicuous of these was the resort to singing as a relief of emotions otherwise difficult to articulate.

"The industrial significance of the Union and its religious suggestiveness were, however, less important than the effect which it had on politics. The revolt of Hodge was the finishing blow to the old régime. It heralded the advent of rural democracy. The politician had never hoped much from the rural labourer. Logically he was of course entitled to a vote. But it was feared he would be as clay in the hands of the potter, in the hands of the squire and the parson. Joseph Arch dispelled that dread. He revealed the labourer as a factor, a real, living, potent factor, in the land. From that conviction sprang the Reform Bill which in 1884 enfranchised the country householders, and placed the constitution of the House of Commons on a frankly democratic basis.

"Great things, therefore, have sprung from that revolt of the serfs, and although many hopes were disappointed, and the millennium is still to seek, who can say that Joseph Arch has not been justified by the results of the great impetus which he gave to the cause of progress at a critical moment?"

The Union was necessary. What power has the poor man if he have not combination? The right to combine belongs to us all. The agricultural labourer has used his right with excellent results. First the grain, then the ear, then the full corn in the ear. First organisation, then higher wages and all which that means, and then the protection and power of the Parliamentary vote. With the franchise the agricultural labourer became politically a free man. And recent legislation, in the direction of allotments, free education, parish councils and so forth, has recognised that henceforth his interests are to be considered. The vote procured him this recognition and legislation; the Union procured him the vote. More than that, the vote is exercising an educational influence and awakening a sense of responsibility which was dormant. The labourer's horizon has widened; he is no longer content to plod on as before; there has quickened in him a laudable ambition to improve his condition ; desires have awakened in him for a higher standard of living, better cottages, more leisure for self-improvement, and some surer provision against sickness and old age.

The supreme achievement of the Union, its culminating point as it were, was the franchise for the agricultural labourer. When that was obtained the Union was no longer politically necessary, and it died a natural death. Should there be agricultural labourers' unions in the future, they will probably be of a purely local kind.

The labourer has now political power ; it remains for him to use it wisely. The legislature, moreover, has placed local machinery at his command whereby he can benefit himself in divers ways. He needs guiding to use this machinery aright, and those who are in a position to do so, should help him by throwing the weight of their local influence into the local scale. It is their duty to help him to help himself and others, to respect himself and others. He must be helped to develop himself on his own lines, and to develop the material resources at his disposal. Adequate education, elementary and technical, is what the agricultural labourer now needs most of all. With education he can equip himself and his children for their lifework and so take a place in the community and fill it—not mis-fill it. Help the square peg to the square hole ; the round peg to the round hole. In the average labourer's family there will generally be found some children who are fitted by nature for work other than that of cultivating the land ; this being so, give them a chance of developing for right use any natural gift or faculty they may possess. Those who have local influence should see that an efficient technical school is within reach of these children, be they boys or girls. Many of course will drift away from the villages to the large centres of population ; many to London. This is inevitable ; but, if they are equipped with a good education, they will play their proper part in the struggle of life, and will become useful and self-respecting members of the community, whether their lot be cast in town or country.

I have noticed that a curious jealousy exists among some agricultural labourers against machinery. But education will bring about a proper adjustment between the agricultural machine and the agricultural labourer. The man will learn how to utilise the machine to the utmost for his own benefit ; with a fuller knowledge he will make it co-operate with him, instead of allowing it to compete with him. Education, technical education, will also teach the labourer to make use of other means of improving his position, which now too often are lying idle by his hands; and it is here that the local owners and occupiers of the land can help him too. Allotments, small holdings, dairies, poultry-yards, gardens, bee-keeping, pig-keeping, and so forth, as well as various local industries and crafts, should be fostered. The housing of the labourers also, alas! too often needs improvement. Village shops might be developed into co-operative stores. In short everything which tends to make the village a centre of wholesome life should be heartily encouraged. Co-operation, on the basis of mutual good will, is what is wanted, for in this way we may come to a better understanding of each other's needs, know one another better and help one another more.

I am all in favour of fostering the local spirit. Make a man proud of, and interested in, his birthplace or locality—make him feel he has a part in it—and you have started him on the road to good citizenship. Some will remain strongly local all their lives; others will broaden and widen from the local basis. The right and natural development is from home to neighbouring homes; then to the homes of the parish, the district, the county, the country, the empire, the world. But everything depends on individual effort; the man must help himself if he is to help others. Surely the career of Joseph Arch, who fought his way up from the plough-tail to a seat in Parliament, is an apt illustration of this truth; and he won his fight, be it remembered, without any of the advantages which surround the agricultural labourers nowadays, and which he was so largely instrumental in securing for them.

I have said there are some expressions of opinion in this book with which I do not altogether agree, though I respect the honest spirit which dictated them. One of them refers to the somewhat sweeping strictures on the country clergy. What they may have been in the days of which Joseph Arch has written I have, of course, no personal knowledge; the dead hand was on the Church in those days, and sympathy with the people was certainly not a strong point with the clergy. As no less an authority than Dean Stubbs has put it: "Popular reforms in all ages and all countries, from the Prophet Amos down to Joseph Arch, have rarely met with much favour from the established authorities in either Church or State." * But it would be unfair to ignore the fact that this reproach has now been largely wiped away,

* "Village Politics," by the Dean of Ely.

and there exists no body of men more anxious to do their duty than the country clergy. There are many landowners, too, both great and small, despite the agricultural depression which has hit them hard, who are most desirous, and have always been desirous, to do all that in them lies to help their poorer brethren, and to sympathise with their needs and aspirations ; and this in no spirit of patronage, but in the spirit of love. I believe this spirit is deepening and broadening every day, and in it may be read one of the most encouraging signs of the times. Whatever may be the immediate issues of the hour, social questions constitute the politics of the future. But these questions will never be settled satisfactorily until all classes of the community are willing to work for the common good.

FRANCES EVELYN WARWICK.

JOSEPH ARCH:

The Story of His Life.

MY FOREWORD.

ALTHOUGH it has been frequently suggested to me that a review of the chief events in my chequered career, during the greater part of which I figured prominently before the public, would prove or interest to those whose lot it is to labour and to toil, and perhaps even to others, I never until now seriously entertained the idea of attempting to write a book. When, however, the illustrious and noble lady whose name adorns the title-page did me the great and unexpected honour to come forward, and most generously offer to edit the work, I could no longer resist.

I am in the sere and yellow leaf; my race is nearly run; my work will soon be over: I may therefore be pardoned for pleading at the outset that a kind and indulgent reading public will view with tolerant eyes such faults and failings as must necessarily appear in the following pages.

It is the life-story of an English agricultural labourer,—of a man who has undergone many and varied experiences, who has borne severe toil, privations, and hardships, and who was blessed with few social advantages or privileges, yet who was endued by Nature with a robust, healthy, and sturdy constitution, a dogged determination, and a steady, plodding perseverance, which culminated eventually in more than ordinary success. Should the perusal of such a "plain, unvarnised tale" act as a spur to effort, or should it encourage the young man reader in a worthy ambition to improve his condition socially, mentally, and morally, this unpretending volume will not have been written in vain.

CHAPTER I.

CHILDHOOD.

I WAS born at Barford, in Warwickshire, on November 10th, 1826. This village, situated on a bend of willow-fringed Avon, possesses a fine old bridge of grey stone, and in its straggling street there are houses still in existence, with peaked gables and projecting frames and eaves of darkened wood, which William Shakespeare may have seen, and even entered. Warwick Castle and the county town are within three miles, and Stratford-on-Avon lies not quite seven miles away; so my country—and I am proud to say it—is Shakespeare's country, and my home, and what was the home of many of my forefathers as well, lies right in the very heart of old England.

Three generations of Arches sleep the sleep of the just in Barford churchyard. They were, every one of them, honest, upright, hardworking children of the soil; good men and true, ancestors any man might be right proud to own. Some of my Warwickshire forbears fought with Cromwell at Edgehill, and in other battles of the Civil War, against tyranny and oppression and for the liberty of the people. I expect that is where I get my fighting propensities from; fighting was in the blood, and I just harked back to those old Roundhead ancestors of mine, who struck many a brave and sturdy blow on the right side.

Within a stone's throw of the graveyard, and nearly opposite the parish church with its fifteenth-century tower, stands the homely cottage in which I first saw the light. It has been in the possession of the Arch family for a good hundred and fifty years. Though repairs and alterations and improvements, including a new slated roof and the addition of a small greenhouse, give it a modern appearance, the open chimney and the black beams in the ceiling of the living-room show its true age plainly enough; so do the black beams of the gable at the back, which overlooks my workshop and my half-acre of garden. My grandfather bought the freehold of the cottage and little garden from a man named Thomas Ashley, for the sum of thirty pounds.

This grandfather was a famous hedger and ditcher in his day, a man who did with all his might whatever he put his hand to; and judging from all accounts he must have put his hand to a lot of things from his youth upwards. He came to hold a very good and responsible position under one of the Earls of Warwick. My grandmother was also employed by the same earl. They lived for several years at the Lodge, Warwick Park. They were a thrifty, hard-working couple, respected and looked up to by their neighbours. It was while they were living at the Lodge that they contrived to save up the thirty pounds. Little by little, coin by coin, they stored up the hard-earned money in what I may call the poor man's Post Office Savings Bank of that day—a stocking.

Well, I have good reason to remember that same old stocking with gratitude—and I do—for out of it came forth, as it were, the cottage and bit of land I call mine to-day.

My grandmother was one of a strong, well-grown stock, born and brought up in Oxfordshire. She certainly was a remarkably fine old woman, standing six feet four inches in height, and she had three brothers to match her ; each of my great-uncles stood well over six feet four. She was long-lived, being nearly ninety when she died, and she kept her faculties up to the last. Although I was only about six years old, I can recall some of her sayings and doings clearly, and very quaint they were.

My father was a Barford man, and my mother was a Warwickshire woman, so I come directly of Warwickshire stock on both sides. My father was a shepherd when he married and brought my mother to the cottage where they lived and died, and where their four children were born—two boys and two girls. My elder brother died young; if he had lived he would have inherited our cottage. My father was a sober, industrious, agricultural labourer, steady as old Time, a plodding man, and a good all-round worker, who could turn his hand to anything, like his father before him.

He was quiet and peaceable by nature, no fighter ; he did not agree with those who were ready to pick a quarrel and stir up strife for a trifle ; on the contrary he was too much inclined to let people take advantage of him. But he could be independent and show a stiff back if it came to a question of principle ; and he had no mind to bend his neck to squire or parson for the sake of their doles, when they wanted him to do what he thought was wrong. Quiet man though he was, he had his opinions, and he could stick to them on occasion. He showed that, to his cost and ours, when he refused to sign a petition in favour of the Corn Laws.

This petition was properly hall-marked by the local magnates ; they sanctioned it, and they put their signatures to it ; but my father was a staunch Repealer, and would have nothing whatever to do with such a document. He was made to pay, and we with him, for his honest adherence to principle. Because he dared to speak out and assert what he believed to be right and true ; because he, a poor labourer, stood firm for Repeal ; because he held on to his opinion, he was a marked man for the rest of his life. He did not turn aside for that though, and try to put matters straight for himself again by currying favour with the magnates ; he just plodded steadily on, doing his own work day by day, rearing his family without reproach, on low wages, and in hard times.

My mother, whose first husband had been a coachman in a gentleman's family, was of a different character. She was shrewd, strong-willed, and self-reliant; always able to hold every inch of her own with anybody with whom she came into contact. In personal appearance she was a fine, big, stout, healthy-looking woman, and I am as like her as two pins. The following anecdote will serve to show my mother's strength of will and determination of character.

In our village we had a most despotic parson's wife, a kind of would-be lady pope, and one day she took it into her head to issue a decree. She gave out that all the girls attending school were to have their hair cut round like a basin, more like prison girls than anything else. My mother put her foot down, and said she never would allow her daughters to have their hair cut in such an unsightly way. When she heard this, the parson's wife became very nasty; and she could be uncommonly nasty when she chose. She proceeded to make things very uncomfortable for my mother; but she had met her match, and more, in the agricultural labourer's wife. My mother fought it out inch by inch, and though she had a tough fight of it she won in the end. But the parson's wife never forgave her for it. My father, if he had been left to himself, would have given in at once, for the sake of peace and quietness —he was against offending the "powers that be" in a general way—but my mother pulled too strong for him. She went out and did battle, but from that time my parents never received a farthing's-worth of charity in the way of soup, coals, or the like, which were given regularly, and as a matter of course, from the rectory to nearly every poor person in the village.

But though this was an unfair deprivation and a real hardship besides, with wages at nine shillings or, at the very most, twelve shillings a week, my mother would not let it trouble her; she was too independent for that. There was no cringing, no time-serving, and no cant about her. If ever there was a practical, just, devoted, and good woman she was; but cant and talk for talking's sake she could not abide. She did not hold with quarrelling for quarrelling's sake either. She always used to say to me when I got into a bit of a quarrel, and that was not seldom, "Oh, my boy, that won't do; he who would have friends must show himself friendly"; and all through my later life I have never gone anywhere without making friends, simply by following out her teaching.

There was another principle which she fastened on my mind, and that was self-reliance and self-help. Over and over again she would say to me, "What you can do for yourself, my boy, when you grow up to be a man, never let anybody else do for you"; and I have kept that advice before me all my life. She was a fine woman, and if ever a man truly loved and admired his mother I did! The training I had from her—the teaching, the example, and the advice—was the training that made me, and shaped my life.

She was a great admirer of Shakespeare. She used

to talk about him very often, and she was well versed in his works. She would read bits aloud to me of an evening, and tell me tales from the plays. On Sundays she used to read the Bible to me in the same way, and tell me stories from it. Shakespeare and the Bible were the books I was brought up on, and I don't want any better. I have heard and read a good deal since then, but I have never come across anything to beat them.

She was also a splendid hand at writing letters. A great many of the poor people who had children and relatives away from home, but who could not write to them, used to come to my mother and ask her to write their letters for them. She did it with pleasure ; she was always willing to help her friends, and even her enemies if they wanted help. There was nothing vindictive or mean about her, she had too large a heart for that. A more upright, capable, kindly, and motherly woman never drew breath ; her heart was full of sympathy, and her brain of resource. You might count on her giving the right kind of help at a pinch ; if you were in a difficulty she was always ready to come to the rescue ; and if you happened to be in a tight place she would generally manage to find a way out.

Before her marriage she had been in domestic service at Warwick Castle ; she was a first-rate laundress and an excellent nurse, and she did not hide these talents in a napkin.

I may truly say that my sisters and I owed our lives

to her twice over, for she saved us from being starved to death one winter. It was 1835, the winter of the Repeal of the Corn Laws. I was about nine years old. I well remember eating barley bread, and seeing the tears in my poor mother's eyes as she cut slices off a loaf; for even barley loaves were all too scarce, and especially with us just then. Because my father had refused to sign for "a small loaf and a dear one," he could not get any work whatever for eighteen weeks. He tried hard to get a job, but it was useless; he was a marked man, and we should have starved if my mother had not kept us all by her laundry work.

It was a terrible winter. No one who has not gone through it, or has not witnessed something similar, can realise *how* terrible it was. The scenes I witnessed then made an indelible impression on my mind. I have often told the Tories, "You caused the iron to enter into my soul very young, and you will never draw it out. It will remain there till I die." That barley bread got into my vitals.

There was corn enough for everybody—that was the hard, cruel part of it—but those who owned it would not sell it out when it was so sorely needed. They kept it back, they locked it up; and all the time the folk were crying out in their extremity for bread,—crying out to men who hardened their hearts and turned deaf ears to the hungry cries of their starving fellow-creatures. To make as much money as they could, by letting corn rise to famine prices, was all the owners of it cared about. "Make money at any price" was their motto. They belonged to the class of men who always try to turn to their own profit the miseries, the misfortunes, and the helplessness or their poorer neighbours. They grew fat at the expense of their fellows. Those who ruled in high places, and had the making of the laws in their hands, were chiefly rich landowners and successful traders, and instead of trying to raise the people, create a higher standard of comfort and well-being, and better their general condition, they did their best—or worst—to keep them in a state of poverty and serfdom, of dependence and wretchedness. Those who owned and held the land believed, and acted up to their belief as far as they were able, that the land belonged to the rich man only, that the poor man had no part nor lot in it, and had no sort of claim on society. If a poor man dared to marry and have children, they thought he had no *right* to claim the necessary food wherewith to keep himself and his family alive. They thought, too, every mother's son of them, that, when a labourer could no longer work, he had lost the right to live. Work was all they wanted from him ; he was to work and hold his tongue, year in and year out, early and late, and if he could not work, why, what was the use of him ? It was what he was made for, to labour and toil for his betters, without complaint, on a starvation wage. When no more work could be squeezed out of him, he was no better than a cumberer of other folk's ground, and the proper place for such as he was the churchyard, where he would be sure to lie quiet under a few feet of earth, and want neither food nor wages any more. A quick death and a cheap burying—that was the motto of those extortioners for the poor man past work.

Being a little chap at the time, I did not realise all that—it was not likely—but I remembered what I saw with my own eyes and heard with my own ears. About the time of the Repeal things had got so bad that they could hardly be worse. The food we could get was of very poor quality, and there was far too little of it. Meat was rarely, if ever, to be seen on the labourer's table ; the price was too high for his pocket,—a big pocket it was, but with very little in it ; next to nothing most days, and sometimes nothing at all ! In many a household even a morsel of bacon was considered a luxury. Flour was so dear that the cottage loaf was mostly of barley. Tea ran to six and seven shillings a pound, sugar would be eightpence a pound, and the price of other provisions was in proportion. If fresh meat is still scarcer than it should be in the labourer's cottage to-day, he can at any rate get good wheaten bread and plenty of potatoes ; but in the twenties and thirties he had neither wheaten bread nor a plentiful supply of potatoes to fall back on. In the country districts generally potatoes were exceedingly scarce. In our own neighbourhood there were none to speak of ; only one man near us grew them, and he hoarded them up. With corn at a prohibitive price, with fresh meat hardly ever within their reach, with what potatoes there were hoarded up and not for their buying—you see, that potato-hoarder was only following the wicked example of the corn-owners!—what, in the name of necessity, were the people to do? They could not grow potatoes; they had no allotments then, they had no hope of them, and the bulk of the labourers had no gardens.

Well, these people—people, mind you, who were clearing and planting and tilling the land, who were putting their very lives into it—in order to keep body and soul together, and some kind of roof other than the workhouse over their miserable heads, were driven to steal the food they could not get for love or money. Yes, would-be honest Englishmen were forced to become common thieves. They stole turnips from the fields, potatoes when they could get them, and any other edible thing they could lay hands on. You see, they were ravenous; they were starving. I have no doubt that if our Warwickshire earth had been eatable some of these poor sons of the soil, like the Andaman Islanders, would have tried to nourish themselves on it, so hard pressed were they. They were rendered so desperate through hunger that they defied the law and its terrors every day.

As they were unable to procure fresh meat honestly, they stole that as well. Poaching became so prevalent that it is hardly an exaggeration to say that every other man you met was a poacher. It is my deliberate opinion that these men were to some extent justified in their actions; they had by hook or by crook to obtain food somewhere, in order to enable themselves, their wives, and their children to live at all, to keep the breath in their bodies. Necessity knows no law but its own. I have always been one for keeping the laws of the land and upholding them as far as possible; but how can I blame these men because they would not sit still, and let the life be starved out of them and theirs? They would not; so they risked their liberty, the next dearest thing they had—though it was a poor enough liberty at the best—in their endeavours to obtain food. The horrors of those times are clearly and vividly before my mind's eye even now. It is as if they had been burned and branded into me. I cannot forget them.

There is one thing, however, for which I shall always be thankful, and the thought of it is like a bright spot in that dark, black time. I am glad to say that, even when things were at their very worst with us, my father was never obliged to go out and steal food. We grew carrots and turnips in our garden, and we had not to pay anything out for rent. There was always some money coming in. There was my father's wage, which varied from eight to ten shillings a week, and during those eighteen weeks, when he was without work, my mother, as I have already said, turned to and managed to earn sufficient to keep our heads above water—above ground rather! No, though it is true that things were as bad as bad could be with us, all through that bitter, hard winter my parents remained both honest and independent. They had a long, tough fight of it, but they kept their heads up bravely; they stole from no man, nor did they take alms from any one ; they never sank down to the level of the thief and the pauper. It had never been my mother's policy to take alms. She was always willing and ready to accept a kindness and to return one, but she did not wish any one to help her while she was able to help herself; and when she had finished her work she wanted to draw her money, and spend it at her leisure and as she liked, without interference from anybody.

Numbers of people used to go to the rectory for soup, but not a drop of it did we touch. I have stood at our door with my mother, and I have seen her face look sad as she watched the little children toddle past, carrying the tin cans, and their toes coming out of their boots. "Ah, my boy," she once said, "you shall never, never do that. I will work these fingers to the bone before you have to do it!" She was as good as her word—*I never went to the rectory for soup.*

My mother, as might be expected, was not in favour at the rectory from the first. She did not order herself lowly and reverently towards her betters according to the Church Catechism. She had no betters for the matter of that,—not in Barford. She would not duck down to the rector's wife just because she happened to be the rector's wife, and she was not properly and humbly thankful for coals and soup. She showed plainly that she put a value on herself as a free and independent woman, and she would not stoop to beg favours of any one, let it be squire or parson or rich farmer. Threatening and bullying would not make her budge an inch—just the contrary. She had a good sound head on her shoulders, and when once she had thought a thing out and made up her mind about it she would stick to her opinion through thick and thin. The lady-despot at the rectory did not want to have anything to do with a woman of that kind; a woman with grit, and a good stiff backbone, had no business to be in the village at all, she thought. That a labourer's wife should ever have dared to stand up against her sacred authority was gall and wormwood to her.

Of course, if my mother had been a strong churchwoman, and a regular churchgoer, things would have been all the other way. If she had been ready to conform to the Church as by law established, the rector and his wife would have put up with a good deal of independence, and would have overlooked a lot of plain-speaking about other matters. But she was not appealed to by the Church service, and she did not hold with the Church teaching. It was not that she was an irreligious woman—very far from it; but there seemed very little practical religion in the Church in those days, and it was quite enough for her if preaching and practice did not go together. All men are equal in the sight of God, but if the parson preached that doctrine he did not act up to it in God's House. In the parish church the poor man and his wife were shown pretty plainly where they came among their fellow-creatures and fellow-worshippers—men and women of the same flesh and blood, and of like passions with themselves, however superior they might seem to be in the eyes of the world because they were rich and high-placed. In the parish church the poor were apportioned their lowly places, and taught that they must sit in them Sunday after Sunday all their lives long. They must sit meekly and never dare to mingle with their betters in the social scale. It was an object lesson repeated week after week, one which no one could mistake, and it sank deep into my mind.

I remember a thing which made my mother very angry. The parson's wife issued a decree, that the labourers should sit on one side of the church and their wives on the other. When my mother heard of it she said, "No, 'those whom God hath joined together let no man put asunder,' and certainly no woman shall!"

I can also remember the time when the parson's wife used to sit in state in her pew in the chancel, and the poor women used to walk up the church and make a curtsey to her before taking the seats set apart for them. They were taught in this way that they had to pay homage and respect to those "put in authority over them," and made to understand that they must "honour the powers that be," as represented in the rector's wife. You may be pretty certain that many of these women did not relish the curtsey-scraping and other humiliations they had to put up with, but they were afraid to speak out. They had their families to think of, children to feed and clothe somehow ; and when so many could not earn a living wage, but only a half-starving one, when very often a labouring man was out of work for weeks at a stretch,—why, the wives and mothers learned to take thankfully whatever was doled out to them at the parsonage or elsewhere, and drop the curtsey expected of them, without making a wry face. A smooth face and a smooth tongue was what their benefactors required of them, and they got both. It was only human nature that the poor "had-nots" should look up to the "hads" and be obedient to their wishes ; especially when the "hads" gave to the "had-nots" out of their abundance, dropped a few pence into the wife's hand when the husband's pocket was empty, or sent the family enough for a bite and a sup when the cottage cupboard was as bare as Mother Hubbard's.

With bowed head and bended knee the poor learned to receive from the rich what was only their due, had they but known it. Years of poverty had ground the spirit of independence right out of them ; these wives and mothers were tamed by poverty, they were cowed by it, as their parents had been before them in many cases, and the spirit of servitude was bred in their very bones. And the worst of it was the mischief did not stop at the women—it never does. They set an example of spiritless submission, which their children were only too inclined to follow. Follow it too many of them did, and they and their children are reaping the consequences and paying the price of it to-day.

I can remember when the squire and the other local magnates used to sit in state in the centre of the aisle. They did not, if you please, like the look of the agricultural labourers. Hodge sat too near them, and even in his Sunday best he was an offence to their eyes. They also objected to Hodge looking at them, so they had curtains put up to hide them from the vulgar gaze. And yet, while all this was going on, while the poor had to bear with such high-handed dealings, people wondered why the Church had lost its hold, and continued to lose its hold, on the labourers in the country districts! It never had any hold on me—in that, I was my mother's son also. I never took the Communion in the parish church in my life. When I was seven years old I saw something which prevented me once for all. One Sunday my father was going to stop to take the Communion, and I, being a boy, had of course to go out before it began. I may here mention that the church door opened then in a direct line with the chancel and the main aisle, so that anybody looking through the keyhole could easily see what was going on inside. The door is now more to the side of the church, and out of direct line with the chancel. I was a little bit of a fellow, and curious. I said to myself, "What does father stop behind for? What is it they do? I'll see." So I went out of church, closed the door, placed my eye at the keyhole and peeped through, and what I saw will be engraved on my mind until the last day of my life. That sight caused a wound which has never been healed. My proud little spirit smarted and burned when I saw what happened at that Communion service.

First, up walked the squire to the communion rails; the farmers went up next; then up went the tradesmen, the shopkeepers, the wheelwright, and the blacksmith; and then, the very last of all, went the poor agricultural labourers in their smock frocks. They walked up by themselves; nobody else knelt with them; it was as if they were unclean—and at that sight the iron entered straight into my poor little heart and remained fast embedded there. I said to myself, "If that's what goes on—never for me!" I ran home and told my mother what I had seen, and I wanted to know why my father was not as good in the eyes of God as the squire, and why the poor should be forced to come up last of all to the table of the Lord. My mother gloried in my spirit.

I have heard, difficult as it is to believe, that much the same thing goes on in several villages even now, notably in Wiltshire. Perhaps the difference between the rich and the poor may not be driven home in so marked a manner in country churches as it was in the thirties; but if it is not, it is because they are afraid of us now, and dare not show up in their true colours. The dragon of caste is only scotched, not killed; he is a tough, scaly old monster, and many a sturdy blow will have to be struck at him yet, before he wriggles his last. He has been wounded in the fight;

we have fought with him, and some of the life blood has flowed out of him, but he is only lying low ; his mouth is there and his teeth are ready, and if we give him the chance, he will turn and bite as hard as ever he did.

My father was a very regular churchgoer. Wet or shine he would be in his place of a Sunday; he went as regularly and as steadily as a wound-up eight-day clock. I used to puzzle my little head over it. I used to say to myself, "Why ever does father go and put up with such treatment?" I suppose he kept on going because he had been brought up to it. To church he had always been accustomed to go, so to church he went. And there were other working men like him in that.

My mother was different. To do a thing just because she had done it before was not her way; her reason, her judgment, and her will were always active. She did not agree with Church teaching, and she did not hold with parsons' ways. She did not say, "Whatever is, is right"; she thought that a great deal of what was, was wrong. She was a dissenter by nature and by conviction.

There was no chapel in our village, but when I was about fourteen years of age some dissenters began to come over from Wellsbourne. They used to hold meetings in a back lane. When the parson got wind of it, he and his supporters, the farmers, dared the labourers to go near these unorthodox Christians. If we did, then good-bye to all the charities; no more soup and coals should we have. And it was no idle threat. If that was not religious persecution I should like to know what was! They knew they had the labourers under their thumbs, and so they put the screw on when it pleased them. Of course we had long ago seen the last of the soup and the coals; they had been stopped when my mother fought over the hair-cutting. I well remember going with my mother to listen to these dissenters. They used to preach under an old barn in the back lane. Rough and ready men were they, dressed in their fustian coats, earnest and devoted to the truth as they saw it, good men all—they have gone home now. God rest them!

CHAPTER II.

BOYHOOD TO MANHOOD.

WHEN I look back to the days of my boyhood and live them over again in memory, I can see what a lot of truth there is in the well-known saying, "The hand which rocks the cradle, rules the world." It is my opinion, however, that pretty nearly everything depends on the kind of rocking. If the hand which rocks is a weak and unsteady one, why, then the poor babe will be jerked and shaken, and his walk through life will most likely be jerky and unsteady too; he will be more or less of a wobbler and a shirker, he will not march straight and steady to his mark. There will not be much of the ruler about him; he may reckon on being trodden down, and other folk will rule him.

They used to say and believe that fairies, good and bad, came to the cradle of the new-born babe with gifts. Well, I don't think there are many who believe that nowadays, but like all those old tales there was some sort of a truth behind it. My mother was my good fairy, in a manner of saying. She gave me the right-down good gifts of a healthy body and a strong brain, and she passed on to me some of the qualities for which I can take no particular credit to myself, such as sympathy with my fellow-creatures, integrity, and steadfastness of purpose. She rocked her cradle so firmly and so well that she rocked in as much of the good as she could manage, and she rocked out all the bad she could get at, and she got at more than a little. All her life she taught my sisters and myself by her precepts and her example; she educated us in the true sense of the word. She did her part towards making fair scholars of us by supplementing what instruction we got at the village school, and she continued to teach me in my spare time after I left. At that time a child was not qualified to begin his schooling until he was six years old; there was no such blessed thing as an infant school. A child could run loose about the village in "poverty, ignorance, and dirt," till he reached the regulation age; and after that also. There were no Board Schools, with their sixth and seventh and eight standards; there were no School Board Inspectors and grants, then. A village boy was given the bare chance of picking up a few scraps of rudimentary knowledge—the three Rs, as we used to say—or of going without. He could take it in or leave it out; and, knowing what stuff the ordinary village boy was made of, he did what any one might have expected—any one, that is, with an ounce of sense in him—he either left the little learning out, or he more often than not took it in all wrong. The teaching in most of the village schools, then, was bad almost beyond belief.

"Much knowledge of the right sort is a dangerous thing for the poor," might have been the motto put up over the door of the village school in my day. The less book-learning the labourer's lad got stuffed into him, the better for him and the safer for those above him, was what those in authority believed and acted up to. I daresay they made themselves think somehow or other—perhaps by *not* thinking—that they were doing their duty in that state of life to which it had pleased God to call *them*, when they tried to numb his brain, as a preliminary to stunting his body later on, as stunt it they did, by forcing him to work like a beast of burden for a pittance.

These gentry did not want him to know; they did not want him to think; they only wanted him to work. To toil with the hand was what he was born into the world for, and they took precious good care to see that he did it from his youth upwards. Of course he might learn his catechism; that, and things similar to it, was the right, proper, and suitable knowledge for such as he; he would be the more likely to stay contentedly in his place to the end of his working days.

The majority of the schools were parsons' schools; we call them voluntary now, but parsons' they are still, and they will remain so to the end. I should like to see them swept away from off the face of the country. I hope I shall live to see that day ; but as they seem to have had a new lease of life given them lately there is not much chance of that ! I never had any sympathy with this kind of school, and it is not in me to have it.

The school in our village was one of the parson kind, but luckily for us youngsters it was a downright good one. For that we had to thank our master ; it was entirely owing to him. I can truthfully say that our master all those years ago was, master for master, a better one than the man they have there now. Our man was sensible and practical above the common, and he had the true interests of his scholars at heart. He knew how important it was that during the very few years of schooling we could have, we should be taught what would prove of most use to us in every-day life. He flatly refused to waste his time and ours over the catechism and other useless educational lumber of the same sort, to the exclusion of what it was so much more necessary for us to know. He was determined that he would make boys fit to do something to earn their living when they left school ; and he stuck manfully to that determination. He was as excellent a teacher as a poor boy could wish to meet with, and I shall never forget what I owe him. It would have been difficult to beat him at reading, writing, spelling, arithmetic, and mensuration. I was only able to pick up the rudiments of these with him, but I picked them up so thoroughly that I never let them drop again. My master saw to it that the foundation was well and truly laid, and I was thus able to build up, later on, safe and sure, and by degrees, a solid little structure of knowledge on the top of it. I began to attend when I was six, the eligible age, but I was obliged to leave before I was nine, so that I had barely three years of regular schooling to start me on my way in life. But if the dark doom of the labourer's child fell up on me betimes, I did not let the black cloud of ignorance settle on my faculties. I started right away, not only to keep what knowledge I had gained, but to add more to it. I bought books, and studied hard, and educated myself, when I came home of an evening from the fields, or from following the plough; so that with the help of my mother and my books—books purchased out of my scanty wage—I managed to pick up piecemeal what was then considered a fair education. I was wonderfully fond of my books and my writing. I did not want to go into the street and play with the other boys; I stayed indoors and stuck to my self-set lessons. My mother would set me copies, give me writing tasks, and sums to work out. She was always ready to help me, willing to explain a difficulty, or smooth out a knotty point, if she could. She was as anxious that I should get on as I was myself.

I was a youngster of nine when I began to earn money. My first job was crow-scaring, and for this I received fourpence a day. This day was a twelve hours one, so it sometimes happened that I got more than was in the bargain, and that was a smart taste of the farmer's stick when he ran across me outside the field I had been set to watch. I can remember how he would come into the field suddenly, and walk quietly up behind me ; and, if he caught me idling, I used to catch it hot. There was no sparing the stick and spoiling the child then ! This crow-scaring was very monotonous work, and many a time I proved the truth of the old adage about Satan finding mischief, for idle hands. My idle hands found a good deal to do, what with bird-nesting, trespassing, and other boyish tricks and diversions. But if those days spent in the fields were rather monotonous, they were at any rate wholesome, and I throve apace. I had fresh air to breathe, plenty of room to stretch my young limbs in, and just enough plain food to nourish a growing boy. Had I been a miner's son, I might have been in those days slaving my wretched little life away in the depths of a coal mine, breathing foul air, herding with other children of my own age or younger still, dragging load after load of coal up ladders, or sitting behind a door in the pitch dark for fourteen hours at a stretch. I knew nothing of such a cruel, brutalising, demoralising child's life as that. I had the sky over my head, and if there came wind and rain and stormy weather, there came sunshine too. And I had the trees to look at and climb, hedgerow flowers to pluck, and streams to wade in. " Nature's feast of changing beauty " was always spread out before me ; and, though I did not think much about it in that way, still I was taking it all in without knowing it.

I must admit, however that, if this sort of work did not prove harmful to robust boys with a sound constitution like myself, it played havoc with the weakly ones, and set loose all too soon the sleeping dogs of disease, the fell dogs of consumption and bronchitis and rheumatism, which devoured them wholesale when they should have been in their manhood's prime. If I had been cursed with a rickety body, if I had been ill-nourished and insufficiently clad, and had been obliged to stand in a new-sown field shivering on an empty stomach, while the cold wind blew and the chill rain poured down in torrents and soaked me to the skin, I should probably not be living to tell this tale to-day. If I had survived, ten chances to one, it would have been in the shape ot a crippled martyr to rheumatism or a wheezy victim to bronchitis: I should have been a broken-down, doubled-up, worn-out old man. The sickly son of an agricultural labourer had as little chance of growing up to a healthy manhood as had the sickly son of a miner or a mill hand: it was a regular case of extremes meeting in a vicious circle. If he got past the bird-scaring stage he had the carter and the ploughman to contend with, and their tenderest mercies were cruel. They used their tongues and their whips and their boots on him so freely, that it is no exaggeration to say that the life of poor little Hodge was not a whit better than that of a plantation nigger boy.

I kept at crow-scaring for about twelve months, during which time I worked for several farmers. My first employer was a big, burly man, fairly well-to-do. He came to grief, however, through his extravagance. He did not look after his business properly, and, to make matters worse for himself, he married a London lady who would be very gay, would have everything after the London pattern, so she very soon brought him down. Here I may say that this is but one instance out of many which have, from time to time, come under my notice. There were too many farmers and farmers' wives of this sort in my youth, and it is my candid opinion that there are more of them about now than ever there were, and no one has any kind of use for them. Farmers' wives nowadays are ashamed to go to market to sell their eggs and butter as they used commonly to do. They want to play the piano, dress fine, make calls and ape the county gentry, and of course the farms will not stand it. How can they? And the farmers too want to hunt, and shoot, and play the fine gentleman at ease. Then, when these would-be swells find their cash run short, they cry out that it is the labourers who are extravagant and thriftless, who want too high a wage, who do too little work, and are bringing the land to ruin!

Why do not these farmers, with their wives and families, draw in, and turn to, and live according to their means, instead of being above their trade? Let the farmer give up his hunter, let his wife doff her silken gowns, her furbelows and her fal-lals, let his daughters drop their tinkling accomplishments, and let them give their time, their attention, and their money to the farm, as it is their clear and bounden duty to do. If they do not give the farm their care and personal attention, the farm will give them up. That is a dead certainty. This was what happened to the first farmer I worked for. My father, by the way, worked for this same man.

From crow-scarer to ploughboy was my next step, with an accompanying increase in wage of twopence a day. Three shillings a week was that amount better than nothing, but it was a small contribution to the common family fund ; it was not sufficient to keep me, let alone buy clothes. We should have been in a very bad way if my mother, by her laundry earnings, had not subsidised my father's wage. My clothing was of the coarsest. I had to go to school in a smock-frock and old hobnailed boots, and my work-a-day garb was the same. The sons of the wheelwrights, the master tailor, and the tradesmen were just becoming genteel, and used to dress in shoddy cloth. These peacocky youngsters would cheek the lads in smock-frocks whenever they got the chance, and many a stand-up fight we used to have—regular pitched battles of smock-frock against cloth-coat, they were, in which smock-frock held his own right well. The lot of the ordinary ploughboy was not an enviable one, and I, in common with the other lads at the plough tail, had a rough time of it. Some of our carters were brutal bullies ; and they liked to make us dance a quickstep to the tune of the stick and the whip—cutting capers in more ways than one! The head carter was so fond of this kind of tune and caper-cutting that he would be at it on the smallest provocation. He was a cruel flogger, and the very sight of him was enough to set some of the lads shaking in their hobnailed boots. Many a time and oft in the dark and early hours of the morning has little Joe Arch, the ploughboy, trudged up the lane, "creeping like snail unwillingly to work," with his satchel on his shoulder, containing, not books, but his food for the day. This would be a hunch of barley bread, with occasionally an apple baked in paste of coarse wheat-meal. Apple-dumpling day was a red one in my boy's calendar. When I had such a dainty bit in my bag it seldom stayed there many minutes. Although I had despatched a hearty breakfast before starting, out would come the dumpling. "Just to have a look at it, and to see if it is so big as mother generally makes them," I would say to myself. Then I would turn it about and admire its size. From handling the dainty to tasting it was a sure process. "I'll have one little bite—only a nibble," I would say. When I had got my tooth into that dumpling Adam with his apple wasn't in it; it was a case of "once bitten soon gone." Then I would hurry on to make up for my dawdling, with only the hunch of barley bread in my wallet, the joys of the dumpling behind me, and before me the day's drudgery with perhaps a thrashing thrown in.

When I was between twelve and thirteen years of age I could drive a pair of horses and plough my own piece. It was a proud day for me when I drove my first pair and got eightpence a day wage. This kind of work is generally called "gee-oh-ing."

I quickly became an efficient geeoher, and proved then, as I have often done since, the truth of the old saying, "Where there's a will there's a way." I geeohed with a will, so the way of promotion was not long in being reached. There was a wealthy banker and Justice of the Peace in the village, a great hunting man, who kept six or seven horses. I began to drive a pair of horses at plough for him; and after a bit, thinking I suppose that I was a smart, likely lad, he took me into his stables, made me a sort of stable-boy, and gave me eight shillings a week to start with. Here was a rise for a lad, who was set on rising as fast and as much as he could. In time my wages went up to nine shillings a week, and I was able to be a real help to our little household, and lighten somewhat the burden of care resting on my mother's shoulders. But this was the high-water mark; and if my wages were higher than they had been, my working-day was a longer one. I had to give my money's worth, and I gave it, good measure, as I have always done. I would stick like a limpet to my books of an evening. "Not an idle minute" was my rule. There were no slack half-hours for me, no taking it easy with the other lads. To make more money, to do more, to know more, to be a somebody in my little world was my ambition, and I toiled strenuously to attain it. There was not much in the way of amusement going on in the village to distract my attention, and draw me out side our home. The village lad had two kinds of recreation open to him. He could take his choice between lounging and boozing in the public house, or playing bowls in the bowling alley. That was all. There were no cricket or football clubs, no Forester's meetings. When they did start a sick benefit fund, of which, by the way, I am still a member, the parson, the farmer, and the leading men of the parish did their very best to put it down, to stamp it out with their despotic heels. The parson refused point blank to preach a sermon in aid of funds for it. His parishoners had no right to start such a club, he thought; it was a sign that they were getting too independent, that they were learning how to help themselves, which was the very last thing he wanted them to do, whatever he might say and preach to the contrary. That a labourer, who had fallen out of work through illness, should be supported, even for a time, from a common fund over which the rectory had no direct control, was gall and wormwood to the parson. Worse still, the labourer's wife would not be so ready to come to the rectory back-door, humbly begging for help. Worse and worse still, she and the children might slip out of the yoke of Church attendance altogether, if rectory charity were no longer a necessity. No; this sick club was the thin end of a bad wedge, and it must be pulled out and broken up without delay.

We labourers had no lack of lords and masters. There were the parson and his wife at the rectory. There was the squire, with his hand of iron overshadowing us all. There was no velvet glove on that hard hand, as many a poor man found to his hurt. He brought it down on my father because he would not sign for a small loaf and a dear one ; and if it had not been for my mother, that hand would have crushed him to the earth, maybe crushed the life right out of him. At the sight of the squire the people trembled. He lorded it right feudally over his tenants, the farmers ; the farmers in their turn tyrannised over the labourers ; the labourers were no better than toads under a harrow. Most of the farmers were oppressors of the poor ; they put on the iron wage-screw, and screwed the labourers' wages down, down below living point ; they stretched him on the rack of life-long, abject poverty. I can remember the time when wages were so low that a man with several children was allowed parish relief. He was forced to accept this degrading kind of help, for he could not have brought up his family without it. Let him work as hard as he would, he could not earn the wherewithal to do it. The labourer who had a big family was blamed for it, and treated accordingly. I know for a fact that, when some of the men had a large number of children and were unable to keep them, the parish authorities used to take several of them away and put them in the workhouse. It was a disgraceful state of things, from which there seemed no loophole of escape. Parents pauperised because of their children, children pauperised from their youth up because their fathers, however willing, were not able to feed and clothe them. Is it to be wondered at that the people, more often than not, flung prudence, and thrift, and steady industry, and good conduct to the four winds? Who dare blame them and cast it in their teeth? The poor man who accepted the sop of parish help, which was cast to him as a bone to a dog, felt that life's heavy burden had been made lighter; he was relieved from sickening worry, he was no longer obliged to watch his children fading out of life before his miserable eyes. And so it was that men, born to be free, and willing to be independent, were turned into parasites. If a man was sober and prudent and industrious, what reward had he? What return did he see for the exercise of such difficult virtues? Why, even if he had managed, by the most strenuous efforts, to keep himself afloat on life's stream, he was almost bound to see his little raft of independence slowly, surely drifting on to the mudbanks of pauperism at the close of his voyage. Yes, after all his labour and toil, that was to be the end of him; there he would be stranded, there he would die, there would be his grave. Could a freeborn, self-respecting Englishman meet with a more bitterly cruel fate than this? The mere prospect of such a fate was enough to drive many a man into a downhill course of thriftlessness, recklessness, and hard drinking. What did he care then, if at the end of his rollicking road the poorhouse door would be yawning wide to receive him? He couldn't help that, he had given up trying. He drowned the thought in his glass, and chalked up his score with a laugh, and went down a bit faster.

Some of the farmer's wives were in sympathy with the people, but only a very few of them. I will not condemn the lot wholesale, for some of them were kind, especially to the labourer's wives when they had babies. All the womanhood in them came well to the front at such times; they would give milk, and nourishing food, and clothes, and they gave with a kind hand and a warm heart. I wish I could say as much for their husbands. They must have had their good points like other men; but what kindliness they possessed was like the other side of the moon in relation to the earth, it was always turned away from the agricultural labourer. The picture of them, which was bitten deep into my memory when I was a growing lad, is a bitter, black one. They impressed themselves on me as taskmasters and oppressors, and my heart used to burn within me when I heard of their doings, and when I saw how the men who toiled so hard for them were treated like the dirt beneath their feet. I observed, and listened, and remembered, and stored it all up for future use.

I went on working in the stables until I was about sixteen, and then I started mowing for the same banker. He used to pay me eighteenpence a day for what he would have had to pay another man half-a-crown. I knew this well enough, and the thought of the extra shilling which should have been in my pocket and was not, rankled and continued to rankle, though I kept pretty quiet about it at the time. In the succeeding summer I joined a gang of mowers, all in the banker's employ; we worked from five o'clock until seven, but not a farthing's increase on my wage did I get, though I was now as expert with the scythe as the best mower among them. I felt the injustice of this treatment more and more keenly, but I dared not speak out,—the time for *that* had not come, and I could not risk the loss of my earnings, for my father was in receipt of only eight shillings a week just then. We had to practise the strictest economy in order to keep the wolf of hunger at bay. That wolf is the poor man's familiar; he would be on the prowl round the labourer's humble home from Monday morning until Saturday night—ay, and on Sunday too. He was a ravenous, profane beast, having no respect for the Sabbath day to keep it holy. He was always snapping, and snarling, and growling round the corner. Because we had no rent to pay we fared better than many, but manage as my mother might, we seldom got a taste of fresh meat more than once in the seven days.

It was at this period that a crushing blow fell upon our little family: my mother died. It was an irretrievable loss, a terrible grief to me. Mother, teacher, councillor, guide, and familiar friend—she was all that to me, and more. Oh, if only she could have lived to see me in Parliament, what a proud and joyful day it would have been for her! This sad event took place in 1842.

I stayed on in the old home for a while and took care of my father, but I was more than ever bent on improving my condition and earning a better wage A man from another part of the kingdom introduced a new style of hedge-cutting into our county. I very soon found out that he could make a tidy bit of money by it, so I set to work at once and learned how to do it. The banker in whose employ I still was let me try my prentice hand, and I practised this new style on his hedges, improving steadily year by year. Then hedge-cutting matches were instituted—"hedging matches" they called them. The first time I competed I gained a prize; the second time I again won a prize; and the third time I carried off the first prize. Then a championship match was arranged, all the head prizemen for many miles round being asked to compete. I entered the lists and won the first prize of two pounds, a medal, and the proud title of "Champion Hedgecutter of England." I had made up my mind that I would master everything I took up, and I was determined to take up everything which would further the one aim and object I had in life then—*i.e.*, the bettering of my own position by every honest means in my power. The winning of this championship is an instance of how I succeeded. Soon after this "glorious victory," I went into different English counties, and also into Wales, hedge-cutting. I got good jobs and very good money, and was in great request. Not only was I a master of this branch of my craft, with men working under me, but, as I had taken to mowing when sixteen years of age, I had now become a master hand at that also, and had almost invariably a gang of from twenty to twenty-five men under me in the field. This was my reward for having caught slippery old Father Time by his fore-lock. I made some very good mowing contracts with large graziers; they would give me six and seven shillings an acre. The farmers were not so liberal by half, as they seldom paid more than three shillings an acre. Still, taking one contract with another, I did well and could put more money into my pocket than I had ever done yet.

The Midlands and South Wales was my beat, and I kept my eyes and ears wide open, while going my hedge-cutting and mowing rounds. I saw that there was a smouldering discontent among the different classes of agricultural labourers with whom I was brought into contact, but they did not make any effort to improve their position. I would ask the men who worked under me, whether they were satisfied with their condition, and their answers were almost without exception in the decided negative.

But there it ended. Discontented as they were, they lacked the energy to better themselves. They would grumble and complain by the hour, but they would not budge an inch from the place and position in which they found themselves. The fact was, very few of them could write a letter, so the majority were afraid to go from home, because they would not be able to communicate with their friends. This inert mass of underfed, overworked, uneducated men was stuck fast in the Slough of Despond. Practically, they were voiceless, and voteless, and hopeless. I realised this, and I pondered over all I saw and heard as I ranged far and wide over the country on Shanks' mare. I laid it up in my heart against the day of wrath to come ; the day, still far distant, when I should find my voice and make of it a trumpet, wherewith to sound forth through the length and breadth of the land, the woes and the wrongs of the agricultural labourer.

I now worked my way back to Barford, and at last found myself once more in the old cottage. I had gained both money and experience, I had travelled over large tracts of my native land, I had been tried as a labourer and had not been found wanting ; as a mower, as a hedger and ditcher, I had more than held my own with the best. Wherever I had worked I had given proof that I was not one of the hopeless, helpless nobodies. I was conscious of increased strength, and vigour of mind and body ; I had learned where I stood among my fellow-workers, and consequently I was more than ever determined to carve out an upward path for myself, and be a somebody in the world of working men.

CHAPTER III

WAITING THE CALL.

IT was early in the forties when I made my way back like a homing pigeon to the old Arch roof-tree. I was now a stalwart young man, nearing the end of my teens, a true chip of the old block. There was nothing of the shamefaced prodigal son about me when I set foot in my native village once more, and returned to my father. I had not been wasting my wages in riotous living, and then been reduced to feed on swine husks because I had not a penny piece left to my bad name. No; it was young Joe Arch the worker, not Joe Arch the wastrel, who tramped home from his travels with money in his pocket, money enough to have bought and paid for a fatted calf on his own account, wherewith to give his father a treat. I had been journeying to and fro on the face of a fine broad bit of English earth, seeking what wages I could earn, what work I could get, and what facts I could devour. I found, I got, I devoured, every morsel which came in my way. I read, marked, learned and inwardly digested, as the prayer book says somewhere, all I could lay my hands or ears or eyes on. At the same time I was taking in a supply of facts which would not be digested—tough facts about the land and the labourer, that accumulated and lay within my mind, heavy as a lump of lead, and hard as a stone. No matter what I did, whether I was working with my hands or my head, that mass of indigestible facts was always in the background, worrying and bothering me. I got no peace ; it worried and bothered me more and more as each year went by.

When in Wales, I remember comparing the condition of the Welsh agricultural labourer with that of his English brother in the Midlands, and especially in Warwickshire. It was all in favour of the Welshman. He could obtain a decent cottage at a low rental, and as a rule he could get a strip of garden with it. Fruit was plentiful, and you could get as much good cider as you wanted to drink at about a penny a quart. The majority of the men owned at least half a score of prime apple trees, some had more, and occasionally you would see a little orchard containing as many as forty trees in full bearing. There was no doubt about it, and I saw it with a heavy heart, the Welshman had a better time of it, a more hopeful lot, than his English brother.

There was another thing which my travels showed me plain as a pikestaff, and that was the real value of our little freehold property. I had been proud of it before, now I was thankful for it as well. In one

English county after another I saw men living with their families—if *living* it could be called—in cottages which, if bigger, were hardly better than the sty they kept their pigs in, when they were lucky enough to have a young porker fattening on the premises. These garnished hovels, for such they were with their outside trimmings of ivy and climbing roses, were garnished without, but they were undrained and unclean within, so that the seven devils of disease and vice had possession, and flourished like weeds on a dunghill or toadstools in a cellar. And these precious hovels would be the property of a farmer, or a squire, or some other Dives of the neighbourhood. Even if a labourer did scrape enough money together to buy the roof over his head, he very soon found out that the roof was not for sale—not for him, at any rate, the privilege of owning a bit of house property. Oh, no; the labourer might live in his garnished hovel on sufferance, he might bide there at Dives' good will and pleasure, or he might be kicked out bag and baggage, at a week's notice, if Dives so chose. Try as he might, the labourer could not get at the land either. In parish after parish he could not lay so much as a little finger on one rood of it; he could neither buy nor hire it. Landless, and all but roofless, these men were, hundreds and hundreds of them. When I used to see how terribly bad things were with them I would say to myself, "Well Joe, you have something to be thankful for, when all's said and done. You mayn't be the young Queen Victoria in her palace, nor the Earl of Warwick in his castle; but your father is king of his cottage and lord of his mite of land, as his father was before him, and as you will be in your turn, please God."

By the way, if a poor knight of labour had the right to carry such a useless article as a coat of arms, I would have an old stocking figuring on it, fine and large!

Glad as I was to get back home, the old place did not seem the same without my mother. We missed her badly at every turn. I learned then that the working-man's home is no home at all, if there is not a good housewife within doors. Let his wife be a slattern, and a wilful, careless waster,—well, then, before very very long, there will be woeful want stepping in, bringing angry words and worse behind, and driving love like smoke up the kitchen chimney; let his home be hugger-mugger, and it is only a man in a thousand who will not step down to the public-house for an hour's comfort and enjoyment after his day's labour is over. Who will cast the first stone at him for doing it? Not I—though neither my father nor I went that way. We put up with inconveniences of all sorts, and tried to get along as best we could, rather than run the risk of having dishonest people about us, plundering right and left when we were safe away in the fields. I worked at hedging and ditching and draining, at fence and hurdle making, at any and every job which would bring in good money: it was all in the week's work, and in the evening I would keep pegging away at my books.

When I was in my twenty-first year a gentleman, who was going to travel abroad, asked me to accompany him as his servant. I jumped at the offer. I was eager to go, I wanted to see more of the world and what life was like in foreign parts, and I might not have such a chance again. But when I told my father about it he implored me not to leave him; he said he was getting old and feeble, and that he had nobody but me in the world to look after him. I could not forsake the old man after that; it would have been a cruel thing to do; and I thought too, that, if I did go abroad, it was more than likely that I should not get the comforts I was able to get at home. So I said, "All right, father, I won't leave you in the lurch; I'll stay." There was nothing for it then but to marry and settle down, for we could not go on as we had been doing. It had been a makeshift kind of a life at the best. So it came about that, in 1847, when barely one-and-twenty years of age, I took unto myself a wife. She was the daughter of a Wellesbourne mechanic; she was in domestic service in the village when I met her. We soon settled down comfortably in the cottage, where seven children were born to us, six of whom are still living.

My wife was not the woman my mother was. She was no scholar, and she did not think over questions and have a firm opinion about them as my mother did; and I felt the difference almost from the first.

She was a good, clean wife, and a good mother; she looked after my father well; she was always attending to her home and to her family; but she was no companion to me in my aspirations. My father noticed this, and often used to say, "Joe, she is hardly a companion for you." She had not any idea of rising in the world; she wished to stop in the place where it had pleased the Lord to call her. She thought, "As it was in the beginning, is now, and ever shall be, world without end. Amen." Those were not my mother's sentiments, and they were not mine. Then, she never could bear my going away from home to work. Over and over again I used to say to her, "What on earth is the good of my stopping in the village earning nine shillings a week with four or five little ones to keep, and bread eightpence-halfpenny a loaf, when by going away I can earn forty shillings a week, and can send you home twenty-five shillings?" But, oh no, I must stop at home with her. It was natural enough I suppose, but it was foolish. We never could convince her that I was right in going, though we tried very hard to make her see as we did about it. Of course, she was never alone; she had her children to look after, and father, who was at work close by, used to come home to his meals regularly. She taught her children how to work, and in this respect she taught them well; but she could not train them for better positions in life. What extra education they had I gave them myself; she could not. She meant well, and she did well, as far as she was able; she was a good, honest woman, who acted up to what lights she had. She was a Nonconformist, and on that point we were at one. I flung Churchgoing over early in life, from religious conviction. I did not believe in Church doctrine, as preached by the parson. I did not believe either in ordering myself "lowly and reverently to all my betters," because they were never able to tell me who my betters were. Those they called my betters I did not think my betters in any respect. Like my good mother before me, I was a Nonconformist by nature and by conviction. I began to be in open sympathy with them from the time when I went with my mother to hear the Wellesbourne men preach in that old barn up the back lane, which I have already mentioned. A chapel was built in the village in 1840. The Wesleyans happened to get hold of a piece of ground, on which an old butcher's shop had formerly stood; they built a chapel on the site of it, and there it stands to this day. It was supplied by local preachers. Very soon after my marriage I began to take an active part in local preaching, and other doings of the Nonconformist community. My religious views are strong ones. I cannot bear cant—I despise it. I believe in practical Christianity. I would not deceive a man, if I knew it; and as for wronging a man, I can say with an easy conscience, if I were going to die the next minute, that I have never wronged a fellow-creature intentionally, in my life. Yes, my religious views are strong ones; but I don't want to talk much about them, for I hold that a man's religion should be more in his life than on his lips. If it is in his life, it will take him the best part of his time to live up to it; and if he feels a strong call to preach, as I did, there is the circuit open to him, and the chapel pulpit of a Sunday.

By this time I had formed my political opinions. When I was only about eighteen years of age, I made up my mind to be a Liberal, and I have stuck to the party ever since. I expect the Tory barley bread I had to feed on got into my bones and made me a Liberal! It has had that contrary effect on more than one man I have come across. Then, as a lad, every time I earned a penny by doing odd jobs or running an errand, I would buy some old papers. These were originally published at fivepence-halfpenny. I used to read Gladstone's and Bright's speeches in them, and from these I formed my opinions. But it was a case of like to like; I got what I wanted in the speeches, they gave me reasons for feeling and thinking in the way I already did. I should have been a Liberal, even if there had been up to then no such word in the language. I should have thought and felt as I did, even if I had never heard of Gladstone and Bright. I could not help being one. Liberalism was in me to start with.

The stage of my life on which I had now entered was a busy, a varied, and a trying one. I had a young and increasing family to provide for. Though my habits were frugal, and my wife showed herself a marvel of economy and good management in the house, I very soon saw that I must put my best foot foremost, and tramp farther afield than Barford. My wife objected, but I was determined that my children should be brought up decently; that they should have plenty of plain wholesome food; as good an education as I could get them and give them; and a fair start in life. If they did not have this it would not be my fault, but my misfortune. So off I set on my travels. Hard work, good wages, rough quarters, strange companions, long journeys and long absences—such was the programme. When in Wales I would preach in chapels among the mountains, and more than once I have 'held forth' in my everyday clothes. The Welsh cotters gave me a warm welcome and the right hand of fellowship wherever I went. Many a little token of their hearty good will have I carried off with me. Working, preaching, and reading whatever books or papers I could pick up, I would find my way home and settle down for a while to much the same kind of life in the village.

My mother had fought a good fight with the "powers that be." It was my turn now to stand up for my rights, and those of my children. I had some tremendous fights, especially in connexion with the schooling of my children. I remember well the following incident:—One day my second daughter went with me to Warwick. I went to do some marketing and to buy some new tools. While there she saw a hair net studded with white beads. She took a great fancy to it and said, "Father, do buy that net for me." I saw no harm in it, so I bought it for her. It cost ninepence. The little maid was only about nine years old and was therefore naturally very proud of her hair-net. On the Monday morning nothing would suit her but she should put this hair-net on to go to school in. Off she trotted with it, as pleased as Punch. Well, the parson's wife went down to the school that morning and saw my child with her hair-net on. Up she marched to the child and said, "I shall not allow you to come to school with a hair-net on—we don't allow *poor people's* children to wear hair-nets with beads, and, if you dare to come to school this afternoon with that trumpery on, I shall take it off and teach you a lesson." I happened to be working close at home just then, and when I came in to dinner I found my child crying. I asked her what was wrong and she told me what the parson's wife had said. It made my blood boil. Tradesmen's children were to be allowed to wear buckles on their shoes, and feathers and flowers in their hats, while the poor labourer's child was not to be allowed to wear a hair-net with a few beads on it! My wife was for giving in to the parson's wife, because she did not want to have any bother and unpleasantness; but I happened to be made of sterner stuff. I told the child then and there to keep her hair net on, and I took her back to school myself. I saw the schoolmistress, and I said to her "Mrs. —— what's the matter with my children?" "Matter, Mr. Arch?" says she; "there's nothing the matter, there are no better behaved children in the school." "Then," I said, "what is the meaning of this?" and I went on to tell her about the net. She said she had never made any such rule, it was the parson's wife who had made it. Then I told her to tell the parson's wife, if she came into the school that afternoon, that if she dared to take the hair-net from off my child's head I would summons her at Warwick, as she had no more right to take the hair-net off my child's head than I had a right to steal my neighbour's goods. This settled the lady; for when she came into the school that very afternoon the schoolmistress told her what I had said. "Oh," said the parson's wife, "that Arch is a horrid man. He is a firebrand in the parish," but she never attempted to touch my child.

They had a very bad system, which I later on was instrumental in breaking up. When a father had a boy old enough to go to school, he had to go to the parson and get a ticket before the boy was allowed to enter the school; and the mother had to go to the parson's wife to get permission for the girls to enter. This was another of their numerous dodges to keep up the power of the parson. But I upset that. I had a little grandson up from Wales. I got my wife to clean his boots and trim him up nicely, and then I told her to take him to school without first obtaining a ticket. To the school she took him right away.

"Have you a ticket?" asked the schoolmaster. Said my wife, "Oh, my husband said I was not to get one." "Then I cannot admit the boy," said the schoolmaster. My wife brought the boy back and told me what the schoolmaster had said. Here was my opportunity. I knew the Act, I had read it through and through. The Act said to me, "You must get your boy educated." Said I to the Act, "With the greatest of pleasure, and whatever is due and required to be paid I will pay; but to go to the parson to ask whether I may carry out the provision of the law I never, never will!" So I just told my wife to take the boy to the school again on the following Monday morning and to tell the schoolmaster that, if he refused the child admission, I would at once write to the School Authorities and ask them to summon me before the Bench at Warwick. My wife went down and told him this. "Oh," said he, "that will never do. I will accept the boy on my own responsibility. He can come in now." After that we were not troubled very much about tickets. They knew better than to fight it out. They knew they were in the wrong, that they had not half a leg to stand on; so they kept quiet. They would have dearly liked to drive me out of the parish, neck and crop.

I had another tussle with the parson. There was a sort of village charity, the outcome of an agreement made many years ago with one of the Earls of Warwick. There used to be a right of way across the park; it was the shortest cut to the town, and the Earl offered to give two hundred-weight of coal every year to each working man in the village. This was to buy us out. The villagers agreed to it, so it was a fair bargain. My birthright was sold long before I was born; still, the coals were there to claim if I chose, and I did choose. For two or three years I did not have any, but one day when they were distributing these coals I happened to be at home, and I thought I might just as well go for my two hundred-weight. So I got my barrow, and went to the man who was giving them out. "I have come for my coals," I said.

"Oh," said he, looking at me, "have you?" "Yes," I said, "and I mean to have them too." He looked at his list. "Your name is not down on my list," said he. "Oh," said I, "it's not, is it? Who makes out that list, I should like to know?" "The parson," said he. "I thought so," said I. "Well I have come here to do business, let there be no sort of a mistake about that. It is now about a quarter past one—if I do not receive an order to fetch my coals by three o'clock, I am going across the park; and, if they summon me, I will tell the reason why. All the world hereabouts shall know why I went." I said no more, but went off. I had said quite enough, however, for before three o'clock had struck, up comes a lad with a message, "Please will you come down and fetch your coals." Down for my coals I went, and had no more bother about it.

My fights for the liberty of the subject and my struggles to preserve the freedom and independence of myself and my family did not stop at the parson. I had four pitched battles with the Bench at Warwick over the vaccination of my children, and I beat them every time. I defended my own case, for I knew the Act pretty well and so had no need to employ a lawyer. I remember the Bench remitted the fines, but

I had to pay seventeen-and-sixpence costs. The fines amounted in all to about four guineas. The Chairman of the Bench was a rigid Tory, and he knew I was a labourer ; so I had nothing very nice to expect from him. The doctor used to attend at the village school, and the women were in the habit of carrying their babies there to be vaccinated. I put my foot down over this vaccination business, and said straight out that I did not intend to have my children treated as if they were cattle. Every time I was summoned the Court was crowded ; sometimes the Chairman had a job to keep order, for there was so much feeling stirred up. The Bench adjourned the first time, and set the policeman and the registrar to make enquiries as to whether anybody else in the village resented the law. I was not going to be behind-hand in the matters and I also got a friend to go round making enquiries. We found out that there were a hundred and twenty-five children not vaccinated, yet I was the only criminal. It came out afterwards that this was one of the parson's tricks. He knew my children had not been vaccinated and he could not let pass such a chance of having a dig at me. I must have walked two hundred miles over that case. I was then working about twenty-five miles from the Court, and I did the journey eight times—four times to the Court, and four times back to my work.

The second time I came up before the Court the chairman said, "Why have you not had your children vaccinated ?" I said, "Because my children are healthy, and no hereditary disease can be traced in their ancestors for many generations, and I am not going to have their blood tainted now by the filthy matter which is too often used for vaccination purposes." I then asked the chairman, as he said the law compelled me to have my children vaccinated, whether my children belonged to the law or whether they belonged to me, and whether, if the law were that their ears were to be cut off, I must needs obey? Said I: "If I do have my children vaccinated, and if they become ill from the effects of it, and become disfigured for life, as many a poor child does, will the State maintain and keep them?" The answer was "No." "Then," I said, "I shall certainly not allow my children to be vaccinated." "But," said the chairman, "you are the only one in the village who will not have it done." "Who told you that?" I asked. "The registrar," he said. "Perhaps," said I, "you know how the registrar does his business. If not, I will tell you, because it is quite time you did know. That man goes to a public-house keeper, and asks him to find out all the children that are born, and what their names are to be. When the registrar has obtained this information from the public-house keeper, he enters the names of the children in the public book. I do not allow my wife to lower herself, by going to a beer-house to inform them she has a baby, nor do I intend to so lower myself. If my wife has a baby, it is the duty of the registrar to keep a record of the fact. It is not the duty of a father or a mother to go down to a public-house and inform the keeper of it, so that the registrar may save himself any trouble." Well, the chairman had nothing to say on this point. It was a crying disgrace that such a state of things should be permitted.

Of course, all this disputing and contending with the high and mighty ones helped to spread my name abroad, and there was not a parson or a squire in the countryside who loved the sound of it. If they could have stuck a gag in my mouth, gagged I should have been in a jiffy. If they could have clapped a muzzle on me, muzzled I should have been before I could say "Jack Robinson!" But they could neither gag nor muzzle me. They gave me the bad name, but they couldn't hang me. They, and others of the same kidney, wrote me down a contentious brawler, a dissenting wind-bag, and a Radical revolutionary; but not one of them could say I was an idler who neglected his family, and left them to shift for themselves. The fact of my being a steady, industrious, and capable workman was a stumper for them; they could not get over that. My little house and garden were kept in good order—apple-pie order, I might say. The garden was choke full of fruit and vegetables in their season, and I raised as many flowers as I could find room for. When my father died, in 1862, I took off the old thatched roof of the cottage, and replaced it with one of slate, put in windows, and made it as smart and comfortable as it is to-day. I had to wait until his death to make these improvements, because the old man would not have it touched. He used to say, "You may do what you like to the old place, Joe, when I am gone, but while I'm above ground it must stay as it is." He could not bear to see the things about him altered, and I respected his wishes.

Every year now my interest in politics, and in all that had to do with the land and the labourer, was growing stronger and stronger. I remember that we had no election contests at first, but at last a candidate of the right colour came along, and there was a bit of a commotion; our rural waters were troubled; but not to much purpose then, for the Tories beat us by a fifteen-hundred majority. Still, the fight had begun, and what Liberals there were had waked up, and were pulling together. At the next election we decided to put up two men. Before, it had been a sort of three-cornered fight; two on the Tory side, and one on the Liberal. We ran our men in by twenty-seven votes. I stumped the country for our side, and took an active part in the Liberal cause. The squire I mentioned was a Tory, and he came and asked me to vote Tory, but I absolutely refused to do it. I thought to myself, "You little know Joe Arch, if you think he's going to play the part of a political Judas for any master born." But he had not done with me. This great squire—he was a very rich, influential man—sent for me to go down to his house when my work was over, in order to canvass me. I went down, and after some talk he said to me, "Do your Liberals find you employment?" "What has that to do with my vote?"

I said. "I sell you my labour, but not my conscience; that's not for sale."

"Oh!" said this big, strapping, six-foot man.

"Now look here, sir," I said; "I sat second horse behind you for several years, and I have worked in your stables, but since I have been out of your stables have you ever given me a sovereign without my having given you a sovereign's worth of good labour? No! You know I have always given you a sovereign's worth of labour for every sovereign you have given me, and therefore why should I give you my vote because I sell you my labour?" "Then," said he, "Sit down, Joe, and have a glass of sherry." Down I sat accordingly, and drank sherry until I could hardly see my way out, for I was not used to such drink at that time. As I was going out of the room the squire said to me, "Let's shake hands." So we shook hands. Then he said, "Arch, I admire you; you can be trusted anywhere, and with anything. I knew that before to-night, but I thought I would canvass you. I told the lawyer I was going to canvass you, but I expected this result."

We had open voting then, and the following day I went to poll behind the man for whom I was then cutting hedges; he was a farmer. The Conservative candidates were not liked by the farmers, for they were landlords of a bad kind. When my employer met me outside the Corn Exchange, he said:

"Which way did you vote?"

"Liberal," said I. "And how did *you* vote?"

"Oh, Tory," said he.

"Now look here," I said, "you would have liked to have gone my way only you dared not. And, though I have voted Liberal, you dare not sack me; because you cannot get anybody else to do my work."

He said nothing then—they were a couple of home truths he had to swallow as best he could. But the next day he confessed to me that I went to poll a political free man whilst he went as a political slave. "I should have lost my farm," he said, "as, being open polling, it would have been noted if I had voted Liberal as my conscience directed me."

Here was a nice state of things. I thought to myself, "Yes; every word of it's true, and I wouldn't be in your shoes—they cost more than mine, and it's a kind of price I wouldn't pay if I had to go barefoot." This happened during the election of 1868. At that time, such was the strength of Tory tyranny and terrorism, very few of the farmers or the labourers dared serve on the Liberal Committee; they were afraid, and with reason, that they would lose their farms or their work, if they did. But I never troubled myself on that score, I continued to take a prominent part in local politics, and I have been ever since in connection with the organisation of the Liberal party in that part of the country.

By this time I had got a great deal of influence in the village. The big-wigs found out that I was a labouring man they had to reckon with; that, if they tried to tread on my toes, I trod back with my hob-nail boots; that I had a voice and a hand and a head which matched, and more than matched, theirs. My neighbours found that I was no cracked bell; that, whenever I was hit, I rang true for liberty and the rights of the people. They knew that, though I preached on a Sunday, I was no humbug on a week-day. If I told them in the chapel pulpit that I hated shams and loathed oppression, that I earnestly believed in the higher destinies of man in this world as well as in the next, and that I had a deep and tender sympathy with the sorrows, the struggles, and the aspirations of my fellow-men,—if I told them all this and much more, in the pulpit, each working day made it clear to them that these words did not come glib from my lips, but warm from my heart. I knew their difficulties and the hardships of their lot, because I had shared that lot and faced the same difficulties. Yes; I tried to practise on a week-day what I preached on a Sunday to my brother labourers.

Times and again I have had as many as from twenty-five to thirty men working under me, and have had to pay them their wages. Never once did I stop any of their pay for being late, although by doing so I could have made a fair amount of money. During the whole of my labouring career I discharged only one man. If a man did not do his work properly I used to say to him, "Look here old chap, you couldn't get these wages elsewhere, so set to work and learn to do it properly"; and to do them justice they generally took my advice in the right spirit, and put in much better work from that time forward. A wise word spoken in time makes the working wheels go round; and a wise word will be a dam to stop a flow of foolish ones, if you know just when to say it. "Waste words, and you waste time; waste time, and you waste wages," I used to say. When a gang of men are bark-peeling, one man chattering will put all the others off work; and that means a biggish loss of money in a short time. When I undertook a lot of contracts for the Government for oak felling, peeling and squaring, I was in honour bound to see that it was not defrauded; and also, as I had to pay the men their wages, it was to my interest to see that I got a fair day's work for a fair day's pay. So I used to put it to them this way: "The man who wastes his time, and the time of his mates in idle chatter plays the fraudful fool; he cheats the Government, he cheats me, and he cheats himself." They knew I spoke the truth. They could never say that I shirked while they worked. I would do my share of timber squaring with the best man in the gang; very few could beat me with an axe, for I could cut almost to a hair's breadth anywhere I liked. The men respected me accordingly—I was a master at their own trade. They saw too that I had their interests at heart; I proved it to them by the way in which I treated them.

By the end of the sixties and the beginning of the seventies, I had bettered my position as a labourer all round. I did not work then for farmers at ten shillings a week! I used to obtain large ploughing jobs at from two shillings to three-and-sixpence a day ; but the farmers would cut me down to the two shillings whenever they could. I did not see the force of that, and I let them know it. I used also to get work as a carpenter's labourer from a friend of mine, who was a builder and carpenter. He is alive now, and is one of my greatest friends. He used to send for me when he got very busy coffin-making, or putting on roofing, or making church work. I could do very useful work for him, for which he always paid me well. Then my skill at hurdle-making and gate-hanging would come in handy at odd times. Being a good all-round man I was never at a loss for a job.

But, if things were going well with me at the beginning of the seventies, they were going from bad to worse with the agricultural labourer generally. In our part of the country his poor little tide of prosperity was at its lowest ebb. Things were so bad with the men that they were beginning to grow desperate. The trodden worms, which had so long writhed under the iron heel of the oppressor, were turning at last. The smouldering fire of discontent was shooting out tongues of flame here and there. The sore stricken, who had brooded in sullen anger over their wrongs, were rising to strike in their turn. The men were murmuring and muttering the countryside round, but they wanted a voice ; they spoke low among themselves, but they were afraid to speak out. They were sick of suffering but they had no physician. I took note of it all ; I had been taking note of it for years ;

and I had thought out the remedy. There was only one remedy, and that was *Combination.* The men were weak—if they would be strong they must unite. I saw the day drawing steadily nearer and nearer, when the wretched units of labour would be forced to unite, driven to combine. I saw the time surely coming when, as one man, they would waken to the fact that "Union makes Strength." When that day came I would be ready to help them, willing to speak for them. So I bided my time; I knew it must come.

In 1872 that time came, and it found me ready.

CHAPTER IV.

THE CALL COMES.

WHEN 1872 began I was in my forty-sixth year, an experienced agricultural labourer in robust health, active in mind and body, master of my work in all its branches, in full employment and earning good money. The house I lived in was an English working man's castle of the right sort—it was my own, every stick and stone of it. No lean minion of the law had the right to lay so much as the tip of a parchment-finger on it, and I had no horse-leech of a mortgage fastened on to me draining the blood of manliness and independence out of me. The bread I earned by honest sweat was, crust and crumb, my own; and I could stand up and look the whole world straight in the face, for I owed no man anything, not so much as a copper farthing. My plot of land was no waste field either; it was a fruitful garden if ever there was one; every square foot of it was tilled, planted and watered, and I raised more fruit, flowers, and vegetables off it than I had any use for.

Inside my house I had a good wife to keep it clean and neat, to cook the victuals, which, if homely, were plentiful, and to attend to my wants and make me comfortable. Outside it I had earned the confidence of men in my own walk of life ; they knew me for a fellow-labourer with a plain-speaking tongue in his head, a heart in the right place, and a good will towards them, and the day was now close at hand when they would make proof of me. I had earned the distrust and dislike of my so-called betters, but I did not care one jot or tittle for that. I knew I was as bad to their taste as a dose of bitters or a jorum of Epsom salts, and when I thought of that I chuckled. One old farmer used to say I was the most dangerous man that ever went on a farm, as I was always talking about combination to the labourers, and spreading discontent far and wide. So I was, and the farther I could spread it the better I was pleased. I would speak a few words to this man and a few to that, trying to stir them all up, and make them see where the only remedy for their misery lay ; in season and out of season I was at them, dropping in the good seed of manly discontent ; and I made sure, too, that most of it was not cast on to stony ground. I daresay the employers likened me to the enemy who came by stealth and sowed tares ; but that was not my view of it. I considered that I was sowing seed which, if properly looked after, would sprout up into the bread-yielding wheat of Union.

Although I had reached a pretty prosperous condition of life in 1870 and 1871, things were still going from bad to worse with the bulk of the labourers in our neighbourhood ; in fact, they had got so bad that they could hardly get worse, and I knew that the men in other parts of the country were in the same plight. After the harvest of 1871 had been reaped, and the winter had set in, the sufferings of the men became cruel, and when the new year of 1872 opened there seemed to be only two doors left open for *them* : one was the big door of disgrace which led to a life of degradation in the poorhouse; the other was the narrow door of death, which perchance would lead to a freer and happier life beyond the grave. When such a choice as this was all that was left for many an honest labouring man, who will dare to blame them because they refused to make it ! Their poverty had fallen to starvation point, and was past all bearing. They began to raise their heads and look about them; and they saw that if they would keep life in their bodies, and rise out of their miserable state, they must set to and force open a door of escape for themselves. Oppression, and hunger, and misery, made them desperate, and desperation was the mother of Union.

I had spent years thinking the matter well out; I had pondered over it when at work in the wood and the field; I had considered the question when I was hedging and ditching ; I had thrashed it right out in my mind when I was tramping to and from my day's toil; and I had come to the conclusion that only organised labour could stand up, even for a single day, against employers' tyranny. I told many a man that, in the course of talk, but I was determined not to make any attempt to start the Union myself. I saw it was bound to come; but I also saw that the men themselves must ask me to help them. My part was to sit still and wait; about that I was clear; so I waited.

I had heard that some few men were stirring at Willey and Weston, and that one or two of them had asked for higher wages, saying they meant to have better pay, as it was their right. Many a time I had cried out within myself, like the souls under the altar mentioned in the Book of the Revelation, "How long, O Lord, how long!" When this good news reached me I said to myself, "It won't be long now. They are raising their voices at last! the day is at hand." And it was so.

The day was February 7th, 1872. It was a very wet morning, and I was busy at home on a carpentering job; I was making a box. My wife came in to me and said, "Joe, here's three men come to see you. What for, I don't know." But I knew fast enough. In walked the three; they turned out to be labourers from over Wellesbourne way. I stopped work, and we had a talk. They said they had come to ask me to hold a meeting at Wellesbourne that evening. They wanted to get the men together, and start a Union directly. I told them that, if they did form a Union, they would have to fight hard for it, and they would have to suffer a great deal; both they and their families. They said the labourers were prepared both to fight and suffer. Things could not be worse; wages were so low, and provisions were so dear, that nothing but downright starvation lay before them unless the farmers could be made to raise their wages. Asking was of no use; it was nothing but waste of breath; so they must join together and strike, and hold out till the employers gave in. When I saw that the men were in dead earnest, and had counted the cost and were determined to stand shoulder to shoulder till they could squeeze a living wage out of their employers, and that they were the spokesmen of others likeminded with themselves, I said I would address the meeting that evening at 7 o'clock. I told them that I had left nine shillings a week behind me years ago, and as I had got out of the ditch myself, I was ready and willing to help them out too. I said, "If you are ready to combine, I will run all risk and come over and help you."

I remember that evening, as if it were but yesterday. When I set out I was dressed in a pair of cord trousers, and cord vest, and an old flannel-jacket. I have that jacket at home now, and I put a high value on it. As I tramped along the wet, muddy road to Wellesbourne my heart was stirred within me, and questions passed through my mind and troubled me. Was it a false start, a sort of hole-and-corner movement, which would come to nothing, and do more harm to the men than good? If a Union were fairly set afoot, would the farmers prove too strong for it?

Then I thought of what I was risking. If I were a forward figure in this business, and things went all wrong it might be the ruin of me. I remembered the Labourer's Union in Dorsetshire, started in the thirties—what had become of that? Poor Hammett had had to pay a heavy price for standing up with his fellow-labourers against the oppression. He and five others had been tried in 1834, and sentenced to seven years' transportation. The law had said that, when forming their little Agricultural Labourers' Union, they had administered illegal oaths. The plain truth of it was that, for daring to be Unionists they had been sent to the hulks in Australia. What matter though such a storm of anger had been raised by the shameful punishment that a free pardon had been granted them after about two years. They had been terribly punished. The disgrace and the indignities they had been obliged to put up with could never be wiped out. They were martyrs in a good cause, and I honoured them; but I did not want to be a martyr, I wanted to win alive and kicking. The law could not send me to the hulks; but there are more ways of torturing and ruining a man than one, and I knew that if the law could catch me anyhow it would. Those brave Dorsetshire labourers had paid a heavy penalty; they had suffered bitterly; that little Union had fallen to pieces, and the last state of the poor labourer had been worse, far worse, than the first.

What if the Union we meant to start in this corner of Warwickshire to-night should fall to bits like a badly made box? There was no saying what might happen. The men might be in earnest, but could they stay? Could they stand it out? Had they grit enough in them to face the farmers as freeborn Englishmen demanding their just dues, when they had been cringing to them so long? And what was a handful of poverty-stricken, half-starved, agricultural labourers going to do against so many of these powerful employers and rich oppressors! No Union I was sure could do any real good, or make any lasting improvement in the men's condition, if it was to be confined to a few men in one county. It would have to be a thumping big Union, with hundreds in it heartening one another for the glorious struggle before them. It would have to be a Union whose members were drawn from every county in England, and bound into one great unit by a common desire and a common hope.

The off chance of failure was present with me, as I trudged forward through the slush that chill February evening. But soon my spirits rose again. Was not the time fully ripe? Yes, I knew it was. In my heart I felt surely, surely, that the time of harvest was come. Those three men who had tramped to Barford that morning, and had called me to come over and help them, were but the firstfruits of it. Oh, there was going to be a grand reaping, and a glorious gathering in—the grandest, the most glorious the agricultural labourer had ever put his hand to in England for ages.

Why then should I despond and be cast down? Why should my soul be disquieted within me? Was I not marching on my way to lead my fellow-men out of the house of bondage, to deliver them from the hand of the oppressors? What if the beginning were small—would it not swell and grow greatly? What if the labourers were weak as bruised reeds? They should band together and bind themselves round with the strong steel of Union, so that they should stand up as one man in their strength to confound the mighty. Shoulder to shoulder they should go forward to strike a blow for freedom, to fight a good fight for life and liberty. When thoughts such as these burned in me like live coals, I said, "Joe Arch, what you have got to do is plain, and there must be no skulking and running away from the work which has been set you to do. You mustn't play the coward, you must play the man. You have got to trust in the Lord and in the power of His might, and speak out strong for Union." At that I took courage, and went forward with a bold heart.

When I reached Wellesbourne, lo, and behold, it was as lively as a swarm of bees in June. We settled that I should address the meeting under the old chestnut tree; and I expected to find some thirty or forty of the principal men there. What then was my surprise to see not a few tens but many hundreds of labourers assembled; there were nearly two thousand of them. The news that I was going to speak that night had been spread about; and so the men had come in from all the villages round within a radius of ten miles. Not a circular had been sent out nor a handbill printed, but from cottage to cottage, and from farm to farm, the word had been passed on; and here were the labourers gathered together in their hundreds. Wellesbourne village was there, every man in it; and they had come from Moreton and Locksley and Charlecote and Hampton Lucy, and from Barford, to hear what I had to say to them. By this time the night had fallen pitch dark; but the men got bean poles and hung lanterns on them, and we could see well enough. It was an extraordinary sight, and I shall never forget it, not to my dying day. I mounted an old pig-stool, and in the flickering light of the lanterns I saw the earnest upturned faces of these poor brothers of mine—faces gaunt with hunger and pinched with want—all looking towards me and ready to listen to the words, that would fall from my lips. These white slaves of England stood there with the darkness all about them, like the Children of Israel waiting for some one to lead them out of the land of Egypt. I determined that, if they made a mistake and took the wrong turning, it would not be my fault, so I stood on my pig-stool and spoke out straight and strong for Union. My speech lasted about an hour, I believe, but I was not measuring minutes then. By the end of it the men were properly roused, and they pressed in and crowded up asking questions; they regularly pelted me with them; it was a perfect hailstorm. We passed a resolution to form a Union then and there, and the names of the men could not be taken down fast enough; we enrolled between two and three hundred members that night. It was a brave start, and before we parted it was arranged that there should be another meeting at the same place in a fortnight's time. I knew now that a fire had been kindled which would catch on, and spread, and run abroad like sparks in stubble; and I felt certain that this night we had set light to a beacon, which would prove a rallying point for the agricultural labourers throughout the country.

The news of the meeting soon spread like wildfire, and publicity gave great help to the cause. The result was that, when I got to the chestnut tree on the evening of February 21st, a fortnight later, I found a bigger crowd than before, and I think we had nearly every policeman in the county there as well. They thought there would be a disturbance, but they need not have troubled themselves on that score. I have always preached restraint, and advocated keeping within the law, if possible. Now, more than ever, did I feel called upon to plead for moderation, and I told them in the plainest terms that, if they had recourse to violence and riot and incendiarism, or if they wantonly destroyed any kind of property, they must not look to Joseph Arch to lead them. I would be a peaceable Wat Tyler of the fields, but I would be no rioting leader of the riotous. Neither I nor they should wear handcuffs and see the inside of a gaol, if I could help it. We had come there to strike off the rusty old fetters that had crippled us, and our fathers before us, not to forge new ones for ourselves. We had come there to gain our freedom by lawful means, not to lose what little we had by lawlessness. We were going to stand up for our rights, we were going to ask for our just dues, and we were resolved to have them ; but from first to last we were going to act as law-abiding citizens, not as red-handed revolutionaries.

That meeting was as orderly a one as any man could wish to take part in who respected himself and others, and the police had nothing to do but look on and listen, while an agricultural labourer hit the nail of tyranny on the head with unsparing blows. Many a nail was hammered hard and fast into oppression's coffin that night !

A lot more joined after the meeting, and in my opinion these horny-handed sons of toil who gave in their names for Union were like the old Barons at Runnymede, for they put their sign and seal as best they could to the Magna Charta of the English Agricultural Labourer. How my heart glowed and swelled with joy as the men came in to us ! Here were some hundreds of my despised, crushed and downtrodden fellow-workers daring to stand up at last like independent men, and pledging themselves to look the farmer fair and square in the face and say : " Give us a fair day's wage and we will give you a fair day's work ; if you won't pay fair, we won't work ; if you starve us, we will strike." And any one who saw their faces and heard their words would never have had a doubt but that they meant to strike a stout blow for the cause, and not one blow either. " Dogged does it " and " strike or die " were their sentiments, and I rejoiced to know it.

We let neither grass nor weeds grow under our feet after this, I promise you. A small committee was got together, a secretary was appointed, and we set actively to work. Notices were served upon the farmers asking for sixteen shillings a week, with a week's notice if refused. We first thought of asking eighteen shillings; but from an average wage of twelve shillings to one of eighteen shillings was too much of a jump up, and no farmer would be likely to fork down another six shillings every week for the asking. An average increase of four shillings a week was more reasonable, and more likely to be granted when the farmer found he would lose his men if he did not give it. But it soon turned out that they would not hear of the sixteen shillings either; for, when the men went for their wages on the Saturday following, the farmers refused to grant it, so the men came out on strike. The shepherds and waggoners who were engaged by the month, and who had a shilling a week more than the ordinary labourer—they worked a seven days' week for it—did not come out. It was the twelve shillings a week labourer who struck; twelve shillings was the average, but there were men getting nine and ten shillings; and some were earning on an average not more than eight.

In a very short time there were a hundred men out in Wellesbourne alone, and nearly another hundred from the neighbouring villages. On the Monday after, there was hardly a labourer in Wellesbourne who went to work as usual. Men who for forty and fifty years had never known what it was to have a free day, hung about idle, and did not know what to do with themselves. These poor fellow-workers of mine did not know what to do with a holiday when they had taken it. All work and no play during a lifetime had turned Jack, the agricultural labourer, into a dull John Bull. But, dull as he might be, he had sense enough to know that once out he must bide out till the employer came to terms with him. Many a man and woman that Monday morning felt that there was a grim struggle before them; that they and their children might have to suffer pangs of hunger even worse than those they had endured in the past; that things might go so badly with them, that they would be driven from their homes, and have to be like wanderers on the face of the earth, seeking work and perhaps finding none.

But every man who had put his hand to the Union plough meant to stick to it till the Union work was done. Not a man Jack of them would yield and turn back now. That was the stubborn spirit abroad among them. There was not a pound's worth of silver among the lot who came out on strike in Wellesbourne, and till funds could be collected for their support, they had to get credit from the shop for the barest necessaries. Kettle broth, and tea made from crusts burnt black and scraped into the pot to give a little colour to the "water bewitched," was no new food and drink to the half-starved labourers; it was what they and their children had been fed upon year in and year out; but the bit of bacon could be no longer counted on. A rasher of bacon at the middle-day meal would put some heart, if not much strength, into a man; now he had to go without, or borrow it from the shopkeeper. The worst of it was, that owing to the miserable wages paid the men they were nearly always in debt to the shop a week a-head—this system of dealing was called "one week under another," and it meant that the greater part, if not the whole, of the labourer's wages were spent each week before they were earned. How could a man in such a bondage of debt as this call himself free, or feel free? No, there was always a little millstone of debt hanging round his poor weak neck, and he was a very lucky man who could rid himself of it before death took him. But they had struck for freedom now, and more were striking every day.

I was going from place to place as hard and as fast as I could, addressing meetings and forming branches of the Union. All that stirring time I felt as if there was a living fire in me. It seemed to me that I was fulfilling a mission; that I had been raised up for the work. Had not the vision of it been before my eyes for twenty years! There was a strength and a power in me which had been pent up and had been growing, and now it flowed forth. The people responded nobly to the call. I declare that, as I look back on those days, the only words which properly describe them are the words of the prophet Ezekiel when he speaks of his vision in the valley of dry bones: "So I prophesied as I was commanded: and as I prophesied, there was a noise, and behold a shaking, and the bones came together, bone to his bone. And when I beheld, lo, the sinews and the flesh came up upon them, and the skin covered them above: but there was no breath in them. Then said he unto me, Prophesy unto the wind, prophesy, son of man, and say to the wind, Thus saith the Lord God; come from the four winds, O breath, and breathe upon these slain, that they may live. So I prophesied as he commanded me, and the breath came into them, and they lived, and stood up upon their feet, an exceeding great army."

The people seemed to me to rise up like that when I went and spoke to them at this time. At one place forty-five men gave in their names, and a branch was formed in less than five minutes. Branches were formed at Barford, and Radford, and Cubbington, and Fenny Compton, and many another village and township in the neighbourhood. Then the movement spread on and on, into no less than eight counties. The men of Oxfordshire, Herefordshire, Leicestershire, Somersetshire, Norfolk, Northamptonshire, Essex, and Worcestershire rose to their feet in their valleys of dry bones, and stood up for Union. Then the whole country was aroused and was ringing with the news. All the leading papers took note of this strange thing; they could no longer ignore the fact that a great moral and intellectual awakening was in progress among the down-trodden peasantry of England.

There was anger and amazement among the powers of the land—the lord, the squire, the farmer, and the parson—when they saw these serfs of the soil girding on their manhood, and heard them refuse to starve any longer on nine and ten shillings a week. Toilers in the north and in the south, in the west and in the east, stood still to watch and listen. Here were the lowest of their brethren, those who had been dumb with fear and stricken to the earth with want, holding themselves like men, and bracing themselves together for battle with the powers of darkness seated in high places. Their voice was gone abroad with no uncertain sound, and the noise of their moving was heard afar off. The grand day of awakening had fully come.

Then the employers took counsel together; they were beginning to quake in their shoes. They tried threats first; threats had served their turn in the past, when a labourer here and there had opened his mouth to ask for more wages, threats would soon cow the labourer and teach him that his right place was to sit quiet and be thankful for what he had. The peasant might mop and mow before his lord like a monkey, but he stood up as a man at his peril. Yet the peasant continued to stand up, his poor, bent back growing stronger and straighter every day, and the high and mighty employer glared at the astonishing spectacle in powerless wrath; he got as mad as a hornet, and as savage as a bull of Bashan. These fine gentlemen had not a single serf to bully and crush, and dance a devil's dance on now; no, they had combined men to reckon with, men who, in union, were strong with the strength of a giant.

It was not very long, either, before the employer found that, when he had done his worst, he was but a poor sort of giant-killer; for the more blows he showered on him, the more that terrible Union giant thrived and waxed strong. To his terror, he learned that the giant would not be propitiated by false oaths, and deluded by lying promises into laying down his arms; that he could not be lulled to sleep by specious words and smooth speeches, so that he might be throttled and killed; but, that on the contrary, this redoubtable giant had his eyes wide open, that his cudgel was grasped firmly in his mighty hand, that he was ready to strike blow after blow for freedom with it, and that his teeth were sharpened for a bite at the hand which had starved him, and which was now stretched out to bestow on him a treacherous caress. Though the employer approached him softly, with honey on his tongue, the giant knew there was poison as of asps underneath it—yes, this new son of man turned with loathing from the Judas that would have betrayed him with a kiss.

And the powerful ones talked with one another about this new thing. The lords of the land, the hostile lords of Brobdignag, eyed it superciliously through the microscope of their own self-importance, and said, "What strange creature is this? Ah, some miserable little insect. It may do damage. Some one should kill it." That was how the lords looked at the Union man in those days.

Said the squire, swaggering up to it, "What new

vermin is this? A dose of rat-poison's the thing. Bury it out of sight and make manure of it," and swaggered away again. Said the parson, "Surely it is an evil spirit or a devil, let us flee from it"; and the parson fled as fast as his black coat would let him. Said the farmer, "We can't take stock of this thing anyhow. It's a breed we've no use for—it's dangerous. Catch it and knock it on the head"; and he stood growling. These lords and squires and parsons and farmers could not kill the Union giant; they could not even scotch him; but they tried hard to put a quick end to him.

By the beginning of March, the farmers all about were grumbling and growling at the top of their voices. Spring work had been delayed on account of the continuous rain; the weather was now fine and dry, but the men were got so fine and small, that the farmer could not see them on his farm. Out they were, and out they would stay till they had the wage they wanted.

The employers thought that, when they refused the sixteen shillings, the men would be starved into submission. It was soon evident that they had made a mistake in their tyrannical calculation. Day followed day, and the men did not come creeping humbly back like whipped curs to heel. Then the employers laid their angry heads together—they were as hot as red pepper with rage—and they declared that, if the men would not bend they must be broken. One of their schemes was to discharge the whole of the labourers in the district. "For," said they, "if all are out they will be in such a state of distress that they will not be able to help each other as they are doing now. The men who have not yet struck are contributing to the strike fund out of wages given by us—well, we are going to put a stopper on that little game. Lock out the lot, and then they will have to knuckle under."

But things did not turn out as the farmers thought they would; they could no longer work their wicked will unchecked on a miserable handful of labourers who would sink unnoticed in a local struggle. Hodge the Unionist was up for a bout with Jack his master, and the ring looking on was as big as all England. The press gave tongue, and then there was a hue and cry all over the country. The *Daily News* did us yeoman service by sending down Archibald Forbes, the famous war correspondent, to collect information and write up the subject. He went round to several of the villages with me to see the condition of things for himself, and when the first of his powerful articles appeared he came to me with a copy of the *Daily News* in his hand, and said, pointing to the article, "Now you won't want for money."

He spoke the truth too; practical sympathy was stirred by them, and the money we sorely needed flowed in from unexpected quarters. The *Daily News* has been a true and staunch friend to the labourer all through, and I should like to put it on record here that I consider we owe the paper a debt of gratitude for the service it rendered the Agricultural Labourers'

Union in 1872. Those articles opened the eyes of a large section of the public to the gravity of the struggle going on in South Warwickshire at that moment, and materially helped to turn the scale in our favour at a critical time.

The strike was now in full swing. The farmer had beckoned to the labourer and patted the hard bed of servitude in vain; all their patting and wheedling could not persuade the men to come back and lie down on it. Skin and bone had had enough of flinty couches. Said the labourer, "Give me the sixteen shillings a week and I'll make my humble bed my own way. It won't be a bed of luxury, but it'll be a bed I can rest my aching bones on. If you don't I'll walk off to where I can get what I want."

Then the farmer began to hit out right and left with his arbitrary fist, and the word was passed round among them that every Union man was to be knocked flat and jumped on. At Radford and Wellesbourne and other places near, they were turned out of their cottages; about Harbury and Snitterfield, they were discharged, and the masters all over the neighbourhood followed suit. One well-known gentleman who occupied an influential position in the county, made his agent serve notices on all his Union tenants about Walton and Wellesbourne. He also called a meeting in the interests of the employers. These kind gentlemen agreed among themselves that the Union fostered a spirit of discord, and that the demands of the strikers were excessive; and it was resolved that in the interests of the men themselves, they should be dissuaded from joining the Union, and that those of them who had been foolish enough to join, should be strongly advised to withdraw. Spoil the Union piecemeal was their policy; but they found we were wide awake, and declined to be spoiled. Some employers said they would advance wages from twelve shillings to fifteen shillings; but they did not wish to give the additional shilling, because it would look as if they had been forced to it by the Union. One landlord, Lord Leigh, granted an advance to fifteen shillings, and a good many offered fourteen shillings. The question now was, "Is it to be fifteen or sixteen shillings?"

Canon Girdlestone wrote in a friendly spirit advising compromise and conciliation. He said the Warwickshire labourer was already better off than many of his kind. We did not dispute the fact that the bulk of the labourers in Devonshire got only eight shillings a week, that few or none got more than nine shillings, and that bad cottages and high rents were the rule there. It was all too true; but to our thinking, this only showed that the sooner they had the Union all through Devonshire and such benighted regions the better for Hodge.

The London Trades Council took up our cause. It offered help, and it called on workmen of all classes to support us. It was pointed out to the artisan that by assisting his brother-toiler to stay in the country on better conditions, he would then not be so likely to crowd into the towns, and his purchasing power would most probably be a good deal higher. "Help your brother and you help yourself" was the moral of it.

On the Good Friday of 1872, about six weeks after the formation of the Union, we held a great demonstration and tea meeting in the public hall, Portland Street, Leamington. It made a tremendous stir, and people came flocking and streaming in from miles round. Crowds of poor labourers with their wives and children marched into the town, headed by their village fife and drum bands. Leamington had never seen such a sight in all its born days; and those who saw it and took part in it are not likely to forget it. Wellesbourne was to the fore as usual. John Lewis had seen to that. He was one of the very first men in the district to help set the Union going, and he was no laggard now. He sent messengers off to scour the neighbourhood, and he got a bell and went round like a town-crier, summoning the people to a tryst under the old chestnut tree at 8.30 a.m. on Good Friday morning. At the appointed time men and women came tramping up dressed in what of best they had. A poor best according to rich folk's notions no doubt, but smock frock and fustian jacket and shabby gown covered brave English hearts, beating high with hope of the good times coming. That little band of stiff and bent and battered men, stunted and toil-worn, with their thin and haggard wives, were no coneys—a sorry and a feeble folk. No; they were strong in Union as they took the road this March morning, with stout and trusty John Lewis at their head. They marched away, singing this rhyme as they tramped into Leamington:

"The farm labourers of South Warwickshire,
Have not had a rise for many a year,
Although bread has often been dear;
But now they've found a Union."

And so they had, as all the world was soon to know.

It was a busy day for me, if it was a proud one. I took the chair at the Organising Committee which sat in the room downstairs. They elected me organising secretary at a small salary, and Henry Taylor, a Leamington carpenter, was elected paid secretary, on the condition that he gave up any office he might hold in another Union, and joined ours. We wanted neither outsiders nor professional Trades Union men; we knew our own business and we were determined from the outset to manage it in our own way. "Hands off!" we said to any outside meddler who wanted to poke a finger into our Union pie. We then drew up the following Rules:—

1. The name of the Society shall be the "Warwickshire Agricultural Labourers' Union."

2. Its object is to elevate the social position of the farm labourers of the county by assisting them to increase their wages; to lessen the number of ordinary working hours; to improve their habitations; to provide them with gardens or allotments; and to

assist deserving and suitable labourers to migrate and emigrate.

3. In all questions of dispute about remuneration of labour, an attempt shall be made to decide such dispute by arbitration between the Union and the employers of labour.

4. The Board shall have power to make arrangements for arbitration as regards the price of labour; to take charge of all disputes between employers and employed; to make arrangements for supporting members when out of work; to help labourers to migrate and emigrate; to suspend, fine or expel any member who shall violate the society's regulations, and shall have such other powers as may be necessary to accomplish the objects of the Society, and shall avail itself of all requisite provisions under the Friendly Societies and Trades Unions Acts.

5. The Board shall hereafter decide how many hours, not exceeding ten, shall constitute a day's work, and all over-time shall be paid for at the rate of fourpence per hour, and all Sunday work shall be paid for as overtime, except in such cases as the Union shall direct.

6. Labourers' work shall cease by four o'clock on Saturdays, except in such cases as the Union may direct.

7. The Board shall consist of one delegate, elected by each branch numbering not less that fifty members, and three members of the Leamington Trades' Union; but the last-mentioned members shall not have the power of voting.

8. The Board shall meet monthly at Leamington to transact the business of the Society, and special meetings may be convened by the secretary and chairman jointly at two days' notice ; nine delegates to form a quorum.

Rule 9 provided for the election of a chairman, secretary, treasurer (who must find security), two trustees, and a professional auditor.

Rule 13 provided that there should be a yearly meeting at Leamington, at which the Board shall submit a report and balance sheet (audited) for approval.

The contributions to the Union were fixed at sixpence entrance fee, and twopence per week subscription.

We had got through a good afternoon's work by the time all was settled, and we had the evening meeting still before us. Oh, what a meeting that was !

Many of the Trade Unions took part in it, and nearly every tradesman in and around Leamington was there. The gentlemen of Warwickshire were conspicuous by their absence, but the people had been pouring in, and pouring in like a flood, till the hall was as full as it could hold ; and then they overflowed into the street, and thousands more joined the overflow. They called for me to come out and address them ; so out I came, and Forbes took the chair and we held a meeting there. When I stood up in my moleskins, I faced such a crowd of my fellow-creatures as I had never before set eyes on. It was a flood-tide of humanity which swayed and heaved as far as I could see in the gas-light; it extended right away down Windsor Street.

The spectacle of those waiting thousands was enough to touch the heart and fire any man not made of wood and stone. It fired me so that I felt I had got the strength of ten men in me. My heart went out to every listener there, and that made my voice reach them too. I told them what a struggle I had had, how I had fought my way up, bit by bit. I wanted them to know that I had been through what they were suffering now; that I was no professional agitator, but a working agricultural labourer, who was acquainted with their griefs from personal experience, and who was convinced that their one chance of social salvation lay in Union; that if they meant to have a living wage instead of a starvation one, they must combine and unite to get it. It was their due; for when a man gave his master honest work, he had a right to honest money in return. It was no matter of compliment or favour between master and man, but of fair dealing and bargaining. I wanted the men to act rightly by themselves and their wives and little children.

Years ago, when I was a young married man, my master had said to me, "Eighteen-pence a day is all I'll give you." I had a wife and two children, and I knew my duty to them before God, because of the vow I had made to her at the altar, to be, to do, or to die, to keep them. I knew that eighteen-pence a day would not keep them, and I struck. I knew I got into bad report for that, and in consequence I had to put on clothes on Monday morning, and never took them off again till Saturday night, and I went where I could get higher wages. Sometimes I could not get anything but straw to lie on, and once I slept for nights on corded wood. The Union offered the men a shorter way to a living wage than the slow road I had been forced to take. And why? Because I was single-handed. I could never have gone as far as I had done, if I had not had a great deal in my favour. I put it all before them, and I urged every working man and woman present to join the Union. Through it and through it only would labourers' right prevail against employers' right. While I spoke I felt I was carrying the people along with me. It was a splendid meeting.

Inside the Hall the people heard capital speeches from gentlemen who were in sympathy with the cause. Among the principal speakers were Sir Baldwin Leighton, the Hon. Auberon Herbert, Mr. E. Jenkins, M.P., Dr. Langford of Birmingham, and Jesse Collings. A labourers' friend at Birmingham sent us a donation of £100, through Mr. Dixon, M.P. When this was announced there was a tremendous outburst of cheering, and when a note from this unknown friend was read out the cheering was louder than ever. He wrote to us, "The right to form the Union must be fought for to the death." The people caught up those words like a battle cry. It was just what we were all feeling that night inside the hall and outside it. With one voice we shouted, "The right to form the Union must be fought for to the death!" The labourers of Warwickshire who had assembled in Leamington on that Good Friday evening tramped back to their poor homes strong for Union. Yes, the dumb had found a voice at last; the despairing were filled with hope; the downtrodden slave had become a man again. Their forefathers had stood up for the threatened liberties of England, and with scythes and pitchforks and clubbed muskets had beaten back the King's Life Guards till the cannon mowed them down. The men of Warwickshire, in the year of grace eighteen hundred and seventy-two, meant to stand up like soldiers, and fight or die for the Agricultural Labourers' Union.

CHAPTER V.

FORMING THE UNION.

THE Leamington meeting was a startler to those gentry who had blinded themselves with blinkers, and made themselves hard of hearing with cotton wool, and had sat at ease in the lordly chair of the scornful. It burst like a bomb among these proud lollers and made them jump with rage. There was a fine clattering and chattering from one end of the county to the other ; such a noise and a to-do as if the skies were falling in on them, and the ground was crumbling away under their feet. In a manner of speaking the ground they trod on had become alive, and had risen up against them, and given them earthquake shocks, each stronger than the last, till after the big one at Leamington they stood up shaking. But we were not idling our dear-bought time away, listening on our doorsteps to the hullabaloos : not a bit of it ; for they might clatter and chatter till their tongues ached, as long as they left us free to finish the work we had set our hands to. Six weeks we had been at it almost night and day, and we were hard and fast at it now, pushing ahead at racing speed, covering the ground on our own conveyances as if we were walking and talking for a wager. So we were; we had staked our little all—our widow's mite—on the Union, and it was fight or fall with us. We did not mean to fall and lie flat; we meant to stand up and wrestle and strain every sinew till the day was ours. "More money and men for the Union!" was our battle cry now.

We had made an appeal to the country for funds; we now sent out circulars to all members of Parliament, and to the Trade Unions throughout the country as well. In a very few days cheques ranging from £50 to £100 began to come in. The response was quick as it was generous. That golden stream caused fresh life to flow through our veins. When the lock-out commenced we had only five shillings in hand and that was in coppers, pennies and half-pennies contributed by some of the labourers; most of them had not a farthing to their name.

I remember once, after a meeting under the old chestnut tree—Archibald Forbes was there, also the Hon. Auberon Herbert and Mr. E. Jenkins—how we adjourned to John Lewis's cottage to transact business in those early Union days. We had a solitary light to lighten our darkness, and the committee stood on the stone-flagged floor. We had two teacups to hold the money. I and another member received the books from the local secretaries and advanced what cash was needed. The books contained the list of names of all the Branch members, also of those out of work, and a record of the number of days in the week on which any had got work. When this statement had been made in full the secretary received the total amount for his particular branch. We allowed about nine shillings a week for each family when we could. Well, such was the staunch feeling for the Union among the members, that those who had been fortunate enough to get work in the second week of the strike and lock-out, paid in something for the others, though they were not bound by any of our rules to do so. That is but one example of the self-sacrifice and brotherly kindness which prevailed amongst us. Yes ; we were strongly knit together by loyalty and good will, so it would have been a strange thing if we had not won.

I remember, too, a stirring meeting at Southam early in April. I addressed upwards of three hundred labourers and their wives on the bowling green there. It was a good place for the unskilled labourers to be drafted to, as there were stone quarries and lime works in the neighbourhood. At that time I was all for migration, from one part of the country to another. I did not want to see our best men taken out of the country. I knew that there was room and work for all, if only some gumption and common-sense were exercised by the labourers and their leaders in settling and arranging with the right masters in the best places. I believed that work could be found then, without much difficulty, for six or seven hundred men, at wages ranging from twenty to twenty-five shillings a week. If the worst came to the worst we could send as many out of the country. Emigration agents, with the best intentions no doubt, were prowling around, picking and choosing the most likely, and tempting them across the sea. I set my back stiff against the emigration door as long as I could, but men were slipping through, for there was hope on the other side of it; land and life and liberty might be theirs in the colonies, and the mother country had given them stones for bread, and for drink the cold water of workhouse charity.

Some of the discharged men were migrating to other localities. Gentlemen came in search of hands for the cotton mills, and others wanted labourers on the railway works. The North Eastern Railway offered work for drivers and horsekeepers at one pound and twenty-three shillings a week A good many went North and some emigrated to New Zealand. The labourer, through the Union, was now able to break the chain of poverty, fear, and debt, which had tied him by the leg to one place. He would hobble off elsewhere, and soon he would learn how to walk erect—a free man. The employers kept locking-out the men and refusing to come to terms with those who had asked for the rise. There were some two hundred men on strike in the Leamington district alone. But I should like to honourably mention one employer who was a noble exception to her class in our neighbourhood. Miss Rylands, a Wellesbourne lady, took the better part ; when she received notice from her labourers she sent for a gentleman from Birmingham, asked him to arbitrate, and on his award she increased their wages without more ado.

I was holding meetings wherever I could get men together, and we met mostly out of doors. I remember addressing over four hundred in an orchard at Harbury. Sometimes we gathered under a tree, sometimes in a field ; now it would be in an orchard, and the next might be by the roadside. We met by sunlight and moonlight and starlight and lantern light—the sun in the sky or the farthing dip—it was all one to the Union man at that time. When we were assembled we often led off with a song or Union ballad such as the following :—

STAND LIKE THE BRAVE.

(*Adapted by* G. M. Ball.)

O workmen awake, for the strife is at hand;
With right on your side, then with hope firmly stand
To meet your oppressors, go, fearlessly go,
And stand like the brave, with your face to the foe.

Stand like the brave, stand like the brave;
Oh, stand like the brave with your face to the foe.

Whatever's the danger, take heed and beware,
And turn not your back—for no armour is there ;
Seek righteous reward for your labour—then go
And stand like the brave, with your face to the foe.

The cause of each other with vigour defend,
Be honest and true, and fight to the end;
Where duty may lead you, go, fearlessly go,
And stand like the brave, with your face to the foe.

Let hope then still cheer us; though long be the strife,
More comforts shall come to the workman's home life;
More food for our children; demand it, then go
And stand like the brave, with your face to the foe.

Press on, never doubting redemption draws near—
Poor serfs shall arise from oppression and fear;
Though great ones oppose you, they cannot o'erthrow
If you stand like the brave, with your face to the foe.

We would start that to a rousing tune, and sing it with a will all together. There was another which was a great favourite; it was called "The Fine Old English Labourer," and it went to the tune of "A Fine Old English Gentleman," as follows:—

Come, lads, and listen to my song, a song of honest toil,
'Tis of the English labourer, the tiller of the soil;
I'll tell you how he used to fare, and all the ills he bore,
Till he stood up in his manhood, resolved to bear no more.
This fine old English labourer, one of the present time.

He used to take whatever wage the farmer chose to pay,
And work as hard as any horse for eighteenpence a day;
Or if he grumbled at the nine, and dared to ask for ten,
The angry farmer cursed and swore, and sacked him there and then.

He used to tramp off to his work while town folk were abed,
With nothing in his belly but a slice or two of bread;
He dined upon potatoes, and he never dreamed of meat,
Except a lump of bacon fat sometimes by way of treat.

He used to find it hard enough to give his children food,
But sent them to the village school as often as he could;
But though he knew that school was good, they must have bread and clothes,
So he had to send them to the fields to scare away the crows.

He used to walk along the fields and see his landlord's game
Devour his master's growing crops, and think it was a shame;
But if the keeper found on him a rabbit or a wire,
He got it hot when brought before the parson and the squire.

But now he's wide awake enough and doing all he can
At last, for honest labour's rights, he's fighting like a man;
Since squires and landlords will not help, to help himself he'll try,
And if he does not get fair wage, he'll know the reason why.

They used to treat him as they liked in the evil days of old,
They thought there was no power on earth to beat the power of gold;
They used to threaten what they'd do whenever work was slack,
But now he laughs their threats to scorn with the Union at his back.
This fine old English labourer, one of the present time.

If a squire or a parson or a farmer had passed by on the other side while we were singing this song or others like it, his ears would have told him that the English labourer was awake to his wrongs, and meant to have his rights at last. Yes, poor Hodge was sitting up and rubbing his eyes after his long sleep, and he was getting on to his feet and shaking himself and pulling himself together, and was walking about and was talking over things with his mates. "We won't be worms much longer," the men were saying, not under their breaths as if they feared stone walls might betray them, but they were using the manly voice their Maker had given them.

The movement was flowing over the country like a spring tide. The men of Denham in Buckinghamshire joined in hundreds. There was agitation in Norfolk, where the men struck for shorter hours; there was a lock-out at Long Sutton Marsh, and very soon the wages in that district advanced to two shillings and threepence and two shillings and sixpence a day. Men in Dorsetshire were striking; the labourers about Shaftesbury and Blandford came out asking for a rise to twelve shillings a week. The state of the labourer in that county was as bad as it could very well be.

The men of Gloucestershire and Worcestershire were moving and meeting. The wages there were from nine up to twelve shillings a week, and I daresay the average would be about ten shillings. Rents were high, from four to six pounds a year, and the accommodation was miserable. They worked very long hours all over this part. A man would start at five o'clock in the morning, and he did not leave off until dark ; often he was at it till very late, and cases were frequent where the men had a day's work that went nearly round the clock twice over. Of course here, as in other places, the carters had a seven days' week ; many of them having from five to ten horses to look after. For a man to be free of debt was the great exception, and not the rule. At one meeting I asked the men present who were not in debt to the shopkeeper to hold up their hands, and when I looked there was not one single hand held up. The curse of debt lay heavy on the agricultural labourer wherever I went, and who was going to blame them?

Take the case of a man getting what was at that time considered a good wage for the labourer in most places, thirteen shillings a week. A Barford man would have to pay for rent one shilling and sixpence, if he had something of a family and lived in a decent cottage. He would spend about nine shillings on bread, loaves being sevenpence-halfpenny each ; potatoes were at the rate of four shillings and sixpence for eight gallons, flour about twelve shillings a bushel. If there were two children at school that would be a regular out-going twopence a week.

It is easy to see that a man's expenses were bound to be greater than his earnings. The family lived on potatoes, dry bread, greens, and herbs, kettle broth, and tea which was coloured water ; there was a bit of bacon for the man now and then, but fresh meat would come like Christmas, once a year. Perhaps one of the boys might be earning about three shillings a week at ploughing, another getting a little for bird-scaring, and sometimes the wife herself would go into the fields, but she could only go if the family was small and running on its own legs—if there were several young ones and a baby in the cradle she was forced to bide at home. There was the wear and tear of clothes to be reckoned. In nine cases out of ten the bread bill had to wait for clearance till harvest bounty, when for about a month the man would earn about one pound a week. What chance had that family of being strong and healthy? Low living made poor blood and poor bones and poor flesh. If the father got a leg sore and was laid by with it—and that was no rare thing—the family would have to go on the parish till he could get about again. Many an honest striving man was no better than a wrung dishclout before he was half through his day's work. It was no uncommon occurrence for a decent, self-respecting labourer to find himself, after a working life of sixty years, brought down to parish help at the bitter end.

I knew of such men and their wives, who had worked early and late, toiling and moiling and patching and contriving, who had reared a large family of sons and daughters, who had kept themselves to themselves, and showed a brave front to misfortune, and had never had a farthing of parish relief the whole time, and yet who, in their honourable old age, were driven to go on the parish when they began to fail. The Union said, "We're going to stop this."

All through April the labourers were rising, and the farmers were standing out, and the clergy were taking the matter up. The Vicar of Harbury convened a meeting in support of the Union, and there was a parson here and there who went with us openly; but the majority were against us, and others blew now hot now cold, and flew round like weather-cocks as squire or farmer or villager grew strongest at the moment. These shining lights of the Church as by Law Established were but poor farthing rushlights to the agricultural labourer. The Farmers' Club threatened us, but the young Union had fastened its milk teeth in the farmers' jaws, and did not mean to leave go. Some of the farmers were all for advertising; they wanted to import Scotch and Irish labour at cheap rates, because the season was advancing, and our men were leaving the neighbourhood, and unless the employers granted the rise they were not likely to be such fools as to come back again.

Some of those gentlemen who had the good of the cause at heart warned me against having anything to do with professional agitators; Mr. Bromley Davenport, M.P., was one of those who cautioned us, and there were others who said, "Arch, don't let this movement be complicated by Trade Union interference." I had made up my mind to keep clear of them all; I was not going to let them have any control over our affairs if I could help it. Our movement was well started before they took any notice of us. When I met with one of the Trade Union men down at Whitnash I had already founded eight of our Branch Unions. Letters were now coming in by the gross from all parts of the country, asking for help and advice, and inviting me and Russell to come and start branch Unions. We found ourselves with an immense job on hand. I remember how our Executive Committee sat the whole day through—it was, I think, on April 10th—in the Primitive Methodist Chapel at Wellesbourne, settling what further organisation was necessary, and making plans for larger united action. We divided the country into two districts, North and South; a secretary was appointed to each, and a staff of speakers was told off to lecture and carry on the campaign. As thousands had joined us, and more were coming in every day, we felt that the time had come for establishing the Union on a wider basis.

It had grown to be a national movement and it was high time it had a national name. The idea was to concentrate and consolidate the County Unions somewhat on the lines of the Farmers' Agricultural Chambers, all of them to converge in one central body, which would assemble at some appointed place. We accordingly decided that we would call together a great congress to be held at Leamington towards the end of May, in order to establish a National Agricultural Labourers' Union. This was to take a mighty big stride forward, but we considered that facts warranted our making it.

Agriculturists were officially recognising an agitation which had been going on for two months. At a special meeting of the County Chamber of Agriculture, held at the Shire Hall in Warwick, the Earl of Denbigh advised employers to confer with the labourers, and see if they could not between them come to some satisfactory settlement; for, as it was, things were at a dead-lock. Some of the farmers now began to declare that the ground had been cut from under their feet by the labourers.

We knew nothing about that; but it was pretty plain we were making farmer and landlord sit up and take stock of us, and our doings and askings. They declared that they could not increase the men's wages to any extent, as rent depended on the value of the poorest land that could be cultivated profitably, and that the effect of any great rise in wage would be to throw the poorest land out of cultivation.

The employers were agreed that better dwellings should be provided, and that many of the cottages were not all they should be; but, said they, "Look at our side of the question; unequal local taxation prevents the landlord from investing capital in better cottages, and so improving his property." They talked away and argued and discussed, and said something must be done, but what that something was to be they did not exactly know. Others said that it was only to be expected that the labourer would ask for some sort of rise in his wage, because there appeared to be a general increase of prosperity in all kinds of trade throughout the country, and that the agricultural workman knew this, and wanted to share in it; also, that in some form, direct or indirect, he was bound to benefit with the rest, though the advantage might not be permanent. They asked us to send some delegates to a conference, but we declined. They proposed that the Union should appoint three representatives to meet three landowners and three tenant farmers. Russell wrote back that our executive committee would be glad to know a little more about the properly appointed representatives, and what qualifications they were supposed to possess. He wrote, too, that the resolution of the Executive Committee was, "That in view of the present incomplete state of the formation of the Agricultural Labourers' Union, this meeting is of opinion that the proposal should be postponed for the present." Russell's letter was dated April 29th, 1872. We were not going to be hurried into action to suit the convenience of the employers.

The County Chamber of Agriculture held another meeting at the Warwick Shire Hall early in May. Said they to themselves, "Something must be settled, and that soon, or where shall we be?" This labourers' agitation is really a very serious matter indeed. Look at this Union, its success is quite extraordinary, it has extended into all the adjoining counties, and in a few weeks it is to be expanded from a mere County Union into a National one, by means of a great congress of representatives. Owing to migration and the state of the general labour market, wages are still going up; they have already risen from twelve to fourteen and fifteen shillings; and this Union is insisting on having sixteen shillings, and it says that if the sixteen shillings is withheld the men can get twenty-three shillings, and even twenty-seven shillings by taking train to the North. This is terrible; if we delay, wages may go higher still. We must show the Union that we are willing to come to terms, that we even court reconciliation, but we must be careful not to pledge ourselves to particulars."

It was clear the employers meant business. Most of the prominent members of the Council were present, including about thirty tenant farmers and several influential landowners. They sent an answer to Russell's letter, saying that the Chairman and two other members of the Chamber of Agriculture would be willing to meet any three members appointed by the Committee of the Agricultural Labourers' Union as their representatives. The employers were all for conciliation now, and they went so far as to consider the labourers' feelings! They declared that the Wellesbourne farmers' resolutions placarded about the country, intimidating men from joining the Union by threatening to turn them out of their situations and cottages, was most illegal, inconsiderate and uncalled for.

Here was a change! The Chamber was now advocating piecework; and also payment of wages in coin, instead of partly in coin and partly in kind. Said these gentlemen, in their new-born consideration for the welfare of the labourer, "This practice of paying wages in kind prevents a just estimate of the value received by the labourer, induces unreasonable demands on the part of the employed, affords facilities for impositions by unscrupulous employers, leads to improvident habits, and increases intemperance."

All very true, but why did these gentlemen not find this out before; or if they had found it out, why had they not taken action? Such was their tender feeling for the labourer *now*, that they agreed to ask the farmers to pay the men their wages the day before the local market, so as to give them an opportunity of laying out their money to the best advantage. A new day was dawning for Hodge indeed!

Just after this I presided at the first meeting of our board of directors. It was held in the Temperance Hall at Leamington, and some five and thirty delegates from the county branches put in an appearance. Our chief business was to make all arrangements for the coming Congress. The Board was greatly assisted by the valuable counsel of Mr. E. Jenkins, of the Middle Temple, a member of our Finance Committee. I remember what cheering reports were put in. Contributions were coming in from every side, and the total amount already reached the figure of over £800.

About four thousand men were enrolled in Warwickshire alone; Lincolnshire had between three and four thousand in Union; Cambridgeshire had over two thousand, and Huntingdonshire the same.

It was resolved that a National Congress should be held at the end of the month. We decided to accept the offer of a preliminary conference with the representatives of the Chamber of Agriculture: I and two others to represent the Union. We appointed Jesse Collings, E. Jenkins, J. Arnold, and E. Haynes, Union trustees.

As there was now only a handful of labourers out on strike in the Wellesbourne district, we resolved that, subject to the necessities of the Warwickshire Labourers' Union, such subscriptions as came to hand should be held in trust to assist our brethren in other parts. We were of opinion that the Union funds should be for the general benefit of the agricultural labourers throughout the kingdom—those who were in the Union, of course—and we decided to take the opinion of the congress on the subject. It was certain that we ought to be regularly empowered to draw on our funds for general migration and emigration purposes when needful. The contributions were general, and the Union was becoming general too.

We meant to hold an evening meeting in the Temperance Hall as well, but so many wanted to attend that we decided to have it in the circus instead, where there were seats for about three thousand people. We sent out hasty announcements by hand-bill and crier, and in spite of the heavy rain there was a large gathering, and the meeting was a most enthusiastic one. It put fresh spirit into all of us. Later on in the month we had a good meeting at Buckingham. Then came the great day of the Congress—May 29th—when some sixty delegates attended. Invitations had been sent to every county in England and Wales, requesting the Unions to send up two or more *bona fide* representative farm labourers, that they might take part in forming a National Union, the aim of which was the general improvement of their brethren. Some of the delegates came very long distances, the expenses being borne by the local Unions. They met to discuss such points as the raising of wages, the lessening of working hours, the improvement of cottages, the securing of suitable allotments, and the aiding of emigration. Influential and experienced gentlemen were invited to read papers on the second day. We wanted high and low to join in throwing light on the subject, with a view to taking legislative action. "Act, act in the living present" was our motto.

G. Dixon, M.P. for Birmingham, was in the chair, and among those present on the platform were Sir Baldwin Leighton, Hon. and Rev. J. W. Leigh, Rev. J. J. Trebeck, Rev. C. F. C. Pigott, Dr. J. A. Langford, Rev. A. O'Neil; J. Campbell, J.P. (Rugby),

W. G. Ward, H. Pratt, Sec. of the London Executive Committee, Jesse Collings, and A. Arnold. Letters of sympathy were read from the Hon. Auberon Herbert, Professor Fawcett, M.P., Lord Edmond Fitzmaurice, M.P., Canon Girdlestone, and others.

Dr. Langford reported on the progress and condition of the Union. There had been some thirty village meetings, attended by a total of twelve thousand one hundred labourers and others; sixty-three branches had been formed, consisting in all of four thousand six hundred and seventy-two members. About a hundred and fifty men had been helped during the strike, and had been assisted to migrate. Some two hundred labourers had emigrated. It was calculated that in all there were between forty and fifty thousand in Union.

I should mention here that a Union movement had been started in Herefordshire in 1871, nearly a year before ours. It began in the village of Leintwardine and it was backed up by the rector. It spread over six counties in a very short time, and when our Congress sat it had been so successfully worked by T. H. Strange, the secretary, and by others, that there were about thirty thousand members in it. The watchword of the Herefordshire organisation had been from its commencement, "Emigration, migration, but not strikes." This West of England Union had sent surplus labour to Yorkshire, Lancashire, and Staffordshire, where the wages averaged sixteen and seventeen shillings; and some men, about forty, I think, had been emigrated to America. Before this movement began the average rate of wages in Hererordshire had been from nine to ten shillings ; in Gloucestershire the average was nine shillings ; often a man's wages did not amount to more than eight shillings ; and that not for "wet or dry," so that his earnings might not reach seven shillings a week sometimes. No sooner had this Union caught on than wages in Herefordshire rose on an average two shillings a week, and all over the six counties there was improvement, though there was plenty of room for a great deal more. In Wiltshire and in Dorsetshire particularly, there was much more to be done in the way of a general levelling up.

Well, here we were at the end of May 1872 with a strength of nearly fifty thousand, and I consider such a splendid force of Agricultural Labourers, banded together in one common cause, justified us in putting on record the faith that was in us, which we did as follows :—"The Committee believe in the justice and righteousness of their cause, and have the firmest faith that Divine blessing will rest upon it."

Our delegates also proposed, seconded, and adopted the following resolutions :—

"That a complete list of the public subscriptions be printed, and that the hearty thanks of the Conference be hereby given to all who have contributed to the funds of the movement, or otherwise promoted it.

"That a National Union of Agricultural Labourers be formed in each county or division of county, and that the National Agricultural Labourers' Union shall consist of representatives elected by such district Unions.

"That the Council of the National Agricultural Labourers' Union meet at Leamington at least twice a year, and that the expenses of the representatives so attending be paid by the various district Unions.

"That the Executive or Managing Committee of the National Agricultural Labourers' Union shall consist of twelve labourers elected annually at a meeting of the Council of the National Agricultural Labourers' Union.

"That such Executive or Managing Committee shall meet at Leamington at least once a fortnight.

"That the following twelve labourers constitute the Executive of the National Agricultural Labourers' Union *pro tem*: J. Arch, E. Russell, G. Allington, T. Parker, J. Biddle, J. Prickett, J. Harris, E. Haynes, H. Blackwell, G. Jordan, B. Herring, G. Lunnon, and E. Pill."

In the afternoon we again met for further settlement of the constitution of the National Agricultural Labourers' Union, and the following were some of the resolutions adopted:—

"That a committee be formed of gentlemen favourable to the principles of the National Agricultural Labourers' Union, for consultation and advice, but without the power to vote; such committee to be invited to act by the Executive Committee.

"That the Executive Committee of the National Agricultural Labourers' Union be requested to draw up the rules of the Union, and obtain such aid as may be necessary, and submit such rules to the first general meeting of the Council for approval.

"That the Executive of the National Agricultural Labourers' Union be empowered to procure the necessary offices and paid officers, and other help for the transacting of the business of the Union.

"That Mr. J. E. M. Vincent be requested to act as the treasurer of the National Agricultural Labourers' Union.

"That the funds of the National Agricultural Labourers' Union be invested in the names of the following gentlemen as trustees :—

"Jesse Collings (Birmingham); E. Jenkins (London); A. Arnold (Hampton-in-Arden) ; E. Haynes (Ratley).

"That all payments made by the treasurer be based on resolutions of the Executive Committee signed by the chairman and one of the Committee members.

"That the repayment of money by the trustees to the treasurer shall be on authority of a resolution of the Executive Committee signed by the chairman and one other member of the Committee."

The Executive decided to select for a committee of advisers, such gentlemen from the London and Birmingham Aid Committees as they thought would be most useful.

Hodgson Pratt, secretary of the London Central Aid Committee asked us how his committee could best assist the movement ; he, and indeed all those from outside who attended, showed a spirit of most hearty goodwill.

It warmed my heart when I saw the delegates come in. I was able that proud day to give the hand of fellowship and a true Union greeting to men come up from Herefordshire and Bedfordshire and Shropshire and Wiltshire, from Dorsetshire and Gloucestershire and Staffordshire, from Yorkshire and Norfolk and Suffolk and Bucks and Nottinghamshire, from Northamptonshire and Worcestershire and Huntingdonshire, and from distant Radnorshire. Never had there been a gathering like unto this. When I stood up there with all these brethren gathered together in Congress, while we sang Russell's spirit-stirring Union hymn as with one mighty voice, I said within myself, "Joseph Arch, you have not lived in vain, and of a surety the Lord God of Hosts is with us this day."

In my speech I told them that we must have frequent meetings for consultation and discussion, that we might keep up the spirit of good fellowship and put heart into one another. There must be no local jealousies, no self-seeking, no isolation; we must stand and act together, if we would not fall to pieces like a bundle of sticks without a binder. The Branches and Districts would work in concord through a common representative and Executive Committee. A Central Fund was the stand-by of the great trade societies, and so it would be of our National Union; we were bound to have a central common treasury. Every member was clearly to understand that the Branch was to remit its fund to the District ; that each District would remit three-fourths of the receipts to the National centre ; and that if any Branch or District failed to do this, it would have no kind of claim on the general resources of the Union. It was essential that money matters should be regularly organised on the soundest possible basis. The fourth part, which the Districts were to be allowed to keep back, was to be spent at the District Committee's discretion in meeting current expenses and promoting the general objects of the Union.

For the working expenses of the various Branches we recommended an Incidental Fund, which could easily be kept going, if each member would make a small payment. I urged all members to act with great caution and referred them to Rule 10 which ran like this :—"All cases of dispute between members of of the National Agricultural Labourers' Union, and employers must be laid before the Branch Committee to which such members may belong ; and should the Branch Committee be unable to arrange the question to the mutual satisfaction of the parties interested, in conjunction with the District Committee, recourse shall had to be arbitration. Should the District Committee be unable to arrange for such arbitration, an appeal shall be made to the National Executive Committee for its decision. Any award made by the arbitration or by the decision of the National Executive shall be binding on all members of the Union; and in no case shall a strike be resorted to until all the above means have been tried and have failed."

That shows plainly how we felt and intended to act on the strike question. "Don't strike," I said, "unless all other means fail. Let peace and moderation mark all our meetings; let courtesy and fairness and firmness mark all our demands. Let us exercise patience in the enforcement of just claims; let us fraternise, let us centralise, and all will go well with us; and we shall surely prosper in the glorious work we have put our hands to. With brotherly feeling, with a united front, with every District welded into a great whole; with a common fund to which all shall contribute, and on which all shall have the right to draw, the time will not be distant when every agricultural labourer shall have what few have yet enjoyed—a fair day's pay for a fair day's work. Nine and a half hours, exclusive of meal times, as a day's work, and sixteen shillings a week pay are not extravagant demands. Brothers, be united and you will be strong; be temperate and you will be respected; realise a central capital and you will be able to act with firmness and independence. Be united, be sober, and you will soon be free."

United action for our common freedom—that was the sentiment of the Agricultural Labourers' Congress which sat at Leamington; and which, by its action in organising the Union on a national basis, marked an important epoch in the history of the movement, and started it forward on a fresh career of struggle and of triumph.

CHAPTER VI.

PROGRESS OF THE UNION.

THE May Congress which inaugurated the National Agricultural Labourers' Union was so much more of a success than any of us had expected that not a few were nearly carried off their feet by surprise, so to speak. It roused more feeling for and against us than ever. Our friends cheered us on with right good will ; and I do not think I am using much of a figure of speech when I say that our enemies went about gnashing their teeth with spiteful rage, and grinning like the dog mentioned in the Psalms. They might run around grinning and gnashing and foaming as hard as they pleased as long as they did not cross our track ; there were some of us who thought that if they did they would be served as the cow was by the engine, it would be a bad day for them ; the big Union engine was now going along at full speed with plenty of fuel to feed it, and it would just run over them, and would never so much as know it had done it. But you may be sure we had no time to waste in cock-crowing when once Congress rose. We had got our work cut out for us on a large scale ; there were no inches about it, miles made the measure.

We had listened to able papers from the united gentlemen, among whom were the Hon. Auberon Herbert, M.P., who gave us one on the Game Laws, which was growing a very hot subject; it had long been a sore one ; Sir Baldwin Leighton who, though a Conservative landlord, treated garden and meadow allotments from a fair and liberal point of view ; the Hon. and Rev. J. W. Leigh, who took co-operative farming as his subject ; Mr. Butcher, of Banbury, who gave us a capital paper on co-operative stores ; Jesse Collings, who took education ; and Rev. H. Solly, who took village clubs and reading-rooms. We wanted to get all the information we could from trustworthy sources, and from friends who were honestly interested in the movement; but at the same time we did not mean to be led away into starting all sorts of schemes before our own proper work was done, and was securely established. I was not going to have the cart of agricultural reforms stuck before the Union horse ; though from the time of the Congress onward there was a body of men inside and outside the Union who kept urging us to adopt such a topsy-turvy way of driving to destruction.

"No, thank you," said I. "I'm for reform as much as anybody, but it's got to be the labourer first, and reform all round after."

"Oh," said some, "but you can do both at the same time. You can raise the labourer and push forward reform—the one helps the other."

"Not a bit of it," said I. "Reform away as much as *you* please, but I'm a practical man, and I'm not such a fool at this time of day as to try sitting on two stools at once. And I'm not going to entice any fellow-worker of mine to play such a down-falling game either."

"Oh," said some, "but then the Union must not sink into a mere organisation for Trade Union purposes—this is a great moral uprising which promises to have the most beneficial result on the country at large."

"Very good," said I; "so be it, with all my heart. I hope it *is* moral, and I should be sorry if it did not have beneficial results on the country at large, but charity must begin its good work at home; when the home work is well done it may go and work abroad. It may work away then like one o'clock, and my blessing will go with it. But there's no blessing attached to those who try to run before they can walk. We've got to take a step at a time and that a steady one; we'll run on to reforms of law and land fast enough, and sure enough, when we're ready. It's a poor shoemaker who can't stick to his last. Well, to raise the wages, shorten the hours, and make a free man out of a land-tied slave is *my* last, and to that last I'll stick as tight as beeswax for the present. Raise a man's material condition to the level of self-respecting decency and the moral will rise too. Give the agricultural labourer the chance of making his home life like a well-tilled freehold plot, and the seed of morality will soon show its head above ground; and if well watered and tended, it will grow into a sturdy and thriving young plant, and no one need fear but that God Almighty will give the increase. But keep a man living like a hog and he'll have more or less the mind and the morals of a hog; and what's more, if you drive him hard, he'll be like an English Gadarenean swine; a drink devil will enter into him, and drive him down a steep place into the sea of death and destruction."

We had the Union plough well started, and the team was pulling straight and strong, and all together, and I should have been a queer kind of a ploughman if I had let half a dozen ploughshares be tacked on to mine. There were furrows in plenty to be turned over in the English agricultural field, and there was room for a dozen good drivers with teams and ploughshares to match.

Union meetings, meetings everywhere, was the order of the day, and we had to be on the sharp look-out to keep professional Trade Unionists from the towns in their own places. I was not going to have our folk made light-headed with wrong notions, so that they would be leaping over the hedge of the law into a jail. Said a good friend of the cause, "We must have a care that Hodge does not blossom into an Anarchist." I did not intend that he should, though.

I had no special fancy for fiery blooms of that sort. Wherever I spied out a blossom of anarchy and arson I said to myself I would nip it in the bud; and nip it I did, sharp as a November frost or a pair of scissors.

Of course I was called an agitator; so I was, because everyone who stirs people up to do things is an agitator, but those who so named me attached a bad meaning to the word. I was agitating for the right and not for the wrong; I was no "Arch Apostle of Arson," as some one chose to call me. The Bishop of Gloucester (Dr. Ellicott) was one of my worst enemies in the early days of the movement. He wanted me, and those like me, ducked in the horse pond. He was at a dinner one day and the question of our agitation came up. He did not say in so many words that I ought to be ducked in the horse pond, but he spoke in a sort of parable. If I remember right, he said with reference to me, "There is an old saying, 'Don't nail their ears to the pump, and don't duck them in the horse pond.'" The sentiment of his remark was a downright incitement to riot, in my opinion. I paid the bishop out several times over for that saying, for it was a wrong spirit for a bishop to show. I remember on one occasion, when I was at Gloucester, I said in the course of speech, "I have a good mind to lay a heavy indictment against the bishop. He appears to believe in adult baptism which is contrary to the doctrine of the Church of England." Unless I am mightily mistaken, Dr. Ellicott repented in episcopal sackcloth and Lenten ashes for that little speech. It was in the early autumn of 1872, I think, that he showed which side he was on. As to the parsons generally, I never expected them to have much sympathy with us. Their stock argument against the Union was that it was "setting class against class." This was their poll-parrot cry. "Oh yes," said they, "the men have a perfect right to try and improve themselves, and we will help them; but the Union is setting class against class."

It was in the autumn of this year that a considerable number of men emigrated to New Zealand on very favourable terms; they went out on railway contract work for the firm of Messrs. J. Brogden and Sons. The idea of emigration was taking more hold of the men than I liked. But migration was a different thing, though sometimes when I urged migration they would say, "We don't want to leave the old county, if we can find work and a living in it. We can't all migrate North, and to those places where the wages are good. If we do we'll have wages going down, or we'll be turned off 'not wanted,' and then where should we be? Wages are so low in most of the other parts of the country that, if we did move, it would not be to better ourselves." There was too much truth in it.

Early in December a great meeting in our favour was held at Exeter Hall. The citizens of London wished to publicly show their sympathy with us. Samuel Morley took the chair. He was a first-rate man and a substantial helper of the Union. He gave the first £500 cheque towards the support of the Warwickshire men. Among those present on the platform were, Sir C. Dilke, M.P., Sir C. Trevelyan, Sir John Bennett, Mr. Mundella, M.P., Archbishop Manning, and T. Hughes, M.P. I, and Ball, and Mitchell represented the town.

Charles Bradlaugh was there, too, and I should just like to say a word about him. I first came across him at a meeting in the Town Hall at Northampton, when I spoke. The next time we met was on this occasion at Exeter Hall. I got to know him very well and was very friendly with him. He was a fine statesman, and before he died he gave proof of it too. In his way he worked hard for our cause. His sceptical ideas went against him, and the majority of people were horrified at him. I was not; and I can truthfully say that, though he and I had many interviews and conversations, he never once broached the subject of religion, or aired his sceptical opinions to me. He always took care to keep them well in the background. Also, I never heard him allude to them on any platform. I honoured and respected Charles Bradlaugh; he had a great struggle all through his life, but he fought like a man for what he believed to be the right. He was a man of principle, a big-hearted man; and a good many of his traducers might have taken a few lessons from him with a great deal of benefit to themselves. In the course of my career I also met Mrs. Besant several times. When Bradlaugh held a great indignation meeting in Trafalgar Square to protest against the use of brute force, I went up to London to take part in it. Mrs. Besant was in the room where the committee were making all the necessary arrangements, and it was there I first saw her. She often spoke, and most eloquently, on behalf of our cause. At that time she held the same views as Bradlaugh. I think she lost a good deal of her influence when she took up with Theosophy, but I dare say she then influenced a different class of persons.

At this Exeter Hall meeting Cardinal Manning spoke up nobly for us. The testimony, at such a time and in such a place, of a man so respected, and who occupied such a commanding position in his Church, was of the greatest value to the Union. He said that the agricultural movement was not an act of insubordination, nor were the promoters of it mischievous agitators, and that the men who had asked him to speak at this meeting had said, "We are resolved to attain what is just, and we will attain it only in a God-fearing and law-abiding way."

I remember he told us that he believed he was the only man present who could say that he sat as chairman of a rural vestry in 1833—4, and saw doled out to the labouring man, the gallon of flour and the shilling a head, which was given according to the number of his family. He also told us that he had had an acquaintance with the labouring men of Sussex, extending over a period of seventeen years; and he remembered the first introduction of the New Poor

Law Amendment Act, with all its precipitate applications, which had caused untold misery and suffering. Yes, Manning, both as Church of England parson, and as a Roman Catholic priest, ever proved himself the working man's friend. He was a practical friend to us, for he sent us a subscription of £10 in 1878, and again one of the same amount in 1879. He also publicly testified to my good faith and was a true friend through thick and thin.

There had been an electoral reform conference held at St. James's Hall in November, at which I was present. Joseph Chamberlain presided, and the voteless condition of the agricultural labourer was discussed. It was again mentioned at this December meeting. I believed the vote was as certain to come as sunrising, but we had not made it a plank in the Union platform yet; the time was scarcely ripe for it. When we three labourers stood up to speak in our turn, we stuck pretty close to our subject—the labourer. I remember how Ball, who was a Lincolnshire man, told them that as a child he had worked for twopence a day, and that he had been obliged to go to work hundreds of times on a breakfast of bread and hot water, and as for dinner—well, a herring and a bit of bread had to do duty for *that*. Owing to the Union, things were looking a little brighter in Lincolnshire at the end of 1872; wages had risen, which was something to the good; but on the other hand, cottage accommodation was very bad. The small holdings were being broken up, for the small holders generally were in a ruinous condition.

Then the cottages fell into the hands of bigger proprietors. When a man was put into a cottage the farmer of whom he rented it, or the landlord of whom he held it, would say to him, "If you live here you work for me, and if you work for me you will have to take what I choose to give you." If the man was not told this in so many words, it practically came to the same thing. There was no doubt that the whole land question wanted a thorough overhauling; and many were convinced that the problem would never be solved till the day came when land would be owned in the same way that other property is owned, when it could be transferred and dealt with as easily as consols or railway shares.

Mitchell, who was a Somersetshire man, told them a little of his experiences, too; and they had been bitterly hard. He was frightened away from the plough-tail when he was about nineteen. He slaved at farm work from 4 a.m. till 10 p.m., and often longer, and frequently not more than two pennyworth of victuals would pass his lips the long day through. Slave as he might, his tyrannical employer was never satisfied. Wages would run in those parts from six to seven shillings a week and stop at eight or nine shillings. There were old men whose wages did not go beyond a miserable five shillings, and when they had paid one shilling and sixpence out of that for rent, they made a close acquaintance with half-starvation. One poor old man said he was so hungry most days, that he often did not know what to do to get along. The ordinary breakfast would be a tea-kettle broth—that is, bread in the breakfast pot with hot water poured on it; for dinner there would be a few potatoes, some bread, and occasionally a bit of bacon, but the bacon was most often seen on the father's plate while the rest had to feed on the smell of it; then for supper bread again, and perhaps a small bit of cheese. Here was high living for a working-man! The cottage accommodation was a disgrace to civilisation; and this, not only in Somersetshire, but all over the country. As many as thirteen people would sleep all huddled up together in one small cottage bedroom. A well-known country clergyman, the Rev. Mr. Fraser, afterwards Bishop of Manchester, who gave evidence before an Agricultural Commission held in the sixties—it extended, I think, over the years 1867-8-9—stated that it was impossible to exaggerate the terrible state of things then existing; they were so bad physically, socially, economically, morally, and intellectually, that it would be difficult to make them worse. Well, in 1872, at the end of that year of grace, this particular disgrace to Christian England was as rampant as ever it had been. And I think among the worst sinners in this respect I should name the class of small proprietors. Most likely they had not the money—in fact, we know that the bulk of them had not the wherewithal—either to improve and enlarge the cottages they owned, or to pull them down and build new and better ones. So the labourer and his family were forced to sleep in one room—it makes my blood run cold when I think of it—while squire and parson, and oftentimes farmers, had commonly more rooms than they needed—they had plenty of room at any rate for decent living. Spare rooms and suites of apartments, the squire, and the landlord, and the wealthy employer had at command, while the labourers on their estates were herded together like beasts of the field, or worse.

I gave the audience some of my early experience also; and I had something to say about the farmers as well. I was the candid friend of the farmer then, and in my opinion I have never been anything else. I knew well enough that many tenant farmers had injuries to complain of as well as the men, and I did not want to see the neck of the farmer under the foot of the labourer; not at all, there should be no neck and foot business about the relationship between the two. Farmers as a class had been fearfully oppressed. In my own country the custom was that the farmer should hold his land upon a twelve-months' notice. Say that a man rented a farm and improved it greatly during a five years' tenancy; would he be able to rest secure, and confidently reap the fruits of his labour? Oh dear no; soon would come the landlord, have the land re-assessed, and impose an extra five shillings an acre on it. The farmer had to pay this or go; and how, when he had been so fleeced, could he raise the labourers' wages when they asked him to give them a shilling or two more a week? He had to cut down his expenses to make good the extra iniquitous rent; and you may be sure that in this paring process the poor labourer got most of the cutting; he was shorn close to the skin.

Farmer and labourer had improved the land together, but the landlord took the increase thereof. And now the farmers were so bat-blind to their own best interests, that they were trying to crush out the Union. It was a foolish and short-sighted course they were taking; but the majority made themselves deaf as adders then, and for a long while after. Indeed, I might say that at this present time too many of them are bat-blind and adder-deaf still.

Over and over again I have tried to show them that here in England the interest of labourer and farmer is at bottom one and the same—is, was, and ever shall be, while the land system continues on its present basis, and there are such men on the earth as landlords, farmers, and hired labourers. I say that the farmer and labourer are the Siamese Twins of the agricultural world, and he who would tear them asunder and put them apart is their most deadly enemy. Every farmer, who by word and deed denies this vital fact and cuts himself off from the life interests of the labourer, is his own assassin; he will very soon find that he has dealt himself a suicidal blow. To commit suicide is the act of a fool or a madman; every one in his senses will agree to that I should think. Well, not only have scores and scores of farmers in the past behaved like fools and madmen, but they are behaving so still. By stopping up their ears, which were dull enough before, so that they became deaf to the voice of reason and common-sense, they made themselves no whit better than the horses and mules without understanding; they turned themselves into their own worst enemy, and it served them quite right when they had to pay through the nose for their folly. They paid in the past, they paid in the early years of the Union, they have kept on paying ever since. They do not seem able to learn a simple lesson—simple as A, B, C, or the multiplication table. I said at that meeting:

"The farmers are afraid of the labourers combining, but they are not afraid of our strong arm when they want us to work, nor of the blessings of life we have toiled to procure them. I do not wonder at the kicking of the landlords, who see where all this will push them by-and-by; but I am surprised, very much surprised at the poor farmer. I pity his poor brainless head. I say to the farmer, 'The labourers are your best friends, yet you take them by the neck and bundle them into the street, and the landlord pats you on the back and says, "Oh, you have done it so nicely, do it again," and you go away and do it again.'

"I warned the farmers ten years ago, when they formed their Chamber of Agriculture, to take care and see what they were about, and they pooh-poohed me as only an agricultural labourer, who could not possibly know anything of the farmer's business. Well, now they are finding themselves in the ditch. We will try and pull them out by means of our much despised Union. But I would have farmer and landlord take heed of a labourer's warning. The Union will prosper and the Union will win, and woe be to them who oppose it. Our motto is, 'United to protect, but not combined to injure'; but we will fight tooth and nail for the Union, if we are driven to it by those who, in their own interests, should be on our side. If things go on as they seem to be going now, Lord Derby will not prove to have been so far out, when he said there would be two masters to one man. I say, 'You will get your toes pinched as sure as you are born, if you don't keep a sharp look out, and mind where you are walking.'

"I speak from an honest and manly heart to landlord and farmer on this question. I am not one who strokes a man down the back because he is a gentleman, nor do I speak evil of him when he is out of hearing after giving him a mouthful of smooth words. I'm no back-biting cringer, nor do I cherish bitter feelings against any—there is no dumb, black dog in me—so I say right out here and now to the landlords of this country and to the tenant farmers, that if they continue to make our Union men suffer in the way they have done, if they mean to turn them away from their employment, starve them, and drive them into the streets, leaving them without shelter or with only 'the hillside for their bed, and the broad canopy of heaven for their curtain,' then landlord and tenant farmer will live to rue the day on which they were born.

"What have we to thank our country and its

Government for either? Parliament spent some twenty millions of money to wipe out slavery in the West Indies, but how about the slaves at home? We who have been white slaves, and those of us who are white slaves still, are driven to desperate remedies. I say that, it our country means to go on treating us as mere machines in the hands of a money-mongering few, we will leave her, let her fate fall how it may. Waves of men have rolled from her shores to foreign strands, and waves of men will follow. Yes, the tide of labour will ebb away from these island shores, and agricultural England will be left bare. Those who have toiled in the sweat of their brow to make her fruitful will leave her to barrenness. They will forsake in sorrow and anguish of spirit her who has been to them no nursing mother; they will go from her, they will depart and will return no more."

Emigration was beginning to stare us full in the face, but I wanted to keep it in the background as a last resource. I remember we passed a resolution at this meeting declaring the present condition of the agricultural labourer to be a national disgrace, inimical to the best interests of the nation. That resolution was nothing but God's own truth.

At the end of December the Warwickshire Labourers' Union was formally affiliated with the National Agricultural Labourers' Union at a meeting held at Leamington, when Mr. G. H. Ward of Perriston Towers presided. There were some sixty-nine or seventy delegates present. They represented the branches of the Warwickshire Union, which consisted of about six thousand two hundred members. The reports were cheering, for wages had been raised one, two, and, in some cases, three shillings above the average wage given before the Union made its power felt; the farmers were giving in. Still there was more to be done in this direction, for the highest wage seldom reached fifteen shillings; it was sometimes fourteen shillings, but the average was thirteen shillings; and there were still far too many places in which the average wage was eleven shillings; occasionally it was down at ten shillings, and even nine shillings.

Since May we had forwarded some two hundred and fifty men to other parts; some had been migrated and were working at more remunerative employments, some had emigrated, and thus the so-called surplus labour of the districts on this side of England had been reduced. But in spite of improvement, cases such as these were all too common.

A carter would come and say: "My wages are twelve shillings but I have no perquisites; I have to work fourteen hours a day six days out of seven, and on Sunday I have to put in half a day's labour."

A shepherd would say: "And look at me, I got ten shillings for a week of seven days, and I lost time in bad weather; out of this I had to pay one and sixpence rent for a cottage with two bedrooms, and now here I am, sacked because I've joined the Union."

A farm labourer would say: "My poor wages are

seven shillings a week, and I lose money on bad days; my rent is one shilling and threepence, and I have to pay out one shilling and threepence halfpenny a month for club money; how is a man to keep alive and going on it? I'm most always hungry, and I can't keep decent clothes on my back, not even of a Sunday, and my family has to make the best shift it can. 'Tisn't life at all, and I often wish I was out of it."

What man, with no better chance before him than dragging out a miserable existence like this, would not have wished the same?

We had done wonders in 1872. When I look back now on that first year of our Union's life, I see clearer than ever what a grand start we had made in less than twelve months; but as I reviewed our progress then, when '72 was nearing its end, and considered that there were still many hundreds of our brethren scattered over the land who could cap and match these tales of grinding misery, it seemed to me we had done next to nothing. We would have to be up and doing in 1873, and I said to myself that the motto for the coming year must be, "Press forward, push onward, rise upward without ceasing."

The New Year which dawned on the first of January 1873, brought stormy times along with it. Early in the year some labourers held a meeting in the village of Littleworth, near Farringdon, in Berkshire. An ill-conditioned farmer made a fuss, and so three leaders of the meeting were summoned before the Bench for having caused obstruction on the Queen's highway. This was all nonsense, and only a pretext, because the Primitive Methodists had been in the habit for years of holding meetings on the very same spot. The three men were convicted, and there was a to-do all round the neighbourhood.

"Oh," said we, "this is too much; we are not going to let the right of meeting together in the open be taken away from us without a struggle. This is a case for the Union to take up and fight out. We will call a test meeting, and if we are summoned for obstruction, so be it. We will go before the Bench and conduct ourselves as law-abiding, peaceable citizens should; but we will have the best legal advice at our backs, for we have Union funds to pay for it. The Bench will find we are no longer poor, ignorant, unprotected labourers, to be browbeaten and bullied and put upon; we will give them a Queen's Counsel to tackle, and we will stand by to see what they make of the job."

So we arranged to hold a test meeting towards the end of March, and it was a tremendous one. On the appointed day the big Market Place at Farringdon was more than half-filled with labourers. John Charles Cox, J.P. (he is now a minister of the Church of England), took the chair, and upheld us splendidly. Mackenzie and I, and also two or three well-known gentlemen, were in a waggon drawn up by the side of Cox. Very soon after the proceedings commenced, the superintendent of the police appeared on the scene, just as we had expected he would. He asked us to break up the meeting and disperse, as we were causing an obstruction; but we were doing nothing of the sort, for we had taken particular care to keep the crowd all round us compactly, so that people could walk or drive about easily. He said our meeting was illegal and must be dissolved at once. We civilly refused to go; thereupon he asked for our names and addresses, which we of course gave, and when he had taken them down we were allowed to finish our meeting without further molestation.

Two or three of the magistrates down there, however, were very bitter against me—I believe they would have hanged me if they could—so but a few days were allowed to pass before they sent me a summons to appear before the Bench. Cox and Mackenzie had summonses served on them also. Off we went to Farringdon on the morning of April 15th, to get our case tried. We had Fitzjames Stephen, Q.C., to defend us; Mr. E. Jenkins, our constant friend, was retained, and the case was entrusted to Messrs. Sheen & Roscoe, London. As I was entering the Court, the superintendent of police, a regular old Dogberry said to me, "You will catch it hot this time; they mean to give it you stiff." "Well," said I, "let them; but if I am convicted I am not going to leave the Court unless I am handcuffed. If I've got to go, I go as a felon. You can take me to Reading gaol if you will, but before I go there I shall telegraph to the House of Commons."

By one o'clock on that Tuesday morning the Court was packed. The trial lasted over an hour, and then the magistrates retired to consider their decision ; but might have saved themselves the trouble of going through that piece of formality, for we had won the day. We had got a surveyor to make out a plan of the Market Place, and the boundary line of the space covered by the crowd was plainly marked on it. The surveyor proved beyond dispute that there was plenty of room for anybody to walk or drive round the crowd, so they could not obtain a conviction on the ground of obstruction in fact.

There was one particular magistrate who hated me and the Union and all its works, and he was as mad as a hatter when he saw how things were going. Then Fitzjames Stephen proved that we had a parliamentary petition down for consideration on our meeting programme ; and as the Bill of Rights protects from imprisonment all assemblies of English citizens who meet for the purpose of petitioning the House of Commons, this settled the matter. We could not be sent to prison ; but of course I did not know what trick the Bench might not have up its sleeve. I knew that the magistrate I have mentioned would convict by hook or by crook if he could. I heard afterwards that he did stick out against us as long as he had a leg to stand on, but he was compelled to climb down at the finish. When the magistrates returned to the Court, the Chairman said, "We have decided not to convict you this time, but you will be bound down to hold no more meetings in Berkshire."

"I shall not accept that decision," I said. "I am going to hold a meeting to-night about three miles away."

The magistrates did not know what to say, and finally they dismissed the case, and I held my meeting that night without let or hindrance.

While we were in Court there were about four hundred labourers outside armed with sticks; and although I begged them to keep quiet and not to strike a blow, they said that if the police brought me out in handcuffs, they would go for the policemen and smash them. I am certain they would have done it too, for there was very hot and bitter feeling aroused among the men. The magistrates dared not leave the Court by the front entrance; they slipped away by the back door, and in that they showed their wisdom, for if the men had caught sight of them there would have been a row on the spot.

The Union won a great victory and we exulted over it. We had good reason to rejoice, as every public building in those parts was closed against us. It was a decision which strengthened our position very much and cleared the ground for us in more senses than one.

Then there was the shameful Chipping Norton affair, which roused the indignation of the whole country, as well it might. Sixteen respectable English working women were committed to prison with hard labour. It happened this way.

At Ascot, in Oxfordshire, some men were locked out. At this time there were small strikes going on here and there in the county. Some Union men working for a farmer or two would ask for Union wages. They would give notice on the Saturday that they wanted the rise the next week. If the farmers held out and refused it, the men would leave on the following Saturday. There was a small local strike on at Ascot, and the carter of a farmer there, named Hambridge, joined the strike without giving the usual notice. Hambridge summoned him and got the costs. Then Hambridge called in outside labour, got over, I think it was, two men, from a village in the neighbourhood. Of course this made the bad feeling ten times worse; it was not dropping oil on troubled waters anyway. These Ascot women, who had husbands out of work, thought they would drive the men away when they came. It was but natural that they should object to outsiders slipping into their husbands' shoes, and they wanted to show the farmers that Ascot folk, women though they might be, were not going to stand by and see their bread and butter pass to strangers without some sort of protest. So when the men came in, out marched the women and mobbed them. The women dared them to enter Hambridge's field. The only blows that they struck were tongue blows, though I heard that some of them carried sticks. Hambridge took the matter up, and the women, seventeen of them, were summoned before the magistrates at Chipping Norton.

The presiding magistrates were two clergymen—squarsons, as they called them. In their evidence the labourers, who were strapping men and not likely to be frightened and hurt by a parcel of women, gave evidence that, so far from being set upon with sticks, they had been invited by the women to come back to the village and have a drink. In fact it was plain enough to any unprejudiced person that no physical injury was attempted; at the most there might have been a little hustling, but these stalwart labourers after saying "No, thank you," to the offer of a drink—it was the poor women's tempting bait—went to work on Hambridge's farm under the protection of a police constable.

Of course the women pleaded "Not guilty," and the reverend magistrates retired to consider and consult. They were a very long time about it. Then they came back into Court and passed sentence on sixteen of the women; seven were to be imprisoned with ten days' hard labour, and nine were to have seven days' hard labour. Here was a sentence to be passed by clergymen of the Church of England, on respectable working women, some of whom had children at the breast!

We had been prepared for the infliction of a fine, and one of our men was in Court with the necessary money all ready. He thought he would only have to hand over the sum named by the magistrates, and the women would be free ; but imprisonment with *hard labour* was what none of us had bargained for. When this scandalous decision was known, Chipping Norton was turned upside down ; and as Holloway—he was chairman of the Oxford district of the National Agricultural Labourers' Union—said, "If I had not been present, violence would have been committed." The people were raging, for no one had the least idea that such a law existed as was now brought to bear on them with such terrible force. It fell on them like a thunderbolt from the blue. There was a riot in the town that evening, and I believe the police there had to telegraph for assistance not knowing how far the people might go. The authorities thought discretion the better of valour, for instead of waiting till the morning as was usual, they had the women driven to Oxford in a brake, and they were locked up in Oxford Gaol at about six o'clock in the morning.

The press took the matter up, and the action of the Bench was unanimously condemned. One pressman who was sent down by a leading London paper to inquire into the matter said, "Act 34 and 35 Victoria, c. 32, which is an act to amend the Criminal Law relating to violence, threats, and molestation," did not allow the option of a fine. The magistrates might have allowed the women to stand out on their own recognisances, binding them "to come up for judgment when called upon," or they could have left out the hard labour.

The feeling was intense; we were roused to a man; petitions for the immediate release of the women were sent up to the Home Office, and our Leamington Committee acted at once. I, and also Attenborough, issued an appeal to the county and the public. The result was subscriptions amounting to eighty pounds came in—five pounds of the sum in pence—and we arranged that the sixteen women should have five pounds apiece presented to them on their release from prison. When their sentences had expired we got two brakes with four horses in each and went to meet them as they came out of Oxford Gaol, and took them right into Ascot, headed by a band of music. When we arrived in front of the house of the ringleader of the farmers, I gave each of the women five pounds.

I remember we had a crowded meeting at Chipping Norton—there were nearly three thousand around the waggon; and there was an indignation meeting held in the evening, when we declared that we must have (1) extension of the franchise; (2) repeal of the Criminal Law Amendment Act; (3) appointment of stipendiary magistrates. It was high time that the clergy should be removed from the bench. The resolution carried was, "That clerical magistracy is most unsatisfactory; and in order to secure a better administration of the law, it is considered absolutely necessary to establish a stipendiary magistracy, on account of class influence on the present administrators."

I had long been of this opinion. I had seen too

much of this class influence on the Bench and had felt it too. I heard that the parsons' friends got up a kind of counter demonstration to express their sympathy with the poor persecuted prosecutors. Well, it was the opinion of every right-thinking person at the time that these clerical magistrates had thoroughly disgraced themselves, and had shown what spirit they were of. By their decision they lowered themselves in the opinion of all Christian people; and those of us who had felt bitter against the parson and all his works, felt more bitter than ever; we said, "Not a single solitary parson shall sit on the bench to deal out left-handed judgment, if we can help it."

It was a bad and a discreditable day's work those parson-magistrates did at Chipping Norton, both for themselves and their like; and those responsible for it were down in our black books for many a month, aye and many a year after. What man among us, let alone our wives, could forget that sixteen honest and respectable labourers' wives had been cruelly sentenced to imprisonment and hard labour? We said, "An insult has been passed on every working man and woman in England. Would such a punishment have been meted out to sixteen of the farmers' wives in the neighbourhood? Never; the parsons would not have dared to do it. These Church of England gentry have too often trampled ruthlessly on the labourer in the past; but we had our own Union now, and they could trample on us no longer. I held then, as I hold now, that clergymen have no business on the Bench, and I am glad to see they are becoming fewer and fewer. It is a matter of common knowledge that clerical magistrates are always the hardest and most severe, and yet they call themselves ministers of One Who always tempered justice with mercy.

CHAPTER VII.

THE GAME LAWS.

IN the May of 1873, I gave evidence before a Select Committee on the Game Laws. Sir Michael Hicks Beach was present, and George Ward Hunt was in the chair. I suppose they had me up before them as being a representative man of my class. Well, on that occasion, I made myself the Agricultural Labourers' mouthpiece, and they got more home truths than some of them liked to swallow. I remember that they tried to find out what the labourers thought on some other subjects. Owing to the Union, Hodge had grown to be something more than a nonentity in the landlord's eye; his poor poll had popped up above the employers' horizon, and they were beginning to get very curious about him. This Hodge had feelings and opinions of his own, no doubt; perhaps they had better know just what they were in good time, and so be prepared for the evil day, which might come all too soon, when Hodge would have a *vote*. Then he would no longer be only a dumb, human man, a son of Adam on a level with the earth he tilled, and with no more voice in the ordering of affairs than the horses and sheep he tended. He would be a political man with a voting voice; and what was still more dreadful, there would be a great many of him.

Yes; this Hodge was growing up fast now to political manhood, and the landlords must examine the creature and see what stuff he is made of; how much blind side he has got and how much right side, so that they might be sure of catching hold of him, and gripping him well, and then bringing a little paternal pressure to bear on him—all for his own good, of course.

Said the Tories, "If Hodge will not sit quiet and be paternally governed by us, he will have to be paternally persuaded; but rule himself he cannot, and must not. What with the Elementary Education Act of 1870, and the Ballot Bill of 1872, we shall have to look sharp after him and his ways; and if he gets the vote he will be kicking over the traces altogether, so we must take him in hand in good time, and train him in the way he should go, that he may vote as we wish, because of course *we* know what is best for him."

I had taken notice of what landlords had been saying and doing for many a year; I do not say that all the landlords were cast in the same mould or made of the same metal—no; there were some who were our true friends, who were no wolves with a sheepskin thrown over them—but the majority of them were against us in their hearts, and a number of them showed openly that they were all for their own class,—that they and their kind came first and second and third, and Hodge nowhere. I knew the class pride and the pocket pride of them, so when I came up before the Committee I had made up my mind that I would not be drawn. I was determined to keep to the Game Laws, and they pretty soon found out that evidence on that head was all they were going to get out of me. I could speak, but I knew how to keep my mouth shut and my teeth locked up tight. Teeth-locking was a trade I had learned early in life. If I had been a weak and fearful man, like scores of my class, I might have got lock-jaw when in the presence of my "betters," and "the powers that be." The timid labourer did, and his masters thought that he was so dull and slow that he had next to no wits, and so had nothing to say. That might have been so with many—and small wonder at it—but there were hundreds who could speak out and up when they were by themselves, but who had learned the trade of mouth-shutting and teeth-locking as soon as they could talk, and before they knew what bird-scaring was. A man with the weight of many masters on him learns how to be dumb, and deaf, and blind, at a very early hour in the morning.

I gave the Committee what information I could on the subject they were there to inquire into. I repeat it, with additions, because a good deal of it holds equally good now. I told them that the agricultural labourers strongly objected to the Game Laws. I said, " We think such laws are a great scandal to the nation ; we feel very hot about it and it is spoken of at all our meetings ; I and others have spoken very strongly against them lately, whenever we have had the chance. The day that the Poaching Prevention Act of 1862 became law was a black day for the labourer ; from that time onwards he might at any hour be subjected to the indignity of being assailed and searched by the police officer."

I remember that, when the Act was first brought to bear, I myself was compelled to make a definite and positive agreement with my employer, in regard to perquisites I had when I was at work. When wood-felling and timber-cutting I always liked to have a basket of chips and dead wood to carry back with me; it was a customary perquisite. I understood that the new law allowed a police officer to seize me and search me, if he saw me after dark with anything which aroused his suspicions. As I did not give over work while it was daylight in the short days of winter, that of course exposed me to the chance of being way-laid by a police officer and being searched for game. The very thought of such an indignity made me, and the other labourers as well, exceedingly angry, and I determined to take what steps I could to prevent myself getting into trouble. I made this wood perquisite a matter of bargain between me and my employer, so that I took it as a legal thing. I knew well enough that the word of a police officer is generally believed before a working man's: that I couldn't help. I knew too, that if an employer thought well to prosecute a man with wood found on him he could do so, unless there was a thorough understanding between man and master. That thorough understanding I took care to have wherever I went.

Two women in my village suffered through this matter of perquisites. It has been the custom in our neighbourhood, ever since I was a boy, that if a woman was cleaning turnips in a field she might take two or three, once or twice in a week. Farmers did not object, as a rule, and I have often seen women when turnip-cleaning put some into their aprons before the employer's face; it was an understood thing. Farmers have made such offers of turnips to me, and of course I have taken them; I no more thought of refusing them than I would have thought of refusing to put my week's wages in my pocket. After the Act came into operation the police set upon these women—respectable, honest, married women—searched them, brought them before the magistrate at Warwick, and charged them with stealing turnips. The police prosecuted and gave evidence, and the women were fined. It was a very great shame, and the village people were very bitter and sore about it. If tidy, decent, hard-working mothers of families were not safe, who could be? Before this Act passed a working man might trudge home at night in peace, carrying his little basket or his bundle of perquisites; but after it became law the insulting hand of the policeman was hard and heavy upon him. 'Twas as if so many Jacks-in-the-Box had been set free to spring out on the labourer, from the hedge, or the ditch, or the copse, or the field.

There was a man arrested in 1866, within forty yards of his own house. He had got two or three sticks which he had picked up in the road going along. They had been blown out of the hedge and lay on the highway, so he put them in his inside pocket, for they were only bits. A policeman jumped out on him and caught him by the collar and said, "I have a strong suspicion that you have game." The man said, "I have no game."

"What have you in your pocket then?" said the policeman.

"You can soon see what I have got," answered the man, and he showed his inside pocket in which were the few sticks.

The policeman then said, "You must go along with me; I must lock you up."

At that the man began to be a little bit resolute. He felt as I should have felt when the police officer said he would lock him up, and they had a little bit of a tussle in the road. After that I suppose he was charged with resisting the police. They took him off and locked him up that night. He had his hearing the next morning and the case was adjourned to the following Saturday, but there he was kept two or three days, and was not bailed out. Our blood was up at all this; so we collected evidence in the village, and employed a solicitor for him—we found the money to do it—and the man was discharged. I knew him well and had worked with him, and I had never known him dishonest in my life. The whole affair was a burning shame. And it was not the only case of the kind that came under my own notice.

There was the case of my own brother-in-law. He was walking home from Warwick to Barford, a distance of about three miles, along the highroad. It was near Christmas time, and he had been to buy the week's groceries. He was a bit late, which was only natural and to be expected; for I daresay he had not got home from work till six or half-past six—the usual time—and when he had had a wash and a cup of tea it would be something after seven in the evening. Then he would have to walk into Warwick, and do his business, so he would be on the road home about ten o'clock at night. Well, as he was walking innocently along, a policeman stepped out of the ditch and laid hold of his collar, and said, "What have you got in your pockets?" My brother-in-law said, "I have nothing there but what is my own. I have been in to Warwick to buy the week's groceries." The policeman let go, but of course my brother-in-law was very angry, and so were we all at such an indignity. This was what a decent, law-abiding man was exposed to when walking along the Queen's highway on his own private business. How were we to know that we had a legal remedy for such treatment as this? We were ignorant of the law, we feared the law, and

I think we had good reason to, considering the way it was often administered. We did not know that the law says if a constable stops a person when he has no reasonable cause to suspect him of having come from land where he had probably been in search of game, the man so stopped might county-court the constable for undue search. I did not know it myself till the Committee told me such was the law. But suppose my brother-in-law had county-courted that policeman for undue search, the chances are that the police or the magistrates would have found a way out, and the policeman would have got off scot free, while the labourer would have had a black mark against his name for ever after.

After a bit the police made so many mistakes that they grew a little more cautious. Lord Leigh, chairman of the bench at petty sessions, reprimanded them in one or two instances for bringing up cases where there was no real ground for suspicion. But there was, speaking generally, far too much partiality and strong prejudice and class feeling prevalent among the magistrates. I believe Lord Leigh and some others that sat upon our bench always did justice; those we knew, and we said among ourselves, "Oh, if I was to be brought before the bench I should prefer so-and-so, and so-and-so, to try us. Justice would be done; even if the day went against us, we should be sure it was the fault of the law and not of the way in which it was administered." Yes, we are not such fools as not to know a just man when we see him, whatever his rank and standing in life may be. And to a just man, who administers the law justly, I take off my hat.

Why, a policeman in the neighbourhood of Coventry told me, that if a certain gentleman was on the bench, he never dared to take a case of poaching before him unless the evidence was very clear. When that particular gentleman was not there he brought up several cases where there was only slight suspicion, but he got convictions. "We picked our customers in the magistrates," he said.

Then there was a case but last year in the county court. I know of a man who sued a labourer for damages because he did not fulfil his week's work; he had left it at a very short notice. Well, the labourer had to pay a certain amount for damages. But that very same master, only a fortnight ago, discharged a man at a minute's notice. The man sued his master for a week's wages, but the judge nonsuited him, and it was the same judge in both cases!

The only proper remedy for this sort of thing is to have stipendiary magistrates, for they could come and judge a case on its merits. What is a judge but a man after all? The county court judge makes but a very small circuit. He lives in the very centre of magisterial influence; magistrates are the friends of game preservers; and these game preservers are sure to be landlords, with a great deal of influence. If a county court judge gets his table well supplied with game from his preserving friends, he would be something more than human, I think, if he was not hand-in-glove with them. I don't wish to imply that they would judge unjustly of set purpose, or knowingly deliver wrong judgment, or go against the law of the land; but I do say that they would naturally favour their own class, and their own friends, where the law gave them a chance of doing so. I don't know much law, but I have had experience enough of it to be certain that there are plenty of loopholes of escape, which a clever and competent lawyer can slip through by the skin of his teeth, as it were. And the way they do slip and wriggle through astonishes a plain man. I should like to see the magistrates taking circuits, and knowing no game preserver, no landlord, no poor man, till the case is brought before him on the bench. I do not see, for my part, how we can have even-handed justice dealt out in any other way. When a poaching case comes up before them, some of the magistrates seem to lose their heads altogether.

There was a man who most brutally ill-treated his wife, and the punishment he got was a fine of ten shillings and costs. In the very same place, and just a week after, a man was brought up for poaching, and he was fined one pound and costs. He was charged, I think, with aggravated assault on the keeper as well; but, allowing for that, look at the difference—just double punishment in the poaching case! This is one instance among very many of a similar sort. We labourers notice it, and of course we are riled and sore; there is a lot of smothered anger among us at the present time, and there will be till the law is altered.

As to the prevalence of poaching since the Prevention Act came into operation—well, I do not profess to give an opinion; generally speaking, I can only speak with knowledge of my own neighbourhood. When I was a lad, there used to be a gang of poachers in our village; they went out at night as regularly in the seasons as others went to their day's work and their harvesting. There were, I believe, four or five, or maybe more, of them. The gang broke up some years ago. One or two are still alive, and following constant work; the others are old, or dead. A professional or gang-poacher generally gave it up when he was about fifty or so, because he began then to get stiff, and lost his speed. Poaching means very quick work, and, to succeed at it, a man is bound to be a fast runner, agile, and quick-witted. A little poaching goes on still about my neighbourhood, I regret to say; some few men manage to work by day and poach by night, but such a burning of the candle at both ends quickly tells on them; some will do a bit of rabbiting, say two nights a week, so that they can do their ordinary work all right. I know of one man who did this, and he said he had bought his cow with the money he got for the hares and rabbits and birds he had caught. Still, the younger men now value their own manhood more; they think that a man should work by day and not prowl by night, and I quite agree with them. Times have changed since the thirties and forties and fifties, and men have changed with them.

The bitter, bad days of my youth are, I hope past

for ever; a man was often driven to poach, then, if he wanted to live; now, owing largely to the Union, the rate of wages in South Warwickshire—in what I call my corner of old England—has risen to fourteen shillings, fifteen shillings, and sixteen shillings; risen to a living wage, tight fit though it may be, if a man has a large family to provide for. I am most proud and thankful to be able to say that, for the last winter or two, we have not had a man out of employment the whole year through; every single one has been able to get a job here or there. Before the Union started, the general rule was, no constant employment, and an average wage of nine to ten shillings, sometimes eleven shillings. I have known of labourers who were in the habit of taking a gun with them when they went to work, and as they were going along the road, or perhaps crossing by a field path, if a hare or a rabbit came in their way they would shoot it and bring it home for the wife's cooking pot; and if they had not procured a little fresh meat for themselves in this way, they would never have tasted it at all. That was before the law was passed, forcing a man who carries a gun to take out a licence. If a labourer is bent on poaching now, he uses other weapons and instruments; but poach he will and can if he has a mind to. To my thinking there will be poaching till the Game Laws are abolished. They have done untold harm to the labouring man.

For instance, a farmer would sometimes say to me, "If you see any man setting snares, or in any way destroying game, and if you know who he is, and will report him to me, I will give you ten shillings." Such an offer as this was common enough, and it made tattlers and tale-bearers of the men who wanted to earn an extra ten shillings if they could. It was demoralising, because they had no sympathy with the law, but quite the contrary: I might say that their sympathy with it was limited to a chance of getting an extra ten shillings whenever they could spy on a brother labourer and report him. Then the keepers—who were often turncoat poachers themselves—would be quite ready to buy game eggs of a labourer. Some time since a keeper came to me—he had charge of a sort of preserve, not a regular one—and he said, "If you find any pheasants' eggs, bring them to me and I will give you one-and-sixpence. I will give you the same money whether you bring only half a dozen or half a score." It was a temptation, and this was by no manner of means a rare case; men were tempted like this here, there, and all about.

I remember I once had an opportunity of being a game watcher; but I refused the offer, because I like my bed, and it does not suit me to expose my head for the sake of hares and rabbits. There's far too much made of game, and a pheasant is more of a pampered creature than a peasant, any day of the week. If that isn't turning things backside foremost, what is? Game, game! We have heard too much about it, and had too little of it. Game and their keepers have been as bad as an Egyptian plague to many an honest man. Why I have been watched by a gamekeeper myself; regularly stalked I have been. After draining or hedge-cutting, when I have finished my work at night, he has gone right along my work and beyond, to see if I had put any game or traps there, and he has looked into every hole to see if I have committed myself. The keepers as a rule are men who want to get up cases, and they do not care where they get them from. That keeper, if he had put a hare in one of those holes beyond where I had not cut, and I had gone the next morning and begun my day's work and had unfortunately picked it up,—although I never put a wire there,—he might have watched and come down on me and prosecuted. Keepers have been known to play such dastardly tricks on labourers. I am of opinion that these men would be considerably better if they had hard work to do. They say the best poacher makes the best gamekeeper, and it is more than likely. But neither the police nor the keepers nab many poachers. Sometimes a farmer is reluctant to prosecute a man caught with a hare or a rabbit on him; but to a certain extent the police will compel him. There was such a case, where a man stepped out of his way and fetched a rabbit out of its hole. The police saw him and summoned him. The farmer who rented the land said, "I don't want the man summoned. You had better let it drop"; but the policeman said he should summon the man, and if he did not he should never bother about the hares and rabbits on his farm after.

I gave the committee, before mentioned, examples from my own knowledge of how labourers are made to suffer unjustly, owing to these laws.

"Last Thursday," I said, "I saw a man who was made to pay £1 9*s.* 6*d.* because he was getting some liverwort for his afflicted wife. He went into the wood where it grew; it grows by the sides of dykes in woods, and I have often got some of it myself, and other herbs which are very essential to the health of a growing family. I have always used them for mine for years. No doubt the man should have asked leave, I grant that, but I daresay he never thought about it; he only thought of the liverwort. He went just inside the gate and was picking the herb when up marches the keeper, apprehends him, and summons him for trespass in pursuit of game. On that charge the man was tried, and he had the option of paying, or going to prison for twenty-one days. Why, I myself would have got over a gate to procure adder's-tongue or a herb of that description if necessary, and that without a second thought. This man's case is only one of many, there are plenty such."

I said that, "An honest labourer would think nothing of knocking over a rabbit in the daytime, if he saw it and it came in his way, and neither should I. I don't see any harm in it, because in my opinion ground game is wild. The plain truth is, we labourers do not believe hares and rabbits belong to any individual, not any more than thrushes and blackbirds do. I should not inform against a man who knocked over a rabbit or a hare. Has the hare or the rabbit a brand on him for purposes of identification? If I found a stray loaf on the road it would be mine, and so with a rabbit or a hare. But if I found a loaf or a sheep, and they were branded, then of course I should take steps to restore them to their rightful owners."

One of the Committee raised the question of a likeness between game and spirits, and I said there could be no comparison between the two. "Who," I asked, "has ever seen game with a duty stamp on it? I suppose there is a Government stamp upon all spirits that duty is paid for; well, if a man defrauded the Government of the duty on certain spirits so stamped, he would know perfectly well that he was cheating the Government. The stamp would be there to point the moral. Then who ever heard of a cask of spirits running here and there and eating? A hare does though, as many of us have found to our cost. Such a hare may have gone and got his breakfast in my garden, and then after having a feed at my expense, and perhaps doing some damage as well, he may course off to my employer's farm and have another meal at *his* expense. That hare might go coursing and eating from farm to farm, and who is to know where he comes from and whose property he is supposed to be? All I can say is, if I could catch that hare and kill him, I would, and I would carry him home and jug him, and have a tasty meal off him."

To see hares and rabbits running across his path is a very great temptation to many a man who has a family to feed; besides, there is a propensity in every man to look at what he believes to be nice and tasty, let it be winged game or running. He does not believe, either, that it has been created exclusively for one class of the community; and so he may kill a hare or a rabbit when it passes his way, because his wages are inadequate to meet the demands on them, or from dire necessity, or just because he likes jugged hare as well as anybody else. If a man sees unstamped temptation running along before him on four legs he'll run after it on his two, and will knock it over if he can, and take it home and make a feast of it. I should not consider him a guilty person if he did, but he would be run in to prison and run up before the bench in no time, if the police officers or the gamekeeper caught him.

When a game preserver lays the charge, and a game preserver is on the bench, what chance has a poor labourer who has unfortunately stepped out of his way to kill a hare; what chance has he of getting off, poor fellow? Why, none of course. And it is a serious, a very serious, thing, because even if it is a first offence —it should not be counted an offence at all, I think —the man is looked on as a poaching vagabond by all the employing class round about. It is true that his neighbours do not desert him. I myself have taken such men along with me, as good men to work as ever took a tool in hand, but who after such a conviction could not get employment from the farmers. Well,

I have gone with them from one end of the village to the other, to farmer after farmer, but nobody would give them a job. They have not had a farthing in their pockets, and what were they to do? "Oh," they would say, "there's nothing for it but to go back to poaching, and we'll go the whole hog." If it is a first offence a man should be let off with a caution; but I don't see why he should be brought before the bench at all, though I suppose it is heresy to say so.

I remember taking with me on a contract job a man who had been up before the magistrate only once, and the farmer for whom I was working came up to me and said, "You must get rid of that man."

"Why?" I asked.

"Oh, the keeper has been round and I know he would not like to see him at work here. You had better get rid of him or it will cause a noise."

That man had to go then and there, though I was very reluctant to part with him. Even if a labourer does get employment after a poaching conviction, he is watched and suspected; he is looked on as a suspicious character, and the sooner he makes his exit from that village the better, because to live under such spying and suspicion is morally bad for the man; it makes him sour, or reckless and hopeless, and he says, "All right; if I'm to be a marked man I won't be a marked man for nothing," and he goes poaching, out of recklessness and devil-may-care misery.

There was a case which made me very angry. Some boys belonging to our village were going along together ; there were two or three of them, the biggest lad a youth of about twelve. A leveret came through the hedge, and the lad took aim at it with a stone, and by chance hit it ; it was quite a speculation. What should one of the boys do but run off to the farmer, who happened to have the shooting on his own farm. The boy sneaks to the farmer, who comes to the other lad and makes him give up the leveret. I don't complain of that ; but that farmer was heard to say, "Ah, if that boy had been a bit older I would have sent him to Warwick for a month." Suppose the lad had been sixteen years of age, and had incautiously thought, "There is a hare, I'll have a throw at it," and had hit it and knocked it over ; he would have been immediately apprehended, his prospects would have been blasted, and there would have been nothing for him left to do but to go away from his home and his parish. He would have gone with a cloud on him, and if he did not happen to be independent and resolute, he might be ruined in character as well. And what for ? Surely a boy is of more account than a leveret !

I have worked, and I would work, with a man who has been convicted of knocking over a hare or a rabbit, but I should not care to go to work with a man who had taken a hen off a roost. If the poacher was a good workman, it would be all right in my eyes and in the eyes of the other labourers ; but let a man who had stolen a hen off a roost be ever such a good workman, I should have nothing to do with him ; I should keep clear of him and avoid his company, because he would be a felon. What is more; if I saw any man steal six-pennyworth from an employer of mine, I should at once report the man.

I have never poached myself, not once; but I take no particular credit to myself on that account. I am glad I can say truthfully, as I said to the Committee then, "Gentlemen, I never poached, but I don't glory in it." Why for should I? This I know: Suppose I am had up before the magistrates on some slight charge not in any way connected with game, and I see sitting on the bench in close proximity to the magistrates a certain squire, on whose property I had once happened to knock over a hare or a little rabbit. If that squire recognised me, as he would be sure to do, he would tell the magistrates, and they would be very likely to inflict on me the heaviest penalty in their power. The case taken on its own merits might have been trivial; but I should have to bear the whole rush of the law, because the magistrates were friends of this squire who had a bitter feeling against me. This is no imaginary instance, for such partial judgments and unfair punishments have been far too common, far too much a matter of course.

I have also witnessed the strong feeling of game-preserving landlords against small or large tenants who interfere with game. I have known farmers who have been boycotted by their landlords simply for destroying game; regularly sent to Coventry they have been, as if they had committed some crime or outrage against humanity. Farmers have been great sufferers; I know this, and I have seen it. During my travelling up and down the country I have seen fields all over rubbish. I have asked the reason, and the answer would be, "Oh, it's on account of the game." Some of these fields had not been cultivated for two and three years; there were several such fields in the neighbourhood of Wells, and also around Cromer. Not only there either; for in my own time, when going to work in different parts of the country, I have seen a great number of crops that have been eaten down by game, and fields where rubbish has grown up faster than the crops have. In my opinion, and it is a deliberate one, cultivation of crops throughout the country has been lowered considerably, and some land has been thrown out of cultivation altogether, by the plague of game.

I do not think the preservation of winged game is so detrimental to the interests of farmer and labourer as that of the ground game is. For instance, if a man takes and plants a twenty-acre field, and there is no ground game to play havoc with the crop, it would perhaps grow fifteen or sixteen bags of three bushels each per acre; but if there were a number of hares and rabbits eating off it continually, the man might not get above ten bags. Then of course he could not afford to pay his labourers so well, nor would he employ so many. The farmer has to pay the same rent for the field, and if he finds his crop so messed about and spoiled he loses spirit.

It is a general rule that game farms are badly cultivated. When harvesting is on, we labourers always had an eye to the rabbits. If one was started, you would hear a cry of, " Run him down, knock him over, run him in ! " and we always do, if we can, just as we should knock over any other wild thing which was good eating. The farmers are often very sore about this custom. They will perhaps bring three or four men, and shoot all the rabbits they can. I remember a certain field where the farmer and his friends would come ; when we got down to a particular corner of it, they would stand there with their guns and shoot away wholesale, and not leave one rabbit for us. After I had been served that trick, when I began to work in the morning I used to look out for myself. If I started a rabbit and it ran among standing corn I would run it in if I could, but of course I would be careful of the corn, for I should have to cut it, and and as every one knows it's a miserable job to cut trampled corn. There are many who are not so careful, not out of malice or wanton carelessness, but because the rabbit goes so fast that they follow on as fast as *they* can without thinking, till it is too late. Then the man has to pay after his fashion as well as his master.

I have said more than once in public, that on account of the Game Laws many a farmer was obliged to take land at a disadvantage or he could not get it at all ; and not only that, the right of shooting is often reserved, and men come on the farms, break the fences, destroy the crops, shoot the rabbits and hares the farmers have made fat, and go off with their spoil, grinning at the poor farmer, who has to bear it as best he may.

Labourers have suffered too in their humble way. Most of the villagers in my neighbourhood have allotments and gardens, which, to the poor man, are as important as the farm to the farmer, and they have found that hares and rabbits are very destructive to little crops. I told the Committee that I had just lately asked a policeman whether, if I wired a hare on my garden he could apprehend me, and he said he could report me, and if the Commissioners thought it a case that would be convicted they would empower him to summon me. I had the policeman's statement *verbatim* in my pocket. The Committee said the policeman was mistaken, that the law was not so. But that, unless I assign away my rights to do so, I may capture a hare or a rabbit on the land I occupy, and nobody can punish me for it where there is no preservation of game. If the policeman was wrong, how were *we* to know? The labourer has mostly to learn *his* law by bitter experience. There was nothing said about game on the allotments in our part of the world. I occupied twenty perches of land unfenced. Of course no man would go to the expense of putting up a wire fence against hares and rabbits which some one else might claim. Why, at that rate, he might be asked to put up a deer fence! I know only too well that our gardens are very much liked by the hares; and there is a feeling abroad among us, that if we meddled in any sort of way with the game, or it was known that we had killed any on our ground, we should soon hear of it, and have notice to quit. A labourer may have some nice young cabbages coming up, and they may be done for by the ground game, but he is afraid to move actively in the matter, for he feels as if "Notice to quit" is being shaken like a rod over his back all the time, when it's a question of game. Labourers looking at their little gardens will see their greens and broccoli eaten, and will say, "Just look here what a mischievous affair!" If some one says, "Why don't you catch them?" "Oh," they will say, "it would not do, we should lose our land." We feel that we must be very careful; that we must not commit ourselves.

I said to the Committee that we, on our part, had our allotments from year to year, paying twelve months in advance; mine I had had eight years. I had been careful never to knock over a hare on my allotment field, I should have been a marked man if I had; and if the police had come about it I could not have answered for the consequences. A man with any of the Englishman in him won't stand knocking about. I was extra particular after the start of the Union, both for my own sake and on account of the credit of the cause. In 1871, if I had been placed before the magistrates of the county of Warwick in a case of larceny or felony, I might have been leniently dealt with; but after the start of the Union it would have been another pair of shoes for me.

They would have dealt out to me the utmost rigour of the law. So I had to be wary and look to my goings.

I told the Committee I did not want to see game exterminated. I want to see it reduced. A man may preserve game on his own ground if he wishes to—far be it from me to wish to interfere with the liberty of the subject—but he must keep it on his own ground and not let it go spoiling other people's, and making promiscuous meals at the poor labourer's expense. A man may breed twenty thousand hares if he so choose; but they should be bred for his own sport and not for our plague; they should be kept on his own grounds, and not be running and skipping about and doing injuries to the helpless tenants. Catching is having as far as game is concerned. It comes pretty much to this, it is partly a question of identification and partly of feeding. I should say to a preserver, "Have your stray game and welcome, whether it is the sort that flies through the air or runs on the ground, if you can identify it. If a partridge comes picking about in my garden or allotment, or a hare runs about nibbling, and you can point to a brand or a stamp on them and say, "There, that's my mark, and so is that," I should say, "Very good, remove them to your own land and the quicker the better; but as they have damaged my good stuff I must ask you to make compensation—just compensation and not a farthing more, for I don't want charity."

But, if the preserver could not identify them as

his beyond dispute, I should say: "Then they are wild and astray; they have been feeding at my expense; I am going to put them in my pot, and feed on them; they will make very good eating."

Or, suppose I am walking along the public road, which is everybody's property, and which I, with many others, help to keep in repair by contributing to the road rate, and I see a bird or a hare or a rabbit; it may belong to Brown or Jones or Jack Robinson for aught I can tell, and it is wild on the highway. I think I should be quite justified in catching that hare and killing it. That is my view, and it is the view of agricultural labourers generally, however much some of them, through fear, may pretend to the contrary; and that view will not be altered while the Game Laws remain in force. My remedy—I don't consider it perfect—is to abolish the Game Laws, which are an abomination in our eyes, and to make the law of trespass strict; but anyhow let the Game Laws be done away with. I should like to see game free, as free as it is in America; and that day of freedom will come yet, though I may not live to see it.

I was very glad to have my bit of a say to these gentlemen about the Game Laws, not that in my opinion special committees and commissions, Royal or otherwise, do much practical good. They ask questions, and draw up reports, and issue Blue Books. There is a lot of talk, and there is a sight of printer's ink and papers used up after the talking is over-past; then perhaps a little Bill gets dragged through the two Houses of Parliament. There is too much sitting and talking, and not enough pushing and acting. They are better than nothing; but they are lame kind of things when they are going at their fastest. The Ground Game Act of 1880 has done something for the farmer, but we do not want all this tinkering at a worn-out kettle; we do not want a little letting out here and there of this legal strait jacket, and a little granting of this and that right to shoot ground game, when we believe that ground game is wild and ought therefore to be free. Pheasants are on the increase, I hear, and they will go on increasing while there are rich men who can afford to preserve and breed them. Well and good; so much the better for the market in the end. They are dainty eating; and so they ought to be, for they are fed and guarded and kept close, better than many a poor man's children can ever be. I should like to see the day when a plump, well-fed pheasant would be within the reach of the labourer's purse, but that will not be in my time. The whole question was a sore and burning one with us in 1873, and it rankles still.

There was another thing I was glad of; I showed the farmers once more that I was their friend, and that when giving evidence before influential landlords seated together in a place of power, I was not afraid to speak up in the interests of the farmers as well as of the labourers.

At most of the meetings I addressed during this period, I spoke a great deal of the tenant farmers' condition, and I spoke to them also. I remember addressing some six hundred farmers at Dorchester fair and they listened most attentively. My interest in their affairs was growing stronger the more I looked into the whole question of land tenure and rent. I found, and on good authority, that a quarter of the whole class had no security whatever for the investment of any capital. A paper of their own had said that at that time there were some four hundred farmers nearly bankrupt, and another four hundred who only managed to hobble on at all by the good will of the landlords.

Of course, if this was a true statement, and I believe it was not an exaggeration, then the farming interest was the most depressed and most insecure of any great industrial branch of employment in the kingdom. Farmers had their vote, and now they had the ballot; political power was theirs, but for all that, instead of using it to advance their own rightful interests, they would crawl snail-like to the feet of the squire, and vote as they were bid. The ballot was getting safer, and there was less intimidation and spying, and fewer attempts were made to mark a man down in a note-book according to the way he voted. I know for a fact that, in those early days of the ballot, the Conservatives started what we christened the "Tory Ticket Dodge." When an election was on, there would be Tory agents stationed at the entrance to the polling place with note-books in their hands. Up would come a farmer to vote. "Your ticket, please," says the agent. If the farmer had one, and gave it up, it showed publicly that he was a Tory. If he had not a ticket telling him to vote for the Tory Candidate, the agent would put a black mark against his name in the notebook. If the farmer's name was not known to him he would take good care to find it out. It was a disgraceful attempt to make the ballot of no use; but these Tory agents and their note-books soon had to make themselves scarce. Since the Ballot Act had made voting safer, and so strengthened the independence of the voter, and since the Union had been started, the labourers—the more thoughtful men among them—were asking themselves why they should not have the vote also. A shorter working day and a little better food were giving some of them the time and the spirit to consider, and to resolve that they would not long be politically non-existent if they could help it.

CHAPTER VIII.

MY VISIT TO CANADA.

ABOUT this time I was contemplating a visit to Canada and the United States. Meanwhile I took a short run over to Ireland, and made myself acquainted at first hand with the condition of the people. From that day forth Home Rule was down strong on my programme. The lowered condition of the farmers, their attitude to us, and the question of emigration for the betterment of the labourer, were forcing themselves on our attention. At one big meeting —it was at Newbury, if I remember aright—I was moved to speak strongly on these subjects, more especially as I was shortly going to Canada with a view to putting labourers' emigration on a sound basis. I told them at the meeting that some three hundred thousand had emigrated from our shores during the last year, and this represented forty millions worth of bone, sinew, and muscle. I was going to Canada and the United States in August, but if I found there farmers who bought and sold, and had both sides of the bargain, I should say: "Stop where you are, chaps; the crows are as black there as in England." But if I found that country across the water the true home of the working man, where a labourer was free to make his own terms; if his boy could sit down on the same form with the boy whose father has got wealth, and could read out of the same book and write on the same slate, and where the poor man had the same political power as the classes above him; then, if farmers here would not treat their labourers like men, let the working men follow me, and I would lead them across the broad Atlantic to the fruitful fields of America, with its ninety millions of acres yet untilled.

It was a question I had neither shelved nor muzzled, but I had appealed to the farmers again and again. Though I had advocated the rights of the farmer as much as those of the labourer; I had met with insult and contempt in return. Farmers had locked out our men by scores and hundreds, till we had been compelled to raise two thousand pounds from the public to save the men and their families from starvation.

I considered the farmers guilty before God and man; and I said if they began to play that dodge again I would make them before that day twelvemonth know the worth of a man. I wished to treat them with the utmost courtesy and friendship; I had fought their battle before the Game Committee of the House of Commons, and they knew it. I had depicted the farmers' wrongs as vividly as ever I had those of my fellow-labourers. I had shown the great landlords of the country that they were doing an injustice to farmers as a class; and yet, in face of my humble advocacy and honest statements, they had tried to put their heel on the necks of my coadjutors and myself.

All this had only put me more on my mettle; it had not frightened me. Some of the foolish farmers in my part of the country had said the Union would only be a nine days' wonder; but one who had known me from a boy had said: "If Arch has got anything to do with it, before you can make him loose his hold, you will have to cut his head off." It was the truth, too. When I saw some six hundred thousand tillers of the soil in slavery and mocked, I would traverse America from end to end, if I lost my life for it, in trying to raise my fellow-labourers to better things. I was not afraid of walking, if there were no other means of transit open to me; for I had been a Methodist preacher twenty-five years, and had walked seven thousand miles on my own conveyances to preach, and had never had a sixpence from the State. And whether I preached to peasant, to peer, or to prince, I should preach alike to one and all the same grand old Bible doctrine:

"Let Cæsar's due be ever paid
To Cæsar and his throne;
But consciences and souls were made
To bow to God alone."

I had never in the course of my life bowed a single muscle in my neck to the monster of oppresion, and I was not willing that any man should. I would go cringing to the feet of no mayor, public officer, farmer, or landlord, while Almighty God stretched above our heads the broad canopy of the bright blue sky, and under our feet the green sward. Those of us who had been accustomed to what some people called ranting preaching, were prepared to take our stand where thin-skinned gentlemen would feel a delicacy in treading. We would tread firmly and we would march very far. We did not ask for miracles, we only asked for what was possible and right.

I said: "Place the labourer in a free market, in good surroundings, under happy conditions; invest him with his rights; give him a moderate stake in the soil of two or three acres to till for himself. Let landlord and labourer and farmer shake hands, the cordial handshake of good fellowship; let them pull in one boat and let them have an eye to each other's interests; let England be the land where this shall come to pass, and then, should a foreign foe rashly put foot on English soil, the stalwart labourers of England, well fed, independent, honest and industrious, would rise up in their thousands, and would march out to fight for country and for Queen, and the world would be made to know that on the face of God's broad earth there is no better soldier than the English labouring man.

"But much as I love my country—and no man could love her more—if I see within her men who are slaves; men allowed to pine, and sink to death and the grave; men denied the common necessaries of life, who yet spend their lives in unremitting toil for the millions above them; I shall raise my voice and use my influence on both sides of the Atlantic till England, the rightful mother of men and not of slaves, shall be driven to consider her ways and be wise, and treat her industrial population as she ought. Let England be the fruitful mother of men, the nursing mother of heroes; then may her banner be waved proudly aloft, and no man would more delight than I to see stamped on her insignia that which she should ever carry waving in the winds of the world:

"'England—the pride of the ocean, the first gem of the sea.'"

Emigration as a complement to migration was the next piece of work I had to tackle; there was no getting away from it. Though thousands of acres here were lying uncultivated, and thousands more were only half tilled, yet we could not find work for hundreds of our men. Emigration agents were busy, and they hankered after the English labourer, who had the reputation of being the best of his sort. We had been discussing the matter at our meetings for some time past. The Canadian Government wanted men; many had already gone, and hundreds of our people were now turning their faces towards the American continent; but neither they nor the Executive of the Union wished their exodus to be a wild-goose chase.

They came to me and said: "We want you to go over first and look at the country, and then come back and report to us, so that we may know what prospects there are of our being able to better ourselves."

I said: "I'm very willing to go."

I was then given an official mandate from the Union to "proceed to Canada and to make myself acquainted with the condition and resources of the country as a field for emigrants of the farm-labourers' class." This direction and request expressed the wish of eighty thousand members of the National Agricultural Labourers' Union and not only of them, for there were thousands of labourers who had not yet joined the Union, but who—and I am proud to quote the words —"looked upon Joseph Arch as their natural and incorruptible representative in the eyes of the world." The Allan Line offered me a free first-class passage out, and the White Star Line offered to bring me back. I accepted both offers.

I started from home on August 27th, 1873, going from Leamington to Liverpool. At the latter town I met a deputation of the Trades Societies in the evening, and they gave me a cordial reception and expressed their full sympathy with the object of my journey. Arthur Clayden, a member of the Consultative Committee of the National Agricultural Labourers' Union, accompanied me. On Thursday, August 28th, we went on board the *Caspian*, Allan Line steamer, Captain J. Trocks being in command, and we loosed from Liverpool about 2.30 p.m.

I remember how kind and attentive Captain Trocks was. I was a bit upset for three days, for we had a tumbling sea and variable winds, so he let me have my meals on deck, and told off his cabin boy to wait on me. There were two or three distinguished Canadians among the passengers. After I found my sea-legs I enjoyed every knot of the voyage. I remember passing by the rocks of Newfoundland and New Brunswick on our left, and Labrador on our right; the scenery on both sides was splendid. When we left the rocks behind we steamed up the Straits of Belle Isle, with the Island of Anticosti in view; then through the Gulf of St. Lawrence to Father Point, where a pilot came on board to guide us safe into harbour. On the right from Father Point is the Island of New Orleans. For more than a hundred miles I noticed, as we steamed along, beautiful cottages, bright little homes standing in the midst of small farms. These holdings were mostly the property of the French settlers. I noticed that the farming was slovenly, and I heard that these settlers were much behind the times in their agricultural methods. As I looked at them I thought of what the English labourer could do, if he had such a chance of acquiring a bit of land. The scenery was a feast to the eye on both sides.

On Sunday, September 7th, we steamed into the harbour of Quebec beneath a bright sun and surrounded by some of the finest scenery I ever beheld. We landed safe and sound at St. Louis about 1 p.m. At about 3 p.m. we crossed the St. Lawrence by boat, and went to the St. Louis Hotel, where we were met by Mr. L. Stafford, the Emigration Agent, who paid us every kind attention. I can well remember how glad I was to get a quiet night's rest.

On the Monday morning, after a refreshing sleep, I felt a new man, and I set to work without loss of time. I met the editor of the *Quebec Mercury* and then I went to call on Mr. Lesage, Deputy Minister of Agriculture and Public Works for the Province of Quebec. The interview was a long and satisfactory one. Mr. Lesage listened with the closest attention to my plans, and we discussed a practical emigration scheme. The idea was to supplement free grants of land with some provision for immediate starting in life of the man without capital. A rough home would be built, seed would be supplied and a portion of land would be cleared. The cost of this to be repaid after the third year or so by annual instalments, extending over say ten years. This seemed a feasible and sensible scheme. I left Mr. Lesage feeling very cheerful, and I said to myself: "This is a promising start; cheer up, and go ahead!"

I also inspected the Emigrants' Home, an extensive pile of buildings, clean, airy, and commodious, erected by the Dominion Government for the temporary accommodation of emigrants, and placed under the capable direction of Mr. L. Stafford. As many as a thousand people could find shelter here. The women had a lofty wing set apart for their especial use, there were admirable lavatories, there was a capital laundry, and ample cooking accommodation. Upstairs the large rooms were fitted with sloping, sleeping benches. Altogether, I was surprised and delighted with the Home. It looked like business.

On Tuesday, September 9th, I visited the King's Bastion, which is some three hundred and seventeen feet above the level of the sea; also Wolff's monument, which is near the city gaol. In the afternoon I again waited on Mr. Lesage and got my railway papers.

On Wednesday, 10th, I received an invitation to dine with Lord Dufferin that evening. During the day I paid a visit to the Huron Indians, and was very much interested in what I saw. The men make snow-shoes and manufacture leather articles, and the women execute very fine work for ladies. In the evening, Lord Dufferin sent a carriage and pair with attendant servants to fetch me, and the guard fired a salute when I entered the citadel. The dinner was a splendid one, and I relished it very much. There was a brilliant assemblage to meet me, and I had the opportunity of conversing with several public men. I had to go rather early, and for that I was heartily sorry. No one could have been more kind and courteous than Lord Dufferin was, and I fully appreciated the honour he did me, and through me the working men of old England.

It is my opinion that, if all the Colonial Governors were like Lord Dufferin, we should have no difficulties and no 'strained relations' with our colonies. I do not say this because he treated me so well, though of course that counts in my judgment, but because he was the man I found him to be—a man of catholic tastes and sympathies, a scholar, and a gentleman. A more honest man, with views more simple and genuine,

I never conversed with in my life. He was a worthy representative of our Queen, and he treated us right royally. He was good enough to order the Colonel of his Life Guards, Colonel Denison, to take me and Clayden round the country, and show us the ropes. The Government paid all our expenses. It showed plainly that our mission was regarded as of high importance, and we were treated as persons travelling on business of public moment.

On Thursday, September 11th, Clayden and I, having been provided with the requisite passes and credentials, started by the Grand Trunk Railway for Sherbrooke and the eastern townships. We travelled the whole day through wonderful scenery, and I remember we were well shaken up in the train. I got a rapid view of the country as we shot through it. Often and often during the tour I wished for eyes in the back of my head, and at each side as well, for I was eager to see everything, and to pass nothing by either. On Friday, September 12th, we started for Stanstead, a village some forty miles from Sherbrooke. We passed through several villages and by a number of farms, and I did not much like what I saw. The farmers looked care-worn and toil-worn, and this was partly owing to the rough life, but more to the scarcity of labour. As I looked at some of them I thought to myself: "A jolly-faced, beef-fed English farmer is a Merry Andrew by the side of his scarecrow of a Canadian brother. The burly Englishman can take life pretty easy when all's said and done; he can jog to market comfortably on his stout cob, or bowl along in his gig, and do his bit of business in the market, and have his dinner at the ordinary and his chat, and then jog comfortably home again to his wife and his supper. His farm isn't so big, but then he can have it well under his eye, if he wants to; and there are labourers and to spare, if he likes to employ them and pay them a fair wage. But out in these eastern townships it is a very different tale."

Labour was terribly scarce. A man owning some three or four hundred acres would have one hand, or at the most two; and miserable, haggard, lank specimens of humanity they would be, with the hopeless look you see on a man's face when he knows he has more work before him than he can hope to overtake. The farmers hereabouts seemed to have but one idea in their heads, and that was to see how much work they could squeeze out of the hired labourers. I had a little conversation with one of these owners of hundreds and hundreds of labour-starved acres. He said the labourers' hours were from sunrise to sunset during five months of the year, and from six to six during the remainder, and he said he did not think there ought to be any difficulty in getting more labourers over.

"Oh!" said I, "don't you just wish you may get them?"

"But," said he, "look what good pay we give; a dollar and a quarter a day, and board and lodging!"

"I can't help that," said I, "good pay or poor pay,

you want not a man, but a slave. Well, since the Union has been started the English labourer is more determined than ever he was to be a true Briton, and as you know, 'Britons never, never, *never* will be slaves.'"

That farmer dried up; he knew it was the truth. He looked surprised when he should have known better. They say the self-made men among them are the worst task-masters and the hardest drivers. No doubt the struggle they have undergone has hardened and embittered not a few of them. There seemed to be good openings for young farmers with moderate capital, however. One enterprising man, a farmer of the right sort, had shown what could be done. Within six months he had sold ten head of cattle, of his own raising, for some ten thousand guineas; and for one splendid animal, which had gone to England, he got three thousand guineas. This was something like business.

When at Stanstead I visited the Methodist chapel, a splendid building erected in 1856. I also saw the new College in course of building. I remember what a rough buggy ride of forty miles we had, through village and bush. I think we started at five in the morning, and when we reached home again about six o'clock in the evening I was all spattered with mud, and regularly tired out. A visit we paid to Scottstown was more cheering. Mr. Scott, a Glasgow man, was the moving spirit of this new and thriving settlement. He had bought some thousands of acres, and had erected a saw-mill on the Salmon river, which I thought a first-rate plan. There were over a hundred Highlanders hewing down timber, and the engine driving the timber-saw was a sixty horse-power one. Later on they meant to use water power.

Everywhere was a spirit of industry, common sense, and enterprise. Mr. Scott said he would build a cottage for each settler and family, and grant them an uncleared plot; also, he would buy the felled timber from the man, thus enabling the settler to clear his land and get ready money as he went along.

I had a long ride with Scott—a shrewd Scot if ever there was one—and I was much struck by the immense resources of this part of the country; the land was splendid and was crying out for cultivation. The owners are chiefly French Canadians, and they cannot hold a candle to a Scotch or English farmer of the better class. After visiting Lennoxville, we made our way to Sherbrooke again, and then took train to Montreal. As we rushed along we had a fine view of river, and mountain, and fertile valley; it was truly a magnificent country. We put up at the Donegana Hotel, and I remember we could not make head or tail of the French language, which was the one used. It was so much gibberish to me. We reached Montreal on September 16th, and we went to a Provincial Agricultural Show there, and the Committee received us very well. I saw some splendid specimens of shorthorns; in fact I never set eyes on better. There were a few fine South Downs and some very good horses on view. The cereals and roots were remarkably fine, too.

They told me, and I soon saw it for myself, that the soil in this part is wonderfully prolific. One man had grown, he said, thirty tons of Indian corn, and nearly the same in root crops, to the acre, and he could get enough off one acre to keep a cow for a whole year. Here was a land of plenty! Why, it was a vast mine of agricultural wealth. There were farms of one and two thousand acres, well cleared, lying waiting for the farmer. All this made me realise how ignorant the average Englishman, more particularly the labourer, is of the immense natural wealth of Canada. Seeing is believing, they say; well, I saw, and could not but believe.

I had an interview of quite four hours with Mr. Pope, the Minister of Agriculture, a shrewd, intelligent, and practical man. While in Ottawa I had several important interviews with heads of departments. I had more than one with Mr. Lowe, Secretary of the Agricultural Department; and Sir J. A. Macdonald, then Prime Minister, gave me a most cordial reception. He very strongly urged the colonisation of Manitoba, where there were millions of acres waiting for the settler. It was plain enough that in this country there was lack of labour and loads of land. I took care to see something of the sights as we went from place to place; but, business came first and pleasure after. We got to Toronto on September 25th; a long, tedious journey of four hundred miles. I remember that Colonel Denison met us at the station and took us to the Queen's Hotel, and we were the honoured guests of the Provincial Governor during our stay in Ontario. Both the Premier and the Attorney General gave us a warm welcome, and we dined with some of the chief men of the City at Government House.

The practical result of our visit here was very satisfactory and promising. The Dominion Government and our Union would co-operate systematically, and so make certain of a regular and continuous supply of first-class English agricultural labourers. A registry was to be kept, and a list of wants and requirements was to be regularly sent over to our Union to be distributed.

That piece of business done, we had a bit of pleasure. We took a trip to Niagara Falls. It is a sight I can never forget; it was stupendous! it was sublime! As I gazed at that mighty mass of rushing, roaring, foaming water I could but exclaim, "O Lord, thou layest the beams of Thy chambers in *mighty* waters!" What waters they were! It was a most glorious, a most solemn, almost a terrifying spectacle. Never did I realise, till that day, how small a thing is man when brought face to face with the mighty forces of Nature. It was an overwhelming sight, and one which I would not have missed for worlds.

From Niagara we went to Pelham township, driving through a fruitful land of orchards and vineyards. We went to an Agricultural Show at Fenwick, and met a number of prosperous farmers. There were magnificent apples, pears, grapes, and melons ranged on tables in long rows, and there were some of the finest specimens of beets and swedes any man could wish to see. There were splendid teams of horses here, and also at an Agricultural Show at Hamilton, where we met the mayor and town council. Indeed, both these shows were a treat, and were a credit to all concerned. In this district of Pelham there were some thirty thousand acres of fertile land divided among three hundred owners. The average was one labourer to each farm, and so of course the land was labour starved. At least half-a-dozen labourers more on each farm were required. We noticed that the farmers in these parts drove very light traps, which could go at a great rate, and so cover long distances in a short space of time. As the distances from place to place are very long in a thinly settled country, I suppose it was another instance of old mother Necessity and her daughter, Invention.

At Hamilton I remember the Trades Unions gave us a capital supper and a very pleasant evening, during which they presented me with an endorsed address. We went over the Wanzer sewing-machine factories, and fine ones they were.

On October 2nd we returned to Toronto and lunched with the Lieutenant-Governor of Ontario and the provincial Cabinet. I remember we had a sharp debate. In the evening I had an interview with Mr. Lowe, of a satisfactory character, and the next day we started on a tour through the Muskako district. We travelled on the Northern Railway to Washago, through woods brilliant with the tints of autumn. I had never seen such colours on the trees at home. We went up the river Muskoka to Bracebridge, enjoying fine bracing weather.

Bracebridge consisted of a few streets which were nothing but hard mud tracks, the houses were built of wood, and the people were ragged, and poor-looking. There was no air of prosperity about this township. We drove to Huntsville next day, some twenty-five miles through a wild forest track. It was a rough, uncultivated country, and only fit for rough hardy men. As they said: "The land here pretty well takes the life of a man, and these great tracts are little better than white elephants." One farmer who had had to carry on a hand-to-hand struggle with the Indians, and had often gone in hourly fear of his life, said that, after years of constant hard labour, he had only managed to properly clear forty acres. Ordinary clearing meant cutting the trees down within about three feet of the ground, and clearing away the felled timber. When a man cleared his stumps away too it showed he was going ahead properly. I know we could not help saying: "Well, if our men at home would work as hard and live as hard and leave the drink alone, and *had the same chance of owning their land*, there would be no call for them to forsake their native country, as they are doing and wishing to do."

Why, some of the poor labourers of Wilts and Dorset were rich, by comparison, with these owners of hundreds and hundreds of acres, but—and it was a mighty big *but*—the labourers had no hope of rising, and these toil-worn men were working their *own land*, and what would be the land of their children after them. They were not pouring their labour away like water into a pail without a bottom. The hardships in Canada were the voluntary hardships of free men toiling for themselves and their children.

While in the Bracebridge and Huntsville districts I went into the woods, and the lumberers found I could swing an axe with the best of them, and they offered me high wages to stay.

"Oh, I've another axe to grind," I said, "and I must lumber along to other parts."

The Huntsville country was a fine one for fishing and shooting, and did not belie its name. I remember the church there was a log one. When I got back to Toronto, I again had an interview with the Premier, and laid my plans before him, and then I went to the Great Northern Railway Office to meet a deputation, and had I remember a very long and sharp debate on the emigration subject. I also saw some friends who had come out and who were doing well. On October 8th we visited Paris, and there I found an old schoolfellow, and several friends from the old country. This schoolfellow had done uncommonly well. He had been twenty-five years in Canada, and now he owned his house, and had some two thousand pounds out at interest. He was foreman of extensive flour-mills, the property of the mayor, with whom I lunched. I remember we met some of the leading men at the mayor's house, and we heard stories of the early struggles and trials of these pioneers. It did my heart good to see master and man flourishing and working away side by side, each respecting the other in good fellowship.

We saw the Agricultural Show, too, and drove over Mr. Brown's farm. We had a beautiful drive to Bowpark, through a country as different to Huntsville and Bracebridge as night is to day. The farms were in a high state of cultivation, and the land looked like a fruitful garden. It was a great temperance place; tea and coffee and iced water were our drinks. The air was as bracing and as good a pick-me-up as sparkling cider, so no wonder drunkards were a rarity. This Bowpark farm was a splendid one of some nine hundred acres. The soil was alluvial deposit, and it was nearly enclosed by the Grand River; it was a picked spot. The cattle were the pick of their kind too, and the Berkshire pigs beat any we had come across in the old country.

"Oh, yes," I said, "a man may be a king among farmers out here, if he only drops the fine gentleman, and puts mind and muscle and money into his business. Let some hundreds of Englishmen with a nice bit of capital, and go and grit, and youth as well, come out and serve for a year or so under a successful emigrant farmer, and then take up their own farms and employ good English labourers, who can have land of their own in turn, and then emigration will be as good as a tale come true."

We travelled to London next in a Pullman's car, and a deputation of the Town Council received us in the station, gave us tea, and showed us round the city. I went to see the oil works and sulphur springs in the neighbourhood, and here and all around I noticed the general prosperity. Poverty was not to be seen; only comfort and abundance in this western district. It was a bit like the Promised Land we thought, and I wanted to plump down and settle there myself. The old friends I met gave me some valuable advice and information, and they said: "Oh there's no doubt but it's a good land for good men. If a sober, honest, hard-working man comes hereabouts he can be a landowner. He can have a good farm of his own, a well-built house, money out at interest, his children well educated; and, what's more, they may, if they've got it in them, rise to good positions in the State. There's nothing to stop them. They may rise and rise if they have a mind to; if they've the will, the way's all open."

Aye, that was what the labourer at home wanted, an open way to rise up and up, if he had the wish and the brain and the grit to do so.

By the time I got back to Ottawa on Thursday, October 23rd, I was nearly used up; but though I was so tired and had travelled all night, I had breakfast, and went to see the Parliament opened. It was a grand display. I remember the place was so full we had hard work to get a bed. On Friday, October 24th, I went down to the Parliament offices and had a final four hours' interview with Mr. Pope and Mr. Lowe. It was as satisfactory as could be wished. The Government was fully prepared to co-operate with the National Agricultural Labourers' Union in an extensive emigration scheme. They wanted me to accept an appointment under the Dominion Government in England, and they offered me a much larger salary than I ever got from the Union; but, in the first place I never was an office-seeker, and in the second—though it came a long way first in my mind—I was bound heart and soul and body to our Union and our cause, so I said, "No, thank you."

It was agreed that a book of warrants for assisted emigrants should be forwarded to the Leamington office, so that in future adult members of the Union would be entitled, on the recommendation of their President or secretary, to a grant of about forty-five shillings towards the passage out. It was a great point gained when Mr. Pope said he would take my signature or the secretary's, instead of a clergyman's or a magistrate's, to the forms of application for assisted passages.

I had promised to bring out the following spring a hundred picked men and their families and see them safely through to their lots, if the Ontario Government would co-operate by clearing a portion of their free grants and helping them to build cottages, so that work would be found at once, together with enough capital to start and go along with.

I had also arranged with the Government Emigration Agent at Toronto that a registry of applications should be kept for such men as might prefer service for a time, and that a list of places with full particulars as to working hours, wages, and accommodation should be kept, and should be certified to as genuine by the reeve of the town whence the application came. We thought more men might go to Toronto, as there was a demand, and then they might settle themselves on the land later if they wished.

So, after having settled all this, I could leave the Dominion feeling that something had been done, and that our mission had not been in vain. We started for New York on Saturday, October 25th; but owing to the lateness of the season, and the unsettled state of affairs in New York, we made up our minds to investigate the United States of America more fully at some future day, and start to old England on November 8th, by the *Republic*, White Star Line.

When at Brooklyn I took the opportunity of hearing De Witt Talmage preach; and he gave us a most telling discourse on the text, "*He began to be in want.*" I preached myself in one of the Primitive Methodist Chapels there on Sunday, November 2nd. During my tour I was able to preach at a good many places, and to take part in prayer meetings.

There was a thing that made me very angry while I was in New York. I may say—and I do not say it from vanity; there was nothing to be vain about, for it is the way of the people over there, who like what is new and will make a noise over it—that I was regularly besieged by interviewers; papers heralded my coming, and the day after I got to the city nearly every New York paper had a description of me. What made me angry was a hoax played on me and the citizens by some sort of a Working-Man's Union. Some-one said to me: "Do you know that your coming was announced two months ago, and also that you would address a monster meeting of working men in the Coopers' Institute?" The papers spread it abroad, and at the appointed hour thousands were assembled; and I was told that an entrance fee was charged.

"Who," I said, "got up this infamous hoax?"

"Oh, the Central Working Men's Union, or some such organisation"

"Then," said I, "I'll have nothing whatever to do with them," and to that I stuck. When one man after another besought me to address them, I said, "No, you have acted dishonourably towards the public, and whatever may be your American customs, we in England know only two things, right and wrong. You had no authority for publishing my name as a speaker at your meeting. You did not even know where I was, and yet you deliberately advertised me all over the city, and so associated my name with an imposition. I wish you good morning, gentlemen; I'll have nothing whatever to do with you."

So I gave the New York Trades Unionists the cold shoulder—the coldest I had got—and I am of opinion they richly deserved it.

On Monday, November 3rd, we set off for Boston

at the urgent request of a deputation of citizens. I remember, on the Tuesday I went to Reedsferry to meet some old friends, and spent a very pleasant time with them. On the Wednesday they gave me a downright splendid reception in Faneuil Hall at Boston, when I spoke for more than an hour. Wendell Phillips was in the chair, and there was a number of prominent politicians present. The Hall was beautifully decorated for the occasion, and no man could have asked a more hospitable welcome. After the meeting, at which there were over four thousand present, I went to a banquet at the Adam's House Hotel, got up by the Trade Societies. It was a very nice affair indeed, and I enjoyed my dinner. I am not above saying that I am every inch a John Bull in the latter respect; I have said so before, and I will say it again. I do not care where the dinner is—it may be in Windsor Castle (though I have only taken light refreshments there at the Queen's Diamond Jubilee Garden Party to Members of Parliament), or in a labourer's humble cottage—but if it is a good one, I thank God for it and fall to. I am a good trencherman as they say, and so every healthy hearty working Englishman should be.

The Mayor of Boston drove us to see the chief places of note, and I visited, among several others, Senator Sumner, the poet Longfellow, and Jeanie Collins the philanthropist.

On Friday, November 7th, I was back in New York, said good-bye to friends, and went on board the *Republic*. The next morning at 8 a.m we started for home in pouring rain. We encountered some very rough weather, and I remember only too well the great waves rolling over the deck with terrific fury. One went over my head and smashed one of the boats in. The storm lasted about thirty-six hours.

On Tuesday, November 18th, I rose at 8 a.m. and went on deck. It was a beautiful morning, and calm. As we entered St. George's Channel I caught sight of Old England, and I had a good look at her, and as I looked, the poet's words came into my mind :—

> "Breathes there a man with soul so dead
> Who never to himself hath said,
> This is my own, my native land!
> Whose heart hath ne'er within him burned,
> As home his footsteps he hath turned
> From wandering on a foreign strand?"

Ah! the heart of Joseph Arch burned within him; and I am not ashamed to say that a tear came to his eye too, when he saw the old country once more over the tossing waves; "England, old England, the home of the brave and the true and the free," rose before me once more, and about 12 p.m., November 18th, 1873, I again set foot on her shores.

CHAPTER IX.

MY VIEWS ON EMIGRATION.

WHILE I was away in Canada I had left the Union in charge of a vice-president who had been a right hand to me all through. When I came back I took up my special work again, and made a report on my tour and its results. Clayden had been sending home some capital letters to the *Daily News*—our old and faithful friend among the big London Dailies—and they were afterwards reprinted in his little book, "The Revolt of the Field." Directly I landed I put myself in communication with the Union, and on December 1st we had a meeting of the Executive Committee at Leamington. In the evening we held a great meeting at the Circus, and I gave an account of my stewardship to an audience of about four thousand people. The Rev. F. S. Attenborough presided, and with him on the platform were the following:—Messrs J. Campbell, R. W. Collier, H. Taylor, A. Clayden, Ball, Edwards-Wood, J. E. M. Vincent, E. Russell, C. R. Burgis, E. Haynes, R. G. Sweeting, G. T. Haigh, and W. G. Ward.

I made a long speech, and I told them that, for a long time, I had been one of those who could not see that emigration was the right thing, and was strongly opposed to it. Now I had been brought to see things differently, although when I commenced the agitation in 1872 it was to better the condition of the farm labourer in the land of his birth. I said, "I love my country; but I love my countrymen better. The name of a country is nothing to me, if she leaves her countrymen out in the cold. The name of a nation is nothing to me, if she leaves her honest working-men to live upon starvation wages and die in the wards of the workhouse." Because I loved my country I was cut to the heart by the knowledge that the flower of her labouring men were being driven away from her, and I said to myself: "So be it; if they've got to go, let them go to an English colony, that they may be Englishmen still. Canada is calling for our men; let them then go to her, and she shall be their mother by adoption, for Canada is England's loyal daughter." I said to them: "I think I showed myself a true-born Englishman by going to Canada. I had many pressing invitations to go to the States before I went there, but as an Englishman I went first to that land where the British flag waves." There was a thing which Clayden and I noticed, and in one of his letters he says: "It is a somewhat significant fact that even the smallest village has its drill sheds for the use of volunteers. Canada is prepared, and can take care of herself. Any one who has seen the tens of thousands of lithe, active, intelligent, well-disciplined men of Canada, and has witnessed the innumerable proofs of their patriotism, loyalty, and respect for the parent institutions, will never again have one moment's uneasiness respecting its future." It was true then, and I believe it is just as true in this year of the Diamond Jubilee of Her Most Gracious Majesty Queen Victoria—God bless her!

It was a loyal and a prepared Canada in 1873: it is a loyal and a prepared Canada in 1897. I told them that night that I also was the same man as I was on February 7th, 1872. I said: "I fear no man's frown; I court no man's smiles; but I will have honesty, truth, and justice between man and man, whether it is between prince and prince, or beggar and beggar." I went over as an officer of the Union, as a representative agricultural labourer, and all the honour done to me was done to the Union and to the men I represented. I said: "His Excellency, the Governor-General, who is the Queen's representative there, gave me the right hand of fellowship, and listened as attentively to what the representative of the farm-labourers had to say as if I had been the Archbishop of Canterbury." I felt honoured, but I was not uplifted.

"I found a few old Tories in Canada," I told them; "but I must say, for the honour of the different public men of Canada whom I was introduced to, and with whom I had conversations, that a more business-like and a more honourable class of men, as business men and men ot responsibility, I never met with. But my business was not to curry favour with officials; my mission was to do business with them; and when I laid my programme before them, they said they would consider the question, and let me know."

In two letters I had, one from Mr. Pope, and the other from the Hon. Mr. McKellar, chief of the Department of Public Works, Ontario, I received the fullest assurance that the Government of Canada, both Provincial and Dominion, would do their utmost to facilitate the emigration of the farm-labourers to that country, and would pledge themselves that the members of our Union emigrating there should be properly looked after and cared for.

The audience cheered, I remember, when I gave them that assurance. There had been, as there always is, and ever must be, men who had said, "Oh, be careful, be *very* careful about sending men to Canada. Look at the Brazilian fiasco; take warning by that." I told these cautioners that it was no good throwing the Brazilian scheme on my shoulders, for I had opposed the emigration of those poor men. Lord Carnarvon, too, rose in the House of Lords to ask a question concerning the poor emigrants who were "suffering in Brazil as the victims of that merely capricious man."

In the first place I was not a capricious man, and in the second, I had nothing to do with the Brazilian mess. I went on to tell the audience something about the plans we had made, and what they must expect if they went out. I said: "I will give you my plans with regard to the free grants of land offered by the Government. There may have been some misunderstanding and some misconception with regard to those free grants of land. I am satisfied of this: if any man goes out there thinking that, because he has got a thousand pounds or two in his pocket, he is going right out into the bush to make his way there, and have a lot of powdered-haired flunkeys to wait upon him, he will be terribly taken in. I visited, not only those towns that had been settled some thirty or forty years, but those districts which had been opened only about ten months. I was determined to see what bush-life was, and what a lumberer's shanty was. I have stripped to my shirt and chopped the trees, and I can tell you that, in sunny England—the land of the free, as they call it—I have suffered ten times more hardships in the rural woods than any Canadian suffers in his shanty in the pine forest. More than that; I have suffered these hardships for sixteen and seventeen shillings a week, for which a lumberer of Canada offered me forty-five shillings. The honest, industrious, hard-handed farm labourer is just the boy to do it; and any English farm-labourer—when the Government have carried out their plans which I am promised they will do directly, and for aught I know they may be already building shanties for Englishmen—who goes there will have a shanty, and a comfortable one; for I insisted that they should be built in a way by which chastity, virtue, and decency should be maintained. Perhaps you may say that is strong—what right had you to insist on that? But I say that the mission on which I was sent was not one of a frivolous nature or character.

"I wanted the prosperity of my fellow working-men to be enhanced. I wanted to see them on lands where their children could be well educated; I wanted to see the morals and virtues of these people cared for. Let me say, too, that, if anything has given me greater pleasure than another, it was that in the remotest district I visited—which I may say was twenty miles beyond the confines of civilisation—I found the log-hut built by the workmen themselves, in which they assembled every night in the week for their mental improvement and religious purposes, and where, on the Sabbath day, three times they assemble to bow before the Throne of our Creator. Then, during the week these places were used as schools for their children. As an Englishman, I value the morality, the virtue, and the chastity of my family; and where I could not take my dear boys and girls, I would not advise my fellow-labourer to go. But I say this to-night, that, if I had not upon my shoulders the responsibility that I have in this country with regard to this movement, and if the farm-labourers of England will release me from my responsibility, I will take with me my wife and family, and will go to Canada; for it is a better land than England. I am not come here to play the part of hypocrite. I did not go to Canada to play the part of hypocrite. Some of the papers have said I was 'sold,' that the Governor-General of Canada had bought me, and that I induced others to go where I would not go myself. But I say again, to-night, that, if the farm-labourers will now release me from my responsibility, Joseph Arch is the man that does not fear bush life, but can wield his axe as well as any man, and he will go to Canada to-day.

"Now, fellow working-men, these are plain facts; they are simple statements. Next Spring, the Government of Canada will send over to our office the number of cottages they have built, and the number of allotments they have cleared. Now, I wish to be clear on this point. The Government is prepared to build a comfortable and decent log-hut for a man and his wife and family, to shelter him the moment he arrives. They will also clear from five to six acres, and they will find you the seed to plant it. The moment you get there, you may begin to put your spade in the sod. I will not tell you that every stump will be out; but I will tell you that on some of these stump lands I have seen some of the finest crops of corn growing I ever saw in my life. The Government, I repeat, will find you seed; they will find you from five to six acres of land ready for the deposit of that seed; and as soon as you have got your land, and at any time find your strong arms idle, the Government will take up every day, every hour, of your spare time, and will pay you the equivalent of five shillings a day for working on the colonisation roads. More than what I have said—beyond that five or six acres of cleared land, you will have a hundred acres uncleared given to you free, and the sooner you can clear that the better. But here I would say, for the information of persons present, that if you think of going to settle upon these free-grant lands, and of cutting down every stick upon the land, it would be a mistake. I should like to see some of the timber left, and I will tell you why. I pointed out to the Government the imprudent conduct pursued with regard to cutting down timber. They had driven it so far away from the towns that it costs a large price to obtain it.

"Now, with regard to hired labour. I met with bodies of farmers who said they wanted English farm-labourers if they would come out. I wanted to know what would be about the price they would give for that labour. They said they could not talk about that; but I replied, 'You must tell me there or thereabouts.' Some farmers told me candidly that, if they could get good English farm-labourers, they would give them at the least twenty dollars a month, or £1 a week, besides their board, a good cottage to live in with their wives and families, rent free, all their fuel found for them, an acre ot land attached to the cottage, and the run of a cow among the farmer's cows. I tell you, gentlemen, this is not mere theory. I went to a friend of mine, who sat beside me in Barford school, and he told me that every man had got his cow; and he took me round to show me what a splendid cow his man had got. With regard to food allowances, what did I say to the Government? I said, 'Gentlemen, I would rather you would pay these men in hard cash, and let them sit round their own tables at home.' I believe in family fraternity ; and if there is anything that does my heart good, it is when I can sit at the table with my dear wife and family with a good joint of meat. For my part, though, I never saw a leg of mutton on my table since the day I was married.

"But I saw plenty of joints in Canada, plenty of great lumps of beef in working-men's houses ; and I do say seriously, that it is the ambition and glory of every loving father, whether he works in a smock-frock or not, if he has a father's heart, to sit at his own table and cut the food for his own family. Nothing delights him more. As an Englishman then, it appeared to me that it would be better in Canada, if the farmers were to pay the wages in full, if they unanimously said they would rather pay good wages and let the men be in their own homes.

"Now for a few facts. I went into the city of Toronto and met one of our Union men, who left Hertfordshire, and who landed in the month of May last—he, his wife, and his wife's sister. They all went to work, and I found that, up to about October 2nd, the woman had sent her father—who was then on the parish at Hitchin—ten dollars to comfort him, and they had saved one hundred dollars into the bargain. I met also three of our poor Dorsetshire slaves. They are not slaves now. One of them, Charles Davies, because he had dared to join the Union, and had got his wages raised from ten to twelve shillings a week, was told that he would have his allotment taken from him. He said, 'I will go to Canada'; and to Canada he went. He went to Paris, where some of my old schoolmates live to-day. How did I find him? Not the poor poverty-stricken man he was in Dorsetshire. He was at work upon the Great Western Railway of Canada, at five shillings a day. He had got five cords of splendid firewood, all his own, to face the winter with. He had twenty bushels of prime potatoes that he had bought, and he had got them all in his cellar; for, mind you, they have got cellars in their log-huts. 'Now then,' says he, 'Joe, you come down to-night to our house, and spend an hour or two with me.' I went down to his house, where he had with him his two fellow-labourers from Dorsetshire, who only went out last April. Since then, one of them has paid the fare for his wife and family to come out. I went into the house, and what did I see? I saw on the table a lump of roast beef weighing about sixteen pounds. He said, 'This is not all, Joe.' 'Well,' I said, 'let us see the whole.' He took me into the pantry, and there hung a quarter of beef. Said he, 'I gave five cents a pound for it'; that was twopence-halfpenny. 'Now,' said he, 'come here'; and he showed me a couple of pigs that he had given a dollar and a quarter for (five shillings), which, I am satisfied, in the English market he must have given twenty-four or twenty-five shillings ror. 'Now,' said he, 'that is all my own.' It was clear that neither men nor women in Canada need starve; and that is only one of the scores of cases that I witnessed.

"But now I must give you just a little about the dark side of what I saw. You will bear in mind that I am not going to speak disparagingly of any particular district. I speak of things just as I found them. In the Eastern townships there were three of our Union men who were not receiving the wages they expected to receive; but I must tell you that the men seemed in good spirits. I will tell you what they said, 'We are not paid as well here as up in the Western province, but we do not mean to despair. We are in the country, and it is big enough to move about in.' They never talked that way in England, because they never had anything to move about with. I happened to be with the man who engaged them, and I believe him to be a good man. 'Now,' said I, 'how is it these men are not getting the wages they anticipated getting?' Well, of course there were several excuses, but I would not admit of any excuse. They wanted to make me believe that the English farm-labourer in Canada had to work for a few months on rather low wages in order to learn his business. I said, 'Well, gentlemen, you are talking to one who was a farm-labourer from nine to forty-seven years of age, and you tell me I have got to come to Canada and pay a certain premium for my apprenticeship at forty-seven years! I will not believe it, and I will not have it.' I went up to one of the farm-labourers and asked, 'Is this man a good labourer?' The reply was, 'He is a very good labourer.' 'Then,' said I, 'pay him the full amount of his wages.' I did not leave it there. I went down to the Ottawa Parliament, and laid the case of these men before the Minister of Agriculture. He wrote down to that neighbourhood, and the last time I saw him, I was told that the men had got their rights. That was what I saw, and all I saw, of the dark side of the question, and that is not much to make a bother about.

"What is that compared to the dark side of the labourer's picture in England? What is to be said of poor Gooch, the victim of the spleen of the farmers of Bedfordshire? And yet we are told by the great Leviathan, the *Times*, that we can have justice if we like. There are some people perhaps who are anxious to settle this question, and to solve the problem of the English farm labourers. If the landlords of this country would do as Sir John Pakington suggested at a very early stage of this movement at the Worcestershire Chamber of Agriculture, they would solve the problem at once. But we are not content with Sir John Pakington making speeches to Chambers of Agriculture; we want him to put his sympathy into a practical form. He has the land, and we ask him to set the example. Now, I maintain this, that the problem to be solved is connected with the very strength of the farmer's position in this country; and I say that, if our programme is not very speedily carried out, many of the farmers of England will do what the chairman said they would, 'Weep for the crust they wasted in years gone by.'

"Now about our Union programme. We do not want to carry it out as it was carried out in my poor father's time—about 1838 and 1839—in the village of Barford. I can remember the circumstances which happened when I was a boy. The men wanted some land which they could plant with vegetables. They got the land; but how much was doled out? Half-a-quarter of an acre, and for this they had to pay at the rate of £3 8*s.* 6*d.* an acre, while the farmer on the other side of the hedge, paid only thirty shillings an acre. We must have some different process to that. I say, Let the farm-labourer have from three to four acres of land, to cultivate for himself and his family, at the same price as the farmer. But I say also, Give to the farmer, too, security for what he puts into his land. Members of Parliament have talked about what they believed would solve the problem, and the landlords talk about solving the problem. I say it would be a good thing. We want it done; and we want it done between this and next Spring. I do not want to see my fellow-labourers leave the country. I do not want to see the bone and sinew, which are to make this country rich and wealthy, leave us; but I say this, that if the farm-labourers of England are to be treated in the future as they have been in the past, I would say to all honest, industrious men, willing to work: 'Throw down your tools and go to the country which will give you wages, and give you land and opportunities of independence.' Now, is there anything unfair, is there anything dishonest or unjust, in my request? I ask, Would not the artizans in the towns be better off if the farm-labourers had got land to till? What is the reason why your vegetables come so scarce into the market? Because the land is held in large plots, and the farmers are too proud to cultivate vegetables on it. There is no class of the community which would not be the better by it, as well. There has been a dispute as to the increase in the yield; but we have the case of land at Long Itchington yielding only fifteen bushels, which now that a working man has got it yields sixteen bags. The landlords would be wise if they would do something to settle this question. They have done nothing yet; but we will agitate until they have done something—until by emigration the men have left the country, and the lands are left to till themselves.

"The Chairman wishes me to say a word or two about the emigrants' homes in Canada. I must tell you that I visited every emigrant's home in every town I went into, and I found everything that a humble working-man need wish while he is travelling through the country. I inquired very closely as to where they put the men, and where their wives and families. They said, 'We put them in that room; there, we put the single young men; there, we put the single young females.' And I say that in the Dominion of Canada, they have in their emigrants' homes displayed the greatest caution and respect for the virtue and chastity of our farm-labourers' wives and families, when they get there.

"Now, I just want to say a word or two upon another point, and that is with regard to my plan of the labourer having some land to cultivate for himself. There is a great deal said about the heavy taxation of the country. I see the Chambers of Agriculture are discussing as to what they shall do with their poor paupers. Well, if I was a member of a Chamber, I should make a proposition that the men should have some land to till for themselves. A gentleman said to me the other day, 'Why do you not teach these men to be provident?' 'Why,' I said, 'do you talk like that? How can a man be provident who has not enough to live upon?' What a monstrous thing to ask a man to save when he does not get enough to find his family bread! Why, it is mocking us. What I say is this, 'Put the men in the position to be provident; and, if they are not provident *then*, blame them.'

"Now, what I want to say in this country is that the farm-labourer, instead of being a forced burden upon the taxation of the country, and on the pockets of the people, should be allowed to make his way for himself by being put in a position to do it. When a man has three or four acres of land, I ask how many of such men, when they come to the downhill of life will become chargeable on the parish? How many will want to go to the parish doctor? Farm-labourers with three or four acres of land would scorn the action of becoming paupers. You would do the same as I did to the parish doctor when he came into my home and wanted to cut my children for the cowpox. I quickly showed him the door. Let the labourer have three or four acres of land, and he will not be a pauper. I appeal to every honest son here, whether he would under those circumstances be summoned before the Board of Guardians to pay a shilling a week for his poor father or mother in the Union Workhouse, if he had three or four acres of land to cultivate? If my plan were carried out, you would not have five per cent. of the poor agricultural labourers' parents in the Union that you now have. They would teach themselves to love them and take care of them."

I finished my speech by thanking the Trades Societies, and acknowledging the obligations our Union was under to them for their friendly aid and advice. Then I ended up by saying, "I tell my opponents that, while I can raise my voice and there is a single link of slavery left upon any single agricultural labourer in England, I will agitate this question until he is free."

During the discussion after, some questions were asked about the winters in Canada, so I said, "I tell you that I have seen men, my own schoolfellows, who have been eighteen, nineteen, and twenty years in Canada, and they tell me that they like the winters of Canada better than the winters of England; and I am sure that any man with the will to work has no need to feel the Canadian winters more than those of the old country. It's true I have not been in Canada during the winter, but I have been with truthful men, and have made the closest inquiries into the matter, and I am perfectly satisfied on the subject."

The following resolution was unanimously carried:—"This meeting desires to congratulate Mr. Arch on his mission to Canada; and, seeing that emigration has become a necessity to the labouring classes as a means of advancing their interest, this meeting is pleased to know that the Government of the Dominion of Canada is prepared to bring the matter to a practical issue by co-operating with the National Agricultural Labourers' Union."

"Thorough does it," was my motto whilst in Canada, and I soon convinced my audience that I had not been on a pleasure trip. They saw I was no work-scamper. The reception I met with that day, both at the Committee and at the evening meeting, was most gratifying to me. It was a good wind up to what had been a very anxious time; though I got all the enjoyment and benefit out of it that I could. I had, however, been on the strain and stretch from the moment I sailed for Canada in August till the close of that first of December; and I can tell you, I felt when it was well over that I had earned my night's repose; and I took it, too. Now in these later days, when my warfare is ended, I look back on that Canadian tour with great pleasure; I would not have missed going for a pot of money. I was living and learning every minute of every day, and I fulfilled my mission to the best of my ability. I remember I had some fine fun with the farmers over it, and I made several of the cantankerous ones wince. The mere fact of my being received so well was bitterness and gall to them, and I could not resist rubbing it in a bit when I saw how they took it. I told them that an English farm labourer was of some account in Canada, that he was reckoned a very valuable article, that the farmers there wanted more of such a good thing, and that if he was not exactly worth his weight in gold, it was because he was worth more, and that he could turn into a farmer himself if he had a mind to.

The farmers made wry faces at all this and some of them blustered away; but they dared not say much, because I had been to see for myself, and they had not. I proved once more the truth of the saying that knowledge is power, and the more of that sort of power I could get the better, for it was very useful to a labouring man fighting our Union battles. Then some would say to me, "Well I suppose as you were sent over on an emigration job, that was about all you did." "You are mistaken there," I would say; "I killed a good many birds with my stone, just as many as my stone would kill, in fact. And if I did most of my bird-killing in Canada, it was not because I had no chance of knocking over a turkey buzzard or two in the States—or a spread-eagle for the matter of that. Why I had not been in Canada five days before a deputation of wealthy men crossed the frontier from the States, and wanted me to go back with them at once. But it was Canada first, where the English flag waves; and the United States another day. "Oh," some would say, "but you can't have seen much of the country tearing through it at the rate you did, and on Union business too." "Oh, didn't I?" I would answer. "I got a firm grip of the country as I went along; the rivers, mountains, lakes, and forests I saw are fixed in my memory, and will remain there as long as memory lasts. And I took care to see something of its aboriginal inhabitants, too. I went into four or five Indian settlements, and slept in their wigwams; and I never took a revolver with me, nor was I ever in any way molested.

"What's more, I preached in the log huts of forest clearings, and in the stone-built chapels of town and city. I drove miles through country fertile as a garden of Eden, and tramped with lumberers to their daily toil in the vast and lonely primeval forests, where civilised man has never trod before. I dined with the great of the land and supped with the humble: I fared like a prince in gorgeous palaces, and I fed like a labourer in humble shanties. I met old friends, and I made new ones. And wherever I went in my journeyings to and fro in that great and prospering country—a country I was proud to call an English colony—I met with hearty welcomes and good cheer, and many an honest 'God speed you,' warm from the heart, sent me on my way rejoicing. I set more store on the friendliness and good will of my fellow-men in Canada than all the rest put together. We want more of it in England. When landlord and farmers and labourers, when employer and employed, can sit down together, and rise up together in a spirit of good fellowship, then the millennium will be at hand, when it is said the wolf and the lamb shall lie down together; but to my thinking the wolf has got to become lamb-like, or else, if we try it on too soon, the lamb will be there, but he'll be inside the wolf, and the beast of prey will be master of the field."

Then some men would say, "Well, Arch, what conclusions have you come to about Canada and emigration to there?" "Well," I would say, "the conclusions I have come to are, that the colony offers splendid opportunities to a man who is prepared to face a rough life. He has plenty to eat and plenty to drink. He rolls his bed down in a big shanty, and before he turns out to work in the morning there is always plenty of good meat, bread, and coffee for him; he has not, like his English brother-labourer, to commence work on an empty stomach. The lumberers supply their men with very good food. The standard of living is far higher than it is in England, the rate of wages much higher, and the cost of living much cheaper. Clothing, however, is rather dearer. In the winter the clothing is all lined with flannel and the trousers are stuffed into waterproof top-boots. It is a rough and ready life, but there is plenty, and above all there is *hope*. A man there may rise, and the knowledge puts life and spirit into him. He says to himself, 'I may get on if I've a mind to, and I *have* a mind to'; and on he goes, felling, and clearing, and planting, and reaping, and building, and flourishing, he and his family, like a patriarch of the olden days in a new land. Why I would go myself to-morrow, if I could."

At this they would say, "Oh well, if what you say is true, and you would go yourself to-morrow, there's something in this emigration after all."

My saying I would go myself influenced a number of men. "If you would go but can't, why, we can go and will," they would say; and they did, scores of them. For some time after this, the emigration went on steadily; but then, as now, I only looked upon emigration as a disagreeable necessity, not as a thing to be recommended. I could not bear to see our best men pouring out of the mother country when I knew we wanted them badly.

I consider that it is largely owing to this emigration movement that we have such great tracts of land in England out of cultivation now. The best men have been drained away steadily for years, and the result is, that to-day, in this year of 1897, it is becoming very difficult to find practical labourers from thirty to thirty-five years of age. We have only boys and old men left; the best have gone abroad, and as far as I can see they will continue to go whilst land and labour are divorced. Migration not emigration is the cure I cry for now, as I cried for it in 1873; but with migration must go partial redistribution of land and readjustment of land tenure. Free the land of the legal fetters that hamper its transfer, and you help to free the labourer and put him on his feet. If he finds he has a bit of English soil to stand on he will soon say : "I am going to stay in the old country ; there's hope for a man here now. Life is worth living, so I won't emigrate. I will stay on the land when I have the chance to call a morsel of it mine ; and I will prosper, and so help to make England prosperous too."

Yes, I say, let the labourers migrate if they will ; but do not let them emigrate while there is English land for them to settle on, and to till, and to live by. Let the labourer live on the land and by the land ; then England will keep and not lose him, and I say that a good English labourer is well worth the keeping. In the name of our country's prosperity then, let us keep him.

CHAPTER X.

MORE WORK FOR THE UNION.

I HAD been on my travels abroad, now I was on the stump at home again; and if there were stormy times for the Union in 1873, there were fighting days and desperate struggles in 1874. We had commenced the fight on February 7th, 1872, with five shillings, and we won it in April 1873, with a balance of £800 on deposit in Lloyd's Bank. That was very well and very good; but we had not only to stand our ground, we had to go ahead. Go ahead we did; and during 1874 the movement extended all over the country, and I was sent for from east, and from west, and from north and south. I pretty well boxed the compass, and I worked like a slave. In fact, all through these early years I spoke on an average at five or six meetings a week. We could not do much in the north; about Newcastle and those northern districts the men were much better paid, and they said, "The Union is a good thing, but we are well off and can get along without it." The Union was strongest, and kept so, in the Midland, Eastern, and Western counties. In 1874 we had the great Suffolk lock-out! there were some four thousand men thrown out of work. The farmers, naturally enough, were angry with the men because they asked for an advance of wages, so they locked them out as they had done elsewhere, their main object being to kill the organisation. We made a second appeal to the country and to the Trade Unions. I started off and travelled through the North of England, and in a month and four days—I worked desperately hard day and night, till I was about done up—we collected just over £3,000. Then we held a great demonstration in the Pomona Gardens, Manchester, and Manchester took the matter up splendidly; even the Bishop, Dr. Fraser, took sides with us, which in my opinion was a very brave thing for a prominent dignitary of the Church of England to do, but then he was a man as well as a bishop. A good many other towns backed us up as well, but none of them so enthusiastically as Manchester. Many wealthy merchants were present at this meeting, and at its close cheques to the value of £340 were placed in my hands for the relief of the distressed labourers of the Eastern counties. The outcome of it all was a triumph for us, because the National Agricultural Labourers' Union was established on a firmer, and a broader basis than before—on a truly national one.

I had a bit of a tussle with Bishop Fraser of Manchester, and it happened in this way: I had been addressing a public meeting in the Temperance Hall at Leicester. Just before that I had been reading the papers, and had found that a great number of men were deserting the army—it was estimated six hundred a week—and we could not get five per cent back again. The majority of them went off to America, and as soon as they landed there they were beyond the reach of English law altogether. We found also that the emigration agents were very busy—far too busy—taking our best men away from the villages; shiploads were going off every week. At this Leicester meeting I happened to say that I thought we were approaching a very serious crisis in this country, and that I had seen, in a cartoon, Disraeli standing on a landing-stage watching hundreds of labourers leaving our shores, and John Bull was represented asking him the question, "Is it wise to drive these men out of the country?" "Oh!" says Disraeli, "it does not matter, they have no votes." We had an old Unitarian Minister in the chair, and I turned to him and said: "Look here, Mr. Chairman, as an Englishman I must protest, and most solemnly protest, against this driving of the best of our men out of the country. Surely most of my audience have read history! If so, let them think seriously of the time when one of our Kings devastated the Isle of Wight and turned it into a deer forest. What happened? France sent her men over and sacked the Island, knocked Carisbrooke Castle into ruins, and laid waste the whole of the Island. What if our country is devastated in the same way! What if the cold and envious eagle eye of some foreign potentate were to be cast over our little sea-girt isle! What if he had a large army at his despotic command, and seeing our soldiers deserting us, our labourers leaving us—we know that the rank and file of the British Army is recruited from the ranks of the labourers—what if, seeing this, he fell upon us like a wolf on the fold! What if he invaded this country, sacked it, and cut off the heads of these hard-hearted landlords, who are responsible for so much of the mischief, until the streets ran with blood! I, for one, sir, should never weep a tear."

This had the same effect as a bolt from the blue, and the Bishop of Manchester got hold of a paper containing a report of my speech. Two nights after this Leicester meeting, I was due at Manchester for the first time; it was when the great lock-out was on. When I got into Market Street—that was where I had been directed to go—I found a committee of gentlemen there who had been to the bishop to ask him to take the chair for me that evening at the Town Hall; but he had just been reading my speech, and he said he could not do it for a man who talked like that. "I thought you said he was a local preacher," said the bishop. "I should like him to justify that statement." It was put in black and white that I was to justify my statement by the Word of God.

Well, at the meeting, after the preliminaries had been disposed of, I said: "Mr. Chairman, I have been called upon to justify the statement I made the night before last, by the Word of God. I will soon do it. I have been called the modern Moses: I do not lay claim to the piety nor the pathos of that ancient patriarch, but when he delivered the children of Israel from bondage, and they came to the Red Sea, what happened? The Egyptian Army was behind and the Red Sea in front. Moses smote the waters with his rod and, contrary to the laws which govern liquids, they parted, and the children of Israel passed through. The Egyptian army was mightily incensed at this, and dared to follow them into the chasm of the deep; but Moses saw them, and as soon as the last of the Israelites had passed safely over on to the other side, he waved his rod back and the waters rolled on and engulfed the Egyptians. Then, when he saw the Egyptians lying dead along the shore, what did Moses say? Did he tell his followers to go on their bended knees and weep? Did he tell them to put on weeds of mourning? No! He bade them take their harps and timbrels and sing unto the Lord, for He had saved them from the Egyptians."

That was my answer from the Bible to the Bishop of Manchester. He sent a special reporter to the meeting, and when he read the report he said, "Well, this is a marvellous reply; I should not have thought him capable of it. That man must read his Bible. Now I am perfectly satisfied that the labourers are in the right hands."

Then he wrote a letter to the *Times* entitled, "Are the farmers of England going mad?" I got complimented from all parts of the kingdom on that speech. They have not forgotten it in Manchester to this day. The last time I was down there several people said to me, "You have not forgotten the Bishop, have you?" Bishop Fraser was a fine man, and an honest and a well-meaning one. The operatives and the people knew he was their friend, and when he died he was deeply and sincerely mourned by the thousands of poor in his diocese. He was a wonderfully liberal man, considering his cloth and his lawn sleeves. I wish some of the parsons about had taken a leaf out of his book, and had tried to be a bit more after his pattern; for, as a rule, I found the cut of their clerical cloth was not on true Gospel lines, but very much to the contrary. I was continually having tussles with them; if they did not—the bulk of them—oppose me openly, they either did nothing one way or the other, or they stuck in my way like a rock, or stood, like a stone wall, blocking up the path to Union.

I can remember how the parson at a little place in Oxfordshire bitterly opposed me. He did not oppose me in a fair hand-to-hand fight; instead of debating the matter properly in public, he kept close at home and sent his curate to do his dirty work. Perhaps it was just as well for him that he did stay at home, for I verily believe the people would have tried to lynch him if he had come out, he was so unpopular in his parish. The curate, when he arrived at the meeting, began, as they always do in such cases, to riot a little bit; but I shut him up with, "Look here, young fellow, you just try and behave yourself till I have finished. You have been to college and ought to have learned good manners; I have not been to college, but I will give you a fair hearing." I can tell you he kept pretty quiet until I had finished; and then I asked him to come up on the platform and say what he had to say. After a little hesitation he got up and began in the usual affected clerical manner, "Labourers and friends, Mr. Arch, you know, has not been giving you the right doctrine. He must know that the law of supply and demand must rule the wages market. Now, if there are more labourers here than are required, you must work for low wages," and so he went on for some time.

When he had finished I said, "You are a curate, are you not?"

"Yes."

"Well," I said, "you ought to be the very last man to preach that doctrine. How does your class stand to-day?" I pulled a copy of the *Daily Telegraph* out of my pocket, and said, "I noticed here that a very large meeting has recently been held in London, to discuss the best means of obtaining money to buy clothes for the children of poor curates. There are some three thousand like you in England to-day, out of work. Bring your labour into the market on the same law of supply and demand, and see how you fare; we can get plenty like you at nine shillings a week."

"I want to go," said he.

"Sit still a little longer," I said; "you are in good company. When you leave here, go and learn the first principles of Christianity and fair play. Your wives and children can go begging; the labourers' wives and children cannot. Would it not be a wonderful thing to see half-a-dozen curates going through this village, with their pulpits on their backs, asking for a job?" This was enough for him. He did not stop to say he wanted to go, he went; he cleared off just as hard as his legs could carry him.

I used to consider it a real treat to be able to make short work of a parson or a curate of this description. There was another parson I remember who worried me. Those fellows—that particular brand of parson—used to haunt me more than anybody else; they were ten times worse than the squires; they nagged so. I held a meeting one night at a village about two miles from Heyford in Oxfordshire. The next morning I went to Heyford Station to catch my train, and continue my journey. When I got there I found the station crowded with emigrants just off to America. A little curate came up to me and said, "Is your name Arch?"

"Yes; and what's your name?"

"So-and-so. Have you seen the *Banbury Guardian*?"

"Yes."

"Did you see that they called you a 'tallyman'?"

"Yes."

"You are going to reply to it, I presume?"

"No. It takes me all my time to reply to wise men; I have no time to answer fools." That settled him—he soon cleared off the platform.

But I am bound to say that, if the parsons and their weakling curates nagged and worried, and tried a little word-scratching when they could, it was the farmers who were the most abusive. Not all, be it understood, any more than all the parsons—there were enlightened exceptions in both classes. I used to catch it very hot from the farmers when in railway carriages. Very often when travelling they would recognise me, and would get into the same carriage, and go for me. I used to be frightfully abused, and more than once I have been threatened with assault. I remember an instance: It was Smithfield Cattle Show week, and I got in at Leamington with some farmers. They had come from a considerable distance to Warwick and then changed, and were going on to London. There were four of them in the carriage, but they did not know me. By the way, it was just when the emigration agents were working their hardest, and were taking our men away by the shipload, and a great deal was being said on the subject. Well, these farmers began to talk about "that fellow, Arch"; so I sat still as a mouse and listened. One said, "Look here, he's making a thousand a year out of these poor emigrants; poor fools, he's selling them like cattle to the foreigners." So they carried on for some time capping one lie with another. At last, when we got to Ealing, I turned to the farmer next to me—he was an old man, between sixty and seventy years of age, but he was the worst of the lot for abuse—and I said to him :

"Do you mean to say, old gentleman, that Arch makes a thousand a year out of selling emigrants?"

"Yes," was the gruff reply.

"Can you prove it?"

"Yes, I can."

"Do you know Arch?"

"No."

"Well, I am the man; and I am going to make you prove what you say."

At that he looked as mad as an aged March hare.

"Now look here, old fellow," said I; "as soon as we get to Paddington I am going to have you locked up, and" (turning to the others) "I insist on you gentlemen bearing witness against him."

When I said this the old chap got properly frightened.

"Oh, don't make a fuss, don't try to lock me up," he said. "I want to go to Smithfield."

I tormented him for some time, but at last out of pity I said, "Poor old fool, for that's what you are, it seems, I will let you go this time; but I will tell you what I'll do; I will come to your place and hold a public meeting, and I will tell the men how I frightened you."

"Oh Lord! Oh Lord!" he cried. "Don't tell the men, for it's more than I can do to manage them already."

But I affected to be stern and unbending, and I

left him. I do not think the old fellow had a very pleasant trip to the Cattle Show!

He and his like were spreading lies broadcast about me, and the emigration, and the Union; and the worst of it was, like all lies, a few of them stuck pretty fast, as such mud will, and I was a good deal worried and bothered by them later on, too.

I well remember another encounter I had with some farmers. I was going to Cambridge from Bletchley Cattle Sale, and four or five of them got into the carriage where I was. They did not know me. The Union and Arch were the topics of the day, and the conversation naturally turned on them. They were a particularly fine selection of bullies—a choice lot—and they started slating me for all they were worth. One said I was a worthless humbug; another said that I was a cadger; another said that I made two thousand a year at the game, and so on. They credited me with all the vices and none of the virtues of this world. Hanging was too good for me by half. Well, after a time, and without making myself known, I joined in this beautiful conversation, and I asked one of the farmers how he knew Arch made two thousand a year. He seemed to resent the question, and started bullying, and was going to knock my head through the carriage. On my informing him that, as I had only one head I meant to take care of it, and I should not allow myself to be treated in that way; also, that if he started that game, I should in self-defence have to start punching his head, which

I did not want to do, he got very wild, and mad as a bull of Bashan. He rampaged like a lunatic and fairly lost his head. At the next station he got out, and I asked him if he would give me his card as I should like very much to correspond with him.

"Card! I ain't got no card," he growled, with a face as red as a beet root.

"That's a pity," said I, "but perhaps you would be so good as to take mine. Here it is."

I handed him one, and he took it. When he saw the name on it he rapped out an oath and made a dash at me. The train, however, was moving, so he was held back, and the last I saw of him was a picture—he was stamping up and down the platform like one possessed, and regularly foaming at the mouth with rage. He was in a pretty taking! There were three commercial travellers in the carriage with me, and they said they did not know how I managed to keep my temper, considering the bullying I had had. I told them that it did not trouble me, as I did not think it any good to lose my temper and fall out with people, who were at the least half-lunatic.

This was the sort of way the farmers went on, and hardly a week passed at this time without some such ruction. The sound of my name would set their tongues clacking; and if the lies they passed on had turned into stones, all I can say is there would have been enough for road-mending, and heaps to spare. The sight of me would start them off puffing, and prancing, and snorting, and crying, "Ha, ha!" like thc war-horse in Job; they would gnash their teeth and butt at me like rampaging unicorns. And they were not the only ones I had to contend with, besides the parsons and the squires—though as regards the squires, I seldom, if ever, fell foul of them personally, as they generally sent their flunkeys to say their nasty things for them—but I have also had plenty of scrimmages with village shopkeepers. I remember one I had at Pillinghurst, in Sussex. I went down there to address a public meeting, or rather to test the right of public meeting, and when I got to the village I found four or five hundred labourers wandering about and forty-two policemen, if you please, in charge of a sergeant, to keep order. I had just come back from Canada and had a Canadian suit on, so nobody recognised me. I, however, made myself known to two or three and the secret was soon gone.

Well, we proceeded to the village green—a fine open space—and a gentleman from Brighton wanted to take the chair, and he did so. He said he had heard there was going to be war so he had come down to see the fun. Up I got on to a stool, and I started the meeting. Up came the sergeant of the police and said, "Move on; you can't stand there."

"Are you aware," I said, "that any Englishman can stand on any public ground, and deliver a speech in favour of a petition to the House of Commons? I have a petition here for the House of Commons, and you must not touch me." I knew my law on that point, after our previous experiences.

The farmers who were present stood dumbfounded and made no further opposition. We proceeded with our meeting, and while I was speaking a butcher, whose shop was within twenty yards of the green, came up and bullied me. But while he was trying the bullying game on with me, some one else was playing a different sort of game with him ; some one just slipped up and stole a leg of pork from his shop. This too, within twenty yards of two-and-forty policemen ! The butcher did not hear the last of that leg of pork for some time.

They say that threatened men live long ; if that is so, then I ought to be a second Methuselah. And talking of threats reminds me that, once when I was going to address a meeting at a small country place, I was told on arriving, "You had better look out ; the squire, I've heard, is going to turn the fire-hose on you and make you dry up your spouting."

"Oh," said I, "is he indeed ! It'll take more than the play of his fire-hose to dry me up. Let him come, and I and my mates will give him a fiery welcome.'

But that was all the squire did—nothing came of it. I expect when he got wind of the determined attitude of the labourers he thought discretion was the better part of valour. Those who meditated a watery welcome decamped, taking their hose with them. The men would stand no nonsense, and no tampering with me either. You see it was not merely because I was Joseph Arch, it was because I represented the Union to them, and they knew I was toiling almost night and day to further their interests.

But I met with ingratitude and insult and opposition inside the Union. In 1874 rather grave accusations were brought against me by certain persons. They charged me with malversation of funds, among other things. One member of our Consultative Committee was very bitter against me, and some of the others also. He was made to pay for the unfounded charges he made, because his name was expunged from the Consultative Committee, and the Committee passed this resolution :—"The attention of the Consultative Committee of the National Agricultural Labourers' Union, having been directed to certain charges made by Mr. —— in the public press against the Executive and its officers, is of opinion that such charges are groundless, and cannot for a moment be sustained; and expresses its unabated confidence in both Mr. Arch and the other officers."

I suffered a great deal at the time from these misstatements; they hurt me far more than anything outsiders could say, or did say. I shall quote here from a letter which J. C. Cox wrote to the *Labourers' Union Chronicle* of September 19th, 1874. "The character of Joseph Arch is too pure and true to suffer in the long run. I have seen, and learnt, and heard more of that man than, probably, any one else out of his own rank of life; and I fearlessly say that, if I was to be asked to point out the man of all others on God's earth at the present moment, whom I believed to be absolutely incorruptible and true as steel to the work before him, I should unhesitatingly lay my hand upon the shoulder of honest Joseph Arch. Many is the cheque and banknote which that man has received from admirers, intended for his own private use, and which he has, to my knowledge, in his own quiet way, handed over to the general funds; and if self-aggrandisement was his object, as Mr. —— implies, he might have retired from the business of an agitator long ago on a comfortable competence. Did Mr. —— never hear of him refusing the handsome salary of the Canadian Government, on Sir Edward Watkin's farm? And I know of several other like opportunities that have never been made public."

What vexed me so much was that I knew the Union was certain to suffer for this disunion; a house divided against itself is bound to come to grief, and I felt very sore at the thought of outsiders scoffing and pointing the finger of scorn at us and saying, "Look, for all their talk about Union they can't keep united among themselves!" Instead of brethren working together in unity, it looked as if we were going to split in pieces; and at that thought my heart, stout as it was, would sink within me. Only those who have studied the subject, or have done such work as I put my hand to, can understand what difficulties I had to contend with from those very men I wished to help. It was not merely the prejudices of landlords and farmers and parsons I had to overcome; there were prejudices as blind, backs as stiff, and ears as deaf, within our own borders. There was a man who showed that he understood my difficulties in this respect; that was Thorold Rogers. He was a fine fellow, a genuine and a sincere man. He took an active part in the Union work soon after it began, and he followed it through to the end. This is what he says in Vol. II. of that valuable book of his, "Six Centuries of Work and Wages":

"Some years later, Joseph Arch, a Warwickshire peasant, undertook the heroic task of rousing the agricultural labourer from his apathy, of bearding the farmers and the landowners, and of striving to create an Agricultural Labourers' Union. I believe that I was the first person in some position who recognised his labours, by taking the chair at one of his meetings; and I have been able to see how good his judgment has been, how consistent his conduct, and how prodigious are his difficulties. I believe he has done no little service to his own order, but I conclude he has done more for the general interests of labour, if only by showing how universal is the instinct that workmen can better their condition only by joint and united action. And it should be said, that other workmen, trained for a longer period in the experience of labour partnerships, have aided, and that not obscurely, the undertaking in which Arch is engaged.

"The difficulties in creating and maintaining a labour partnership of agricultural hands, are very great. In the darkest period of their history, artizans, even when their action was proscribed by the law, still clung together, had common purposes, took counsel, though secretly and in peril, and struck against oppressively low wages.

"But for three centuries at least, agricultural labourers have had no organisation whatever on behalf of their class interests. I shall have written in vain if I have not pointed out how effectively the employers of rural labour contrived to enslave and subdue them. It is hard to see how any one could have hoped to move them. But even when they were moved, it was still more difficult to make the units cohere. I remember that an eminent clergyman of my acquaintance, now deceased, told me that when he first took a country living—some of Arch's kindred were among his domestic servants, and he was entirely friendly to Arch's policy—nothing struck him more painfully than the evident suspicion with which the labourers in his parish met kindness. He said that he very early despaired of their confidence, for he noticed that invariably any trust he showed in them was distrusted, was supposed to be tendered with the object of overreaching them. I do not comment on the experiences which must have induced this habit of mind in them, but simply say that this was the material with which Arch had to deal.

"I am willing enough to admit that my clerical friend's position was more awkward than that of other persons. But though, being one of their order, the advocate of an agricultural union occupies a more independent and more confidential position than the intelligent parish clergyman. The temper of the peasants must be, even to an enthusiast, no easy instrument to play upon. He has to combat with the persistent apathy of despair. He has to contend with the sluggishness of ignorance. He has to interpret the habitual mendacity of distrust. He has to rebuke the low cunning with which the oppressed shirk duty, for only those who are worthy can take a good part in the emancipation of the English serf. I well remember that a friend of mine, earnestly anxious to better his labourers on his model farm, gave them high wages, regular work, and showed them infinite consideration. At last he despaired and sold his property, because they thought him, in their poor puzzled way, a fool; and he found that he had made them worse knaves than he found them.

"Again, such a man, constrained to be a leader of men, is obliged to assert an authority, and exercise a decision which others, inevitably less informed, cannot understand, and are loath to submit to. This difficulty is universal. The most awkward persons to deal with when debate is needed, are two mobs, one of uneducated, and the other of fairly educated persons; for the former are generally suspicious, the latter generally conceited. Neither will concede to the expert unless there is danger, or till patience wearies conceit. The greatest difficulty we are told, even with the comparatively well-trained artizan, is willing obedience to necessary discipline. It is said that the ill-success which has attended various schemes of co-operation, has been due to the disinclination of operatives to obey the necessary orders of one who is of their own order, whom they have invested with authority. They will obey an overlooker whom their employer selects, even though his rule be harsh and severe ; but it is not so easy to induce them to acquiesce in the directions of those whom they could depose at their pleasure. But the difficulty is greater the less instructed persons are, and the less familiar they are with the process by which the reality of liberty is achieved,—by the sacrifice of a portion of liberty itself. I have heard that in Mr. Arch's efforts he has been constantly baffled for a time, by revolts from the necessary authority with which the manager of a labour organisation must be invested.

"Again, the scattered character of the agricultural population must needs be a great difficulty in the way of adequately organising them. The heads of a trade union in towns can summon their men speedily ; and take action, if action seems desirable, promptly. But it is far more difficult to manipulate the scattered elements of an agricultural union, especially when the hostility to it is so marked, as has been generally shown, and the opportunities of giving effect to that hostility are so numerous. I do not believe that the mass of peasants could have been moved at all, had it not been for the organisation of the Primitive Methodists, a religious system which, as far as I have seen its working, has done more good with scanty means, and perhaps, in some persons' eyes, with grotesque appliances for devotion, than any other religious agency.—The poverty of the agricultural labourer is a serious bar to the organisation of the order.—The economies of the Agricultural Labourers' Union are rigid, the expenditure is cut down to the narrowest limits. I am persuaded that the jealousy which the farmers feel and the resentment which they express against Arch and his Union are a mistake. The first condition under which a workman can be expected to be honest and intelligent, efficient and effective, is that he should have a sense of self-respect. Half a man's worth, says the Greek poet, is taken away on the day that he becomes a slave. The increase in the labourer's pay, if it be obtained, will be much more than compensated by the moral education which he has got by submitting to discipline and by understanding the principles of a labour partnership. When working men make a free contract,—and they can never make such a contract as individuals,—I am persuaded that they will make more intelligent and more beneficial bargains for the use of their labour, than they ever will if they are hindered from corporate and collective action, or remain under the impression that their wages are fixed without any discretion on their part, or are constantly called upon to defend or apologise for what they believe is their undoubted right —a right which no consistent economist would dispute.

"The public is profoundly interested in the efficiency and the independence of the working man. By the former the industrial success of the country is guaranteed and secured. In the latter, there lies the only hope that we shall ever be able to realise in our day what the trade guilds of the Middle Ages aimed at, and in some directions unquestionably secured—the character of the workman, as contained in his moral and professional reputation, and the excellence of the work which he turned out, to say nothing of the practical refutation of social fallacies. Among the members of the Agricultural Labourers' Union, sobriety, independence of public charity, and education are conditions. The Trade Unions of London and other large towns do not perhaps exercise the moral discipline over their members which they might do if their fellows more generally enlisted in the system, and which they will do, as they get stronger and better informed. But I am abundantly convinced that the English trade unionists include in their numbers the most intelligent, conscientious, and valuable of the working men."

I have quoted all this, because I endorse it and know it to be the truth, and because I consider the opinion of such a man as Thorold Rogers very valuable ; it is the opinion of a man who has given much time and thought and trouble to the labour question—he is no ignorant hotheaded tattler ; and if he did take a side it was after he had thought the matter well out and considered it in all bearings. What he says about sobriety, independence of public charity, and education being conditions of our Union, is the truth. We went strong on all three points. I do not object to a glass of beer, or something hot of a cold night ; but

I do say, let there be moderation in the enjoyment of the drinks of the earth. Use them and enjoy them as we would and should any other good thing, but do not let them get the mastery over us. Often and often have I spoken on this subject at our meetings. I would say, "You know as well as I do that there is one great evil to be removed from among the labourers of this country, namely intemperance. No one could be more disgusted than I am when I see a drunken working-man. I do not wish to criticise you as to how you should spend your money, but I do ask you to keep in your pockets the pence, and shillings too, you are only too ready to waste in beer. I do not place all the blame on the labourer," I would tell them, "far from it; it is with the Government the chief blame rests. A system has been introduced into this country, by the selling of intoxicating liquors, which victimises, paralyses and pauperises mankind. Of course it bears hardest on the poor; if a poor man is found by the roadside drunk, there is no remedy but to take him to the station house; but if the squire's son is found in such a position, or gracefully reclining in the ditch, it would be readily attributed to the fact that he was suffering from dipsomania, and he would be gently conducted to the ancestral home." I knew—none better—what dire temptations the poor agricultural labourer had, to drink more than was good for him.

There was one very general temptation which came round regularly with each harvest season, and was the cause of much mischief and misery and riot. This was the harvest frolic, as it was called ; and it took place at harvest-home time when the corn was gathered in. After a harvest supper, which the men had either at the farmer's own house, or if he could not manage it, at the public-house, and where any amount of eating and drinking went on—not the hearty eating and drinking of hungry but self-respecting men; but a regular gorging of victuals and swilling of beer, and something stronger too—after all this, the men, half-drunk, and stupid or riotous from the feast, would start off the next day and go round begging for tips and nips. They would stop at the publics on their way and have another drop to carry them on ; and what with "drops" here and there and all along the road, nine out of ten of them would be in a disgraceful condition long before the day was out. Then they would quarrel among themselves, and they would go home too, and give the wife a black eye or a beating, and turn the place upside down. This harvest frolic was a bad old custom, and was the cause of many going astray and getting into trouble. The worst of it was, too, that the more respectable men were pretty well forced to get drunk then—it was the custom, so they had to. A frolic like that would just be the last straw to a man trying hard to keep a sober head on his poor shoulders ; and it would push some weak-headed youngster, trembling on the verge, right over the precipice of habitual drunkenness, right over for bad and all ; for he would get into some mess, lose his self-respect, and go the whole hog after, with a worthless wife like a millstone round his weak neck to help drag him down to the bottomless pit of pèrdition. Many such cruel cases have there been.

Many an honest, right-down, good fellow I have also seen overcome by drink, because he was suffering from the pangs and the gripes of an empty stomach ; many a poor, half-starved, overworked man have I seen sink into a drunken sot and a hoggish beer-swiller, because he could get no sort of comfort in his wretched home, and had no hope of ever being anything but a slave and a pauper. The law, of course, could not consider and stay to inquire into all the causes which had brought him to such a state ; the law has only time to be just, it cannot spare time to be merciful ; and if a man was brought up charged with being drunk and disorderly, it would say, "Fine him," or "Put him in prison," or both. I do not say the law is wrong. What I do say is, that the law should be applied to rich and poor alike ; that the liquor laws should be altered and amended, and that the poor labourer should have his conditions, his surroundings bettered. Change a man's conditions and you change your man. Give a man the chance of rising as far as it is in him to rise ; but you must begin early with him just as you would with a young sapling or any growing plant. Take a man while he is young and tender, and train him ; put the best into him and draw the best out of him just as you would do to a valuable plant or any growing thing with life in it.

It was because I and others felt so strongly upon this

point that we made education such a plank in the Union platform. I knew from bitter, cruel experience how hard it was to get even a working-day sort of an education, and it was strongly borne in on me that if the labouring man did not get himself educated somehow there was no hope of his rising to manly independence. Now we had the Elementary Education Act of 1870 in operation, I felt that we were in duty bound to take every advantage of it we could —that we should be false to our trust if we did not, that we should be shortsighted fools and no wiser than madmen if we did not make full use of such a priceless blessing. Over and over again I used to say, "If you want your dear children to have a fair chance of rising, of bettering themselves and enabling them to better their surroundings in time, you must see that they are educated—not only stuffed up with a little or a lot of useless knowledge and facts, but taught what is likely to prove useful to them, so that they are put in a fair way to start well, and on the right lines of their life journey. Yes, start them fair on the right lines, and if they have the go in them they'll go; some will go like a parliamentary train, and some will go like an express, each according to his way, but they'll *go*." There were too many of us who had stuck in the mud, and stuck fast for life. The children were not going to stick in the mud of ignorance if I could help it. Ignorance is the blockhead mother of misery to my thinking. Half, aye, and more than half, the difficulties I had to contend with in my Union work were due to the dreadful ignorance I had to encounter among my fellow labourers. They were obstinate, suspicious, and stupid, because they were so ignorant ; their brains were ill-nourished and so they were dull ; their uncultivated minds were like dark lanterns with a rushlight inside ; they did not know how to think a thing out, and they did not even know how to try. Hundreds of these brothers of mine in the country districts were sunk in brutish ignorance, and time and again I used to feel after I had been speaking to them and trying to reason with them till my voice was hoarse and I was nearly worn out, that I had been as good as knocking my poor head against a thick stone wall.

Headaches and heartaches and throataches, many a one, they gave me. I could not blame them as I should blame the present generation if they behaved in the same way, because the old folk had not the privileges the young folk have had since 1870. Children were employed till the law compelled them to be sent to school, and when the father was able to earn so little who can wonder at it? Boys, as soon as they were big enough, would be sent out into the fields, just as I was. Some would say, "Oh, it is a good thing for the boy ; he will get into working ways early and learn to be a good farm hand." But there were others, and those were the most respectable and the best men who would say, "There is no need to set a boy to work on a farm till he is twelve or thirteen, if only his parents are able to keep him at school and get along without his earnings."

A boy was supposed to spend five years at school, but generally he would spend about three, and then not attend regularly. There were night schools it is true, but at their best they were mostly makeshift sort of affairs. The boys would often attend them in the slack winter months from November to March, or they would put in their day schooling then, but the irregularity and the poor teaching did not give the ordinary lad a fair chance of getting even a decent elementary education. Then, many of them were at work all Sunday as well, and the farmers who employed them did not trouble themselves about the education of their labourers, young or old. Work was all they troubled about, and the consequence was the boys were often nothing but young heathens, and were made stupid with toil before they had a chance of getting what wits they had sharpened up a bit.

I remember that the ordinary payment for school was twopence a week, sometimes it would be only a penny, sometimes it would be as much as fourpence, and for a better school it would be sixpence; there was no system worth speaking of. Of course, if a lad could earn money—and some managed to earn a pretty fair amount, as much as eightpence and tenpence a day—the parents were only too thankful. But the worst of it was, not only was the boy missing his small chance of being a fair scholar, but he would be almost his own master when he was not at all fit to be. He earned money enough to be independent of his mother, and ten chances to one he would get into all sorts of mischief, and there was no one to control him. His master did not care, as a rule, what he did out of work time. Oh, it was a very bad state of affairs!

Then the gang system was in full force when I was a young man, and indeed right on into the sixties, though it was then beginning to die out. I have always been opposed to this form of labour organisation. There were private gangs and public ones; small ones and large ones; fixed ones and wandering ones. Sometimes the gang would consist of one man and three or four children working under him; they would go turnip-singling and bean-dropping. Sometimes there would be a mixed gang of men and women weeding and picking "twitch"; some would consist of women only. The potato gangs would be among the largest. You would see a line of women and children of all ages placed along a furrow at irregular distances; the piece allotted to each would vary a little and was called a "stint," and all the potatoes in that furrow would have to be picked up before the plough came down the next one. Behind the line would be two or three carts, and the men with them would empty the baskets in. Such a gang would frequently number as many as seventy, and there would be a man walking up and down behind them superintending. Generally he was a rough bullying fellow, who could bluster and swear and threaten and knock the youngsters about and browbeat the women, but who was nothing of a workman himself. Pea-picking gangs were generally very large, consisting of four and five hundred women and children. The language the women, and the children too, would use was beyond belief. Women who could get no decent indoor work, or who were rough and coarse and bold, would take to gang work, and instead of considering the poor little children by the side of them, these unnatural women have been known to teach the children vile language, and to encourage them in wickedness. There was no limit as to age, and I have seen little mites of things in potato fields who were hardly old enough to walk; and I have seen poor little toddlers set to turnip-singling when they should have been indoors with their mother.

There were regular ganging villages near and about Leicester and Nottingham, and, as was to be expected, the ignorance among them was very great, was a disgrace to a civilised country. It was a cruel and a thoroughly bad system; it was all wrong. The children should have been at home or at school, and the women should have been minding their houses, or should have been in domestic service, or working at some trade suited to women. I am glad to think it more or less a thing of the past. Of course it was not all bad; some of the private gangs working for a respectable farmer would be made up of men and women and children in his regular employ, and would only form into gangs at certain seasons when combination of labour was an advantage. But, generally speaking, the system was a bad and an injurious one. Directly, and indirectly, our Union put a spoke in its wheel. We advocated the regular attendance of the children at school, and we tried to raise the moral standard in the home. "Give your children a good education and a decent home, and make them members of the Union later on," we used to say. Sometimes I used to feel as if I was on a bank I had climbed up, and was pulling other labourers and their wives and children out of a Slough of Despond, till my arms ached fit to drop off, and my head was swimming, and my legs were shaking under me. But I, and my mates standing by me, kept on pulling and tugging with might and main ; we did not stop longer than to fetch our breath, and then we set to work pulling and tugging again. And I may say, and do say without bitterness now, that the "thank-yous" we got for our pains were not as plentiful as blackberries.

CHAPTER XI.

THE DAWNING OF THE FRANCHISE.

ALL through the seventies the Ark of Union was storm-tossed; now it would sail along on the waves of fair weather, now it would be rolling in deep and troubled waters; but through storm and shine, in fair weather and in foul, it still sailed on, and I still stuck to my post. It had to suffer attacks from foes without and from traitors within. I had to bear what I may call the slings and arrows of outrageous slander, assassin stabs in the back of my reputation were dealt me, my character was defamed, and the purity of my motives was called in question by those who should have known me better. Self-seekers and place-hunters strove to knock me down, trample upon me, and cast me overboard—but the fate of the fallen angels was theirs, and it was they who fell and were cast down and thrown over, while I stood firm, and true friends stood by me and struck many a doughty blow in my defence. Cast down in spirit I often was, and sore at heart, but never—no not when the storm was at its highest, or the fight waxed hottest and fiercest—did I lose heart altogether, and fall a prey to ugly old Giant Despair. I never saw the inside of Doubting Castle, though I won't say that I have not peeped in at the door. There were days, too, when I have said to myself, "Why, the poor Union Ark is a worse vessel to sail in than the venerable old patriarch Noah's—his was choke full of wild beasts of all sorts as well as human beings, but they all lived in peace together, they had a little millennium all to themselves, in fact —and yet here were we in these nineteenth-century days of civilisation fighting like cats, and dogs, and tigers." In my opinion these traitors to the cause were no better than heathen savages and cannibals, for what were they doing when all is said and done, but trying to swallow each other? It was a cruel shame and a bitter disgrace, and I felt it to the marrow of my bones when outsiders twitted us and pointed the finger of scorn at us, and hooted. And you may depend they did that, for there were malignants about in plenty, just as there were in olden days. All the same I went right on and I made myself as blind as I could to the scorn-pointing finger, pointed it ever so scornfully, and as deaf as I could to the voice of the hooter, hooted he ever so loudly.

The numbers in Union and the cash in hand fluctuated of course, but, speaking roughly, there was on the whole an increase through the seventies. Up to the end of April 1875 the members numbered

58,650—this was the total returned for 38 districts with 1,368 branches. In 1874 the total income was £21,000, and in 1875 it was £23,130. The expenditure for reliet in cases of lock-outs and strikes during 1874 was £7,500, and in 1875 £21,400; this increase was owing to the great lock-out in the Eastern Counties. Over £6,000 was spent for migration and emigration purposes; nearly 2,000 men had been assisted to emigrate to Australia and New Zealand, 500 to Queensland, and nearly 4,000 were sent to Canada. Over £26,000 was received from the various Trades Unions and the general public. Law expenses and other liabilities came to £690. The cash in hand in 1875 was £4,150. By the end of 1875 we had about 60,000 men in Union, and over £7,000 in the bank. Of the thousands who went to Canada and our other colonies I can only say that the bulk of them were picked men; the drones of course would not go—not they—so they were left more or less on our hands, and there is not a doubt of it but that they proved a drag on us.

A parallel case is, I hear, going on in Wales; the Canadian Government is going to take out about a thousand ot Lord Penrhyn's miners, the very flower of Welsh working men. It is a lamentable thing that such men should be forced to leave the native land they love so well, because they dared to maintain their right to combine. What is worse is that, while our best workmen are being driven out of the country, we are letting the riff-raff and the refuse of other lands pour into England. I am very strongly opposed to the immigration of alien paupers ; as a man who has the best interests of his country at heart I am bound to be. Owing to bad treatment at home, several thousands of our best men emigrate every year—this is bad enough in itself—but instead of this relieving the congested state of the population, we get in about three times as many worthless pauper aliens, foreign Jews, vagrant Italians, etc., the scum of their own countries, three of whom cannot do the work of one honest Englishman. Brassey always said he could not find in any nationality three men who would answer to one good English navvy. With regard to emigration generally, I think, if people in this country find it a hard task to get along, and if they have friends in the Colonies who are willing to look after them until they can make a fair start for themselves, by all means let them go. I do not blame them for going, but I blame the system which permits of their being starved out of the country, and which lets in the rubbish, so to speak, of other countries. I know how I felt it when, at about the time the Union was started, a great number of tradesmen, carpenters, glass-blowers from Lancashire—especially the latter, and in fact the majority of the best skilled labourers—took advantage of the cheap rates and emigrated.

Still, in spite of drones, and strikes and lock-outs and other difficulties, we went on progressing through 1876. A number joined us that year, when they found that by so doing they had a better chance of getting good wages. All through 1877, 1878, and 1879 we managed to keep the wages well up, and so were doing one of the chief bits of work we were organised to do. If there were drawbacks in one direction, there was a steady keeping up to the mark in another; we were all alive—our very quarrels and dissensions showed that, and the thought used to bring me a little cold comfort at times—and we were growing. We were making our power felt, and a Union man who wanted legal or other help, if his cause was good, had not to ask in vain.

For instance, we took up and agitated the case of Luke Hills, who was carter to a certain farmer and landowner at Cuckfield, in Sussex. Hills had been convicted under the "Master and Servant Act" for breach of contract. He had hired himself for one year, but leaving before the expiration of that time, his master had him arrested and taken before the Petty Justices, who convicted him and fined him £5. His employer had claimed £9 damages. Of course Hills could not find the money in the fortnight allowed him for payment, and he was committed to Lewes gaol for three months. It was proved afterwards that Hills had never made any such contract, and that when his master engaged him he had merely made an entry of the transaction in his note book. There was no definite contract, and Hills never understood that there was. This way of dispensing Justices' justice raised a great deal of indignation throughout the country, and well it might. The question was raised in the House of Commons, and Sir Richard Assheton Cross, the Home Secretary, ordered Hills to be released after he had suffered a month's imprisonment. The conviction was both unjust and illegal—no agreement was proved, and Hills never knew there had been any; there must be more than one party to an agreement, which should be duly signed by both parties, and duly witnessed and stamped.

There was another case of imprisonment which roused a great deal of feeling, for it was a very cruel one. Samuel Dawson, a farm labourer aged fifty-seven, whose wages averaged twelve shillings a week, was sent to Bedford gaol for two months with hard labour by the Sharnbrook Justices, because he could not pay one shilling a week towards the maintenance of his parents. Dawson served his time and came out of prison on August 10th, 1875.

It was a cruel business, and it touched scores and scores of labourers on the raw, for this question of maintaining parents was a burning one. It touched me, because I knew from personal experience how hard put to it a man can be to make both ends meet, if he has a wife and a young family and even one aged parent dependent on him. My father was a ratepayer for thirty-two years and never troubled the parish for a farthing. When the poor old man was taken ill, of course my wife had to attend on him. She was pleased enough to do it, and she did her duty by him as a good daughter-in-law should ; but she had her little family to see to, and she had been accustomed to bring in about two shillings a week by going out charing, and so help to keep the pot boiling. The growing children were hearty and wanted a lot of food. It was a serious thing for us just then to lose that two shillings a week, and to have to provide little extras for my father into the bargain. All the money he had by him now was just a few shillings, and that though he had toiled hard, and lived hard, and kept himself respectable all his life. So I said to my wife, " There's nothing for it but going to the guardians and asking them to give me a little help." I did not like it, but I went. The overseer had said he thought the parish ought to assist me a little as long as I had my father ill on my hands, considering I had a pretty large family to support, and he advised me to go before the board. I went and I said : " Gentlemen, I don't want you to support my aged father, but I should be glad if you would give my wife one-shilling-and-sixpence a week towards nursing him, as she is cut off from her charing. What I ask is less than my wife's earnings, and it is nothing to the expense of my father's illness." Well, they refused me that, and said that my father could go into the workhouse, and I could pay one-and-sixpence a week towards his expenses.

My blood boiled up at that. What ! my honest, respectable old father turned into the workhouse to end his days—never ! I up and said to these gentlemen,

"I'd sooner rot under a hedge than he should go there!"

And he did not go—he died under the old Arch roof-tree, and he breathed his last breath in my arms. We managed to make his last years comfortable somehow; but I know this, that after all was over, and my father was decently and respectably buried, I was in debt £10, and I had extremely hard work for twelve months to get out of it again. I felt it bitterly at the time, and I should have been something less than a man and a dutiful and affectionate son, if I had not. Of course, when the strain was off I could say to myself, "Joe Arch, I am glad you had no parish help, not a stiver,"—but I shall never forget the day I went before the guardians to ask for it, and they refused it. It was a day of humiliation and anger for me. And mine was but a test case. I can honestly say now that I am not sorry I had to bear that bit of trouble, because, not only was I sharing the common lot of my fellow-labourers, but I could, therefore, truly sympathise with those in a like case. There were numbers then and later, up and down the country, in just the position I was in, and who were treated in the same way. It was short-sighted policy on the guardians' part. There were scores of hard-working married sons and daughters who, for the sake of two shillings a week, and a loaf outside the house, would have been enabled to take care of their aged parents at home, and see them decently buried. If they were put into the house they would cost the rates at least another shilling a week; more, if, as has been calculated, it costs the ratepayers from three shillings and ten pence to four shillings a week per adult. Then, if a man with his wife, and say six children, went into the House, they would be better off there than they would be outside; if the man could only earn eleven or twelve shillings a week in wages. When this could be the state of affairs it was in my opinion, as good as offering a man a premium to become a pauper.

I never have advocated indiscriminate outdoor relief; very far from it. I wish I might live to see the day when every working man in England will be beyond the need of asking for such degrading help, because he is able to earn fair wages and be a self-supporting member of this great community. Still, in such cases as mine, the Poor Law administrators should have tempered judgment with mercy, and granted me a little discreet and temporary help. I happened to be a strong man, so I pulled through—it was a hard job, though—but for one who could, there were hundreds who could not, and for want of that little, and in my opinion deserved help, they broke down. A respectable man broken down, who has, as it were, the back of his self-respect and independence snapped in the middle, is a sight to make angels weep, and what is more, he becomes a drag on the community in the end and a burden on the ratepayers. A man with natural affection would put up with a great deal before he would let his old father die in a pauper's bed in the workhouse.

There was a little poem written by John Harris, entitled, "The Dying Labour-Lord," from which I shall quote a few verses, because it shows what the feelings of the labouring man was on the subject, and will be always, I hope :

High over the whispering pines
The rooks in flocks were flying,
As in the cell of a lone poorhouse
A labour-lord lay dying.

His frame was of a giant mould,
Which time had partly broke;
His breast, his shoulders, back and sides
And limbs were like limbs of oak.

Now the mighty man was low,
His life was feebly flying;
Old age had bound the village hind
And the labour-lord lay dying.

Men passed along outside;
The rich, the great, swept by,
But none enquired for the labour-lord
Who was so soon to die.

He oft had tilled their fields;
He oft had reaped their grain;
The profits swelled their shining hoards,
But his the crushing pain.

He gave to them his youth,
His manhood's golden prime;
And now they leave the labour-lord,
Wrecked on the strand of time.

None could compete with him
To cut the granite rock,
To guide the plough, or wield the scythe,
Or shear the fleecy flock.

He was an honest man
As ever delved the sod;
Misfortunes came and turned him here
To die alone with God.

Yes, it was the unfortunate pauper, not the drone pauper, our hearts bled for. I firmly believe in the apostolic injunction, that if a man will not work, neither shall he eat. The drone, high or low, whether robed in lordly purple or clothed in labouring fustian, should be forced to work, or left to feel the pangs of deserved hunger. The born drone and the willing drone should have a taste of the spare rod of starvation and a spell of hard labour; but the honest man who wants to work, and who cannot get employment try he ever so, or who through misfortune is reduced to the condition of a drone, that man should have a helping hand held out to him, so that he may rise to his position as a worthy worker in the industrial hive, and feel once more a manly, independent spirit rise high within him. The Union had done, and was doing, much to make this possible. We were keeping up wages, we were protecting labour against the oppression of capital, we were educating our people by means of speeches and papers, we were awakening their intellectual life and making them reason and think. We were working hand-in-hand with the Act of 1870, and now we were making another step forward: we were beginning to agitate for the extension of the borough franchise to the counties. That was a long and a persistent agitation, extending from about 1875 up to our triumph in 1884.

We sent up petition after petition to the House of Commons, and those kept our men busy and also helped to keep them united. They would pick out a man in the village, give him a few pence, and send him tramping round the county for signatures to the different petitions. I myself took one up to the House of Commons which was about seventeen yards long. Mr. Dixon presented to the House the petition from eighty thousand farm-labourers in favour of household suffrage in the counties. I was in the House when Trevelyan introduced the Bill, and Lord Hartington walked out.

On the motion for the second reading of this Household Franchise Counties Bill, Trevelyan proceeded to move it in a very able speech. In it he said : "We draw a distinction almost unknown in any constitutional country or in our own colonies, and which did not exist even here in its present invidious and aggravated form before 1867, between the inhabitants of towns and those of rural England. We brand our village population as if they were political pagans, because four hundred years ago, one of the worst Parliaments that ever sat in this country robbed the county inhabitants of their votes on the ground that (to use the very words of the Act) 'being people of small substance and no value, they pretended a voice equivalent with the most worthy knights and esquires' —so we keep up a difference between the town and county franchise because in 1429 a parliament of Henry VI. was afraid of our rural population."

I was bitterly disappointed when the Bill was defeated in 1875 by a majority of, I think, one hundred and two. But of course we only kept agitating more and more, and the franchise was a front plank in the Union platform from this time onwards.

We met with the usual opposition from farmer and parson, aye and from dissenting minister too ; for it is a true word with reference to any cause that, " he who is not for us is against us." And those who openly befriended us, or even were known to have listened to us, had to suffer. I heard that Mr. Easton, for instance, who stood in the Liberal interests, largely owed his defeat in the West Suffolk election of 1875 to his having subscribed to the Union, and also to his known sympathy with our cause. The farmers were mad with him for that, and said, " Oh, if Easton is the labourers' friend he can't be, and he shan't be, ours." The Conservatives made the most of it of course, and there was a rumour spread about that I was going round with him as a sort of right-hand man and backer up. Well, he lost the election. I do not say it was wholly owing to his known sympathy with us ; but that had a great deal to do with his defeat. As to the dissenting ministers who turned the cold shoulder of indifference and distrust on us—well, I said my say on that matter on more than one occasion. I remember speaking out at a meeting in 1875, and I said :

" I am just going to say a word or two with reference to the class of men who really could not have been ignorant of the grand result of this movement—I refer now to the ministers of the gospel. I don't ask, Are they of the Church or are they of Dissent? I am myself a dissenter, and I have asked ministers of the denomination to which I belong,—'Why do you give us the cold shoulder as you do? Has the Union made us less reverential towards God than we were before it began? 'No!' 'Has it made us more drunken, dissipated, and wretched than we were before it began?' 'No!' 'Has it made us less loyal to our country, less true to our trusts, and less honest to our employers?' 'No!' 'Has it made us less intelligent than what we might have been?' 'No!'

"It is a fact, an undeniable fact, that before 1872 there were thousands of our honest, hard-working farm-labourers, who didn't know a letter in the alphabet; who attended our churches and chapels, and to whom the Bible was a sealed book; and why? because they could not read it. But now there are thousands of these men, who, by virtue of this agitation, and by virtue of themselves, have begun to read; and now, instead of finding hundreds of them wandering about the lanes on the Sabbath day, you will find them in the bosom of their families reading the Word of God—that Book they never knew a syllable of before. And I say, if I know anything of my Bible and the teachings of Christ, of His Spirit and Character, at the great day of account these ministers will stand condemned for leaving the agricultural labourer to find his own way to heaven, when they ought to have tended him and taught him that themselves. I have had conversations with a great number of Dissenting ministers, and Church ministers too, upon this matter, and I don't say that we have not found them in many places really and truly sympathising with us—I mean especially the dissenters—but then they daren't speak out their minds. Let a Dissenting minister come into your town; let him settle down in one of your chapels—I don't know how many you have got—and let him dare to say a word in favour of the movement, and on the side of the poor man who is down in the ditch, then you will find the little capitalist and deacon down upon him like vultures—and yet they do it in the name of godliness and Christianity and love to mankind.

"If there is a minister here—I don't care what your creed or denomination may be—but, if you can show me a single instance where your Master, whom you profess to teach, turned the force of His influence to go with the strong and to crush the weak, then I will say you are right in what you do. But while I cannot find a single instance where He would turn his attention to such dastardly, and mean, and unchristian conduct, and you are mean enough to do it, I shall certainly enter my protest against you; and I will make England ring with the hypocrisy which is blinding the eyes of men, and leading thousands down to hell. I know there are a great many who want to frame hosts of excuses for their neglect on these great points I have alluded to. True religion fears the frown of no man—no, never. True religion shirk its duty, and pander to the crotchets of the money-monger? No, never! I tell you, my brethren here to-night, that this agricultural labourers' movement has shown the dark deeds of a corrupt and so-called Christianity more than anything that has been started could do.

"Now I will just give you one instance out of the many that have come under my notice, with regard to the great sympathy and honesty of clerical men. I was travelling in a railway carriage, and a minister was in the same carriage with me; but, of course, he didn't know who I was. We got into conversation about one thing and another, and at last I introduced the labour movement. He was very pleased indeed to find it had been done so remarkably well—to find it had been conducted so peaceably; and his firm conviction was that it was in a very great measure attributable to the very good and sound advice that their leader, Joseph Arch, had given them.

"I said, 'Sir, you express yourself as pleasantly surprised at the conduct of the labourers, but I confess I am disappointingly surprised with you as ministers for having treated them in the way you have.'

"'Well, but you know,' he said, 'as ministers we have got to be very watchful.'

"They have—for their money! Well, in reply to his views on the question, I said, 'Now, sir, look here. You say you have got to be very careful and watchful; you didn't know which way the movement would turn; you didn't know what shape it would take; you thought perhaps it would result in breaking machinery, and setting fire to ricks, and everything that was wrong and violent and bad. But sir, do you mean to tell me that if you had fear of anything of that sort, it was not your duty, when you knew the labourers were going to assemble on their village green, to have been there first on the spot and have advised them to go right. Do you mean to tell me that you have done your duty in keeping at home, and letting these men go on, and then say, 'Aha, that's just what I expected you would do'?

"Well, having hit him rather plain and straight, he said that now, as long as it had assumed the shape it had, ministers generally were beginning to be favourable to the movement, and he had no doubt for a moment, that they would as a rule come round, and give it their best assistance and advice, and guide it properly.

"I said: 'Sir, I beg your pardon; if in the hour of our ignorance, when you dreaded us, we had common sense to do right and have done it, I tell you now—you and the rest of the ministers of all denominations—as we have done without you in the past, we will do without you in the future.'"

So much for ministers in this matter—there were too many Laodiceans among them, and they got from us the treatment they richly deserved. On another occasion, when speaking in Lincolnshire with reference to a franchise petition, which was going to be sent to the House of Commons, I said I considered that to keep somewhere about a million of hard-working and honest Englishmen out of their rights as citizens was dangerous to the interests of this country; and that while these agricultural labourers and rural artizans were void of the rights of citizenship there was something radically wrong which needed immediate reform, if the country was to be made and kept secure. Why I wanted the farm-labourers and other workmen to have their rights was this: it was all very well for a tyrant minority to hold a lot of poor dupes in ignorance and slavery, and treat them as a tyrant and despot like the Shah of Persia would; but when the subjects of that tyrannised country became intelligent and thoughtful, then I did not care who the tyrant was, nor where he lived, nor what his power—the arm of that tyrant must be broken down by the force of the intelligence of the people over whom he had tyrannised. What then for the agricultural labourers?

In 1871 the farmers could meet these men with a terrible threat, if they dared to stand erect. I myself had been the subject of some of these threats; I had seen my brother labourers stand and tremble like an aspen leaf shaken by the smallest breeze of wind, at the dark look of the employer. And what was the cause of all this? Was it that they had not within them the hearts of men? Was it because they had not the brains of men? No; it was simply because they had not the pluck of men, or if they had, they dared not develop it. These things, however, were changed; and to any of the middle or wealthier classes who were present I would say, that upon the success of this Union movement would depend the success of our country. Let the movement be blighted; let majorities or minorities, or farmers, or landlords, try to blast it, and at the same moment that they had blasted the hopes of the men who were the bone and sinew of the nation—that very moment, I did not care what their army and navy might be, they might write up on the chalk rocks of their nation, "Ichabod," "Ichabod," for their glory, of a truth, would have departed from them.

This agitation which had caused so much uneasiness in the midst of certain parties, was an agitation which I considered every right-minded man ought to have welcomed with some degree of satisfaction, even though he might not approve of its every principle. There was a time when men talked under the hedges as to what means they should adopt to elevate themselves from the thraldom and slavery in which they had been plunged. I ventured to say this: that, if the tenant farmers in this country had not in the end met them in 1872—thousands of my brother labourers, honest, law-abiding citizens—they would in time have been met by the fire of the incendiary, and the knife, and the barricade. It was utterly impossible to keep these men in slavery. God had designed the freedom of mankind, and if it had been in the arrangement of His Providence to have tamed the pride of Belshazzar by the destruction of his empire, He could have done it in His might. Never, too, until the farmers exerted themselves to secure for the labourers the franchise would the labourers assist them in passing a respectable

Tenants' Rights measure. Nay more, failing the help of the farmer, the labourers would turn upon him and would concentrate their attention on the Land Question, demanding the cultivation of the soil where it was now waste, and increasing the productiveness of it where it was now comparatively barren. I considered it an important hour in our national history. When the history of the nineteenth century was written, as with a pen of iron in letters of eternal brass, it would be seen before the great judgment bar of God that this great movement was holy in its purpose, righteous in its design, and honest at its core ; and God who had blessed it thus far would bless it in the future, if we acted like honourable men ; and thus would be seen the hand of a gracious Providence, in wiping away from our so-called Christian country one of the foulest, and blackest, and direst spots that ever stained it—the poverty, and suffering, and slavery, of the agricultural labourer.

I spoke all over the country for the Franchise, at our Union meetings principally. I saw, too, that the day might come, when the next bit of work my hand would find to do would be to speak for my fellows in the Parliament House of the nation. I had never seriously considered the question of my entering the House of Commons until in 1874, Mr. W. E. Forster, in his speech on the Franchise Bill said, "I should very much like to see Mr. Arch in the House of Commons now."

In 1877 I was asked to contest two seats, Southwark

and Woodstock, but I refused them both. In the first place, I felt the time was not ripe; and in the second, I was sure that I could do better work outside; also, I thought if I was sent to Parliament then, somebody would be sure to spoil the work already done. The Cause came first with me from first to last, whatever malicious enemies might say to the contrary. The very idea of my entering Parliament roused the anger and jealousy of several Union officials; of course, they gave various reasons and some plausible excuses, but the real reason was plain enough,—they were jealous, and they could not bear the thought of my going so far up the ladder and leaving them behind. There were ticklish times for the Union just then, owing more to inside dissensions than anything else, and I knew without any telling that my place for a while longer must be, not on the floor of the House of Commons, but on the platforms of district and branch Union meetings, at sittings of Committees and at Union Council Boards. But all the while I kept the franchise ball rolling, and the franchise petitions going round and up to "The Honourable the House of Commons of Great Britain and Ireland in Parliament assembled." A sure sign that the franchise agitation was a genuine and deep-rooted one was the fact that the men sang franchise songs at their meetings; sometimes they would start with a well-known Union one, but just as often in the later years they would sing some political verses as well. Here is one that was a favourite:

THE FRANCHISE.

There's a man who represents our shire
    In the Parliament House, they say,
Returned by the votes of farmer and squire
    And others who bear the sway;
And farmer and squire, when laws are made,
    Are pretty well cared for thus;
But the County Member, I'm much afraid,
    Has but little care for us.
So we ought to vote, deny it who can,
'Tis the right of an honest Englishman.

Whenever a tyrant country beak
    Has got us beneath his thumb,
For Justice then he ought sure to speak
    But the County Member is dumb.
Whenever the rights of labour need
    A vote on a certain day,
The County Member is sure to plead
    And vote the contrary way.
So we ought to vote, deny it who can,
'Tis the right of an honest Englishman.

We ask for the vote, and we have good cause
    To make it our firm demand;
For ages the rich have made all the laws,
    And have robbed the poor of their land.
The Parliament men false weights have made,
    So that Justice often fails;
And to make it worse, "The Great Unpaid
    Must always fiddle the scales.
So we ought to vote, deny it who can,
'Tis the right of an honest Englishman.

CHAPTER XII.

FOES FROM WITHIN.

BUT if we were singing Union and franchise songs at our meetings we were singing tunes of a different sort as well, and they were not songs to be proud of. Why, some of our conferences and meetings might just have come out of the Tower of Babel, there was such a confusion of tongues; officials trying to cry one another down, and trying to push one another out, and struggling to get the upper hand, beset us on every side and gave the enemy cause to rejoice. However, when the confusion was "worse confounded," as one of our poets says, I used to say to myself, "Never you mind, Joe, just you keep going ahead. The cause won't be the worse for it in the end. If the Union is founded on the bottom rock of Truth, the Union will stand. It's no impious Tower of Babel, but one of Freedom's Forts, and we've got to hold it. A free tongue and a free press are the rights of all. Let's have free discussion and fair play out in the open. Truth's but a poor candle if daylight puts it out." But discussion is one thing; abuse is another. Discussion is one of Freedom's children; abuse is the offspring of tyranny and hate, and should be stamped out as you would stamp out a viper.

We had the press for and against us, of course. In 1872 *The Labourers' Union Chronicle* was started, and was conducted by J. E. Matthew Vincent. It was entitled, "*The Labourers' Union Chronicle*: an Independent Advocate of the British Toilers' Rights to Free Land, Freedom from Priestcraft, and from the Tyranny of Capital"; and it had a great influence on the movement in its early stage. The next paper we had was entitled, *The English Labourers' Chronicle*. The Property and Organ of the National Agricultural Labourers' Union, combining *The English Labourer*, and *The Labourers' Chronicle*.

This paper was started by a gentleman, because a few gentlemen of means said the labourers wanted a paper to ventilate their grievances. They invested in the paper and the Union also contributed part of its funds to give it a good start. The labourers took it in and it went well for a considerable time. It stopped through lack of funds caused by the outside subsidies being withdrawn. This was the only paper subsidised by the Union. Others, however, were started in Lincolnshire and Kent, but they were purely local. Both of these papers have long been defunct. They all played a useful part and dropped when their day was done. I know, though, that the editors had no beds of roses—

I do not suppose any editor has that, but some of the labour paper editors had beds that were no softer than harrows. I did not envy them their worrying work, for they sometimes did not know which way to turn. One would say, "Oh, you publish too many of So-and-So's speeches," or, "You do not publish enough of them," and so on. I remember when the Rev. F. S. Attenborough was editing *The English Labourers' Chronicle*, for years he was nearly driven distracted, what with this person and that trying to make him edit the paper as *they* wished. At our Annual Meeting in May 1878, held in the Lecture Hall, Weigh House Chapel, Fish Street, London, when he read his report he said:

"Without solicitation on my part, you asked me twelve months ago to edit your newspaper. I undertook the duty in the determination to discharge it to the best of my power. The duty has proved to be the most difficult and anxious with which I have ever been concerned. In discharging it I have had to deal with many persons, and with more opinions. The conflict between these opinions has been my greatest trouble. Some friends have asked me to publish fewer of Mr. Arch's speeches. Others have blamed me because I did not publish more. Some have urged me to give prominence to teetotal matters; others have said that if I did they should give up the paper. Some have complained of the presence of district news, others of the absence of it. Some have asked me to blame given persons, others have asked me to praise them. Some have thanked me for the paper as embodying every excellence, others have assured me that it has been scarcely worth reading."

This statement was well within the mark, and is only a sample of what labour paper editors, at any rate, have to put up with. I wrote an article every week for the *English Labourers' Chronicle* for two years, giving a history of the first four years of the Union movement.

Among the various matters that came up for discussion, was the Castle Bytham Farm business. To put it straight, and I should like it to go straight, there were four men in that part of England who had nearly spent themselves as public speakers ; I may say that three of them had absolutely done so. Then this farm was to let ; the Union at that time had some funds on hand and the Executive Committee met and decided to take it. I was attending a series of meetings down in Surrey then, and therefore was not present, and knew nothing about the matter until I came back. The whole thing was carried through by the vice-president, who took my place when I was away. He was one of the four men I have referred to, and they wanted to get this farm. They got it, and the Union had to find the funds wherewith to cultivate it. This I strongly objected to, as I did not see why a few men should get a good living out of a farm run by the money of the labourers who had no land of their own. This was the ground on which I based my objection. Besides, we were not entitled by Act of Parliament to buy more than one acre of land out of the funds of the Union, and they had taken fourteen acres, and hoped, if you please, to add another fourteen to it in a few years' time. Well, under the Trades Union Act this was illegal. No doubt the object of this Act was to enable trades' unions to hold land for office purposes, but not for the purpose of tilling land. As our solicitor said, "When the Union comes to take plots of land and to enter upon co-operative farming it is undertaking business entirely different from that set forth in your rules, and under the Trades Union Act it cannot be done." It was suggested that the Executive Council should take steps for the formation of a society under the Industrial Societies Act, an Act which, said the solicitor, "enables societies like yours to engage in any kind of trade whatever, including of course the acquisition of land, and there is consequently no limit to which such a society may not carry its operations." I took no part whatever in the proposal to start such a society, though there were others who did. We got out of this Castle Bytham transaction, but it cost us a good round sum to do it. We had to deal with a person who, as may be imagined, wanted his pound of flesh—however, we did get out of it. The fact was, a lot of the men were craving for the land; as some one said, they were properly "land mad," and in 1875 there was a regular split on the question. A number of the hasty and too eager ones, thought the Union was going to do everything for them all at a stroke ; they were just like a crowd of greedy, impatient children, and they either would not, or could not, get it knocked into their stupid heads that we had to go steady and go sure before we tried to go fast. We were not a set of conjurers.

It is always the case in any movement of this kind, but that reflection comes later ; at the time I was very much troubled and annoyed, because I knew I was doing everything in my power to help them on to the land. What was such a handful as we Union officials against so many of the high and mighty ? When there was a question raised in 1878 about the Charity Lands, I came forward. A deputation of our members, in which I was included, waited on the Home Secretary, the day before our Annual Council meeting. Mr. Shaw Lefevre, M.P. introduced me. I said then, that the education question was one great reason why the wishes of the labourers with respect to the Charity Lands should receive careful consideration. The labourers were now very properly compelled to send their children to school, but it so happened that in many instances this provision diminished the weekly earnings of the labourer and his family, as some of his children were earning a few shillings a week. Any decrease in the family income where the labourers earned but eleven or twelve shillings a week—and, in spite of all the Union had done, there were many such cases still—proved a serious drawback ; and it was therefore highly desirable that any advantage, which the labourer was entitled to receive in respect of land, should be augmented rather than diminished. The agricultural labourers were eminently qualified for using a little bit of land to the best advantage, and, if such plots could be handed over to them, they might increase their incomes some three or four shillings a week, which would enable them all the better to comply with the provisions of the Educational Act, and send their children to school.

There was another point I brought forward : I said that the agricultural labourers strongly objected to the present provision in the Education Act by which Boards of Guardians were authorised to pay the school fees of the children of indigent parents. They believed that it brought them into contact with the Union in a most undesirable manner, and tended to pauperise them, by breaking down the feelings of self-respect and dislike to the Union Workhouse, which it was desirable to foster in the minds of the working classes. Also another advantage likely to arise from providing a bit of land for the labourer was, that it enabled him to make a little provision for sickness, bad times, and old age, on which occasions he was not so likely to apply to the parish, and in that way there would be a considerable saving to the poor rates. These were points we felt strongly about, and as spokesman for my fellows I made the most of the chance. These Charity Lands were nearly all let as farms until we got the vote. The vote broke the back of that ; I knew it would, and I always told the men so. But they found waiting a hard job, as who does not ? And my experience is, that the more uneducated a man is the worse hand he is at waiting, because he is as unreasonable as a baby.

For a while the numbers fell off, but then again more would join. During 1877 there was some decline in numbers, largely owing to the great depression of trade and commerce, and those districts which stood nearest the commercial centres felt the effect of it most. For instance, Hereford and Worcester had declined more than other places, because they were on the borders of South Wales where the coal and iron trade had been so bad. Men had gone into these districts, and then when slackness set in they came back again to their own districts, and in some instances, they actually went through the various districts proclaiming that the Union was a failure. Then, again, many fell into arrears and were thus lost to us; often, poor fellows, through no fault of their own.

This matter of arrears depended a very great deal on the activity of the branch secretary. If he kept looking the men up, and kept in touch with them, he would generally get his money. In hay and in harvest time the men would often be away from their homes for five, six, and seven weeks, coming back late on the Saturday night, and leaving again either late on Sunday night or early on Monday morning. The secretary had to catch them when he could. It was not that in most cases the men were unwilling to pay up; it was that they would forget, or spend the money in other ways, without considering. A district secretary's post was no sinecure, and a man who undertook it was bound to have his whole heart in the business and put self last. He had to be strong, too—a regular willing horse. It was a post that tested a man all through, and many and many a district secretary came out nobly—they tramped and talked and worked like heroes. But, as was sure to happen, there was dross among the gold; there were self-seekers, and there were the unstable and weak-kneed. The discontented made their voices heard, and like the daughter of the horse-leech they kept crying for more salary, more power, more consideration. "More, more!" was their cry.

When there was a question of cutting down their salaries in 1878 I stood up and said I had no sympathy whatever with such a thing as that. Nor had I—not a jot. There were grumblers, who said office and management expenses were far too heavy. Well, I was only too willing to have the organisation worked on the most strictly economical lines; for not only was I always opposed to waste of my own substance, but I was still more opposed to the waste of other people's. "Waste not, want not," was an excellent Union motto, but it wanted supplementing. An organisation was like a living machine, and it had to be kept going, and if the oil of money was lacking it would come to a stop and fall to bits, for in its motion was its life. That was where an organisation of human beings differed from a mere machine—what was rust in a machine was breaking up in an organisation. The fact was that a desperate attempt was being made by malcontents—and also by some of the short-sighted, well-meaning members, in hopes of bettering things—to federalise the Union. I said to them then, "What do we find in federalism in such cases as ours? Why, we find that the federalists are like so many Kilkenny cats, scratching each other to pieces to see who shall have the most power." I said, too, "If you wish to have your organisation complete, do not let it degenerate by means of bickerings and misunderstandings from its present high position. You are proposing to reduce the salaries of your officers; but why on earth did you not give me notice to reduce my wages?"

I told them, too, that every hour spent in wrangling cost upwards of £5 to the funds of the Union, and that sensible men would never behave in such "penny wise, pound foolish" fashion. There were those who wanted to knock me over, who wanted to cripple and paralyse the central body, and get the districts to federate.

"Oh," they said, "centralisation means despotism."

I, if you please, was the Napoleon of the despotism, a man of iron and brass who would crush them into nothingness. I kept on telling them that they could vote me out if they chose. I was kept there by their votes and I said:

"If the right man is not at the head, put him there; and if you send me about my business I shall always trust and pray that the National Agricultural Labourers'

Union may be truly national, and not a collection of local Federal Unions."

There was another thing I told them too, I said: "I know as I travel the country through—and I think my experience on the work of unions and unionism is as wide, and my information as great, as that of any man in the room—I have met with not a few of the leaders of the great organisations throughout the length and breadth of England, but I do not find that while they deplore, as we all deplore, the fact of stagnation—I say I do not find them coming forth in their Councils and saying, that their Unions are going to the dogs in two or three years. They have their organisations, and to a great extent those organisations are similar to our own."

The Chairman of this Council (Mr. Macdonald, M.P. for Stafford) who had a much greater experience than any of us, cautioned us against splitting our Union into sections, and he advised us, as a man who had forty-five years' experience in connection with Trades' Unions against our six years' experience, not to divide ourselves. "We have heard a great deal," he said, "about centralisation being despotism, but let me refer you to the great lock-out in 1874, and allow me to say that if it had not been for the National Union, you would not have had a Union to-day." I said also, "With regard to your executive committee, which is charged as being the embodiment of centralised despotism, I can tell you that I have never seen a question of a grant brought before them, but that they have always been anxious, as far as lay in their power, to grant a cheque, no matter whether it was for a strike or a lock-out or for working expenses."

"Let me tell you this," I said; "I have not a very high opinion of one district having plenty of money and another district being in poverty." I told them, too, that if our Union had suffered somewhat during the past twelve months, it had not suffered a tithe of what other unions had suffered. "We have got to pull a long and a strong pull altogether, and put our shoulders to the Union wheel, for we have a great deal of organisation work to do yet. If we are to reform our Union, it must be by perfecting the details of our machinery." I was enraged at the self-seeking, and squabbling, and back-biting, and that far more for the sake of the Union than for my own.

And then, as my custom as ever been, I spoke straight. If I have to hit, I hit as straight from the shoulder as I can, a good, honest, English, knockdown blow. "Face the foe, and don't fear the fall," was my motto. I did not mince my words fine with the labourers either. I told them at the different meetings, and whenever I got the chance, that if they did not care for better wages, if they did not want redemption from bondage, beer, ignorance, and tyranny, they might stay as they were, and be degraded serfs all their days, and die in the workhouse; we had done what we could, and would go on till we dropped trying to make men of them, but drop we too, soon should, if they did not join in and lend a willing hand. "One and all it must be, so one and all let it be," I said over, and over, and over.

The malcontents were at it harder than ever in 1879. They wanted to form the Federal Unions into districts; each district to have a president, and so forth, and each district was to send up so much for my support. I refused it, because the moment they stopped the supplies I was done. I told them so. I saw that my enemies had waxed so bitter against me that they intended to kick me out, their toes were tingling to do it; but I was not going to be kicked out—my work was not done, nothing like done. I was determined that if I was to go, I should be dismissed in an open, above-board manner; but that was just what my enemies did not want. They tried to hustle me off the Union platform, they tried to push me out of the president's chair. All I can say is, they did not know Joseph Arch when they tried that game on. I had desperate hard times in 1878 and 1879, but there was comfort brought to me, too, when I found so many members staunch to the Union and to me.

I remember a great meeting we had on the seventh anniversary of the Union. We held it under the old chestnut-tree at Wellesbourne. It was a pouring wet day and the roads were in a fearful state, but notwithstanding that, between two and three thousand assembled, many walking seven and eight miles through mud and slush. An open waggon was our platform; it was drawn up against the trunk of the old chestnut and lit up with tallow dips. As some one remarked,

"There's little light from those dips, Joe, but there's plenty of grease."

"Enough light to see by, and more than enough to hear by," said I. From the top of the chestnut tree a Union flag proudly floated like the banner in the poem "Excelsior." George Mitchell was voted to the chair. I was a bit fagged out when I stood up, but once started I went ahead like a house afire. I know this: I carried the men with me, for they stood like one man during my speech which lasted a good hour and a half. I was greatly moved; I can remember now how all strung up I felt.

I began by saying: "Seven years ago to-night I responded to the call of a deputation of Warwickshire agricultural labourers to come here and speak to you on the question of Union. I felt the importance of my position at that time, and I see the face of a labourer in this gathering, who said to me after the first meeting had been held, 'You have lighted a torch which I have no doubt will light the whole country up before long.' When he made that remark to me I felt I had undertaken a work, which, if that prophecy were fulfilled, would require the most indomitable determination, the strictest integrity, the most sterling character and perseverance to carry it out; but to-night I feel I have a responsibility which I had not at that time. I felt it to be a great responsibility to start the Union, but I feel it to-night to be a greater responsibility to defend it against its internal enemies."

I went into the history of the Union and into details

of the internal struggles, and into the personal insults I had had put upon me. "But," I said, "when fourteen thousand and more of my countrymen rally round the standard of the Union, which, seven years ago, we raised on this memorable spot, I can well afford to stand against the calumny of the calumniator ; I can well afford to smile at the opprobrium and contumely cast upon me."

I reminded them of our triumphs as well as our struggles. "When 1874 set in," I said, "you then fought one of the greatest battles—and when I say greatest, I mean in proportion to our genius for fighting, and I also mean in proportion to our skill in carrying on a battle—therefore, on that score I say we fought, as agricultural labourers, the greatest battle that ever was fought by working men in England. The country at that time rushed to your rescue with about £25,000 ; but you fought for the right to combine, and you won a grand and a glorious victory.

"In 1875 you are well aware that it was said Joseph Arch tried to wreck the Union ; but when mistakes of a serious character are made, I am determined to ferret them out. I feel the dignity of my character, though a farm-labourer born and bred, as much as the Prince of Wales does. Though it might sever me from my nearest and dearest friends, I will never allow the highest power a man has, and that is his character, to be foundered in the mire of treachery. If to bring mistakes to broad daylight ; if to unearth a mistake for the satisfaction of tens of thousands of men; if to speak the truth, and dare to stand single-handed, as I did in the Birmingham Council—if all this be the cause of wrecking your Union, I would far sooner see it wrecked on the sands of truth and justice, than that it should be buried in the mire of selfishness and trickery.

"As you know," I went on to say, "my character was libelled in the vilest manner week after week for something like eighteen months. I was advised to take counsel's opinion upon one of the very worst of these libels, and counsel returned his opinion that it was a very good case, and that I should make my opponents suffer; but he said it would cost a sum of money to start the action. I then said, 'Very well, let it drop; for, if the character of Joseph Arch cannot defend itself without taking hundreds of pounds of the labourers' funds, then let him die in ignominy and disgrace.'

"The last May Council (1878) came, and a committee was then formed to inquire into a cheaper method of working your Union. That committee drew up their report, and I was instructed to call a general meeting of representatives from every district, to consider their report. The committee decided upon nine out of the ten recommendations submitted to you. Some of the very men who voted for the acceptance of nine of these resolutions, went back into their districts and told their members that if these resolutions were carried, it would do the Union more harm than good. I ask, Was that constitutional? I think not.

That committee was formed from every district, and it authorised me to call a council in London. I felt certain there would be a little bit of antagonism, but what was at the bottom of this antagonism? I unhesitatingly say it was because it was the wish of your president and your committee, that these resolutions should be placed in your hands, and not in the hands of the district representatives. I said, 'Let every member of the Union have a chance to speak upon them.' Was not that constitutional? Then you are told that I want to form a Union of my own, and that I am a despot. Now, let us look where the despotism lies.

"In these resolutions it was said that you members should have the entire power of fixing the salaries of your officers, which power you have a right to. I voted heartily for that. It was also proposed that you should fix the salary of your president, and that you should have the power to elect him or send him away. Was not that true constitutionalism? But what about the men who, at the London Council would not let the votes of their members be known; who said they came there to represent their districts? Why, out of fifty branches in one of those districts I hold forty-five to-day. Those men went there to represent themselves. Who, I ask, is the despot? The country at large shall read what I am saying to-night, and let the country give the verdict."

I went into the question of the circulars which had roused a great deal of feeling. I had issued one, and my action had been stigmatised as unconstitutional. I said, "Well, with regard to this circular—it has gone, and why did I issue it? I should have returned from the London Council on the Thursday, but your chairman who is always so generous as to find me a home for nothing in London, knows that I was too ill to return from London on Thursday in consequence of the abuse I had received. On the Friday I got home and I found there was a circular which had been issued by the Oxford district secretary, from 'The Strand, London.' It was concerning a meeting on Federation or separation. I regard the Oxfordshire men with as much respect and sincerity as I do you men of Warwickshire. I looked at it and I said, 'If that is your game, to split the Union, I will take the bull by the horns.'

"On the Saturday night, after I had finished my correspondence which, as you may imagine, was rather large, I wrote out my circular, forwarded it to Leamington to get it printed, which was done; and it was forwarded to the Oxford district before the district secretary had an opportunity of carrying out his designs. What! Am I, at the head of your movement, to bow to every dog that barks; to tamely submit to every word of insult? Never!"

I went into the different points, but I came round again to the main point, which was centralisation *versus* federation. I said: "Centralise your funds. I should like you to send your funds to the central office. Let your district secretary be your agent, and let him be looking after your interests; let him audit your accounts, and let your general secretary receive the moneys at the central office. You may depend upon it that your Union will never be sound at the core till you have these reforms. Let the district committees be all unpaid men. Let your Executive be unpaid men. Let no outsider have any voice in your Council ; it is your cause, and manage it yourselves. Have some good *bonâ fide* labourers on your Executive Committee. Send unpaid men to the Council I beg of you. If you send the same men, to a great degree my mouth will be gagged again ; my hands will be tied."

"These are some of the measures of reform we propose; they may startle some of my friends, but I am not a weak man myself. It will require the most determined perseverance on your part, and the closest unity of action, and the widest possible discussion, if these things are to be brought about. I will be plain and honest with you. If you do not think me the right man in the right place, if you think I am not worthy of your confidence —I tell you sincerely and honestly, if it should be your will and pleasure to vote me out of office I will take off my hat and will say, 'Gentlemen, you had a perfect right to do it.' If you think that my salary is too high, it is in your own hands ; but if the salary you offer me is a starving wage, it is not a question with me, 'Can I get more?' for I could have done that before to-day ; nor is it a question with me how much I can get; but the question is, 'Can I live and maintain my family, and travel through the country, and expose my constitution and health for the wage?' If it is a wage that I cannot do so upon, I will deal truly with you, and say it is so low that I must get something else. You be honest with me and I will be honest with you. I tell you candidly that, whether I am a despot or Napoleonic, I will not stand humbug from either officers or men."

I think by the time I finished every man and woman assembled under the old chestnut tree saw plainly just how things were, and it was brought home to them that they must centralise, or the Union would split in pieces. I remember there was a cry for the old Union song, beginning "When Arch beneath the Wellesbourne Tree." It did me good to hear how heartily they sang it. There was such a hand-shaking after, that I thought to myself, "Seven years of hard labour, Joe, brings a reward with it; hearten up and make ready for seven years more."

I had need to, for there was plenty of fighting yet to be got through. I know there were times when it used to seem to me something like mockery at this period, if we opened a meeting with such a song as the following:

> Welcome to our Union meeting,
>   Friends and strangers, old and young:
> Farmers, tradesmen, labourers greeting,
>   Every hand, and eye and tongue,
> Every name to-day is "Brother";
> All our creed is—love each other.

All the same it *was* our creed and we were striving to keep true to it.

My theme now was—Unite and centralise; economise and popularise. In fact, I wanted the maximum of reform on a popular basis. When I was presiding over the Warwickshire District Annual Meeting at Leamington in April 1879, not long before we held our Annual Council, I told them that I (and others with me) was going straight for reform. I said I had hoped that the Committee which was appointed last May, and the resolutions which they sent out to the branches, would have been the means of stopping the expenses which they were obliged to incur in calling such meetings as those throughout the country. There might be, I said, some men who differed from me in opinion, but I had given the question very careful consideration; and, having submitted it to figures, I found that our officers, from first to last, could be elected with considerably less expense, by adopting the circular plan and allowing every member in the Union to have his vote.

I was a great advocate for a man, let him belong to what organisation he might, having his direct and individual vote for or against any great question affecting that organisation of which he was a member. I said: "During the past seven years I have presided over a considerable number of representative meetings like the present, and questions of great importance have been brought up from different branches, which the representatives of other districts knew nothing whatever about. I have sometimes wondered how these men could really vote upon questions which neither they nor their members had ever for one moment considered, and I therefore have come to the conclusion that the most democratic and the most thoroughly English way of doing business—especially in a great organisation like this—is not to place the responsibility upon the shoulders of one man, whom they may send to record his vote for them, but for every member to give his vote from the first to the last."

That was the way I wanted the Union to be governed. "Of course," I said, "we have been compelled to call this meeting, and we shall be obliged to call another General Council, but I very much grudge the expense. The necessity of calling the meeting has been brought about, not by the desire of the members throughout the Union, for I may say that their first vote on the question of lessening the expenses of holding large representative meetings was overwhelming in majority, but because their wishes, and desires, and votes were set at nought on the 21st of January last in London." The federals had been the peace-breakers, they had been wilful wasters in more ways than one—that was the opinion of a great number of our men. Numbers wanted the popular vote in the branches when they understood that by it they would be able to elect whom they liked to do their business, from the president down to the least official among them.

At our Annual Council, held in London in May 1879, we calculated that those assembled represented some twenty-three thousand labourers in Union, and in spite of appearances, there was reason for congratulation. To begin with we numbered in our Union some of the most intelligent labourers—the pick of the men ; then those who had fallen out had done so because of the general depression ; they were, the bulk of them, with us in spirit and fellow-feeling, and were only waiting for better times when work would enable them to be Union men once more. It was an undeniable fact, too, that in many parts of England, where wages had been kept up to twelve and thirteen shillings a week, they would have run down to nine and ten if it had not been for the Union. It was true that a number—a large number—of our men had been obliged to submit to a reduction of one shilling a week ; but they were only sharing in the general depression, and it was not as much as other organisations had been obliged to submit to. Things were hopeful, there was no gainsaying it, and things I knew would look more hopeful still, if wisdom and discretion ruled our counsels. We had to aim at making and keeping the Union national as we had aimed at first ; to have a good centralising fund ; to encourage the placing of the management in the hands of unpaid men ; and to give every member a direct vote. And we ultimately did decide to try for simplicity in arrangement, economy in management, and representation in government. I said again and again that the members must never forget that what they had to do was to represent an organisation ; to support it if weak, and to eliminate, if possible, anything in its constitution which operated against the prosperity and good of their republic. What affected the left hand affected the right; what affected the head affected the whole frame. It was necessary, therefore, to look earnestly and diligently to the parts, since it was the correct adjustment of the parts that constituted the perfection of the whole.

It had been widely reported that the Union was going down; nevertheless it was alive and vigorous still, and I had never seen good men so energetic as they were now. Where false friends lived branches had been broken up, and in some places societies of fifty or sixty had been formed. It was obvious, however, that these must die out, from the impossibility of making local what could only succeed as a national and universal scheme. I told them that the history of trades associations taught us something in 1851. They were split up into little factions; consequently there was no unity of force or action, and the result was the masters easily beat the men. Whilst we stand at one another's backs we are strong; if we separate we ensure defeat. The central organisation of the Union had twenty-three thousand odd members, in connection with which a Sick Benefit Society had been appended with a fund now approximating to £4,000. Other advantages would be developed in due course, if the Union remained true to itself.

But there were malcontents crying out for concessions never contemplated by the Union. Some were asking for land. It was amusing what got into the labourers' heads sometimes. One official told me he had been asked for money to buy an old thrashing machine! Why, if such calls were recognised the Union might close its books at any time. I had been denounced as obstructive to the interests of the Union and its members. My obstruction was that I had objected to the spending of funds contrary to the object for which they were designed. An application had been made to me for £500, for the purpose of obtaining a farm. A gentleman would have advanced the money on my security but not on that of the Union. I could not clearly see the justice of being made responsible as a private security, simply because I belonged to the Union. Conditionally those who wanted the farm might have had it; but their own action deprived them of the chance, and for this I had been put down as an obstructionist. Well, all these misunderstandings would work themselves out in time. I could say from experience—travelling as I did in all parts of the kingdom—that the feelings of Unionism, and the principles of Unionism, were growing in the minds of the farm-labourers of the country. I knew only too well that there had been enough to check the warmest desires, and to blight the brightest hopes, but I was glad—thankful—to say that all the efforts to damp our desires and blight our hopes had failed. They might have succeeded with a few, but very soon, like the repentant turncoat, they would be singing "The Backslider's Lament." I was confident that the labourers, taking county for county, were more determined than ever to stand by their grand old Union.

I spoke in this strain at meeting after meeting; warning, exhorting, encouraging, as far as in me lay. I remember there was a song which was rather popular at this period; and I will quote it as illustrative of the prevailing spirit of the men:

All hands to the rescue, our Union's in danger,
By sham friends in our ranks, which we plainly can see;
So swelled with ambition, their togs it won't fit 'em,
They vainly would climb to the top of the tree.

There is this one and that one, a third, and yet more,
Who legislate for themselves, regardless of we;
But we, their paymasters, now fearlessly tell them
That, though once we were blind, we can now very well see.

They have grossly insulted our leader and pleader,
A man of far greater fame and renown,
Whose slippers they all are unworthy to carry,
Or even his stockings or garters to town.

Away with all tailors and president-railers,
"Peace and retrenchment" our motto shall be;
With Arch, for our leader we never can mend him,
Let all that would spurn him from us ever flee.

"Peace, retrenchment, and reform," was our motto that year; and in spite of foes from within and without, I was ready to lead the van of our Union army on to victory.

CHAPTER XIII.

THE LAND AND THE LABOURERS.

THE land question, as well as the franchise, was just at this period pressing itself on our attention, and it was no wonder, for the agricultural depression had been, and was, so great, that a Commission was being held to inquire into the terrible state of affairs. Of course the Union was affected; though I may truly say it was solid, more solid than ever, but here and there men were dropping out. They had got into their heads the idea that once their wages were up, they would not only keep up, but would never go down any more. The farmers had been telling them so; of course it paid them to make the men believe that, and the men, like silly sheep, believed them. Well, they had to pay sharp and dear for their credulity. What was the first thing we heard?—this was during 1879 and 1880—why, that the farmers of Worcestershire had decided to drop the wages of their labourers two shillings a week! This was a big, a terrible, drop for a man earning only eleven or twelve shillings. When I heard the bad news I said, "Oh, now they will perhaps value their Union at its true worth. Big drop or little drop, it's all one; the men will just have to submit. They would not join the Union, or have fallen away from it, and so they have nothing to help them. They refused to pay twopence a week into the Union, which would have cost them nine shillings a year, so now they have to submit to a drop which will cost them £5 4*s*. a year. We have heard before of people being penny wise and pound foolish, but in this case the labourers have been penny wise and five pound foolish, and I say, 'Serve them right.'" The Staffordshire labourers, who behaved in the same foolish way, had to put up with a similar drop.

Farmers were down on the men whenever they got the chance, and a great deal of petty meanness they showed. I remember a case which occurred in 1876 as an instance of what I mean. There was a certain farmer at Shanklin. He had a dispute with a labourer named Coombs, who thereupon left his master's service. The farmer summoned Coombs to Newport for leaving his employment, and the case was dismissed. A second time the farmer summoned him for £1 damages for leaving the horses in the stable, and a second time the case broke down. So, to spite the labourer, the farmer goes and ploughs up his potatoes! However, at the Newport County Court he made the discovery that he could not do as he liked with a labourer's property; at any rate, if the labourer was a Union man, and could so procure proper legal assistance. The judge denounced the farmer's conduct, and declared he had been guilty of as gross an act of trespass as was ever committed. The farmer was condemned to pay at the rate of three-shillings-and-sixpence per rod for twenty-four and three-quarter rods of potatoes, £4 3*s*. 2*d*., and costs, including plaintiff's counsel's fee. It was rather a heavy bill for the gratification of such spiteful meanness.

Again and again men would be discharged for being Union men. There is one case which occurs to me; it took place when the Union was in its early days, but it was typical of what went on all through the seventies. This case was a good deal quoted. A farmer discharged one of his men for joining the Union —a man he could easily replace he thought—but he had a shepherd whom he could not so easily spare. He went to the shepherd and said, "John, have you joined the Union?"

"Yes, Master, that have I."

"Ah, well now I've got a sheep's head at home that I was going to give you, but now it'll go to a better man."

"Very well, master."

"And John, my wife bought a frock for your little girl, but that'll go to some one else."

"Very well, master," said the shepherd once more, and then off stumped master tyrant.

This sort of tyranny was still going on; but the farmers were suffering themselves, some of them as much as their bitterest enemies could wish. Things had been going down hill with them for a long time past. I remember in the autumn of 1878 how bad things were in Norfolk ; the farms there were quite thirty per cent. worse, productively, than they had been in 1872, and many of the farmers' crops were mortgaged to the bank.

In Dorsetshire, again, many of the farms were in a state of scandalous neglect. On one farm three brothers, all farmers, were seen in a field of theirs, cutting down the thistles and docks with scythes. Another farmer in the same county sent his men into a field to plough, but as he had not provided them with gloves and gaiters they had to come out again. Mowers were sent to cut down docks and thistles in some of the fields. When they had cut them and carted them away, they were sent in to plough the land ; but the roots proved too strong for them, so men and plough had to retire. Fields choke full of thistles was no uncommon sight. In county after county there was this terrible, this lamentable, blot of neglected, weed-covered land.

At a meeting in the spring of 1878, I said, "At the present time there are 897,000 acres less growing crops in England than in 1870, and 2,606,000 fewer sheep than in 1874." I also said, "The present average of money spent on the land is £5 10*s*. an acre, and this, it has been shown, is insufficient to nourish the land. If, instead of investing in Turkish bonds, men had spent their money on the land, they might now have saved the farmers from a state of bankruptcy. Mr. Mechi, a well-known authority, said that £10 an acre at least ought to be spent on the land. At the present time £225,000,000 is invested in land, but according to Mr. Mechi, £211,000,000 more ought to be spent on it. If this were to be done, the soil of England would take 50,000,000 more labourers to cultivate it."

"Is the farmer," I asked, "doing all he can for the land, or instead, is not the farmer who, a few years ago, kept twenty-five or thirty milch cows, now content with four, and are not seven fat beasts now sold off a farm where there used to be sold twenty? At the present time we send out for eighty-five million pounds' worth of food for the people of this country, for there is only enough produced in it to feed forty out of every hundred. The farmers have sixty more customers than they can find food for, and yet they say trade is bad!"

I remember saying as far back as 1875 that, if the farmers did not get a good Tenants' Rights Bill within the next five years, four out of five of them would be cracked up, and I was not so far out. If the farmers had their weepers on in 1875, they have kept them on pretty well ever since, and they have had enough to make them mourn. Why, in my own county it was reported in the spring of 1879 that there were over a hundred farms to let, amounting to a twelfth part of the entire county. It was the same sad story in other counties. Landlords were offering reductions of rent amounting to ten, twenty, and even thirty per cent.; but the farmers in many instances refused even this. Bad seasons, coupled with want of proper security for their outlay, proved too much for dozens of poor tenant farmers. In a long speech I made on the subject at a labourers' meeting at Abbot's Salford in October 1879, I said:

"I have always been a firm believer in the dignity of labour. Whatever that labour may be, if it tends to benefit the country and increase its happiness and welfare, the men thus employed are England's greatest noblemen. But, unhappily, labour in this country has never met with its proper share of honour, or been rewarded with the remuneration, which in my judgment it ought to have had. Although you have been told that labour is something inferior to capital, I maintain on the other hand that capital is inferior to labour. What is capital? As John Stuart Mill put it, it is the accumulation of labour, and if labour has thus begotten capital, labour ought to take the first position in the country. Surely the child should acknowledge its parent with respect! I say capital is the child of labour and it is a dangerous thing for the interests ot any community when the child begins to strangle the parent.

"You have heard a great deal about the organisations of working men, and it may be that they have not always acted so wisely as they should have done; but what class of Her Majesty's subjects do you find perfect? Why, it is a certain fact that even by the highest Trade Union in the country, the House of Lords, great mistakes have been made; and if labouring men in the past have happened to be sometimes in the wrong, why should their organisation be decried by capitalists whom their labour had made rich!

"Whilst in Edinburgh a few weeks ago, I was surprised to hear a statement, more reliable than the information the Government gives the country on its foreign policy, that during the last year the various Trades Unions in Great Britain have, in relief for sickness, benefits at death or accident, payment to members out of employment, and some outlay on strikes, spent no less than a quarter of a million sterling. Not a penny of this vast sum has ever passed through the Mansion House, nor has any member of a Trades Union ever asked Her Majesty to patronise the fund. It has been raised by the horny-handed working men, without any aid, and such a result is an honour to you. I am happy to tell you that the Labourers' Union is growing, that its funds are in a prosperous state and increasing; every month shows our enemies, who asserted we were dead, that they have been telling falsehoods, for here we are still alive. I shall now move the adoption of the following petition to Parliament, from the inhabitants of Abbot's Salford and the neighbourhood:

> 'That your petitioners, seeing the large amount of uncultivated land in this country, and the conditions under which millions of acres more are held, are compelled to come to the conclusion that there can

> be no permanent improvement in trade or in the condition of the people until we have a sweeping reform in the land laws, and this meeting therefore urges upon the people of this country the necessity of vigorous agitation upon the land question until such measures are passed in Parliament as may meet the requirements of the people.'

"I believe when Parliament meets, hundreds of such petitions will be presented. The landlords and farmers of England probably never dreamt, six or seven years ago, that the labourers would take this important question in hand. For centuries we have, as a class, been immensely docile, and if a labourer grumbled at all it was like the Irishman, 'as loud as possible to himself.' It was not because there was no need for complaint, it was not because there were not justifiable grounds for grumbling; but such was the hard lot of the farm labourer, that if he dared to speak out he very soon had to skedaddle somewhere else, and not unfrequently he was driven out of his native parish. In addressing you to-night I shall endeavour to give you what in my judgment, as a farm-labourer, is one of the main causes of the present agricultural depression. But what have we got to do with it?

"Well, we had the impudence to want to be represented upon the Royal Commission. Oh, for shame on these Billycocks! Do you not know that you are represented in the House of Commons as fairly as any other class? You have the landed proprietors, who understand all your wants; and when in that august assembly any question crops up affecting your interests as labourers, they will give it 'their calm and serious consideration.' I have closely watched the course of political events ever since I was a boy, and for the life of me, I cannot see that any single question affecting the agricultural labourers has received the 'calm and serious consideration' of the county representatives, except the poor laws; and their main object in considering them seems to be how nearly they can starve the poor without quite killing them. In all legislative movements we have, as a class, been totally ignored. At the present time there is a depression in agriculture, and yet the most important class, the labourers, are not allowed a representative upon the Royal Commission to inquire into the causes of depression. I say we are the most important class; because, if all the landowners in the county emigrated next week, it would be nothing like the loss to the country that it would be if the labourers left its shores.

"I do not, I can tell you, intend to be shut out on this question. But I will ask you, if there had been no Union, would the labourers ever have dreamt of making an inquiry, or even expressing their opinion on the present depression? Without our organisation would the press have recognised us as it does now, and record our meetings? We shall also make the Tory Government recognise us. We will show them that they cannot have it all their own way. You have heard that the cause of agricultural depression is the bad seasons we have had. There is no doubt a great deal of truth in that, but what has made the bad seasons tell upon the farmers is the fact that their land has not been properly cultivated. You may go from Dan to Beersheba, and the Royal Commission can sit till they are as old as Methuselah, and when they have searched the whole creation they must come to the conclusion that the tenant farmers, to a large extent, have to thank themselves for the present agricultural depression. What has been the policy of the tenant farmers throughout the kingdom for the last twenty years? I know, and you as labourers know, and we don't want a Commission to tell us. Their policy has been to do with as little labour as possible, and the labour they did employ was never paid for sufficiently to enable the men to do a good day's work. They have half-paid labour, and the result is half-fed labour. If a farmer's team of horses is not more than half-fed, he cannot expect them to do full work, and it is just the same with the labourers. Year after year, the men who have sowed and reaped the corn have known that, independently of the seasons, the crops have not been so fruitful as if proper labour had been put into the land. This is the very root of the evil from the labourers' standpoint.

"But there is a disadvantage under which the farmers labour, and that is the short and uncertain tenure of the land. If a farmer lays out £1,000, or £2,000 on his farm, he does not know that he may not be called upon to pay an increased rent; and if he does not think proper to pay interest on his own capital, he has notice to quit, and some one else is ready to give the landlord the advantage of the tenant's money. What power has the farmer to compel the landlord to pay for unexhausted improvements? I do not blame the farmers so much for being sparse with labour under such circumstances; but I do blame them for being such noodles as to take land upon such conditions as will allow the landlords to step in at any time and filch their capital. I dare say I shall be called an agitator, and be charged with setting class against class; but I am here to tell the truth, and if there is any tenant farmer here, let him deny anything I have said.

"When this movement was started, noblemen and landed proprietors used to invite me to discuss the question with them in London. It was amusing to hear them talk. They said that all these matters were regulated by the law of supply and demand; that with the present patent machinery and mechanical appliances, farmers could do with far less labour than they used to do; and that it was of no use my thinking of labourers getting high wages so long as they were so thick on the ground. My experience as a labourer is that, for the past twenty years, not half enough labour has been employed on the land. Just to show you that these wise men know nothing of the question, let us judge of their opinions by results. Take their patent machinery and mechanical appliances, that were to enable them to do without the strong arm of the labourers, and to send them to Jericho if they had nowhere else to go to, where have they landed the farmer to-day? They have landed him on his knees at the foot of Queen Victoria, as a humble suppliant, and saying, through the mouth of Lord Yarmouth: 'If it please your Majesty, will you please give me authority to go down to the House of Commons and tell that august assembly that you have consented to a Royal Commission to inquire into the miserable state of the tenant farmer, and to tell him how he is to pay £100 with £75 cash?' If the farmers had not listened to the twaddle that the earth could be tilled by machinery alone, and that the Almighty had not made living beings to till it, they would not have been in their present position. If some complicated machinery is invented, and the landlords applaud it, the farmer buys it at once.

"There is another matter which has much aggravated farmers' difficulties, and that is foreign competition. I was much struck by reading a speech of Lord Beaconsfield in which he said reciprocity is dead; and if he had told the truth, he might have added that it is buried, and that although he has educated his party in a great many matters, it is more than he or all English Toryism can do to raise it to life again. Reciprocity is buried, not with 'a sure and certain hope of resurrection,' but never to rise again: and all the Tories in Christendom will never dare to tax again the poor man's loaf. The farmers want a cure for foreign competition: well then, they should grow more food for the people at home. If people could buy bread and beef and cheese from our own farmers, they would of course do so; and if they grew a sufficient quantity of food for the people, they would not go to other countries for it. We send a hundred millions of British capital every year to the various colonies and the States of America, to produce food which might be grown at home, and yet farmers allow the Americans to have our labourers and to take the steam out of our markets.

"It does not need a man two months, let alone two years, to get at the root of the mischief. This foreign competition has been an awful bugbear to the farmers, but it was a great blessing to the workmen during the past winter. Let us thank God for Cobden and Bright. The fruit of their labours has been seen in thousands of homes which have been blessed with the cheap loaf. It may be said that the farmer is not responsible for foreign competition; but we must remember that they have foolishly sent thousands of men across the Atlantic, to grow beef and corn to send here to compete with English produce. When the movement started there was a terrible hullabaloo, and many farmers said they would sack their men and not employ a single Unionist. They have carried out their promise, and now they are reaping the reward of their foolish policy. I believe they have not yet got to a tenth part of what they will have to suffer. No less than seven hundred and fifty thousand men, women, and children have, during the past seven years, left this country for other lands.

"You have a right to ask who were the men who went? They were those with the most courage, and those whom the farmers could least do without; those who could and would turn their hand to anything. The very men that the farmers said seven years ago they would starve into submission, are those who are now helping foreign growers to compete with the farmers at home. These men would never have had the means to emigrate unless the Union had helped them. I have heard that, in various parts of the country, the farmers have threatened to pinch their labourers this winter, and to reduce their wages to ten shillings a week. Will that help the farmer out of his difficulties? Will that enable him to grow larger crops? Will that stop foreign competition? No! and God will avenge the oppressor. I believe that the succession of bad harvests are a visitation of the Almighty upon the farmers for their treatment of their labourers, and upon a luxurious and dissipated aristocracy. I believe in a God of Providence, and as sure as the sun rises and sets, He will avenge Himself on the oppressor. The farmer must not be too confident. There are broad fields in our colonies, with thousands of acres of virgin soil, only awaiting the labourer to till them, and large companies are being formed to induce the best men to emigrate. Only lately a telegram was received in Ireland from New York, stating that in America they are prepared to find £50,000 to send out Irish tenants to a country where they will have brighter prospects, better laws, and freedom for all. They were invited, in fact, to go to the grand States of America, the home of justice and liberty. All the English farmers who have any pluck at all are going out, and when they get to their destination, they will want farm labourers to till their fields.

"An intelligent tenant-farmer recently told me that it would be a sorry thing for England if this tide of emigration once set in in earnest to the States. The men who travel know the real state of the case; but, unhappily, too many farmers only know the price of pigs, and what was paid for beef and wheat at Evesham market, and if they go from this district to Birmingham market, they think they have been all over the world. Twenty years ago and now are widely different. The labourer then was a dull, docile being; but to-day he stands up and demands to be recognised as an Englishman. He claims his political rights; and I may say, for the comfort of the farmers, that their land reforms and their prosperity will never be consummated till they and their labourers go together to the ballot-box to send the proper men to represent them in Parliament.

"It is a very remarkable thing that, if the landlords in Parliament have any new tax, they put it on the shoulders of the poor farmers. I am inclined to think that when the tax-collector comes round for money to pay the horrible butchers' bills in Afghanistan and Zululand, Sir Stafford Northcote, if he wants the full tax, will in many places in this country have to take it out in thistles. Between this place and Warwick station, and especially along the line from Alcester, there are not five fields in sight of the railway fit to put autumn seed in. If there are, let any farmer point them out to me. If justice were only done to the land the people would have their food forty per cent. cheaper than it now is. If the farmers really carry out their threat to sink the wages, there will be no alternative for the labourers but to go to the workhouse, where they will cost the ratepayers four shillings and tenpence a head, whilst at home they would be satisfied with three shillings to keep their children. By making a man, his wife, and four children paupers, the farmers would have to pay about twenty-four shillings a week, whilst fourteen shillings was all they would give the labourer for his work. Will a state of things like this make the farmer wealthy and the poor man contented? We have in the United Kingdom, according to the Board of Trade returns, twenty-seven millions of acres of waste land that will amply repay cultivation.

"Who is to find the £25,000,000, which has been expended by the Government in blood and murder? What will England benefit by the Afghan war? And what will we get from the Zulu campaign except a large elephant's tusk? Just in the same way, we got a tremendous booty from Ashantee in the shape of an old umbrella. I care not what position you occupy, whether you are farmers, shopkeepers, publicans, or artizans, I call upon you to rise in the majesty of your manhood and say that, whilst agriculture is declining, and the full produce is not got out of the land, and whilst there are twenty-seven millions of acres of uncultivated land, you will not allow the bone and the sinew of the country to leave our shores, nor £25,000,000 to be wasted in useless wars ; that you will hunt to the ground the authors of a blood and thunder policy, and place in their stead men of intelligence and wisdom, who will see the greatness of the nation, not in a blustering and wicked foreign policy, but in the happiness and prosperity of the people."

It was a long and an important speech this, and one I had carefully prepared. I remember that at the end of it I gave a mock Tory address, mimicking a certain Conservative parliamentary big-wig. I did it on the spur of the moment, and I finished up with the following adaptation of a well-known hymn :

From Chatham's pleasant mountains,
  From Aldershot's bare plain,
Where the British flag floats proudly,
  And the lion shakes his mane;
From barracks and from mess-room
  Resound the bugle's notes,
Calling to arms to cross the sea
  And cut some heathen throats.

What though from every pulpit
  We daily Christ proclaim,
And bend before the Prince of Peace,
  And worship in His name
In vain, in adoration
  We bow before the Throne;
Those heathen are possessed of lands
  Which we must make our own.

What though our souls are lighted
  With wisdom from on high!
Shall we to men benighted
  The Gatling gun deny?
Proclaim it, oh! proclaim it
  To Afghan and Zulu!
This is the way we Christianise
  And teach them who is who.

Blow gently, blow, ye breezes,
  Let the war smoke upward curl,
While bathed in blood and glory
  Stands forth our Premier Earl!
But weep, oh! weep for England,
  And bow the head in shame;
For sullied is her honour,
  And tarnished is her name.

I felt very strongly about these wars, and the awful expenditure of blood and men and money. It was a waste of God-given gifts I could not stand silent and contemplate. As I said elsewhere, "The Government has been kicking up a row abroad on purpose to stop legislation at home; we will therefore kick up a row with the Government by putting in a Liberal and a Peace one when the next election comes." I said too, "Agriculture is depressed, and will be so long as there is a landlord Parliament. Hundreds, I may say thousands, of honest working men are wanting to get a respectable living by the labour of their hands, but that privilege is denied them. The result of this lack of labour is that we have hundreds and thousands of mothers almost starved to death, and I have no hesitation in saying that the pinchings of hunger which tens of thousands of poor, dear children suffered this last winter will have sown the seeds of decay in their youthful systems, which will bring thousands of them to a premature grave before this day twelvemonths. We are not only murdering Zulus, but the innocents at home, and yet Englishmen can stand by, quiet as lambs, and see millions of their hard-earned money wasted in bloody murder, while at home tens of thousands are having their constitutions sapped to the core through it."

I also said, "I say to you labourers, join our noble Union. Stick to it like men when you have joined it; and if people in better positions turn up their noses in contempt never mind. Our numbers are great enough, our intelligence is powerful enough, and when we get the vote, we shall show them that our votes are numerous enough, to cast aside this war policy, and to bring back to England her peace, her commerce, and her prosperity."

I could not help feeling that this agricultural depression was a natural judgment on the farmers for their treatment of the labourers. They had, in their criminal folly, recklessly cast from them the best men—and a good farm-hand is a very good thing. This is what Thorold Rogers said at a meeting we held at Oxford in 1878; and he knew what he was talking about. He said: "Let me say a word or two about the functions of a first-class farm hand, and I am quite certain that there are many in this room who will agree with me. Suppose I ask a man whether he thinks it is an easy thing to drive a straight furrow over a ten-acre field, and to carry his furrow from one end of the field to the other, and from this side to that without any 'wobbling' in his work. What would he say? Why it is as hard work as painting pictures, and a man that has not had a good education in this direction is as incapable of learning it, except after a long and painful course of training, as is a man who paints pictures. Let me ask you about shearing a sheep. It is a much easier task to clip a boy's head at a barber's shop than to shear a sheep, and nothing is more artistic than a clean, well-sheared sheep. Then how about rick-building. You may depend on it that it is, on the whole, harder to build a rick well than a house well. My impression is, too, that the art of making a rick is peculiar to that part of England which lies between the Trent and the British Channel. I have spoken of three high arts possessed by a good farm hand. Now, how about making a ditch and a hedge! This is no easy matter; and it requires a considerable amount of skill to be able to make a line straight across a fifty-acre field, and do it to the particular point, having laid the drain-pipes in such a way as not to allow a break in the outfall of the water.

"Well, if you set to work, to compare the work of the agricultural labourer who possesses the five or six qualifications I have mentioned—and I am perfectly certain I could make them up to a dozen—with the work of an ordinary artizan who receives thirty-five shillings a week, the agricultural labourer, as far as regards the varied nature of his accomplishments, is conceivably superior to the artizan. Every one knows in manufacturing places it is constantly the business to get those hands who can do one particular thing with the greatest exactness and rapidity, but in agricultural work the best man is he who does the largest number of things with the greatest rapidity. I do not grudge the artizan his thirty-five shillings; but I want to know why the agricultural labourer should not get as much, too."

He went on to say that for five hundred years the legislature had been striving to reduce by force of law the wages of the agricultural labourer. In the beginning of the reign of Queen Elizabeth, who was a clever and an able woman, but who was obliged to consult some people about her, the legislature of the time contrived to pass a law which really did more to degrade the labourer than anything that could be imagined. In the fifth year of her reign it was decided that the Chairman of Quarter Sessions in every county should fix the wages which the agricultural labourer should receive, and mighty low they fixed them. They had the power, not only or doing this, but of punishing anybody who gave more or asked more than was fixed, and the consequence was the agricultural labourer was left entirely to the mercy of the employers.

There was another thing he said, which I had often said myself. "I suppose a labourer, among other accomplishments, knows a little about sheep and pigs, and is pretty well aware that if a sheep or an ox is starved, his carcass is not improved. Well, on the whole, the healthiest condition for the human being also is when he has enough to eat. But there is a higher consideration than his physical health, and that is his moral growth ; and it is quite certain that a man who has no prospect, no hope, nothing to get but what is absolutely necessary for his daily maintenance and those depending on him, cannot develop those virtues which a man should possess. Along with a good physical strength and a good moral growth there comes a conscience ; and one of the first directions which the conscience of a man takes in the work he is set is that of giving true value for the wages he receives. You may depend upon it an underpaid farm-labourer will no more have the inclination to do a good day's work than he has the power to do it, and when you have raised his condition by giving him the power you will also bestow upon him the inclination."

I remember he also said that a great squire who lived near Oxford had told him he was extremely thankful that the Labourers' Union had come into the parish, where he owned every inch of land. It had raised the men to a higher level, and in some districts this Union, led and guided by Joseph Arch, had been the cause of the diminution of pauperism ; and the great service he had done was not denied by persons of intelligence, and only repudiated by persons who were fools. Of course I thought that was nothing but the truth ; not because

I was Joseph Arch, but because I was leading our Union. If the farmers had had the sense to lend us a helping hand, when their hour of trial came, we would have stood side by side with them, and helped them—aye with might and main, and instead of cursing the Union they would have blessed it; but the turnip-headed farmer turned his back on us, and he has lived to rue the day when he did it.

CHAPTER XIV.

THE CAUSES OF AGRICULTURAL DEPRESSION.

IN the spring of 1880 I contested Wilton as a supporter of Gladstone, my opponent being the Hon. Sidney Herbert. Wilton was a pocket borough under the control of the Earl of Pembroke, who owned the estate, and whose nominee alone it was supposed could win the seat. The borough had for over twenty-four years sent a Liberal to Parliament, so it was looked upon as a Liberal borough; but in 1877 the nominee and warming pan gave up the seat, having accepted the "Chiltern Hundreds." Then Mr. Sidney Herbert, the earl's brother, a young man of twenty-two, was run out as an Independent candidate, promising to follow in the steps of his father, the late Lord Herbert of Lea. As there was a good deal of uncertainty as to Mr. Herbert's politics, and as the earl, the nominee, was a Conservative, the Liberal party consulted, and the result was a contest. Mr. Norris of Bristol was the Liberal candidate, but he was defeated, and so the "Independent" took his seat in

Parliament, and upon every important division voted with the Government, including the "cat."

The Liberals were very angry at this, and as the borough was an agricultural one, the Wilton Liberal Society invited me to stand; and I said I was willing, but that I could not pay my expenses. If they could be guaranted I would come down and fight my best against Tory landlordism, war, bad trade, starvation, and the "cat." A gentleman hearing of the money difficulty said, "Let Mr. Arch come; I'll willingly pay all his expenses;" so down I went, and an exciting time of it I had. We held our first meeting in the Temperance Hall, Monday, March 22nd, 1880, and things were lively—a bit too lively. Considering the behaviour outside, I wonder I got through this, my first, address as a political candidate without bodily harm. While I was speaking there would be crash! bang! and stones, great big ones, would fly through the smashed windows into the Hall. So bad was it that they had to put up window-boards inside, and in spite of precautions several of the audience were badly hit. The roughs outside hooted and howled in a most disgraceful manner; but for all the howls and the stones I finished my speech to the end as I set out to do.

There was a great deal of feeling in the country, largely among the agricultural labourers and artizans and small shopkeepers, about the Zulu War, and I alluded to it in my speech.

I said: "In the *Daily News*, some few months ago, I read a statement which made my blood almost boil in my veins. It was a letter from their special correspondent, and had reference to the unhappy affair at Isandula, a spot visited four months after the unfortunate affray. He says: 'A strange dead calm reigned in this solitude of nature; grain had grown luxuriantly around the waggons, sprouting from the seed that had dropped from the loads and had fallen in soil fertilised by the life-blood of gallant men. So long the grass in most places had grown that it mercifully shrouded the dead, whom for four long months we had left unburied.' And who were the unfortunate men whose bones were left there bleaching in the intense heat of an African sun? They were chiefly the sons of agricultural labourers. And what a thought for the mother whose son had been engaged in that sad conflict—the thought that the child whom she in pain bore and in anguish brought forth, whom she nourished in his boyhood, and hoped to have seen grown up to have formed and to have played some significant and useful part in the body politic, had lain weltering in his own life-blood on an alien shore, and his body had been open to the penetrating sun four months."

I also referred to the "cat-o'-nine tails," and I said: "I cannot forget that large and enthusiastic meeting which I attended in Hyde Park last summer to protest against the use of that monstrous instrument of torture. It is all very well for the people who reside in rural villages or in large towns to say that the soldiers themselves do not require its abrogation! Let us converse with the soldier, and what do we find? I have embraced every opportunity of ascertaining their opinion upon the matter, and I have never found a single soldier of the rank and file yet who ever attempted to bolster up the system; except to this extent, that, if you give it to the rank and file, give it to the officers too, when they disgrace themselves."

The feeling among the labourers about the abuse of the "cat" in the army was very strong. There were all sorts of stories going about; one was, I remember, that a young man, the leader of the Rifle Band and who was popularly known as the "Pride of Winchester," had been flogged to death with this instrument of torture in Zululand, within three months of his leaving home. There were all sorts of terrible tales, exaggerated no doubt, and sometimes untrue; but many of them beyond a doubt had too much brutal truth at the back of them.

There was another thing I alluded to in that speech—the question of the ballot and of secret voting. I said: "With regard to the ballot, I will not say a word deriding the powers that be, but if any gentleman tells you working-men that the ballot is not secret, he knows he is telling you a falsehood. I understand that, at the last election at this borough, which was in 1877, farmers were seen at the polling-booth with books professing to take the electors' names and telling them, 'Oh, we shall know how you vote.'"

Now just let me give you my experience with regard to the ballot. At the election of 1874—the General

Election—I went to record my vote. There were three gentlemen standing in the schoolroom when we went to poll, who had been telling working-men who happened to have votes, "We shall know how you vote. Mind what you are doing; you will lose your place; be careful."

They had been carrying on that little game nearly the whole day, so after recording my vote for the man I believed would go to Parliament to do the most good, I turned round to them, and as respectfully as I knew how, said, "Gentlemen, can you tell me how I voted?"

They looked very sheepish at me. I repeated:

"Gentlemen, can you tell me how I voted?

"Now," I added, "I am surprised at three gentlemen like you standing here and telling falsehood after falsehood for the purpose of intimidating the working-men. Why didn't you tell me when I came into the schoolroom you should know how I voted?"

"Oh," said they, "you are too old."

Well, I would simply say to the working-men here, "Be too old for 'em."

I finished up my saying: "Now, before I sit down, allow me to exhort every elector here—don't use intimidation, and don't be intimidated. Let us, if we are Liberals, fight the battle honestly and nobly as men. The Liberal cause of England requires no falsehoods to bolster it up. Men like Mr. Gladstone, Lord Hartington, and Earl Granville, want no secret intriguing to give them a standing in this country

They have won it, not by trickery, not by 'scientific frontiers,' not by a series of Oriental surprises, not by depressing its trade, but they have won it by dint of indomitable perseverance for their country's honour, and by their strict integrity. And they will win again with a grand and triumphant majority, and we shall yet see this old England of ours what she deserves to be—noble, happy, and free. If it be the will and pleasure of you electors of Wilton to record your votes in my favour, don't for a moment think I am absolute perfection. I am liable to make mistakes, as are other men. Don't for a moment conceive I am an angel. If you do you will have a wrong conception of me. But meet me on the ground of a man and an Englishman. Meet me in the political area as a thorough Liberal, and, if by your votes I have the honour to represent Wilton in Parliament, believe that the name of Joseph Arch will never be disgraced, either on the floor of St. Stephen's or throughout his native land ; but he will live and die an honest, true, and earnest Liberal and Englishman."

I remember we held another meeting under a great tree at Netton; and a most successful one at Coombe Bisset, when I spoke to a listening throng in the light of the full moon. The farmers tried to annoy me at one or two meetings ; but we kept them down. There was some intimidation too, we heard ; farmers putting on the screw with a view to preventing their labourers voting for me, and one labourer was actually threatened. The legal adviser to the Liberal Committee told the men plainly that any farmer who discharged a man for not voting as he wished, or who threatened to deal with a labourer in an unpleasant way for the same cause, was liable to six months with hard labour, and perpetual disfranchisement. Lots of the men were frightened hêre, and in other places, by the farmers, and of course they did not know how the law protected them.

There was one point on which I took my stand from the start, and that was, " No canvassing." I said : " I do not wish it. I regard the vote as a sacred trust, and I disdain to extract, by means of a canvass, that which the law directs is to be done in secret. Canvassing is, in my opinion, a mean subterfuge. Its object is to get at a man's vote in an indirect way, and I shall keep clear of it."

I shall quote here what the *English Labourers' Chronicle* said, because it expressed my own feelings, and also those of the labourers at my back. " Whatever may be the result of the election at Wilton," it said, " one thing we shall always be able to point to with feelings of justifiable pride. Mr. Joseph Arch is the first candidate who has had the moral courage to contest a constituency without resorting to the questionable practice of canvassing the electors, with the view of ascertaining the way in which they intend to dispose of their votes. That is something of which Mr. Arch will ever have reason to be proud." I do not know about pride, but I felt I was doing right, and as I would have others do to me in a like case.

I lost the election, but I was far from being disheartened. On the contrary, I was astonished to find how politically wide awake the labourers were becoming. I said to myself, "Never mind, Joe; better luck next time. You'll tread the floor of St. Stephen's yet, as the representative and the mouthpiece of your fellow-labourers. The time is not ripe yet; but it's ripening fast. Look alive, then, and don't waste a minute. Stir up the men; for once they get the franchise, they will send some one to speak for them in the Assembly of the Nation." And I went around stirring them up.

Here is a specimen of a petition of ours about the county and borough franchise :—

> "To the House of Commons of Great Britain and Ireland in Parliament, assembled :—The humble petition of the undersigned delegates of the National Agricultural Labourers' Union sheweth, That your petitioners, representing the opinion of the unfranchised farm labourers of the kingdom, feel it to be a monstrous grievance that they, who are the producers of so large a portion of the national wealth, and who are heavily taxed in proportion to their means, should have no voice in the imposition of those taxes, and that they should be called upon to obey laws in the making of which they have no share, laws which have been made for them by other classes unacquainted with their wants, laws which in many an instance press most unevenly and unfairly on those who are the

> poorest paid subjects of the realm. That your petitioners are of opinion that the vote is of the greatest value to those who are the poorest and therefore the most defenceless, and they earnestly implore your House to grant them this right ; for they feel that they are at present treated as aliens in the country of their birth, and are compelled to seek in other climes for those constitutional rights denied to them at home. Your petitioners hear that a Bill has been introduced into your House by Mr. Trevelyan for the assimilation of the county and borough franchise, and they therefore pray that this Bill may be passed into law during the present session."

At our Annual Council that year I said : "We now have a Government in office which will listen to our requests. It is a Government, I am pleased to say, that the National Agricultural Labourers' Union has helped to place in power. This has not been done by the votes which our men possess, but by the circulation of the paper amongst the £12 voters in the counties, and which has had an immense influence in winning them over from Conservatism to Liberalism. The day is not far distant when we shall have our political rights as householders in the counties." We had to wait four years longer for it though ? But it took the working-man in franchised boroughs twenty-five years to get his vote.

After all I was called before the Royal Commission

to give evidence, and I came up twice. The first time was on August 4th, 1881; the second time in December of the same year. The Duke of Richmond and Gordon was president, and I remember I made him rather wild. When he asked me the question as to what was the cause of the depression, I told him that I thought the reason of the present depressed state of agriculture arose from three causes—*i.e.*, not sufficient labour employed, rents too high, and not enough money put in the land. He then asked me whether I knew the tenant farmers had no money. I told him I did not think they would ever be likely to have any. I had been reading a book on the subject, and from it I learned that the landlords had raised the agricultural rents of England twenty per cent. in eighteen years on the tenant farmers' profits. Something like ten and a quarter millions had to be paid away to the parsons in the shape of tithes. How then were the farmers to have any money, with the parsons on one hand and the landlords on the other? Why, they were topped and tailed like turnips!

I remember, too, one of the Commissioners said to me, "I am paying fully sixty per cent. more for my labour since you began this Union."

"I am very glad to hear it," I said, "but it proves one of two things. If you are paying sixty per cent. more for your labour than when the Union was started, you were either paying miserably low wages before it began, or you are paying very high wages now. Which is it?" He would not tell me.

Of course they wanted to know all about the Union, and I told them that though it was not perfection, it supplied a want, and was in my opinion a necessity. I gave them some details. I said: "Our headquarters are at Leamington, and we have a general meeting every year. The officers are now elected by a popular vote, and rules are made by the representative assembly—that is, so many branches are formed into a district; each district has the power of sending so many representatives in proportion to the number of its members, and these representatives make the rules. The rules are then submitted to every branch for the consideration of every member, and as they pass them so the representative gathering accept them. Rules are drawn up by a special committee. Representatives of the local unions are voted for, either by ballot or openly. Each branch has a paper sent it, 'Whom will you nominate as your president, your general secretary, or your district officers? or whom will you appoint to sit on the executive committee?'"

I could not help thinking of our early efforts at organisation and our little beginnings, and contrasting them with the organisation of 1881. Our numbers were on the increase now; there were some twenty-five thousand, spread over twenty-two counties, in Union. Though the farmers had scoffed at us, they had found it expedient to start a sort of a union of their own. We never feared it, for it was not a real thing—it was a rope of sand. I knew very little about it, as regards rules and management, etc. But I do know something about the farmer's inconsistency, and the following is a case in point. When a labourer, one of our members, wanted the recognised wage of—at that particular time—thirteen shillings a week, the farmer, if he was a member of the Farmers' Union, was compelled by the laws of his union to refuse to pay him this wage. The farmer had to advertise for a non-Union man to whom he often had to pay eighteen shillings a week, in addition to which he had to lodge him. So that, in order to spite our Union, farmers often had to pay eighteen shillings a week to, and lodge, a bad workman, instead of paying thirteen shillings a week to one of our men.

But this silly state of things did not last long. The farmers subscribed to this precious Association for a time, but as they got rather sharply twitted about it, they soon dropped it. Like a bubble it quickly burst. I believe the chairman of the farmer's sort of Trades Union, which they called a "Chamber of Agriculture," was generally, if not always, some great local landowner. Well, of course the chairman was considered. I need say no more. He practically gagged the meeting over which he presided.

I told the Commissioners that I did not agree with the Farmers' Alliance, which much resembled our Union. I said: "The time has come when labourers will not be mocked. We have heard a great deal of the identity of the labourers' and farmers' interests. I have always believed in it, but the identity has not been properly realised. The Chairman of the Alliance wrote to me that he was thoroughly satisfied that the interests of the labourers were bound up in the Farmers' Alliance, and that they were going to send a deputation to Mr. Gladstone. I immediately wrote back as courteously as I knew how, and I offered to get up a deputation of labourers, and let farmers and labourers go to the Premier together, and show that we had this identity of interest. Of course that was not allowed. Well, is that not mocking us?"

There was too much humbug and shilly-shallying and blundering about these Farmers' Unions and Alliances, or whatever they called them. I had no kind of patience with them. I told the farmers they must not look to the landlords to redress their grievances. In 1873 and 1874, when the labourers were trying to push their worthless selves into notice, the landlords said that landlords and tenants must row in one boat; well, they rowed in one boat till the bottom was out and it was water-logged. I said again and again to the farmers: "You must strike out into a new line of politics. You have been ploughing in the same furrow until your plough has not only got never a share, but you have never a share to put on it. Your political power is not more than two thirds of what it was in 1874, because so many of you have had to give up your farms. Well, you must bestir yourselves, and join hands with us and find a remedy—you will never do it alone, and the landlords will not lift a little finger to help you. Don't count on them. Join in with us, and the sooner the better."

Then as to the tithe, I used to tell them that I thought the law on the subject should be altered, but that if they took a farm, and agreed with their eyes wide open to pay so much in tithe, they ought to do so. I do not think now that tithes should be abolished altogether as a charge on the land, but they should be applied to relieving the parish and road rates. They should not, however, go to the parsons. Let those who want parsons pay for them. I pay for mine. Should tithes be abolished, the landlords would very likely raise the rents. In fact, the farmers will never be really safe till they get an Act passed fixing the scale of rents.

Then there was the question of security. I said to the Commissioners that the very fact of the tenant farmers holding their land on the present conditions is to my thinking a proof that they have no commercial brains in their heads. "Custom," I said, "has bound the farmer's mind, and he has not gone with the times. A large quantity of land is let to-day on the condition that the tenant farmer may put whatever capital he likes into the soil, and when the landlord thinks well to notice him quietly out of it, there is no clause in the agreement that will allow him to claim compensation for the money he has put in. For the last twenty-five years farmers have farmed to leave instead of to stay. I have heard them remark, 'Well, you know we farm to leave, and that's all about it.' The present system gives the farmer no guarantee that justice will be done him. His position is only safe paternally and not legally. And I for one do not believe in living under any one's patronage."

Of course agricultural depression did not spring up like a mushroom. From 1857 to 1875 the value of land in England went up enormously. Caird said that in 1875 the farmers were paying £9,000,000 more for land than in 1857. Who had made it valuable? Not the landed proprietors but the extension of capital brought in by the hand of industry. It seemed to me that the landed aristocracy owed a great debt to the tenant farmers and the agricultural labourers. But when the value of the land increased, their gratitude showed itself in a singular fashion—they raised the rents. The Agricultural Holdings Act was not favoured by the farmers—they called it a sham, because it was permissive where it ought to have been compulsory. I used to tell the farmers at this period, "Oh well, if you will be children you must take the chastisement of children." They let themselves be bested, and only grumbled or acted in a left-handed sort of a fashion.

Then again I advocated very strongly and persistently the abolition of entail and primogeniture. It had undoubtedly helped greatly to starve the land. I said, "I do not think people should have the power to tie up the land for more than one life." Entailed estates in my pretty wide experience were less well cultivated; and on such estates I have known many farmers pining for material to repair their fences, and they could not get it. These estates were dilapidated because the life owners were frequently crippled for want of ready money, and they had to provide dowries and sisters' settlements off the land which they could not do as they liked with. Land could not be sold freely, for, in a manner of saying, the dead bodies of centuries lay upon it, dead hands gripped it and held it as in a vice.

In my opinion, and in the opinion of hundreds, it was high time these feudal laws were abolished, and land transfer made as easy and quick as the buying and selling of an ox or a sheep. "Free the land from the dead hand," I used to say, in speech after speech. "Let the land circulate; let more share in it; give the labourers a chance. The farmer ought to be in such a position that, if at some future time he wants to make the land he has tilled his own, he may do so by fair purchase. I do not preach confiscation, I do not encourage thieving; but let the farmer have a chance of paying for the land if he wishes to do so." "You farmers," I used to say, "have grandchildren and great-grandchildren occupying land tilled by their ancestors; they have been paying rent for generations; and yet you are no nearer making a single yard of it your own than were your ancestors."

The land system is rotten, and the farmers are foolish. The land was labour-starved, and they held the threat of machinery over the ignorant labourer's head. I said to the Commissioners: "The farmers have used machinery as a sort of weapon over the backs of their labourers. I heard of a certain farmer who boasted for years at a market ordinary that he bought a reaping machine but he never used it, and he said, 'It has paid me a good percentage, keeping it in my coach-house to frighten the labourers with.'" He was one of many, too. As to machinery, I never had any objection to it as supplementing the labourer, but I consider it requires a strong complement of men, and must have them, if farming is to succeed. I always said I never wished any sort of legislative interference with machinery, unless the farmer makes a machine to eat the bread when it is baked! I said: "I think so far machinery has been at least a partial failure; it has been made too much of. I can take you across clay hills in my own neighbourhood to-day where I have cut crops of sixty-two, fifty-five, and fifty bushels of wheat upon an acre, harvest by harvest; and some six or seven years before these bad seasons set in, even the last four or five years, I cut over the same ground—though they were good seasons—not more than twenty, twenty-five, and in some cases not more than fifteen bushels. This was where they had been applying scientific machinery and leaving the labourer out of it. Mr. Giffen's figures will tell you that on the large farms the crops and the stock have not been so productive as on the smaller farms, where there is scarcely any machinery used."

Then as to labour-starving the land. Why, there were farms of five and six hundred acres with only two men and a boy to work them; there were such farms in Warwickshire, Dorsetshire, and Worcestershire—some of eight and nine hundred acres on which for a considerable time no horse's foot had been put to plough, nor a man's foot to hoe and clean, nor a single grain of corn grown. Many farms were thrown up, or were scarcely touched, and like the sluggard's garden, the thistles and weeds, the docks and the briar, grew apace and no man checked them. The farmers were much to blame for not using more labour, and also for not paying their men according to their worth.

I said to the Commissioners: "It has been a great mistake farmers have made ever since I can remember, that they have not given the best men the best price. Twenty-seven years ago I was putting in a large drain for a farmer; it was six feet deep, and he was paying me one shilling and sixpence a day, and was paying another man forking 'twitch' on the same land just the same price. I asked the farmer for two shillings and sixpence—I judged my work was worth it—but he refused to give it, so I just struck then and there.

"Then, again, an employer of mine told me years ago that I was worth twenty-four shillings a week on any farm. I said, 'Why don't you give it me?' 'If I were to give you twenty-four shillings, Arch, my labourers would be dissatisfied, and I should also incur the displeasure of my brother farmers.'

"Now why should I not have had that twenty-four shillings? I should have earned it to the full, because I could make gates, and hurdles, and hedges, and stack and thatch buildings and ricks, and shear, and drain, and mow. I say that, if the other men had seen me get that twenty-four shillings, they would have said, 'Oh, it's some use learning things and buying tools.' Tools are very expensive things for us to invest in. I have spent as much as £20 in tools in my lifetime. If I was a farmer, and had a superior workman at work, and he was getting twenty-four to twenty-five shillings a week, and another man said, 'I think I can do as well,' I should say, 'Then I will set you a job, and you shall have a try'; and if he could do the work, he should have the same money. Give the men a chance of doing better if they can."

I said, too, that I strongly advocated piecework where practicable; it was much fairer to both man and master. Then again, for years and years the farmers had said they were to fix the price of labour—"We fix the wages, my men, and you have got to take what we choose to offer you." However, the Union knocked that little bit of injustice a smart blow. The farmers who paid their men properly, and employed sufficient labour, had a better chance of pulling through a hard time. Those who labour-starved the land were simply, "labour wise and land foolish," and they began to find it out too late. Those farmers who had cultivated their land well, had enriched it and not spared labour, could afford to retrench in a very bad season without sinking. Their invested capital showed up its worth in the day of scarcity.

But whatever was said it always resolved itself in the last resource to this—better security, more freedom. The farmer's hands were tied by fear of a twelve-months' notice, and the landlord's hands were too frequently tied by the law of entail. I said at this period: "The land has been kept for a number of years under such a series of restrictions, and of so binding a character, that now we have the agriculturalists in such a position as cannot be found in any nation under the sun, I believe, with something like twenty-five per cent. of the occupiers of the land turning bankrupt, or on the brink of bankruptcy."

Land, land : that was what we were all thinking about and talking about, and the idea of an Allotment Act was in the air. Jesse Collings was taking the matter up after his fashion in the House—he was Member for Ipswich—and at a big meeting I was at in December 1881 we had a petition on hand in which it said : "Your petitioners view with grave concern the uncultivated condition of much of the land of England, and the consequent distress amongst the unemployed labourers, and respectfully but most earnestly pray your honourable House to pass the motion of Mr. Jesse Collings in favour of peasant proprietorships, which they believe would practically remedy the existing evils."

When before the Commisioners, I said : "If you want the labourer to rise, if you want him to get above being a pauper, if you want to make him self-reliant—we have been too dependent a class—if a man can make a good profit out of his quarter of an acre (and I know some men will make it more than others), let him do so. If that man could take an acre or a couple, and by that means save himself from pauperism, let him. I think it is highly desirable that the labourer should not be limited to a quarter of an acre, but that you should let him have some scope for his ability. A labourer should have a good quarter of an acre attached to his cottage; and if he can cultivate it and get enough out of it to take another half-acre it would be a wise step for any landed proprietor to let thrifty and persevering men have it. Those, of course, who do not properly cultivate their plot should not be allowed to keep it on.

"And I think the same rent should be charged to the labourer as is charged to the farmer. The rule, however, is to charge the labourer excessively; to make him pay twenty-five, thirty, and even forty per cent. more for his land than the farmer does. I have gone exhaustively into the question. A farmer will pay at the rate of thirty shillings an acre for land which the labourer has to pay for at the rate of five pounds per acre. This is land let to the labourer in addition and apart from his cottage garden-land, on which the men grow vegetables for their families.

"Take my own village, or Hampton Lucy, or take a number of villages in the west of England I have gone through; there is the field of allotments, and they have been paying from five shillings to eight shillings, and eight shillings and sixpence to ten shillings for twenty perches. Now five shillings for twenty perches equals two pounds per acre, and yet a farmer on the other side of the hedge will get his for twenty-five shillings. If the landlord can afford to let allotment-land at twenty-five shillings per acre to the farmer, he can surely let the labourer have it at, say, thirty shillings.

"Bad seasons affect the little plots or land just as much as the larger. I know that, owing to the bad seasons, labourers have had to pay for the vegetables they were unable to raise on their plots. I think 1879 was, taking it all round, about the worst season we ever had in my experience. I know that in my own garden, which I cultivate well, the produce was not worth so much in 1879 by about £3 10*s*. or £4 as it is worth to-day. It is a fact that labourers suffer just as much as the farmers, and more, because of their very limited resources, in bad seasons. It is another example of what I have always taught, that when you come down to facts the interests of labourer and farmer are identical.

"Then, again, a labourer should have good security for his plot. He puts good labour into it, and clears it, and improves its value. I know how my father suffered—he had his allotment shifted four times in the course of his life. The labourers were put into a field in very bad condition, such that no farmer particularly cared to cultivate it; they held it for three or four years, and got it thoroughly clean and capable of bearing anything, and then they were shifted on to another.

"I consider that granting land is the only practicable way by which labourers can extricate themselves from pauperism and serfdom. I say, let a thrifty labourer be a small farmer if he can save enough; sufficient land should be open to him at a reasonable rate. I think, as things are, that it would be a great blessing if some of the farmers could be upset, as they have more land than they can cultivate, and here are labourers crying out for it.

"Let the labourer raise himself by the land. I teach the farm labourers never to be satisfied while there is a chance of advancing in life. To teach a man to be content to stick in the mud, is to teach a man to curse himself. I think we should increase within his mind a just discontent for every year of his life, to make himself a better man, and go one better every year he lives."

"Yes," I used to say to the men, too, "stand on the land and rise on the land." Now legislation was taking up the matter, and in 1882 the Allotments Act was passed.

CHAPTER XV.

I ENTER PARLIAMENT.

ALL during 1882 I spoke a great deal on the land question and on the franchise. Of course the Allotments Extension Act was very much discussed. Howard Evans was the real author of the Act, though he said the question was first stirred up by Mr. Theodore Dodd, the son of an Oxfordshire clergyman. Mr. Dodd wrote some articles on the subject, and he declared that the Act of William IV. applied to all local charity lands. Of course, there had been a lot of talk in different parts about these lands; and Howard Evans, when travelling about the country for the Union, saw that something had to be done. Many of our district secretaries got hold of the county charity reports and began to agitate. When the trustees were applied to about the lands they generally made both their ears conveniently deaf. Then the Charity Commissioners were applied to and they would have nothing to say to Evans, and showed him the door. Evans got a Bill drawn up and Sir Charles

Dilke promised to lay it before the House ; he did so, but it ended in being dropped. Then, after the election of 1880, Jesse Collings took up the matter. We all knew the labourers were divorced from the land, and that this was neither good for them nor for the country.

As soon as Parliament opened in 1882 Jesse Collings pressed on the "Charity Lands Bill"—a boon to the rural labourers it was meant to be. The Act was originally intended to give the labourers a cheap and easy remedy in the nearest county court. The moment, however, we attempted to apply it, the Charity Commissioners made all the difficulties they possibly could. They were not friendly to the Act, though they were obliged to administer it. As Evans said : "The tricks resorted to by some of the trustees are simply infamous. In some cases they have let the land on a long lease so as to evade the Act ; in others they have, contrary to law, charged exorbitant rents ; in others they have, contrary to law, refused to let except to farm labourers, and sometimes only to farm labourers who are householders ; in others they have ignored the Act altogether ; in others they have illegally demanded half a year's rent in advance." There were so many complaints, that Jesse Collings asked for help to start an Allotments Extension Association. I must say that Evans worked like a slave over this Act, and he wrote on it in our paper, and gave extracts from the Charity Digest.

I did my part by speaking on the subject. I told the men that they must see to it, and have the pluck to move themselves, for they had to force the hand of the Charity Commissioners. In many and many a village the charity land had been diverted from the purpose intended and enclosed in the farms, and when a poor man wanted a piece of land he had perhaps to pay the parson at the rate of £3 or £4 an acre for it.

I had to stir them up about the Union, too. Reports got about that the Union was dead, or next door to it. In an article I contributed to the *English Labourers' Chronicle* at the end of 1882, I said: "What are the labourers' hopes for the coming Christmas? They have let the Union go down, and instead of getting thirteen or fourteen shillings a week, they are receiving ten." I also said: "I ask, can any labourer who has read the *English Labourers' Chronicle* sit down to his Christmas dinner on Monday, December 25th, 1882, and not say that the Union, assisted by such men as Mr. Jesse Collings and Mr. Howard Evans, has enlightened his mind?"

"In some parts of the eastern counties an attempt was made to keep harvest wages down," I told them, "notwithstanding there was more to cut and gather. The men being strong in Union in many parts gained a ten shillings advance on their wages of the previous year. But in some parts of Gloucestershire, Wilts, Hants, Berks, Somerset, yes, and even in some parts of Warwickshire, they have been obliged to take whatever wage the farmer chose to pay."

Of course the Union was strong in parts, and where it was so it was very strong. As usual, I came in for any amount of abuse because of my notions about the land question ; but I pegged away all the same, and I said : "Let them write till their pens are worn to a stump, until their ink-bottles are dry, and until their fingers ache, and their arms also to the shoulder ; but, so long as I see millions of my fellow-countrymen, who have to eat to-morrow the bread they earn to-day, and who have to struggle hard to keep the wolf from the door—so long as I see them suffering as they do ; so long will I labour to remove the cause of that suffering, and the great evil which I believe the land laws inflict upon the country. The landlords say, 'Touch these laws, and our political power will wane and wither.' I say, if that be so, however great the calamity—and it would not be great—for the sake of a prosperous trade, for the sake of a secure agriculture, let their political power wane and wither ; but perish the laws that have so long been a hindrance and a curse to the country."

At this time the question of the labourer's cottage accommodation was a great deal talked about. It was always cropping up, and little wonder. Scores of the cottages were nothing but garnished hovels at their best when I was a boy ; they were much the same in my young manhood, still the same when I was working for the Union and many are not much better to-day. In the sixties the overcrowding entailed a condition of things among the agricultural labourers which made a man blush for his country. Again and again I spoke out on this subject. I cannot think what the country clergy were doing not to have called high Heaven to witness on the terrible things going on in the parishes. In some cases the accommodation in labourers' cottages was so limited, that whole families of seven, eight, and nine, of both sexes, lived and slept in one room, and the sanitary arrangements were appalling.

Well, in 1881, when I was before the Commission, I had my say on the matter of bad cottages, and also on the question of cottage right. I said: "I think if the farmer is going in for tenant right, which of course I hold with, that there should be legislation to grant the labourers' cottage right." I knew of farms myself where the cottages were let with the farms, and of course it bound the men hand and foot. I said: "I never would live in one of those cottages myself. When a cottage is let with a farm, a man is compelled to labour on that farm from January to December." I knew of a case in 1872, but seven miles from my own house, in which, when the junction railway passed through the district, the railway companies were offering three shillings and sixpence to three shillings and tenpence per diem, and young, strong men, who were at work on this land for eleven shillings, left it; but they were pretty quickly told that unless they came back for twelve shillings they should leave their cottages. I said then: "Why, this cottage question has been going on forty years, to my knowledge."

I always thought this a shameful injustice. I said to the Commissioners: "The principle of cottages on farms being at the farmer's mercy is not sound at bottom.

If I, as a labourer, rented a cottage from you, and paid my rent, I would not be bound by you or any man living to labour as he wished. Let the farmer go into the market for his labour, the same as any other employer of labour. If a labourer," I said, "has a proper notice to quit, well and good; but I call it a monstrous injustice that he should be driven out of his cottage on a week's notice." I said, "Both tenant farmers and labourers have a precarious holding; it should in both cases be made more stable."

I know, too, that in my own village I strongly opposed overcrowding and indiscriminate sleeping. I called the attention of the Nuisance Inspector to the matter, and he soon stopped it. He made the farmers, in some instances, build new cottages with proper sleeping accommodation. There ought always to be, in my opinion, two bedrooms at the least; three bedrooms should be the general rule, because, even if a man has to pay a little more rent, his sons can then stay at home longer, and so help to keep the house going. Besides, it would have another effect: if the sons were comfortably accommodated with their parents, they would not be in such a hurry to make hasty marriages while only lads, as is far too often the case.

I will quote here from an article on the Franchise, which I contributed to the *Nineteenth Century*; because it touches on the question from another side. I said: "We are asked sometimes why we urge our claims so strongly. Is there anything in a vote which will do you any good? Do you believe it to be the panacea for all the ills you have to bear? Well, let us see. Have we in our own rural villages the same sanitary arrangements as there are in our enfranchised towns? It is true there are in some parts nuisance inspectors, but there are many—very many—villages where there are no sanitary arrangements at all? I must not name villages; any one who travels must observe the bad sanitary condition of the rural districts. But whoever brought a Bill into Parliament to compel the great landowner to properly drain his cottage property?

"There are, it is true, many improvements needed in our towns, but they have the means in their hands to rectify them. If an enfranchised town is suffering from bad sanitary arrangements—it may be the local squire or lord may object to certain measures the town authorities have seen fit to adopt—where do they apply? Why, to Parliament, where they have their representatives. But how is the rural workman, without a vote, to make himself heard on a matter of this kind? He may call the district inspector in, but what follows as a rule? It may be he complains of some nuisance which may emanate from his rich neighbour's neglect; if so, if he cannot ply his trade to profit without begging the custom of his rich neighbour to keep his trade going, no matter how bad the nuisance, he must hold his tongue or be prepared for the consequences.

"And while such laws exist as the law of primogeniture and entail, it will be more or less the policy of the present owner to get as great a rent as he can, while doing as little in the shape of improvement as he can. Only the other week in Wilts I saw cottages unfit for human beings to live in; fast going to decay, and the sooner the better; but will the present owner build more? Question!

"During the last twenty years how many of our cottages have been pulled down, and more built to replace them? thus driving the farm labourers into the towns, and in tens of thousands of instances robbing the land of their useful labour. Had the labourer been enfranchised half a century ago, the land as well as the villages would not have presented such a serious picture of dilapidation. Of course there are exceptions to this rule.

"Then there is pure water. It the water of a town is bad, means are set on foot to improve it; a town water Bill is brought into the House. And yet in many of our villages the water is not fit for human beings to drink; but who is to call the attention of the legislature to that? Some one may raise the question; but not until the vote is extended to every householder in the counties, will that question receive its due consideration—not only good drainage and good water, but good and decent cottages. Why is there an Artizans' Dwelling Act for our large towns? Why are the inhabitants to say where the law should take effect and where it should not? Why not an Agricultural Labourers' Dwelling Act? He would have had his Act the same as the artizan, but he had no vote. When the same right to send men to Parliament as the artizan in town has is given to the labourer, he will no longer be content to live in a fever den. He will no longer be content to drink impure water."

I had made up my mind that, if the cottages remained in their bad condition, it would not be because I had failed to have my say on the subject.

For a good many reasons I was very glad when I saw the last of 1882. From 1878 up to that year I had a very rough time of it at the hands of certain persons who had been inside the Union, and who wanted to bring about my downfall. In fact, they followed me everywhere like a lot of sleuth-hounds.

In 1883 I was chosen President of the Birmingham Radical Union, and we kept agitating for the franchise harder and louder than ever. In 1884 we got it. Next to the famous year of the start of the Union, the year which saw the agricultural labourer enfranchised was the great year of my life. We had a vote at last; we were now politically alive and existent, and there were those amongst us who intended to use that existence to the utmost of our power in pressing forward our best interests. I told them at Kenilworth in 1885, where I attended a meeting in support of Mr. P. H. Cobb's candidature for the Rugby division, that from the time I was ten years of age I made up my mind that, if the day should come when I could make my voice heard, I would make it heard against the landocracy of this country. I had made it heard, and I had by no means done; for now I hoped soon to be in the House of Commons to give the landlords a word or two about the periodical increases of rent and a few other things. In the autumn of 1885 I remember speaking at a great demonstration of miners at Burslem. Thomas Burt, M.P., president of the Miners' Union, was there, and he and I sat on the platform together. Burt is a very fine man, a solid, straightforward party politician; and being a working-man and a representative of the miners, he was particularly interesting to me. I was great friends with him, and I am proud to say so. That Burslem meeting was a downright good one, and they gave me a very hearty welcome.

In the November of 1885 came the general election and with it my chance of entering Parliament. I was told that the working-men of North-West Norfolk had been holding meetings at their branches and had determined to have me as their candidate. They asked me to contest the seat, and promised, if I would stand, that my expenses should be paid. They sent for me to go down to the Blackfriars Hall at Lynn when the candidates were selected. There were two Liberal candidates for the vacancy; Sir Bampton Gurdon, whom the well-to-do and upper classes wanted to return, and myself, whom the labourers wanted to represent them. I went down, and when the poll was taken I polled exactly double the number of votes Sir Bampton did. I therefore stood in the Liberal and labouring class interest. My opponent was Lord Henry Bentinck. In my address to the electors, I said I would support the extension of Free Trade to all articles of food; a measure for conferring local government by boards upon county districts; the complete reform of the land laws; compensation for improvements in the soil; total abolition of the law of distress; power to government or local boards to acquire land at reasonable purchase value, and to relet the same in allotments; disestablishment of the Church; free, secular elementary education; Sunday closing of public houses, except to bona-fide travellers; abolition of perpetual pensions; substitution of arbitration for war; and equal laws for all parts of the United Kingdom.

Lord Henry Bentinck was a young man and of course trained in a very different school; with the best will in the world he could not possibly enter into our feelings and understand our particular needs. The two millions of new voters wanted some one of their own class to speak for them. I was ready. The voting took place at Lynn on Tuesday, December 8th, 1885, and the votes were cast up on the Wednesday, when it was found that I was returned by a majority of 640. I polled 4461 votes, and Lord Henry Bentinck 3821. There was a great scene when the poll was declared. I remember how put about the Tories were, for a Liberal had not captured the seat for sixty or seventy years. They sent a troop of men down to one of my meetings to cripple me. They gave them five shillings and a gallon of beer each; but it so happened that a new line was being cut to South Lynn, and all the navvies knew me—the majority of them had come off the land on to the line. One day the ganger went to Lynn to draw the money to pay the men, and on his way he called in at a public house, and overheard the men who had been sent down by the Tories discussing the best way to pay me out. That night he told the navvies what he had heard, and they all attended my meeting armed with sticks. When the Tory crowd commenced to set about me, the navvies went for them and thrashed them most unmercifully, and the Tory roughs, with the navvies' mark on them, were regularly cowed and slunk off out of the way. I remember I rode through Lynn to the Town Hall in a donkey cart; and after the poll had been declared, when I rose to thank the electors for the honour they had conferred upon me, I said that while my opponents with carriages, horses, servants, and all their aristocratic paraphernalia, had failed to accomplish their object, Joseph and his brethren had accomplished *their* object with a donkey cart. The humble donkey had drawn me on to triumph and a majority of 640.

The day I entered Parliament as Joseph Arch, M.P. for North-West Norfolk, was a proud one, but pride was subdued by responsibility. Joseph Chamberlain and Jesse Collings were my sponsors. Chamberlain was smiling all over his face, I remember; if I was smiling, it was an inside smile at the thought that my entry marked the triumph of our enfranchisement. I took my place in the Council Chamber of the nation as the representative of the labourer and of the Prince of Wales—the Sandringham estates are in the North-West division—and I said to myself, "Joseph Arch, M.P., you see to it that neither the Prince nor the labourer has cause to be ashamed of you." I did not put on a black coat—I aped nobody—I wore my rough tweed jacket and billycock hat; the same I generally wore at my country meetings. As I was, so I wished to be. A few weeks after I entered Parliament Mrs. Peel, the wife of the Speaker, sent me an invitation to take tea with her. I went, and found her very nice and interesting, and the Speaker very friendly. He gave the first Levée in morning dress, and I also went to that. I met with a great deal of friendliness from different people with whom I was at this time brought into contact. When I went down to Leamington in January to attend the annual soirée in connection with the Liberal Working Men's Club, I told them that, though a club which was being formed in London had written to ask me to become one of its vice-presidents, I did not intend to waste my time in London clubs. My place was within the walls of the House of Commons when important business was before it. There I should sit and listen, and there I should speak when the proper time came. I said, too: "The return of the twelve working-men's candidates is only the beginning of brighter and better days for the working classes, and you may rest assured that when the carpenter, the glass-blower, the man from the forge, and the agricultural labourer put their shoulders together within the walls of St. Stephen's, they will scatter so much Radicalism that a great number of gentlemen will catch the dreadful disease." I said, too, that I meant to wear my ordinary dress in the House, not to make myself conspicuous, but because I was determined to do like the Shunamitish woman of whom I read in the good old book, and who had great opportunities of enriching herself—I would live and die with my brethren.

I rose to make my maiden speech on January 26th, 1886, in which I opposed Mr. Chaplin's Allotment Bill. In this speech I said: "When I read the speech of Her Most Gracious Majesty the Queen, which expressed sympathy with the distress that was prevalent, not only in trade but in agriculture, I took it certainly to mean this—'You are in a terribly poverty-stricken condition. Your lot in life is hard. You are without employment, and without money, and consequently must be without food. I know your lot is hard, but I have no remedy.' It seems to me something like this—that, supposing as an individual I were suffering intense bodily pain, and I sent for a medical adviser; he looks at me, he sees me writhing in agony, and he says, 'I have not a single ingredient in my surgery that I could apply to assuage your pain.' Would it not be natural enough to me to seek the advice of some more skilled physician? It Her Majesty's Government have no remedy for this distress, then, I think, the country will very soon look out for another physician, who has a practical remedy already to hand." I went on to say: "Honourable gentlemen have said that about a quarter of an acre is sufficient for a working-man in a village. There may be some working-men, such as shepherds and carters, who perhaps would be contented with a rood of ground; but I venture to say that a very large number of the labourers in Norfolk—and I am speaking now from my own experience in that county —would only be too glad if they could rent an acre or two at a fair market price. On the other hand, I do not find any human or Divine law which would confine me, as a skilled labourer, to one rood of God's earth. If I have energy, tact, and skill, by which I could cultivate my acre or two, and buy my cow into the bargain, I do not see any just reason why my energies should be crippled and my forces held back, and why I should be content as an agricultural labourer with a rood of ground and my nose to the grindstone all the days of my life." I said: "I cannot understand for the life of me why, if an English workman can, by thrift and industry and care, manage to secure to himself and his family a cow, he should not have the opportunity for doing so. The Amendment of the honourable member for Ipswich (Jesse Collings) means that. We do not ask for borrowed funds, or for the land to be given us, and we have no desire to steal it. What the Amendment asks, and what I ask honourable gentlemen on both sides of the House, is whether the time has not come when these thousands of industrious and willing workers should no longer be shut out from the soil, and should have an opportunity of obtaining a fair foothold, and producing food for themselves and their families?

"Why are these men out of work? Is it because the land is so well cultivated that no more of their labour is required? I travel this country from one end to the other, and I have an idea I know when land is cultivated and when it is not, as well as any gentleman in this House. I say, fearless of contradiction, that there are tens of thousands of acres of land waiting for the hand of the workman; and what this House ought to consider and aim at, is to use every legitimate means to bring the land that cries for labour to the labourer as soon as possible. I am addressing in this House large landed proprietors, and will any honourable gentleman attempt for one moment to deny that the best cultivated estate is the best for the landlord?

"When I look at this question, I go almost out of the region of party politics. It is not a landlord's, a tenant farmer's, or a labourer's question; it is the question of the people, and they will very soon make it their question. We are not Socialists—not in the accepted meaning of the word; but to a certain extent we are Socialists, because we are social beings. We like social comforts and social society, but we have a great aversion to social society paid for out of the poor rates. An honourable gentleman said last night that it was beyond the power of the honourable member for North-West Norfolk to raise wages. I thought it was equally impossible for landlords in this country to force up rent. We have always been told that the price of labour would be regulated by what it is worth in the market. That is just what land has got to be. My idea of justice in land is this—that it I have to sell, as a tenant farmer, my produce extremely cheap, then I say the rent of my land should be extremely cheap.

"But the time has come for, and this Parliament has been elected very largely to carry out, some just and wise measure, not only for the improvement of the tenant farmers—and Heaven knows they want something, many of them—but for the benefit of the labourers, and for the benefit of the country. When I look around on this side of the House I see several honourable gentlemen—a fair number of Liberal members—who have been returned by the votes, very largely, of the agricultural labourers. They know that during the contests in various divisions the labourers expressed a very great desire for land to cultivate for themselves. They naturally concurred with that idea; but I have never heard any Liberal candidate promise the labourers 'three acres and a cow.' For myself, I never made such a vain promise."

The fact was, I considered "three acres and a cow" all moonshine. The Allotments Act was a miserable failure until the labourers got the vote, but since then thousands of acres have been put into their hands. In my opinion allotments ought to be compulsory. I fought Mr. Chaplin three times across the floor of the House over that Bill.

I supported Gladstone's Home Rule Bill. It was thrown out on the Second Reading, and so we were brought face to face with another election. As every politician knows, the Liberal party split over it, and the Gladstonian Liberals stood on one side and the Liberal Unionists under Hartington, Goschen, and Chamberlain stood on the other, rejecting what they called the new policy. I went with Gladstone, for I believed in doing justice to Ireland ; but I was never—not for a single instance—a Separationist. Freedom and justice in Union was my motto. The feeling was very bitter at this election, and there was fatal division in our ranks. The polling for our division took place on July 9th, 1886, and Lord Henry Bentinck was returned by a majority of twenty votes. Of course, apart from other things, I had to fight against heavy odds. To begin with, I could not leave my place in Parliament, and I had no machinery in the shape of carriages, the Primrose League, and great territorial influence, to put in motion, even if I had wished it. Then the "three acres and a cow" fallacy did me a good deal of damage, for too many of the labourers expected to have them at once.

Gladstone took a very warm interest in my election, and sent me a telegram on the day preceding the poll. I remember, as I was driving along past a hayfield, the men recognised me and the driver pulled up. I shouted to them, "Been to the poll, lads ?"

"Yes, walked there and back this morning," they shouted back.

I jumped down, pushed through the hedge, and gave round copies of Gladstone's telegram. They read them, and then they stuck them on their forks and waved them, giving me a hearty cheer.

As I passed by another place I got into a crowd of Bentinckites, and had to encounter a regular volley of abuse and groans, with only a cheer or two. As I crossed the railway at Massingham the porters shouted that they were all for me. I made a speech on the green to over five hundred men and women, and I made another at Rudham. When I left I was escorted by about three hundred men and boys, singing an election song and beating a drum.

When the poll was declared there was a tremendous yell of joy from the Bentinckites. I made a short speech, and I said: "Though I am defeated, I am not disgraced. I hope Lord Henry will advocate in Parliament those measures which I myself would have supported had I been returned. In the meantime be not dismayed, for before long I shall come back and claim the confidence of my fellow-labourers." Though I often wished that my work was done, and I could go back to my cottage home in Barford to labour in peace, I felt I could not leave my work half done; that as soon as ever I had the chance I must again raise my voice in the people's cause in the Council Chamber of the nation.

I did not waste time crying over spilt milk, for directly after my defeat I started off on an electioneering tour through Norfolk. I also visited Lancashire early in 1887, on an educational, political tour, and began with an address at Caton on the land question. We had a splendid meeting, and among other things I pitched into Chaplin's Allotments Bill. I said that, "As an agricultural labourer I looked upon it as a perfect insult to me, and what was an insult to me was an insult to my class. I did not intend the labourers and the working men of England to be bamboozled with such a miserable Bill. If a working man in any village required half an acre of land—and he was not to have any more—he was to be compelled to get four ratepayers to sign a requisition to take to the county magistrates 'in petty or general sessions assembled.' 'Why,' I said, 'who would be the four ratepayers to sign the requisition?' I asked a noble member of the House of Commons whether four ordinary farmers would be induced to sign, or four tradesmen, say the blacksmith, the butcher, the grocer, and the baker in a village? They would not sign it, for the simple reason that, as soon as they set themselves up to do anything for the social elevation of the agricultural labour, they would be boycotted.

"I told Mr. Chaplin, coming out of the House of Commons, that I would make his Bill stink in the nostrils of the nation before I had done with it. Suppose there were four persons, however, who had the courage to sign a requisition for another person to rent half an acre of land. They get up the requisition and make it duly suppliant in tone, and they take it to the county magistrates 'in petty or general sessions assembled.' But the third clause in the Bill distinctly stated that these magistrates should have the power, if they thought fit, to refuse the application if they did not consider it satisfactory—that is, you know, giving it 'their most serious consideration.' Well, I insisted on a division upon the second reading of the Bill, and I beat Mr. Henry Chaplin and his Conservative friends by a majority of fifteen, and so far his Bill lay dead.

"Look at it in another light. Why should any working man be treated any less courteously and considerately, because he is poor, than a gentleman? If I was a gentleman and wanted a farm or a large house, do you think I would stoop to go and ask four ratepayers, say in Caton, to sign a requisition for me to take to the magistrates and ask their permission whether I was to have this farm or house, or not? Certainly not. But the case is no different from that of a working man who wants to rent a piece of land. My claim is a common-sense one, and it is this, that if there are sixty or seventy men in a village who want to rent land let them go direct to the landlord and have done with it, and leave the magistrates to officiate as the rabbit-killers. Don't you think I did right in helping to defeat that Bill? I think I did."

I spoke out about State-aided emigration. I said: "We have a great deal said now by some of our landed proprietors about adopting a scheme of State-aided emigration. They want Government to 'copper down' about a million of money to send the surplus labour out of our country to other countries and the colonies. They tell us it is not 'emigration' but 'colonisation.' I was asked to sit upon a Board of Directors for promoting this scheme, and I said, 'If you are going to emigrate Bishops and Deans I would be on your Board of Directors to-morrow.' The men who go in for

State-aided emigration are those who have made such a wonderful clamour about the Irish Question. They want to put their hands into the pocket of the State to emigrate—whom? If you are going to emigrate the drunken loafers out of your towns—the cadger, the idle fellow, who won't work at all—I say that the colonies don't want that class of man. If you are going to emigrate the most intelligent and the best workmen, the men with the most skill and the strongest muscles and the highest courage, then I ask, Can we as a country afford to lose them? I say, Certainly not. I cannot understand State-aided emigration unless it is to emigrate those who 'toil not, neither do they spin.'

"There is another phase of the question that I would like to draw attention to. A good many agriculturists have grumbled to me about the low price of produce, and they said, 'Gladstone's a lot to do with it, and you have helped'; and I have said, 'Thank God, the people's bread is a bit cheaper then.' But I said also, 'You have made this rod for your own back. Go back to the year 1874, when about four thousand men in the Eastern Counties and others in Dorset and in Wilts were locked out, for the abominable crime of daring to unite together to better their social position. These men were wandering about your villages willing to work, and you refused them. Then your colonial emigration agents came over, and they took thousands of the most plucky and most intelligent of your workmen away. You would not let them till the land here for you, and now they are cultivating land of their own with perfect freedom in the colonies; and these men, whom you drove from their homes in England, are now your competitors there, and fifteen thousand miles away are sending to England in countless shiploads the corn which you cannot produce.' "

I said too: "We are told through the papers that every year we have to send about a hundred and twenty millions of money to foreign countries for eggs, butter, cheese, meat, bread, and so forth, for food for the people of this country. Yet, notwithstanding this enormous outlay, you have hundreds of thousands of men, women, and children in this country who are not more than half fed. Compare those facts with this—we have thousands of acres of land in this country that are not tilled, and that would repay tilling if the 'Dead Hand' were taken off, and if the cultivator had fair play; and would it not be wise in us therefore, instead of sending away a hundred and twenty millions of our hard-earned money for food, if we raised, as we could raise, more than one-half of that amount at home, if the land was only tilled? It has been going on for years within my recollection, that the smart lads of our country villages find out that there are better markets for their labour than to work upon the land, and they rush off, as they have done by thousands, into your large centres of industry.

"And now that trade is a bit depressed you are told that you are over-populated. It may be said that you are over-populated and that trade is depressed, considering the demand for the articles you produce in trade; but how on earth can British agriculture be truly said to be in a depressed condition when there is a demand every year for a hundred million pounds' worth more of agricultural produce than we can supply? Talk of supply and demand! As far as this is concerned the farmers of this country have got the game in their own hands, if they will cease to be Tories and take a right view of their own interests and those of the nation! It is a serious mistake for farmers to send landlords to Parliament to look after farmers' interests. You may just as well expect the cat to guard the cream."

I also said: "It is said a man has a right to do what he likes with his own. That is not true. You cannot put a nuisance under your neighbour's window or where you choose; you cannot put a pigstye where you choose; you must do nothing which is an injury to your neighbour. Take the same idea and carry it into our landed system. Take my own little property of half-a-quarter of an acre, the productive power of which was valued by a competent gardener at £6 a year. If there were a hundred men in my village who owned the same quantity of land and cultivated it, they and the neighbourhood would be the richer by £600 annually. But if I and my neighbours happened to have a pocketful of money, and because of that neglected to till our land, there would be, in the first instance, a loss to the community of £600 annually; but that would not be all.

"These men would go into the neighbouring market with their money to buy what they wanted, and would buy up the produce which should be available to those who had no gardens—the poor artizans of the town. I say this, that if we dared to rob the public in such a way, and competed with the man who has no garden and but little money in his pocket, then the Government ought to step in and say to me and my neighbour, 'If you won't cultivate this land, here is the full market price for it—you must either cultivate it or sell it, one way or the other, because you have no right to waste the public food.' This may be rather Radical doctrine, but I maintain that it is pure Conservatism. I mean to say that I am a far better Conservative than Lord Salisbury, and for this reason—I wish to create the greatest possible wealth out of the land. It is a Conservative measure to place a lot of industrious working men upon the land, and produce from the land all the wealth it is calculated to produce, for the inhabitants of our towns and for the prosperity of the whole country."

I wound up my speech by saying: "The few thoughts I throw out to-night are for your interests and the interests of the whole country. Society is like a great building. You cannot remove the foundation stone of a building without moving all that is above it, even to the top. Just so with society. Let the lower classes of society rise and become thrifty, and provident, and happy, with plenty to eat and plenty to do, with good wages fairly earned, and then every other class of society will be raised, will be strong and happy in proportion. I want you working men to set your heart upon these things; and when the next election comes let no bribe, no intimidation, no temptation lead you from the path of duty; and if you do that duty honourably and well, though you may not realise all that you hope for yourselves, this at least you will do—you will leave to posterity after you, to your children and your children's children, a brighter and a better heritage than it has been your lot to receive."

When I was speaking at Badsey, in South Worcestershire, I told them that I had worked for fifteen candidates and written for twenty-nine, and how it had hit me hard when these men I had helped voted against Gladstone and Home Rule. I had rather an exciting meeting at Broadway, I remember, in the August of 1887. It was held in a field, and shortly after I began to speak a balloon in the shape of an animal, which had been set up in a field some distance off, floated over the meeting, and several of my opponents—I had a good many there—raised a cry ot "Oh, look, here comes the cow!"

I said, "I know very well what you mean. I am not surprised that the calves first spied out the cow!"

In the February of 1888 I spoke at Southam, in my county, to a splendid meeting. I dealt with the Irish question and the detestable coercive policy of the Government. I was as hot as fire about it. I had been most careful to sit through the debates on it in the House, and I said to the meeting, "I sat close to the feet of Mr. Gladstone when he delivered his three hours and twenty-five minutes' address upon the Home Rule question, and if I live I shall sit there again."

I also said: "It is one of the happiest things for England, Scotland, Ireland, and Wales, that Mr. Gladstone introduced his Home Rule Bill. Why are the Irish people so law-abiding, in spite of the greatest possible persecution? How is it we do not hear of explosions of dynamite and shooting of landlords? It is because of the Home Rule Bill; and when I sat at the feet of our great political Gamaliel, and listened to his words, the thought flashed across my mind, 'Ah, Mr. Gladstone, you are raising a star of hope in the horizon of Ireland, and whether this Bill is passed or not, this star will shine on and on till poor Ireland is free.'"

I spoke also on the Fair Trade question. I said: "I want you to examine logically this Fair Trade dodge. I don't think they will try it on in my division again. They got it pretty well when they tried it on there in 1885. But in Warwickshire I find there is a number of gentlemen who are trying this dodge upon you. How will it act? Suppose one of you men with your family consume twelve quartern loaves weekly. If Fair Trade raised the price twopence a loaf, your bread bill for the week would be increased two shillings a week. But then the farmer will say, 'I could afford to pay you two shillings a week more money.' Well, if I were at work for a farmer, and he said that to me, I should say, 'Is that all, sir? Can't you give me more than that?' Bear in mind that if Fair Trade makes your bread cost you two shillings more, you ought not to rest satisfied unless your wages are raised at least four shillings a week. I will tell you why. The shoemaker will charge you more for your shoes; the tailor will charge you more for your clothes; and the butcher will charge you more for your meat; and you will never get bilious through eating beefsteaks. You won't see a leg of mutton on your table very often. Beware of this. I want you to see that it is very easy to draw you into the net, but it will be difficult to get you out when you are in. I don't want you to get into the snare.

"I was recently addressing a large meeting in a manufacturing district, and I said to the manufacturers: 'Suppose the food of your operatives is raised thirty per cent., they will immediately come down upon you for an increase of wages thirty per cent. Suppose for instance they do this, and the present Government put a tax on imports of ten per cent., the foreigner will then put a tax upon your exported goods of say twenty per cent.; and knowing you cannot do without his bread-stuffs, he will say, "Very well, if you don't like that we will manufacture our own goods." You will lose his trade with you, and still be obliged to buy his goods. If you want to ruin your manufactures put on the taxes at once.'"

The points which covered the Fair Trade Controversy were—any tax put upon goods imported into this country would have to be paid by the English consumer and not by the foreigner; protection could not be limited to any one single article. If corn were protected, the manufacturers would ask for their goods to be protected also. And also the cry for protection was simply a landlords' cry, started and kept up for the purpose of maintaining rents at their present high position, and enabling them to ride about in their carriages. This was the way a speaker at the meeting put it.

For some time past I had been in bad health and suffering a great deal at times, so it was often as much as I could do to get through my meetings and keep the political ball rolling. But now, as ever, I kept pegging away and toiled on. Enemies were still on my track, and I had to face another accusation about our Union funds. Major Rasch was reported in the *Daily News* as having put a question to the First Lord of the Treasury respecting the Agricultural Labourers' Union, couched in these words:

"Whether the Government would take steps to prevent misappropriation in connection with this body?"

Well, as you may guess, I was up in arms on the spot. We had a correspondence on the subject, in which Major Rasch did not come out well. Another thing; the very allegation made by him was the subject of a judicial inquiry in the Court of Chancery in November

1887, when Mr. Justice Stirling, after reading the affidavits of all the parties to the suit, decided in my favour. He declared the charges were false, and made without the slightest foundation.

Sir Selwyn Ibbotson wanted me to send all the books and vouchers, and everything in connection with the financial arrangements of the Union, to a firm of chartered accountants in London. I replied that I had nothing at all to do with the books or the accounts of the Union, this department being in the hands of the committee and secretary. But, even if I had, I should certainly decline his request on these grounds: (1) That from the commencement of the Union we had submitted the accounts every six months to two chartered accountants in Birmingham, which they had audited and found correct, and it would have been an insult to those gentlemen if we had placed the accounts in the hands of London accountants to audit again. (2) That, provided I should feel myself at liberty to send the accounts of the Labourers' Union to the accountants he suggested, would he kindly send me the balance sheet of his estate, so that I could see that he was sound and solvent? That was my answer, and I did not hear anything further from Sir Selwyn Ibbotson.

As for me personally, I never received any money on behalf of the Union; I was only a hired servant year by year. At the Annual Congress the labourers elected their president, and they elected me They paid me so much a week and my travelling expenses.

I travelled for them for about twenty-four years on those conditions. I received no contributions, and the only moneys I paid away in any shape or form were my own travelling expenses, which they refunded to me in due course. During the whole time I was connected with the Union I had nothing at all to do with the financial accounts. The Union paid my Parliamentary expenses. My salary was so much, and my expenses were so much, which amounted in all, taking one week with another, to between £4 and £5 a week.

When I went to the House of Commons they allowed me my expenses in addition to my salary. My election expenses came to about £800; they were found for me by subscriptions from wealthy men. From 1876 to 1879 my salary was £3 a week, and from 1879 to the time the Union collapsed it was £2 10*s*. The cause of the reduction was this: when the wages of the labourers began to be reduced they cried out about the salaries of the officials, and said that these also ought to be reduced. The majority of the officials did not like this, and did their best to keep their salaries up—it was natural enough—but I was willing to take ten shillings a week less, and told them so. The labourers accepted my offer, and the other officials had to come down also. After the year 1884 the Union began to go down, largely owing to the fact that an important part of the work was done (though by no means all); the men had the vote; it was as if they had a wide door set open before them, and they thought that they could get all they wanted by means of their representatives in Parliament. They did not understand how slow a thing reform is, and there were too many of them who thought they had only to ask and they would receive—three acres and a cow, for instance. I myself felt at this period that the main thing to be done next was to get a hearing in the House of Commons. We had our vote, and we were not to let it rust. Well, I was not rusting out through these years, and I never worked harder in all my life at speechmaking than I did in 1887 and 1888. I did not spare my lungs, nor my throat, nor my legs, nor my head; and my heart was as warm for the cause as it had ever been.

CHAPTER XVI.

AT THE END OF THE DAY.

AFTER County Councils were created by the Local Government Act of 1888 I stood for County Councillor for the Wellesbourne division; and though squarsons and squires, landlords and money-bags, were leagued together against me, I was returned by a majority of thirty-four. My opponent was Mr. Cove Jones, a magistrate, who of course had great influence behind him. He had carriages at his service, I had "Shanks's mare"; he had the Primrose League to work for him, I had a few trusty friends to speak for me. I did not canvass; I merely addressed three meetings from the distance of the platform. After the victory I received many kind letters which were as balm to me, for I had to submit to a regular torrent of scurrilous abuse from enemies and false friends. It was a bitter experience. Many of them were so prejudiced against me, and looked at all my doings with such jaundiced eyes, that I gave up trying to right myself with them. I was not going to play the part of the miller in the fable, and I consoled myself by saying, "Never mind; fierce is the light that beats upon a prominent man, and many are the clods of mud pitched at him. Go ahead as before, and let snarling dogs snarl and bark till they bark their bark away; they'll only hurt themselves most in the end."

I sat in the County Council till the end of 1892, and attended regularly. I was appointed on various committees and was able to do good work, more particularly on the Highways, Roads, and Bridges Committee. I liked the work and regretted having to give it up; but needs must when illness drives, and work elsewhere called me away.

Not long after this I unveiled a bust of Mr. Gladstone at the Bingley Liberal Club, and in my speech on that occasion I said: "I can say that, as a working man, I think no man has stronger claims upon my sympathy, support, and affection than Mr. Gladstone. When the election of 1880 came we had him placed at the helm of affairs. Although I was twitted by weak-kneed Liberals and Tories that he would never concede the franchise, my faith in his honesty, in his sense of justice to the people, and in his love for the people, was not in the slightest degree shaken by these jeers. I was perfectly certain that he would enfranchise my class. In taking off this covering to unveil to you the bust of this great statesman I can say, fearless of contradiction, that he lives in the affections of thousands of men, aye, tens of thousands, who dwell in our rural villages in humble cottages, and who, I believe, whenever a wise Providence shall call him aside from this scene of action, will mourn his loss with a great and profound depth of feeling. I do not believe that Mr. Gladstone or any other living being is free from mistakes; but of this I am certain, that whenever he has made a mistake and has found it out, he has been honourable, he has been manly enough to acknowledge it, and has done his best to rectify it."

I had the honour, by the bye, of paying Mr. Gladstone a visit at Hawarden Castle in 1884, and I was received by the Rev. Stephen Gladstone, Vicar of Hawarden. It was a red-letter day in my life, for I hold my political chief in the highest honour. He is a very great man indeed, and when I was brought into close personal contact with him I realised it more than ever. He is one of the mighty men of the earth.

We held our eighteenth annual council this year, and we had to present a very unfavourable report. The fact was, the Sick Benefit Society was pulling the Union to the ground. I had always been against it. A lot of the workmen who were getting advanced in years—men of sixty years of age and thereabouts—began to feel that they would like to start such a society in connection with the Union. I objected to it at once, and the harpies who were around me tried to divorce the men from me, by telling them that I wanted them all to go into the workhouse. My reason for objecting was that I did not want the men to embark upon an undertaking which I foresaw they could not possibly keep up, and they found out in the end that I was right. I only wish I had been wrong. I paid into the society all the time it was in existence, but I had nothing from it. They tried to make a whip out of that affair wherewith to flog me, but it was no good.

The society was started in 1877. At that time district benefit societies were springing up in different directions, so ours was started, and men of sixty were eligible for membership on payment of an entrance fee of one shilling and sixpence. In addition to that, members of district sick benefit societies, irrespective of age and standards of health, were taken over in a lump, provided they had funds amounting to £1 per member. Then the standard of entrance fees was fixed at one shilling and sixpence, a sum preposterously low; in fact, men who would have had to pay £1, and even more than that, for admission into a Court of Foresters or an Odd Fellows' Lodge, were admitted into our society for one shilling and sixpence each. The admission of men over and above that age, where other societies have found it safe, and indeed necessary, to draw the line, resulted in the enrolment of members who were almost constantly on the funds. So it came about that for almost every ten shillings paid in, twenty shillings had to be paid out. Then the neglect of enforcing a proper entrance fee, the amount of which should have been regulated by the age of the applicant, deprived the fund of considerable sums. The basis of the fund was false hopes, and so it was bound to collapse; but, unfortunately, it helped greatly to kill the Union too.

I told them at the annual meeting that the Sick Benefit Society had neither been the handiwork of myself nor the present committee. It was what the members themselves had made it. Two years before we had been obliged to impose a levy of one shilling and sixpence per member. At that time, other societies, owing to the great amount of sickness, had also been obliged to impose levies varying from one shilling to one shilling and sixpence a week.

In 1888 the council and the executive committee sat till nearly midnight to see what alterations were advisable, with the view of saving the society from a collapse. The reforms then adopted were directed to be embodied in a circular, and submitted to the members for their approval. Neither the council nor the committee could do more. What was the result? The members refused to sanction what had been done, and there was consequently no alteration. I told them that I had gone carefully into the measures of reform then proposed, and had the men accepted them, the funds in hand would have been from £1,000 to £1,600 more than they were. That reform need not have lasted more than two years, or three at the outside; after which, they could, if they had thought proper, have reverted to the previous system of grants.

That refusal—and that refusal alone—had forced the council of the Union, to report a very large outlay in connection with the sick funds, considerably more than in any former year.

I said that the council would have to face the question like men, and if they did so they would see what had been the cause of the increase in expenditure. They all knew that when the funds were locked up in Chancery that the parties who locked them up professed to be extreme friends of the Union. Well, this was what the papers said: "The gentleman who did that was the only guardian of the labourers, and the president and the executive council were a lot of extravagant spendthrifts, who were running away with the Sick Benefit money, and wasting it in all that was bad." They now all knew that instead of that having consolidated the Union, the idea got abroad that the Sick Benefit funds were being improperly spent, and, as a consequence, a very large number of young men, who would have been paying members to this hour, became alarmed and left the fund. The consequence then was that we were left with the aged members on our hands; and as the sickness among them was necessarily greater than among the younger men, the demands upon the Union funds had largely increased, while the contributions had decreased. So that instead of benefiting the old men, the locking up of the funds had done them irreparable mischief. I told them I had paid into the fund nearly £40, and never drawn a farthing.

Another thing which had militated against us was this. In some villages a notice had been received by the men of a reduction in their wages. The men at once recognised the value of their Union. They appealed for help ; I responded and went to their aid. Sometimes a new branch of forty or fifty members was raised and the reduction notified did not take place. But perhaps in a month or so the branch was again broken up, and when the reason was asked, the answer was given, "Oh, we have read such and such things in the papers about the Union funds, and we don't know what to think." All these reports did us a great deal of damage when we could ill afford to stand it.

Then there was the Widows' Relief Society, which was started in 1881 at two places; but it soon fell through. My name was printed on the papers and pamphlets of the society ; but that was done without my consent, and I strongly objected to it. I opposed this society, simply because I did not see how it could be properly worked. All this worried me greatly and helped to keep me in bad health. We were being found fault with in certain papers, first for this and then for that. Why had the Union touched politics? Why had there been such a Sick Benefit Society? And so it went on ; and of course all this affected our numbers most seriously. I wrote on the subject, to try and stem the tide, and showed how wages invariably fell back to the old rate, or nearly so, whenever the branch in that particular neighbourhood broke up. I begged the labourers to combine once more, and win the ground they had once so nobly fought for and had so foolishly lost by their own indifference.

From 1875 up to 1885 the Union had comparative peace, and moved steadily and calmly on; but after the 1885 General Election the Union was all wrong. It was venomously assailed by men who up till then had declared they were its very best friends. The truth was, some of these vipers were furious because they could not get the labourers to send them to Parliament, and they tried with all their wicked spite to howl and hoot the Union down. They wished to crush it out of existence. They tried to smash me up over and over again. They kept repeating that I misappropriated the funds, and of course some thought it might be true. I told the men once that my private diaries from 1872 onward could be inspected by a practical accountant any day, and that I had brought into the funds of the Union by my own individual efforts £14,000; a sum four times greater than any that had been paid out for services rendered.

I would not have gone into this miserable question here, but for this—it shows what I had to go through; that being president of a Union was not all sunshine and honey; there was plenty of gall and wormwood forced to my lips by those who were no better than Judases. I am not the first, nor shall I be the last, while human nature is what it is, to bear the brunt of such cowardly and persistent attacks on name and fame; but I can honestly say that what distressed me most was the injury they did to the Union.

In 1890 the Union, largely owing to the indefatigable efforts of Mr. Walker—he pushed it hard and fast, and never spared himself—began to look up once more. The morphia of lying and misrepresentation of myself and others who were working hard in the cause laid the majority in many villages in Norfolk and elsewhere fast asleep. For four years delegates and officers had been like so many John the Baptists crying in the wilderness without avail ; but in 1890 the men began to wake up once more. The fall in wages touched them up and made them jump into Union. I spoke a good deal on Union just at this period, but the strain and anxiety were beginning to tell on me. I held up as long as I could and got along through 1891 ; but in the spring of 1892 I had a very serious illness, which it seemed to me I should never be able to shake off. I was regularly done up, worn out, and pulled down. The thing that cheered me was to hear of our progress.

By the time the General Election was on I was up and about again, and felt strong enough to warrant me in coming forward once more as a candidate for my former division. In this election the Liberals captured four seats in our part, my own and three others. I felt so confident that I should be returned that, when the business of the last executive committee was concluded, I said, "Gentlemen, that's the whole of the business, and when I meet you again at our next committee meeting I shall be Member of Parliament."

Well, I was returned by a majority of 1089. The Tories were completely staggered by it. In 1885 several of the local gentry lent me horses and carriages to take voters to the poll, though

I used a "dickey cart" myself; but in 1892 they would not lend me a wheel. They all turned against me because I voted for Home Rule. On polling day the men came in and polled for me well, and the old women lent their donkey carts to bring them in. When the High Sheriff saw the figures, he was so much annoyed that he refused to declare the poll, and the under sheriff had to do it. I then went up to the High Sheriff, held out my hand and thanked him for the very able way in which he had conducted the count. He shook hands with me, then deliberately pulled his handkerchief out of his pocket and wiped his hand. After that I just went up, shook hands with him again, and told him I was perfectly satisfied with the state of the poll, if he was!

Before the figures were declared there were ten carriages and pairs from Welbeck Abbey drawn up by the Assembly Rooms, awaiting the result of the poll; five minutes after it was declared, lo! they were all gone. The High Sheriff, I remember, was white with rage. When I left the Town Hall there was a tremendous crowd outside. Policemen were there in force to see that I was not crushed to death. I noticed five big, burly fishermen walking behind me, and when I got to the first donkey cart they laid hold of me and lifted me in and started hurrahing, and the crowd took it up; and then the donkey was started off and I was carted round the place, the people cheering all the time. It was a splendid ovation—right down splendid.

After that I went to the Liberal Club and addressed a meeting from the balcony; there were between seven and eight thousand people there. I noticed several prominent Conservatives in the crowd, and after thanking my supporters and agent, I addressed myself to them. I told them I hoped the election which had just taken place would teach them a lesson which they would never forget. In 1885, when I had the patronage of several of the local gentry and the loan of their horses and carriages, I won by 640; in 1886, when my opponents had all the forces of Welbeck Abbey and all the forces of every baronet and squire in the division to help them, they managed to beat me by 20 votes. "And now," I said, "I have stood the test again without the support of any of those gentlemen who have turned out to be Tories, and what has happened? Why, Joseph and his brethren have licked you in a donkey cart—a glorious licking this time it is too!" Well, after this the Conservatives cleared out of that meeting as soon as they could. The enthusiasm was tremendous, and the people shouted and hurrahed and sang songs:

Shout a loud hurrah! boys,
Raise your voices high,
Arch is going to Parliament
With a grand majority.
Shout hurrah! boys.

They sang this and "For he's a jolly good fellow," etc. How they did shout, bless their hearts! There was riding and running all the country-side round.

One man I heard of mounted his grey pony directly he got the news and rode from house to house spreading the glad tidings: he was a shoemaker, and he had his sleeves turned up and his apron on—he could not spare time to titivate. Oh, there was a regular to-do! My welcome back to Barford I shall never forget. My wife and I travelled down from London, and at Warwick we had a fine reception. A procession was formed at the bottom of Broad Street, and the Warwick Town Band struck up a lively tune when our carriage stopped. I got out and into another, and the men pushed and pulled it along. There was a large flag behind it, and also banners with inscriptions on them. I made a speech, and we had speeches and great cheering, and then off we drove to Barford and up to the old cottage. There we had more speeches and cheering and handshaking—it was a reception to uplift a man.

I forgot all my rough times then, all my struggles; I only remembered I was Joseph Arch, M.P. once more, the chosen representative of the agricultural labourers, and that by a glorious majority. It was a thumping victory for us and no mistake, and the labourers had done a splendid stroke towards breaking the back of the clerical and the territorial influences in the rural districts. They had got to see that what I had been telling them for years was the truth, that the ballot-box is the only weapon they possess, and by properly using it they can outwit the squire, the parson, and the land agent, with more effect than by holding arguments.

A pressman came to interview me just after the election and I told him what I thought, and what I meant my future policy to be. I said: "I tell you frankly, neither the Tory Allotments Act (1887) nor the Small Holdings Acts are of much, if any, good to the labourers. Our men realise that, and it is why they wish the Liberals to deal with their wants. After the Irish question is got out of the way we must have Parish Councils. By conferring upon these councils the control of the charities, and the administration of the Poor Law, many of the abuses at present existing will be disposed of. These councils, too, must take over the matters of rating and education in the villages. Then, above all, they must have the power to compulsorily acquire as much land for the labourer as he wants at the same rent as land is letting in the district. The labourers must, moreover, have conceded to them the right to sell their improvements if they choose." I was strong on the point that the meetings must be held in the evenings, so that the men could attend, otherwise parson and squire would manipulate them. There was another thing I said: "Hodge never forgets his friends and never forgives his enemies. He has been waiting like a tiger in his lair for the past six years, and now that he has sprung upon the Tories he pretty well frightens them out of their Conservative wits."

While I was up in London attending Parliament the Union was being actively worked in Norfolk and Essex. More than twelve thousand had joined during

1890-91, and some hundred and eighty-nine branches had been put in working order; but I saw that the work of the Union was practically done for the time being. It was a sort of final flicker up before the candle went out, and my Parliamentary duties left me no choice but to look on. I was now moving in the political sphere on my fellow-labourers' behalf. In February 1893 an article of mine appeared in the *New Review*. It was entitled "Lords and Labourers," and I wrote it in two goes of six hours each. Lord Winchilsea had broached the idea of forming the National Agricultural Union, which was to be a combination of landlords, farmers, and labourers. I opposed this because I thought the wolf and the lamb could not make common cause together, and I therefore warned the labourers not to have anything to do with it. In my opinion it was simply a Tory dodge to get the control of affairs into their own hands.

In this article I said: "The ranks of selfishness and class privilege are broken and routed, but the enemy has not yet given up the contest in despair. He is wise enough to abandon his old attitude compounded of tyranny and neglect, and now he comes fawning and smooth-tongued, saying, 'We are your friends; we wish you well; our interests are one; let us make common cause; join us in defence of our common livelihood.' This is the attitude which the landlords, and, following their example, the tenant farmers are taking up to-day. While I have breath I will raise my voice to prevent my brethren the labourers from falling into this skilfully baited trap. The labourers' interest is that of the farmers! He should join with them in defence of a common livelihood! Yes, when the mouse can lick the cream from the cat's whiskers!" I went on to say: "The British farmer is still the same selfish, stubborn animal that he ever was, and God help the labourer who has to trust himself to his tender mercies. We are told agriculture is so depressed that there is no longer a living to be made out of the land, and unless the labourers join with landlords and farmers to obtain legislative reforms there will soon be neither work nor wages left for them. I agree with the French minister who said he would be prepared to abolish capital punishment if the assassins would lead the way. When I can see a sign that landlord and farmer are prepared to consider the claims of labour, when I can assure myself that these new-fangled schemes and unions are something more than a plot to make the labourer pull the chestnuts out of the fire for the benefit of these autocrats, then I may be prepared to give the scheme a favourable consideration.

"At present I must confess that to my mind the evidence tends the other way. On one hand I read the words of my Lord Ravensworth, who says that for the salvation of agriculture it is necessary that all three classes interested in it should band together, and that as a preliminary step to this holy alliance the labourers must consent to a reduction in their wages all round. On the other hand, I see our old friend, Mr. James Lowther, openly advocating a duty on corn! A holy alliance truly! Increased rent, more money to waste in London frivolities for the landlord, more hunters for the farmer, and more silk gowns for his wife; and for the labourer, less wages and a dear loaf—the rich to be filled with good things, and the hungry to be sent empty away! My best thanks to these gentlemen who have so discreetly let the cat out of the bag.

"Lord Winchilsea, the proud parent of the embryo union, is more astute. *He* does not commit himself to heroic reforms—his words are softer than butter. The reforms, to obtain which it is necessary to establish this proposed gigantic organisation, and to induce the ermine robe (with many a dainty shudder, without doubt) to embrace the fustian smock, are harmless, not to say trivial: the decrease of the burden of taxation on land, a revision of railway rates, and a better system for the collection and distribution of agricultural produce—which last grand reform, as I shall shortly show, it only requires a little energy and enterprise on the part of the farmers themselves to secure. A fortnight ago these three reforms comprised the whole of his lordship's programme.

"But it seems he has discovered that the tea he is providing for the labourers is not sufficiently sweetened; therefore he has, within the past week, dropped another lump of sugar into it. The latest addition to the programme of the Agricultural Union is a sliding scale of wages for labourers dependent on the price of corn. When corn rises five shillings a quarter the wages of the labourers are to rise concomitantly threepence a day. Bravo, my lord! When once the door is open to concession—even a crack—pressure from without may very soon fling it wide. I do not despair of seeing our sultans of the soil, in their eager angling for votes, swallowing wholesale the programme of the Agricultural Labourers' Union. But I should very much like to have the details of the scheme from Lord Winchilsea. What about the grazing and dairy districts? Are the men who are employed there to tend cattle—are the shepherds and the horse-keepers to share in the benefits of this sliding scale? If not, there will be pretty general discontent among them supposing the price of stock or dairy produce rises while that of corn sinks. If they are to share in it, the proposal at once stands out in its true light as a bribe to catch votes in favour of a measure intended to raise the price of corn—that is, stripping off the frippery of language and looking at the naked fact, in favour of Protection. For not one of the remedies proposed, except Protection, makes for the raising of the price of agricultural produce. Revision of railway rates, reduction of the burden of taxation on land, better methods of collection and distribution, all purport to benefit the agriculturist, by cheapening the cost of production, not by increasing the price of produce.

"A precious benefit for the labourer this last truly! Raise the price of his bread a penny a loaf, and give him an additional eighteenpence a week! And suppose, instead of rising, the price of corn falls while our noble lords are carrying out their Protection agitation? Are the wages of the labourers to *fall* threepence a day for every five shillings' fall in the price of wheat? Presumably so; otherwise the proposal would amount to stereotyping the rate of wages at present obtaining in the country.

"This, then, is the halter which the noble Earl of Winchilsea and his henchmen are hoping to put round the necks of the labourers as they go to the polls. 'Vote for the candidates of our union,' they say, 'for those only who will promote measures tending to raise the price of corn; if you do not—if you reject our programme and vote for the "cheap loaf"—you will cut your own throats, for you will bring about a fall in your own wages.' It behoves all true friends of the labourer to speak up. The proposal is so spurious and so fair-sounding that I cannot conceal from myself that there is danger that the flies may seek the honey-pots.

"It is no wonder landlords are anxious for the return of Protection. In the course of a close observation of agricultural matters, extending over a long series of years, I have found it an invariable rule that whenever the price of corn rises rents rise also; but I have not observed any proportionate increase in the labourers' wages. Under Protection the landlord would improve his position, the farmer would, at the least, maintain his, while the labourer, who is least able to bear loss, must inevitably suffer. Under these circumstances, can I, as one of his own flesh and blood, allow him to be cozened into a partnership which means ruin to him without raising my voice to warn, and, if possible, to save him?"

I said too, that "We who had worked and toiled to raise the condition of the British labourer would not cease from our endeavours to tear off the smiling mask of plenty with which the authors of this Union's being have covered the grinning death's head beneath, until we can say, 'Surely in vain is the net spread in the sight of any bird.'

"The labourer," I said, "is the child of the soil—the others are parasites who have affixed themselves to it; and before agriculture can become prosperous again they must go." I went on to say that the "squire must have his London house; he must entertain 'the county' in a sumptuous and ostentatious manner; he must find money for his sons to spend three or four years of idleness and extravagance at Oxford or Cambridge, or a longer period in a cavalry regiment; he must give marriage portions to his daughters. To do all this the money must be wrung from the land; to give it the land is starved for want of cultivation, and the labourer, who is the least able to protect himself, is kept in penury.

"The tenant farmer," I went on to say, "is no less to blame than his landlord. I have no hesitation in saying that no man can farm at a profit unless he and his family are willing one and all to give close attention and hard work to their business. But the modern farmer must hunt and shoot, he must go to evening parties, play cards, and smoke and drink with his friends, while his wife dresses in silk, reads novels, and plays the piano. Hence only the merest outlines of his business are attended to, and those 'inconsidered trifles' which turn a loss into a profit are utterly neglected.

"Let the farmers," I said, "once become manufacturers as well as mere producers of raw material, and Lord Winchilsea's desire for a better system of collection and distribution of produce will speedily become an accomplished fact without his lordship's interference."

I also said: "High rents, charges on the land—*i.e.*, mortgages, jointures, tithes, etc., and a desire for luxuries on the part of landlord and farmer, with its consequent inattention tc business on the part of the latter—I believe lie at the root of the present serious condition of agriculture." I said: "The vampire land-starving farmer is in, and has been allowed to lay field to field, to take three or four farms perhaps, each one of which ought to afford a good living. Those farms are the second curse of agriculture which must be done away with. The system had a political origin. The Whig or Tory owner of a dozen farms found some of his dozen tenants opposed to him in politics. Therefore his policy was to 'boil down' the constituency by reducing the tenants to the lowest possible number."

"If landlords were wise," I went on, "they would get rid of the land-starving farmer, and return to the old system of farms from fifty to one hundred and fifty acres. We are not without object lessons as to the great results to be obtained from small holdings of land. In the village of Barford I have been able to obtain for the men a number of small holdings of land, from one to three acres in size, with astonishingly good results. In by-gone days the County Court officer was a familiar figure in Barford ; he has not been in the place for several years. There is not a careful man in the place who has not got one pig or more in his stye, and a more manly, independent set of fellows could not be found in the land. They are under obligations to nobody, and they fear nobody. One man, who is not, as a labourer, much more than half a man, told me that even in this last year of scarcity he obtained sufficient wheat off half an acre to supply his family with bread till the winter was over. Where is the tenant of four to six hundred acres who could say that his land produces in like proportion? Even at the present low price of corn there is a handsome profit to be obtained when this quantity is grown."

I wound up by saying : " We must make the profits of his own skill and energy secure to every man ; we must get rid, by free sale, or otherwise, of burdened estates ; and we must have a class of farmers to work the land who are industrious and attentive to their business, who will work, themselves and their families, instead of playing at being ladies and gentlemen.

"Nemesis is at the door of those who in their selfish ease and soft living never regarded the cry of the poor.

Ruin is upon them, and they will fall unmissed and unregretted, to give place to a newer, brighter state of things. I do not in the least regret the blight which has come upon the present agricultural system of England. Sharp diseases require sharp remedies, and if only the present depression can make a root-and-branch affair of the fungus-growths of feudalism and class privilege which have for centuries choked the tillers of the soil, I for one shall count it gain. But I will never, if I can help it, permit the labourers to be drawn into a trap, however daintily baited, which has for its object the bolstering up of a pernicious system. It was a saying when I was young, that if you saw the fox's brush sticking out of the earth you might be sure the fox was at home. The brush of my Lord Ravensworth and that of Mr. Lowther are plain for all to see, and I think I can see the tip of that of my Lord Winchilsea."

As you may guess, I was full up to the brim and overflowing with my subject when I wrote out this article for the *New Review*. I was not going to have the men bamboozled without trying to stop the lordly game. No, it was too much of a good thing, and I could not sit quiet under such a proposal. Not only my tongue should speak, but my pen should be a point to show the labourers what a Jack-o'-lantern was being dangled before their eyes by the smooth-tongued gentlemen who advocated this protectionist union. It tickled me a good deal to watch the tactics of Lord Winchilsea and Mr. Henry Chaplin and others of the same kidney. Why, after all their talk about the evils of agitation and unionism, they were nothing but aristocratic agitators and Unionists themselves. It suited their convenience now to adopt the methods they had tried to cry down. They laid themselves out with honeyed smiles and buttered words to entrap Hodge; and why? Because Hodge had a vote. Well, Hodge has the ballot-box, too, and he has learned how to use it as a free man should.

I have, as I said before, but little faith in Special Committees and Royal Commissions, but there was one to inquire into the condition of the poor which I hoped might achieve something. I sat on it, and the Prince of Wales was also a member of this Commission. I should like here to bear testimony to the invariable kindness and courtesy which I have received from His Royal Highness. Among other things the Prince of Wales sent me two tickets for the opening of the Imperial Institute; he sent me his good wishes with them, and that pleased me most of all. I am his member, you see in a manner of speaking; and I will say this—should I be spared to see him King of England, he will not have a more loyal subject in all his vast dominions, in all his great empire, than Joseph Arch of Barford, the agricultural labourer who has had the honour of representing his division in Parliament. I was representing it in 1893; and at the last election, when so many big guns went by the board, I was chosen to represent it again—once more I was the Prince of Wales's own M.P. So I am Joseph Arch, M.P. for the North-Western Division of Norfolk still.

The introduction of the Parish Councils Bill was

another day of triumph for me. I said to some one with whom I was discussing the matter, "The Bill is a great stride in the right direction. It is going to revolutionise our villages; it will give England back her vanished peasantry, and add immensely to the prosperity of the country. These are surely great things to set against the loss of their influence by the squire and the parson, who have squandered away their chances of binding the labourer to their interests by assisting the farmer to grind him into the dust."

And now as to the Union—the starting and the leading of which I look upon as my real life-work, the great thing I was specially set apart to accomplish by the help of that All-seeing, All-knowing Providence which overrules the destinies of men and all things—*its* work was, for the time being, accomplished, and so it died a natural death. For about the last four years it has been practically non-existent. The men had got the vote, they were getting on the land, their path was being smoothed for them, and so they thought they no longer needed their Union. Well, time will show.

As I sit here in my little cottage at Barford and review the past, it seems at one minute a long look back; at another it seems but yesterday that my grandmother sat in the chair I am sitting in now—a chair which is over a hundred years old—and I stood by her, a little chap of six. And there is the old eight-day clock which my father bought in Leamington more than fifty years ago. He, I have heard him tell, carried home the case over his shoulder, and my mother trudged at his side with the works in her market basket. I can see my good mother cutting the barley bread for us, with tears in her eyes because there is so little of it for the children who are so hungry. I can see my father step in at the door, come home from his work for a bite and sup of whatever is going. I can see myself tramping off in my little smock-frock, clapper in hand, to scare away the birds; then jumping the clods at sixpence a day; and so on, right away on to the great year of 1872, when I held that first meeting under the Wellesbourne chestnut-tree on the February evening which saw the birth of the Agricultural Labourers' Union.

I know that it was the hand of the Lord of Hosts which led me that day; that the Almighty Maker of heaven and earth raised me up to do this particular thing; that in the counsel of His wisdom He singled me out, and set me on my feet in His sight, and breathed of the breath of His Spirit into me, and sent me forth as a messenger of the Lord God of Battles. So I girded up my loins and went forth. It was from the Lord God of Battles I came, that there might one day be peace in the land. Only through warfare could we attain to freedom and peace and prosperity; only through the storm and stress of battle could we reach the haven where we would be. I was but a humble instrument in the Lord's hands, and now my work is over, my warfare is accomplished.

But there is a great work still to be done in the

century that is close upon us, and I call upon the young men among us to rise up in their strength and do it. Let them set their hands to the plough and never falter, never look back. Let them face the day that is dawning, and let them go forward with stout hearts. There is none so lowly, none so humble, none so poor, but he has his work to do; and it is a bit of work set for him, and no one else can do it but he himself—to each man his appointed work.

To the future of the agricultural labourer I look forward with confidence. I know—none better—that all is not glittering gold in his lot; but the bettering of that lot, the brightening of that lot rests with himself. When I began he had nothing. Now he has the political telephone of the vote, his Board Schools, his County Councils, his Parish Councils. I say, then, here are the means of betterment and progress lying ready to his hand, if he will but use them with discretion and manly, independent judgment. I am all for self-help. Let the labourer think and reason, let him use books and every chance of improvement that comes in his way; but let him never be ashamed of his work, of his calling in life. If he honours his own manhood, if he honours his labour, if he honours all other men and all other honest workers, he will be honoured in his turn, and his labour also. Do not let him ape any man; let him be himself, and let him aim at being himself at his best. That is what we have all got to aim at—to be ourselves at our best.

"The land for the people" is the goal the labourers

are working for. What I want to see is, when a labourer has no work to do for others he has something to do for himself. He can attend to his allotment and grow fruit, vegetables, and keep a pig for himself and his family, so that when the winter comes round he will have, like the busy ant, a good store laid up to keep them all going till the spring comes round.

Get on the land, I say, but by your own help—I do not believe in State-aid and land nationalisation. Get on a bit of land at a fair average rent, and then do the best with it—that is what the labourer should do. As a last extremity I would employ compulsion, but only so. Self-help and liberty, order and progress—these are what I advocate. I think that in the course of time new ideas will spring up—they are bound to do so—and when the labourers' present legitimate grievances are satisfied they will settle down to steady progress Present-day Socialism will die a natural death sooner or later. To my mind the Socialism of the future will consist in the improvement and upward tendency of the strength—physical, moral, and mental—of the rural and urban population of England.

A great, a very great responsibility rests with the press of the country. I say to that press collectively: "Do not abuse your power, do not shirk your responsibility; but use your power, face your responsibility, and be a beacon of light and leading to the agricultural labourers. Teach them to be steady, industrious, sober, and independent; teach them to take advantage of every turn of the tide, and to be for ever striving to get nearer the goal of improvement, the goal of perfection. Point the way to them, and keep pointing."

Will there ever be another Agricultural Labourers' Union? If it should be found necessary to form another, the new one will, I believe, differ in many important respects from the old; for the times are changing. But now as ever union means strength, and disunion means weakness. Combine, co-operate in manly independence, that is the main thing; help yourselves and help others, that is the point; the machinery will then take care of itself. There is a union coming, a mighty union, but I shall not live to see it in its glory. I see the beginning of it though. And here to my mind is one sign of it—that the noble lady whose name adorns the title-page of this book should have displayed such generous and unprejudiced impartiality as to edit the Life of Joseph Arch.*

Yes, it is a sign of the grand union that is coming, when prince and peer and peasant shall combine and co-operate for the good of one and all. It is a union that will be as big as all England; it will be as big as the empire; and some day it is going to be as big as the whole world. The world in union! That is what is coming, that is what all must work for. I shall not live to see it, but as sure as the sun shines in

* I want this to stand; I don't want it edited out.—J.A.

the heavens the great and glorious day when the world will be in union will dawn at last. In that sure and certain faith I lay down my pen and bid my readers farewell. A last word I would say to all; it is this—Courage, and work for union! the union of the world.

INDEX.